The Election

The Election

Richard Warren Field

The Election

Copyright © 1997 by Richard Warren Field

 Infortainment Publishing Company
P.O. Box 571752
Tarzana, CA 91357-1752

HTTP://WWW.INFORTAINMENT.COM

This book is printed in the United States of America on acid-free paper.

The Election is a work of fiction. All events described are imaginary. Aside from background materials referring to both public figures and historical persons, all characters are also imaginary.

First Printing, November 1997

10   9   8   7   6   5   4   3   2   1

Library of Congress Catalog Card Number: 97-93231

Field, Richard Warren
            The election / Richard Warren Field
                p.   cm.
            ISBN 0-9652287-0-3

For my children,
>   Michelle Elizabeth and
>   Ryan Joseph,
>   and for their children.

The "Regenerating Biosphere" future, humankind's next and potentially greatest era, will come to fruition more during their generations than during mine. This will occur especially when we rediscover the power of freedom and creativity that built the United States into a great nation, and that can be harnessed again to take us to this new, inspiring, and ultimately essential way of living.

ACKNOWLEDGMENTS

In today's fiction venue, with the craving for "page-turners" and "good reads," it is essential to call upon an experienced editor for guidance. My thanks to Upton Brady, who greatly helped an author prone to using more where less would do.

My thanks to my children, who serve as a never-ending source of inspiration.

A complex project of this sort, with detailed research necessary to supply as much realism as possible to the story, requires a great deal of time and commitment. For me, such a commitment would have been impossible without the unswerving support of my wife Carrie, who took on more than her share of the mundane so that I could be creative.

Prologue

"You're going on trial for murder," Elwood Kaplan reminded his client Will Runalli, as they sat in a functional, drab conference room of the San Luis Obispo County courthouse. "I don't think our newly elected President will be interested in helping you."

"You mean you don't think we can convince the President that 'boys will be boys,' and 'all's fair in love and politics?'" Runalli was barely five feet tall, and hyperactive. Though now grey-haired and paunchy, he still maintained the boyish, cocky demeanor that earned him the nickname "munchkin" or "munchkin-mouth."

"They'll throw the key away," Kaplan told him gloomily. "You're charged with masterminding a political assassination. You allegedly had the victim murdered to put your own candidate into the Presidency."

"All right, counselor, I'm no dummy. I understand the situation. Give me a legal opinion. What're their chances of hanging this on me?"

"They have a sleazy star witness who they made a very generous deal with. We'll get the jury to hate him, and to hate his testimony, enough to create a reasonable doubt. If we do that, you walk."

"So here it is," Runalli announced dryly, as if ushering in the opening of a theatrical production. "The trial of Will Runalli, epilogue to the wildest election in United States history. Lucky me. I'm this month's entertainment spectacle. This month's circus act."

Kaplan allowed himself a slight smile. "You're this month's villain."

Will Runalli took the detached, almost mocking cynicism of his attorney in stride. "The villain? It's not the worst role. Ever heard of Machiavelli? An Italian guy. Known for hardball politics. Anybody remember the good-guy politicians from that era?"

"There was more than one Machiavelli around during this election," Kaplan commented, now beginning to enjoy the conversation.

"Only one Michael Edwards," Runalli stated, with a suddenly icy, loathing tone.

Kaplan smiled.

"Michael Edwards," Runalli repeated again. "Why did that son-of-a-bitch have to chase the Presidency *this* election? This was going to be my year, my big come-back. Instead, I'm rotting in a prison cell—can't even make bail."

Kaplan smiled again, savoring an irony. "Didn't Edwards actually help keep your man in the race at one point?"

"Yeah. That was a long time ago. Before someone decided a Machiavelli like me needed to be involved in this thing." Runalli's tone became increasingly sinister. "Before Edwards had to deal with his own skeleton-in-the-closet scandal. Before the assassination attempts." Runalli broke into a chilling smile. "I should have joined forces with *those* guys."

"Well, we better go in."

Runalli nodded, and they walked into the packed courtroom together.

Part One

The Decision

Chapter 1

Early November, The Year Before the Election: Friday
New York City, New York

"You SLEAZY SON-OF-A-<BLEEP>! You <BLEEPING> <BLEEP-bleep>! You sure worked overtime to dig up this <bleep>ing <bleep>!" Democratic Presidential candidate Senator Victor Parker stopped as suddenly as he had started, but continued to glare at the subject of his tirade, veteran television reporter Don Samuelson. Victor Parker's usually very dignified public persona made his outburst even more newsworthy.

Samuelson was unable to suppress completely a subtly arrogant smirk from creeping onto his face as he waited for Parker to regain his composure and finish responding to Samuelson's question.

A reporter asked no one in particular, "What is it?"

Parker disdainfully flung a photograph into the crowd of reporters with a flippant flick of his wrist. "Mr. Samuelson here did a very clever job of setting me up," Parker replied, less angrily, but with rage still seething. "He got me to swear that I have always been faithful to my wife, that I would never patronize prostitutes, and then came up with this photograph of me, alone at the funeral of a prostitute, about four years ago. This isn't even a newspaper photo—he had to badger the poor girl's family to come up with this piece of slimy reporting.

"But I'm going to disappoint you, Mr. Samuelson. It's not at all what you think. It's true—this was a lady I was intimately involved with. But that was *in college, before* I was married. She took a bad fork in the road. She turned to drugs, prostitution, and then suffered an agonizing death from AIDS. When I became aware, I tried to help . . ." Parker started to choke with emotion, but seemed to use his lingering anger to fight back his tears. "And I stood by her as a friend." He paused, measuring his words more carefully now. "Maybe I shouldn't have tried to keep it quiet. But it seemed at the time like a personal matter that had nothing to do with politics, or my fitness to lead. I might add that I *still* feel that way. I hope this clarifies matters for you, Mr. Samuelson."

The videotape clip ended and World-Wide Broadcasting System anchorman Michael Edwards now appeared on the television screen. "That was a recap of our lead story, the shocking outburst of Democratic Presidential candidate Victor Parker. No viewer in this country could have any doubts what the bleeps in our soundtrack covered." Edwards had the ability to embrace the television camera with his intense, dark blue eyes. He saw millions of individual viewers, and spoke to each of them separately, but all at the same time. This talent had driven WWBS's 6:30 p.m. news to the top of the ratings.

Ted Jessup, the producer of the WWBS Evening News, stood in the control room, surrounded by busy technicians. Jessup was a long-time friend of Michael Edwards, about ten years older than him. While Edwards' looks seemed to get more distinguished with age, Jessup was simply aging, with a bulging mid-section and retreating grayish-brown hairline to prove it. As the producer, he had essentially completed his job for the broadcast. It was now up to everyone on the veteran staff to carry out their assigned duties for the meticulously timed half-hour broadcast. Edwards was the glue between various taped segments—he tied stories together, brought the broadcast in and out of commercials, and supplied enough background information on each segment to make it understandable to the viewer. Jessup was watching the broadcast complacently, almost not listening, as he now did most nights.

"It was patently obvious to this reporter that Victor Parker was misled into an ambush interview by Don Samuelson, a reporter for one of our competitors," Edwards stated sternly.

"What did he say?" Jessup asked, taken by surprise.

No one in the control room answered. They were all busy, and assumed Jessup had asked a rhetorical question.

"Senator Parker lost his temper when he realized how he had been set up by previous questions," Edwards continued. "And the questions that triggered the outburst were absolutely out-of-bounds, unfair, and ridiculous. During the 1992 election, we had the spectacle of marital fidelity emerging as a major campaign issue, with tabloids leading networks into inquiries of future President Clinton that ignored accepted standards of privacy and decency. But today, Mr. Samuelson lowered those standards even further. He actually asked this potential national leader questions about a college romance that occurred over twenty years ago, before marriage, with a woman who long after their association became a drug addict, then a prostitute, eventually dying of AIDS."

Jessup's jaw dropped. He grabbed some papers lying on a table next to him. He read them frantically. "This is not what he's supposed to be saying . . ." he said to no one in particular.

"What did this exercise in smutty reporting have to do with this potential candidate's qualifications to lead this country?" Edwards asked the television audience.

Jessup stared out of the control booth incredulously and asked rhetorically, "Michael, what the fuck are you doing?"

"Mr. Samuelson's reporting tactics have resulted in a sound bite that could haunt Senator Parker, possibly destroying his chances for the Democratic nomination," Edwards continued, oblivious to his producer's irritation. "Ironically, the senator recovered from his outburst and explained his outrage convincingly. But the attention-grabber was that profane, angry fifteen seconds. In today's bite-driven news atmosphere, that's considered 'great television.'

"Mr. Samuelson will have you believe that his questionable tactics have revealed some hidden character flaw in this man. He will believe that he as a journalist has done us all a great public service. He will see this as a proud moment in his career."

Jessup again spoke to his anchorman, knowing Edwards couldn't hear him, but because saying something was less painful for him than saying nothing. "Michael, you cannot declare war on another network without producer approval."

But Edwards was moving to the climax. "I have to ask—do we want a President who does *not* lose his temper when confronted with blatant unfairness? Can we continue to choose our leaders on the basis of fifteen second sound bites manufactured by reporters like Don Samuelson? This country, this *world,* has problems that need attention. We need visionaries who offer solutions to problems, not perfectly-poised, press-resistant, public-relations puppets.

"I'm asking these questions tonight. If you agree that these are important questions, I implore you to address your concerns to Don Samuelson, his network, and all reporters like him. Let's hold them accountable, the way they want to hold our political leaders accountable.

"Good night, my friends, and thank you for bringing us into your homes this evening."

The voice-over announcer came on the air. "This has been the WWBS Evening News with Michael Edwards in New York." The music swelled behind the credits, and the evening's broadcast was over.

Michael Edwards smiled as he collected his papers. He savored a brief moment of calm before the probable storm.

And Ted Jessup stormed into the area quickly.

"That is *not* what I approved," Jessup scolded.

"I know. The version you approved was general. I decided the piece would be better if it was more specific."

"You should have cleared this one through me, too."

"I didn't want to put you on the spot. If someone gets mad, let 'em get mad at me."

"Michael," Jessup lectured, "this is my news show. I'm responsible."

"You and I have spoken about reporting tactics like this. I know you agree with me."

"You—" Jessup gathered his thoughts. Edwards was right. They had spoken about this subject and he did agree. "There are ways to . . . This should have been discussed."

Edwards now used silence as his best weapon, smiling as Jessup struggled to chastise him.

A young female assistant approached them. "Telephone."

"That's gotta be upstairs calling me," Jessup guessed.

"Uh, no sir," the nervous young assistant corrected. "It's . . . Donald Samuelson . . . for Mr. Edwards. He sounded a little upset."

Jessup raised his chin with satisfaction and looked at Edwards.

"To hell with him," Edwards replied. "Tell him you can't find me, or I'm in a meeting—yeah, tell him I'm in a meeting. I promise to call him tomorrow."

Jessup looked at Edwards disdainfully as the assistant walked away.

"Well, I *am* in a meeting," he told Jessup insistently, but with a tongue-in-cheek tone. "With my boss. He's chewing me out. Not doing a very good job of it, but that's what he's doing. It would be insubordinate to leave in the middle of his reprimand to take a call."

"Michael, you don't seem to understand the—"

"Let me handle Samuelson," Michael reassured. "Seriously, Ted, I'll take care of it."

"Like you did tonight?"

"No. This'll call for some diplomacy."

"Nice idea."

"So are we done with the reprimand?"

Jessup sighed frustratedly. "Michael, step into my office," he said as his eyes narrowed.

Edwards was taken by surprise. "Your office," he repeated quietly. "Your office? Really?"

"Yes. Right now."

Edwards shrugged and got up from his chair on the set, then walked out of the room, turning toward Jessup's office.

"Not *that* office," Jessup called out impatiently as he followed. "My after-broadcast office."

"Your—" Edwards turned and looked at him puzzled.

"Up the street."

Edwards' face transformed from confusion to understanding. "Oh, *that* office."

Jessup looked back through the doorway at the broadcast set and saw the same young assistant picking up a ringing phone. "Before my call from upstairs *does* come."

✪ ✪ ✪

JESSUP'S "AFTER-BROADCAST" OFFICE WAS THE PARK AVENUE BAR AND GRILL, situated on the bottom floor of a tall office building in the midst of some of Manhattan's prime office space. It was the kind of place where you could take off your tie late in the evening, but it better be an expensive tie. Jessup was a well-known, long-time patron of the plush, dimly lit but meticulously maintained establishment. He had been well aware of the stereotype of the hard-working, hard-edged, hard-*drinking* news producer. So in the mid 1980's, as he began to rise at WWBS, keenly sensitive to appearances, he had an understanding with the Park Avenue Bar and Grill bartenders that his drinks were to be mostly ice and water. Though Jessup was now less sensitive to such considerations as he became more secure in his position, he had never changed the arrangement.

"So I can tell the brass on the eighth floor that you'll have this thing with Samuelson straightened out by Monday?" Jessup asked as he put the scotch on the rocks he had just sipped back on the table.

"Sure, why not," Edwards replied nonchalantly as he sipped a brandy.

"You have been such an arrogant asshole lately," Jessup complained.

"Slamming Samuelson today for his scummy crap was doing my job," Edwards stated firmly. "That egomaniac has been giving us all a bad name with his catch-them-off-guard journalism for too damn long."

"Sure, but I remember a Michael Edwards who could lay out a reprimand so subtly that the target barely knew he'd been taken down."

"And that subtlety may be clever, but the hammer over the head is the only way the other guy really gets the word."

"Okay," Jessup replied, nodding his head in surrender. "But you may have outfoxed yourself with this one. Your 'hammer over the head' could save Senator Victor Parker, keeping alive one of your most formidable rivals."

"Now you?" Edwards asked wearily. "I'm not a candidate, Ted."

"Really. Don't you have two tapes in your office labeled LOS ANGELES/APRIL 3RD and JEFFERSON ISLAND/SEPTEMBER 7TH? Who's going to deal with—"

"I don't know," Edwards answered impatiently. "But I don't see how it could be me."

"A lot of people are telling pollsters they think it could be you . . ."

Edwards squinted through a suspicious smile. "You?"

"I don't think *anybody* can do that job." He paused. "But if someone can, it might be a guy who started an economic revolution in his spare time while becoming one of the most admired reporters and commentators in the country."

"An 'economic revolution?'"

"Don't get modest on me—I know you too well," Jessup said smiling. "That 'economic revolution' shit was written up in financial magazines all over the country."

"A lot of hype. People in the media are always hyping."

Jessup laughed.

"You know, I lambasted Mr. 'I'm-all-ears' Perot in 1992 for what I said was *his* arrogance. That guy, buying the American Presidency so he could magnanimously hand it back to the American people. What a clown! I said Perot was starting a disturbing trend—rich guys buying political offices as a hobby. Someone'll go back to those tapes at that little bitty local station in California and nail me with those statements."

"Expect Samuelson to be first."

"I'm going to straighten everything out with him, remember?"

"That's right." Jessup smiled. His face then twisted as he considered his next comment. "I'd vote for you," he finally said quietly.

"You're supposed to talk me out of this . . ."

"Los Angeles/April 3rd: Officer Barry McDowell. Jefferson Island/September 7th: the photo that made the cover of every major news publication in the universe."

"Jessup, you're a *jerk*," Edwards replied, but not in a tone as angry as the words.

Jessup's face broke into a satisfied smile.

Edwards grudgingly returned the smile.

☼   ☼   ☼

The Same Day: Friday
Santa Barbara Channel, Five Miles off the Coast of California

"Hooo boy, that Edwards goes after publicity like a cockroach after rotting muck," Beauregard Hunter drawled, as he and his assistant, Tyler Rhodes, watched the end of the WWBS Evening News broadcast. They sat in a small recreation room built on top of a state-of-the-art oil-drilling platform just off the shores of Santa Barbara County in California.

Beauregard Hunter made a craggy, elderly appearance, looking every one of his seventy-three years of age. His down-home drawl and cheap country-western clothes belied the focused mind that had made him a top executive in the oil industry for over forty years. Only his elaborately embossed cowboy boots hinted at his enormous wealth.

"You know, boss, there are three other networks you could watch," Rhodes reminded Hunter light-heartedly.

"Yeah, I know. But that damn WWBS has the best evening news," Hunter admitted through a begrudging grin. "I still don't like that Edwards guy—I don't like his opinions or his politics. And I don't like the idea of him running for President, that's for damn sure."

"He won't run," Rhodes stated confidently. "And so what if he does? He's got no political connections in either party."

"But he's got lots of money," Hunter reminded him. He stood up as he used the remote control to turn off the television set. "Speaking of lots of money, this place here looks good."

"Sure does."

They walked out of the room into an area that connected the modules of the platform structure, a small hall of green painted metal. After walking a few steps, they arrived at an elevator where Hunter pressed the button to summon it.

"Took us over ten years of wrangling with fish-hugging, coast-loving, bleeding hearts and regulators, but we got it done," Hunter commented triumphantly. "We're finally pumping oil from out here, right next to one of our biggest markets in the world. Low transport costs—just pop it over to our refineries along the L.A. coast, and out to the pumps. We're gonna make a fortune for twenty, maybe thirty years."

"It's a great coup, sir. And after all the flak you got for the expense of it, for the litigation, then the construction—the stockholders should be on their knees thanking you for fighting so hard."

Hunter smiled broadly. "And since I'm one of those stockholders—what a headache, answering to all these fools. Aw, hell. Remind me again, why did I take this company public?"

"To make a billion dollars."

"Oh yeah." Hunter smiled sardonically.

The elevator arrived. They stepped in and pressed "H" for "helideck." The elevator started up.

"Only way we'll get screwed on this thing is if people decide they don't need so much oil," Hunter stated smugly.

"Not likely."

The helideck was painted with the striking blue and green colors of the company logo, and was especially impressive from the air. A single high, narrow, triangular tower rose from the ocean in one corner of the platform, looking like the Eiffel Tower. The rest of the platform structure sat on a flat base, comprising a jumbled maze of large steel rectangular compartments, giving the entire structure a jagged, asymmetrical appearance.

Sharp gusts of wind blasted cold air into the faces of Hunter and Rhodes when they stepped out onto the helideck.

Hunter stopped to look over the platform again. He had been to offshore platforms before, and was aware that this was the most sophisticated, best built and most expensive one he had ever seen. "Hell of an investment," he finally commented to Rhodes.

Rhodes nodded. He could tell that there was a lingering thought or problem nagging at Hunter, and he knew they wouldn't leave until Hunter articulated it.

"That son-of-a-bitch Edwards has got some idea that the country can get along with less oil."

"Him again?" Rhodes asked with slight disbelief. "He can't—"

"He can't hurt us from the anchor desk? That's what you think? I'm just a silly old coot worrying about nothing?"

"I didn't say that. But I can't see him getting any real power, or getting into any kind of a position to hurt our efforts. He's on the outside looking in. He—"

"But if he runs and wins, he'll be on the *inside*."

Rhodes was amazed at how long this discussion had lasted. He dismissed the concern. "I don't see that happening."

"You believe in coincidence?" Hunter asked.

Rhodes smiled. He knew what was coming. He'd heard it before. "I know you don't."

"Son, I got my start not far from here, near Bakersfield, actually near a place called Taft. Had a cousin stall his car out there. I was finishing up my Navy stint, just after the end of the Ko-rean War, at a place on the coast out here called Oxnard. I had to drive all night through winding roads to get my cousin. But instead of grumbling and cursing about it, I looked around. And that Taft area looked a hell of a lot like some Texas oil-fields I'd worked at before the war. So I hired a geologist, then mortgaged everything I had, and a few things I didn't have, to buy every option I could get my hands on. I hit gusher after gusher. Was that a coincidence, that my cousin broke down out there? Yeah. To someone who's not paying attention."

Rhodes continued smiling as he nodded.

"There's some reason I saw that Edwards on TV tonight, and he got me pissed off. Too much at stake, son. I've been playing in the big leagues too long to let a hunch go by without a second glance."

Rhodes still wasn't sure what Hunter had in mind.

"I know," Hunter continued obliquely, almost conversing with himself. "He can't be elected. No way; no chance." Hunter shifted from reflective to decisive. "Get those overpaid, over-taught, brainiac, M-B-A futuristics kids you talked me into hiring—get them busy on this. I want a report on Edwards. Get 'em to do some of those scenario things they do. Can he get elected? If he does, what will he want to do? They can base it on all his bullshit—there should be plenty of it for them to sift through. And, will he be able to do what he wants if he *does* get in?"

"Okay."

"I already know some of this. I'll see if they get it right with what I *do* know, so I know if I can trust whatever else they tell me." Hunter paused as he flashed a mischievous gleam. "'Cause if I need to do something to protect my flanks . . . I've got a buddy with connections that would scare the stiff pecker off a horny bull. Maybe I'll get him working on some preliminaries . . ."

"I'll get our staff futurists on it."

"Good. Now let's get back to Texas. Oh, and tell the people who put together these platforms that they did a damn fine job."

"I will."

They moved quickly to the waiting company helicopter and boarded.

☼   ☼   ☼

Early November: The Next Day, Saturday
New York City, New York

"DID YOU SEE HOW THE TIMES IS PLAYING THIS?" MICHAEL EDWARDS asked his wife Teresa disgustedly. They sat at the kitchen table of the Edwards' First Avenue apartment, in their robes, reading the morning paper as they munched muffins and sipped grapefruit juice. This was a pauper's quarters compared to their homes in Connecticut and California, but it was convenient to the WWBS studio. "They're portraying this as a cat-fight between TV news reporters, and turning it into a criticism of TV news in general."

Teresa smiled and shook her head. "They've always thought of TV news as inferior to print, so you shouldn't be surprised." Though Teresa was now over fifty, she was barely heavier than she had been at twenty, and had a classically beautiful face that Michael thought time had refined. During the late 60's, she had won a major regional beauty contest just so she could decline her title and denounce the beauty contest as sexist. She had married Michael Edwards in the early 70's, with many broad goals which had gradually been subordinated to the concerns of raising their three children, Heather-Lynn, Keith and Pauline, who were all now either on their own or away in college. "Irritating, but certainly predictable," Teresa said, finishing her thought.

"'Petulant,'" Michael quoted with disbelief. "They called my commentary 'petulant.'"

Teresa smiled again. "It was. I mean, it was right on the mark, but it was . . . grumpy."

"I sounded 'grumpy' on the air?"

"Michael, you've been a damn grouch off the air for the last three, maybe even six months—ever since you gave up your position at Omni-Vee. Sooner or later, you were going to carry your mood into a broadcast."

"What're you talking about?" Michael set the paper down and glared at her incredulously.

"Little things. Like I've been asking you to call Sy back for over a week. And every time I do, you—"

"He wants to nag me about some investment bullshit."

"He seemed to think it was important—stuff you have to approve and sign."

"I know what he's calling about," Michael told her impatiently. "He's worried whether or not our investments will clear us two million, or six million, or ten million dollars next week. He bores the crap out of me."

"You should at least call him back and tell him he bores you."

"Is this what we've become, Teresa? We *hate* yuppies, but we're the yuppiest of them all. Fat and happy, rich and richer . . . A couple of hippie to yuppy sell-outs."

"Excuse me," Teresa objected, now losing some patience. "Neither one of us is 'fat,' no one has 'sold out' anything, and you are certainly *not* happy."

"What the hell happened to us, Teresa? We marched against the Viet Nam war. We thumbed our noses at our materialistic parents. We made love on beaches and in forests all over northern California."

Teresa smiled.

"All of this money garbage is my father's measure of success. We were supposed to make the world a better place. Instead, I have the damn Midas touch. My father wins. I'm successful, by *his* measure, not mine."

"Michael, you make it sound like you were trying to make money," Teresa lectured back. "I don't remember you doing anything just to get rich. Your anchorman position, your documentary and book, Omni-Vee . . . You just did them all very well, and sometimes when you do that, when you give lots of people something they want, you end up making a lot of money. It's society's way of rewarding the productive."

"So the world really does run the way our parents say. We build a better mousetrap, and get rich. The money means we're successful."

"No Michael, that's not what I mean. Sometimes you need to use your money to do something good, to 'make the world a better place.'"

"Oh yeah," Michael countered cynically. "The Rockefellers and the Kennedys have been very good at that kind of thing."

"That's not what I mean either." Teresa paused, seeming frustrated. "Michael, you know what you need to do," she finally said.

"You mean use our millions to run for President," Michael stated flatly, addressing the issue they had been dancing around. He shook his head disgustedly. "Every one of those projects I took on in the past felt absolutely certain to be successful. And I controlled the key elements. This one I know in my gut is doomed."

"Even with the other projects, you agonized over them before you moved ahead. You analyzed the Omni-Vee thing until you drove me nuts."

Michael nodded. "I did. I admit it. You kept saying 'do-it, do-it, here's an idea about this, and that.'"

"You analyze and agonize over routine decisions. You've changed political parties so many times that you can't even go after a party nomination."

"But there was always a reason. You know that. At first, I didn't vote. I felt the system was corrupt. Then, I signed up for the Peace and Freedom Party."

"Michael . . ." Teresa tried to interject.

"But that froze me out of the 1972 primary, and the dumb-dumb Democrats nominated unelectable George McGovern. So I decided that even though the major political parties were establishment puppet shows, I would always pick one so I could have a vote in the primaries."

"Michael," Teresa summoned more forcefully.

"I went Republican in 1976 to vote against right-wing cowboy Ronald Reagan. I was four years off on that one. I went Democrat in 1980 to vote for Teddy Kennedy against Carter, before I discovered he wasn't a real Kennedy, and way before I discovered *none* of them were real Kennedys. I ended up voting for Anderson in the general election. Then I—"

"Michael," Teresa finally interrupted forcefully enough to get her husband to end his self-justification. "This is exactly what I mean! Who goes through all that?"

"No one," Michael admitted sheepishly.

"So I know you have to analyze this thing to death. But before you decide against it, I have a question for you. Suppose this Midas touch of yours, that has caused all these millions to fall in our laps, is for one purpose—for you to get into a position where you really can 'make the world a better place?' And suppose you don't try to do it? What does that make you? Another fat-and-happy yuppy, or something a lot worse?"

Michael drew a deep breath. "Teresa, I'm not sure what it would do to me to get into a fight like this and lose it."

Michael could see in her face that Teresa did not understand.

"I'll spend most of next year preaching what I think we need to do, asking the American people to adopt my ideas, spending most of my time with people who will believe in my vision and want us to implement it. I don't know what it will do to me if I have to walk away after the year's up, without the opportunity to put any of those ideas into action. On the book, the documentary, even Omni-Vee, I had ideas and put them into action. With this, I'll be running around the country for almost a year, begging to have the opportunity to try my plans of action, with the probability that I'll never get a chance to use them."

"Well, what will it do to you if you don't even try?"

Edwards smiled. "I'll turn into a lovable curmudgeon—I'll keep all the players honest with my caustic wit."

Teresa shook her head with a weak smile that evolved into grimace. "You don't do the 'lovable curmudgeon' thing very well at all. You're obnoxious, not lovable. And I didn't marry a curmudgeon. I married a man who really wants to 'make the world a better place,' who has taken charge of his surroundings and made things happen."

"I think this one will be too much . . ."

"Michael, you have to do this. I understand everything you're saying. And I'm very much afraid of what it might be like to live with you if you take this on and lose. But not to do it will ruin you as a person. You're right. You're not a fat-and-happy yuppy. This is the new challenge you've been looking for. To walk away from it would mean you are no longer who you've been for the last thirty years. And you know better than anyone how fluky the public stage is. You're not likely to get in this situation again. They'll find a new savior to drool over by next month." She paused, and Michael could see she was searching for the argument that would finally convince him.

"I'll make it even more personal," she continued. "What are you going to say to Barry McDowell, star of LOS ANGELES/APRIL 3RD? And what about the Jefferson family from Florida, and JEFFERSON ISLAND/SEPTEMBER 7TH? How will you explain to them that you didn't even try, that it was too much effort to fight for your ideas?"

"You want to do this, don't you?" Michael asked with a sly smile.

"Of course *I* do. But I'm the plunger. You're the cogitator, the analyzer, the contemplator. Before you jump into a pool, you need to know the temperature of the water, the chlorine content, when it was last cleaned and the wind velocity to make sure you land in just the right spot. I just jump in. I'll find out the temperature when I hit the water. I'll find out where I've landed when I come up for air."

"And you're ready to plunge."

"You couldn't start this up soon enough for me."

Edwards nodded slowly. "I think you may be right about this. I need the next challenge. But I won't do it as an exercise in futility." He paused. "Drew Saroyan owes me a favor. I'm going to ask him to meet with me and—"

"Discuss this thing to death."

"At least into a coma, yes."

Teresa groaned, but knew that this was progress.

"The bottom line is that if he can chart some kind of a strategy, a practical path toward victory, something I can visualize coming to fruition, then we'll take that plunge. If he tells me it's hopeless, then we'll stay dry until a better bet comes along."

"Okay," was all she said. Michael suspected she would still not give up trying to convince him, even if his talk with Drew Saroyan came to nothing.

Chapter 2

Early November: The Following Monday
Washington, D.C.

"YOU BEEN TRYING TO CALL ME?" MICHAEL EDWARDS ASKED DONALD Samuelson as he approached Samuelson's table at the G Street Cafe in Washington D.C., just up the street from the Capitol Building. Samuelson was sitting with three other colleagues, just about to bite into a sandwich for lunch. He was short, dark-haired, with a round face and a slight New England accent.

Edwards' surprise appearance stopped him in mid bite, but he tried, mostly successfully, to recover. "Yeah. Don't you know how to return a phone call?"

"Sometimes. I'm returning this one in person."

"Four days later." Samuelson started to bite into his sandwich again.

"First chance I had to come down here. I figured I'd catch you off guard at your favorite eating place so you'd have a tougher time gathering yourself to ream me out."

Samuelson again stopped short of biting into his sandwich. "Don't count on it."

"You wanna talk or not?" Edwards challenged. "I've got a table over in the corner. You got something you wanna say to me? Come over and put your fanny into a chair. Now, you can bite into your sandwich." Edwards turned abruptly and walked toward his table.

Samuelson turned to his lunch companions. "That son-of-a-bitch," he grumbled. He grabbed his lunch plate, but then put it back down. "Let him stew a few minutes." Samuelson finally bit into his sandwich.

Edwards enjoyed chopped lobster in a rich red cream sauce over rice as he sat reading, occasionally glancing up to see if Samuelson was coming over. He started to take another bite of his meal, then smirked as Samuelson approached and sat down in the empty seat at the two-person table. Edwards finished his bite, then reached into a basket of French bread, taking out a piece. He trained his eyes on Samuelson and nodded his head, continuing to smirk. "Bread?" he asked with mocking courtesy as he extended the piece of French bread.

"You have a slow news day last Friday?" Samuelson demanded, ignoring the offer.

Edwards replied as he buttered his bread. "Not really. Cheap shots at politicians with national reputations always make good news."

"And cheap shots by anchormen against their colleagues make pretty good stories too. Hell, you saved the senator's butt. He's looking like a martyr to media cruelty—a paragon of sincerity and righteous indignation. Are you on his staff now?"

"I spoke out against unfairness. You—"

"That guy should have been ready for me. He just showed he's not ready to play in the major leagues."

"That's not your call."

"I'm not making the call. The American people will."

"We can't keep choosing our leaders this way. We're ending up with bland resume leaders whose main strength is that they can handle assholes like you. Where are the visionaries going to come from if—"

"I don't want to hear your little editorial again. I'm just warning you, don't start a war with me. I want an apology."

"Oh, right," Edwards countered sarcastically. "You'll wait until the year *three* thousand for that."

"Then I'll wax your ass, Edwards."

"This is not personal. Don't take it that way. I'm not attacking you. I'm attacking *tactics* of yours, and others, who—"

"I didn't hear you mention any others."

"You and others in our profession," Edwards continued, "who are turning politics into garbage."

"Here's the fact, Edwards," Samuelson told him through a simmer. "You're starting to get caught up in all this hype that you should run for President. Even I've said some nice things about you, which I now thoroughly regret. You know how it works. The media might get carried away building someone up. But when the idiot starts to take the shit too seriously, and fancies himself God almighty, we'll take him down just as fast—hell, *faster*."

"So you're going to come after me? Is that what you're saying?"

"Not 'personal,' Edwards," Samuelson said, with a mocking emphasis on the word "personal." "I'll do it as a public service, to remove a pompous opportunist with delusions of grandeur from the public's admiration."

"You could try," Edwards acknowledged casually, "and you just might be able to make me another victim of a media barrage. And things will go on. Look at the clowns this system produces. President Kenneth Hampton. Senator Victor Parker. Wally Trewillinger, Roy Highland. These are the guys we have to choose from because your tactics drive off people—"

"Don't rehash that commentary again," Samuelson insisted. "Look," he said quietly after a momentary silence, "if you want to avoid a real war with me and my network, you'll do another commentary. You'll clarify that you were not attacking me personally, that you just disagree with me over tactics."

Edwards nodded. "Okay. I'll go along with that. Not because you threatened me, but because it's the fair thing to do. I'll also mention we aired our differences and do a pep-talk for the integrity of the media in general."

"Fine."

"Hatchet buried?"

Samuelson was cagy. "Maybe. You'll have to wonder. I'm telling you, I don't like being harangued for doing my job."

"Welcome to the big leagues, Samuelson."

Samuelson smiled mischievously as he got up from his chair. "I'm gonna enjoy it if you decide to run for President."

"Does this mean you won't vote for me?" Edwards asked with a mock whine as he stood up.

"You never know." Samuelson paused. "But I do appreciate you having the guts to come down here and talk this out with me." He extended his hand.

"Yeah," Edwards acknowledged as he took Samuelson's hand and shook it. "Look in on my broadcast tonight."

"Count on it." Samuelson walked casually back to his seat.

Edwards delivered a carefully crafted commentary that evening. He also made certain his audience knew he was clarifying and not apologizing.

☼   ☼   ☼

The Next Day: Tuesday
West Hollywood, California

"OKAY, YOU'VE FINALLY GOT THE REPORTS," PARKER STATED GRUFFLY. "Which speech do I give to these people?" Senator Parker and his chief campaign aide, Nicholas Mueller, met briefly before a fund-raising appearance in the banquet room of the Bohemian restaurant. They sat in a small, messy office, reluctantly lent to them by the owner of the Bohemian. The interior of the restaurant itself was elegant in a tacky, Hollywood way, looking better on film, or in brochures and magazines, than in person, like a talk show or game show set. The owner hesitated to allow outsiders into the office because its shabby condition was so contrary to the chic public image the restaurant enjoyed. But this was a $5,000 a plate dinner—a favor to these customers was hard to refuse.

"You know how I feel about that quitting speech under *any* circumstances," Mueller insisted firmly. Tall, thin, with short, straight, brown hair and studious-looking, black-rimmed eyeglasses, Mueller was Parker's long-time friend and campaign manager for his last four elections, all victories. At heart, a child of the 60's, he still considered himself a practitioner of the peace, love and understanding ethic, alive, as he saw it, among contemporary liberal Democrats.

"Just give me the results," Parker ordered.

"Not really that bad," Mueller told him, pleasantly surprised, as he shuffled some papers, preparing to expand his answer. "They point to—"

"Don't spin it for me," Parker said impatiently. "Just give it to me straight."

Mueller nodded, then smiled slightly. "Okay. You lost a little. But Senator, you're still the Democratic front-runner, and you'd still beat President Hampton if the election was held today."

Parker squinted in disbelief. "I lose my cool on TV, curse out a reporter, and just 'lose a little?'"

"It's Edwards." Mueller smiled. "Talk about spin—he spun this thing better than we could have done it ourselves. When he went after Samuelson and called him smutty and slimy, he distracted everyone with the story of battling super-reporters. A lot of people are talking about *that*."

"So Edwards has saved me?"

"That's why we took so long to finalize our poll results," Mueller told him. "We ran it twice. The second time, we asked if people had seen the Edwards commentary or were aware of it. Of those people, only two per cent already supporting you changed their minds. And over eighty per cent said your . . . your burst of temper, would not have any influence on whether they'd vote for you."

"So I'm giving a fund-raising speech—we're still in the hunt."

"We're still in the *lead.*"

A smile slowly crept onto Parker's face. "Edwards." He shook his head. "You know that son-of-a-bitch is going to run against us."

"I don't think so," Mueller dismissed. "It's not really his type of gambit."

"Really? It's flashy, public . . ."

"You think he'll go third party?"

"That's the only way he could do it," Parker assured Mueller confidently. "And I'm telling you, it would be just like him."

"A third-party run is almost a sure loser. The *best* he can do is be a spoiler. It's a long-hours, low-odds proposition."

"The word is, he's got a meeting set with a high-powered political consultant," Parker sprung on Mueller smugly.

"What?" Mueller was genuinely surprised. "Who?"

"Maybe Will Runalli . . ."

"That guy?" Mueller asked with squeamish disbelief. He shrugged. "Maybe the munchkin-mouth could be of some use to Edwards. But he's a hardball player. Edwards is a smoothy."

"Good combination."

"You sure it's Runalli?"

"I don't really know," Parker told him. "I was teasing you a little. Runalli has actually been contacting *us.*"

"Oh no," Mueller blurted out apprehensively.

"Don't worry. We'll reward Edwards' good deed for us by recommending Runalli to him."

Mueller smiled.

"Well, I better go out and pitch the cause," Parker observed. "Thanks to good old flashy, handsome-to-die-for Michael Edwards, we've got a campaign to get on with."

They left the office and headed to the banquet room.

☼   ☼   ☼

Mid November, The Year Before the Election: Monday
New Orleans, Louisiana

ZACHARY FADIMAN WAS THE LONE DINER IN THE PRIVATE BANQUET ROOM
of "Le Cochon Rouge" restaurant on Bourbon Street in the French Quarter
of New Orleans. He sat at a table in the back of the expensively elegant
room, with his back to the back wall. Rows of empty tables, covered with
fresh place-settings, sat between Fadiman and the main entrance to the
room. A tuxedoed waiter placed his dinner in front of him. He looked
approvingly at the sliced lamb covered with a creamy mint sauce.

"Good," he told the waiter. Fadiman spoke precisely and
unemotionally, rarely smiling. This get-to-the-point manner, combined with
hard work and well-calculated moves, had built Fadiman Industries into
one of the most successful weapons suppliers in the world.

The other man with him, standing slightly to his right, was not eating.
He was big and burly, with a totally shaved head and a calculating manner
not unlike Fadiman's. He might have been in his forties, but his age was
obscured by his lack of hair and the mirrored glasses he wore. He held a
cellular telephone in his hand.

The phone rang. "Yeah?" answered the burly man. He heard the
response, nodded, then said to Fadiman, "He's here, alone." The security
man asked into the phone, "His tail?" He listened then commented to
Fadiman. "The DEA tail is with him, but won't be able to track him in
here without blowing cover."

Fadiman nodded. "Tell them to show him in."

The burly man spoke into the phone. "You can bring him back."

The door of the banquet room opened and Ernesto Enriquez
swaggered in. He was dressed in a perfectly tailored European suit,
without a hair out of place. Fadiman, who had never met him face-to-face,
was surprised at how young he was—probably only in his late twenties.

"Mr. Fadiman," he greeted amiably, as he extended his hand.

Fadiman stood up, impassively took Enriquez' hand and shook it.

"Such precautions were not necessary," Enriquez chided gently as he
looked over at Fadiman's security man.

"You wanted to see me," Fadiman told him coolly. "I'm here."

Enriquez sat down at the table across from Fadiman. "You can take
my money for weapons, and for investments, but you don't like to sit down
with me?"

"You may be a good customer, and these days, they're hard to find.

But I don't care for your line of work, and I don't like you teaching kids to blow up police vehicles."

"Those 'kids,' as you call them, make very loyal street soldiers, and they don't get long prison sentences if they are caught. And I'm involved in many businesses, Mr. Fadiman—I own stock in some of yours."

"I can't control whether you buy stock in my publicly traded companies."

"I thought you were my friend. Maybe I should start taking my business to the French, or the Czechs, or the Russians," Enriquez countered, clearly becoming angry.

"Fine. They're a hemisphere away, and their stuff isn't half as good as what you can get from me. So—"

"Okay, okay."

"Look, we need each other," Fadiman conceded. "But I don't like to advertise our relationship."

Enriquez' opening politeness had eroded to a business-like tone. "You've made your point."

"So why is it you wanted to see me?"

"I always follow your politics," Enriquez explained, "because I need to see if it will affect my businesses. I am very disturbed by talk about this Michael Edwards running for your Presidency."

Fadiman shrugged. "So?"

"He could be very bad for my business."

Fadiman scowled dubiously. "I watch the guy," he said nonchalantly. "He's a great businessman. And he's not running yet. All he's said about your business—" Fadiman interrupted himself in mid sentence as he realized what Enriquez was worried about. "I get it," he said smiling. "Yeah, I can see how his approach might be a big problem for you."

"He's my worst nightmare. And I'll bet that some of his ideas will upset other businessmen in your country."

"Possibly. Who cares?"

"Aren't we all interested in a favorable business climate?"

Fadiman shook his head. "This is what you wanted to see me about?" He snorted. "If he runs, it'll have to be as a third party candidate. And these third party guys never get in. He'll make a bunch of noise, then end up in the back pages while Hampton gets reelected. And Edwards' approach to your . . . business—the American people will never buy it."

"Do your other friends, like your oil friend Hunter . . . does Hunter worry about him?"

"I have no idea," Fadiman lied.

"Mr. Fadiman, I *am* worried about this Edwards. And dealing with this kind of problem is something I would rather not do alone."

"There's no threat."

"I'm looking to make contact with businessmen who feel as I do. Will you pass my name along? I can be of immense help in ways that—"

"Reekay, don't get into things you don't understand."

"I would consider it a personal favor, as a very good customer, if you would pass my name along," Enriquez said more firmly.

"Why not?" Fadiman agreed easily, sensing Enriquez' growing irritation, and not willing to argue with him.

"And help me meet with those who share my concerns?"

"Sure, if they want to . . ."

"I sincerely hope your friends, like Mr. Hunter, will not be shy about making contact with me if they feel we can be of mutual benefit to each other," he said seriously, emphasizing each word.

Fadiman nodded, but didn't reply. He didn't like what seemed to be an implied threat.

Enriquez stood up. "Well, this is what I came to discuss. I'll look forward to hearing from you."

They shook hands.

Enriquez nodded, allowed a slight smile to come onto his lips, then made a brisk exit.

Fadiman turned to his security man. "Punk."

"But a dangerous punk," the security man added. "I'm not sure this meeting was a good idea."

"I know it *wasn't*," Fadiman agreed. "But I had no choice. He's one of my best customers right now. You know that son-of-a-bitch paid over ten times the market value of some of my most expensive high-tech stuff without even negotiating the price?"

"Those guys are drowning in money," the security man observed.

"While most of the governments of the world, including our own, are bankrupt, or verging on it. But no matter how much money these drug-punks get, they're always scheming to get more . . ."

The security man nodded.

"And I know there's more to his game than what he's saying. He's way too worried about all of this for a drug punk."

"You want me to check that out?"

"Yes. Very discreetly. I don't want to get blind-sided by this jerk, and if I know what he's *really* up to . . ."

Fadiman's security man nodded again. "I have some good sources in

South America."

"Good." Fadiman grinned briefly. "Hunter has asked for us to lay some groundwork on Edwards."

"Really."

"Yeah. I've got some ideas. I'll run them by you later, after dinner." The security man nodded.

Fadiman continued eating.

✷   ✷   ✷

Mid November, The Year Before the Election: Thursday Washington, D.C.

"THIS IS PRETTY FUNNY," PRESIDENT HAMPTON CHUCKLED AS HE reviewed a two-page, stapled document handed to him by the director of his re-election campaign, Covington Klondike. Both men were dressed casually for this informal meeting in the Oval Office. The President sat behind his neat desk; Klondike sat across from him. The President laughed out loud as he read further. "This is good." President Hampton was an attractive, muscular man, with wavy light brown hair.

Klondike smiled. When he graduated from Hastings Law School almost 40 years before, and took the best offer received from a prestigious Washington law firm, he had no idea how his career would evolve. But when the firm assigned him to a new client, young politician Kenneth Hampton, Covington Klondike quickly became Hampton's main attorney, and their association continued almost uninterrupted, right up to the day Hampton took the oath of office for the Presidency. Klondike was a large, flabby man with a few black and grey hairs left on his otherwise bald scalp.

"Uh, Cuv, this little gem can't get to the media," Hampton told Klondike, with a more serious tone.

"It won't," Klondike assured. "There were just a couple of us who put this together, kind of as a jumping-off point for discussion of the competition."

"Okay," the President acknowledged. "Then let's go over it. See what we might want to get started on . . ." He placed the document in the center of his desk where they could both refer to it simultaneously:

REELECTION CAMPAIGN - The Contenders

The Democrats

Senator Victor Parker: The Maryland beanpole, the
liberal's liberal and Democrat's Democrat. He's the
front-runner: has the Democratic connections and
resume to take the nomination (Junior Counsel to the
Ervin Watergate Committee in early 70's, Under-
Secretary of State under Carter and Secretary of
Education under Clinton). Has the ability to spread
the liberal fertilizer and make the stench smell sweet
long enough to win. He's the top competitor.

Mayor Jeffrey Jefferson: The former black panther and
Mayor of Newark has found respectability. He's even
taller and thinner than Parker; makes the Maryland
beanpole look like the Maryland crab. Great orator.
Nothing to say. A black leader, not a national leader,
no matter how many times he throws his hat into the
Presidential ring. Could get on the ticket as VP as a
politically-correct ethnic choice.

Senator Roy Highland: Republican in the Democratic
Party. Will try to out-Republican us and say he's the
more populist choice. Too jowly and southern-sounding
(from Florida) to win the general. Too offensive to
the hard-core bleeding heart wing of the Democratic
Party to win nomination, though he will get some
middle-of-the-road support and give Parker somewhat of
a bad time.

Governor Jane Teppleson: "Plain-Jane." Plain-looking,
dull-talking. Had a decent record as Governor of
Connecticut. Good at getting some things done through
hard work and negotiation. But her robotic style
should remind voters of Dukakis of 1988. Too boring to
do much. Could end up as VP choice as a politically-
correct gender choice.

Congressman Wallace Trewillinger: Professor of the
irrelevant, hero of the grampa-spectacle, bow-tie, and
suspender industries, winner of Captain Kangaroo look-
alike contests. Also the choice of eggheads, but
incapable of capsulizing views into digestible bites
for the popular media. His views will confuse almost
everyone; the media will pulverize his long-winded
treatises into incomprehensibility. Thinks long career

as professor and consultant on foreign relations, and just one term as Congressman from Massachusetts, qualifies him for President. Will not appeal to Mr. and Mrs. Middle America. Will get knocked out of the race early.

The Republicans

President Kenneth Hampton: Our fearless hero. Deserves a second term with more cooperative Congress. Good golfer. Great campaigner. Polls pessimistic right now, but a long way to go. Will kick rears in November.

Vice President Frances Willis: Will she or won't she? Only her bleeding heart fellow frumpy female constituency knows for sure. Politically correct gender VP choice for us last election. Turned out to be the worst team player since Brutus stabbed Caesar and Delilah shaved Samson. Can't take away the nomination, but could do damage with a challenge.

"So Parker's the guy to beat, and he's still in the race," President Hampton observed.

"Yeah," Klondike agreed. "I think he's the only one of these clowns who can beat you. But he leads in the head to heads right now, and he's the Democratic front-runner. Maybe most importantly? He's way ahead of the others on the fund-raising."

Hampton nodded. "I'd rather have one of these other people, but I think we can handle Mr. Parker. Hopefully they'll beat each other up for a few months. And hopefully Willis doesn't get into this thing and try to beat *me* up."

Klondike smiled.

"What about a third party?"

"I don't think we'll have one this year. I've got to tell you, we could use a liberally-oriented third party candidate to suck up some anti-incumbent votes away from—"

Klondike's cellular phone rang. "It's my private line," he told the President, implying that the call could be important.

Hampton nodded his approval for Klondike to take the call.

"Hello?" Klondike's expression became suddenly serious. "Okay . . . No . . . No, I'll talk to you more later . . . Yeah, I'm in a meeting . . . Yes . . . Bye."

Klondike exhaled a long breath as he ended the call and slipped his cellular back into his front shirt pocket. "We have another candidate."

"Willis," Hampton said quietly.

"Yup. She'll announce tomorrow."

"We've got to get her out of this thing as quickly as we can," Hampton told him, now coldly serious.

"I know. I'll get our best people working on it."

President Hampton picked up the candidate summary, and allowed a slight smile to creep onto his face as he reread the section on former Vice President Willis. But his smile disappeared as he finished reading. "Any other copies of this?" he asked.

"I'm not sure."

"Make sure this is the only copy." President Hampton folded the document in half and stood up. The meeting was over.

☼   ☼   ☼

Mid November: The Next Day, Friday
New York City, New York

"GOOD EVENING. FORMER VICE PRESIDENT FRANCES WILLIS HAS announced that she will challenge President Kenneth Hampton for the Republican nomination," Edwards told his news audience buoyantly, with a subtle tone of drama and excitement in his voice as he began the evening's broadcast. "She has taken this unprecedented step because she is dissatisfied with President Hampton's approach to various recent issues, as she detailed in her announcement, made at 1:00 today in Chicago, Illinois."

A short videotape excerpt of the announcement now ran. Frances Willis was dignified though not pretty, slightly overweight with pleasantly-styled frosty brown hair. She stood at a lectern in a fairly large auditorium. "I cannot stand by while my party betrays its constituents, constituents whom *I* implored to vote Republican for President in the last election," she insisted firmly. "This is not just about women's issues, though the veto of the Day Care Subsidy Bill, and the continual attempts to ram Supreme Court nominees down our throats who have no respect for a woman's right to control her own reproductive organs, are definite indications of President Hampton's disregard for the concerns of most of the women in this country. But the President also continues to support big business over small business, profits over the health of people in places that are fouled and filthy, and abstract economic double-talk over desperate homeless citizens living in the streets."

The excerpt ended.

Edwards continued. "So President Hampton will now have a challenge from within his party, which confronts him at a time when his approval rating is at its lowest point in over two years. President Hampton originally chose Frances Willis to balance the Republican ticket during the last election, but signs of strain between the two began to show even during the campaign. Some of her less conservative views, such as her pro-choice stance on abortion, gave her compatibility problems with the President. The rift widened after they took office, culminating with Frances Willis's unprecedented resignation earlier this year. This challenge has to be especially troublesome for President Hampton, since the conventional wisdom is that Frances Willis's presence on the ticket may have made the difference in his narrow defeat of his Democratic opponent last election. After Congress confirmed Burt Dooley, the long-time Republican Congressman, as interim Vice President, neither President Hampton nor Vice President Dooley made any public commitments that Vice President Dooley will remain on the ticket. So the Republican Party appears to be in a state of some confusion at the present time.

"With Frances Willis's announcement today, the slate of candidates running to secure the Democratic and Republican nominations for the upcoming Presidential election appears to be set. Andrew Talbot of our Washington bureau will help us take a look at each of these candidates. Andy?"

Michael watched the monitor as it cut to Andrew Talbot, a young network reporter who was not only bright and hard-working, but had great presence in front of the camera. "Thank you, Michael."

Andrew Talbot rendered a bite-driven, well-organized presentation on the candidates, in the best tradition of television news. Edwards himself had delivered similar reports in the past. But tonight, as Edwards watched, he felt more and more disgusted as he saw each candidate reduced to oversimplification. How many viewers would rely on these incomplete and hopelessly cursory capsules to decide which leader to choose? Even more upsetting to Edwards was the realization that those candidates who could reduce their messages and identities most effectively into these capsules were the ones who would have the most success in the electoral process. Unfortunately, the skills it took to capsulize themselves successfully did not transfer at all to the work of actually fashioning effective policies to deal with the complex challenges facing the country.

But Edwards actually found he enjoyed the last part of Talbot's report:

"This election year, many of the experts are saying that the problems of the country are too overwhelming and complex for one person to grasp and deal with. They also argue that the system is becoming unworkable, with the President as the only nationally elected leader, charged with governing the entire country, while the representatives elected to Congress are obligated to place local priorities ahead of national ones. So many experts have concluded that one-term Presidents, and an escalating anti-incumbent attitude toward Congressional representatives and whatever party is in power, will continue to be common. The voters, frustrated with a lack of progress by government in solving the nation's complex problems, will routinely vote incumbent Presidents and Congressional representatives out of office.

"These seven candidates will be dealing with that reality. Aside from small straw polls, their first major test will be at the Iowa Caucuses on Monday, January 22nd, followed by the first full-blown primary in New Hampshire on Tuesday, February 15th. Until then, everyone can run with the optimism of being undefeated, though untested. Back to you, Michael."

"Thank you, Andy. A federal judge in New York ordered the early release of 36 more inmates from Attica State Prison today due to overcrowding beyond federally mandated guidelines. This was the third such release in the last six months, despite near-violent protests outside the Federal Court . . ." Edwards finished the rest of the broadcast, with the show proceeding almost exactly as planned, down to the second.

✿   ✿   ✿

"GREAT BROADCAST," JESSUP TOLD EDWARDS AS HE WALKED ONTO THE set at the conclusion of the show.

"Thanks," Edwards answered with a perfunctory smile.

"I think Andy did a nice job of profiling the candidates. He's improving every day."

"Oh yeah," Edwards quipped sarcastically. "He pulled out those sound-bites flawlessly—he did a beautiful job of trivializing all of the candidates, in the best tradition of TV news."

Jessup heaved an irritated sigh. "What're we supposed to do? A two hour special on them? All three viewers who would tune in would be asleep before it was over."

"Yeah. That's our alibi. Blame our audience. They're too stupid—their attention spans are too short . . ."

"You know, all of our research shows that—"

"I know," Edwards interrupted irritably. "That's why Ross Perot's amateur productions drew such huge ratings in 1992."

"This research is—"

"Yeah, I know, very scientific." Edwards paused. "I would just like to know what all this does for LOS ANGELES/APRIL 3RD, and JEFFERSON ISLAND/SEPTEMBER 7TH."

"That's not our job."

"So we always say."

"You have a suggestion?"

"Yeah. I'm going home." Edwards got up from the set as he grabbed his papers.

"If you can think of a better way to do this . . ."

But Edwards had walked away.

"Well, I think that was a nice broadcast," Jessup called out to everyone who could hear him.

Edwards heard Jessup's words. He emitted a knowing, fatalistic smile as he cruised over into his office. He tossed the papers he was carrying onto his desk, and grabbed his briefcase, determined to make a quick exit. But he stopped—he was forgetting something.

Edwards walked over to a filing cabinet and opened it up. Two videocassettes sat on top of stacks of other books and papers. Edwards pulled them out. He didn't have to check them—they were the only videocassettes he kept in this filing cabinet. But he did anyway. They were labeled "LOS ANGELES/APRIL 3RD" and "JEFFERSON ISLAND/SEPTEMBER 7TH." He pulled them out and put them in his briefcase, shoved the filing cabinet drawer shut and left quickly.

Chapter 3

Just After Midnight, the Following Morning
New York City, New York

"I'LL GET IN DEEP < BLEEP > FOR SAYING THIS," POLICE OFFICER BARRY McDowell stated bluntly, "but we are *losing* this war. I don't care how many numbers the President wants to trot out. We are *losing*." Michael Edwards sat bleary-eyed in the small bedroom of their apartment that he used as his study. The lights were all off—the room was dark except for the flickering of a small 13-inch television monitor, part of a combination videocassette-television, and a computer screen sitting to its right, both on the computer stand. He was watching "LOS ANGELES/APRIL 3RD," specifically, the interview he had conducted with Officer McDowell that had captured national attention after it aired. As he heard the word "losing," he felt a jolt of determination, and his hands moved quickly to his computer keyboard, which clattered as his fingers energetically translated his thoughts into words.

"Do you think this attitude is generally shared by—" But Edwards' interview question was cut short as the momentum of McDowell's emotions carried him past listening to Edwards' next question.

"You know what they told us?" he continued, with his eyes glistening. "When we told them we would need weapons and training to counter what the drug gangs have now? They told us it's not in the budget."

Teresa poked her head through the doorway and gently interrupted.

"Michael, you've got Drew Saroyan coming here tomorrow morning."

"I know," Michael acknowledged quietly as he stopped his fingers and then the tape for a moment. "What time is it?"

"Letterman just ended. So it's—about twelve-thirty."

Edwards smiled. "Letterman? You're not watching After Hours on WWBS?"

"Maybe tomorrow night."

"It's not on Saturday nights."

"Oh darn," she wisecracked sarcastically. "What're *you* watching?" But as she glanced at the television screen, she answered her own question. "Again?"

Edwards grinned. "Again . . . *still*." He looked over at the videocassette boxes he had brought home, which now sat empty on his desk. "I decided to organize my basic ideas for Drew, so it's on paper, and it's easy for him to see how everything tracks."

Teresa nodded her understanding and stifled the impulse to tell Michael he should try to get some sleep. She left the room.

Michael finished inputting the thought Teresa had interrupted, then resumed watching "LOS ANGELES/APRIL 3RD." He recalled how he had convinced Ted Jessup that the events occurring in a small cul-de-sac of South Central Los Angeles were compelling enough to send the WWBS anchorman out to the area for comprehensive coverage. None of the other networks had even featured the events the day they had happened.

The startling events had resulted from what was supposed to be a record drug arrest, the product of brilliant and meticulous police-work by the DEA and LAPD working together. They had determined that ten million dollars worth of uncut cocaine had come into the United States and was on its way to a South Central neighborhood for distribution. They had allowed the shipment to proceed into the neighborhood because the leaders of the South American drug cartel involved in the shipment were scheduled to be on hand for its arrival. Not only would they seize a record quantity of contraband, but they would also apprehend major foreign players, in the United States, and in possession of enough contraband to put them away for more than a few lifetimes.

This Los Angeles neighborhood had been completely taken over by drug-trafficking. At the end of the cul-de-sac were three houses linked together in a single structure that looked like a cross between a fortress and a drive-thru restaurant. It was evident that at one time in the recent past, these were separate, single-family houses. Now they were forged together for quite a different purpose. Along the block, leading up to the end of the cul-de-sac, was a series of houses on both sides of the street. Arson and other forms of violent intimidation had been used to buy, or appropriate, homes on the block for the drug dealers. Police detectives were frustrated since they knew exactly what had happened, but could not get terrified witnesses to testify at prosecutions. This operation meant vindication was at hand. Three LAPD battering rams and a fleet of well-armed police officers moved into the area, along with DEA operatives—the mood was almost euphoric. Officer Barry McDowell felt it. He was familiar with the area as a patrol officer. And he was thrilled that he would be a part of the force about to deal with this notorious pocket of crime and corruption.

But when the police moved in, they found themselves fighting for their lives, as anti-tank missiles were launched into the battering rams, then into the police and police cars. Gang members for the drug cartel had taken up positions in the houses flanking the sides of the cul-de-sac. Police were trapped between overlapping fields of fire in the street. Any ideas of taking possession of the cocaine or the cartel leaders were abandoned quickly. The police fled for their lives. The National Guard came quickly into the area the following day, but by then, the area had been abandoned. The cost of a block of real estate in the declining South Central area of Los Angeles was just a cost of doing business for the drug cartel. They would find another cul-de-sac, and open up another drive-thru drug-mart.

For Officer McDowell, the shock of being so completely outgunned by criminals was bad enough. But his most poignant recollections came as he saw a heartsick, sweaty, smudge-faced boy of no more than eleven emerge from one of the houses flanking the cul-de-sac. A stray missile, poorly aimed, had devastated the house across the street. The boy looked in terror toward the smoldering ruins across from him. He was a dark-haired, Hispanic boy, wearing a blue bandanna around his head. He broke into sobs and tears rolled down his cheeks as he called out softly and plaintively: "Pepito." Police officers, including McDowell, trained their weapons on him, but he was obviously not armed, and nearly oblivious to the threat of the police. McDowell was stunned with how young this boy was. His surprise would multiply geometrically later that night when he assisted rescuers as they pulled the body of the boy's nine-year old brother, "Pepito," from the charred, smoky bricks and wood of the house across the street. An errant missile had been launched from the house the sobbing boy emerged from—Pepito's brother had killed him.

"The city, the state, the feds—they're all bankrupt." McDowell continued his response during Edwards' interview of him. "We can't afford to go at these guys weapon for weapon. So we'll write off parts of the city—that's when I told them we were losing the <bleep>ing war."

Edwards let him run long with this statement. McDowell's heartfelt, strong emotions were powerful television, and his revelations were dramatic.

"'Don't tell anyone you think we're losing, or we'll take your badge.'"

Edwards started to follow-up. "You mean they threatened to fire you if you—"

But McDowell was still in mid-tirade. "Mr. Edwards," he added sternly, "my father fought in Viet Nam. He told me how the government kept <bleep>ing with the casualty numbers to make it look like we were winning. We *lost*. And that war really messed up my father—I don't think he ever got over it. Now they're doing the same thing with this war on drugs. Well I won't take it! They can have their <bleep> damn badge!"

"So you're resigning from the force?"

"You got ears! I'm not going to <bleep>ing Viet Nam. Even when it has come to me! <Bleep> that <bleep>!" McDowell stormed away from the interview.

Edwards and McDowell eventually became friends. Edwards was intrigued with the street-wise son-of-a-Viet-Nam-vet who had single-handedly assaulted the "war on drugs" strategy and claims of success. Edwards helped McDowell get a book on drug enforcement strategies (and their failures) published by recommending McDowell to a literary agent. But Edwards was painfully aware that though McDowell had survived, there were still cul-de-sacs in the nation's cities that were little more than tribute ceded to powerful drug-lords.

Edwards rewound the tape. The "war on drugs" had been going on in one form or another since he was a boy. From the hippie drug culture of the 60's to the brutal gang violence of the 90's, the policies concerning illegal drugs had gotten more destructive. The situation was clearly not improving—it was deteriorating. Edwards exhaled a deep breath. He had stated frequently what he thought was the only logical and obvious way to "win" the war. But no one in power was even on the right track. Would it take his candidacy, and his victory, to implement his answer?

Edwards pulled "LOS ANGELES/APRIL 3RD" out of the videocassette machine and inserted "JEFFERSON ISLAND/SEPTEMBER 7TH."

Michael Edwards and WWBS had been ahead of this story. Hurricane Justine was due to hit south Florida in slightly over 24 hours. By all predictions, this promised to be the third storm of catastrophic proportions to ravage the Gulf Coast during the previous decade. And this one had the potential to be the worst of all of them. So WWBS, including Michael Edwards, had come south to Florida to highlight preparations for another round of climatic wrath for this beleaguered part of the country.

The other major networks concentrated on Miami. But Michael wondered about the Florida Keys. At first, he thought of looking at Key West, but he discovered what he thought would be an even better story.

Edwards and the WWBS crew went out to Jefferson Island, a few miles west of Islamorada Island. Islamorada Island was one of the islands linked by the Keys bridge, boasting a World War I memorial, along with typical Keys tourist resorts. But Jefferson Island was privately owned by Violet Jefferson-Clarke, and reachable only by a short boat-ride from Islamorada. Rather than focusing on the typical stories of how large communities and businesses were gearing up to face the meteorological onslaught, Edwards and Jessup felt that a woman guarding her island from the elements made a more poignant, personal story. She was an impressive personality, an elderly but energetic lady, related by blood to Thomas Jefferson. She supervised the sandbagging operations on the island that had been in her family for eight generations as she gave a spunky interview to Michael Edwards. They sat on the porch of her colonial-style mansion, not far from the island's best beach, and the only structure on the small island. The island was approximately a half mile across, and five hundred yards up-and-down. It was flat—there was a slight rise constructed for the house.

The storm would turn out to be one of the worst ever recalled in the area, even in the context of the ferocious storms that had occurred during recent years. Sheets of wind-whipped rain flooded coastal areas, inflicting widespread damage despite precautions, and killing almost one hundred people. Huge waves rose up and pounded the Keys, knocking down even heavily fortified coastal structures. Water inundated most coastal areas, with structures either eroded by the fury of the waves, or even dragged right off the coasts into the sea. The Keys bridge was seriously damaged and submerged in several places.

WWBS had the footage the other networks had—the shots of palm trees bent at awkward, strained, sideways angles by the winds, and the aftermath shots of pockets of devastated buildings and inundated regions. They could run those shots and not lose a rating point, or risk having their coverage labeled as inadequate.

But Edwards knew that the Violet Jefferson-Clarke story was the type of angle on the storm that would distinguish WWBS. He had laid the foundation for the story. Now he would follow-up with the story's ending. The audience would hunger to know what had happened to this stubborn, admirable woman.

"Where's the island!?" Edwards yelled to the pilot over the loud noise of the helicopter rotors as they circled. One cameraman accompanied them in the small helicopter, which was cramped and uncomfortable.

"Supposed to be right here!" the pilot replied.

"You sure your heading was correct?" Edwards asked frustratedly.

"Absolutely!"

Edwards slumped back irritably. His great human angle on this story was disappearing because of what appeared to be a chopper pilot's bad navigational abilities. He stared out over the water sternly as he pondered what to do. The helicopter continued to circle, decreasing altitude.

Edwards spotted something. "Get closer to the water!" he requested.

The chopper moved slowly down toward the water and began more circling. It was ten minutes later that Edwards saw what he had just glimpsed earlier. The jagged edges of the roofless walls from the Jefferson Island mansion were protruding a few feet above the still choppy waters of the surface of the ocean. Jefferson Island was now under water. And Violet Jefferson-Clarke had disappeared with her island, never to be found. Another circling got them close enough to see beneath the water. Edwards could see the broken, toppled, piles of sandbags that were supposed to keep the water from engulfing the island.

"That *is* the fucking island!" Edwards told the chopper pilot.

Edwards had little trouble convincing Ted Jessup to get underwater photographers into the area. That evening, WWBS led with stunning footage of the stately colonial mansion on Jefferson Island before the storm, followed by footage of the same mansion, photographed with crystal clarity, as it stood roofless and disintegrating under water. The pictures were even a financial success for WWBS. Three major news magazines ran both images on their covers, with the "before" image on the left and the underwater "after" image on the right. One magazine ran the cover caption "Are We Entering the Greenhouse Century?" Another read "The Disappearing Coasts." And the third simply showed in bold script the dates of both pictures, taken two days apart. True, most of the island reemerged above water over the subsequent weeks. But this image stood for more than just the fate of this one island in the Florida Keys. And Edwards discussed its significance in broader terms during his commentary that evening.

"Flooding has been a recurring nightmare all over the world in recent years," Edwards told his audience. "Experts worry that south Florida, the Mississippi River delta near New Orleans, and the Galveston area near Houston, Texas, may all be under water in the next 50 to 100 years. Major floods have ruined property and lives all along the Mississippi River three times in the last ten years.

"Around the world, similar catastrophic floods have occurred in this decade. Bangladesh has had three major floods in its low-lying regions, accounting for half a million deaths as the swelling population has caused poorer citizens to expand into marginal areas of the Ganges River basin almost certain to flood. Catastrophic flooding has hit Egypt's low-lying areas along the Nile, and the entire area may be vulnerable to even a moderate storm. Floods have also devastated significant areas of Bangkok, Thailand and Venice, Italy in well-publicized storms during the last three years. So this is a worldwide trend. And it brings me to my commentary for this evening.

"One of the issues we hear little discussion of by our leaders is global warming," Michael Edwards said gravely to the camera. "Yet the consequences for this nation, for this *entire planet*, will be cataclysmic if the planet's temperature increases by just a few degrees centigrade.

"A lot of discussions I hear pertain to whether or not there is a global warming trend, or a so-called greenhouse effect. And many remember the late 70's, when some climatologists were convinced that we were entering a new Ice Age. I hope past overreaction to transitory climatic cycles does not lull us into complacency. Because to me, it is obvious that global warming has already begun. We have personally noticed, over recent years, hotter summers, milder winters and weird weather patterns that point to global disruptions in the meteorological status quo. Recorded temperatures in most major cities are following an increasing trend. And a large proportion of the hottest temperatures ever recorded at many locations have been recorded in the last ten to fifteen years.

"But let's assume for a moment that we aren't currently at the beginning of a global warming. I hope that's true. That means nature is giving us some extra time. But by all accepted laws of physics, we must enter a global warming soon. The amounts of greenhouse gases, especially CO_2, dumped into the atmosphere due to the consumption of fossil fuels and deforestation, have increased dramatically. A global warming is absolutely inevitable, based on those verified quantitative measurements. To believe otherwise is to ignore scientific fact completely, saying 'I'll pretend the laws of physics and chemistry don't exist so I can ignore this problem.'

"But we will inevitably be forced to face it. So it only makes sense for us to face this problem squarely *now*, before the sea levels rise and flood our coastal towns, before our farmlands become deserts—before it will be impossible to avoid disruption and tragedy on a scale we can only barely imagine now.

"I challenge our leaders to make themselves heard on this issue. Not with public relations lip service. Bring us answers with vision. Please don't suggest short-sighted solutions like burning natural gas instead of coal because it produces less CO_2. And don't suggest pass-the-buck solutions like resolutions to get Brazil to burn less of its forest or get Third World nations to reduce their birth rates. We must accept our *own* contribution to this situation and take steps to adjust our *own* behavior that contributes to it. This network will enthusiastically cover such proposals to this challenge.

"Good night, ladies and gentlemen, and thanks for bringing us into your homes this evening."

The theme music and credits rolled.

Michael Edwards watched as the television screen turned snowy. His sentiments hadn't changed from that night in Miami when he had delivered the commentary. But again, he now felt he had answers and was certain of the practicality of his solutions. He had stated his ideas, but they had never been taken seriously by anyone in power. People around the country, familiar with his ideas, were asking him to put himself forward as a possible leader of the country. It was unlikely such a groundswell of support would ever self-generate like this again. But what would it take for him succeed? Was it a vanity move, a plunge into ego that would leave him spent and disillusioned when it was over? His meeting with Drew Saroyan would settle his final choice.

Chapter 4

The Same Day
New York City, New York

"So MICHAEL EDWARDS WANTS TO CROSS THE LINE AND BECOME A player," Drew Saroyan teased as Michael and Teresa Edwards greeted him at the door of their apartment. Saroyan's baby face only now showed signs of his fifty years. Michael knew Drew had finally made peace with his workaholic nature, after three divorces. When he took on a high-profile political campaign, nothing else mattered to him. He gained personal satisfaction through the success of his candidates, and had simply eliminated the complications of a personal life.

"I'm not crossing any lines yet," Edwards replied. He and Teresa ushered Saroyan into the living room where he and Michael sat down on a plush couch. Teresa sat on a chair, at a right angle to them. Saroyan put his briefcase down on the coffee table in front of them.

"I know. You just gotta let me savor the irony of this."

"Yeah. We're usually the other guys."

"I'd say often the villains. But all kidding aside, I'll never forget the break you cut for my guy in '96."

"Congressman Nelson's little secret was his own business. It wasn't important to the election—he was going to lose that governor's race in a landslide anyway. What was I going to accomplish except mess up his life to satisfy my ego with an exclusive?"

"But we both know, there are guys in your business who would've jumped on that story regardless. I owe you. This little meeting is a way I can express my gratitude."

"And your input will help me a lot."

"Okay. So you're thinking of running for President . . ."

"Yeah. I'd use my own money to seed it, then rely on contributions."

"With a political party?"

Michael glanced over at Teresa and they shared a knowing smile. "I don't know if that would work."

"He's belonged to most of them at one time or another," Teresa commented, amused.

Saroyan nodded. "I get the picture."

"I think I would be most effective as a third candidate with no party affiliations. My positions on the issues will be a little unconventional—"

"That's what I suspected you would want to do," Saroyan interjected.

"You know me; you know politics. Am I out of my mind?"

"Yes," Saroyan answered immediately. "But anyone who wants that job is out of his mind. You're asking me what your chances are."

"Or what my strategy should be."

"Fair enough. I have some ideas, based on a general understanding of what you stand for. But I need to know what your campaign will be about."

"Okay." Michael Edwards raised his eyebrows, shrugged, and handed Drew Saroyan the document he had crafted the night before.

Saroyan narrowed his eyes thoughtfully as he took the pages. "Okay. Give me a minute."

"Sure."

Saroyan appeared to read slowly and carefully, not rushing his assessment just because Teresa and Michael were waiting.

Saroyan finished reading, drew a deep breath, and without changing his expression, popped open his briefcase and stared at three pages of paper stapled together. He then pulled out a lap-top computer, along with a printer, and quickly punched some information into his keyboard.

Edwards observed curiously and impatiently. What was Saroyan's reaction?

Teresa was wary, as if she felt Saroyan was toying with them.

"I have to tell you," Saroyan told him finally, "that I am impressed. And it is not easy to impress me. It's nice to see how all these ideas you've been expressing fit together."

"Thank you."

"I need you to answer one other question. Is your strategy to win outright, or to get your proposals some national attention?"

"I have a news program that gives me national attention. If I do this, I want to *win*."

Saroyan nodded. "I won't mince words—the odds would be huge against you. But it's not impossible. And I know how we'd do it. We'd start by—"

"'We?'"

Saroyan smiled. "If you do this crazy thing, you will hire me to run it, won't you?"

"You really want to?"

"Yeah. It would be uphill, my biggest challenge in years." He paused. "And for the first time in years I would feel I was working on something I believed in one hundred per cent."

"I *have* impressed you."

"Yeah, yeah, yeah," Saroyan snapped irritably, "and that's enough gushing for today. Now let me tell you the strategy, and you can decide if you really want to go through with this. We need to address three strategy areas. First, we need to decide when and how to highlight your specific views on these issues, and which issues to focus on."

Teresa moved uncomfortably in her chair.

"Your discussions of the deficit and national debt are the least controversial, and the least inspiring. Your environmental program, which from my first glance also looks like a visionary economic program, is *brilliant*, and we will probably want to lead with it. Your 'atomic bomb' of the war on drugs . . ." Saroyan's voice trailed off.

"It's got to be there," Edwards insisted.

"Yeah. But we ought to hold it back. Your doomsday weapon will not be immediately embraced by the electorate. Let's get a following before we spring it."

Edwards nodded, acknowledging and absorbing, not necessarily agreeing.

"Your foreign policy ideas are also good, but ever since the 'red scare' disappeared, people don't get as excited with foreign policy issues. In fact, candidates are often accused of neglecting this country if they focus too much on the problems of the other ones."

"So the environmental program is where we hang our initial hat—good."

"Yup. I read this thing, but now I want you to tell it to me conversationally, as if you're telling a story to a room full of admirers."

"Okay." Edwards thought a moment. "Hello America," he began casually. "In case you haven't gotten the word, the Industrial Revolution is over."

Saroyan smiled.

"The pundits and gurus of futuristics will tell you that we are entering the 'Age of Information.' But this faddish description of the new era is incomplete."

Saroyan nodded.

"People will not eat information, wear information, drive information to work, or use information to fuel their vehicles. The new era will still have to be concerned with how flesh-and-blood humans sustain themselves."

"So that brings us to what Michael Edwards calls . . . ta-da . . ." Saroyan signaled for Edwards to complete the introduction:

"The Regenerating Biosphere era."

"Bravissimo," Saroyan applauded daintily.

Michael grinned, but caught a glimpse of Teresa, who squirmed uneasily as she frowned.

"Now, a Regenerating Biosphere is basically recycling and using renewable resources?" Saroyan seemed less confident with this subject.

"I didn't have time to flesh that whole one out for you," Michael acknowledged. "Basically, the Industrial Revolution was fueled by burning pieces of the planet, and built by ripping up pieces of the planet and shaping them into the materials we needed. For the Regenerating Biosphere era, we will use inexhaustible energy sources that don't require us to burn off portions of the planet. That means those sources are clean, almost non-polluting. And, we will work to recycle materials already torn out of the earth's crust to manufacture the things we need to survive."

"Thank you, professor, I understood that part of it," Saroyan quipped. "It's all that cycle stuff that I'm not sure I follow. In fact, I'm not sure how important it is to bombard the American people with all this abstract theory. It'll be hard to communicate and may bog down your—"

"It's absolutely essential," Michael insisted. "The proposals I will make follow from the theories. People need to know that I'm not pulling ideas out of thin air. They need to know the reasoning behind what I will offer."

Saroyan pursed his lips skeptically.

"What you call the 'cycle stuff'—I think you're referring to linear and cyclical consumption."

"Yeah."

"During the Industrial Revolution, consumption was linear. During the Regenerating Biosphere era, it will be cyclical."

Saroyan's facial expression told Edwards he could have been speaking in a foreign language.

"Okay. Linear consumption: Metal is extracted from the Earth's crust and built into an automobile. When it wears out, it goes to a junkyard. The start of this consumption line is the Earth's crust; the end of the consumption line is the junkyard. Another one: Farmers grow their produce and sell it to consumers, who eat and digest it. Human wastes result, which are then treated and released, often into streams or into the ocean. Start of the line—the farm. End of the line—the sewage treatment plant.

"Cyclical consumption—the metal from the discarded car becomes the metal for the new car through recycling. And the human waste is treated for use as fertilizer, with its nutrients placed back into the farmer's soil at the beginning of the consumption cycle."

"Alright, I get it," Saroyan acknowledged. "But isn't it enough just to offer the American public renewable resources and recycling? Do they need all this cycle stuff?"

"Some won't. But reanalyzing consumption patterns is absolutely essential if we are going to break out of the Industrial Revolution mindset. Right now, economists measure the health of an economy by totaling up natural resources and how well they're being utilized. 'Progress' is quantified by measuring how efficiently and quickly we are burning up our fuels and ripping up the earth's crust, without regard to the side effects the world is beginning to choke on. The cycles will allow a new framework for analysis, for quantifying 'progress' toward a Regenerating Biosphere. We'll look at how efficiently a given material goes through a consumption cycle: How much energy is needed to complete the cycle? How much virgin fuel or material is lost during the duration of the cycle, and has to be replaced when the cycle repeats? And, can those fuels or materials be reduced, once we know what we're using?"

Saroyan smiled cynically. "Some numbers-crunching economist'll win a Nobel Prize for sorting all this out in formulas and graphs."

Teresa exhaled irritably.

"Hey, I hope so," Michael countered seriously. "I hope he invites me to his victory party."

"He better," Saroyan added. "Okay, I'm with you. And most Americans'll agree with the goal. But they're not going to believe it's possible."

"I know. They've been sold on the idea that renewable energy is not feasible. But that's only because we're still trapped in the Industrial Revolution mindset."

"Decentralize power generation."

"Exactly," Michael agreed emphatically, pleased to see Saroyan apparently understood this concept. "So you know about this idea . . ."

Saroyan smiled. "I've heard you speak about it before, but it's one of my favorite Edwards raps. Tell me again—pretend I'm a cynical group of Americans listening to you."

"Cynical. Okay . . ." Michael gathered his thoughts for a quick moment, then began. "During the Industrial Revolution, we burned fuel in large power plants and beamed the power around on a grid to where we needed it. That was fine when we had huge furnaces and wanted to centralize the process in the interests of efficiency, and to contain pollution. But for renewable energy, let's be clear. Renewable energy is basically solar energy. Solar light for electricity or direct heat. Uneven solar heating of the atmosphere, causing temperature differentials, which cause wind currents. This type of energy is available all over the planet, but in diffuse amounts. Why would we want to concentrate it into power plants just to beam it back out again? Each structure should function as its own renewable energy center, capturing what's available right where it is, selling the excess to a local energy storage facility, and then drawing on that storage when extra energy is needed."

Saroyan nodded. "I've heard you give that message in a lot punchier tone," he said, as if criticizing a performer for a disappointing rendition of a favorite song. "We'll get a good commercial going for that one."

"Yeah. We'll remind everyone that according to the Worldwatch Institute, enough solar energy hits the earth's surface every day to supply the current electricity needs of human beings for *ten thousand years*. We just need to capture a small part of that energy, and stop trying to concentrate it when Mother Nature herself is supplying it all over the globe. And we need to tell about the successes using this idea that have already occurred. Like the energy study institute house in the Rocky Mountains that is completely energy self-sufficient. This same bunch has gathered evidence to indicate that if we simply practiced aggressive conservation strategies, we could end the need for foreign energy oil imports. This is *without* any use of renewables. And we'll tell about the school in New Hampshire that is heated totally by solar cells all but ten days of the year, and how at the turn of the last century, a large percentage of homes in California and Florida used solar hot water heaters. You can still see the damn things in pictures of homes from that period! Can you imagine how much more hot water could be heated by these things if we added another hundred years of technology to their designs?"

"Good specifics in there. Now what about recycling? To a lot of people, that's the homeless looking for empty cans."

Michael chuckled. "Study after study has shown that recycling is less costly than mining or some other method of gathering materials—it's cleaner and creates more jobs that are less dangerous. The only reason this gets obscured is because we're still trapped in the subsidies of the Industrial Revolution, which distort—"

"Hold it, hold it," Saroyan requested insistently with a palm up. "Let's keep it in order."

"Okay."

"Now let's say we have the American people sold on the Regenerating Biosphere—"

"You mean convinced?" Teresa interrupted caustically.

"Uh, sure, 'convinced' that the Regenerating Biosphere future is what they want, and that it is feasible," Saroyan said, not allowing the interruption to derail his train of thought. "Now we have to tell them how we get there."

"Right."

"They're gonna smell *taxes*—some big government program with grants, researchers, pilot projects . . ."

"Like oil shale."

"Yeah."

Michael shook his head grinning. "That oil shale mess came about because Jimmy Carter understood that we needed to move in a new direction on our energy consumption, but he thought like a *Democrat*. Get bureaucrats to solve it. Get big government to make it happen. And that never works. The Industrial Revolution wasn't created by government, and the Regenerating Biosphere era won't be either."

"But Michael, you're trying to take control of the most important job in the government. If government won't do it, then why are you trying to be part of it?" Saroyan was smirking, obviously playing devil's advocate.

"Because," Michael told him with emphatic relish, "government will create the climate for this transition to take root and spread, by galvanizing the awesome creative power of the Capitalist system and focusing it on the task."

"I know," Saroyan acknowledged, still smirking. "Governmental Economic Activism." He exhaled a long, trepidatious breath. "True Costs,

True Benefits. I hope we don't strangle ourselves on all this theory."

Michael smiled. "That's why I need to hire guys like you. You'll help me present all this properly."

"If it can be done. Okay, let's run down the basics. You've got two major components of Economic Activism . . ."

"Right. Government as consumer is the first. The Federal Government is one of the largest consumers in this economy—it consumes twenty per cent of the goods and services. So Government would get its suppliers to build structures with windmills and solar cells—with renewable energy systems managed by computers for maximum efficiency designed into them. Government would order electric or hydrogen-powered cars for their huge vehicle fleets whenever practical. You watch private enterprise jump into the picture. They'll try to supply the lowest bids. They'll innovate to create efficiency in their products and lower costs. That'll bring other consumers to these products as prices come down and quality improves. The government has done some of this already. But as President, I'll systematize the process, and make it a priority."

"That's the easy part," Saroyan observed. "There might be some initial higher costs, but in the long run, Government will save money with government buildings and vehicles using renewables."

"But this won't do the job alone."

"Nope. True Costs, True Benefits. Here's where things'll get dangerous, especially if the media chops it up."

"I know," Michael agreed as his eyebrows raised quickly, then lowered. "But this is where we must have the courage to propose the things that will really make a difference. This part of the plan is *essential*, because it will bring about the changes to everyday people that will make a real difference, and ultimately take us to the new era."

"And it's change that people always say they want, but secretly fear."

"Absolutely," Michael said. "That's why I like the term Regenerating Biosphere over the term I hear environmentalists use—Sustainable Future. That sounds very unexciting, a world where we're just scraping by, but not necessarily prospering or hoping for a *better* future. But we *can* hope for a better future. Cleaner and more prosperous. If we can get people to understand, and then really believe this, down to their shoelaces, we will be successful."

Saroyan nodded, first without expression, but then completed his nod as a slight smile crept onto his face.

"I'm making speeches to you now," Edwards observed, trying to read Saroyan's grin.

"Well, I've asked you to," Saroyan reminded him. "I'm just amazed, after all these years of listening to politicians make speeches, that I'm actually enjoying this."

"Should we go over True Costs and True Benefits?"

"Yeah. I saw it on paper. Let me see what it sounds like."

"It's simple. It's government using the taxation system to assess True Costs and compensate for True Benefits. In our Free Market system, the competing self-interests of buyers and sellers are balanced through competition in the marketplace. This system causes the most efficient utilization of the world's resources in the history of humanity. This works, because competing producers of the same product bring their products to market, trying to offer the best quality at the lowest price to maximize their own earnings. The producer who fails to manufacture his product efficiently will sustain higher production costs and will be unable to bring his product to the market at a price where he can make a meaningful profit. This drives inefficient producers out of the marketplace.

"But the system, as it functions right now, fails to assess all of the True Costs of nonrenewable, linear consumption and fails to reward consumers for the True Benefits of cyclical consumption. The costs of waste, depletion and pollution, costs to society as a whole, are not paid for by the individual buyers and the sellers in the marketplace. Society as a whole feels them, but individual economic actors don't."

Saroyan looked puzzled. "Simple?" He shook his head. "I hated economics in school . . ."

"Let me give an example. Someone choosing between a solar-powered furnace, and a coal-powered furnace, is going to look at the individual benefits to him when he decides what to buy. But society would benefit from his purchase of a solar furnace, because he would not pollute the air, or deplete a scarce resource that leaves scars on the planet when they dig it up. The benefits to society are simply not part of the market interaction.

"So when the True Costs of production are not incorporated, we allow inefficiency to succeed. Buyers and sellers are not compelled to make the most appropriate choices on what products to offer and purchase. The market then favors products that damage the biosphere. And that's what's happened. We've never paid for all the costs of our modes of production and consumption. And the ecological deficit has mounted. Now we have a filthy environment of accumulating wastes."

"Thank you again, professor. We may have to present that a little more . . . concisely. Like saying that the coal furnace is cheaper because the cost of the environmental damage done by coal mining is not included in the price."

"That's what I said."

"Sort of. So what do we do about this ecological deficit?"

Edwards shrugged. "That's where Economic Activism comes in. Government assesses the True Costs and True Benefits of whatever modes of production and consumption are chosen. With these costs and benefits appropriately assessed, the Free Market can turn its creative power toward bringing production and consumption into harmony with our biosphere. And Economic Activism exists right now, and did at the beginning of the Industrial Revolution. Some political types will try to say that government is just a neutral regulator of the playing field. But government can't be neutral. By choosing to purchase some products and not others, they're not neutral.

"And more importantly, the government has been giving subsidies through all of modern economic history. Hell, one of our problems is that we're still caught up in the subsidies of the Industrial Revolution. Back then, governments decided that industrialization was in society's best interests; cheap raw materials and fuels were important to make it happen. Industrialization was a True Benefit that needed government support and encouragement. So government gave subsidies to entrepreneurs recovering the minerals necessary to fuel industrialization. Unfortunately, those entrepreneurs have now become powerful special interests, used to their favored treatment. And the governments who originally gave them the subsidies have forgotten why. We have to fix the subsidy schemes that are now outdated. We must make the True Costs and True Benefits allocations work together. Assessing the costs—"

"You mean imposing taxes."

"Yeah," Edwards admitted. "They can dampen the whole economy. So the cost assessments should be phased in over long periods, giving time for new products to develop. And most important, they *must* be accompanied by True Benefit balances. I swear, if I was President, I would veto any attempt by Congress to start up a cost assessment *without* balancing it with a tax credit. I mean, if we tax the use of coal for fuel in a home, we *must* offer tax credits to those who use wind power or solar light and/or heat for energy in their homes."

"Again, we can simplify this. We're proposing we tax some things to pay their True Costs in order to subsidize others that provide True Benefits. And we'll have to be sure we make that linkage repeatedly," Saroyan told him. "If you don't, you'll be portrayed as a candidate who wants to raise taxes, and we can forget it."

"I agree. And I know there have been experts who have suggested that taxes affect environmental behavior. A lot of countries have high taxes on fossil fuels. Western Europe's high gasoline taxes cause the prices there to go up to $3.00, even $5.00 a gallon, encouraging some conservation. But Americans won't take that. And they shouldn't. The government's job is only half done. Basically, it's the stick without the carrot. Americans are absolutely hostile to taxes. They will not support a huge tax increase on fossil fuels unless they can see an alternative to paying that huge tax."

"We will need to say that over and over," Saroyan observed again.

"There's just one other thing I'd like to say. We should let everyone know that we realize implementing a True Costs and True Benefits plan will not be an exact science. We'll call for phasing in cost assessments and reimbursements for benefits, and base the precise numbers on practical considerations. The costs, uh, taxes, should start out small enough to avoid inflicting deep wounds on producers and consumers—the benefits have to be large enough to create incentives. And, the whole thing has to make fiscal sense for the government. By *phasing in* the cost assessments, we give consumers and businesses a chance to adjust to the new priorities." Michael looked at Saroyan with earnest sincerity. "Drew, it is really important to me that we get people to embrace the system. That's the reason we *must* make it clear to the American people *why* these measures should be taken. I want to encourage constructive progress toward a Regenerating Biosphere. I do *not* want to penalize anyone for prior activities, or point fingers and lay blame."

Saroyan nodded, then grinned slightly. He seemed to be intrigued, and maybe even a little unaccustomed to such unabashed sincerity from a potential candidate. "Okay. I see where you're coming from. And I like it, Michael. And the True Costs-True Benefits proposals will, without a doubt, give yet another set of number-crunching economists a shot at the Nobel Prize when they translate it all into something more tangible. But we also have to do the same."

"I know," Michael agreed. "And I am thrashing out some specific proposal ideas; they're not quite ready yet."

"It's when you get to the True Costs portion that it'll get tricky."

"That's why you said we have to link anything about True Costs to True Benefits."

"Oh, *we'll* link them," Saroyan promised him. "But your friends in the media may not oblige us by retaining the link when they do their reports. When you talk about taxing non-renewable fuels, you're talking about taxing gasoline. Don't forget 1996, when gas shot up about 30 to 50 cents a gallon. Everyone screamed bloody murder. That old Bob Dole tried to make a campaign issue out of a nickel of gasoline tax, and had some takers."

"That's different," Michael dismissed. "What made people mad was a suspicion of price gouging—greedy oil interests were suspected of squeezing Americans on the cost of what is considered by most to be an essential expense. What we propose is designed to *reduce,* and eventually *eliminate*, our dependence on their commodity. The True Cost assessment would be gradual, with incentives for alternatives linked. It's different, *totally* different."

"Yeah? A higher price at the pump is a higher price at the pump."

"If that's what you focus on."

"Don't worry, our *opponents* will focus on it."

Michael bristled at what seemed to him to be defeatist pessimism.

Teresa again exhaled with obvious irritation.

"Then I'll make damn sure the entire package is understood," Michael stated sternly, "and that we would never agree to implement it piecemeal."

"Michael, relax," Saroyan reassured. "I'm on your side. I'm just telling you what the problems are going to be. And this is another good reason to lead with your environmental package. It's the most complicated item on your agenda, so we'll get the whole thing out at the beginning, before anyone takes us seriously enough to set the political attack dogs on us. By the time they do, we'll make sure True Costs and True Benefits, taxes and tax credits, are absolutely linked together in the public mind."

Michael nodded.

"So, in a nutshell, we offer the Regenerating Biosphere as the future of choice, and make our case that it is well within our ability to achieve. When they ask how, we tell them we will use the taxation system; through incentives and disincentives, we will cause the Free Market itself to bring about the transition."

"That's a real basic nutshell," Michael observed, now smiling again, "but that is basically it."

"Let me tell you," Saroyan said, "that may be all that a lot of people get. We better be able to put it in terms that simple."

Michael nodded.

"Now let's talk about how you get into this thing," Saroyan suggested. "Your initial problem, no matter how much of a following you gather, will be convincing the voters that you can be elected. If they think you're a sure loser, they won't waste a vote on you. Your own seed money should be used to start a non-profit organization. You go around the country making speeches and proposals, particularly at college campuses. This sets up a grass roots network of supporters who can raise money and build your following. They can also start the drives to get you on the 50 state ballots. That has always been a tough task for third alternative candidates, but we should be able to handle it, given your national reputation. These college kids will be particularly receptive to your long-term visionary approach, and they'll admire your rebellion against the system by running outside established political parties."

Teresa finally perked up, raising her eyebrows and straightening up in her chair.

"Grass roots was Perot's strength. In 1992, he set up one of the most awesome volunteer organizations in the political history of the United States, but then shit all over the volunteers by bringing his 'white-shirts' in to take over the organizations. Then he pulled the rug out from under everyone by withdrawing. And he *still* got 19 per cent of the vote after coming back! We'll handle the volunteers professionally from the beginning, to avoid this kind of awkwardness. And we'll take another page out of Perot's book—we'll hit the talk shows and other pop type forums to publicize your message."

"Sounds very practical," Edwards commented.

"When your strength builds, which it should early in the primaries as the electorate gets disgusted with the other choices, we pounce. And the trend toward earlier and earlier state primaries will really help us. There's a big dead spot between the primaries and the conventions now. We'll announce we are in the race when we know we'll get the really great poll numbers. That will make you a viable choice. The media will have to cover you; they have a tradition of taking third-party candidates lightly, but they couldn't with Perot in 1992 because his poll numbers were so high that he was actually leading at one point. In 1996, they were pretty much able to ignore him. So we have to get in when the numbers are up. Then we brace for the onslaught."

Michael nodded knowingly.

"The onslaught?" Teresa asked.

Michael waited for Saroyan to explain. "Michael knows what I mean," he said. "When he looks like a candidate, they will come after him. The media, the other candidates, any opportunist who thinks Michael's candidacy can be of use. That's when the *real* campaign starts. At that point, it's fundamentals. We would take every possible opportunity to showcase polls that demonstrate your electability. We'd use the media to portray you as an equal candidate to the other two. Opportunities will come up. We will have to exploit them flawlessly and creatively if we're going to have any chance."

"And we'll need to get the good six o'clock news bites."

"Yup, right along with the other candidates. Even what may look like adverse publicity will be better than no publicity."

"I understand that well."

Teresa was openly frowning.

"The third consideration is winning electoral votes, state by state, one by one."

Edwards nodded again.

"I knew a little of what you're about. So I did a quick state-by-state analysis." Saroyan printed out three sheets of paper from the printer hooked up to his lap-top. "I changed it a little after reading your agenda; I moved Florida and some Mississippi River states into higher categories. Florida has had environmental problems, and problems with the drug trade, both issues which will be featured in your campaign. It's a state with an older electorate, and hasn't gone big for third alternative candidates, but I think they could go big for you, if we spend some time convincing them. And the Mississippi River states of Louisiana, Arkansas, Missouri and Iowa have been subject to flooding in recent years, possibly caused by increased sea levels. These voters may believe that the greenhouse effect is starting to flow right into their homes. If they do, you will become viable.

"I've also included a summary of the results of the recent independent runs for President—John Anderson's run in 1980, and Ross Perot's runs in 1992 and 1996." Saroyan handed the pages to Edwards:

TABLE I

State by State Analysis of
the Michael Edwards Candidacy

PRIMARY CORE STATES: (132 votes, 10 states)
New England (35 votes, 6 states): Massachusetts(12), Vermont(3), New Hampshire(4), Connecticut(8), Rhode Island(4)
Far West (72 votes, 3 states): California(54), Oregon(7), Washington(11)
South (special case) (25 votes, 1 state): Florida(25)

POSSIBILITIES: (48 votes, 8 states)
Mountain States (23 votes, 5 states): Colorado(8), Utah(5), Idaho(4), Montana(3), Wyoming(3)
Midwest-Progressive (21 votes, 2 states): Minnesota(10), Wisconsin(11)
Hawaii (4 votes, 1 state)

PRIMARY CORE AND POSSIBILITIES: (180 votes, 18 states... 90 more needed to win)

REACHES: (176 votes, 13 states; 143 votes, 9 states without the "Long Reaches")
Mountain State (5 votes, 1 state): New Mexico(5)
Mid-Atlantic Reaches (74 votes, 4 states): Delaware(3), Pennsylvania(23), New Jersey(15), New York(33)
Midwest Reaches (61 votes, 3 states): Ohio(21), Michigan(18), Illinois(22)
Mississippi River States; Long Reaches (33 votes, 4 states): Louisiana(9), Missouri(11), Iowa(7), Arkansas(6)
Alaska (3 votes, 1 state)

"FORGET IT": (182 votes, 20 states)
Traditional South and "Border" States (98 votes, 10 states): Maryland(10), West Virginia(5), Virginia(13), North Carolina(14), South Carolina(8), Georgia(13), Mississippi(7), Alabama(9), Kentucky(8), Tennessee(11)
Midwest-Traditional (18 votes, 2 states): Indiana(12), Kansas(6)
Farmbelt (11 votes, 2 states): North Dakota(3), South Dakota(3), Nebraska(5)
Western South (40 votes, 2 states): Texas(32), Oklahoma(8)
Conservative West (12 votes, 2 states): Arizona(8), Nevada(4)
District of Columbia (3 votes)

TABLE II

State by State Vote Percentage for
Anderson in 1980 and Perot in 1992 and 1996

	Anderson 1980	Perot 1992	Perot 1996	Total all three
Alabama	1(50th)	11(47th)	6(45th)	18(48th)
Alaska	7(21st)	27(4th)	11(8th)	45(9th)
Arizona	9(11th)	24(10th)	8(32nd)	41(19th)
Arkansas	3(41st)	10(48th)	8(32nd)	21(44th)
California*	9(11th)	21(26th)	7(38th)	37(25th)
Colorado†	11(6th)	23(14th)	7(38th)	41(19th)
Connecticut*	12(5th)	22(21st)	10(16th)	44(12th)
Delaware	7(21st)	20(28th)	11(8th)	38(23rd)
Florida*	5(35th)	20(28th)	9(24th)	34(31st)
Georgia	2(44th)	13(44th)	6(45th)	21(44th)
Hawaii†	11(6th)	14(39th)	8(32nd)	33(33rd)
Idaho	6(31st)	28(3rd)	13(3rd)	47(5th)
Illinois	7(21st)	17(34th)	8(32nd)	32(35th)
Indiana	5(35th)	20(28th)	10(16th)	35(29th)
Iowa	9(11th)	19(31st)	8(32nd)	36(27th)
Kansas	7(21st)	27(4th)	9(24th)	43(15th)
Kentucky	2(44th)	14(39th)	9(24th)	25(42nd)
Louisiana	2(44th)	12(45th)	7(38th)	21(44th)
Maine*	10(9th)	30(1st)	14(1st)	54(1st)
Maryland	8(16th)	14(39th)	7(38th)	29(39th)
Massachusetts*	15(1st)	23(14th)	9(24th)	47(5th)
Michigan	7(21st)	19(32nd)	9(24th)	35(29th)
Minnesota†	9(11th)	24(10th)	12(4th)	45(9th)
Mississippi	1(50th)	9(48th)	6(45th)	16(50th)
Missouri	4(39th)	22(21st)	10(16th)	36(27th)
Montana†	8(16th)	26(6th)	14(1st)	48(3rd)
Nebraska	7(21st)	24(10th)	11(17th)	42(17th)
Nevada	7(21st)	26(6th)	9(24th)	42(17th)
New Hampshire*	13(4th)	23(14th)	10(16th)	46(7th)
New Jersey	8(16th)	16(35th)	9(24th)	33(33rd)
New Mexico	6(31st)	16(35th)	6(45th)	28(40th)
New York	8(16th)	16(35th)	8(32nd)	32(35th)
North Carolina	3(41st)	14(39th)	7(38th)	24(43rd)
North Dakota	8(16th)	23(14th)	12(4th)	43(15th)

State by State Vote Percentage for
Anderson in 1980 and Perot in 1992 and 1996

	Anderson 1980	Perot 1992	Perot 1996	Total all three
Ohio	6(31st)	21(26th)	11(8th)	38(23rd)
Oklahoma	3(41st)	23(14th)	11(8th)	37(25th)
Oregon*	10(9th)	25(9th)	11(8th)	46(7th)
Pennsylvania	6(31st)	18(33rd)	10(16th)	34(31st)
Rhode Island*	14(3rd)	23(14th)	11(8th)	48(3rd)
South Carolina	2(44th)	12(45th)	6(45th)	20(47th)
South Dakota	7(21st)	22(21st)	10(16th)	39(21st)
Tennessee	2(44th)	10(48th)	6(45th)	18(48th)
Texas	2(44th)	22(21st)	7(38th)	31(37th)
Utah†	5(35th)	29(2nd)	10(16th)	44(12th)
Vermont*	15(1st)	23(14th)	12(4th)	50(2nd)
Virginia	5(35th)	14(38th)	7(38th)	26(41st)
Washington*	11(6th)	24(10th)	9(24th)	44(12th)
West Virginia	4(39th)	16(35th)	11(8th)	31(37th)
Wisconsin†	7(21st)	22(21st)	10(16th)	39(21st)
Wyoming†	7(21st)	26(6th)	12(4th)	45(9th)
D.C.	9(11th)	4(51st)	2(51st)	15(51st)
Totals	6	19	8	33

* "Primary Core" states
† "Possibility" states

Rankings apply to the 50 states and the District of Columbia, ranked as 51 voting entities. When states have the same percentage, the higher rank is used.

"I have no chance in *twenty* states," Edwards observed incredulously, as he looked at the list.

"It's best to know that now."

"Maybe this *is* crazy."

"Difficult, but not impossible—that's what I told you," Saroyan reminded him. "Basically, you need to take the 'primary core' and the 'possibility states,' then 90 electoral votes from the 'reaches,' roughly half."

Edwards breathed a deep sigh. He marveled at the precise detail of the presentation. Then he smiled. "That simple, huh?"

Teresa was clearly irritated. She didn't indicate why, but Michael could sense her dissatisfaction as she remained uncharacteristically quiet.

"There's one other thing I'd like to have you fill out if you decide to work with me." He handed Edwards another set of stapled papers. "It's a personal profile sheet for our advance people."

"Profile?"

"Yeah. Silly stuff. But it can be important. Like asking you if there are any foods you hate."

"Why would advance men need to know that?"

"You wouldn't want to show up at a rally, maybe with an ethnic group or a group of core supporters, and have them shove food in front of your face that you hate. You could be caught on camera with a goofy look on your face, or you could offend some people. That's the stuff we're trying to avoid."

"Okay."

Teresa's brows knitted together in an unsubtle scowl.

Saroyan stood up to leave. "Thanks for having me over. You two talk it over. I'm telling you from the heart—I hope we take this further together. But if we do, you gotta decide soon."

"I know. And thank *you*, for all the free political analysis."

"Nelson, 1996. No thanks are necessary."

"I'll be in touch."

"I'll look forward to it."

Edwards and his wife escorted Drew Saroyan out the door, then returned to the living room.

"He'd like to do it," Teresa observed, not indicating clearly whether she liked this or not.

"I know. I was surprised. I expected cynical tough-talk. And he could make a ton more money on a major candidacy."

"He smells *some* money, Michael. After all, we are rich, and he knows it."

"Something about it bothers you . . ." Michael observed, dangling the remark in an attempt to get Teresa to explain her obvious irritation during the meeting.

"Not 'it.' *Him*," Teresa explained.

"Him?"

"Michael, his slick strategies and analyzing your food preferences are what have made politics in this country so shallow and silly."

"He knows how to win."

"And that's his first priority. He'll turn you into one of those politician-puppets we both hate."

"He won't change the message. He never asked me to touch the message. And he—"

"He won't change the message," Teresa repeated. "He'll just tell you when to tell each part of it, who to tell it to, and when to answer questions and when to b-s."

"We can walk into this thing like a couple of wide-eyed neophytes, and tell the world it has to do things our way. Perot did that. He wouldn't listen to what experts told him he needed to do. Maybe we get a footnote along with our 5 to 20 per cent of the vote. Or, we go all out, get all the information we need, make all the right moves, and have a shot."

"I don't like working with guys like him. Beauty pageant operators."

"If we're going to win, we'll have to."

"I know."

"Does this mean you think we shouldn't do it?"

Teresa smiled. "You know that once you start thinking about doing these things, you always end up doing them."

"Like Omni-Vee?"

"Exactly."

"So where do you stand on this, Teresa? Here's your chance. Speak your mind."

"I don't like the Drew Saroyans of the world. Manipulative, slick . . . And I hate politics, with all the catering to everyone, and the phoniness, and the greed and power-people show."

"So we pass on this."

"Of course not," Teresa told Michael with a knowing smile. "You're the kind of person who *should* be running for high office. Just keep me away from Saroyan before I strangle him with his silk tie."

Michael laughed. "Okay. But I won't be able to do this without your help."

"Give me the college kids. I'll get them fired up."

"His strategy is easy to lay out on paper. But when you really think about it, it's almost an impossible task. We have no chance in *twenty* states."

"Which means we have a chance in *thirty*. You think the regular doofus-A and doofus-B candidates don't write off states?"

Michael smiled, then pondered again. "I'll have to give up my position at the network, access to millions of people every night . . ."

"If that was enough, you wouldn't have asked this beauty pageant operator to come over here."

"I know," Michael said reflectively. "On television, we feed out minuscule, truncated rations of truth—bits and pieces of problems, maybe even bits and pieces of solutions. But we never dole out a large enough portion of the truth to give a whole solution to a whole problem."

"That's why it's not enough any more."

Michael exhaled. "But is doing this the answer?"

"Michael, you should have figured it out by now," Teresa told him, with a stern efficiency brought about by impatience. "This is a time when you have to throw away all the logical reasons 'to do' or 'not to do.' You take it on because you believe. You lay it on the line because you know in your gut that if you don't, you will regret it forever. You know that what you believe is right, even if the world may *never* be convinced. You believe in your cause down to the callouses on the bottoms of your feet. You either believe or you don't. Make up your mind, Michael. There is no other question. Practicality is irrelevant. You either believe or you don't."

Michael's eyes moistened. "I do believe."

"Then there is only one answer."

Michael looked at his wife of almost thirty years and felt a deep upwelling of love. "So we're going to hit the water, Teresa. We won't know the temperature, except that it will be quite chilly at first. And we have no idea what condition we'll be in after we hit."

"So?" Teresa replied with a casual shrug.

Michael smiled as he shook his head and picked up the phone.

Drew Saroyan found a message on his private answering machine as soon as he got home. The Edwards candidacy would be launched.

Chapter 5

Late December, The Year Before the Election: Monday
Houston, Texas

"ALRIGHT," BEAUREGARD HUNTER SAID WEARILY, "I THINK THAT wraps it up." He sat at the head of a long oak table in a plush conference room at Hunter Oil headquarters. Tyler Rhodes was sitting just to his right. Six other key executives of the company sat along the sides of the table. They were finishing a long operations meeting, longer than usual because of an oil price hike in the Middle East.

"Uh, Mr. Hunter, the futurist people are waiting," Rhodes reminded him tentatively.

"Oh yeah," Hunter recalled. "Send them in." He thought a moment. "The rest of you can go."

Rhodes stood up.

"Not you," Hunter told him. "You made me hire these people. You don't think you're escaping, do you?"

"I'm just going out to bring them in, boss."

Hunter nodded.

A few moments later, Hunter assessed a young man and young woman, both in their early thirties, as they walked in. Matthew Sticklesby was supposed to be a very intelligent young man, with impressive alphabet soup after his name like MBA and PHD, but he was a nerd. Connie Cook was cocky and confident, not pretty, but pleasant-looking. With less alphabet soup after her name, and probably not as smart as Sticklesby, she was never-the-less easier to talk to.

"Have a seat, kids," Hunter told them wearily, but with a touch of the gracious host in his voice. "And tell me about Michael Edwards."

Almost before they were seated, Sticklesby answered: "I think the keys to extrapolating the potentialities of an Edwards candidacy are on page six in the third appendix of our report—"

"I read the goll-dang report," Hunter interrupted. "I have never seen so many words strung together to say so little."

Sticklesby sank in his chair.

"It's late," Hunter continued. "I need a bottom line."

There was a brief silence in the room before Cook spoke. "The bottom line is this. A Michael Edwards candidacy would be good for Hunter Oil."

Hunter looked at her skeptically, but enjoyed the frank, direct answer. "You're not recommending we send him a contribution . . ."

Cook smiled. "No. But the fact is, there is no way he can get a party nomination. He might try it, but he won't succeed. He does not have the political connections he needs to do it. So he'll either run independent right off, or after one of the major parties rejects him. As a third party candidate, given his politics, he'll take votes away from the Democratic challenger, which will probably be Victor Parker. He might even become the focus of the anti-incumbent vote, neutralizing a source of support for a challenger in any election. This'll all help President Hampton get reelected. And Republican administrations are best for Hunter Oil."

Hunter nodded his understanding.

Sticklesby perked up. "Sir, I think that Ms. Cook's stated conclusion is enlightening as far as it goes. But it oversimplifies—"

"Son, I don't want to be difficult with you," Hunter said with irritation thinly masked by a rudimentary politeness, "but it is late, and I don't want to listen to a lot of on-and-on. I read your report. It *needs* to be simplified."

"Yes sir." Sticklesby sank back again.

"We did do a lot of scenarios for you, and gave probabilities for them," Cook added. "But there's only one dangerous scenario that I believe Hunter Oil needs to be concerned about. If Edwards runs a good campaign and convinces large segments of the public that his views on energy and the environment are correct, then he could be harmful, by getting public support, and therefore political support, for his agenda. The company has made large investments into—"

"Yes, I remember that scenario," Hunter interrupted. "And you did a good job on researching Edwards' views. Very sharp. So, if it starts to look like he can convince a lot of people that he is right about things, he could hurt us, without even winning the election."

"Yes," she agreed.

"Thank you two," Hunter told them. "Appreciate you-all staying around so late tonight."

"No problem," Cook told him.

"We're here for you," Sticklesby acknowledged stiffly through a forced smile.

They both stood and left.

"Well, I think I'll tell my old buddy Zack Fadiman to put things on hold," Hunter commented cryptically.

"You'll tell Zack Fadiman about all their cutesy little scenarios?"

"Hell no," Hunter dismissed immediately. "He'd laugh his ass off if I told him I was paying good money for overtrained bookworms to sit around in offices and write 'scenarios' all day."

"We had to hire—"

"I know," Hunter interrupted abruptly. "Every other energy company has these people. So if we make a bad move, our stockholders'll say 'why didn't you-all have these crystal ball eggheads, the way everyone else has?' Shit. Going public made me absurdly rich, but I *hate* answering to stockholders."

"Doesn't Fadiman have any publicly-traded companies?"

"Not that he pays any attention to."

Rhodes smiled, intrigued with Hunter's reply.

"Zack inherited a lot of going concerns from his daddy," Hunter explained. "And he got one of those rich-boy educations; his parents had other things to do, so they shipped him to private schools all over the world. That's great for networking with future leaders, dictators, rich politicians and even a few future terrorists. And that's how he's taken daddy's weapons business and made even more money. He doesn't care much about his other publicly traded companies. A lot of them are run by old buddies of his, or relatives, so he's not too worried. He let's *them* deal with stockholders. He's got a few specialty companies, private companies, that he spends his time with."

"Weapons?"

"Eccentric weapons. And *security*. Cloak and dagger for the corporation. You know, he works with a lot of large corporations that have bigger budgets for . . . security concerns . . . than many countries."

"Good man to have as a friend."

"No doubt." Hunter's face changed expression as he recalled an earlier thought. "By the way, I like that Cook girl. She's sharp, and she knows how to handle herself. Get her out of that dilettante's job and give her some real work for us."

"I will."

☼ ☼ ☼

Late January, Election Year: Sunday
New York, New York

"YOU'VE BEEN QUIET," DREW SAROYAN COMMENTED TO MICHAEL Edwards as Saroyan drove his blue BMW across the Tri-Boro Bridge into Manhattan. They were returning from a late campaign appearance at Yale. A sea of lights glittered ahead in Manhattan as they left a sea of lights behind them in Queens, with only a thin line of darkness marking the East River.

"Tired," Michael explained.

"It really did go well, Michael. We got even more volunteers, and there were more kids backstage to meet with you. I got a real sense of affection and respect."

"I guess we're finally putting it together."

"Yeah. It's been slow, but I think it's starting to move now. A lot of voters sense we need a third candidate, but they're gun-shy after Perot. In a sense, we're not just bashing the Democrats and Republicans, but also putting you forward as someone different from Perot, with a broader vision, who won't quit once he gets everyone cranked up."

"I definitely sense that too."

"Your wife has been a *huge* help."

Michael smiled. "She's been unbelievable. I haven't seen her with this much energy in twenty years." He sighed and yawned again. "Maybe more than me right now."

"I'll tell you, she is accomplishing a lot by staying behind in New Haven tonight. Some of those kids connect with her almost as much as they do with you."

"She's not a good speech-maker, but in a small group, she's very charismatic," Edwards commented. "It's been great to see this side of her emerge again."

"I've been meaning to ask you," Saroyan mentioned, trying to be nonchalant, but betraying more concern than he wanted to. "I get the feeling Teresa is upset with me about something. If I have done anything to offend her . . ."

Michael smiled broadly, almost laughing. "Drew, you shouldn't take it personally," he told Saroyan. "She just hates what you do."

"What I do? What did I do that she hates?"

"No, I mean she hates your job. She considers it manipulating, and too slick."

"Well the fact is—"

"Don't worry about it," Edwards assured him. "No matter how we explain the necessity of your work, she still won't like what you do. She's a purist. As far as she's concerned, our message is so wonderful that it doesn't need to be packaged. Strategy shouldn't have to enter into it. We should be able to tell the people, and then they'll just vote for us."

Saroyan raised his eyebrows and shrugged. "Well, speaking of strategy, Fleming went for the show, and they're already in production on it. You're one of the three."

"Fantastic."

"I should tell you, he's pissed at me."

Edwards grinned knowingly. "Because you really *are* a manipulative son-of-a-bitch."

"He found out I'm working with you."

"He thought you'd suggested this modern day rags-to-riches, American Dream story just off the top of your head?"

"I don't know what he thought. But I got the sense he was too far along with the program to kill it."

"Rags-to-riches," Edwards mused. "More like middle-class faded jeans with holes in the knees to riches."

"Yeah," Saroyan agreed. "Same with Bill Gates from Microsoft. I think Fleming considered dropping you from the program. But the Omni-Vee story is just too good. And, with all the public attention you've been getting, a story about you is good for ratings. Anyway, his people will call you next week to set up an interview."

"Great."

"The air date'll be a week before the New Hampshire primary. We'll do a poll right after it airs. If the numbers look good, we'll try to get a major national poll to follow-up, then dive in."

"So we're getting there."

"Yup. We're also ready to hit the talk shows. Lloyd Prince is a must."

"He's a friend of mine."

"Give him a call. Try to get on the week of Fleming's special."

"Okay."

✧   ✧   ✧

Mid February, Election Year: Thursday
New York, New York

"THE GUY CAME AFTER ME IN THIS AFTERNOON'S INTERVIEW," MICHAEL told Teresa, grinning as they lay back on the king sized bed in the master bedroom of their Manhattan apartment. They were under the covers, watching the large television set in front of them. The room was dark except for the light of the set. "I think he was getting back at me for what he thought was dirty pool from Drew."

"What'd Drew do?" Teresa asked warily as she sipped a glass of juice, then put it on the headboard behind her.

"He met Fleming for lunch, supposedly just buddy-to-buddy, and suggested this great idea for a network special; modern day rags-to-riches stories. He told Fleming he thought I would make a particularly good story. He didn't make it clear to Fleming that he was working with me."

"Oh boy . . ."

"I handled Fleming okay. It made for interesting television. And the first part was almost like a tribute." Edwards smiled knowingly. "The whole thing will give us a big boost."

Teresa smiled and snuggled up to him. "Then let's watch it."

The show was a news-information special airing at 10:00 p.m. on a rival network to WWBS. It consisted of three twenty-minute segments. The Edwards segment, which aired second, had about twelve minutes on his rise to wealth, followed by a short interview section taped earlier in the day.

The program spent only a small amount of time on Edwards' journalistic career. After all, Edwards was the number-one ranked anchorman for a rival network. And the slant of the program was on how the subjects had built their colossal fortunes. Edwards had not built his fortune by being an anchorman, though his national image hadn't hurt. So little was mentioned about his early career. The show simply chronicled how Edwards had started with literary ambitions, aspiring to be the Jack

Kerouac of the 1960's. He spent his time collecting the life experiences he felt he needed to become a great writer. He was making his living contributing articles to newspapers and magazines when one of those articles on the 1971 earthquake in Sylmar, California led to an interview on some television programs. His talent for description and sincerity on camera was apparent, and he found himself with an offer to be an on-camera reporter for a Spokane, Washington television station.

He accepted the job, with the idea that it would be temporary, until his literary breakthrough came. But his broadcasting skills developed, and he found himself caught in a skyrocketing career that culminated with the position of national anchorman for WWBS. His "literary breakthrough" was to come, and very differently from the way he would have imagined.

When the Berlin Wall came down, followed a few years later by the disintegration of the Soviet Union, Edwards marveled at all the different exotic ethnic groups who had been behind the Iron Curtain, many of whom now seemed to be fighting each other. As a good newsman, then stationed in Washington D.C., realizing these areas could become important to American foreign policy, he sought a book that would give him a historical overview of them. But he couldn't find any that did a comprehensive survey. So he did his own research, first out of a sense of obligation to stay informed, but later out of growing fascination and curiosity. As he read and studied, he realized that *he* might write the overview he had sought previously. He didn't immediately get a publishing deal. But when he went to PBS with an idea for a series on the subject, with an accompanying book, he found he quickly had an acclaimed television series and a best-seller to his credit.

While in the former Soviet Union, traveling from new country to new country for the PBS series, Edwards found himself with enormous amounts of time between on-camera segments. (He had been given a leave of absence by WWBS to do the PBS series. Both benefitted from the situation. Edwards attained a national reputation from the PBS series, giving WWBS an anchorman who would rise to number one.) While in a railroad car, traveling across the hilly plains of Kazakhstan, he came up with the idea for a novel, which he completed about the same time the series began to air. Kazakhstan was now the only country in the world with a native Moslem leader and large Moslem population that had a significant store of nuclear weapons on its soil. His novel was a thriller, centering around intrigues by rival factions to gain control of the country, and the nuclear weapons still under a unified ex-Soviet authority. The plot involved former CIA and KGB operatives working in peculiar combinations to prevent extremists from gaining control of some of the world's most sophisticated and destructive weapons. This book sold extremely well, and a movie deal followed.

At first, Michael and Teresa found charities for their extra money. But Michael had another creative impulse, leading him in a direction neither of the Edwards would ever have imagined.

Michael Edwards was fanatically conscious of what he ate—he always tried to maintain a healthy, balanced diet. He lamented how it was hard to control his diet while out on the road signing books, sometimes in a hurry between engagements. Fast food, even when fast food chains tried to promote themselves as healthy, was never dependable. Some of what should have been the healthiest menu items, like fish sandwiches, turned out to be the ones with the most fatty oil, cholesterol, and salt. During his book tours, he found himself frequently choking down fast food, imagining what he wished he could purchase. The list of imagined menu items grew, and as his royalty checks kept coming, his bank account also grew. He began to dream of starting a chain of fast-food restaurants that would cater to the nutritionally conscious, but keep taste and convenience as priorities.

"I decided to get ahold of a young, energetic manager, experienced with fast food who had come up from the bottom," Edwards told the camera. The broadcast then cut to a pan across the "OMNI-VEE" logo, white letters on a bluish-green background. "I told him we would give everyone working for us a profit-share from day one. They would also have options to buy partnership shares in the business with portions of their paychecks."

Paul Fleming's voice-over then came on. "Michael Edwards then went to independent nutrition experts and courted their *unpaid* support and endorsements."

"I knew that *paid* endorsements would be seen as having little weight with the public," Edwards explained. "So we got these people to look at what we had to offer objectively, and worked at it until we had endorsements, even enthusiastic ones, from most of them."

"Soon America was treated to pita chicken-salads, tortilla pizzas of lean mozzarella cheese and zucchini, and turkey hash sandwiches," Fleming continued as the camera showed the various food items as he mentioned them. "All of these were low in fat, cholesterol and salt. He started with 20 outlets. There are now over 8000." The picture now featured shots of long car-lines, waiting for drive-thru service at a sequence of Omni-Vee locations.

"The management system allowed on-site authority for managers and their employees, so they could tailor marketing to the peculiarities of the local area," Fleming continued narrating. "With the profit incentive driving them, ideas flowed from the bottom, encouraged by upper management. And employees, with the profit-sharing motivation, came to work on time, worked hard, and policed malingering by themselves. Because in the profit-sharing scheme, it wasn't only important if the company as a whole was profitable. Each individual outlet would also share a portion of its own profits. Then each region, and those regional employees, would share a portion of the regional aggregate profit, giving them an incentive to encourage each outlet. The home office operated similarly with the regions. Turnover was almost unheard of. And in the case of a few outlet failures, many employees found themselves leaving the company with substantial financial cushions. One young woman, a counter-person, used her money to go to college, and ended up back with Omni-Vee at the home office in the personnel department.

"When the company went public about three and a half years ago, Michael Edwards found himself ranked as one of the top forty richest in the United States."

A smiling Edwards was now introduced in front of a busy Omni-Vee location. "Omni-Vee? Sort of an annoying name," Edwards admitted jovially.

The reporter, not Fleming, smiled.

"It stands for omnivore," Edwards told him. "And it came to me during the hoopla for WWBS's network television premiere of Steven Spielberg's 'Jurassic Park.' You've got the herbivores and the carnivores. But we humans are both of those things—we are the healthiest when we are *omnivores*."

"But the name was not immediately embraced by everyone . . ."

"God no," Edwards replied with emphatic whimsy. "Everyone hated it, including my wife. But everyone *remembered* it, and after an explanation, they remembered what it meant. Some of the most successful marketing schemes of recent years have involved memorability through annoyance."

"People know what you're selling that way."

"Exactly. And it made me rich."

"And a number of your employees."

Edwards smiled proudly. "We had people who thought they'd taken a menial minimum wage job. Most of them got profit-sharing checks, *significant* ones, after one quarter. And the ones who reinvested? Some of them are millionaires."

"Now the profit-sharing set-up . . ."

"It was set-up on a meticulous percentage basis, outlet by outlet, region by region. We tracked each outlet so every employee could see his or her effect on the bottom line. We even tracked profit by time periods. After awhile, we had lines longer for jobs when they opened up, than for the food. And I'll tell you, setting up a complicated, equitable profit-sharing system like this would have been impossible before cheap computer power. Now? It's a snap."

"Mr. Edwards, I know that money has never been a priority for you. What will you do with all of it?"

Edwards shook his head as he wore a weary grin. "To be honest, I don't know."

His image froze on the television screen. The perspective pulled back to show the frozen image on a large monitor which was in a television studio. Michael Edwards sat across from Paul Fleming, the host of the show, and the man who would finish the segment with a short interview. They sat in soft blue chairs with a table between them. Fleming was a slightly smaller than average man with a freckly complexion, heavily covered with make-up, and sandy brown hair with almost no grey. He had a big deep voice that always sounded authoritative.

"You know now, don't you," Fleming followed-up with a firm and knowing tone.

"I have an idea, yeah," Edwards replied, with a winking gleam in his eye.

"Aren't you really campaigning now?" Fleming challenged.

"For my ideas? Yes. Against the narrow-sighted visions of Republicans and Democrats? Absolutely."

"I mean for *office*. For *President*."

"Not yet."

"But you will be soon. You have a high-powered political advisor working for you full time . . ."

"I don't think it's any secret that I am considering a run for the Presidency. A lot of grass roots support has developed and I—"

"You mean you and Mr. Saroyan have astutely mobilized and orchestrated that grass roots support."

"Mr. Fleming, it is not possible to generate the large following we have now unless the public is responsive to the message. I know your cynicism. I work in your business. But the American public is a lot smarter and less prone to manipulation than many in the media would give them credit for. The American people want new approaches. It started with small but significant support for Anderson in 1980. The expression of dissatisfaction accelerated with Perot in 1992. And—"

"I don't want you to give a speech here, Mr. Edwards."

Edwards smiled. "Fair enough. Ask a question."

"We hear about new ideas. We hear this from every campaign against an incumbent. But aren't you running the risk of being just another candidate of 'new ideas' who offers nothing more than a new face? We—"

"That is a completely incorrect characterization of—" Edwards was smiling, but his voice was firm.

"Let me finish my question. We see that you've got a talent for pointing out the problems and the lack of initiative from the major candidates. Perot had that talent too. But where are your 'new ideas?'"

"I've been expressing them all over the country. But they defy capsulization into short sound-bites. This interview is a perfect example of how difficult it is to present complex problems and solutions in today's media. There is pressure to answer quickly, with a short, quotable catch-phrase."

"So you're going to answer questions by complaining about the media? What an original approach. Is that one of your 'new ideas?'"

"I'm trying to tell you, that if I run, I'm not going to do this the way we handle every election. When we fragment America's problems into infinitesimal subdivisions of issues and sub-issues, we end up solving little problems for short spaces of time while either ignoring or even worse, creating bigger problems in the long run. That is why we are drifting, because we—"

"You are sounding more and more like a candidate for office," Fleming quipped cynically. "You are becoming adept at speaking without saying anything."

Edwards smiled mischievously. "And you are following the usual media pattern—first, you truncate peoples' answers into meaninglessness, then turn around and accuse them of not having good comprehensive answers. So let's cut through the typical pattern, and I'll tell you what I'd like to do. I want to focus on where the United States is headed in the near and distant future, what kind of compelling future is possible, and how we will get there. That can't be expressed in a quick answer, but I can outline a few principles. The United States of the future needs change its orientation toward the environment, and lead the world to what I have called a Regenerating Biosphere. This can be done without government creating reams of regulations. Because the United States also needs to rediscover capitalism, and the principles that created such an awesome economic transformation and prosperity in such a short period of time."

"How does that translate into specifics?"

"Well, as an example, we are still using subsidies that apply to the Industrial Revolution, which is now over. During the Industrial Revolution, we—"

"I don't think the American people are interested in a history lesson. It appears obvious—"

"We need to know how we got where we are so we can create an inspiring vision of where we're going," Edwards continued with a smile and a friendly tone, but with a voice full of strong conviction. "When you cut me off, and try to force my approach into your bite-obsessed expectations, you—"

"Michael Edwards, sounding more like a candidate every day," Fleming said, obviously moving to end the interview. "I'm sure we'll hear more from you. You have proven yourself capable of fresh ideas on many diverse subjects. Our final segment is about a man who focused on one area fanatically; computer software. The story of Bill Gates and Microsoft when we return."

The program went to a commercial.

Teresa looked incredulously at Michael. "What was Fleming's problem?"

"I asked him, not in those words," he told her. "He told me that Saroyan had manipulated him and that he wasn't going to be a cheerleader for my candidacy."

"What a jerk."

"He didn't hurt me. If anything, he helped me by being so obviously contentious. I got some good biographical publicity, and hinted at more to come."

Teresa nodded.

Edwards smiled and they cuddled. They kissed once, softly and affectionately, then drifted into sleep.

An hour or so later, a high whirring sound roused Edwards from out of a deep sleep. He groggily looked at the digital clock on the headboard and was surprised to see how little time he had been asleep.

Teresa stirred. "Let the machine get it," she mumbled with irritable grogginess.

"It's the private line," Michael reminded her. Their private phone number, available only to a very small handful of people, rang with a different tone from the regular line.

Michael picked up the phone. "Hello?" he said with a scratchy, just-awakened voice.

"It's Ted. Did I wake you?"

"Ted. What the fuck is going on?"

"I *did* wake you. Uh, I need to talk to you—it's urgent. But . . . I didn't expect you to be asleep. First thing tomorrow morning will do. Eight o'clock. No. Make it 7:30."

"Okay."

"Sorry I woke you." The phone clicked.

"What did he want?" Teresa asked, still groggy and irritable.

"An urgent conference. I gotta go in early tomorrow morning."

"Urgent?" Teresa groaned.

"I'll find out about it tomorrow morning. Let's go back to sleep."

Teresa didn't argue.

✿   ✿   ✿

Mid February: The Next Day, Friday
New York, New York

"YOU WANTED TO SEE ME?" MICHAEL EDWARDS ASKED AS HE ENTERED Ted Jessup's office.

"Yeah," Jessup replied, with hesitancy and a twinge of regret in his voice. "Have a seat."

Edwards sat down. He could tell his friend was about to tell him something that he wouldn't like, and that the task was not a pleasant one.

"Laswell saw the show," Jessup told him somberly. "We spent a good hour on the phone last night talking about it."

Edwards nodded and smiled. "Okay. Assessing the competition?"

"Not quite." Jessup paused to be sure of his wording. "Laswell thinks you're sounding too much like a candidate. He's getting nervous about your objectivity as our anchorman, the credibility of the WWBS news department. I couldn't really disagree with him."

Edwards nodded again. "Ted, what's the bottom line?"

Jessup drew a deep breath and heaved a conflicted sigh. "Laswell says you either need to announce that you will not be running for President, or you need to . . . step down."

Edwards raised his head and brought his index finger to his jaw. "I really do understand his concern." He thought a quick moment. "How much time do I have?"

"Something needs to be done, pretty close to right away."

"You gotta give me a few days."

"I need an answer for Laswell before tonight's show."

"Tell him I'll step down. But tell him I need a little more time. Tell him I won't do any more commentaries."

"I hope he'll buy that."

"It's fair, Ted. Will you at least try to sell it to him?"

Jessup smiled. "I think I can."

Edwards paused uncomfortably. "We have to keep this strictly confidential. Just you and Laswell. News that I'm stepping down would practically be an announcement."

"It wouldn't be in *any* of our interests to let the news leak out."

"Thanks." Edwards stood up and left the room. He needed to make his own urgent call, to Drew Saroyan.

☼   ☼   ☼

Mid February: One Week Later, Friday
New York, New York

"JANE TEPPLESON'S WITHDRAWAL FROM THE DEMOCRATIC PRIMARIES now leaves six candidates still contending for the Presidency," Andrew Talbot told his viewers as he wrapped up his report on the evening's lead campaign story. "Wallace Trewillinger's narrow victory in the New Hampshire primary has boosted his prospects. Parker's narrow loss was a disappointment, but still a strong showing considering he was out of his own region and in Trewillinger's back yard. Jefferson and Highland admittedly did not focus a lot of effort in New Hampshire—their key tests with voters will come later. Two Republicans are still battling, but President Hampton's 68 to 32 trouncing of Frances Willis seems to have canceled out the former Vice President's surprising victory in the Iowa Caucuses.

"Aside from Governor Teppleson's announcement, this was a fairly quiet day for the Presidential campaigns, on this get-away day for the President's Day long weekend. Michael?"

"Thanks, Andy," Michael Edwards acknowledged as the evening's newscast cut back to Edwards on camera. He addressed the television audience with serious sincerity. "As Andy just said, we now have six candidates left vying for the office of President. You have heard me implore them to face the major issues that confront us and offer creative, visionary solutions."

Jessup, who was standing in the control room, suddenly became puzzled. He quickly raised his notes for the evening's broadcast to eye level.

"I have become convinced that we need to challenge assumptions ingrained into the political establishment, to break our growing sense of stagnation," Edwards continued. "The major parties simply are not going to do that—that is obvious. So I humbly offer my candidacy for President as a step, hopefully a broad consequential step, in that direction."

Jessup's eyes bulged in disbelief. "He's going to announce this on the air? Now? On my news show?"

No one in the booth responded. What could anyone say?

"That means I will be resigning my position here, effective at the end of this broadcast, to run for President of the United States as a third alternative candidate. What will I be talking about?" Edwards asked rhetorically as he began to elaborate.

"Shit!" Jessup blurted out. "He's giving a campaign speech!"

"My campaign will look back and examine how the United States became such a powerful and prosperous country. We will then apply the concepts of capitalism and freedom that brought us to the pinnacle of success, and come up with some surprising, common-sense answers. We will apply these concepts to energy and the environment and find ourselves drawn to an era of clean fuels and a less littered world as our economy takes the leadership role in moving beyond the Industrial Revolution to the next great era for humankind, what I call the Regenerating Biosphere. We will apply principles of freedom and equity to the problems of crime and punishment—I will, in the very near future, outline what I believe is the atomic bomb of the so-called war on drugs. We would gain immediate victory over our enemies in that conflict, allowing us to focus our efforts on its true victims. We will apply capitalism and common sense to issues like health care, trying to deal with fundamentals *first*, instead of focusing on tangents when essential problems remain unapproached.

"Freedom and personal responsibility are the keys, the twin common denominators of every proposal my campaign will offer. Over much of this century, we have traded some of our precious freedom in exchange for giving up some of our personal responsibility. But that trade has caused us to drift away from what made this country great. When we let others take care of us, and take responsibility for us, we necessarily give up some of our own personal freedom."

Jessup hoped this was all. "Not fair, Michael. Cheap shot. We don't allow unedited campaign speeches on this show . . ."

"So let me prepare you for some fresh approaches—they may seem unconventional at first," Edwards continued, obviously unable to hear Jessup's objection. "But a fair assessment will show them to be full of practicality, so obvious that you will wonder why politicians in power have never suggested these ideas. I won't try to answer that question. But together, we will break this political stagnation and move ahead.

"Thank you for your kind attention, in the past, as I brought you the news, and now as I try to make some. Good night, ladies and gentlemen, and as always, thank you for bringing us into your homes."

Theme music and credits dominated the television screen as Michael Edwards collected the papers at his on-set desk for the last time.

☼　　　☼　　　☼

"YOU ASSHOLE," TED JESSUP CURSED QUIETLY AS HE ENTERED EDWARDS' office. Edwards was packing his belongings.

Edwards smiled. "I gave you guys a great scoop on a dead news day."

"Bullshit," Jessup countered. "I know it's bullshit because I just tried that line on Laswell and *he* told me it was bullshit. You picked a dead news day on purpose. You'll get more mileage out of this today."

Edwards smirked. "Let Laswell stew," Edwards said good-naturedly. "He pushed us along ahead of schedule. We wanted to announce after a good poll. We're still only in the high teens. We wanted to be in the twenties."

"I feel so sorry for you," Jessup commented sarcastically. "Wait until we get all the requests for equal time."

"I'm a candidate now," Edwards told Jessup mischievously. "This is a win-win for me. If someone makes a fuss, I get all kinds of publicity, tending to indicate the other candidates are worried about me. And if they ignore it, I get away with it."

"I know," Jessup replied grudgingly, "and you couldn't tell me about it because I'd have to say yes or no . . ."

Edwards shrugged a smile. "I'm glad you understand."

"Oh sure." There was still a twinge of sarcasm in his voice. But then he almost sounded serious. "Hell, maybe I should abandon this sinking ship too. Don't you need a real sharp media advisor?"

Edwards wasn't sure if the question was serious. If it was, then he suspected it was more wish than practicality. He looked his friend in the eye, in case this was a serious question. "This won't be a cake walk. The odds are heavily stacked against me. And the whole thing could collapse in a moment. We're also talking about a lot of time away from home, long days, and terrible pressure. Ted, I know you haven't had a hundred per cent health lately . . ."

"All right." Jessup knew Edwards had given him the only reasonable answer possible.

They were silent a moment.

Jessup's eyes watered. "I'm gonna miss you."

"Yeah." But Edwards' voice caught. He cleared his throat. "Listen, I do have a way you can help me where you are right now. I'm not sure whether I'm out of line asking . . ."

"Ask me. I'll let you know if you're out of line."

"You know I'm going to be making a lot of bold proposals. We both know this sound-bite oriented media will be tempted to quote me out of context to get sensational airplay. I'd like to know there is one network I could rely on to get it right."

"You're *al-most* out of line," Jessup replied. "If anyone starts to sense that this network has become an obvious advocate of your candidacy, our credibility will be dumped into the East River. We'd have to handle this relationship very carefully."

Edwards nodded.

"I'd also like some way to justify it journalistically."

"Okay. You have a key informed source in the Edwards campaign—me."

Jessup smiled and nodded. "I believe I could live with this arrangement." After a momentary pause, Jessup remembered something else he wanted to tell Edwards. "By the way, there's a young kid I know who would make a great media advisor. He admires you totally; I think he's seen more than one of your talks. And he's one of the sharpest media guys, even at his age, that I've met in a long time. He's young, no major responsibilities; he'll jump at the opportunity and kick ass for you."

"Okay. Give me his name. Drew and I will look him up."

"Good." Jessup picked up a piece of scrap paper and wrote Oscar Lusman's name, address and phone number. After he finished, he handed the piece of paper to his friend. "Take care of yourself, Michael. The other comments? I already made them the other night."

"I know." The two men started to shake hands, but ended up hugging.

✿   ✿   ✿

Mid February: The Next Day, Saturday
Hollywood, California

BRADFORD "SLICK" NAYLOR USHERED A YOUNG WOMAN INTO HIS cluttered, musty, one bedroom apartment in a run-down section of the eastern part of Hollywood, about five blocks south of Sunset Boulevard. He was a tall thin man, in his fifties, with a rugged face and long, filthy, grayish-brown hair, dressed in dirty jeans and a torn heavy metal T shirt.

The timid young woman hesitated as she entered the apartment. She had the potential to be very pretty, but her gauntness flattened the curves of her shape and her weariness sapped the vibrancy from her face.

"The bedroom's through that door," Naylor told her tersely as he motioned ahead and to his left.

She walked into his bedroom, where she saw an unmade bed with dirty sheets on it.

Naylor threw the newspaper he carried into the apartment on the floor next to the bed. "Come on. If this is the only way you can pay, let's get to it."

The young woman slowly and nervously removed her blouse revealing an emaciated upper body.

"I don't have all week," Naylor told her impatiently.

She quickly took off her jeans and underwear in one motion and stood in front of him without any clothes on, trembling.

"Worth a couple of rocks," Naylor informed her matter-of-factly. He went to a nearby locked box and pulled out a vial of two crack cocaine rocks. "You get these rocks after I get *my* rocks *off*." Naylor laughed, pleased with his joke.

He quickly removed his clothes as the sad girl got on the bed and lay face up.

"Come on, spread 'em," he ordered.

What happened next took no more than thirty seconds.

Naylor got off of her and rolled her off the bed. "Go on, take your rocks. Close the door on your way out."

She grabbed the vial, put on her clothes and left.

Naylor picked up the newspaper. He looked bored with the front page until he spotted a headline below the fold that stated "Anchorman Edwards Announces For President." Naylor now read that article with enthusiasm.

After a few paragraphs, he reached a section featuring a poll showing 17% of potential voters supporting Edwards as their first choice for

President. He slowly placed the newspaper on the bed. "Well I'll be damned. My man Michael goes from news to politics. I think the time has come to cash in. Yup. Time for me to cash in on the good old days."

He leaned back with a victorious grin on his face.

Part Two

The Campaign

Chapter 6

Mid February, Election Year: The Next Day, Saturday
Washington, D.C.

"OKAY, CUV," PRESIDENT KEN HAMPTON DEMANDED, "WHAT DOES this Edwards crap mean to me? Is it possible this guy just signed me up for four more years?" The two casually dressed men were in the midst of a working breakfast at a small table in the Oval Office.

"He might have," Covington Klondike replied as he smiled. "Our own poll has it Hampton, 42; Parker, 39; Edwards, 18. Without Edwards, it's Parker, 53; Hampton, 47. There's a long way to go to November, but it looks like Edwards'll take more away from the Democrats than from us."

"Good. Any way to encourage him?" President Hampton stuck a fork into some scrambled eggs and put a large bite into his mouth.

Klondike smiled again. "Right now, we just leave him alone. Definitely don't attack him, whether we agree with him or not. And when possible, we refer to him as one of your opponents."

"Does he have a chance of winning?"

Klondike snorted as he sipped some orange juice. "Hell no," he dismissed confidently. "He's a flake."

"A flake?" President Hampton questioned incredulously as he stopped his fork in the middle of cutting away another bite of eggs. "He's almost a billionaire."

"No," Klondike corrected. "He has many millions, but not a billion. He's kind of a dabbler—dabbled in writing, in fast food, and now he's dabbling in politics."

"He's a pretty good dabbler from what I can see . . ."

"He's in over his head now. But he'll serve our purpose." Klondike took a bite out of his buttered whole wheat toast.

"He'll split the dissatisfaction vote," Hampton observed wryly.

"Yup. And that is exactly how he might just get you back here for another four years, Mr. President."

Hampton smiled and raised his glass of orange juice. Klondike then raised his glass, and they tapped their glasses together in a silent toast.

☼   ☼   ☼

Mid February: The Next Day, Sunday
Anaheim, California

"THE HAMPTON ADMINISTRATION HAS UTTERLY FAILED TO FULFILL ANY of the promises Ken Hampton made when he took the White House away from the Democrats," Victor Parker orated as he came to the end of his speech at a banquet hall in the Anaheim Hilton. He was campaigning in southern California's usually conservative Orange County, well aware that early support from this area for Bill Clinton in 1992 informed the electorate that the Republicans were in trouble. "Once and for all, we must tell him we've had *enough*. I'm the man to do that for the Democratic Party. No candidate still in the race has the experienced voice or long list of credentials to do it more effectively. With your help, we will prevail in this important mission. Thank you."

Parker moved off the podium smiling and waving as applause echoed throughout the room. He was quickly joined by Nicholas Mueller. "We're due up in L-A in an hour," Mueller told Parker as they walked hurriedly out of the hotel and into a waiting limousine.

The doors to the limousine shut just after Mueller and Parker sat down together in the back seat, and the limousine sped quickly away. "Okay," Parker told Mueller, "we've got an hour to chat. You've had a day to look at this Edwards thing. What's the story?"

"Bottom line? The consensus is that he is not good news for us."

"Clinton had Perot in 1992. Edwards'll be *my* Perot."

Mueller shook his head. "Perot took a lot of right-wing votes with him. Edwards is different. He'll pick off more of the left wing, especially the young liberals who never call themselves liberals."

"So what do we do?"

"For now, we ignore him. We hope he goes away. If we go after him, we give him credibility. But that probably won't be enough." Mueller hesitated. "We've got to get our own support base under control. Our own party could be our worst enemy."

"Yeah," Parker agreed grimly.

"We shit all over each other through the primaries, then struggle after the nomination to put Humpty-Dumpty back together again to win the general. But only Clinton and Carter have been able to do it since the 60's. So what we need," Mueller recommended, "is to keep the factions of our coalition from grand public gestures of defection. Because if it looks like significant segments are jumping off the bandwagon, and Edwards starts to look like a good place to put the anti-Hampton vote, you will not take this election. You might be fighting to stay out of third."

"Sounds like a job for Will Runalli."

Mueller became silent. "That's not funny," he finally said gravely.

"I wasn't joking. The guy has been around forever. He knows the little secrets, how and when to twist arms, and he has one of the most stuffed rolodexes in the business—"

"The guy is a professional slime-ball," Mueller commented bluntly. "The only time I had the misfortune of dealing with the man was about fifteen years ago during a Michigan senatorial race. He had the winning Democratic candidate. And to assure that, he ran one of the scummiest campaigns I have ever seen."

"This is no time to worry about personalities," Parker stated. "My time is *now*. *President* of the United States. If Runalli is what I need, then I can't hesitate about it. We'll keep him at arm's length for now. We'll use him—only if we need him." Parker paused. "I wonder if he'll go for that . . ."

Mueller nodded fatalistically and reluctantly admitted, "He'll jump on it. He hasn't been involved in a national election in a long time and I understand he wants back in badly. I'm not the only one he's rubbed the wrong way." Mueller thought a moment, then shrugged. "Okay. Let's bring him in as a consultant. We'll have him report to someone under us, to keep that 'arm's length' you mentioned."

"Good," Parker agreed.

Mueller heaved a sigh and leaned back in his seat.

✩   ✩   ✩

Late February, Election Year: Tuesday
Orient Point, New York

"BOSTON WHEN?" EDWARDS ASKED REFLECTIVELY AS HE STOOD ON THE back deck of Drew Saroyan's yacht, watching Orient Point on the north coast of Long Island fade into the distance. The cluster of small vessels at the harbor area faded as Saroyan's yacht separated from them. It was a cool, slightly overcast day. Drew Saroyan's yacht moved over the gentle ocean currents, making slow but steady progress across Long Island Sound between the north coast of New York's Long Island and the southern coast of New England. The water in the sound was quiet, undulating in small waves, like a sheltered bay, or even a large lake.

"We'll be in New London before the day is out. I've got a car and driver there to take us out to Newport for the night. We'll be a quick drive from Boston for your first big speech," Saroyan explained.

Edwards drew a deep, refreshing breath as he turned to face Saroyan. "This was a great idea. Nippy, fresh air." He smiled. "A little bite in the air always gives me a lot of energy."

"Me too," Oscar Lusman acknowledged as he joined them and handed them each a cup of steaming tea. Oscar Lusman's thin blonde beard with patches of no growth made his baby face look younger than his twenty-five years. "You've gotta check out the web site stuff I just finished on the lap-top. This thing is gonna be awesome."

"Your fancy, bells-and-whistles web site? The one we just talked about?"

"Yup. And I've got it set to go on CD ROM. We can also give away CD ROM's with the whole thing on it."

Edwards grinned at Saroyan. "He's quick. But I think he's also going to be expensive."

"It didn't cost that much. I got three computer geeks I know to design and program it for free. The costs of the discs—maybe a dollar apiece."

Edwards nodded, impressed.

"For those primitives still not on the net, or without a CD-ROM, we should do an ongoing series of infomercials," Lusman continued. "We'll take tapes of your speeches, or appearances on talk shows—whatever looks good—as part of a high-energy half-hour presentation. We'll use your spoken words as voice-overs for other pictures. And we'll keep updating it as the campaign progresses. These things are surprisingly cheap, compared to buying time on network TV, and if we handle this right, we'll still cover most voters likely to choose you. So this speech in Boston—"

"Wait a minute," Edwards interrupted skeptically. "Some of those infomercials are pretty silly. We don't want to start looking like a bunch of late-night hucksters."

"There's a risk of that," Saroyan agreed. "We could run polls to make sure it isn't backfiring. But I like the idea. We can control the message without being at the mercy of network TV."

"Research indicates that people watch and respond to a lot of the better infomercials," Lusman added. "It's kind of a politically correct thing to hate infomercials. But when you talk to people, it seems like everyone has seen them."

"Before 1992, talk shows would have been considered demeaning for candidates," Saroyan added. "But with the networks' influence diluted by a hundred or so cable channels in most homes, we gotta be creative and reach out from wherever we can be effective."

"Okay, let's try it," Edwards agreed, shrugging. "This is the sort of thing I'm paying you guys for." Edwards then asked uneasily, "How's the money?"

"It's slow," Saroyan told him with a subdued tone of voice. He sipped his tea. "The problem is that people know you're rich. They might be sympathetic, even inspired by your message. But they don't see why they should reach into their pockets, when you can finance this thing yourself."

Edwards looked grim. "I don't want it to be said that I bought the election. I'm spending . . . what, about eight million to get it started? But that's supposed to be seed money . . ."

"Michael, you may have to make a decision," Saroyan told him seriously. "Fund-raising for third candidates is hard enough when supporters know their candidate is strapped. This is a tall order."

"What we should do is make this an issue," Lusman chimed in enthusiastically. "That financial support is a show of support for you."

Saroyan looked puzzled.

But Edwards picked up the train of thought. "Ladies and gentlemen," he began with sincere earnestness, as if addressing an imaginary audience, "my approach—" He stopped himself. "No." He continued. "Our opponents will try to paint me, uh, *portray* me as a rich man purchasing the Presidency. We have to neutralize this argument. Your cash contribution, even five dollars, when added to the contributions of others, will build grass roots financial support that will speak loudly to your fellow citizens."

"That's good," Saroyan nodded. "Put something like that in the infomercial," he told Lusman. "Only don't have Michael making the appeal. Have some supporters that look good on camera. Let them explain it."

"Okay," Lusman acknowledged.

"Fund-raising is not our biggest problem right now," Saroyan told them with quiet frustration. "The damn Democratic primaries. The media is zoned in on those things, because there's nothing the American people love more than a good contest."

"But they also get bored with a bad one," Edwards added knowingly.

"That's why the best thing that could happen would be for the primaries to be decided quickly," Saroyan emphasized.

"Looks like the Republicans are going to oblige us," Edwards commented.

"Yeah," Saroyan agreed. "Hampton hasn't looked back since New Hampshire. But those damn Democrats—now *Jefferson* pulls an upset."

"Maybe we could help someone along a little bit," Lusman suggested.

"What?" Edwards asked, perplexed and suspicious.

"Short of stuffing ballots or engaging in some other unsavory activity, I'm not sure how we'd do that," Saroyan responded, dismissing the suggestion.

"Seriously, I have connections that could dig up some dirt on these guys. Then we just feed the one we want to win with the—"

"Hang on there," Edwards interjected with a wary grin. "I admire your enthusiasm, but I think we ought to concentrate on our own problems."

"Okay," Lusman replied as he shrugged.

Saroyan quickly added his own clarification. "Oscar, leave those types of strategy things to me. After Boston, get out to the west coast and put together a good opening appearance out there."

"Yeah," Lusman acknowledged.

Edwards looked out to the horizon. "A lot of water out here," he told them reflectively. "Sure seems calm right now." He turned to face them both. "I'll bet in November, it's a lot choppier."

✿   ✿   ✿

Late February: The Following Thursday
Boston, Massachusetts

"IT FILLS ME WITH A SENSE OF PRIDE AND HUMILITY TO SPEAK TO YOU here in Boston, a city that exemplifies the spirit of American tradition in a state that has produced some of the most progressive leaders and visionaries in this country's history," Michael Edwards stated powerfully from his lectern in the long banquet hall of the Oxford Hotel. The hotel was just across the Longfellow Bridge from MIT and not too far east of Harvard. Its colonial architecture matched the style of the proud houses of nearby Beacon Hill.

But the Edwards campaign had not chosen the location of this important speech for the high-rent attributes of the area. The hotel was an easy distance from two major universities where Edwards had generated a particularly large amount of excitement. The banquet hall, which held 1500, was filled to overflowing with standing room only. Saroyan and Lusman had deliberately chosen a location too small for the anticipated crowd so the television coverage of the speech would show a crowd so large that it was almost unmanageable. The ploy was successful, though crowd management personnel at the hotel were unhappy with what they perceived as bad planning.

"So I have chosen this occasion to outline the proposals of my campaign for dealing with environmental and energy issues, two subjects that are intimately intertwined. This speech will deal with precise legislation for moving us ahead to the Regenerating Biosphere era, using the principles of Economic Activism guided by the concepts of assessing True Costs and rewarding True Benefits. These deal with economic incentives, the best way, history teaches us, to realize the political will. That's because economics deal with what people have, and how they provide for their families; those concerns drive human behavior at its most basic level. Economic incentives created the Industrial Revolution, and they will also take us to a Regenerating Biosphere."

Manuel Contreras stood in the back of the hall, alternately glaring and sneering, trying to look inconspicuous. But even after removing his blue silk tie, he was blatantly overdressed and out of place in his expensive three-piece suit. Contreras was a husky, heavily-muscled man, with a dark, pock-marked face.

"There are two areas I would like to discuss specifically, where government policy has actually moved us away from the goal of a

Regenerating Biosphere by retaining outdated subsidies," Edwards continued. "First, let's take a look at nuclear power. Here we have a filthy, expensive and dangerous industry that government continues to subsidize. We must end all subsidies immediately!"

The crowd applauded.

"Included would be the immediate repeal of the Price-Anderson Act. This legislation limits the liability of nuclear power plant owners in the event of an accident. I wonder how many of our citizens, particularly those close to nuclear power plants, are aware that in the event of a major accident, the owners of the plant would not have to pick up the full costs of their negligence? Let them obtain insurance for their operations, if they can. If they can't, then that is the economic system's way of preventing a dangerous technology from functioning in the marketplace. Government should not be in the business of stepping in to change the rules so this dangerous enterprise can continue."

The crowd applauded again.

Charles Handel entered the banquet hall quietly, through a side door on the right side of the hall. He closed the side door behind him cautiously, trying not to be noticed. This side entrance put him at about the mid-point of the length of the hall. Handel was dressed casually, in jeans and a dark, plaid cotton shirt. He was in his late 30's, with dark black hair and about a half a week's stubbly growth of beard. He glanced quickly over at Manuel Contreras, confirmed he was there, then glanced away. But he kept Contreras in his peripheral vision.

"The other example of counter-productive government subsidies pertains to oil companies. Our whole society is heavily addicted to this fuel for its very operation. And the cost of this addiction is mounting environmentally, financially and in our foreign policy. Yet we continue to subsidize the consumption of this resource, not even paying for its true economic cost! This creates the illusion that alternative energy sources are impractical as they struggle to compete with a subsidized and familiar energy source. So, I am proposing that after a three year grace period, all oil company subsidies be phased out over the next five years."

More applause sounded.

"Related to this is how we deal with the controversy of off-shore oil drilling. Again, if we permit off-shore oil drilling, we must not subsidize these activities by limiting the liability of energy companies in the event of an accident. For activities currently underway, I will support a gradual lifting of the ceiling of liability until there is no further ceiling."

Charles Handel pulled out a cellular phone and punched in a number.

"This is unit seven," he said quietly. "He's . . . I've tracked him to . . . you won't believe it; he's at the Edwards campaign rally at the Oxford."

"Has he made any contacts?" asked the voice on the other end of the phone.

"No. He's just watching."

"Any assistance needed?"

"Not inside. A unit should be ready to pick up the tail when he leaves."

"Acknowledged. Is he packing?"

"Unknown."

"Continue surveillance. Out."

"The next four proposals are proactive measures designed to lead us to the Regenerating Biosphere era," Edwards stated. "First, government should offer tax credits to all homeowners, landlords and businesses who maintain their buildings using renewable energy systems. These credits would also apply to energy conservation technologies, including computer systems installed to optimize efficient consumption, because not using energy benefits society as a whole as well. And, we should phase in True Costs assessments by slowly escalating taxes on all non-renewable energy sources used in buildings of any kind. We would base these taxes on the scope of environmental degradation caused by the involved energy source. Natural gas is a cleaner and more plentiful non-renewable energy source, and therefore would be taxed less severely. Coal is probably the filthiest of the fossil fuels, and therefore would be taxed the most severely. Low-interest or no-interest government loans would be made available for those structure owners who can demonstrate a financial hardship in paying for the necessary changes."

Manuel Contreras turned and walked toward the right side of the hall, where Charles Handel watched from. This side was much more crowded because the side doors were used by latecomers to enter.

Charles Handel saw Contreras's turn in his peripheral vision. He did not immediately look toward Contreras, to avoid capturing his attention. Instead, he surveyed the crowd, first moving his head away from Contreras's direction, then slowly moving back to where he could look right at him.

Handel turned his head back toward Edwards as he slowly pulled out his cellular phone. He now had more people near him, and had to speak quietly, and efficiently. "Unit seven, reporting," he said, almost in a whisper.

"Report."

"Believe subject is armed—handgun."

"Contacts?"

"None."

"You think Enriquez would send his top enforcer out to hit Edwards at a crowded rally?" the voice asked incredulously.

"Doubt it. Would seem stupid—wasteful of his best man."

"Agreed. Keep an eye on him."

"Out."

Contreras sneered irritably as he noticed how congested the right side area was. He stopped at the right rear corner of the hall.

"Second," Edwards continued, "I am proposing that anyone purchasing an electrically-powered car, or any vehicle fueled by a clean, renewable energy source, any time starting from the date of the legislation, would be entitled to twenty per cent of the purchase price as an income tax credit. And, any automobile manufacturer producing and selling electric cars on a large scale to the public will be largely exempt from taxes on those profits for fifteen years. I have specified the electric car because there are now prototype electric cars that travel up to 80 miles per hour and go 200 to 250 miles before they need to be recharged. With the sudden huge market for electric cars that this program would create, private enterprise will certainly improve on those numbers.

"Of course, if a competitive hydrogen car, solar-powered car, fuel cell car, or even a hybrid-vehicle emerges that is clean and non-polluting, or considerably less polluting, the producers and consumers of those cars would be entitled to appropriate tax credits. And we would formulate the legislation to account for those options.

"What we must do is stimulate the Free Market to bring about these changes. Right now, we have government bureaucracies ordering manufacturers to build electric vehicles and sell a certain number of them. This sounds like government-control reminiscent of the old planned economies in the now-extinct Communist governments of eastern Europe. The governmental technocrats of our own bureaucracy are at war with the auto company executives over the feasibility of this mandated merchandise. The tax-credit, tax-incentive approach uses the drive of the profit motive to encourage work on these new technologies.

"If the so-called big three auto producers don't want to get into the production of these vehicles, some enterprising entrepreneur will, knowing that the government is there helping to create a market for his product. Maybe a fuel cell car, or a hydrogen-powered car, invented by some tinkering genius in his garage, will accomplish these objectives more competitively than the electric car. The computer revolution of the 1970's and 1980's started in some garages.

"And this approach also allows for interim technologies like hybrid vehicles. Some of these vehicles run on electric power for the first 50 miles, then switch over to gasoline. Since most trips people take are under 50 miles, this would significantly reduce gasoline consumption and pollution. So we would give partial tax credits for purchasing these vehicles, and give people incentives to purchase them by raising the cost of gasoline.

"Because also accompanying the tax credits, I am proposing an increase in gasoline taxes of ten cents a gallon every year for the next fifteen years. It is interesting to me that a gasoline tax has often been considered and implemented, based on the argument that our taxes on gasoline are lower than Europe's or Japan's. But have we ever questioned why those countries have higher taxes? Not just to fill the treasuries. They know the effects of these taxes on the marketplace.

"An important comment needs to be made about these proposals. If the electricity for cars is produced by coal, oil, or nuclear power, then this transformation will be of no real benefit in our goal of attaining a Regenerating Biosphere. We would have to enact some form of my first proposal for this second proposal to have its desired effect."

Contreras yawned disgustedly, clearly bored with Edwards' remarks. He turned and walked along the back of the banquet hall, now moving toward the left side.

Handel turned slowly to look at Contreras. Now that Contreras was moving away, Handel was able to focus on him more thoroughly. He again dialed his cellular phone. "Seven. There is no doubt. He's packing."

"Crap."

"Do we move in?"

"It's too soon." The voice on the other end was clearly conflicted and frustrated. "We have only nailed down part of the Enriquez operation. We need a few more weeks at least."

"I know." Handel knew the problem and didn't need to be reminded of it. He needed instructions.

"What's he doing?"

"Hard to talk. He's still in the back—moving to left side . . . less crowded."

"Continue to report."

"Need instructions. Need to set up move-in *now*, if that's our option."

"We'll assess here and get back to you. Out."

Handel exhaled with irritation. Contreras was moving away. The farther away he moved, the less capability Handel would have to intervene and prevent whatever Contreras was planning.

"A third set of proposals would be designed to change this society from a commuting society to what Alvin Toffler has called the 'Electronic Cottage,'" Edwards continued. "With modems and fax machines, added to dramatically developed telephone technology, there is no reason for large segments of the population to leave their homes for crowded freeways taking them to regimented office situations. This is an archaic holdover from the factory concept of the Industrial Revolution.

"There are numerous benefits to this transformation. I'll mention two. We would reduce traffic by eliminating commuters, saving fuel and reducing pollution. And, parents would require less day care, with more flexibility in setting up day care. Working parents could spend more time with their children, strengthening family relations.

"Again, this has not occurred because there are no marketplace incentives moving us toward the change. Who pays for workers to commute? Usually not the employer, who uses the labor of those employees to create goods and services. The employee bears those costs, which have no influence on the bottom line. So there is no incentive to reduce or control this True Cost of production.

"To apply Economic Activism to this situation, first, there should be federal legislation that will compel employers to pay a fair pro-rata share of their employee commuter costs. We would phase in this commuting cost-sharing, and probably exempt small businesses. Second, as companion legislation, there would be generous tax credits for all costs associated with setting up employees in their Electronic Cottages, which we would define as employees able to complete their full-time jobs while only commuting a maximum of twice a week. And employers would receive continued tax credits for all employees who remain in an Electronic Cottage arrangement."

Handel's cellular phone beeped.

"Seven," Handel answered with quiet anticipation.

"Is contacting security an option?"

Handel already had considered this idea and had a quick answer. "No secret service here. Unarmed rent-a-cops. They'd have to call in the real thing, which could blow our operation."

"What's the situation?"

"He's still in the back, at the left corner."

"Sounds harmless."

"For now . . ."

"Keep us informed. Out."

Handel sighed irritably. It appeared to him that the strategy was to do nothing until there were no other options except to continue doing nothing.

"This brings us to a specific, exciting, and genuinely possible future for America," Edwards told his audience enthusiastically. "I see a typical American worker getting up in the morning preparing to go to work in his electric car. He has charged up the batteries for that car using electricity produced by the solar cells and windmills mounted on and around his home. Or, he might use his alcohol-powered vehicle, with the fuel distilled from organic wastes collected and processed at his home with all battery and fuel-distillation processes activated by a computer-controlled smart house. He's commuting today, but he normally commutes only twice a week. His fax machine, modem and telephone make him very effective right from his home the other three days of his work week. And because so many others are only commuting two days a week, he has less traffic to deal with, as he commutes through a cleaner city."

Contreras appeared to be so bored he was about to doze off. He smirked and shook his head, then started up the sparsely populated left side of the hall.

Handel quickly grabbed his cellular phone. "Seven. He's on the move. Toward the front."

"Move in to an intercept position."

Handel gritted his teeth. "I wish you'd told me this was a possibility. I'm out of position now," he said quietly, but obviously frustrated.

"Do your best."

"Yeah."

"Out."

Handel knew that trying to cross through the crowd would be nearly impossible, and too conspicuous to have any chance of success. He needed to move down the right side of the hall to the back, then circle around and follow Contreras's route. But he needed to be subtle. A sudden move circling around in the middle of Edwards' speech would almost certainly attract attention.

Handel moved slowly toward the back of the right side of the hall, watching helplessly as Contreras sauntered up the left side of the hall toward the front row.

Contreras stopped at the front row. Handel had worked his way to the back of the hall, and had moved about half way toward the left side, where he would start forward. But he had to stop when Contreras began to look carefully around the room. Contreras's purposeful stare told Handel that he was sizing up the security situation. Contreras seemed interested in determining whether his move to the front had generated a reaction from any security personnel.

Edwards continued his speech. "Fourth, I am proposing that we expand the current Department of Energy to the Department of Energy and the Environment. We would authorize this department to begin a program of labeling products and services which will lead us to our goal of a Regenerating Biosphere. We would seek representatives from industry, and from consumer groups, to participate. This should be a wide, collaborative effort, non-partisan and non-political. These green tags would be easily detached by the consumer and retained. Consumers would then use the tags when they file their Federal Income Tax returns to claim tax credits for using these beneficial products. This is another possible way of reimbursing consumers for the True Benefits of environmentally conscious choices.

"Some specific products that merit these green tags would be reusable cloth diapers, products made from recycled materials, products made from materials that can be easily recycled, and products made from chemicals that are not harmful to the environment. Of course, we would not limit our list to these examples.

"Industries producing products with the green tags would also receive tax benefits, since we would ask them to print and attach the tags. We should also grant tax credits to all businesses that specialize in recycling. A major part of converting this society from an industrial base to a Regenerating Biosphere is changing the source of our raw materials from the earth's crust to our own discarded trash. Any company especially devoted to that enterprise deserves all possible rewards from government in exchange for the huge benefits their enterprise brings to our society.

"To move toward a Regenerating Biosphere, we must assess taxes on certain types of products and processes. These would include the myriad of plastic disposable items that do not easily reassimilate into the environment, such as disposable diapers, plastic razors, food wrappers and bags. These would also include products consisting of environmentally harmful chemicals, and produced with processes that generate environmentally harmful side effects."

"Seven," Handel spoke quickly into his cellular phone. "If I close on him now, he'll make me. Please advise."

"What is he doing?"

"Watching Edwards. And looking over the area real close."

"Hold your position. If he does something suspicious, move in and take him."

"I'm in the back—he's in the front," Handel stated bitterly. "I need some back-up. But don't send them barging in here."

"How did you get so far out of position?"

"How did I—" Handel cut off his angry, incredulous repetition of the obnoxious question. "We can discuss that later. Advise on the status of my request for back-up."

"Back-up will be coming. Out."

Handel's lips scrunched into an angry circle on his face. He'd wait for Contreras to turn back to the front, then try to move closer. But he knew Contreras had position. There was a good chance that Contreras would be able to do whatever he planned to do. Handel would probably be limited to mopping up after the fact.

"These proposals," Edwards said, "are based on the underlying goal of moving to a Regenerating Biosphere by bringing our Free Market economy into harmony with our goal. An Edwards Administration, and even the Edwards campaign, will be flexible on the specifics of applying the concepts. The basic principles will not be compromised. But we will not consider it a defeat if analysis and debate on these specific proposals leads us to modify them, even before the election. In fact, we will draft specific proposals of legislative quality and then allow them to be picked apart. And yes, based on reactions, we might change some of the specifics. In past campaigns, candidates who shift proposals have been considered vacillating or wishy-washy. But in the legislative process, we will most certainly be asked to debate and modify. Why not start now?"

Handel spotted a seat on the aisle, about one third back from the front on the left side. He decided to make a casual, confident move to take that seat. Even if Contreras saw him, Handel would simply appear to be an Edwards supporter taking his seat. He waited for a good opportunity to make his move.

"Let's subsidize the opportunity to recycle and have an energy self-sufficient home. Let's challenge the new Henry Fords of energy self-sufficient smart homes, solar cells, windmills and recycling to *step forward* and to *make their fortunes.*" Applause picked up to its most intense level since the opening section of the speech.

"And what would be the benefit to all of us and our children, and our children's children, if we can accomplish this smooth transformation to the Regenerating Biosphere era? Politically, there is the obvious short term benefit of reducing our current dependence on scarcer energy sources concentrated in countries sometimes hostile to us. But perhaps more importantly, over the long term, is the benefit of transforming the planet from a place where five to six billion people struggle over scarce and dwindling resources, to a planet of inexhaustible prosperity. Cyclical consumption patterns will reduce, maybe even eventually *end* competition over scarce resources.

"This by-product of the transformation is important for our children, and their children. Many nations are trying to raise their standard of living to our level. We are becoming aware that the Earth's ecosphere cannot support an Industrial Revolution in every corner of the planet. As this has become more evident, the nations still attempting to enter the Industrial Revolution era have begun to ask why the United States, with five per cent of the world's population, should continue to consume over 20 per cent of the world's resources. As the question becomes more insistent, even resentful and angry, we will find ourselves either fighting to retain this inequity, or adjusting our standard of living to alleviate it. I like this third alternative, transforming world consumption away from the Industrial Revolution pattern. Let's provide the leadership by starting this transition.

"An example of this is how some nations are trying to eat truckloads of beef because Americans do, or have in the past. We are becoming aware that farming beef is less efficient than producing other forms of nourishment, and that eating too much clogs our arteries. So we have begun to moderate our consumption of beef, despite our traditions of cowboys, and thick steaks. But other nations still chop down their rainforests so they can raise herds of cattle. By beginning this transition, we will do more than just ask them not to make that choice. We will lead by *example*.

"In fact, as we look ahead, we will also find ourselves looking back hundreds of generations to rediscover the wisdom of hunter-gatherers, who before the agricultural revolution, lived in perfect balance with the biosphere. These were human beings with the same intellectual capacity of humans today, who evolved ways of looking at the world, and of operating in harmony with the environment that gave them an equilibrium of prosperity for thousands, maybe millions of years.

"That way of life is preserved among so-called 'indigenous peoples,' like the aborigines of Australia, or the American Indians of this country. Humans of the agricultural and Industrial Revolution societies have considered these people 'primitive.' But as leaders into the Regenerating Biosphere era will look to the ancient wisdom of these so-called primitives, not to turn back the clock, which would be impossible even if desirable, but to translate their lessons of equilibrium-prosperity to our own world. We may find some of these 'primitives' were really quite advanced in some areas of knowledge."

Contreras had been turned toward Edwards for a while. Now was a good time for Handel to make his move. He arrived at the seat and sat in it.

"Uh, that seat's saved," a young, brown-haired male college student in a maroon Harvard sweatshirt told him. "My girlfriend's just out at the rest room."

"Sorry," Handel said as he vacated the seat.

Contreras looked in his direction, attracted by Handel's movement.

Handel headed to the left side door, as if he was leaving the seat he'd been sitting in for awhile. He looked at his watch to give the appearance of checking the time as he left his seat.

Contreras looked away.

Handel went to the door, but did not go through it. Contreras did not glance back in the area, so he apparently was not suspicious of any activity of Handel's. But Handel had moved in as close as he could get.

"Environmentally, every renewable energy source is almost completely non-polluting. Our cities would cease being cesspools of smog," Edwards stated, continuing his explanation of the benefits of his agenda. "Our descendants may well look back at the cities of the last half of the Twentieth Century and compare them to cities of a few hundred years ago with open sewers. This transformation would also dramatically reduce the amount of greenhouse gases going into the atmosphere, beginning to reverse what could be a catastrophic global warming.

"Use of recycling technologies would also end the trash crisis that threatens most major urban areas. And, ugly, destructive, sometimes dangerous mining operations could be curtailed as we recycle materials already mined.

"Economically, our leadership in these new technologies will create new markets and new trading relationships, stimulating our economy. American businesses will come to world markets selling these products. And, as we noted earlier, recycling and renewable resource technologies are more labor intensive, creating a net result of more jobs."

Edwards' intensity picked up. "Some will say 'these solutions may be practical, but not today.' I don't believe the American people should spend one more day than necessary riding in vehicles that pollute our cities, or held hostage by their dependence on foreign energy sources, or facing the consequences of a potential greenhouse century. I want *tomorrow's* energy and resource consumption instituted *today*. With the approach clearly described in this speech, we absolutely *can* accomplish these goals. So I want the naysayers to stop assuming it can't be done! You and I know it *can* be done. One of the first steps is for us to *believe*."

The crowd responded to this exhortation with strong applause.

"With your help, we will install a new vision of our future *this* year, *now,* and march through the first part of the new millennium with our heads held high, as the world embarks on a new era of peace and prosperity. Join me. Thank you."

The crowd jumped to its feet in unison and applauded wildly. Edwards walked down from the podium to the front row of the audience where he began shaking hands. He moved from his left to his right, toward Contreras's position. Contreras waited for Edwards, toward the end of the row, wearing an arrogant, sneering grin.

There was no time for Handel to call anyone. Contreras was going to make contact with Edwards if he wanted to. Handel tried to move quickly toward the front of the hall, but the crowd pushing towards Edwards blocked him. Handel couldn't do anything but witness whatever was going to happen.

Contreras held his hand across his chest. Was he preparing to reach for his gun? Or was he making sure his gun wouldn't be jostled by the crowd?

Edwards arrived at Contreras. Contreras brought his right hand across his chest and extended his arm toward Edwards.

Handel was still at least twenty feet away, with solid rows of people in between. He put his hand on his gun, but did not pull it out of his concealed belt holster.

But Contreras's hand was empty. He let Edwards grab his hand, then engaged in an enthusiastic, almost overly exaggerated handshake.

Edwards continued to greet the few left in the front of the crowd as he headed toward the left side exit, flanked on his right by Saroyan and other campaign staffers.

Handel breathed a huge sigh of relief. "This is seven," he said into his cellular phone.

"Report."

"No threat to Edwards. Subject just . . . shook his hand."

"Say again, seven?"

"Subject went up to the front and shook Edwards' hand, like they were real good buddies."

"Explanation?"

"I don't have one. I'm just relieved he didn't use that gun, because I had no way to stop him."

"Unit seven, where is the subject now?"

"Following the crowd out the south exit."

"Fine." The tone of the voice on the other end of Handel's cellular phone became brittle and tart. "Your back-up is in place and will pick-up surveillance. You report to base. Copy?"

"Yeah," he replied warily. "But he didn't make me. I can maintain—"

"Report to base."

"Yeah, okay," Handel acknowledged unenthusiastically. "But what's with the attitude?"

"Obviously your subject was not there to shake Edwards' hand. He had a meeting with a contact that you failed to notice because you were too busy playing Secret Service. Now report in."

For a moment, Handel considered if this could be possible. But he was certain Contreras hadn't interacted with anyone, not even subtly. "No," he insisted. "It's not possible. And I think this incident *should* be reported to the Secret Service."

"No further discussion at this time. Report in."

"On my way. Out."

And no matter how hard Handel argued, his superiors at DEA were sure Contreras had completed some kind of surreptitious transaction, and Handel had missed it. Handel suffered through a sharp chastisement. And no report was ever passed on to the Secret Service, or any other security entity.

✪   ✪   ✪

"I WASN'T TOTALLY THRILLED WITH THE SPEECH," EDWARDS ADMITTED to Saroyan as they sat at a table in Edwards' plushly furnished room. He had a sheaf of papers in front of him.

"It was *long*," Saroyan commented.

"I know. And I'm glad I left out the technical discussions on 'Retail Wheeling,' and 'Demand-Side Management' and how utility regulations would have to be changed. And our reasons for opposing the buying and selling of pollution credits. It's just that I don't want to underestimate the American public. I think they're a lot more sophisticated than they get credit for."

"You may be right," Saroyan agreed. "And I heard compliments on the speech from people I respect a lot. But no matter how well you speak, speech-making is still a very static way to communicate anything. We'll use the infomercial for the more detailed stuff, where we can make it more entertaining, with graphics and some interesting video images."

Oscar Lusman quickly entered the room. "I've got a summary of the network coverage," he told them excitedly.

"Good. I'll want to see a tape," Saroyan told him. "But tell me the bottom line. Did we get a bite on all four networks?"

"Right after they did their reports on the other candidates," Lusman replied.

"Perfect," Saroyan said with a satisfied smile.

"What kind of coverage?" Edwards asked.

"That could have been better," Lusman answered. "We got mostly some bites of you at the end, without much focus on your specific proposals."

"Yeah, they're prone to doing that," Edwards commented with a knowing smile.

"At least you're getting the coverage, and it's in the context of reports on the other candidates."

"I don't want to be another one of these guys who says he has a campaign of 'new ideas,' but the public never hears what they are," Edwards told them.

"Your old network won't let that happen," Lusman observed with a smile. "They listed the four main proposals with sharp graphics, showed your closing, with a lot of the applause, and even featured a little of your original campaign announcement."

Edwards finally grinned. "My old buddy, Ted Jessup."

"Ted's a great guy," Lusman added.

"What's the latest on the ballot signatures?" Edwards asked Lusman.

"We've got organizations in every state," Lusman replied. "And the signatures are coming in at a good clip."

"Good."

Saroyan stood up to leave. "We'll see how all this plays, and how our first national ads do. Oscar, get me a tape of the first infomercial as soon as you have it."

Lusman nodded as he stood up. Saroyan and Lusman left.

Chapter 7

That evening, Saturday
Boston, Massachusetts

MICHAEL EDWARDS SIGHED AS HE SAT AT THE DESK IN HIS HOTEL ROOM, with pages of notes and speech drafts in front of him. He looked at the digital clock next to the bed which read "10:48." He flipped his pen onto the desk.

He walked over to the phone and called the front desk. "Any messages for me?" The answer was negative. "Okay. Thanks." He hung up the phone.

But when he went back over to the desk, he couldn't refocus his mind on the speech in front of him.

Teresa burst into the room. "I'm finally back!" she told him energetically. "The meeting tonight went great."

"I was wondering—" But Michael was cut off in mid-sentence.

"You cannot believe the enthusiasm of these kids," Teresa continued rapidly and energetically. "They're so committed. I get a charge out of them, Michael."

"I'm real glad—"

"A couple of the girls knew about me in the Miss Pacific Coast Pageant! They wanted my autograph! And they told me I still look gorgeous," she added with a sly smile.

"You *do* still look gorgeous."

"Oh, and I watched your old network's coverage of your speech today with a bunch of kids! They hooted and hollered; the whole student union over at MIT was into it. I think you're becoming more than just a candidate. They're kids. They like to see things get shaken up—adult things like Democrats and Republicans."

"Drew and I have been trying to—"

"The enthusiasm of these kids by itself'll win this thing!"

Michael could not help but flash a satisfied grin. "I think someone else is a little enthusiastic too. I was wondering where—"

"I know I'm late. I probably should have called. I hope you didn't wait dinner for me. I ate a snack at a cafe over near Harvard. I could go for something now. Michael . . ."

Michael didn't speak, because Teresa seemed to stop in the middle of a thought, and he gave her an opportunity to finish it.

But she didn't speak. She walked slowly over to him, finally quiet, but with a look in her eyes that Michael knew well.

Michael stood up and they embraced. She looked into his eyes with a deep, longing expression of limitless love. He hadn't seen this expression for some time. But he also realized that in recent years, after Omni-Vee had become a huge success and the Edwards family had become one of the wealthiest in the country, Michael had rarely conveyed an expression like this to Teresa either. He knew right then that Teresa had been correct when she'd called him a grouch. He really had become irritable and difficult to approach. He wondered for an instant if he would have been open to Teresa's current mood back before the campaign had started. But he didn't wonder for long. Because he was certainly open to her mood now. They kissed passionately.

"Michael, I need a shower. Take off your clothes and join me in the bathroom." She walked away, into the bathroom and shut the door, before he could say anything.

Michael smiled as he removed his clothes and piled them on a chair. As he did, he heard the water for the shower go on. After he was completely undressed, he walked toward the bathroom.

When Michael opened the door, he found his wife under the shower, still fully clothed. Her white blouse clung to her chest. Because it was wet, her lacy bra holding her beauty queen breasts was easily visible. Her nipples poked through her wet blouse. Her blue jeans darkened as they became soaked. She flipped the sandals off her feet.

Michael got into the shower stall. Teresa moved back under the shower spout and gripped it by raising her hands over her head. "Strip me," she implored.

Michael was now in a lustful frenzy. He had not seen Teresa acting this sensually in a long time. Despite all that money and prosperity, they had been bored. Now they had taken on the most formidable challenge of their lives, and they were passionate about each other again. Michael tore off her clothes and kissed every newly exposed part of her body as he uncovered it.

When she was naked and they were both ready to culminate their passion, she suggested softly "Take me on the floor."

She took him by both hands, leaving the shower still running, and led him out of the bathroom to an open spot on the floor near the table where Michael had met with Saroyan earlier in the day. They engaged in intense and fulfilling love-making that is especially possible when both partners know each other so intimately, when they are familiar with exactly what steps to take to bring the other one to ecstasy.

They fell asleep on the floor.

About an hour later, Michael woke up to hear the shower running. He got up and turned it off. He looked down at his wet, naked wife, sleeping contentedly. He pulled the bedspread off the bed, retook his position next to his wife on the floor, and covered them both.

☼   ☼   ☼

Late February, Election Year: Tuesday
Shreveport, Louisiana

ENRIQUEZ WALKED INTO THE NEARLY EMPTY CAFE ADVERTISING "CAJUN Chili," just southeast of Shreveport, off the main road to Barksdale Air Force Base near the smaller Louisiana community of Bossier City. The Red River was in view at the horizon of green, gently rolling hills. Though Shreveport was the second largest city in Louisiana, it was not primarily a tourist area. The local economy relied on the manufacture of gas and oil equipment, and on nearby Barksdale Air Force Base. Enriquez blew on his hands as he felt the cool snap of the northern Louisiana winter outside. It was close to fifty degrees, but Enriquez was not accustomed to, nor fond of temperatures in that range. He spotted Fadiman and walked over to him. He glanced at his watch. "Am I late? I thought I was early."

Fadiman looked at him smugly, then continued eating the bowl of chili in front of him on the worn, unvarnished wooden table. "You are. I was earlier."

Enriquez sat down across from Fadiman. There were two other people in the cafe, and neither of them were waiting at a table for service. One was a friendly-looking, slightly overweight man with grey hair and a stubbly unshaven face, standing behind the cash register. He wore a dirty apron over his denim overalls. The other was a large man, facing away from Enriquez and Fadiman, behind the counter at the grill, wearing a high white chef's hat and a baggy smock.

"So you're still worried about this Edwards?" Fadiman asked light-heartedly as he chewed and swallowed a bite.

"He's talking about the 'atom bomb' of the war on drugs. We know what that means for me. And the last poll I heard of says he has almost 20 per cent of the voters in his pocket. He is bad for my business."

"This is old stuff," Fadiman dismissed.

"Yeah?" Enriquez snapped. "Then you tell me, have you talked to your friends about this? Your oil buddy Hunter. Have you talked to him? This guy is bad for his business too."

"I'm telling you right now, he won't talk to you," Fadiman told him gruffly.

"So you haven't even asked him," Enriquez concluded, low-voiced, but seething.

"No," Fadiman confirmed casually.

Enriquez looked around. "Where's your security buddy?"

"You said I didn't need him."

"That's right. We're friends," Enriquez said smiling. "Be a friend. Get me a meeting with Hunter."

"You know, you keep asking to meet with my 'friends.' But it keeps coming back to Hunter."

"Because I had one of my people at Edwards' big speech about the Regeneration Biosphere, or something, and I think Hunter and I will have things in common. And my friend says security for Edwards right now is a joke. He says he has a way to solve this Edwards problem for me, with no hassles. But he tends to be cocky, and American politics is not his area of specialization. A clumsy, crude mistake would be difficult to take back and could make this very bad. That is why I would like us all to work together. I really want to work with an American on this."

Fadiman stuck his spoon in his chili. He sneered irritably. "Was your man at Edwards' speech followed?"

"No," Enriquez replied indignantly, and surprised by the question.

Fadiman looked coldly at Enriquez. "What you want . . . may not happen."

Enriquez stood up and leaned over Fadiman. "I want you to start acting like a friend on this and try to get Hunter to meet with me," he said with a menacing growl.

Suddenly the cook with the high white chef's hat moved over into the area and stood between the two of them. He slid an order in front of Enriquez. "Chili, my friend?" It was Fadiman's security man, with a bushy dark-haired wig, glasses and a dark moustache.

If Enriquez recognized him, he didn't indicate it. He leaned back, then sat down. He picked up a spoon. "Chili. Sure." He took a bite.

"I'll talk to Hunter," Fadiman told Enriquez with chilly calm. "If he wants a meeting, I'll set it up. If he doesn't, I will contact you through intermediaries, and this is our *last* face-to-face meeting. And don't threaten me again with pulling your business. I'm not sure I want it anymore."

Enriquez nodded slowly, gaining control over the anger he felt. After all, a further outburst of temper would surely end the possibility of a meeting with Hunter. "So I will hear from you," he finally responded, matter-of-factly, as he put his spoon in the chili and stirred it.

"One way or another."

"Then let us finish this fine chili you have brought us so many miles to enjoy together."

Fadiman put down his spoon and stood up. "I'm through with mine," he announced dispassionately. "It's already paid for. Enjoy the rest of yours." He and his security man left quickly.

Enriquez watched as they left. He looked down at the chili he had just stirred and sneered. He put a bite in his mouth, chewed for a moment, then angrily slammed his fist down on the table. The spoon flew out of his hand and hit the floor, jingling with the sound of metal against tile. He pushed the bowl of chili away from him, then got up and left.

☼   ☼   ☼

"HE'S STILL NOT ADMITTING WHY HE'S REALLY AFRAID OF EDWARDS, AND why he wants to talk to Hunter so badly," Fadiman commented to his security man as they drove down a dusty back road in a rented jeep. The security man was behind the wheel—Fadiman sat next to him in the passenger seat.

"Couldn't he really be afraid of that 'atomic bomb' of the drug war?" the security man asked.

"I'm sure he is," Fadiman commented confidently. "But there's more to it. Anything else from South America?"

"Not yet."

"Which tells me he *is* trying to obscure something, or we'd have an easier time figuring out just what all his convoluted banking arrangements mean."

"We'll untangle it," the security man promised.

"I have no doubt. I want to have a clearer idea on this before I involve Beau."

"You're going to involve Mr. Hunter?"

"I'm going to give him the option, yes."

The security man nodded, betraying just a slight expression of his surprise.

☼   ☼   ☼

Early March, Election Year: Thursday
Berkeley, California

"THERE'S A MR. NAYLOR HERE TO SEE YOU?" LESLIE MCSWAIN, A YOUNG volunteer campaign worker told Oscar Lusman tentatively. Lusman was in the small office adjoining the modest campaign headquarters for Michael Edwards in Berkeley, California, near the University of California campus there. It was two blocks west of Telegraph Avenue, and three blocks south of the "Cal" campus.

"What's he look like?" Lusman asked.

"Like a hippie who stepped out of a time machine from the 60's."

"A lot of our supporters from around here look like that," Lusman observed. "Hell, I've gotta see him, I guess. Tell him to come in."

Bradford "Slick" Naylor entered the office carrying a beaten, weathered briefcase. He looked irritable and impatient. He had worn his cleanest and best pair of jeans which had only one tear just below the right knee. And he wore a brand new white T shirt. "I'm here to see Mikey," he said disrespectfully.

"What's this about?"

"I'll tell him."

"Mister . . . Naylor is it?"

"*'Sir'* to you."

"Whatever. Mr. Edwards is very busy. One thing I do is screen his appointments for him. So you're going to have to tell me what this is about."

Naylor nodded and looked around the room. "You hire people here?"

"Do I? Yeah. I have some hiring responsibility."

"Well maybe we don't need to bother him with this. Yeah. Maybe it *is* better I talk to you. Leave him out of it. Like you say, he's busy."

"We have a lot of work for volunteers . . ." Lusman said probing, still not understanding Naylor's purpose.

Naylor grinned mischievously and rolled his eyes. "Volunteer?" he repeated in disbelief.

"You're going to have make yourself clearer."

"Yeah, well I think you ought to hire me as a . . . I think you people call 'em consultants. Like a publicity consultant or something."

"Uh, Mr. Naylor? We don't have any openings for a consultant. I'm sorry you wasted your time."

"Look kid, I'm an old friend of Michael's. Before you turn me out of here like I was some kind of trash, you'd better let me talk to him."

"Just what is it you think you can do for us?" Lusman asked fishing for Naylor's purpose.

"I have some information. What I can do for you is keep it to myself."

"What kind of information?"

Naylor opened his briefcase and handed Lusman a thin file.

Lusman reviewed the contents. There was a page-one newspaper photo of a much younger Michael Edwards, grubby-looking with scraggly long hair, standing among a small group, watching with obvious disbelief as paramedics wheeled away a stretcher covered with a white sheet. The headline read "Honor Student Found Dead of Overdose." Within the text of the article, under the picture, light blue pen had been used to highlight a brief section: "The search continues for whoever sold the tainted heroin to the widely admired coed. 'She came to our city for an education and got hooked on drugs by some scummy drug pusher,' Detective Harold Buntz of the Berkeley Police angrily announced at a press conference. 'We'll find that pusher, and we'll throw him in prison for murder. This is a *murder* case.'" With the newspaper article was a weathered and torn photo. It showed the smiling face of young Michael Edwards, next to a beautiful young woman with long, straight, black hair. "Thanks for a good time and great stuff, Peace and Love, Fiona," was written in neat, curvy handwriting across the front of the photo.

"Do I get my job?" Naylor asked.

"That file doesn't prove anything," Lusman said, trying to sound tough, but not sure he could maintain it.

"No, but I could dig up ten witnesses who'll create such a shitstorm that it won't matter to anyone what's proof and what isn't. He's not the squeaky clean saint you guys are selling him as. I know it. And I can do more than just say it. I figure that's worth something."

Lusman was uncomfortable. He looked at Naylor and narrowed his eyes caustically. "So it doesn't matter to you that this man could well be the answer to a lot of this country's problems."

"You really believe that shit, don't you," Naylor mocked as he laughed. "What are you gonna do, Jack? Trade a cow for three beans? In the real world, they don't sprout up to a beanstalk. They just give you gas after you eat 'em."

Lusman maintained a quiet exterior. But inside, panic hit like a four alarm fire with lights glaring and sirens blaring. A potentially devastating scandal had just confronted him. Would he be able to play in the big leagues and contain this possible crisis, or would he fail and watch the campaign come crashing to an ignominious end? Could he handle this kind of job, or not? He had to decide what to do now. Asking Saroyan or Edwards about the situation would create more problems than it solved. Isn't this what political operatives like him were paid to do? Handle situations like this so the candidate could remain aloof from them? He was responsible for protecting Michael Edwards. He resolved to do exactly that.

"Just what salary do you expect as a campaign consultant?" Lusman asked him coolly.

"I figure a thousand a week."

"Five hundred."

"Don't bargain with me, kid. I'm letting you off cheap."

"Fine. You'll work directly under me. A thousand a week. Give me an address. I'll mail you a check."

"A check?"

"Come pick up your cash once a week at the headquarters."

"You setting one of these up in L-A maybe?"

"This week."

"Have my cash ready there."

"Fine."

Naylor stood up. "Good deal." He extended his hand.

Lusman didn't move. "Get outta here. I don't expect to see you again, *ever*. And after the election is over, so is your 'job.'"

"Yeah. Okay." Naylor smirked as he shrugged his shoulders. He left the office, then left the headquarters.

Leslie McSwain walked in. "What was *his* story?"

"I'm not sure." Lusman sighed. "I hope I handled it right." He looked at Leslie. "He's going to be a consultant for us. We'll be paying him in cash, out of the L-A office, once a week. His name is . . . Naylor, I think he said. He's a . . . media consultant."

"Okay," Leslie answered, not understanding but not questioning.

Lusman drew and exhaled another deep breath. "Politics." He smiled wearily. "What a weird thing for a person to want to do."

Leslie also smiled.

Chapter 8

"As we reported about thirty minutes ago, in a stunning announcement, Jeffrey Jefferson has withdrawn from the race for the Democratic nomination," the newscaster stated on the limousine radio.

Michael Edwards' eyebrows raised as he exchanged a glance with Drew Saroyan seated in the back of the limousine with him. "I'll be damned."

"Mr. Jefferson has also pledged his support to Victor Parker," the announcer continued. "In a brief speech to some of his campaign workers in Washington D.C., he asked them to join him in assuring the nomination of his long-time friend."

Saroyan chuckled. "'Long-time friend.' They shared a dais a few times at some Democratic fund-raisers. There's some kind of a deal going on, like the VP slot on the ticket . . ."

"What does this do for us?"

"In the long run, it helps. The narrower the field gets, the less interesting the competition. The media will get bored with meaningless primaries and look to us for some action."

"But in the short run . . ."

"I wish the son-of-a-bitch hadn't chosen *today* to do this. We'll be lucky to get any meaningful coverage of your first major appearance on the west coast as a candidate."

"Yeah."

The limousine turned the corner into the entrance to Golden Gate Park. Edwards looked out the tinted windows at the grassy patches of the park bordered by tall trees. "The kid did a good job on this one," Edwards commented.

"He's good," Saroyan agreed. "He really had to fight to get the use of this park. The mayor's a Democrat. It'll look *great* on TV. An outdoor rally in a green setting. But with the trees enclosing the area, the crowd won't disappear in the camera frames. You'll look like you're addressing a huge outdoor throng."

They pulled up to the curb next to the grassy area, framed by lines of high trees, where Edwards would be delivering his first major west coast address. At least seven different television cameras took up positions to cover the event. And again, the crowd was clearly a little too large for the location.

As the limo pulled up, the crowd began to murmur in anticipation. And as Edwards emerged, applause began slowly, then built as the crowd realized he had arrived. Edwards smiled. This was really starting to sound and feel like a national political campaign. He felt a rush of excitement. He was taking his best shot, and was off to a good start.

☆   ☆   ☆

"THAT DAMN JEFFERSON PRACTICALLY KNOCKED US RIGHT OFF THE evening news," Saroyan told them as they sat around a table in Edwards' hotel room at the Hilltop Hotel in San Francisco. The room was modest, but there was a large television monitor with a videocassette recorder hooked up to it. Saroyan, with Teresa and Michael Edwards, prepared to focus most of their attention on the television screen as they ate Chinese food off of paper plates.

"We got *some* coverage, didn't we?" Edwards asked rhetorically, but without enthusiasm.

"We got a mention in about a ten to twenty second clip with a voice-over, no live sound, on three of the four networks," Saroyan told him frustratedly. He took a bite of his food, then grunted and threw his fork onto the table. "Give me the Chinese food from New York any day of the week."

"Are you crazy?" Teresa asked contentiously. "This is San Francisco. No city west of Beijing has better Chinese food."

"You must be from out here," Saroyan said.

"I've been living in New York for years," Teresa insisted. "Nothing in New York can touch the Chinese food in San Francisco."

Michael smiled and decided to change the subject. "What did Ted do with it?" he asked.

"Ran about three minutes on it," Saroyan told him with satisfaction. "Good footage of you and the crowd. Then, later in the broadcast their new guy. Talbot?"

"Yeah," Edwards confirmed.

"This guy Talbot gave a real positive commentary on your Economic Activism and True Costs/True Benefits proposals. He compared them to Roosevelt's New Deal, saying something to the effect that it could be a revolutionary concept like the New Deal policies."

"That's beautiful," Edwards commented. "I just hope we can keep it going with only one network giving us any serious attention."

"We're still being treated by the other ones like an entertaining, but not really serious third candidacy," Saroyan observed. "We've got to get them to change their approach to us."

"If you could see the kids, you wouldn't say we're not being treated seriously," Teresa countered. "There is a real word-of-mouth support building with the young people all over the country."

"And the Democrats are down to three," Edwards observed.

"It'll be two real quick," Saroyan added. "Trewillinger couldn't get votes from anyone south of Pennsylvania on Super Tuesday. And he wasn't close to Parker and Highland here. He obviously can't draw votes outside the northeast."

Edwards nodded.

"But Highland and Parker are neck and neck," Saroyan observed pessimistically. "Those damn guys look like they're in for a good, close race." He paused. "You want to take a look at these clips?"

"Yeah," Edwards replied.

At that moment, there was a firm knock on the door.

"Yeah?" Edwards called out.

Oscar Lusman almost flew into the room, brimming with excitement and energy. He held a VHS videocassette in his hand. "I have something that'll bring a big smile to your faces."

"Another clip?" Saroyan asked.

"No. *Better*. This will . . . Well, let me show it to you." He charged over to the machine and inserted the tape.

Edwards watched as he ate, first silently, then incredulously, as the short tape of no more than two minutes concluded. After the tape was over, Teresa looked over at Michael, trying to read his reaction. And she correctly concluded he was squeamish. Saroyan was smiling slightly. But he also read Michael's expression, and toned down his own reaction accordingly.

It was Saroyan who spoke first. "Does Highland know you have this?" he asked Lusman.

"I doubt it," Lusman chuckled mischievously.

"Where did you get it?" Edwards asked.

"A friend of mine from college, sympathetic to us, and close to the Highland family."

"This would ruin Highland, and end this damn primary that is distracting the media," Saroyan observed.

"I don't care," Edwards stated firmly and unequivocally. "Get that thing back to the slime-pool where you got it."

"What?" Saroyan asked with some surprise.

Teresa smiled.

"This is clearly a private family video, and the remarks he makes . . . the guy he's talking to is the jerk, not him."

"It's his uncle," Lusman told them.

"Give it back. Get rid of it," Edwards ordered tersely, clearly indicating he wanted no further discussion of the matter.

"Michael," Saroyan stated patiently, as if teaching a difficult subject, "this tape could be timed so that—"

"I'm running this show," Edwards interrupted sharply. "I will not win this way. This is not up for discussion. Get *rid* of that *tape.*"

There was a brief pause as Saroyan looked over at Lusman and shrugged. "Get rid of it," he repeated to Oscar.

Lusman seemed frustrated. "I guess I just wonder if anyone else will be as generous if the tables are turned."

"They won't be turned," Saroyan quickly stated.

Lusman looked at Edwards, then back at Saroyan. "I hope not. It's just that in this day and age, it seems as if everyone has something that can come out of the past to cause trouble."

"You're awfully young to be so cynical," Edwards commented with a smile creeping onto his face.

Lusman raised his eyebrows and shrugged.

✿   ✿   ✿

"I'M *COMING*," A GROGGY OSCAR LUSMAN INSISTED AS HE PULLED himself out of bed and went to answer the door of his hotel room. A quick glance at the clock in his room told him the time was 3:03 a.m.

Drew Saroyan entered quickly and quietly.

"I want you to set a lunch appointment next week," he told Lusman.

"What?" Lusman asked, still groggy.

"You might benefit from a little contact with one of your counterparts . . ."

Lusman was tired, and the purpose of Saroyan's visit was not clear to him at all. "Sure," he yessed perfunctorily, sleepily and irritably.

"His name is Will Runalli. Don't let him know I'm involved. Tell him you saw him give a lecture on politics and the media, and now that you're with the Edwards campaign, sort of like a colleague, you want to meet with him to chew the fat."

"Drew, what is this about? Why would this guy—I recognize his name, he's an old-time Democratic Party heavy—why would he meet with me?"

"I guarantee he'll meet with you," Saroyan assured confidently. "He's attached loosely to Parker, though that's being kept pretty quiet. He'll try to pump you for information."

"Yeah?"

"And you're a young, inexperienced guy, awed by his presence. You might just slip and mention some of your frustrations . . ."

"Frustrations."

"Yeah. Some of the frustrations of working for a guy who has as much integrity as Michael Edwards."

Lusman's head began to clear. He suddenly understood why Saroyan had awakened him. "And that frustration might include telling him about . . ." He didn't finish his statement.

"Well, you might tell him a story about your frustration, and if he figures out something useful from it, well . . ."

"So if it gets out there, I didn't do it."

"Resist him. Let him talk you into it. Make the guy think he owes you a favor."

Lusman smiled. "I think I'm going to learn a lot from working with you."

Saroyan nodded, acknowledging the compliment. "Oh, and make sure he doesn't get his copy until Trewillinger has dropped out. We want this to *end* the race between these Democrats, not give Trewillinger a chance to take Highland's place as the main competitor."

"What if Parker won't use the tape?"

"Runalli'll talk him into it. And if he can't, he'll find a way to use it anyway."

"Like you have."

"Yeah," Saroyan agreed, grinning. "Good work, getting ahold of that thing."

Lusman smiled proudly. His expression then became more serious. "And Michael doesn't know about this."

"Michael needs an end to these primaries. He knows that. Sometimes you get lucky. And sometimes you romance Lady Luck a little. And didn't he say to 'get rid of the tape?' That's what we're doing . . . just . . . getting rid of the tape."

"I'll set up the lunch."

"Good. I'll let you get back to sleep." Saroyan left Lusman's room.

✩   ✩   ✩

Late March, Election Year: Monday
New York, New York

"OKAY, SO WHAT IS SO URGENT?" MICHAEL EDWARDS ASKED AT 9:00 P.M. as he walked into one of the editing rooms at Fifth Avenue Video Company where the Edwards campaign was working on its advertisements for television. The equipment was first-rate—the surroundings were spartan. Edwards had chosen this company because he knew it had just recently been started by skilled professionals who had long careers with television networks to their credits. He knew he would get competence at a good price.

Lusman and Saroyan were sitting in the room waiting for him.

"You haven't seen Samuelson's broadcast," Saroyan observed.

"No. I watched WWBS."

"We've got the clip right here," Saroyan told him gravely.

Lusman pushed the playback button.

"Thank you, Pat," Samuelson said to the anchorman who had just introduced him. "Besides the major party candidates still in the race, we also have the candidacy of former anchorman Michael Edwards to consider. Mr. Edwards has focused heavily on the issue of renewable resources. But we know little of his positions on other issues. We have no past record in government to refer to. The closest we can come to that kind of scrutiny is to review some of Mr. Edwards' past commentaries. He has taken some rather unique positions:"

Next on the monitor came a series of quick clips with dates printed in front of them:

December 25, 1975

"The Pope should give the world a great Christmas present by condoning all forms of birth control including the free choice of abortion. If he doesn't, he and the supposedly Holy Catholic Church he represents are guilty of being international criminals, guilty of the murders of starving children in Catholic countries around the globe."

September 2, 1974

"Capitalism now fails the citizens of this nation in many ways. Perhaps we should look at the Socialist model of Sweden where the quality of life for citizens is now surpassing ours."

August 5, 1974

"The Watergate scandal and the blatant abuses of power by Republican Richard Nixon, following years of lies and deception from Democrat Lyndon Johnson, indicate that the American political system is on the verge of collapse. We need a new constitutional convention immediately, and no one who has held any major political office should be allowed to participate. The system is rotten to the core. Let's pull it up by the roots and start over again."

The last clip was of very poor quality, with a blurry picture and scratchy sound:

November 30, 1973

"'Man created God,' says Ian Anderson in the liner notes for Jethro Tull's new album, 'Aqualung.' And now God is dead—Nietzsche and Time Magazine had it right. We should not shed even a wisp of a tear for His passing. Because more evil has been done in God's name, than in the name of Satan. Rejoice, citizens of the world! We can now celebrate true love and the brotherhood of all mankind, and womankind, without the divisive distraction of 'God' and his organized religions to turn us against each other."

Samuelson continued. "I'm sure Mr. Edwards will soften his positions on some of these issues. But until he does, that appears to be his record. His current supporters, and those considering aligning themselves with him may want him to clarify himself on some of these rather unconventional positions. Pat?"

"Thank you for—"

Lusman stopped the machine.

Edwards was enraged. "That *slime*. He pulls my most outrageous commentaries over the last 25 years and strings them together! The 'God is dead' one; he *really* had to dig back to get that one, off a tiny college TV station!"

"He is an asshole," Lusman added.

"Yeah, but the asshole may have done us a favor," Saroyan told them.

Edwards frowned in disbelief.

"Publicity, Michael. He's on the second-rated news show in the country."

"But it's bad publicity," Edwards insisted.

"This might have hurt us if it was right before the election," Saroyan explained. "But we have plenty of time to answer this cheap shot. And people will be talking about it. They'll be talking about *your* candidacy."

"I don't think the guy knows how *not* to take a cheap shot," Michael commented.

"Guys at this level don't always play fair," Lusman added.

Saroyan put his arm on Edwards' shoulder. "This guy does," he told Lusman. "I had a candidate going down for the count. Michael discovered that back in the late 70's, he'd gone on trial for child abuse. It was a hung jury, nine to three for acquittal—and a sealed file. The whole thing was part of a terrible custody fight with his wife. The guy was running on a platform of better education for kids in his state. His past would have made a great story. Michael sat on it and let the guy keep his dignity. I doubt I'd be on this campaign if Michael had handled it differently."

Lusman considered Saroyan's remark.

"Let's call it a night, guys," Edwards suggested. "We've got an ad to finish tomorrow morning."

"Number one, this Friday," Saroyan added enthusiastically.

Edwards headed out the door.

☆   ☆   ☆

Late March, Election Year: Wednesday
Portland, Oregon

"SO BECAUSE OF THE DEMANDS OF CAMPAIGN FINANCING, AND THE realities of what my recent setbacks have done to my ability to raise the money necessary to continue, I regretfully withdraw my candidacy for the Democratic nomination for President of the United States," Wallace Trewillinger told a group of supporters gathered in a grassy area nestled among dignified red brick buildings on the Harvard University campus.

Edwards and Saroyan watched an excerpt of Trewillinger's announcement on the evening news in Edwards' hotel room as they discussed the next day's campaign appearance.

"But I am still disturbed by a continuing lack of vision exhibited by the other candidates in my party. I do not intend to endorse unconditionally the Democratic candidate for President. I ask my supporters to seek out candidates that meet their standards; *demand* competence, *demand* real leadership, *demand* something beyond the usual unimaginative approaches to the issues of our time."

"No surprise here," Edwards commented.

"But his lack of party loyalty is," Saroyan added. "This could be good for *us*."

"He's sure going to make the Democratic nominee work for his endorsement."

Saroyan nodded. "We've got to pick up some of his people. We could be on the bubble. We're still hovering around the high teens to low twenties. If we can't kick it up, we're going to look like just another third party candidate with no chance."

"We're in danger of unraveling in that direction now?" Edwards asked, not realizing Saroyan was this worried.

"That damn neck-and-neck race between Parker and Highland is sticking us on the back-burner," Saroyan stated frustratedly.

"Our friend Samuelson got us on the front-burner." Edwards commented wryly.

"Yeah," Saroyan agreed. "He made us look abused, like we'd been hit with cheap-shots, and got people talking about us."

"He'd be pissed to know he helped us."

"What we need now is for a significant number of these Trewillinger supporters to drift to *us*." Saroyan's attention was suddenly diverted. "Hey," he said as he looked at the television. "There's our answer to

Samuelson . . ."

They both looked at the television screen, catching Michael Edwards' first widely broadcast advertisement on the major networks, just as it was beginning.

Michael Edwards was on the screen speaking; the graphic across his chest read "1977." " . . . and a leader will emerge from the Soviet Union, a young leader without the bitter memories of two devastating world wars. He will be less insecure about buffer states on the Soviet border and will reduce tensions with the United States. In fact, before the end of this century, we will find we have more in *common* with the Soviet Union than in dispute. The days of ideological struggle will be over, and our main security problems will be with desperate smaller nations led by fanatic leaders attempting to destroy the status quo."

During this commentary images of Mikhail Gorbachev, the Berlin Wall coming down, and Sadaam Hussein and Iraq's invasion of Kuwait in 1990 appeared at the appropriate moments. The section closed with a headline on an August 4th, 1990 newspaper reading "US and USSR condemn Iraqi invasion of Kuwait." A sub-headline read "Baker and Shevardnadze issue joint condemnation."

A strong full-voiced commentator continued. "Michael Edwards made this statement in 1977, *before* the Soviet Union went into Afghanistan or hostages were taken in Iran. He has been a proven visionary for 20 years. Now he wants to put his extraordinary talent to use for us, leading this nation into a new era."

Shots of Edwards making speeches at rallies to cheering crowds and shaking the hands of his supporters with a broad, confident smile now flashed on the screen.

"Let's put this man to work. It is time to transform America's economy to one that operates on renewable instead of non-renewable resources. Let us embrace a plan that will bring us a brighter future twenty to fifty years from now. Let us reject the short-sighted politics of the major parties in favor of a third alternative. Vote by vote, choice by choice, he *can* win. Voter by voter, *you* will choose. Vote for Michael Edwards for President."

The final frame froze on a flattering image of Edwards reaching to shake the hand of a supporter, with the green, sunny environment of Golden Gate Park in the background.

The commercial ended with references to the channels and times when the Edwards infomercial would be broadcast.

Edwards wore a broad smile. "Looks nice on the air. And the

referrals to the local infomercials—just what we wanted."

Saroyan nodded.

"Where is Oscar? That guy is doing *great*. Not just with the ads, but I understand from Teresa that we have now qualified for the ballot in 16 states, and are a lock to qualify in all of our core states. I'd like to give him a pat on the back, a 'well-done, son.'"

"He's—" Saroyan caught himself in mid-statement, then adjusted his response. "He's on an errand."

"Well he's doing a nice job. This ad might give us a shot at those Trewillinger supporters." Edwards paused. "You saw my draft of the 'atom bomb' speech. That'll get us back on the front-burner."

Saroyan was hesitant.

"You saw how I'm handling it. I'm presenting it as an idea to debate; it will emphasize that we are running a campaign of new ideas."

"No doubt about that," Saroyan nodded. "I'm still not sure about this," he finally said. "But I will admit, I did some demographic checking, and I'm less apprehensive."

"Yeah? What did your demographics show?"

"The part of the population that will not like your approach at all will be those born before 1945, the pre-baby-boomers. I don't think the baby-boomers will be shocked by your suggestion—they will treat it with an open mind. Many might even go along with it. In 1990, between 45 and 50 percent of eligible voters were born before 1945. And that age group votes more reliably. So this would have been impossible then. But now that number has dropped to between 20 and 25 percent. So . . . it doesn't seem quite as politically suicidal as it did before."

"Thanks for the encouragement. I think that's what they mean when they say 'damning with faint praise.'"

"You're paying me for my expertise. But I will admit, I might be anxious about this because my political antennae are still tuned to the 1990 demographics. Let's give it a shot."

"And I think we should do it with a press conference—in *Chicago*."

Saroyan smiled knowingly. "Nice touch. The land of Capone, and the 'Untouchables' . . . Okay. Let's do it. Let Oscar and me set it up." He paused. "I just wish we could get this race between Highland and Parker to end."

"I know. And I know that you're not happy that I wouldn't agree to use that videotape. But sometimes it is important *how* you win."

"You realize that the same guy who fed Oscar could—"

"I don't want to hear anything more about that video, except that

Oscar got rid of it."

"Okay, Michael. You've made yourself clear on this."

"Good. Now I need some sleep."

Saroyan stood up. "Sounds like a good idea." He smiled and headed to the door.

☼   ☼   ☼

Late March: The Following Friday
Albany, New York

VICTOR PARKER FROWNED AT NICHOLAS MUELLER. WILL RUNALLI SAT with them, grinning smugly. The three were the only ones in the Parker Campaign headquarters in Albany, New York—the New York Primary was scheduled to occur in just over a week. It was late, almost midnight, so the rest of the staff had gone home. They focused their attention on a small television monitor, hooked up to a portable VHS videocassette playback unit.

"Is this thing for real?" Parker finally asked, as snow appeared on the screen, indicating the tape excerpt had come to an end.

"Absolutely," Runalli assured them. "I was able to confirm its accuracy," he lied.

"Really?" Parker asked suspiciously.

"It wasn't easy, but we found someone who was there when—"

"Who shot it?" Mueller asked.

"No one knows. Probably a family member. Does it matter? This *finishes* Highland."

"It matters," Parker told them. "If this thing is some kind of stunt, *we* will get knocked out."

"It's no stunt," Runalli assured them. "Look at the people in the video. There's no way anybody could have pulled together actors and actresses that are dead ringers for all of Highland's relatives, then use make-up to get them to look like they should have twenty years ago."

Parker sighed, then gritted his teeth. "I've got Trewillinger still sniping at me, even though he's supposedly dropped out," he said reflectively, but with accelerating irritation. "I've got the press going on and on about all the various factions of the party and how they're dissatisfied with me. And every morning I have to check on what Highland has said about me the day before so I can counter it. This frigging contest has to come to an *end* so I can get this damn party behind *me* as the guy to take Ken Hampton's job away from him." He paused one more time, then finished his thought resolutely. "Leak the tape . . . anonymously."

"I know just the reporter," Runalli told them shrewdly. "The contest for the Democratic nomination will be over in about one week." He abruptly left.

Parker and Mueller eyed each other with some apprehension.

Mueller scowled, flashing a silent "I-told-you-so."

Parker drew a deep, nervous breath.

Chapter 9

Early April, Election Year: Saturday
Chicago, Illinois

"Michael," Teresa whispered as she shook a sleeping Michael Edwards on the left side of the queen bed they shared at their Chicago hotel room. "Michael," she summoned more insistently.

"I have the day off," a groggy Michael Edwards whined, rousing from his sleep, trying to bask in a rare opportunity to sleep in.

"Michael, I think you might want to see this," she told him as she motioned to the television.

Michael propped himself up on some pillows. He woke up quickly as he watched the television screen.

He saw a fuzzy videotape of a living room with candidate Roy Highland, about twenty years younger, standing on the left side of the picture, holding a drink in one hand and an hors d'oeuvre in the other. Next to him, on the right side of the picture, was an older, overweight man, with a slight family resemblance to Highland, holding a can of beer. They were in the midst of a conversation.

" . . . and I'm telling you," the older man said with a pronounced southern drawl, "it's getting hard to go anywhere anymore where you're dealing with a white person. The jigs and the spics are getting all those government quota jobs, and the gooks, the kikes and the camel jockeys own all the businesses."

"Uncle Jim-Bob, you've got your way of looking at things," Highland replied with an amused smile.

"Listen boy, the world's going to hell. You guys in politics can't stop it."

"We'll do our best."

"I'm telling ya, you and I are gonna be the minority real soon. 'Cause these darker complected races breed like cuka-rachas."

Highland smiled. "That may be true, Uncle Jim-Bob. The only way pure bred southern stock like you and I can stay in the majority is to bleach babies at the hospital."

Uncle Jim-Bob broke into laughter. "That's a good one. Put that in your platform, boy."

"I'd have your vote, wouldn't I . . . "

"Yup. And I'd sure as shit buy a lot of stock in Clorox."

"I mean, didn't our ancestors *own* their ancestors?" Highland continued. "What a nerve! Thinking *they* could have any authority over *us.*" Young Roy Highland's tongue seemed to be in his cheek.

"We did own 'em, boy," the older man said seriously, "and we will again."

He held out his beer and they tapped drinks, the can against the glass, as if toasting the statement. The older man wore a malevolent gleam in his eye. Highland smiled casually.

A male voice from behind the camera sounded with a thick drawl, louder and clearer than the other voices on the tape. "Careful, Jim-Bob," the voice joked, "he's running for office next year. He'll be hitting you up for money any minute."

"That's okay," Jim-Bob replied to the camera. "I always got something for my nephew—the Clorox candidate." He laughed. The picture faded down.

The clip ended and the television monitor now featured newscaster Cedric Hart of one of the major networks. "At first the Highland campaign denied that Senator Highland ever made the remarks or that his uncle ever contributed to his current or past campaigns. But when confronted with the tape, Senator Highland angrily accused—"

Michael used the remote control to turn off the set. He was red-faced with accelerating anger. "I told him not to, and he did it anyway!" Michael stated in a seething rage.

Teresa did not say anything, but watched sympathetically.

Michael grabbed the phone and punched "O." "Room 506," he commanded. "Drew? . . . I told Oscar not to use that Highland stuff. I want him fired . . . Don't give me that . . . Talk about what? I told him not to do it and he did it anyway! . . . Sorry, I'm *not* calm . . . You do that . . . In person, right." Michael hung up the phone.

He got up and grabbed his robe out of the closet. He threw Teresa hers. "Better put some clothes on," he said. "My campaign manager is on his way up to 'talk.'"

☆   ☆   ☆

"You can't fire Oscar for this," Drew Saroyan told a still-smoldering Michael Edwards wearily as they sat at a small table, and Teresa lay on the bed nearby in the Edwards' hotel room.

"I will not have representatives of my campaign engaged in this sleazy shit," Edwards insisted.

"I'll say it one more time. This campaign had no direct involvement in releasing that videotape to the media."

"Come on, Drew, I've been a newsman long enough to hear equivocation. You say no 'direct' involvement—what about 'indirect?'"

"How can I comment on that?" Saroyan responded. "If it was 'indirect,' how could I know about it?"

"Don't bullshit me."

"I'm not bullshitting you. I'm being honest. How can I know? Maybe someone else had the tape too."

"From us."

"That isn't at all clear."

"All I know is that the tape leaked right after Trewillinger dropped out. Real fortunate for us."

"Sometimes you get lucky."

"Damn it, Drew, I want to know about everything this campaign does. Don't fuck around behind my back."

"I'm always up front, Michael."

Edwards narrowed his eyes and glared at Saroyan.

"Regardless of how it came out, Highland is history," Saroyan continued. "It's three months before the first convention. The press has no viable races to cover. This is our chance."

Edwards sighed.

"So let's get ready for that press conference Monday." Saroyan stood up to leave.

"No more lucky surprises like that, Drew," Edwards told him quietly but firmly.

"Let's not go over this again," Saroyan said wearily. He walked to the door and left.

"I'm not letting this thing get out from under me," Michael told Teresa.

"I don't like that guy."

"I know you don't. I never had a reason not to trust him—until now. I just hope these professionals I hired don't get us screwed up."

"Do we need them?"

"Yeah," Edwards replied reluctantly. "To really have a chance? We do."

Teresa sighed. She knew he was right, but she still didn't like it.

☼   ☼   ☼

Early April: The Next Day, Sunday
Hollywood, California

"MUTE," "SLICK" NAYLOR COMMANDED AS HE USED HIS REMOTE control to turn off the sound on his color TV set. His apartment was still musty and dingy, but a new 28 inch color television set and stereo system, incongruous with the other junk in the apartment, sat conspicuously in the living room. Also in the apartment, comfortably reclining on a worn, faded bean bag chair, was Delia Fair, a pretty young woman with dark black hair. "Let there be music during the commercial," Naylor commanded again as he used another remote control to turn on the tuner/amplifier.

Loud rock music sounded.

Naylor puffed on a pipe containing a crack cocaine crystal and sipped some brandy. "The good life until November," he commented ostentatiously. He took another puff on his pipe and another sip of brandy. "You know, Dea, this is my kind of movie. Godfather III. Corleones—my kind of people. I think I'm gonna be a Don."

"Don't you have to be Italian for that?" Dea asked.

"Sicilian. It's a state of mind. Ravioli, lasagna, linguine. I'm as good as they are," he said with hostility creeping into his voice. He shifted his eyes with a sinister glare. "You know, Dea, I think from now on, I'm gonna fuck a girl two or three times, then throw her out."

"You've already had sex with me more than that."

"Which means you better start getting damn creative. 'Cause the minute I'm bored, you're gone."

Delia wasn't sure how to react to Naylor's mood.

"Hey, my meal ticket," Naylor said as he saw a 'news brief' broadcast with the image of Michael Edwards in the upper right hand corner of the screen. Naylor quickly turned off the stereo and put the sound back on the television set.

" . . . dramatic poll results showing the public disenchantment with the two probable candidates from the major parties now that Roy Highland has withdrawn from the race for the Democratic nomination. If the election were held today, Victor Parker would get 33 per cent of the vote, Ken Hampton 29 per cent, and Michael Edwards, a surprising 26 per cent, with 12 per cent undecided. The poll has an error factor of 4 per cent. This makes the race for President a definite three-way contest. Edwards has apparently picked up a large number of Democratic supporters from recently withdrawn candidate Wallace Trewillinger. So this election is just getting started.

"In the Stanley Cup Playoffs today—"

Naylor hit the mute button. "Whoa. I think it's time for a raise." He spoke to Delia. "I've been doing some real important consultant work for this guy."

"Hey Slick, give me a toot," Delia requested.

"Fucking drug addict."

Delia moved over to him. "I can be real creative after I have a toot."

"Yeah. That's why I need a fucking raise." He handed a small white baggy full of cocaine to Delia. "I better go see my buddy, Oscar."

☼   ☼   ☼

Early April: The Following Tuesday
Chicago, Illinois

"I WANT TO THANK YOU FOR COMING TO THIS PRESS CONFERENCE," Michael Edwards stated graciously. He looked around the banquet room of the Sandberg Hotel. The conference was well attended, with almost every seat occupied. All the major television networks were there, as well as many other media representatives. Edwards grinned contentedly. "I'll make a statement first—we are distributing transcripts of it to you right now. Then I'll take your questions."

Lusman and Saroyan watched from the back of the banquet room. Teresa was at Northwestern University speaking to some campaign volunteers.

"So what is the 'atomic bomb,' the doomsday weapon of the war on drugs that I keep referring to? To arrive at the answer to this question, we need to make sure we define who the enemy is in this war. No reasonable person would say we are fighting this war against the drug addicts. When we hear our leaders speak about winning this war, they are referring to defeating the suppliers, the *drug-lords.*

"And this is a powerful enemy. We all know that. They buy sophisticated weapons to defend themselves. They use intricate, often expensive transport systems to bring their illegal commodities into our country. They absorb major losses of equipment, contraband and personnel, but still manage to sustain their industry. They infiltrate the highest levels of government, especially law enforcement, using bribes with amounts of money capable of tempting even the most honest and well-meaning public officials. The source of this power? It's quite obvious. *Money.* Huge, staggering, *mind-boggling* amounts of *money.*

"We can remove the source of all their power with one simple, powerful, doomsday weapon. *Legalization.* "

Edwards paused a moment.

"I can hear gasps from every corner of this country. But I also know from my contacts with many diverse people across the country that more people are willing to consider this option than even in the recent past. Major political figures from all positions on the political spectrum have openly endorsed legalization of many currently illegal drugs.

"So I am proud to be the first major political candidate for President to call for a national debate and discussion as to how we can use this weapon. Within my organization, we have some very specific ideas on this subject. But before discussing specific legislation for legalization, we want to tap the huge creative resource of this country. We want to stimulate thoughts and ideas on this, both positive and negative. Because the *negative* comments will serve to keep us cautious as we take this step.

"Let me start the debate with some thoughts of my own on the subject. It is not an accident that I am here in Chicago. Our situation with illegal drugs today is not materially different from the Prohibition days of illegal alcoholic beverages of the 1920's. And Chicago fell prey to the notorious Al Capone, probably the most famous drug-lord of the first Prohibition era. This is some history that I know Chicagoans are not happy to be reminded of, but a history that will make the people of this city more likely to see the absolute parallels between the Prohibition of the 1920's, and the prohibition *now.* We have gangs in every city, vicious gangs that are well-armed, like the gangster mobs of the 1920's. Today's prohibition is not the only cause of gangs. But the drug trade makes the gang more tempting to new members, the stakes higher, and the weapons more deadly, as the gangs battle each other. How did this country deal with the evil criminal empires caused by the first Prohibition era? We re-legalized, taxed and regulated liquor.

"What effect would legalization have on the war on drugs? The price, currently driven to ludicrous extremes by the scarcity created by prohibition, will drop to just above the costs of production, through legitimate competition. That will end the huge profits flowing to the drug-lords, ending their source of power. This will spell their defeat.

"With government now regulating and taxing the drugs, the huge expenditures currently being spent to fight this war can be redirected. After we defeat our enemies in this war, we can redirect our resources toward helping the victims of the war, the addicts. We have said for years that alcoholism is a disease, and that we need to treat alcoholics with compassion. But we throw other drug addicts into prison, or at the very least, turn them into lawbreakers simply for being unable to resist their weaknesses. The taxes on these drugs should more than pay for the increased education and treatment for drug abusers and addicts. Our bankrupted, fiscally struggling government will come out ahead financially on this as well.

"And as long as we're talking about economics, let's talk about the economics of drugs and crime. Hard core addicts who do not have huge stockpiles of money now have to rob and steal to get the money to pay for their habits. The drive of addiction is compelling and fanatic. It turns people desperate, and their desperation often translates into criminal acts against you, or your families, or others in your neighborhoods, *every* neighborhood. With the end of prohibition, drugs would be reasonably priced, and these victims of addiction will not be inflicting their problems on the rest of us. When was the last time someone committed a violent crime to get the money to buy a bottle of cheap wine?

"More economics? What about our inner cities? There are neighborhoods totally taken over by gangs and the drug trade. Other areas are overrun by the crime that the prohibition economy creates. And what do we tell the young inner city male, facing over 50 per cent unemployment in many areas, when he has the choice of wallowing in economic impotence by playing by the rules, or accumulating huge sums of money by selling drugs? 'Just say no?' Easy for *us* to say. Take the drug economy out of the inner cities, and we remove many of the distortions that have created a number of the conditions we see today. We may then be able to address current problems more effectively.

"When I spoke about the 'atom bomb' of the war on drugs, I know many speculated that I meant getting *tougher*. Tougher penalties. Tougher enforcement strategies. But *freedom* and *tolerance* are what have made this country great. We have gone against our nature in conducting this war. We have told people that they cannot take certain drugs because they may become addicted, and because society doesn't approve of those drugs. We have thrown people in prison because they chose to become addicted to heroin instead of alcohol. We have seized property without due process creating a long litany of well-documented injustices, like the grandmother in Oregon who had her house confiscated when she was caught growing marijuana at home to relieve her glaucoma. And in one state, it is now illegal for convicted drug offenders to go to the park, because they might buy and sell drugs there. They can be found guilty of a misdemeanor just for showing up at the park, even if they are walking a dog, or having a picnic with the family. Legalization speaks to the American traditions of freedom and choice. When the activities of others victimize us, then *that's* when we need to get the law involved. Otherwise, let *freedom* reign.

"What scares us about the prospect of legalization? The general fear is that we will become a nation of drugged-out zombies. Our sidewalks could become cluttered with mentally burnt-out, wasted human beings, addicted to cheap, legal drugs. But polls show that over 90 per cent of Americans would not try dangerous drugs just because they were legal. Ask yourself; would you try cocaine or heroin just because they were legal? These drugs were legal around the turn of the century. Cocaine was popular until the public found out about the dangers of it. Then its usage dropped, *before* it became illegal.

"Also, these drugs are not automatically addictive. How many of you know people who have taken these drugs but never got hooked? Some people actually use these drugs recreationally without becoming zombies. Are they criminals? The use of marijuana has been largely decriminalized in some jurisdictions. Did those areas suddenly become stoned societies? Other countries with various forms of legalization have not turned into nations of drug zombies. So we need to examine our fears. Are they realistic? Do they justify this war on drugs we have been fighting, which is also an assault on many of our freedoms?

"Others say legalization puts the government's stamp of approval on the behavior. Does anyone really believe the government favors abuse of alcohol, even though alcohol consumption is legal? Does the government approve of smoking? Again, our tradition is to keep government out of the business of legislating morality. Government doesn't come out and encourage extra-marital affairs. But no reasonable person suggests we go back to the days when adultery was illegal.

"And what is prohibition of these drugs supposed to do for us? Are we preventing drug addiction? Knowledgeable people would tell you we are fighting an even battle, by the most rosy evaluations. Are we preventing availability? Most people in or near a major metropolitan area would probably have little trouble finding illegal drugs if they wanted them.

"What this current prohibition has done is make the drugs scarce, driving up the price. It has made it impossible for the small proprietor to stay in the drug business because of the risks, capital and connections needed. The war on drugs has done for the cartels what they could not possibly have done for themselves—reduced competition so they have an oligopoly. With a few powerful cartels dominating the market, it is easier to set strategies, to make deals to control the market, to set up bribery schemes with huge, nearly irresistible sums of money, and to create power blocs that can intimidate even national governments.

"And the war on drugs of the Reagan Administration almost certainly led to the development of crack cocaine. Drug dealers found their product scarcer, therefore more expensive. So they invented a product that was cheaper, with a smaller quantity needed to make it. Of course, the high wouldn't last as long for the drug user. But drug users could now buy cocaine in quick hits, affordable by anyone who could get their hands on twenty or so dollars.

"And we have prisons full of drug criminals, people incarcerated for crimes primarily related to drug trafficking or drug addiction. These people would not be taking up space in our prisons if it wasn't for prohibition. Federal judges across the country, following Supreme Court decisions, have mandated that overcrowded prisons constitute 'cruel and unusual punishment.' So we are releasing dangerous criminals, rapists, murderers, and other violent offenders, before they have finished serving their sentences, so we can make room for more inmates, many of them drug criminals. Who would you rather see back on the streets? The guy in Michigan sentenced to life for selling cocaine? Or the guy in Florida sentenced to thirty years for rape and second degree murder, but who was out in six years because of overcrowded prisons? Right now, we have three choices: get our bankrupted governments to build more prisons, pass a constitutional amendment repealing the 'cruel and unusual punishment' section in the Bill of Rights, or release some very bad people early. The end of the second prohibition era will ease this dilemma.

"So I have opened this debate. My administration will take a fresh look at this problem, with a strong eye in the direction of ending prohibition. And as we all contemplate these bold assertions, I want us to consider the story of Barry McDowell, formerly of the Los Angeles Police Department. His story began my metamorphosis on this issue. He was a dedicated police officer, one of the foot soldiers trying to win the war. When he saw first hand how the war was really going, he stepped back, then became one of the country's most articulate advocates to end prohibition. I implore you all to discover his story. Contact information is in the published transcript of this statement. And I ask that other courageous soldiers in the war step forward with their stories. I know from personal experience that many of them share this opinion, though for career and personal reasons, they cannot come forward. Here is a chance for everyone to state frank opinions.

"I'll take a few questions."

Edwards pointed to a reporter. "Yes."

"Mr. Edwards," the reporter asked, "you have been labeled by some experts as a one-issue candidate. Is this your attempt to identify yourself with more than one issue?"

"I've heard the 'one-issue' label," he replied. "I don't accept it, because I believe a Regenerating Biosphere formed through Economic Activism covers a wide range of issues. But yes," Edwards grinned wryly, "this will end the one-issue candidate label." He pointed to another reporter.

"Now that it appears Victor Parker will run against Ken Hampton, how will you get the American people to choose you over those two?"

"By bringing my message to the nation. My proposals have more vision and potential for long-term success than anything from the major parties. And I hope to spend this time discussing *issues* with you, not *strategies*." He pointed out another reporter.

"Mr. Edwards," the reporter challenged, "are you seriously telling the American people that between now and November you can gain the upper hand in enough states to win the electoral college. You need 270 votes . . ."

Edwards was becoming frustrated with the process-oriented questioning. But the more frustrated and angry he felt, the more he smiled, and the softer and slower he spoke. It was a technique he had learned in a progressive management class he had asked all his Omni-Vee managers, including himself, to take. "I know how many votes I need. I have personally anchored the coverage of two Presidential elections. The American people will decide whether or not I can win. I'm not going to tell them anything on that subject. I'll present my views and *they* will decide who will win this election." He paused. "I just laid a big one on you guys. There are some tough questions to ask me. Come on. Enough of the 'how-are-you-going-to-win' garbage." He identified the next questioner.

"Mr. Edwards, there *are* difficult problems with this idea. Are you talking about legalization of drugs for minors? And what about pregnant women taking cocaine?"

Edwards smiled. "Now *there's* a *question*. No, of course dangerous drugs would continue to be illegal for minors. Law enforcement would concentrate on the laws against selling to anyone under 18. In fact, we should step up enforcement efforts on the selling of liquor to minors. The number of teenagers killed, drinking and driving, and those they take with them, is a national disgrace.

"The issue of dangerous drugs and pregnant women is a tougher one. I've always believed that the label of 'crime' should apply to activities that victimize others. And though the child carried by a pregnant woman is not yet a separate human being, he or she will be if the woman has chosen to bring her pregnancy to term. Her behavior could then victimize her future child if she chooses to take dangerous drugs. So I'm leaning toward criminal penalties for such activities. But I look forward to the national debate on this issue. Because such laws could set a dangerous precedent, and we need to draw clear lines when dealing with government interference in such a private matter as a woman nurturing a pregnancy." He recognized another reporter.

"Have you ever taken illegal drugs?"

"That's a fair question," Edwards said, nodding. "I was in Berkeley in the 60's. Yes, I took illegal drugs. I smoked grass. But I never did any dangerous drugs. And I have not taken any illegal drugs since the early 70's, almost thirty years ago."

"Did you ever take LSD?" the reporter followed up.

"I never took any dangerous drugs," Edwards answered quickly, then moving to the next reporter.

"So you'll stay in this election all the way to November, even if it looks like you can't win, but will throw it into the House of Representatives?"

Edwards was silent a moment as anger built within him. "I haven't even thought about that," he told them smiling. "One more chance to ask me a real question on my proposals." He called on another reporter.

"Why a press conference for this? Were you afraid this idea would be coolly received by a large audience?"

Edwards breathed in, then exhaled.

"Easy," Saroyan whispered to Lusman as they watched.

And Edwards tempered his response, avoiding the kind of public temper tantrum that he knew had made Ross Perot unpopular with the media, and often made him appear to be a grouchy, cantankerous old man on camera. "No," Edwards replied with a weary smile, "I thought you guys might challenge me with some good questions." He paused. "There are other ways to do this," he told them quietly and calmly. "I'll address the American people *directly*. You can broadcast excerpts from the Lloyd Prince Show to your audience. I'll be on there later this week. Thank you." Edwards left the podium.

Saroyan looked at Lusman and rolled his eyes. They both laughed nervously. "That is one of the most restrained tantrums you'll ever see," Saroyan finally observed.

"It's a good thing he cut it short," Lusman added. "Those questions about his prior drug use were making me very nervous."

"He handled it well."

Lusman nodded in agreement.

☼   ☼   ☼

Early April: The Following Thursday
Washington, D.C.

"IT'S A PLEASURE TO BE HERE," MICHAEL EDWARDS STATED CORDIALLY as he replied to the introduction made by talk-show host Lloyd Prince in his Washington studio. Edwards and Prince sat across from each other in cushy, light blue chairs, with a small white table between them. There was no studio audience. This was essentially a televised radio talk show.

"So," Prince observed mischievously, getting the show started, "you're making your pilgrimage to the talk shows . . ."

"You could say that," Edwards admitted, smiling, unperturbed. "Experience over the last five to ten years has shown that the callers on these shows ask better questions than supposedly professional reporters. Just look at that so-called press conference I had a few days ago."

"It couldn't be that you agree with other media people, that shows like this one and Larry King's over at CNN, pitch slow, fat 'soft balls' to candidates. You network journalists have given us a bad time."

"I never did," Edwards reminded him. "I understood why these shows became popular. Your audience asks about *issues*. They really want to know where their leaders stand on the problems that face the country. They don't try to design questions to confront and irritate. They ask intelligent questions on what we would do if elected. Those aren't 'soft balls.' For the insincere candidate, those are the most difficult questions of all."

"Well, we've got an opening question that is no 'soft ball,'" Prince promised. "Hyde Park, Illinois, you're on the air with Michael Edwards."

"Thank you." The young female voice rushed, from nervousness, but also from intense emotion. "Mr. Edwards, I'm telling you, I was thinking of voting for you. But I can't now. 'Cause you're way off on this drug thing. My brother—heroin ruined his life. He died with a needle in his vein." Her words began to choke with tears. "I wanted to believe in you. But how can you talk about legalizing these . . . poisons?"

Edwards' face registered genuine compassion and sympathy. He looked at Prince. "Now *that* is a tough question, the kind of question that needs to be asked," he said with quiet intensity. "Ma'am, my heart goes out to you. And I can't possibly imagine how you feel right now. But we have to ask, what did this prohibition do to help your brother? His habit probably bankrupted him . . ."

The woman sniffled and sobbed as she spoke. "God rest his soul, he borrowed and stole money from all of us."

"So he was forced to live in a crummy area of town, maybe even homeless . . ."

"That's what heroin, one of the drugs you want to make legal, did to him."

"And he died of an overdose?"

"Yes sir."

"Ma'am, I wish there was something I could do or say to bring back your brother. I'm terribly sorry for your loss. And I don't know . . . I'm not sure I'm going to convince you of anything. But I sincerely believe that if this drug had been legal, he would not have been homeless and destitute, struggling to pay for a habit that had victimized him. And he might even be alive today because he would have had reliable knowledge of the dosages he was taking. Resources now focused on making him a criminal would have been refocused on helping him break free of his addiction. I really do believe that sincerely. And I wish this was a time before your brother's death, so I could prove to you and your family how this new approach is better than what we have now."

"Mr. Edwards, I—" The woman broke down. "Those heroin dealers ought to be skinned alive, *slowly,* right in front of my mother!"

"We'll take away their power," Edwards argued gently. "Their *money*." Edwards paused. "I can understand why you feel the way you do. And I respect your inclination not to vote for me. But give me a second thought. Was heroin the only enemy? Or was he also fighting a law that turned him from a victim into a criminal? I know you will search your heart and vote accordingly. And I respect your final choice, even if it isn't me."

"I—" The caller didn't know what to say. "I will," she finally stammered ambiguously, still choked with sobs and tears.

Prince didn't try to add anything to the emotional exchange. "Pontiac, Michigan," he said, moving ahead to the next caller.

"Lloyd, I'm a regular listener to your show. And I can't believe you're giving time to this *nut.*"

"In what way is Mr. Edwards a nut?" Prince asked.

"For one thing, he's one of these ecology nuts. He wants us all to have solar cells on our houses for 'clean' energy. But we have an unlimited source of clean energy *now.*"

"Nuclear?" Edwards asked.

"That's right, Mr. Edwards." The caller spat out the words caustically. "But you ecology nuts won't go for that, because it's from big business."

"I have nothing against big business," Edwards corrected. "I hope big business starts making huge profits from the large-scale manufacture of solar cells and windmills. The auto industry factories may be perfect places to make windmills. But nuclear energy is without a doubt the filthiest energy source, the most expensive—"

"Only because of all the regulations your buddies have put on the nuclear companies."

Edwards smirked grimly. "Those regulations are intended to assure safe plants. Let me ask you, caller, because I can tell you're familiar with this issue, what do you suggest we do with the wastes?"

"That's easy. Bury 'em."

"Where?"

"Isn't it . . . Don't they . . . Out in the desert somewhere."

"What about your backyard?" Edwards suggested with calm facetiousness.

"Don't be silly."

"They're 'clean' aren't they? So why not?"

"They're *radioactive*. We can bury 'em in canyons in the desert."

"But the people who live in those areas don't want the wastes buried in their backyards either."

"Well they . . . That's just tough. I mean, who lives out there, anyway?"

"And why should we stick future generations with this crap that *we've* left behind?"

"You're just nitpicking. The industry will find a solution, if you just let 'em."

"*Nitpicking?*" Edwards restated incredulously. "Caller, *no* country that uses nuclear power has come up with a permanent answer on where to store these wastes. This is not 'nitpicking.' This is trying to prevent us from piling toxic filth into our biosphere. If the industry really has an answer, we'd all love to hear it."

"No you wouldn't. You'd just nitpick it."

"So you won't be voting for Mr. Edwards," Prince interjected.

"No."

Prince terminated the call as he smiled. "You going to lose sleep over that vote?" he asked Edwards.

"Not over the vote. But I might lose sleep over the mentality, if I find out it's common."

Prince grinned. "Provo, Utah."

The first callers were unapproving and challenging. But as the ninety minute program proceeded, it became apparent that Edwards was winning over the audience, or that supporters were now calling in much larger numbers. Those who opposed Edwards' views found their arguments consistently countered effectively, always with patience, sometimes with eloquence.

Two calls toward the end of the show epitomized the transformation: "Pasadena, California," Prince announced.

"Mr. Edwards, I have to admit, I had no intention of even considering you when you started out," the articulate, confident, female voice of thirty-something stated. "I heard you give a commentary where you spoke disparagingly about the M-B-A mentality. You denounced what you called 'legions of yuppies,' with their Beemers, or their Lexuses, and their pocket cellular phones, who have all gone to colleges to get their M-B-A's. You said they learned how to exploit the world's resources, but nothing about what it will do to our future if we continue to treat our planet like a smorgasbord and a garbage dump."

"That's from a ways back, but I did say those things," Edwards acknowledged.

"I *am* one of those M-B-A yuppies—I own a Lexus and a cellular phone. But, I also own a small computer programming company in southern California," she added, "And I have been trying to set up a telecommuting situation for my employees. The transformation will be expensive, and your tax credit proposal could make the difference for me, as long as it's not a pittance."

"And I'll try to make sure it isn't," Edwards assured. "If you'll look at what I've been saying recently about working with American business, you'll see I've had a definite change of attitude, maybe related to my own experience as an entrepreneur. American businesses all over the country, of all types and sizes, have to be partners in making the transition to a Regenerating Biosphere. The government needs to help you by harmonizing profits and prosperity with a Regenerating Biosphere, through economic incentives, not government programs."

"And that's why I'm now an Edwards supporter. I've had a change of heart too."

"Great," Edwards acknowledged.

"I'm glad I got through to you. Those early callers—I don't think they're indicative of what's happening in this country. Most people I know are excited about you."

Edwards smiled broadly. "Thank you."

"Fort Lauderdale, Florida," Prince said.

"I want to tell the people," the deep, gravelly, older male voice boomed out, opinionated and strong, and also headlong and unrefined, "that ten years ago I would have said Mr. Edwards was *crazy* to talk about making drugs legal. But about seven years ago, I got caught in the crossfire of this < bleep > ing stupid war—"

"Caller," Prince warned, "watch your language."

"I'm sorry. Am I still on?"

"You've been bleeped," Prince told him. "This show is broadcast on a ten second delay."

"Oh." The caller gathered himself. "It's just that—" He was having trouble reformulating his thoughts. "My house got taken away," he finally said.

"Your house?" Edwards asked.

"My son brought some grass home from Jamaica a couple of summers ago," the caller explained. "The police and the Feds tracked him to our house, arrested him, then took my house. It took me a lawsuit and a lot of hassle to get my house back. I was a Viet Nam vet. I was told I was fighting for freedom over there. When I came home, I joined the protesters and told the truth about that war. Somebody's got to tell the truth about this one. In America, they're not supposed to be able to take your house away unless you done something wrong."

"This is your point, isn't it?" Prince asked Edwards.

"Exactly. The due process clause in the 14th Amendment has been conveniently ignored. This guy was guilty until proven innocent. Our Constitution will be a casualty of this war if we keep going this way."

"A-men," the caller pronounced emphatically. "We need this man to bring some sense back to things. I'm voting for him." The phone line clicked as the caller hung up.

Prince's eyebrows raised and a smile crept onto his face. "You're having quite an evening," he observed.

And Edwards did finish an exceptional, effective appearance, one of a series of similar appearances.

✿   ✿   ✿

Mid April, Election Year: Saturday
Houston, Texas

"NICE SHOT," ZACHARY FADIMAN PRAISED AS HE WATCHED BEAUREGARD Hunter's tee shot at the first hole of the San Jacinto Country Club fade almost three hundred yards down the fairway into the distance. Hunter's drive tailed slightly to the right, just to the left of some trees on the right side of the fairway. Hunter was dressed in gaudy, obnoxious green knickers, and a ridiculously loud, bright plaid golf short. Fadiman wore less conspicuous casual attire.

"I hit the ball a ton," Hunter told Fadiman. "And if I'm lucky, I know which way it's going some of the time."

Fadiman laughed. "Well, my drives don't go quite that far." He teed the ball up and took a measured swing which propelled the ball just over 200 yards straight down the middle of the fairway.

They got into their golf cart and sped down the fairway.

"So why would I want to meet with some drug dealer?" Hunter asked casually.

"He figures you guys have something in common. In a way, I can see what his reasoning is. Edwards is attacking both of your livelihoods."

"Edwards," Hunter scoffed disrespectfully. "I saw him on the Lloyd

Prince show. They all were calling up to bury the guy."

"I think you saw just the beginning."

"I wasn't going to watch the whole thing."

They arrived at Fadiman's golf ball. He took out his three wood and took his measured swing again. The ball whistled low and straight, landing about 50 yards short of the green. He got back into the cart and they continued.

"Edwards is doing well." Fadiman said evenly.

"He'll fade, just like the rest of them."

"You're probably right."

"Hampton's one of the best I've ever seen at winning an election," Hunter observed confidently. "He can deal cheap shots that don't look like cheap shots, and he can muck it up like a pro, which is what you have to do to win these days. That Parker is gonna need a mudder to have any kind of a chance."

"Yeah?" Fadiman replied, with a knowing grin. "I think he agrees with you. Because my sources tell me he took on Will Runalli."

"Whoooo," Hunter howled, amused with this information. "That boy is a first-class mudder. This year's election might just be some fun."

Hunter now got out of the cart with a seven iron. He sailed the ball high over the green. "Shit!" he moaned. "That fucker's across the path onto the second tee."

Fadiman smiled. "It's not that bad."

"Ain't that good." Hunter got back into the cart and they continued toward Fadiman's ball.

"Beau, I'm not trying to sell you on this guy. He's a loose cannon who's got some off-the-wall ideas about how to handle things. And I have to tell you, I think there is more to his concerns than what he's admitting. We're digging into that now. We thought he just had some complex cash-laundering arrangements. Now, I think he's trying to buy something more ambitious than a bigger share of the drug trade with his millions. But, you never know how things might develop. What if this Edwards *does* get elected, and manages to cancel all your company's subsidies?"

Hunter grinned. "I'm not fussing about meeting the guy because of his line of work. I've had dealings with some pretty nasty characters in my day. Sometimes when the stakes are high, you have to." Hunter shrugged. "But I don't want to get involved with a guy who could be a little risky—unless it's necessary."

"He could be useful because he has contacts we don't have. If we need something from those contacts, we'd be able to get it without having to reach into the muck ourselves."

They arrived at Fadiman's golf ball again. He used a nine iron to execute a nice arcing shot that bounced and rolled within twenty feet of the pin.

"That's a beaut," Hunter complimented.

"Thanks," Fadiman acknowledged as he got back into the golf cart and they headed toward Hunter's ball behind the green.

"Well, I don't need the risk of meeting with the guy."

"I understand. But I could make a meeting risk free if you change your mind. He's been under surveillance by the DEA every time he's come to see me, but I've set the meetings so there's no way the tail could establish who he's seeing without giving away the surveillance. I keep meeting him in Louisiana . . . maybe east Texas."

"Closer to home for me than for you."

"True . . ."

They arrived at Hunter's ball about 30 yards behind the green. Hunter hit a pitching wedge, but turned the club face in slightly, preventing the shot from rising. His ball rolled almost all the way off the front of the green.

They left their golf cart, carrying their putters. Both putted twice more to finish the hole.

As they rode toward the second hole, Hunter continued their discussion. "You know, this Edwards boy hasn't said anything yet that might mess you up."

Fadiman nodded. "I know. I might even vote for him."

Hunter was amazed with the statement. "You can't be serious. Then why are you-all putting out feelers for an anti-Edwards meeting?"

Fadiman shrugged. "You've turned down the meeting. I figured you would. But the guy asked to meet with you. Shouldn't I at least let you know? In any business, it's good to let the customer know his options, and not to pre-judge what the customer will want."

They moved to the second tee.

"We've been friends for a long time, or I'd think you were setting me up somehow," Hunter stated slyly. "But you wouldn't do that . . ."

Fadiman was truly surprised by the question. "What would be the point?"

"There would be *no* point."

Hunter stepped up to the tee and hit his drive about 275 yards, but it sailed so far to the left that he almost hit someone playing on the adjacent fairway of the fifth hole. Hunter grimaced, then shrugged.

✩   ✩   ✩

"I CAN OUT-DRIVE YOU AND OUT-HIT YOU OFF THE FAIRWAYS, BUT YOU still beat my butt," Hunter joked with Fadiman as Hunter put his arm around him. The two men were taking a seat in the "19th Hole" lounge. A huge big-screen TV was one of the furnishings of the lounge, which was also full of soft, comfortable black leather chairs and clean, shiny maroon tables. On weekends, the TV was tuned to sports. But on weekdays, particularly before the stock market closed on the east coast, the TV was tuned to CNN Headline News, where a constant running tape of stock market activities scrolled across the screen.

"Your putter wasn't working for you," Fadiman observed.

"Get me a drink," Hunter ordered with good-natured gruffness.

"On me," Fadiman agreed.

A pretty waitress, not young, but still shapely and dressed in a brief, tight outfit, came to their table.

"Bourbon, rocks," Hunter told her.

"Get me a Delta," Fadiman requested, referring to a new beer brewed near New Orleans.

"Be right back, gentlemen."

As the waitress walked away, Fadiman spoke. "I've got tickets to see the Astros tonight. I'm telling you, they—"

Hunter's attention was diverted by the television. He motioned for Fadiman to hold his thought.

A caption reading "Barstow, California" appeared on the screen, over acres and acres of twenty foot high panels of solar cells propped up at 45 degree angles on metal stands rising up from the flat desert landscape. They looked like panes of grey glass sticking out of the otherwise empty and arid desert terrain.

After about three seconds, the image slid to the left half of the screen and another caption reading "Livermore, California" appeared over rolling amber hills covered with plastic white windmills. They looked like pearly propellers whipping and rotating in the wind as they extended above the dry grass.

After another three seconds, the image slid to the right of the screen and Michael Edwards appeared. "This is what the large energy companies of this nation want you to visualize when you think of solar power and wind power."

The picture cut to Michael Edwards walking among the solar cells. He continued speaking as he walked: "This looks impractical. Solar cells stretched out over acres in the desert, hundreds of miles from major cities."

The picture cut to Edwards walking among the windmills. He continued speaking. "Windmills fluttering in the breeze, also miles from where the power will be used. These schemes look like the height of inefficiency, almost comically silly."

On the next cut, Edwards was in front of a home in the Rocky Mountains with south-facing windows, and with solar cells shining and windmills whipping on the roof.

"I don't want to demean the efforts of those who have pioneered renewable energy development. Their research efforts will continue to be important. But when publicity focuses on grand, impractical pilot projects; when we focus on solar-powered planes that struggle to cross the continent, or on solar-powered cars that have top speeds of thirty to forty miles per hour, we get an improper view of how close we are to transforming our energy consumption to renewable energy sources.

"I'd like us to look at this home. No, it won't fly across the country, or transport you at zero miles to the gallon. But this home is completely self-sufficient. Computers store excess power from solar cells and windmills, and regulate electricity consumption in the home. Computers also guide the incineration of waste products including sewage. Some of that waste actually ends up being processed into usable, even saleable raw materials, like fertilizer.

"*This* is renewable energy used *sensibly*. And every home in this nation can function this way. We may not be able to build solar cars that will drive across the nation. But in less dramatic fashion, you may well drive your non-polluting *electric* car across town, using electricity generated at your home. This should be our goal. Small, steady steps toward a Regenerating Biosphere."

A strong, full-voiced narrator came on as the camera pulled back to show Edwards in the foreground of the "smart house" he had just referred to, with solar cells gleaming in the sunlight and windmills spinning in the breeze. "Michael Edwards offers a clear, constructive, compelling vision for the America of our generation, and future generations. Vote by vote, choice by choice, he *can* win. Voter by voter, *you* will choose. Choose Michael Edwards for President."

The ad ended with a graphic reading "Edwards for President."

The waitress delivered the drinks.

Hunter picked his up as his craggy face became stern with serious thought. He remembered what Connie Cook (now heading up the research and development department for non-petroleum products), had told him back in December. He watched cynical and jaded businessmen whom he knew, as well as weekend riffraff whom he did not know, interrupt their conversations to pay close attention to the television ad. And the ad made Hunter himself consider the Edwards' option for a fleeting instant. He couldn't deny the effectiveness of the message's delivery. Maybe he did need to broaden his options. "You can get an untraceable meeting between me and that Enriquez fellow?" he finally asked.

"Yeah," Fadiman answered casually.

"I'll talk to him," Hunter told his friend. "Maybe it wouldn't hurt to have a number of contingency plans available."

"Okay," Fadiman replied, nonchalant about the matter, but intrigued with the way events had gone.

Chapter 10

Mid April, Election Year: Monday
New York, New York

"I DIDN'T EXPECT TO SEE YOU AGAIN." LUSMAN'S VOICE WAS FLAT AS Naylor entered his Manhattan office. Lusman saw that Naylor had improved his dress from fading jeans with holes to a tacky polyester casual suit.

"You kept me waiting a long time," Naylor complained. "It's almost eight o'clock."

"I had appointments," Lusman explained.

"I flew all the way out here to talk to you."

"I'm buying the privilege of *not* talking to you, remember?"

"I need a raise. My . . . research expenses keep going up. And I can see in the news you keep doing better and better. That makes my services more valuable, don't you think?"

"There's no more money for you here," Lusman told Naylor tersely.

"I just need another five hundred a week. You know I'm worth it . . ."

"I'm not going to get caught up in this," Lusman insisted. "You've got what you're going to get. Now go back to California and crawl into the muck you came out of."

"Does Mikey know about this?"

"Absolutely not."

"I think I might have to tell him about it, Oscar."

"That would be a very *stupid* thing for you to do," Lusman told him angrily. "And don't call me Oscar, is that clear?"

"I'm on a first name basis with Mikey . . ."

"If you tell Michael about this, he'll trash the campaign rather than pay you off. Then your little deal here is over for sure. So don't hammer me with this shit anymore. You want to keep this thing going, don't you?"

Naylor's eyes narrowed. "So do you. Or you wouldn't be dealing with me. So where does that leave us?"

Lusman drew a deep angry breath. "I'll give you another two hundred a week. Now get the fuck out of here."

"I need a little more than that. Make it two-fifty."

"Two hundred and get out of here."

"You're a real hard-ass, aren't you . . ."

"Actually, I'm a soft touch. If I were a hard-ass, I'd cut you off and dare you to follow through on your threat to make that file public. If you did, I'd make sure you were charged with extortion. But that's a game of chicken I won't play with Michael's campaign . . . for now."

Naylor nodded. "All right. I'll be picking up my twelve hundred a week for my . . . services."

"Don't remind me. Get outta here."

Naylor stood, looked around the room insolently, then left slowly.

As Naylor left, Teresa Edwards arrived. She walked by him as she entered Lusman's office.

"Teresa," Naylor greeted enthusiastically. "How are you doing?"

"Fine," she replied, with the lack of recognition plain on her face.

"Long time, no see," Naylor added.

"Yeah," she answered through a forced smile.

Naylor laughed quietly as he walked out of the office.

"Is Michael here yet?" Teresa asked Lusman.

"He's due in at 8:30," Lusman replied. "There was some good coverage we all wanted to go over."

"I know. That's why I came over."

"Great," Lusman said. "I'll give you a sneak preview." He picked up a videocassette off his desk and took it to the machine hooked to his office television monitor.

"Who was the guy who just left?" Teresa asked. "Am I supposed to know him?"

"You don't?"

"He looked familiar . . . I swear I've seen him somewhere . . ." Teresa pondered as she tried to search her memory.

"Uh, he works with the homeless in Hollywood," Lusman stammered.

"Oh." Lusman could see Teresa's mind was already past this issue.

☆ ☆ ☆

Mid April: The Following Wednesday
New York, New York

"I KNOW WE DON'T SEE EYE-TO-EYE ON THIS," DREW SAROYAN BEGAN AS he and Michael Edwards sat together in a small editing room at Fifth Avenue Video Company. They had just watched and approved the latest Edwards infomercial. "But we have to come to a final decision. You're on the ballot in just about every state now; it's getting essential."

Edwards frowned. He was tired—it was past midnight. He suspected Saroyan had brought up this subject to try to take advantage of his tiredness. "I hate this manipulative media crap," Edwards reminded him. "That's not what my campaign is about."

"But you hired me, and others, like Oscar Lusman, because you want to give yourself a chance to win."

Edwards dropped his chin as he paused in thought. He raised his chin up again. "We have a chance here to show how different we are. That's why a very open, public search for my running mate is important to me."

"Public, yes. But we have to spin this just right. The media is—"

"Spin it?" Edwards interrupted. "Why does it need to be spun?"

"Because the media is going to focus on running mates now, for all three of you. This could be an opportunity for us. The primary season is deadly dull, with two unexciting winners already picked. But the conventions will come soon. Both candidates will get a support bounce out of the conventions, and we run the risk that you will take a back seat."

Edwards sneered and narrowed his eyes. "That doesn't explain why you're spinning this . . ."

"Generating excitement on your possible running mate will help keep us on the evening newscasts. We need to have exciting spins, and enough drama to keep getting good bites."

"I agree with all of that. But when you talk about anonymous leaks of people we have no intention of considering, just to get rumors flying . . ."

"Michael," Saroyan stated with a patient but lecturing tone, "this is the best way to stress that we are involved in an exhaustive talent search for your running mate. By floating names like Ralph Nader, Barry Commoner . . . maybe even John Anderson . . . we can emphasize that we are not limited to one political party, or even to a politician. And you'll be able to deny it all. It'll all be attributed to wild media speculation."

"So with all this spinning you and Oscar have in mind, all this phoniness you are generating, how do we *really* go about picking my running mate?"

"You and I need to talk about who the actual choice is going to be."

"I think our two top choices are obvious."

"I agree. But we've got to approach them very quietly. I've got a buddy who worked on the Trewillinger campaign. I'll approach him . . . feel him out . . . maybe get him to deliver a message."

Edwards nodded. "Do you think Trewillinger would do it?"

"I don't know. Most established politicians won't touch it, because their parties will see it as disloyal. But Trewillinger is late to the game, and considers himself more of an intellectual than a politician. With our high poll figures, he just might be tempted."

"I think Frances Willis is a lot more in tune with me than she is with her own party."

"If we could get her, it would be a real coup. But she's a lot less likely to go for it than Trewillinger. And I don't have any contacts close to her. It'll be difficult to make a quiet approach."

"But why do we need to make a quiet approach?" Edwards asked Saroyan. "We should announce that these two politicians of immense stature are our top choices for the second spot on the ticket. Wouldn't that give the media a story to run with, and emphasize our non-partisan orientation? And it would be up-front, not some manipulative game."

Saroyan shook his head. "We do want to keep the press speculating on who we *could* choose. We want to make this the most exciting and unique election news they're reporting on right up until the conventions. But we must avoid creating even a *slight* impression that we've offered this to everyone in town and can't get anyone to take it." He shook his head as he recalled a memory. "I'll never forget the '72 election when McGovern had dropped Eagleton as his running mate, and then got turned down by what seemed like every prominent Democrat when he asked them to replace Eagleton. That, right there, might have buried him. It told the public that his own party had given him up for lost."

Saroyan was starting to convince him. Was he tired, with a lower resistance to these ideas, or had Saroyan been right all along? And Teresa was not there to scowl and compare Saroyan to beauty pageant operators. Edwards knew the time and place for this conversation was no accident. Saroyan was an expert at manipulation; should it surprise Edwards that he used this talent *on* his clients as well as *for* them? "So if I agree to this approach," he asked with reluctance but growing resignation, "how exactly would it work?"

"We keep the public speculating while we make very quiet approaches to Trewillinger and Willis. We make sure we are never the subject of a public rejection."

"And if they quietly turn us down?"

"We'll hope all the media hype and speculation will bring us a heavy hitter."

Edwards wanted to agree, but hesitated.

Saroyan went on. "I really believe that your choice of a running mate will decide whether or not you keep your candidacy viable, or whether you become just another protest candidate. Look at recent history. Bush lost the 1992 election in part because of his choice for Vice President in 1988. Clinton's chances improved considerably when he chose Al Gore to run with him. And Perot's choice of Admiral Stockdale in 1992, a nice man but ineffective political performer, convinced the public that Perot was just another protest candidate, without the credentials or even the will to take charge of the Presidency. Our choice has to—"

"I know," Edwards finally interrupted, with a decisive tone. "Do it your way. I don't like it, but . . ." Edwards shook his head, disgusted he was agreeing. "Just do it."

"Michael, there will be no lies. We might leak a name that we discussed, say, Roy Highland."

"Roy Highland?" Edwards asked in disbelief.

"Sure. And we just discussed it."

"Yeah," Edwards replied. "I know how it works." He did want to win this election. For LOS ANGELES/APRIL 3RD, and JEFFERSON ISLAND/SEPTEMBER 7TH, he would allow these professional manipulators to bend his comfort zone. What they wanted to do wasn't illegal. It wasn't really even unethical. It was simply part of the insincerity and gamesmanship that Edwards hated about American politics.

"Let Oscar and me take care of it. We'll get you involved when we have someone serious to consider."

Edwards nodded. "Are we done?" he asked wearily.

"Yes."

☼   ☼   ☼

Late April, Election Year: Wednesday
New Orleans, Louisiana

ZACHARY FADIMAN AND BEAUREGARD HUNTER SAT TOGETHER IN THE
private banquet room of "Le Cochon Rouge." Fadiman had again reserved
a table in the back of the room. He was sitting with his back to the back
wall—Hunter sat to his right. Again, the entire room was empty except for
Fadiman and his guest. Both Fadiman and Hunter were eating their
dinners.

Fadiman's cellular phone, sitting next to him on the table, whirred.
"Yeah," Fadiman said as he answered it quickly.

It was his security man, calling from just outside the restaurant. "He
just pulled up."

Fadiman nodded. "Does he have his usual tail?"

"Looks like it. Another car pulled up near him just a few seconds
later."

"Okay. Escort him back here. But don't make contact with him until
he comes inside the restaurant, and you're sure of the status of the tail."

"Right."

The call ended.

"He's here," Fadiman told Hunter.

"We gonna invite him to dinner?" Hunter asked.

"We'll see how things go—probably not."

A few moments later, Fadiman's security man walked in with Ernesto
Enriquez and escorted him to a seat at the table, across from Fadiman,
facing the wall, with his back to the entrance of the room.

Fadiman put down his fork and stood up. "Mr. Enriquez," he greeted
with the slightest hint of a grin on his face, the closest he would come to
being a cordial host. "Let me introduce you to Beauregard Hunter."

Hunter stood and offered his hand. "How you doing, boy," he
greeted, not really asking a question.

"I'm fine," Enriquez replied politely. "I am very glad I can meet you
at long last."

"'At long last?'" Hunter questioned smiling, as he sat back down.

Enriquez took his seat. "I have been pushing our friend here to get us
together. I think you and I may have interests in common."

"What interests?" Hunter asked.

"I am concerned about some trends in this country, this United States
that has made us all so much money. I wanted to share my concerns with

you rich and powerful men."

"You mean you're concerned about our election, and one Michael Edwards," Hunter stated baldly.

"Of course. And I suspect, Mr. Hunter, that you are also concerned."

"Why don't you-all come out with what's bugging you the most?" Hunter drawled. "The 'atom bomb' of the drug war Edwards keeps talking about."

Enriquez smiled. "Since I hope to have some frank words with you today, I will lay all my cards face up. It is true that I have some agricultural interests in Colombia, Venezuela and Bolivia that some governments consider illegal. This is why I have diversified into other investments. I am speaking to you today out of concern for *all* my investments."

"You're worried over nothing," Fadiman assured him. "I keep telling you that."

"I would like to be sure," Enriquez replied.

"How're you-all gonna do that?" Hunter asked.

"I have watched films and read books about powerful men like us pooling their resources to protect their interests. It seems to me this could be a very good idea in real life. We could all be mutually helpful to each other if the world starts to turn in a direction that threatens our . . . prosperity."

"This is a very dangerous conversation, son," Hunter warned him, but very calmly, without a hint of anxiety. "I play hard in my business, but I mostly play clean. I don't mean to be disrespectful to you or where you come from, but this is no banana republic. You don't do violence against leaders in the political system without—"

"Mr. Hunter," Enriquez interrupted, politely but insistently. "Let's not make speeches to each other. The assassination of President Kennedy in the 60's, and the Watergate scandal of the 70's suggest that you are far more like a 'banana republic' than you think. Powerful people play games with the system here too. I don't know the system. But I have considerable means with which to play some very effective games. A collaboration could be useful."

Fadiman was surprised with Enriquez. He was showing some sophistication and ability to match words with Hunter. He could see Hunter was considering Enriquez' remark. He still felt Enriquez was over his head, and he wanted to make sure both Hunter, and Enriquez himself, were aware of this. "Reekay," he understated quietly, "you're right about one thing. You really don't know the system. You have nothing to fear from

Edwards. Attacking him is not worth the risk." He paused a moment. "Are you aware you have been followed by DEA agents every time you've come to meet me this year?"

"That is not possible," Enriquez countered with subdued but obvious indignation.

"It is possible. It's *happening*. You don't even know it."

Enriquez considered Fadiman's statement. He seemed to be pouting.

"The kind of leader who can mess things up for us with a lot of crazy ideas is not gonna come from the Republicans," Hunter added. "It's fat cats like us that own that party. And the Democrats are so chewed up by special interest groups tugging from every corner that they keep sending dinglebutt after dinglebutt up for election. They occasionally break through, like in '76 and with Clinton, but they won't this year."

Fadiman turned to Enriquez. "And the Republicans are perfect for you. They keep going after your . . . product . . . as if they could keep it out of the country. They just make it scarcer, more expensive, and more profitable while eliminating your competition."

"Listen," Hunter chuckled. "I got to admit, if I thought the son-of-a-bitch was gonna get away with canceling all the breaks we get from the government, I'd be hankering to do something. That's why I decided to meet with you. Maybe we will want to work together, but not yet."

"I don't see how you can say 'not yet,'" Enriquez argued, recovering his concentration and confidence. "You've seen the polls, and the documentaries, and ads on television . . ."

"You got a remote control on your TV set?" Hunter asked him.

Enriquez smiled to hide his irritation with this condescending remark.

"Just turn the damn channel if the man irritates you so much."

"Because he won't be elected," Enriquez restated, almost to see if he could convince himself.

"Exactly," Hunter agreed.

"Okay. But you said yourself that you wanted to meet with me in case things change. So I will tell you that I have very good people who could take whatever measures are necessary to remove this Edwards—"

"Hold on there, boy," Hunter ordered, raising his voice. "I do not want to get involved in discussing a criminal conspiracy to 'remove' a political candidate running for office. Just button that talk up, son."

"You mean you don't want to have a discussion like this unless it is necessary."

"No," Hunter insisted. "I mean I don't want to have a discussion like this at *all*."

Fadiman interceded to try to smooth the rough edges of the conversation. "I know my friend well," he explained. "We need to speak hypothetically, generally. . . Any violent action taken against a political leader in any country cannot look like what it is. It can't look like someone took the guy out."

"How would you do it, then?" asked a puzzled Enriquez.

"I am not willing to stay here for this type of a discussion," Hunter insisted as he began to stand up.

Fadiman motioned him to sit. "I think I can provide Mr. Enriquez with an answer." Fadiman now took on the persona of a Socratic teacher as he addressed himself to Enriquez. "What's the best way to rob a bank?" Fadiman asked. "Dashing in with a perfect plan and escaping with the loot?"

Enriquez shrugged.

"If that's what you think, you've missed a whole different alternative. The best robbery is one where the bank officials don't know there's been a robbery. Maybe they think they lost the money, or they never realize it's missing. You can do it by playing the system. People did that over and over in the 80's."

Enriquez nodded and grinned slightly. "This is why I'm glad to meet with you guys. I'm learning a lot from you old pros."

Fadiman emphasized the lesson. "Robbing a bank with a shotgun can be done by any idiot. And prisons are full of those guys. A scheme to do it right takes more time."

"I can see that," Enriquez agreed.

"We'll let you know if your help is needed," Hunter told him. "Otherwise, you will *not* hear from us."

"Maybe I can be the guy with the idea," Enriquez suggested.

"You're in over your head," Fadiman insisted sternly again.

"Maybe," Enriquez said. "But what am I supposed to do if you old pros don't handle this . . . problem?"

"Be smart, Reekay," Fadiman advised quietly. "Don't mess in places where you're in over your head."

Though Enriquez tried to maintain a poker face, the slight squint in his eyes betrayed his dissatisfaction.

An awkward silence ensued. "Well," Enriquez finally said as he stood up. "It was a pleasure to meet you, Mr. Hunter."

Hunter stood. "Thanks for coming by, young man," he said as they shook hands.

Enriquez nodded to Fadiman, then left the restaurant.

"He's just a street-urchin," Hunter told Fadiman after he was sure Enriquez was out of the room, and out of earshot. "He's sharp, but he's still a punk."

Fadiman nodded.

"Well," Hunter said casually, "I'm a hedge-my-bets guy. So, I met him. I don't think I'll be in touch with him again, but . . ."

"He's still a guy we don't know about completely yet."

"Anything new from your investigation?"

"Yeah. He owns a lot of small Venezuelan holding companies. We're checking them out. And my security people have a source that is about to pay off. I expect to have the straight poop on this guy very shortly."

"Let me know."

"I will."

✿   ✿   ✿

Mid May, Election Year: Friday
Hollywood, California

"HEY SLICK," CAMERON CHANDLER SAID AS "SLICK" NAYLOR OPENED the front door of his latest accommodation, a three bedroom rented house between Sunset and Santa Monica Boulevards near La Brea Avenue.

"Cameron. Long time, no see, man," Naylor greeted. "What brings you out here?"

"Like I told you, I need to make a buy. I need some stuff."

Naylor raised his eyebrows and showed Chandler into his living room. He still had a lot of the beat up, worn furniture from his previous residences, but with some new pieces and his new stereo and television equipment. "Why didn't you go see Kevin?" he asked. "I thought he was your man."

Chandler seemed nervous, but Naylor suspected it was because withdrawal was setting in. "Kevin . . . he's light right now, uh, he's kind of out of commission."

"He got picked up."

"Yeah."

"I figured some of his people might come back to me. I'm not exactly rolling in shit. It'll cost you."

"What?"

"Fifteen hundred a bag."

"Fifteen hundred . . . uh, sure."

Naylor narrowed his eyes a moment. He had expected a negotiation. "How many bags?"

"Uh, fifteen hundred, uh, just the one."

Naylor got up. "Wait here." He left the room, and took a long five minutes to return with the bag. With the extra time, he located and put in his pocket a large, recently sharpened, switchblade knife. Maybe Chandler hadn't negotiated the price because he wasn't concerned about paying it.

Naylor put the plastic baggy, full of white powder, down on the table.

Chandler reached into his pocket and pulled out neatly folded, clean bills, totaling approximately two thousand dollars. The bills were meticulously organized with the twenties on top, the tens next, and a few fives after that, all facing the same direction.

"You've become a lot neater with your cash since you and I did business."

"Neater?" Chandler sounded even more nervous. "Oh, yeah. I have . . . I have gotten neater."

Naylor nodded, then suddenly grabbed Chandler's shirt and tore it from his torso. A wire and tape recorder were attached to his body with masking tape.

"You *motherfucker*!" he exclaimed with caustic menace.

"They caught me with Kevin. They said you were a big player now, that you'd been moving up in the world."

"So you turned it on *me*. You *shit*." Naylor's rage was like an extra presence in the room. He pulled the switchblade knife out of his pocket and pushed the silver button on the handle. The long, gleaming, silver blade snapped out. "I'd cut your slimy heart out, piece by fucking piece, *slowly,* but I know your cop friends are on the way. You *fuck*." Naylor grabbed the baggy and used the knife to hack slits through it.

Chandler watched, paralyzed with fear.

Suddenly there was pounding on both his back and front door. "Police! Open up!"

"You'll pay, motherfucker," Naylor promised venomously as he threw the knife into the wall nearby and raced for a side window, crashing through it. He began running, and allowed the powder to filter out of the slits in the baggy as he fled. The expensive powder became just part of the surrounding dust in the air and on the ground.

The police broke through the doors and ran in with their guns drawn. They saw where Naylor had escaped and quickly followed him.

Naylor had a fifty yard head start. He closed in on a street corner in the residential neighborhood. Despite his head start, he was losing his advantage rapidly. The younger and better conditioned police would have him in their grasp fairly quickly.

Naylor desperately glanced around for some way out. He spied a mailbox. He quickly looked at the baggy. It was almost completely empty. He shook it in the air to remove any further contraband. A sheen of white scattered in a brief puff, then settled to the ground. Naylor dumped what was left of the baggy into the box as he kept moving.

Two policemen approached the box as they chased Naylor. "Watch that fucking box!" the taller one said to the shorter one. He kept chasing Naylor.

Naylor swerved onto a lawn, hoping to get to a backyard where he might lose himself off the lighted street into the blackness of night.

The taller policeman tackled him as he approached the gate to the backyard of the residence. Naylor plummeted to the ground, slamming his face into the grass. "You're under arrest, Bradford Naylor," the officer told him brusquely as he yanked Naylor's arms behind his back and put cuffs on him. The officer pulled him off the lawn and pushed him toward the mailbox.

When they arrived back at the mailbox, Ted Weller, an LAPD Narcotics Detective, was waiting for him. "You know you have the right to keep your trap shut and that you can have your lawyer with you before you talk to me, don't you, Slick?"

"Nolo comprendo, no speakee."

"What did you drop in the box?"

"Nolo comprendo boxo."

"Keep that sense of humor, asshole. You'll need it when they send you up for the rest of your shitty little life."

"No way."

"Oh. You do speakee, huh?"

"You got nothing on me, Weller. Go suck this guy's dick," he suggested insolently as he motioned toward the tall policeman who had just taken him into custody.

"I got nothing on you?" Weller smiled. "Do you understand your rights, fuck-face?"

"Yeah. But you ain't got shit. I've got no stash on me."

"So what? Officer Morris and Officer LaValle saw you drop a baggy into this mailbox. As soon as we get a postal guy out here to open it up, we'll have you nailed. And we've got your buddy, whose heart is still in one piece, who will testify you were selling to him. You're going down,

Slick."

Naylor heaved a huge sigh. "I want my phone call."

"Nolo comprendo phone call, scumbag. Not until you get processed downtown."

✿   ✿   ✿

"I DON'T GIVE A FUCK WHAT TIME IT IS," NAYLOR INSISTED INTO THE phone adjacent to the bloc of holding cells. The area stank of concrete wet with urine and vomit. It was quiet, since most of the detainees were sleeping. "You gotta get me out of here," Naylor insisted loudly, shaky with desperate fear. "You got 24 hours or I'm gonna spill everything."

"Don't yell at me," a groggy Oscar Lusman answered from the bedroom of his condo. "You can only play this card once, asshole," he reminded Naylor. "You spill this, and that ends all your leverage."

"I wouldn't be so sure. I might be able to trade it," he blurted out.

"With the Los Angeles Police?" Lusman asked incredulously. "What would they want with it?"

"They got buddies. They might give me something for it. I've got nothing to lose. You lose everything if you don't get me out of here."

"I'll get you bailed out. And I'll get you an attorney."

"He's gotta keep me out of jail. If I'm going down, so are you."

"If I do get you out of this, your meal ticket is *over*. You're off the payroll now . . . Or, I'll just let you rot."

"I still need the money."

"Tough."

"At least give me two weeks severance, you know, 'cause I am one of your consultants."

"Severance?" Lusman's nostrils flared as he exhaled. "Two weeks *severance*. That means *sever. Cut off.*"

"You get me out of this, you got a deal."

The phone clicked.

Chapter 11

"HEY OSCAR!" ATTORNEY JOEL STERLING CALLED OUT FROM A TABLE at the Plaza Deli. The restaurant was located in an office complex in Century City, a pocket of high rise offices, condominiums, and upscale shopping, surrounded by a residential, one-story area in West Los Angeles, near Twentieth Century Fox Studios. The deli was crowded with patrons watching basketball playoffs. Sterling was a mousy-looking man with curly dark brown hair.

Lusman had just entered the deli. He spotted Sterling and moved quickly to his table.

"How was your flight?" Sterling asked as Oscar took a seat.

"Long," Oscar told him.

"You hungry?" There was a half-eaten corn-beef sandwich in front of Sterling, thick with a high stack of thin slices of meat on rye bread.

"I don't know," Oscar replied, looking unenthusiastically at the sandwich.

"You're one of these salad guys," Sterling recalled.

"I'm not a greasy corn-beef guy."

"Greasy . . ." Sterling obviously didn't agree with the description.

Lusman picked up a menu. "They've got a Chinese chicken salad?"

"Yeah. I'm told it's pretty good."

"That's what I'll get."

There was a brief pause as Lusman put down his menu. "Oscar," Sterling started, changing the subject, "what is this case you've got me on?" Sterling's tone was one of surprise, and distaste.

"I can't go into details. But it's real important."

"I gotta tell you, Oscar, this guy is a slime-doggy. He seems to think I've promised you I can guarantee he's going to get off . . . without doing any time."

"Can you?"

"Guarantee he won't get any time?" Sterling asked in disbelief.

"Yeah."

"I can almost guarantee you he *will* do time. He's done time for dealing before. And he's on a wire trying to sell a major quantity of coke. The D-A's office is going for the throat because they think the guy's got powerful friends to sell out; he tells me he might. He says you know something about that."

Lusman sighed nervously. "He can hurt us."

"You mean you and the Edwards campaign."

"Yes."

Sterling eyed his friend closely. "What do you want me to do?"

"We'll pay for his defense, but you are a legal consultant to the Edwards campaign. You are donating your defense of Naylor, pro bono."

"This is sounding very shaky."

"We have *got* to keep this guy out of prison."

"I don't know if I'm the guy for this," Sterling told him. "You need Perry Mason . . . or Houdini."

Lusman lowered his voice, and in tense but quiet words, went further than he knew he should. "You could end up with a very good job in a Michael Edwards administration if you can pull this off."

Sterling didn't say anything out loud, but he was obviously weighing the promise.

"We're doing very well," Lusman told him, following up. "We really could win."

Sterling nodded slowly. "Out of friendship, and for future considerations, I'll do my best. Just make sure and send me some kind of a consulting job to keep the records straight."

"I'll take care of it."

"I still can't guarantee—"

"Can you keep this son-of-a-bitch out of prison until the election?"

Sterling became even more uncomfortable. "With delaying tactics?

Yeah, I can. But if it's not in my client's best interests, and it becomes apparent I covered your ass instead of his, I could be disbarred."

"Submit an appropriate bill for your . . . delicate handling . . . You're a consultant, remember?"

"Yeah."

"We're in the big leagues now."

Sterling smiled. "Is this the big leagues?" He sniffed the air. "Smells more like the out-house."

Lusman shrugged. The waitress arrived and he ordered his Chinese chicken salad.

✿   ✿   ✿

Late May, Election Year: Wednesday
Pasadena, California

"IT IS ABSOLUTELY ESSENTIAL THAT THESE DISCUSSIONS BE KEPT completely confidential," Jamison Tyler Fullbright told Drew Saroyan and Michael Edwards as they spoke at a table in Edwards' hotel room at the Rose Bowl Hotel in Pasadena.

"I agree," Saroyan answered. "Both of our principals could be negatively affected by a premature disclosure."

"So everything said here stays in this room. We have seen a number of leaks on your possible running mate. The fact that this conference is taking place can not leak."

"Understood," Saroyan responded.

"That out of the way, I am pleased to inform you that my principal is potentially interested in running with you, Mr. Edwards."

"I'm honored," Edwards told him sincerely. "I know that Congressman Trewillinger could face considerable criticism from his own party."

"That's true. But Congressman Trewillinger feels that this may be in the best interests of the nation. He won't let party interests interfere with that consideration."

"That's fantastic," Edwards replied.

"We just need to discuss a few details. Congressman Trewillinger feels it would be important for us to spell out his role in the campaign, and in any future administration."

"And I think that's wise," Edwards agreed. "I would see him as—"

"Uh, Congressman Trewillinger has some very specific ideas on this subject," Fullbright interrupted gently, but firmly.

Edwards was slightly irritated with the interruption, and apprehensive about the 'specific ideas,' but he answered politely. "I'm very interested in the Congressman's ideas."

"He finds a great deal to admire in your domestic proposals, and will fully support your proposals to move toward renewable energy sources."

"I would hope so, since it's one of the major keys to my campaign," Edwards said.

"He feels that the best approach for this ticket would be for the two of you to present yourselves as joint Presidential candidates, with you in charge of domestic policy and Congressman Trewillinger in charge of foreign policy. This fits in well with the prevailing attitude in the country, that the job of President of the United States is too big for one man to do properly. In fact, I believe you have made those comments yourself."

"In a commentary a few years ago, yes," Edwards acknowledged. He fought to keep a polite smile on his face.

"So what Congressman Trewillinger wants is to be part of a joint Presidency."

"I see," Edwards said through the forced smile.

"How would you view such an alliance?" Fullbright asked.

"It's quite . . . unprecedented . . ." Edwards answered.

"Not really. In 1980, Gerald Ford and Ronald Reagan toyed with the idea before Reagan took George Bush onto the ticket."

"True," Edwards replied. He looked at Saroyan.

Saroyan smiled. "Perhaps you should give us some time to consider this rather unconventional and unexpected proposal."

"I understand." Fullbright paused. "May I speak candidly?"

"Always," Edwards replied.

"Congressman Trewillinger feels there is much to admire in your innovative ideas, and the high arch and long horizon of your vision. But he believes you will ultimately fail in this effort, due to your lack of political experience and lack of any long term affiliation with conventional political structures. He can help you with both of those problems. But you cannot expect him to join your effort as a subordinate. He must be assured that his talents, not just his attributes, will be used. He does not want to be exploited to further your campaign, and then forgotten."

"I appreciate your candor," Edwards replied.

"Yes," Saroyan added. "You've been very clear in stating

Congressman Trewillinger's position on this, and you've given us a lot to think over. Thank you for coming out here."

Fullbright stood up and extended his hand; both Edwards and Saroyan stood and shook hands with him. "My pleasure." He left the room.

Edwards and Saroyan sat back down. They were silent for a long moment.

"What do you think?" Edwards finally asked Saroyan.

"You can't do what they want," Saroyan told him. "I was trying to think of a way . . ."

"I know." Edwards heaved a frustrated sigh. "It would have been such a coup."

"But he doesn't think of you as an equal, much less the top man on the ticket. This proposal was almost condescending. He'd assume he was taking over the ticket. 'You cannot expect him to join your effort as a subordinate.' You'd have no control over him whatsoever, and you'd look like a flake if even a hint of this joint presidency idea became public."

Edwards nodded. "We can't expect voters to swallow both a third alternative candidate and a joint Presidency, two radical concepts flung at them at once."

"Exactly. And I think he's figuring that your money would rejuvenate his dead campaign. He could push his foreign policy agenda, on *our* tab."

"So there's no way to negotiate this with him."

"Even if we did, his attitude would still be a huge problem. He didn't ask us for our conditions. He stated his. That's no way for you to start a relationship with your running mate."

"I agree," Edwards said softly.

"I'll turn him down quietly and politely, and we sure as shit will keep this little head-to-head out of the public eye."

"The way Fullbright started out, I thought we'd bagged him."

"Yeah."

"What about Willis?"

"I've made some delicate inquiries," Saroyan told him. "I had an old colleague who knows her set up a meeting for an informal chat. I'm still waiting."

"So where does that leave us?"

"We have had interest from some good people. We'll set up an interview schedule and try to select the best one, if Willis is a no-go."

Edwards nodded then sighed. "You know, Trewillinger's response points up a major weakness in this campaign so far. I really haven't come out with any major foreign policy views."

"I know. But right now, foreign policy is not what excites the electorate."

"I want to make a major speech on foreign policy as soon as possible."

Saroyan nodded.

☼   ☼   ☼

Late May: The Following Friday
Pasadena, California

"I AM HONORED TO BE HERE TODAY TALKING TO A ROOM FULL OF PEOPLE who have contributed so much to the development of humankind in the last half of the Twentieth Century," Edwards stated to a packed assembly room at Jet Propulsion Laboratory in Pasadena. "And I am pleased to use this visit with you to announce one of the major priorities of my future administration. I believe one of the proudest accomplishments of our nation during the Twentieth Century has been the lead we have taken in the exploration of space. We have accomplished the dramatic, landing on the moon. And we have accomplished the functional, with satellites for communication that the world has now become so accustomed to."

Edwards went on to tell a subdued but receptive group that his administration would set three priorities to revitalize America's space program: a permanently orbiting space station by the end of his four year term, a moon landing with the objective of scouting locations for permanent settlements, and coordination with the private sector so that a significant portion of the cost of the expansion into space could be paid for by industries making a *profit* from their use of space.

He described space exploration and settlement as an integral element of a Regenerating Biosphere. He detailed technological advances from past space exploration that had benefitted humankind, and listed present benefits from the nation's current space presence. He went on to suggest that some chemical and metallurgical processes might be carried out more simply and cleanly in space. Having access to vacuums and utilizing the advantages of zero gravity would lead to exciting, barely imaginable possibilities in chemistry and materials physics, potentially eliminating the environmental problems now associated with some manufacturing processes.

And he argued that this was the most effective way to employ many of the workers who had been involved in projects for the military, projects that had been scaled back as a result of the end of the Cold War. He also added that while competition with the former Soviet Union over leadership in the development of space technology was over, Japan and the European Space Agency were quickly closing the gap. He felt the United States should be proud to continue to lead in this area, and that it would be a sad day if that leadership role were transferred to other nations or economic blocs, especially when that transfer could also lead to a possible competitive disadvantage in commerce.

"I'm just here to let you know that you'd better all be ready," he continued. "Because when I get elected, there's going to be a lot of work . . . you people will be *busy*."

A little laughter was followed by a lot of applause.

"In the past, I have heard Presidents talk about putting America to work with government funded jobs, almost make-work jobs, just to stimulate the economy. Well, I like the idea of creating jobs in *this* sector. So many new industries were created as a result of our first space race—personal computers and satellite technologies are just a few of the largest ones. So let's get to work reaching these latest goals for humankind in space, so we can marvel at the undreamed of new products that will arise from the effort."

More applause followed.

"I'm glad you could all be here today so I could share these goals with you. And I will enjoy meeting with you again to restate these goals after I am sworn in as your next President. Thank you."

Edwards received a round of applause from most of the crowd, but a reserved one. The scientific approach of many of the audience members led them to be slightly skeptical of Edwards' pronouncements. They had only been aware of his environmental positions before this speech. Some were concerned that he had fashioned a set of promises designed to secure their approval. But as they heard Edwards repeat his pledges and priorities for the space program in numerous speeches after this one, and in his infomercial and television ads, many realized Edwards was sincere. Some even began to consider voting for him.

✿   ✿   ✿

Mid June, Election Year: Thursday
Maracaibo, Venezuela

"FIVE OR TEN YEARS, AND THIS LAKE WILL BE PUMPING FOR *ME,* AS LONG as . . ." Ernesto Enriquez interrupted his thought as he reflected with his closest associate and enforcer, Manuel Contreras. They looked out over Lake Maracaibo from Enriquez' old style Spanish villa, set on a raised hill, back from the western shore of the Gulf of Venezuela. Oil derricks and other structures associated with Venezuela's thriving petroleum industry could be seen from their commanding view of the lake and surrounding lands. A breeze allowed for better visibility than normal, and for a more comfortable climate than the usual heat and humidity that characterized this northwestern section of the Maracaibo Basin in the western Venezuelan state of Zulia. Venezuela's oil industry had transformed this once poor area, dominated by subsistence agriculture on marginal lands, into the most mineral-rich region in the country. The Lagunillas oil field, across Lake Maracaibo on the east shore, just south of Cuidad Ojeda, was the largest in Latin America. Enriquez had found a productive use for the marginal agricultural lands in Zulia—he had established relationships with specially selected local farmers to supply him with coca leaves.

Contreras and Enriquez sipped beers and munched on quesadillas.

" . . . as long as oil and drugs are still good businesses." Enriquez drew a deep, determined breath. "Ernesto Enriquez will very soon be the John D. Rockefeller, the Armand Hammer, the J. Paul Getty—actually, more like the Joseph Kennedy of South America. But I will take it a step further." He smiled fancifully at what he thought was the cleverness of this analogy, then turned to Manuel. "And you, my friend, will find yourself behind a desk running armies, instead of doing my dirty work."

"Softer days are coming."

"Yes, but that *Edwards* in the United States. We need about five more years to finish putting everything into place. Edwards can single-handedly mess us up."

"My plan is almost ready. I can . . . handle the problem for you . . ."

"But it's *not* ready," Enriquez countered.

"The Cubans are holding me up. The plan is set, but they are asking too much money for the weapon I need."

"For Communists, they understand *Capitalism* very well," Enriquez grumbled. "And they know we have the money." He thought a moment.

"I am learning subtlety from my new American friends. But they are too stupid, or too lazy and content to take action."

"So will you wait for them?"

"No. I will make my move. But I will take my time." He smiled. "It takes time to set up a good plan; my American friends have told me this. And I have plenty of time to pick the perfect circumstances; the American election is not until November."

"Are you sure you need to do anything? Don't the American political experts say this Edwards is peaking, that he has all the support he is going to get?"

"That may or may not be true," he said quietly. "Back in 1990, I heard these experts say that George Bush could not fail to be reelected in 1992. And I once heard that in 1980, some big-time television expert called Ronald Reagan 'politically dead' after he lost his first primary to Bush and the other Republicrats."

Contreras was surprised. He almost let an astonished smile sneak onto his face. "You seem to know a lot about American politics," he observed.

"I checked it out a little—enough to know that I don't trust these experts. I don't like risks and possibilities. I like certainties. And I work to assure them."

"So what of my plan?"

"If my idea does not work, then you will contact the Cubans, pay them what they want, and go forward."

"But I am not involved in your idea."

"No." He smiled. "And neither are the Americans."

"Who *is* involved?"

"Zoilo."

"*Zoilo*," Manuel repeated in disbelief. He then flashed a rare grin. "Ah-huh. I think I see how he could be useful."

"Yes. I'll have him ready for when the time comes."

"Good." Manuel raised his beer glass. "To the South American Rockefeller . . ."

"South American *Kennedy*," Enriquez corrected with a smile.

They toasted.

✿   ✿   ✿

Mid June, Election Year: Friday
New York, New York

"Your record is impressive, Governor," Edwards said as he sat behind the desk of his office in his Manhattan campaign headquarters.

"Thank you, Mr. Edwards," answered Governor Stanford Bieber, a tall, thin, dark-haired man of about thirty-nine with some dignifying grey hair at his temples. "I admire what you have been doing, and I feel there could definitely be some compatibility."

"I do too."

"Mr. Edwards, in any important decision, I feel there should be total frankness. Do you agree with me?"

"Absolutely."

"I don't think you have a chance in hell of winning, but I admire what you're doing and I think a lot of what you're saying needs to be said. For me, I—"

"We're trying to win," Edwards interrupted. "We haven't conceded anything."

"Don't worry. That's what I'll say in public if I get on the ticket. But for me, this is a chance for national exposure, being identified with issues I feel strongly about. As Governor of Vermont, I'm not necessarily going to get a lot of national press. Some tell me my party will see running with you as a betrayal. But I'm willing to take the risk to stand next to you and become a household word."

"I appreciate your frankness." Edwards stood up and extended his hand.

Bieber stood up and shook it.

Saroyan suddenly walked into the room. "Michael, I need to talk with you right away," he said urgently.

"Okay," he replied. He turned to Bieber. "I enjoyed our exchange of views. We share a lot of the same vision of the future."

"I'm glad you feel that way."

"We've got some other people to talk to, so we'll let you know."

"I'll hope it's good news." Bieber left the office.

"What is it?" Edwards asked Saroyan, concerned.

"We just got a call from Conrad Nance at the Washington Post. He's asked for comment on a story they're running, on how we offered the VP spot to Frances Willis, and she turned us down."

"What? Drew . . . we didn't offer—"

"No," he responded emphatically. "But we asked her about it. I just talked to Mary Schott, the lady I told you I knew who was close to Willis. She finally got a chance to meet with Willis for lunch today. She started hinting around about it. Then, the way Mary tells it, Willis kind of put her on the spot, and she admitted that she was in contact with me, and that we were interested."

"But we didn't offer it, Drew. So what's the—"

"It's starting to look like we can't find a real high-credibility running mate." He paused. "How was this Governor Bieber?"

Edwards shrugged. "He's better than most of them." He shook his head fatalistically. "I admired his straightforwardness. He admitted what a lot of these guys haven't said, that he wants the publicity."

"But not the office?"

"He doesn't think I can win."

"He told you that?" Saroyan smiled and shook his head. "That is refreshingly frank for a politician. But I'm not sure his honesty convinces me he's the best man for the job."

"He's also too young."

Saroyan nodded.

"Is it time to contact Trewillinger? Maybe see if we can negotiate something?"

"I don't know," Saroyan answered impatiently. He was clearly frustrated with the lack of a desirable running mate. "I'm really trying to avoid that."

"Yeah."

One of the campaign staff, a plain, frumpy, usually soft-spoken, lady, rushed in, then approached them timidly. "Mr Edwards?" she summoned tentatively.

"Yes," he acknowledged.

"Uh, I think Frances Willis is on the phone for you."

"Put her through to my office."

Saroyan and Edwards moved quickly to Edwards' office and closed the door.

Edwards picked up the phone. "Michael Edwards."

"Mr. Edwards. It's Frances Willis."

"I'm glad you called."

"I got a call from a Post reporter, uh, Conrad something . . ."

"Nance?"

"Yes."

"We got the same call."

"I really don't know how he got his information, but I did not understand you to offer me a spot on your ticket at all."

"Um, we certainly didn't make any formal offer." Edwards paused for a moment. Frances Willis had taken a direct approach to him. He decided to return the favor with frankness. "I'm going to level with you."

Drew Saroyan shook his head nervously.

But Edwards was trusting his gut-level instincts—there was no time to debate the pro's and con's with his campaign advisor. "We did send out a friend of my campaign manager to find out if you'd be interested. If you had shown interest, we would have considered making you an offer. Ma'am, I would be proud to have you on our ticket. But we did not want to put you on the spot if there was no interest."

"I understand."

"We did not leak this to—"

"I know where the leak came from; it wasn't from your campaign."

"So we will tell Mr. Nance that no offer was made."

"Yes." She paused. "Mr. Edwards, I—"

"Please call me Michael."

"Okay. Michael, I respect very much what you have been doing. I can't join your ticket as a conventional Vice Presidential candidate. After all, I have already been the Vice President. I have paid enough dues in that position. But I understand from a friend of Congressman Trewillinger that you have discussed a joint candidacy for President. My brief discussion with you here today leads me to admire you even more. I would consider that sort of arrangement."

Edwards turned white as a ghost. He was shocked and alarmed that she knew about the Trewillinger discussion.

Saroyan could see Michael's blanched expression. "What?" he queried Michael.

Edwards pulled himself together. He didn't have time to explain to Saroyan. "I . . . I appreciate what you're saying. We have . . . we are weighing that kind of approach, and will contact you if we go that way." He drew a deep, nervous breath. "Where did you hear—"

"I have my sources," Willis told him smugly.

"Well, I appreciate the call."

"My pleasure. I wanted to make sure there were no misunderstandings between us before I commented on the story."

"Well, thanks again."

"Call me any time, Michael. Good-bye." She hung up.

Edwards hung up. "She knows about our discussions with

Trewillinger," he observed quietly.

"Shit. That means the media won't be far behind."

"She hinted that *she* would consider a joint candidacy."

Now a knowing smile appeared on Saroyan's face. "What did she say when you mentioned the leak?"

"That she knows it didn't come from our campaign."

"Yeah. She knows. Because *her* people leaked it."

Edwards looked puzzled and waited for the explanation.

"When Mary went out to speak to her, she probably knew about the Trewillinger discussions. When Mary didn't mention the joint candidacy option, it probably confused her. So she leaked the story to set herself up to talk to you by creating a common problem. Then, she let you know *she* was interested, but only as a *joint* candidate."

"Jesus," Edwards groaned. "Well, you wanted a circus surrounding this V-P thing, and now you have it."

"Not a *circus*."

Edwards narrowed his eyes, squinting with disagreement.

"Well, not a circus like *this;* completely out of control. We've got to get this running mate situation nailed down soon, before the whole thing starts to look ridiculous."

Edwards nodded in agreement.

✿   ✿   ✿

Mid June: The Following Sunday
New York, New York

"DON'T TELL ME," MICHAEL SAID TO TED JESSUP AS THEY SAT IN A QUIET corner of the Park Avenue Bar and Grill. "You're here to pump me about the running-mate circus."

Jessup smiled. "That's not why I asked to see you, but I wouldn't mind any inside information you want to give us."

"You can say this, from a highly placed source in the Edwards campaign; we are still looking over a long list of good candidates from every walk of life—"

"Don't hand me your bullshit, Michael."

"Okay. Your source tells you this. Two heavies have offered to join the ticket as joint candidates, with a joint Presidency in mind. Edwards has resisted this suggestion."

"Oh, *'Edwards'* has, has he?"

"Yeah. Drew and I decided we could let that little tidbit slip."

"Thanks."

"If you're not here for that gem, what's on your mind?"

Jessup became more serious. "I'm here as your friend. We have a source inside the South American drug cartels. He says your life is in danger."

Edwards smiled. "That's *great*. Can you put that out?"

"Michael, this is *serious*. You need some powerful protection."

"It just proves that I *do* have the 'atom bomb' for the war on drugs."

"Yeah, uh, Michael, this is not a strong enough story for us to go with. We're still working on nailing it down a little better. But I thought you should know. Some very bad, very violent people may want you dead. If they have their way, you will not live to stand for this election."

"I'll get in touch with Secret Service and get them to beef up—"

"I don't want to knock the Secret Service. But you need some supplementary help. These people after you may be the same people who shot off missiles in Los Angeles . . ."

"You think I need a private service."

"Yeah. And I know who might be good."

"You like to select my campaign personnel for me, don't you?" Edwards joked.

"On all of our projects together, I've been the guy who finds the key people. It's an area you're not familiar with. I guess 'cause I'm your friend . . ."

"I appreciate the tip. Who's the guy?"

"Carl Gregory. I met him a few years ago when we were doing a story on professional bodyguards."

"I remember the story. Did we use him?"

"As an anonymous source. He wouldn't agree to work with us any other way. He felt specifics about him would compromise his clients."

"Give me his number," Edwards told Jessup. "We'll check him out. Drew should probably meet him before I decide whether or not to use him."

Jessup handed him a business card. "I mentioned the situation to him. He gave me his card."

"Thanks."

The rest of the evening was subdued between the two friends. Michael was clearly preoccupied. Jessup understood, and gracefully withdrew from their meeting about fifteen minutes later. Michael pondered whether or not he should tell Teresa. He decided that if he got good protection, and had his staff remain vigilant, there was no reason to worry his wife.

✿   ✿   ✿

Late June: The Following Monday
Hollywood, California

"TALK TO MY ATTORNEY," NAYLOR SNARLED ARROGANTLY AS HE answered his doorbell and found LAPD Detective Weller at his front door.

"Yeah. I figured you'd say that."

"So what're you doing here?"

"I thought we could help each other out."

"*You* wanna help *me?*"

"No. I'm looking to help the citizens of Los Angeles, whom I have sworn to 'protect and serve.' But to get you to help *them*, I'm aware there's gotta be something in it for you."

"Whaddya want?"

"Who's paying for the high-priced legal talent?"

"I got nothing for you, Weller."

"What did they promise you?"

"They?"

"Whoever hired the high-priced legal talent for you."

"I got 'em out of the yellow pages."

"They're just delaying the inevitable, Slick. You're going down."

"I think you're supposed to leave me alone when my lawyer isn't here." Naylor tried to be tough, but his nervousness about his situation, and about what Weller was saying to him, leaked into his voice, causing a slight but detectable waver.

"Yeah? Well, you call me if you start to see the light, Slick. Because the delays aren't helping you. They're helping your high-priced friends. They're just stringing things out 'til they figure out how to get rid of you." He placed his card in Naylor's hand. "You call me when you're ready to hand 'em over to us. We'll take good care of you."

Naylor took the card as he squinted. For the first time, it dawned on Naylor that Sterling's requests for continuances to conduct his own investigation into Naylor's arrest might be a delaying tactic. Was Oscar stupid enough to try to string Naylor along until after the election, then let him take the fall? Naylor would be watching Sterling very closely at the next court appearance. He would demand to know what investigation Sterling was completing. If the answers weren't satisfactory, he resolved to become the Edwards campaign's worst nightmare.

✿   ✿   ✿

Early July, Election Year: Thursday
Culiacan, Mexico

"I'M GOING TO KILL TWO NASTY BIRDS WITH ONE STONE HERE," ERNESTO Enriquez told Manuel Contreras as he winked. They disembarked from a small helicopter Enriquez had piloted to an isolated clearing about 80 miles east of Culiacan, capitol of Sinaloa. "We've got to harvest these plants, and I'm going to talk to Zoilo about our Michael Edwards plan."

"You need my help to talk to him?" Manuel asked.

Enriquez smiled. "I think you scare Zoilo. Just take care of harvesting these plants after we leave."

"Whatever you need."

"Zoilo!" Enriquez greeted enthusiastically as he approached Zoilo Metolitican, who was tending a row of tall marijuana plants in a huge field. The field was carefully positioned in a crease-like valley, situated in the low hills of the western edge of the Sierra Madre Occidental Mountains. Tall, forest-like trees bordered the field on all sides, especially positioned to make the multi-million dollar crop difficult to locate from the air without a very close search. The area was mostly rolling brown hills, and the landscape appeared generally dry and brown from the air. But this area had a pocket of green where a stream and a creek supported more vegetation. Some irrigation also aided the agricultural potential of the area. And well-placed bribes with local officials insured that local authorities did not investigate this pocket of green too closely.

"Mr. Ernesto," Zoilo acknowledged. He was a peculiar man, short, very thin, with distant, hard-to-read expressions. He was almost a full-blooded Indian, with Aztec ancestry. Enriquez knew that his view of reality was heavily influenced by old Indian legends he had heard from his parents and grandparents. He was dark-complected, tanned from his work maintaining the marijuana field. "The plants go good, sir. They go real good."

"I'm glad, Zoilo," Enriquez replied. "We both know how important the plants are."

"You understand real good, Mr. Ernesto. They suck the bad air out of the sky. They suck up all the negative energy."

"That's true."

"The earth is dying, Mr. Ernesto. I have dreamed it. I can save the earth from dying and drying up, but only if the plants spread and spread. The bad air and the bad energy is killing us."

Enriquez nodded. "I know. I wish I had good news. But I need you to move to a new place to start new plants."

"We can't do that. Mr. Ernesto, we can't start over. These are the savior plants. The god who burns in the sun came and blessed them. He told me this is our last chance." Zoilo became more and more agitated as he spoke. "The world. I can *save* the *world*. My people—they have waited for me to complete this sacred task. They are waiting for their home to be restored. You must not stop me, Mr. Ernesto. The sun god will burn me to ashes while I'm still breathing if I fail! My people will curse my name for eternity!"

"I'm not the one who is trying to stop you," Enriquez assured him. "It is the Americans who are taking over this land, just like they have throughout history. They have ordered us to leave this land and destroy the plants."

"The Americans," Zoilo repeated in disbelief. "How can the Americans have any power here?" His eyes narrowed suspiciously. "I thought *you* ruled here, Mr. Ernesto."

"I do. But—" Enriquez deliberately stammered, as if confessing the truth reluctantly. "If we do not remove these plants ourselves, the Americans will send great flying flame-throwers to do it for us. And they will not care how much of our land they burn."

"No! We must talk to the Americans! We must explain to them why the plants cannot die!"

"We have tried. I told the American who ordered us to burn the plants about you and your revelation from the gods. He laughed. He said 'I am an important man. I won't waste my time talking to some fool who takes care of plants.'"

"Then he is an *evil* man," Zoilo countered with caustic hate. "You must have some of your bravest warriors destroy him."

Enriquez shook his head sadly. "He has defeated my best. He uses very powerful magic from evil spirits. I have fought him with the best weapons and the strongest fighters. But I have no one to match the evil magic. So . . . we must do what they say and burn the plants, or watch our land burned by their flame-throwers."

"Who is this evil man?"

"Michael Edwards."

"He must *die*."

Enriquez again shook his head sadly. "Not soon enough to save your plants."

"You say you have no one to oppose his evil magic . . ."

Enriquez looked at him plaintively. "I said that. But—" His eyes were imploring.

"Yes," Zoilo told him with confidence. "You have *me*."

Enriquez smiled with admiration. "I do, Zoilo. I have *you*. Son of a holy man. Descendant from kings. The power is within you."

"The sun god spirit flows to me. He has chosen *me* to act for him." Zoilo's eyes flared and his voice became angry. "I am *he*. I am now the sun god on Earth!"

"That's amazing, Zoilo. You are truly an incredible man," Enriquez patronized.

"I will go to this Michael Edwards and *destroy* him!" Zoilo announced, as if he really was an angry god ruling the cosmos. "The evil magic will be vanquished!"

"I will transport you, sun god!" Enriquez promised him. "I will take you to the United States where you can destroy our enemy."

They left quickly.

Chapter 12

DREW SAROYAN WATCHED GLOOMILY AS MICHAEL EDWARDS STUDIED some papers. They were in Edwards' office in the Manhattan campaign headquarters. Edwards sat at his desk. Saroyan sat across from him in a chair.

Edwards sighed and looked up as he pursed his lips intolerantly. He tossed the papers onto his desk. "So?" he challenged.

"We're unraveling," Saroyan explained. "You can see it in the numbers."

"We lost two points. You're acting like we've already lost the election."

"We may have."

Edwards' nostrils flared and he squinted dubiously. "When I was with the media, I always thought you political pros read these polls too closely. Now I'm sure of it. I'm not happy with this, but we haven't lost."

"It's not just the numbers. It's the reasons. Our own poll indicates that the people defecting think you've reached everyone you're going to reach, which makes you a solid third place, someone who can't win. So they're starting to peel off to make the old 'lesser-of-two-evils' choice."

"So we've peaked?"

"I'm not saying that. But people *think* we have. And with the conventions coming up, this is not good timing."

Edwards leaned back and folded his arms in front of him. "So give me some advice," he told Saroyan as he glared at him.

Saroyan quickly realized he was risking Edwards' wrath if he didn't brighten the mood. He looked down at a list of notes. "First," he began resolutely, "we have to get this V-P situation straightened out. We are starting to look indecisive, and—"

"I know," Edwards agreed, not happy to rehash the obvious. "But what do we have?"

"Nothing I'm happy about."

Edwards shook his head. "Is it time to consider a joint candidacy? I mean, if that's our only shot at winning, maybe we should take another look at it."

"I'll make some quiet contacts," Saroyan said with resignation. "We'll have that option ready."

"What else do you have on your list of . . . prescriptions?" Edwards asked.

"I want you to go on MTV. A couple of political candidates this decade have done well there. We need to reach some new people—we've already reached the people who watch talk shows and infomercials. They either agree with you or they don't."

Edwards nodded. "That's a good idea. Next."

"We've got to be heard on other issues."

Edwards narrowed his eyes. "You mean like *foreign policy?*" he asked, chiding Saroyan.

"Yeah," Saroyan replied sheepishly. "We may have carved out too narrow of an identity. Let's put out your foreign policy speech right away." He thought a moment. "At a west coast university—we've been back in this area too long."

Edwards nodded again. "Okay. Good. Anything else?"

"Well, do *you* have any ideas?"

"Not really." He paused. "This is when we decide whether we're really after this. I *am*. So we will fight to turn it back around."

"Good," Saroyan replied. "Oh, and by the way, I have *some* good news. We just got the word on two more states. Now there are only three where you're not on the ballot yet." He stood up. "I've got some work to do." He started out, then turned back. "I almost forgot; have you ever heard of Everett Phillips?"

"The name is familiar . . ." Edwards pondered it. "I think . . . is he a general?"

"Yeah. He's another guy nominating himself as your running mate. I was about to put his letter with the other ones."

"Everett Phillips. I did a story on him in the mid 80's." He paused a moment, then smiled. "I think I'd like to see that letter."

"Sure. What do you know about him?"

"He was a real sharp general, Viet Nam veteran with medals, but with a view that didn't track well with the Reagan Administration. About the same time Ronald Reagan was fussing and fuming about the 'evil empire,' Phillips was saying that we would have a peaceful accommodation with the Soviet Union within ten years. He was telling his superiors, rather aggressively, that our nation's defense needed to concentrate on terrorism and possible adventurism by aggressive smaller nations. What made it tougher for the Defense Department is that he had been assigned to study the Soviet Union and was their own designated expert!"

"You liked him."

"A *lot*. You've got that letter in your office?"

"Yeah."

Edwards got up and they both walked toward Saroyan's office.

"The other thing I liked a lot, but that made him a real maverick, was that he concluded the Soviets would have to make an accommodation with us because their military budget was draining their entire economy, and their nation's resources. The Afghanistan intervention was the last straw, and he knew it. He went on to conclude that *we* had to get more for *our* money, and that *our* government wasn't doing enough to control costs. In effect, he was saying the United States was headed in the same direction as the Soviet Union. This did not make him a popular guy."

They arrived at Saroyan's office.

"So they got rid of him?" Saroyan asked.

"No. He resigned in 1987. That's when I did the story on him."

"Well, here's his letter," Saroyan told him:

> *Dear Mr. Edwards:*
>
> *I hope you recall our interview back in April of 1987. I still have a videotape of the report you did on my resignation from the Armed Forces and remember our contact cordially.*
>
> *I have watched your recent Presidential campaign, first with curiosity, then with*

admiration. I find myself enthusiastically
casting my vote for you, and arguing your
merits to my friends and associates.
I have also watched your public search for
a running mate. I have noticed the wide
variety of talent you have been
considering. I would humbly request that
you consider me for this position. Your
effort is a fight I would love to make my
own.

Enclosed is a brief resume and some
clippings commenting on my public speaking
abilities in recent appearances. I hope to
meet with you soon to discuss this
exciting possibility in person.

Sincerely,

Everett C. Phillips, General, USA, ret.

"This is the guy," Edwards said to Saroyan with quiet excitement. "We can forget about joint candidacies and unqualified running mates with ulterior motives."

"Wait a minute, Michael. Let's talk about this."

"There's no need. *This* is the *guy.*"

"I think we ought to meet with him."

"Of course. But I know him. He won't screw up any interview. He's perfect."

"Let's not get carried away here. Perfect? A military guy? This reminds me of Stockdale. The voters'll remember it too. You'll look like you're going the same route as Perot. And it also reminds me of George Wallace, when he was running as an independent in the 60's, taking on Curtis Lemay as his number two—you remember those guys?"

"Of course. But I'm no right-wing George Wallace, and General Phillips is definitely not the same type of military man as Curtis Lemay. And you may be right; the voters will think of Stockdale, until they see General Phillips. This guy . . ." Edwards shook his head in admiration. "It is really a boost that someone of his caliber wants to adopt our cause as a subordinate. It gives me a personal boost."

"We still need to talk. Is this guy going to help us?"

"Can't you see how perfectly he compliments me? He's got defense experience, foreign policy experience—he's eminently qualified to be a heartbeat from the President."

"What state is he from?"

"Pennsylvania."

"He could help us there."

"Drew, I'm almost one hundred per cent sure I want this guy. I want him in here A-S-A-P, then we sign him up and head into this race strong."

"It's your campaign. Could I at least meet him and have some input before we firm up the decision?"

Edwards saw that Saroyan felt he was making an impulsive decision. Edwards still knew he had found his running mate, but moderated his tone for Saroyan. "Of course," he replied graciously. "I want your opinion. I'm just excited about this guy."

"Hope I am too."

And after a meeting, Saroyan agreed that Phillips was the best available running mate for Edwards.

✿   ✿   ✿

Early July: The Following Monday
Medford, Oregon

"THIS IS A PRETTY STRANGE PLACE FOR THIS TYPE OF A MEETING," Edwards told Lusman as they walked through a forest of gigantic trees along Bear Creek just southeast of Medford in the Klamath Mountains. The trail was well worn and easy to follow. The trees rising on either side of them darkened the already overcast day. Though the meeting was in a location remote from the campaign trail, and took some time to travel to, Edwards found the location refreshing. It was more than just the calming nature of the huge green trees and the silence, except for the slight crunch of footsteps against the trail and occasional sound of birds. The air was also clean and fresh. The pine smell was a pleasant contrast to the smells of airports, city streets, and hotels.

"This is the way the guy wanted to do this," Oscar explained. "He wants to make sure no one links you to him."

Edwards shrugged. "Well, you and Drew seem to like the guy. I just want to meet him before I agree to put him in charge of protecting my life."

"Yeah. You should. We're just about there."

"Is that him?" Edwards asked in disbelief as they approached a rock formation to the left of the trail about thirty yards ahead. He saw a man who appeared to be in his late forties, wearing a khaki, army-style jacket. He had a full beard and long, shoulder length dark brown hair with a few strands of grey. Hair seemed to flow from the entire perimeter of his face. "He looks like a mountain man, or some old 60's hippie."

Lusman smiled. "I think he'd like both of those descriptions. But I'll bet this guy could kill an enemy in more ways than you can imagine."

"Okay. Let's meet him."

Gregory had climbed off the rock formation and moved toward them.

"Michael Edwards," Gregory greeted with a cordial smile as he extended his hand.

Edwards shook hands, smiling and allowing Gregory to complete his greeting.

"I've been an admirer of you since you started your righteous odyssey," Gregory continued. "I'm glad you decided to talk to me about a little guardian help." He shook Lusman's hand. "Thank your friend Ted Jessup for bringing my existence to his consciousness."

"I think he's got some questions for you," Lusman told Gregory.

"He's trying to become the man. He *better* have questions."

"You don't look like a security guy," Edwards observed, deliberately testing Gregory.

Gregory shrugged. "That's my greatest weapon," he told Edwards proudly. "I know how to use almost every weapon now in vogue on the planet. I can spot security problems before they're much more than dots on the horizon. I can get the best inside investigation available to any of us laboring outside the life force. And I'm always at least a lifetime ahead of those looking to return me to the cosmic soup, because I am not what my enemies expect."

Edwards took a moment to absorb the form and content of Gregory's reply. "You apparently run a successful security agency."

"Ever heard of us?"

"What are you called?"

"We're not in the yellow pages. I'm incorporated under the name ZYXWV. But that's for the tax people and paper pushers. We're not called anything."

"How could I have heard of you if you're not called anything?"

"That's my point."

Edwards shrugged.

"I guard people all over the world—important people. I do investigations, handle special assignments. Some things we do may or may not be legal in some of the countries we operate in. I make a good living with my word-of-mouth clientele. I don't need to advertise."

"How did you get into this business?"

Gregory smiled. "I get to keep some secrets."

Edwards was disappointed with his response.

"I'll give you some idea of my life experience. I was a brat in the Nam. I was stoked on the action. When it ended, I was a hired gun at every hot spot I could find. Then, about fifteen years ago, I realized I was chasing the action because of a death wish that had grown as a cancer in my psyche—I got it damaged when I tried to deny my conscience. I landed hard, spent almost three years on Ronald Reagan's streets. My life was wasting away. I was one of those poor vets who never made it back. But when I saw what I was through the eyes of the pitying yuppies, I woke up. I found I had a place in the cosmic plan, protecting the righteous from the evil, whom I had become familiar with in my previous identities."

"You're an interesting fellow," Edwards told him. "And I'm glad you want to be on my side."

"I'm not a guy you want on the opposite side," Gregory added. "I may still be assigned to hell when the spiritual force weighs my pluses and minuses on the scales of judgement at the end of my finite existence on this planet. But if I keep you from getting damaged by a bad seam in the flow, I believe it will balance as a huge positive on that cosmic scale."

Edwards looked at Lusman, then at Gregory. "I'll need to hear specifics," Edwards told him. "I'll want to know *how* you're protecting me."

"The fact is, you really shouldn't know all the infinite little details," Gregory explained. "It would take too much contact to keep you up-to-date on everything, and for me to fulfill my maximum protective potential, no one should know I'm involved in this. The best protection is invisible."

"Will I know you're there?"

"Inevitably, yes, to some extent. But I will use a lot of chameleon operatives to keep an eye on your crowds. We'll have a crowd sized up; the threats pinpointed."

"How about the Secret Service?"

"We'll work with them. But I never let them into an operation completely. Don't worry, I've worked with them before."

Edwards nodded. "Okay. I'll talk to Drew and we'll let you know."

"I recommend you have Mr. Saroyan or this Mr. Lusman here let me know."

"Okay."

Gregory extended his hand. Edwards and Gregory shook. Gregory headed back up into the rock formation. Edwards and Lusman reversed their direction on the trail.

Saroyan and Gregory had already developed an instant rapport. Saroyan had checked Gregory's references and received dazzling praises. And Gregory had also dazzled Saroyan with his inside knowledge of seamy secrets associated with various national and international political figures. So Saroyan's glowing opinion of Carl Gregory convinced Edwards to hire him. And Edwards liked the idea of a security chief who seemed like a refugee from the 1960's. He felt Carl Gregory fit with the tone of his campaign, and with his own roots and sensibilities.

✸   ✸   ✸

Mid July, Election Year: The Following Wednesday
Berkeley, California

"I WOULD LIKE TO TAKE THIS OPPORTUNITY TO DISCUSS FOREIGN POLICY in a Michael Edwards Administration," Edwards stated to his attentive audience at a practice football field on the campus of the University of California at Berkeley.

Edwards presented a comprehensive address, first focusing on foreign policy, then defense policy as an offshoot of foreign policy, pointing out that defense was needed when diplomacy failed to protect the nation's vital interests. He called for the United States to provide leadership and actively participate in creating an international structure of economically interdependent sovereign nations, all materially prosperous through trade with each other, and all resolving differences without violence. He pointed out that economic interdependence was the best method for guaranteeing world peace. As nations relied on each other for material prosperity, they had vested interests in not destroying each other. The economies of these nations would be based on the principles of a Regenerating Biosphere. These nations would all respect the human rights of their citizens, and be formed through the principles of political and ethnic self-determination.

He also discussed what he called the explosive foreign policy development of the millennium. Two of the world's contradictory trends were colliding—globalism and regional diversification. This collision was especially expressed by minority ethnic enclaves within jurisdictions governed by ethnically distinct majority administrations. He cited specific examples all over the world; the Armenian concentration in the enclave of Nagorno-Karabakh within Azerbaijan, the formerly independent nation of Tibet in China, Northern Ireland, on the island nation of Ireland, and on the North American continent, the predominantly French-speaking province of Quebec in Canada, and the Commonwealth of Puerto Rico in the United States.

Even Edwards' most ardent supporters would have to admit that the address started out flat. It might have been a competent intellectual exercise, but as a political speech, it was coming across as vague and uninspiring.

Carl Gregory's operatives were anything but bored. They had the task of protecting Edwards as he spoke to this eclectic, cosmopolitan crowd.

"Some Arab guy is really making a move toward the front," one of the security operatives in the field observed quietly but urgently into a small transmitter on his sleeve.

"I see him," Carl Gregory's voice replied through the operative's earpiece. "He's about six rows from the front."

"The United States has often been called a 'melting pot,'" Edwards told the audience. "But that is not what is happening here. We are really a smorgasbord; a rich variety of diversity, not a melting pot of dull, homogeneous mush. Our nation is full of ethnic enclaves. So why aren't these groups demanding independence? Because there is, for the most part, a belief that the American system, as it is conceived, provides social justice not based on direct discrimination due to ethnicity. Our minority groups can go to the courts, demand justice if they feel victimized by discrimination, and feel that those demands will be heard.

"So in mediating these conflicts," Edwards stated, building his point, "the goal of the United States, and other foreign diplomats involved, should be to assist the opposing factions in negotiating a relationship that gives both sides confidence that social justice can and will be achieved."

The security operative had moved closer to the man who had attracted his concern.

"He's trying to kill all the plants," chanted the dark-complected man dressed in a Middle Eastern tunic and headdress. "He's trying to kill all the plants."

"Weird," the first operative said into his sleeve. "The guy is acting very weird."

"Can you get to him?" Gregory's voice asked.

"Not without knocking over a whole bunch of people, causing a panic and—"

"Is he armed?"

"Doesn't look like it—but I can't really tell. You'd better be ready up at the podium."

"Right. Out."

The operative kept closing in carefully, but could not get close enough to the chanting man to do more than watch.

"Our defense policy begins by identifying America's most likely enemies in the near future. These will be nations and groups who do not share the foreign policy objectives of the civilized world community. These enemies will often be led by individuals with volatile personalities and fanatic goals based on religion or nationalism, with narrow objectives and questionable morality. America's armed forces need to be ready to counter that type of threat, but in concert with other nations in the world community, with unilateral force used only as a last resort.

"In fact, I will promise *never* to commit American troops, American *lives,* to any action where we do not have a clear, concrete idea of what our mission is, how long it should take, and what *precisely* we need to accomplish before we leave. If we make such a commitment—"

The chanting man arrived at the second row from the front. He reached under his tunic.

"He's going for a gun!" the horrified operative spouted into his sleeve. He lunged through three rows of astonished listeners as he dove at the man's legs.

But the man got his shots off, firing wildly, at least five times. Though Edwards quickly ducked, one bullet, the first one out of the gun, grazed his scalp. The wound was not serious, but blood streamed down the side of his head. Edwards held his head and stayed down behind the podium. Saroyan handed him a white cloth. "Son-of-a-bitch got me," Edwards told him angrily.

At this moment, an opportunistic photographer took a picture of Michael Edwards with an angry, determined look on his face.

☼   ☼   ☼

"THE ASSASSINATION ATTEMPT TODAY ON MICHAEL EDWARDS WAS thwarted by his own security people as well as Secret Service agents," Andrew Talbot reported on the WWBS Evening News as the photograph of Michael Edwards, with blood dripping down the side of his head, filled the screen. Edwards looked stronger than bullets, too tough to let an assassin intimidate him. If his foreign policy speech had been overly esoteric and flat, no one noticed.

Michael Edwards, Drew Saroyan, and Carl Gregory sat in a large motor home parked at a private campground in the forested hills south of San Francisco, just west of Redwood City. They had arranged to be the only people camped in the area that evening. Edwards had a bandage around his head.

"The would-be assassin has been identified as Mohammed Zadgar, apparently a Palestinian dissident who illegally entered this country from Mexico," Talbot continued on the broadcast. "No other information is available on him. Sources in the FBI do not believe he is affiliated with any known terrorist organization. Eye witnesses described him as deranged and irrational, possibly mentally ill or on drugs. Zadgar was killed instantly at the scene."

"So that's it," Edwards observed to them. "Some nut-case from the Middle East . . ."

"I don't want to alarm you, Mr. Edwards," Gregory told him calmly but disquietingly, "but there was a fifth man, not part of my security team, who fired a gun at that guy. He melted right into the crowd."

"What?" Edwards asked, puzzled.

"He's the one who killed the guy."

"Okay, so what does it mean?" Edwards demanded impatiently.

"I'm not sure. But this Middle East maniac scenario is too easy. The guy tested positive for coke, heroin and alcohol—not your normal profile of an Islamic fanatic. And the I-D on him? Definitely a forgery. There's more to this."

"What does the FBI say about this fifth guy? Or the Secret Service?"

"They think it's weird," Gregory explained, "but they have a theory that the guy was someone who helped out, then fled. Maybe his gun wasn't legal."

"So they're not on this thing."

"Not to any great extent. As far as the FBI is concerned, the perpetrator is identified, sort of, and killed. They don't have any leads beyond that. But we better stay ready. This storm could be back."

Edwards nodded.

"Not quite so close next time," Saroyan requested.

"You have my word," Gregory agreed resolutely.

A car pulled up to the campgrounds. Gregory pulled his gun.

But he quickly reholstered it when he recognized Oscar Lusman's rental car. There was someone else with him.

Teresa Edwards bolted from the car after it stopped and raced over to Michael.

He stood up. "Teresa?"

She was almost hysterical. "Michael! I can't believe they tried to—" She threw her arms around him as she broke into sobs. "Are you okay?" she finally asked as she pulled her head back, still within their embrace, just enough to see his head.

"A scratch," he said nonchalantly. "But when I saw the barrel of that gun, it scared the crap out of me . . ." Michael squeezed her affectionately, then looked at her mischievously. "We sure are getting under someone's skin. So I'd say we're on the right track . . ."

"Michael! I don't want you under anyone's skin!" she scolded sharply. She hesitated, but finished her thought. "I want you to withdraw from this *right now*," she insisted.

Michael released their hug. "What?" he asked incredulously.

"This is not worth it."

"Teresa, some maniac got close; we've got good people making sure it doesn't happen again. We can't—"

"You just said you were getting under someone's skin," she argued back. "Now you say this is just some maniac."

Michael shrugged. "The truth is, I don't know which this guy was. The guy seems to be from the Middle East. But Ted Jessup told me one of the South American drug cartels is after me."

"Michael! You didn't tell me?"

"I didn't want to worry you. I hired a good security—"

"That's it," Teresa demanded. "Withdraw now, Michael. Right now. It's not worth your life."

Michael Edwards pulled her back to him. As he spoke, he held her. "You either believe or you don't," Michael repeated to her. "That's what you said to me when we decided to do this. And we established that I do believe in what I am offering to the people of this country." He grinned and continued to hold her as he moved his head back to face her. "I believe even more now than before. We knew we'd have to hit this water without being sure of the temperature or the flow of the currents. You can't ask me to run away from the challenge at the first sign of trouble."

"Don't turn this into some kind of macho thing," Teresa argued.

"'Macho thing?'" Michael was irritated. "I'm no coward. But I wouldn't stay in this race just to prove my courage, or that I'm a tough guy. I'm—" Michael decided to make his point with a question. "Do we still believe, Teresa?"

She exhaled an uncomfortable breath. "That's not the—"

"Do we still believe?" Michael asked more forcefully.

Teresa hesitated, then answered. "Of course."

Michael again brought them into a closer embrace, with their heads on each others' shoulders. So Michael did not see the quiet, fearful tears sneaking out of Teresa's eyes as he continued speaking. "You either believe or you don't. There isn't any other consideration. Practicality is irrelevant. You lay yourself on the line because, if you don't, you will always regret it."

Teresa did not reply.

"Those were your very wise words to me."

Teresa sniffled.

Michael again brought them face to face. "I'm sorry. I'm sorry this is—"

"Michael, I'm sorry too," she interrupted, trying to pull herself together. "I should have known better. I won't ever ask you to withdraw again." She paused. "I want to talk to those security people," she told him decisively.

Michael smiled as he released their hug. "Carl?" he summoned. Michael knew Teresa would probably ask questions and make demands for promises that Carl Gregory had already heard from others. But Teresa was entitled to ask these redundant questions. And he knew this might be the best way Teresa had to make peace with Michael's continuation in the race.

Ironically, the fortunes of his campaign got an enormous boost when the next day, the heroic image of Michael Edwards, fearless and angry, holding a bloody white cloth to his head, appeared in sharp clear colors across the country.

✿   ✿   ✿

Mid July: The Next Day, Friday
Los Angeles, California

"STATE VERSUS NAYLOR," JUDGE HAROLD WINSTON ANNOUNCED quietly. "This is the prelim. Is the state ready?"

"Yes, your honor," prosecutor Meg Villalobos replied. She was a dignified, but plain-looking woman of about thirty.

"Defense?" Judge Winston asked.

Joel Sterling spoke—he was already standing up. "Defense will be asking for a continuance at this time, while we continue our own invest—"

"Your honor," Meg Villalobos interjected impatiently. "This will be the third continuance if it is granted. We didn't oppose the other two, but—"

Naylor stood up. "I also object, your honor."

Sterling looked at Naylor in astonished horror. "Sit *down*," he whispered sharply aside to Naylor.

"Defendant, please sit down and be quiet," the judge ordered. "Defense counsel, what are you investigating? This case seems fairly simple."

Naylor had not resumed his seat. "He's stalling, your honor. I want my lawyer to get to work."

"Defendant, if you don't sit down and remain quiet, you will find yourself in contempt," the judge warned more sternly.

Naylor drew a deep, defiant breath, but sat down.

"How is further investigation going to bear on this preliminary hearing?" Judge Winston asked Sterling.

"We need some more time to check the background of the case. The—"

"You've had over two months, counsel."

"And we've waived our right to a speedy trial. So—"

Naylor jumped up again. "Your honor, I'm unwaiving my right to a—"

"Order," Judge Winston barked. "This preliminary hearing begins in thirty minutes. Counsel," he said sternly to Sterling, "get your client under control or *I will*." The judge banged his gavel and quickly walked away from the bench.

As Naylor and Sterling began to leave the courtroom, Naylor turned to Sterling. "You get me out of this *now*, Mr. Fancy-shit attorney. *Today.* If I get bound over, I'm dealing—anyway I can. You tell Oscar. He'll know what I mean." Naylor started to walk away.

"Hey," Sterling called out. "Keep your butt in your seat and button your lip when we get back," he ordered Naylor. "You're making my job impossible."

"Then be a fucking lawyer and stop stalling." Naylor now walked away abruptly.

☼   ☼   ☼

"RELAX. I'M ON A PAY PHONE FROM A NEARBY BAR," STERLING assured. "I'm telling you, you better get damage control ready. Because it's going down this afternoon, and he's gonna get bound over."

"Think of something."

"I'll do the best job of defense lawyering I can. *Maybe* I can stall it out to give you the weekend to get ready. But . . ." He did not finish the thought because he had already expressed it often enough.

After a few moments of agonizing silence, while Lusman tried to figure out some way to salvage the situation, he finally said "okay" to Sterling. "Call me when it's . . . over . . ."

Oscar's mood sank. He swallowed a huge lump, but not in time to stop a small tear from sneaking out of each eye. The end of this afternoon could very well be the end of the historic Michael Edwards campaign effort, and it would be because Lusman could not contain the Naylor problem. How could he break this news to Drew Saroyan and Michael Edwards, men he had grown to admire deeply? He plunged into an immobilizing depression, dreading the next phone call he would get from California. As darkness settled over the east coast, and the two other members of the Edwards campaign staff in this office went home, Lusman didn't even move to turn on any lights other than the small one on his desk.

The phone rang at about seven-thirty, waking Lusman out of a depression doze. It was not Sterling. News had come from the 50th state—Edwards was now on the ballot in all of them. Lusman smiled briefly at this irony. The day Edwards qualified to be a ballot choice for every voting American might also be the day that his campaign crashed and burned.

Lusman didn't call anyone else. He just stayed at his desk.

Chapter 13

The Same Day
Los Angeles, California

"I AM *CERTAIN*," OFFICER MORT LAVALLE RESPONDED, WITH diminishing patience, to Sterling's question, which was little more than a rephrasing of the same question he had now asked four or five different ways. The court session was sparsely attended—Friday afternoons were not popular times for courtroom observers, and Slick Naylor had few friends, none who would be interested in spending a Friday afternoon to lend moral support to him. "The defendant did not just pass by the mailbox. He opened it up and dropped something in."

"Something?"

"As I have said repeatedly, I wasn't close enough to see exactly what."

"So you can't say for certain that he dropped a *bag* in the mailbox, just that he dropped *something* in . . ."

"Your honor," Meg Villalobos objected. "I have been patient. But this question has been asked and answered over and over. We have established through other witnesses that—"

"I object to this interruption, calculated to obstruct the flow of my cross-examination," Sterling countered.

"Both of you come to order," the judge snapped. "I don't care to hear how patient you've been," he admonished Villalobos. "Just make your objection." He turned to Sterling. "And her objection is *sustained*. Enough already. I know what this witness saw and what he didn't see. Is there anything else?"

"No." Sterling moved somberly to his chair next to Naylor at the defense table. Meg Villalobos had meticulously detailed the case against Naylor, and Sterling, despite his best efforts, hadn't even put a marginal dent in it.

"That's our case," Villalobos concluded confidently.

Sterling perked up.

"The state moves that Bradford Rodney Naylor be bound over for trial on the charges as described in the complaint."

Judge Winston nodded. "The court finds that ample evidence has been presented to justify such an order," he stated perfunctorily. "Counsel?" he addressed to Sterling, soliciting Sterling's position on the motion.

"Your honor, we haven't heard from one witness on the state's list."

"Which witness?"

"Cameron Chandler."

Villalobos stood up, showing a slight erosion in her confidence for the first time since the hearing had begun almost an hour and a half earlier. "Uh, Mr. Chandler will be unable to testify."

"Defense wishes to know why," Sterling told the judge respectfully.

"Counsel?" the judge addressed Villalobos.

"He's . . . deceased."

Now Sterling's mind was racing, and for the first time since the judge ordered the hearing to go forward, Sterling saw a chance of success. "So he will not be able to testify at trial," Sterling thought aloud, restating the obvious. "Your honor, we will present a defense, after which I believe these charges will be dismissed. We request a recess—"

"Your honor, we object to any further delaying tactics—" But Villalobos' objection was also interrupted.

"I want a new attorney!" Naylor demanded. "And I have a statement to make about—"

"Shut up!" Sterling whispered caustically, trying unsuccessfully to keep his scolding between them. "You wanna get out of this?" he managed to ask more quietly.

"The contempt citations are about to *fly*," the judge told them through gritted teeth.

"Please let me clarify myself for the court," Sterling quickly told the judge with as much courtesy and deference as he could summon. "I just need fifteen minutes to confer with my client. And I request that all police witnesses remain in the court for the proceedings when they reconvene."

The judge looked up at the clock; it read just past 4:00 p.m. "How long will your defense take?"

"I'll wrap it up before five. I'll submit, then the court can rule."

"Recess granted," the judge told them. He banged his gavel and quickly left the bench.

☼   ☼   ☼

"THESE DELAYS YOU KEEP COMPLAINING ABOUT MIGHT HAVE SAVED YOUR slimy ass," Sterling told Naylor as they entered a conference room and Sterling closed the door behind them.

"What're you talking about?" Naylor challenged.

"I mean they have a serious problem without Chandler. And I get the feeling he died *recently*."

"Yeah," Naylor confirmed with a casual grin. "The asshole got in trouble again and turned snitch on the wrong people, people with a lot of connections inside, who can pay to make things happen . . ." Naylor flashed a sinister smile. "Like accidents. Like the one he had with a shank, cut himself while shaving his ass, cut from his left nipple to his ding-dong."

"Well, his 'accident' was your lucky day."

"Yeah? Explain it to me."

"If you were scamming the guy, and didn't really have any coke, but maybe flour or sugar in that bag, they'd have nothing on you."

Naylor considered the statement. "Except scamming—that's a crime too."

"They don't want you for scamming. And you didn't pull it off. So the best they can do is get you for a conspiracy to defraud. That's a long way from possession of cocaine with intent to sell."

Naylor thought again. "You want me to say I had sugar, or flour, or something like that in the baggy I was selling to Cameron?"

"Only if it's true. I'm not in here suborning perjury."

Naylor smiled cynically. "Of course not." He brought his eyes into a sly squint. "It just so happens I *was* scamming the guy; it was Bisquick, it was Aunt Jemima's Pancake mix—"

"Make up your mind." Sterling rephrased his advice. "Firm up your recollection."

"Pancake mix. But this hokey-shit better work, lawyer, or I'll make Oscar sorry he ever hired you to represent me."

"You do a good job of laying out the bait on the witness stand, and you'll walk out in just about an hour, free of this whole mess."

After a little further discussion, Naylor and Sterling returned to the courtroom, five minutes before they were due back. Sterling was anxious to get to work now.

"Your honor," Sterling addressed the judge confidently, "I would like to start out by making a motion to exclude the tape made by the Los Angeles Police Department. As the court is aware, tape recordings cannot be made without the consent of at least one of the parties. My client did not give consent. And we have heard no testimony that the other party gave consent—"

Villalobos stood up. "We have a signed and notarized consent form from Cameron Chandler."

"I can't cross-examine a consent form," Sterling argued.

"What do you need to cross-examine?" the judge asked impatiently.

"The circumstances under which consent was given, whether it was coerced, and therefore whether the party giving the consent was part of a scheme to entrap my client."

"Entrapment?" Villalobos repeated in disbelief.

"The court denies your motion, counsel," the judge told him. "The court will take judicial notice that they had him over a barrel, that he consented to be taped because he was looking at big jail time unless he cooperated. Law enforcement does this kind of thing every day. That doesn't make it entrapment."

"Then I request that the court also take judicial notice of the fact that any statements made by Mr. Chandler on the tape are hearsay, and not statements of fact that are evidence in this case."

"Of course."

Next, Sterling called all the police witnesses back to the stand and established that none of them had examined the contraband before the sale began. He then established, through investigating detective Weller, that the lab analysis of the torn, empty plastic baggy found in the mailbox did not have enough residue in it for proper analysis. So there was no chemical analysis verifying that cocaine had been in the plastic bag.

Now Sterling called Naylor to the stand. He kept his questioning absolutely sparse: "Mr. Naylor, what was in the baggy you sold to Cameron Chandler on the evening of May 12th of this year?"

"Aunt Jemima's Pancake mix," Naylor replied matter-of-factly.

"Were you in possession of any cocaine on the evening of May 12th of this year?"

"No sir."

"Did you offer cocaine for sale to Cameron Chandler on the evening of May 12th of the year?"

"Not specifically."

"Thank you." Sterling turned to the judge. "We move to dismiss the charges against the defendant. My client states he was not in possession of cocaine. There is no credible testimony to refute him. No prudent jury could fail to find a reasonable doubt."

"Just a minute," Villalobos chided politely as she stood. "I'd like to cross-examine before you rule."

The judge nodded.

Sterling took his seat. He had deliberately made his motion prematurely to irritate Villalobos. If he could get her personally upset with him, he could get her to see the hearing as a test of egos. This might cause Villalobos to act on emotional impulse instead of logic and common sense.

"Mr. Naylor," Villalobos addressed in a disrespectful tone, "are you telling us that Cameron Chandler was offering to pay you 15 hundred dollars for a small baggy of pancake mix?"

"No. That's what I was selling him. He may have thought I was selling him something different."

"Did he check over the contraband?"

"Objection," Sterling interjected with quiet confidence. "Assumes a fact not in evidence."

"Sustained," the judge ruled without hesitation.

"Did he check the contents of the baggy?"

"No."

"He was willing to hand over 15 hundred dollars without checking to see if you were selling him what he thought you were selling him?"

"You guys set up the deal," Naylor replied smugly. "He knew he was buying with you guys watching. I don't think he gave a sh—" Naylor stopped himself. "I don't think he cared whether I was on the level or not."

"What do you mean by 'on the level?'"

Sterling rubbed his eyes.

Naylor watched Sterling, then replied. "I'm taking the Fifth."

"What?" Villalobos reacted in disbelief.

Sterling jumped up and went toward the bench. "Your honor," he asserted abrasively, "it appears to me that counsel is trying to get my client to testify to theft by fraud, in violation of his Fifth Amendment rights against self-incrimination."

"I don't care about a conspiracy to commit theft by fraud," Villalobos countered.

"Well I *do*," Sterling insisted. "It's my duty to protect my client from these sorts of high-handed tactics by the—"

"Your honor," she insisted angrily, "I cannot cross-examine him effectively if I can't test his credibility on what was in that baggy." Sterling's abrasive, combative approach was definitely provoking Villalobos.

"And I must instruct my client to invoke his Fifth Amendment rights for any questions that bear on a possible intent to defraud."

"Fine," Villalobos replied slyly. "I'll give Mr. Naylor immunity for fraud, theft, or any similar crimes that evening."

"Are you sure you want to do that, counsel?" the judge asked.

Sterling fought the smile that was trying to break onto his face. The corners of his mouth edged up slightly, but he brought them back down before anyone noticed.

"Absolutely," Villalobos answered.

"This is on the record?" Sterling asked meekly, playing the part of an outmaneuvered attorney, for Villalobos' benefit.

"It is."

Sterling acted outwardly apprehensive. "Okay," he said to Naylor. "You have to answer Ms. Villalobos' questions." Sterling trudged slowly back to the defense table, continuing to mask his satisfaction that events were proceeding exactly as he wanted them to.

Villalobos turned smugly to Naylor. "I asked you what you meant when you said you didn't think Cameron Chandler cared if you were 'on the level . . .'"

"I mean that I scammed him. I sold him pancake mix that he thought was cocaine."

The bluntness of Naylor's answer took Villalobos by surprise. She paused a moment, then followed up. "You were pretty angry on tape when you found out he was wired . . ."

"I sure was."

"If you were selling him pancake mix, why were you so angry?"

Naylor's face tightened into a sinister squint. "Because no one can tolerate a snitch."

"What about a scam artist?"

"Objection," Sterling interrupted. "Irrelevant."

"Sustained," Judge Winston agreed.

"Why did you run from the police if all you had was pancake mix?"

"I was scamming—that *is* against the law, isn't it?"

"Why did you fling the contraband, uh, the substance into the air?"

"To destroy the evidence," Naylor insisted.

"That you were selling pancake mix?"

"That I was *scamming.*"

Villalobos paused frustratedly, then tried another question. "What were you going to do when Chandler discovered you'd defrauded him?"

"What was *he* gonna do?" Naylor countered.

"Unresponsive," Villalobos said to the judge.

"Objection. Speculation," Sterling added.

"Not really," the judge replied. "It's borderline, but this is cross-examination." He turned to Naylor. "Don't answer questions with questions. What were you going to do when Cameron Chandler determined he had paid 15 hundred dollars for pancake mix?"

"Yes, your honor, sir, I understood the question. But I think it's backwards. It would be up to Chandler to react. I wouldn't do anything until I found out what *he* was going to do. I'd bet he would do *nothing.* The guy was such a weeny."

The judge drew an unsettled breath. He knew the question had opened the door to just this type of a response.

"You're telling this court that Cameron Chandler would just write off 15 hundred dollars?" Villalobos demanded incredulously.

"The guy was an addict," Naylor insisted. "He spent every waking minute trying to figure out where he could get his next load of stuff. Getting back to me would not be at the top of his list—after a few days, he might not even remember I scammed him."

"But wouldn't this ruin his relationship with you as a regular customer?"

Sterling started to object, since the question assumed a fact not in evidence. But he could see from Naylor's expression that Naylor was ready to bury the question. He withheld his objection, and was glad he did.

"*Customer,*" Naylor replied with belittling amazement. "See, that's where you guys have screwed up. You think I'm some big dealer. I guess Chandler did too. Maybe he sold you guys on it. But I don't do drugs. So I don't care about him as a customer. I saw a chance to pick up a few bucks. Doesn't that kind of prove I was scamming him?"

Meg Villalobos could barely manage to say "nothing further," before she worked her way back to her seat.

"Anything further before I rule?" Judge Winston asked stolidly.

"No," Villalobos answered quickly.

"No, your honor," Sterling said confidently as he shook his head.

"Well, I have no choice but to grant defense's motion," the judge told them fatalistically. "There is insufficient evidence here. Charges are dismissed. The defendant is free."

Naylor beamed an arrogant smile.

Judge Winston caught sight of it. "You got *lucky*," he told Naylor bitterly, "and you've got a good lawyer here to help you make the best of your luck. But I suspect you're on borrowed time. I'll see you back here, or in front of another judge, or in the morgue. The system is designed to protect the innocent. We say we let ten guilty go free rather than have one innocent wrongfully deprived of his or her freedom. We are all aware today, that you are one of the ten. Court is adjourned for the weekend." Judge Winston raised up and pounded his gavel, almost simultaneously with his quick departure from the bench.

"Hey man, you pulled it off." Naylor grabbed Sterling's hand and shook it.

"Yeah," Sterling told him as he made a point of wiping his hand on his pants after Naylor had shaken it. "I believe this ends our association, and your association with our mutual friend in New York."

"You bet it does," Naylor agreed readily. "I mean, you guys held up your end real nice. I'll hold up mine. I'm *gone*." Naylor left the courtroom.

Sterling wondered if there was any way to hold Naylor to this bargain. But that was not his concern.

☼   ☼   ☼

THE PHONE RANG IN LUSMAN'S DARKENED OFFICE.

"Lusman," he greeted wearily. But as he heard the news, he smiled. The relief he felt was enormous, like an infusion of pure productive energy. After hanging up, he turned on some lights to supplement his desk lamp. It would take him a few moments of deep breaths to return to reality. He had to reorient himself away from expecting impending disaster. As he regained his perspective, he felt like Ebenezer Scrooge on Christmas morning. He had been spared from a horrendous alternative future. He even entertained the thought that Naylor's arrest was a blessing, because it removed Naylor as a problem.

☼   ☼   ☼

Mid July: The Following Saturday
San Marino, California

"WE ALMOST GOT HIM," ENRIQUEZ SAID AS HE AND CONTRERAS SAT ON the balcony of the second story of Enriquez' Southern California mansion in the wealthy community of San Marino. His mansion was one of a whole block of huge homes on lots, with spacious, green front-yards.

"I had one of my best men there to make sure that crazy Zoilo didn't survive the assassination attempt," Contreras told him.

"I know. Good job. There is no way they can connect Zoilo to us. They think he is some crazy Arab terrorist." Considering that the assassination attempt had been a failure, the tone of the discussion was strangely upbeat. But Enriquez never liked to acknowledge failure. So he always sought some positives, even in a failed situation, to save face and claim success. And on this occasion, he was particularly anxious to save face with Contreras, his chief strong arm, who had not been involved in formulating the plan.

They were both silent a moment.

"Unfortunately, we still have the Michael Edwards problem," Enriquez finally said.

"Yes."

"And Zoilo's little adventure might have made a hero out of Edwards."

"I can go back to the Cubans."

"Yes. Go ahead." Enriquez thought a moment. "But get one of your best men, one not known to American authorities. I have been told . . . You and I might be followed."

"Ernesto, I believe that I should do this myself. The death will not be traceable to me."

"Unless you are followed and detained at the scene. I must insist. Get a good man. Train him well. I have another meeting set with my American friends. Maybe they have come up with a cleaner way to get rid of him. But we'll be ready if they don't."

"Can you trust those guys?"

"Probably not. But I think they can be useful."

"I will contact the Cubans and get things ready."

"Good."

✿   ✿   ✿

Mid July: The Following Sunday
New York, New York

"SO, YOU BUNCH OF GENIUSES, HERE'S OUR MOMENT IN THE SUN. HOW DO you suppose we should manage it?" Victor Parker was in a surly, irritable mood as he sat in a conference room, backstage at Madison Square Garden on the eve of the Democratic Convention, scheduled to begin the next day. The last two times the Democrats had unseated Republican incumbents, in 1976 and 1992, the Democrats had held their conventions in New York. (The 1980 convention, which renominated President Jimmy Carter, who was then clobbered by Ronald Reagan in the general election, was also held in New York.) Five men and two women sat around a circular table, with partially eaten dinners on paper plates in front of them. But only Nicholas Mueller and Will Runalli spoke. The others sensed Parker's mood, and preferred to stay out of the line of fire.

"The convention schedule is in our printed packets, and—" Mueller started to explain.

"I don't give a damn what time everything is going on," Parker told him. "I want to know what we're going to *do*. As we speak, our illustrious platform committee is starting to put together an agenda that will be impossible for me to campaign on. We still have no deal with Trewillinger. We've got commentators from every media center in the country saying that the Democratic Party is too factionalized to produce a real visionary, like *Edwards*." He sneered. "They say we just nominate bland, uncreative guys who can raise money. And *I'm* the *example*."

"We've got—" Mueller started again.

"I mean, look at these God Damn polls. Hampton 31, Parker 29, and Edwards *twenty-seven*. And this is plus or minus *three*. I might be running *third*. Edwards might be *leading*. Ever since those frigging gunshots—he's like a national hero! Hell, let somebody take a shot at me!"

The room was uncomfortably quiet.

"Come on," Parker scolded impatiently. "I'm not serious. But we need some ideas for this convention. We picked Jeffrey Jefferson to run on the ticket weeks ago. We don't even have the drama of a Vice Presidential choice to drive this thing. If we don't come up with something, the media will. And don't depend on their angle to be one we'll like."

Mueller waited long enough to make sure Parker was through talking. He held up a stack of papers. "We have a whole set of lines of attack on Edwards," he told Parker proudly. "The country is really tired of Ken

Hampton and the Republicans. But Edwards is becoming your main opponent by taking away the anti-Hampton vote. So we need to—"

Parker brusquely grabbed the papers out of Mueller's hand and began thumbing through them.

Mueller stopped speaking and allowed Parker to review the material.

"Brilliant," Parker stated with bitter sarcasm. He tossed the papers into the air, over his shoulder. They fluttered in all directions, cascading to the floor. "You'll have us up there in front of millions of Americans attacking a man who almost got killed just a few days ago, who people see as a courageous crusader."

No one argued with Parker.

"I should fire the whole lot of you. Don't you people understand? Americans are *tired* of attack politics."

The room remained silent.

"The best thing we can do for *Edwards* is to *attack* him. The best thing we can do for *us* is to *ignore* him," Parker told them emphatically.

The silence in the room continued. It was Runalli who finally spoke. "Or, we can joke about him," he stated quietly.

Mueller's eyes narrowed in disbelief.

Parker was also skeptical. "Joke about him?"

"Well, not about him. About his ideas," Runalli clarified.

Parker now wanted to hear more. "Okay . . ."

"I agree we shouldn't mention him very often. And I agree that a direct attack on a man who is very likeable to the American people right now would backfire. But we can't leave him alone completely. It doesn't do any good to trash Hampton, if all the anti-Hampton votes end up with Edwards."

"But joking?" Parker asked, still not clear on the idea.

"Humor can be a great tool. Everyone wants to be in on a good joke. No one wants to be the un-hip person who doesn't get it. And jokes are almost always at someone's expense, with assumptions about the target built in. Jokes about his ideas will allow us to build in the assumption that his ideas are laughable. We would praise his courage, while belittling his ideas." There was a skeptical pause. "I'm not a joke-writer," he continued. "But it would go something like: 'We admire Michael Edwards, and his well-meaning attempts to bring new ideas to us. But we don't want cabinet meetings where the first words are "pass the joint."'"

A nervous twitter went through the group.

Parker scowled.

"I told you I'm not a joke-writer," Runalli shrugged. "But . . . How many people will it take to change a light-bulb if Edwards is elected?"

The group waited for Runalli to finish the riddle.

"None," he said. "There was no sun or wind that day. Or, five. One to put in the new light bulb, one to check the windmill, one to check the solar cells on the roof, one to turn on the generator when there's no sun or wind, and one to get an extra job to pay the extra taxes for gas and coal."

There were a few smiles, and maybe a few snickers.

"Well, you're right—you're no joke-writer," Parker acknowledged as he thought a moment. "But I think you have an idea, a better idea than just completely ignoring him. The humor—you're right—it sends a subliminal message that these things aren't worth being taken seriously. They should be sporadic. It can't look like a monologue for the Tonight Show. And they can't be personal. They have to be against his ideas. We also need to praise Edwards for his courage."

The group nodded. Many of them took notes.

Parker cast a brief, approving glance toward Runalli.

✿   ✿   ✿

THE DEMOCRATIC CONVENTION WENT ABOUT AS EXPECTED. Trewillinger finally gave a lukewarm endorsement, though few believed he was sincere. The Democrats attacked Hampton and highlighted their own ideas, many typical of standard Democratic theories, to "move the country ahead to prosperity for all, not just the rich." And the few carefully crafted references to Edwards had their desired effect. Polls after the convention showed a fair, though not spectacular "bounce" for Parker, mainly at Hampton's expense, but also partly at Edwards'. The same poll referred to in the pre-convention meeting now had Parker with 36%, Hampton with 25%, Edwards with 24%, and 15% undecided.

✿   ✿   ✿

Late July, Election Year: Thursday
Williamsport, Pennsylvania

"WHILE THE DEMOCRATS SPENT LAST WEEK ATTACKING THE Republicans, and telling bad jokes about us, we were concluding an exhaustive talent hunt," Edwards told his audience at a lectern set up in a baseball field where the Little League World Series was held annually.

Though much of the town was still landscaped with oaks, elms, spruces and maples, the dense surrounding forests that had once made the town a major timber center were now largely depleted. "I searched for a compatible running mate, someone with skills and talents that complement mine, and someone with a Presidential bearing. I was not limited to one political party or even limited to the political arena. I had the luxury of choosing the best person for the job. I am extremely pleased to introduce my choice, one of your own Pennsylvanians, Everett Phillips."

Enthusiastic applause sounded for Phillips.

"He brings military and administrative experience to our ticket. And as you will soon see, he brings a formidable presence to the podium. So I am filled with pride and excitement as I formally declare the Edwards-Phillips candidacy, and I am thrilled to have the opportunity to present my Vice Presidential candidate for his first address. General Phillips."

More enthusiastic applause sounded as he stepped to the podium.

"Thank you." Applause continued. Phillips beamed a broad smile. "Thank you." Everett Phillips was a huge muscular man of six feet four inches. He was just over sixty years of age and still in excellent physical condition. He had a short haircut, but not a military flat-top haircut. His hair was black and grey in about equal proportions. He was a widower, so there was no wife to stand beside him as he was introduced. "Thank you very much," he acknowledged as the applause continued.

Finally the applause dissipated.

"Michael and I thank you for such a warm and encouraging welcome," Phillips stated authoritatively. He had a low booming voice, commanding in its effect. He would sometimes slow his speech to build drama into his words. "I am extremely honored to be chosen to stand with Michael Edwards, and join him in this endeavor.

"The Edwards campaign has been characterized by frankness. So let me start right off by assuring the current followers of the Edwards campaign that there is no reason to be leery of the title that precedes my name: 'General.' Yes, I come from a military background which means I am a *fighter*. I am committed to this crusade, because I believe Michael Edwards has offered us one of the most important opportunities we as a nation have had in the last fifty years—the opportunity to choose a leader with a constructive vision of the future, and a practical conception for realizing it. This is an opportunity we *must seize*, and I will be out in every corner of this nation imploring every citizen to do so! When this worthy effort concludes in November, and Michael Edwards has been chosen to lead us, I will know that I have earned my place at his side! And together, we will see the *vision* become *reality*! Thank you."

An enthusiastic ovation acknowledged General Phillips' address. He waved, smiled and nodded as the applause continued.

"Nothing like the home crowd," Edwards commented to Saroyan as they also smiled and applauded.

"I don't care where we are, that was a hell of a delivery," Saroyan replied.

A few more moments of applause sounded.

"Good choice," Saroyan conceded.

Edwards smiled triumphantly.

✿   ✿   ✿

Late July, Election Year: Sunday
Port Aranas, Texas

"I KNOW EVERETT PHILLIPS WELL," FADIMAN SAID DISGUSTEDLY TO Beauregard Hunter as they sat on the deck of Fadiman's fishing boat, docked at a small harbor at Port Aranas off the Texas gulf coast. Fadiman had a hired captain and a valet to serve refreshments. They remained below deck. Both Fadiman and Hunter were putting their fishing poles together, anticipating a large haul from the plentiful Gulf of Mexico waters, and waiting for Enriquez to arrive. "He's a fucking pain in the ass. He has no appreciation for a businessman's right to make a profit."

Hunter grinned mischievously. "You mean he doesn't let you pad your bills."

Fadiman looked at Hunter with a serious glare. "He'll reduce my profits."

"I understand," Hunter replied them. "This ticket's not good for *anyone's* profits."

Fadiman nodded. "And I have solid, reliable connections through both parties. I'd be out of the loop with Edwards, and Phillips."

Hunter nodded.

Fadiman's security man arrived, escorting Enriquez.

"So we're fishing today," Ernesto Enriquez said to Hunter and Fadiman as he joined them. Fadiman's security man stood at a far corner of the deck.

"You don't like fishing?" Hunter asked him, with a hint of irony.

"No, not really. It's boring. And I don't like all this traveling out into the boony-docks to meet with you guys."

"Sit down and relax," Hunter told him. "Fishing takes patience. That's why you don't cotton to it."

Enriquez sat down, scowling.

Hunter turned to Fadiman. "You left your electronic fish kidnapper at home," he commented to Fadiman as he grinned.

"I know you don't like it," Fadiman replied.

"Well I don't see much sport in some contraption that reels in the little suckers the minute they bite. You could teach a monkey to do that."

"No sport."

"That's right."

Fadiman smiled. "I've always felt that if technology gave you the edge, that was part of the sport."

Hunter started to reply.

"But I know how you feel," Fadiman quickly added, precluding Hunter's response. "We'll do it your way today. Besides, it would be awkward for me to be pulling out five fish to every one of yours."

"Nice courtesy to the host," Hunter agreed.

"So besides fishing, what will we talk about today?" Enriquez asked impatiently.

"Close calls," Hunter replied casually.

"Yeah," Enriquez added. "That Edwards guy almost bought the big White House in the sky."

"Any idea who did it?" Fadiman said, also casual and undemanding with his tone of voice.

"Some crazy Arab guy, wasn't it?" Enriquez asked.

Hunter and Fadiman were deliberately silent. They focused on preparing their fishing tackle.

"That's what they said on the news," Enriquez added, becoming unnerved with the silence.

Again Hunter and Fadiman did not reply.

"Do *you* guys know anything about the guy who tried to kill Edwards? Maybe we should send his family some roses . . . or some camel feed . . ."

"You want to send camel feed to some Mexican family?" Hunter finally asked.

"Mexican?" Enriquez pretended disbelief.

"That poor crazy Mexican guy dressed up in some Middle East costume didn't fool anyone for an instant," Fadiman stated firmly.

"I don't know," Enriquez mumbled, caught off guard by the subtle but more and more probing inquiry. "What . . . What do *you* make of it?"

Fadiman now focused a piercing glare into Enriquez' eyes.

Hunter stopped fiddling and focused his complete attention on Enriquez.

"I think some stupid out-of-his-league *punk* from South America tried what he thought was a clever plan, and it didn't work," Fadiman told him through a simmering squint.

"You mean me?" Enriquez asked with poorly feigned innocence.

"You're going to try to deny this?" Hunter asked in disbelief. "I am very disappointed in you, son. I thought we-all were gonna work together on this thing."

"We know you were behind it," Fadiman added authoritatively. "Lying to us is a poor way to maintain a friendship."

Enriquez paused in thought a moment. "Okay. I set it up. But I moved on it 'cause you guys were going too slow."

Hunter and Fadiman were again deliberately silent, trying to make Enriquez as uncomfortable as possible.

"I thought you guys'd be proud of me," Enriquez told them. "I'm your star pupil. You know, subtlety. My plan would have removed Edwards without any kind of trace to me, or any of us."

Fadiman stared frostily.

Hunter sighed.

"You learned half a lesson," Fadiman told him caustically. "And you couldn't have given him more help if you were working *for* him."

"I helped him?" Enriquez asked with insulted disbelief.

"Everyone in the fucking country is trying to figure out who conspired to have him killed," Fadiman explained angrily. "You've given the guy his own Oswald, and Ruby, and he's still walking around to soak up the benefit from it. You've made him look like some noble political warrior."

"You blew it boy," Hunter added.

"I almost *got* him!" Enriquez insisted angrily. "At least I tried. If it had worked, you would be *thanking* me."

Fadiman fumed. "If you'd have killed Edwards, you'd have made him a martyr—a man struck down by a deranged maniac while preaching his doctrines to the world. Then we'd be fighting the ideas of a martyr, of a fallen hero, probably picked up by somebody else."

"You have to eliminate the man *and* his ideas," Hunter told Enriquez. "Sometimes that means the body is still walking around, but the threat is gone."

Enriquez sighed frustratedly. "How can you do that? My way is the best way."

"Minor leaguer, small timer," Fadiman observed angrily.

"Hey!" Enriquez countered indignantly.

"You have a thug's attitude toward this, son," Hunter added. "You need to *watch* and *learn*."

"Watch and learn what?" Enriquez demanded. "You guys aren't *doing* anything. When are you going to make some kind of a move?"

"I have," Fadiman told him coolly.

"Son, you gotta listen more carefully," Hunter cautioned. "Work *with* Mr. Fadiman, not around him. You're charging into the middle of things you don't understand."

"Okay. But what *is* our move?"

"We need to discredit the man, to destroy him, to make him look like a flake and a fool," Fadiman explained, less angry but still less patient than Hunter. "If we do that to him, the public will see his ideas as the ideas of a flake and a fool."

Enriquez frowned as he seemed to consider the idea.

"Put out the word on the street," Fadiman told him. "I want any dirt we can find. Even if it's unfair, unsubstantiated or unsavory—we want to know about it. And if it pans out, we'll pay for it."

"That's *it?*" Enriquez asked, disappointed and disbelieving.

"No," Fadiman snapped back. "It's an insurance policy. We have something else in the works."

"What?" Enriquez asked.

"I don't even ask that," Hunter informed Enriquez. "He'll tell us when and if we need to know."

"I need to know *now*," Enriquez insisted.

"No you don't," Fadiman told him.

A tense momentary silence hung over them.

"I've come to you as a friend," Enriquez finally said. "You should tell me what's going on."

"There's a scandal in everyone's background," Fadiman told Enriquez. "Something that will make him look bad. We need to spring it at a time when he can't repair the damage. So you *can* help, by getting the word out on the street for any dirt on Edwards," Fadiman added.

"Okay." Enriquez frowned. "I can be of much more help to you than trying to dig up smutty gossip. But if this is what you need from me, I will help you big operators, you smart-guys who never make mistakes."

Fadiman didn't like the snide tone sneaking into Enriquez' voice, but let it go. "Neither Beau or I have access to the streets. That's where the scandal on Edwards, if there is one, will be likely to come from."

Enriquez stood up. "Well, I hope the fish bite well for you, my friends. I will look forward to our next meeting."

Fadiman and Hunter stood and they politely shook hands with Enriquez. Enriquez was then escorted off the boat.

✿   ✿   ✿

"SO YOU GOT THE DOPE ON THIS FELLOW ENRIQUEZ?" HUNTER ASKED AS Fadiman's security man returned to the boat.

"I have a final report for you. He's a lot more worried about Edwards' energy policy than about his drug policy," Fadiman told Hunter. "My security man will fill you in." Fadiman walked off the deck to the control area where he would make some final checks before starting the boat's engines and pulling away.

"Ernesto Enriquez," the security man stated to Hunter, as if he owned Enriquez by knowing everything about him. "An interesting and very ambitious character—born in San Cristobal, Venezuela, where he grew up, as Pedro Perez, son of a poor laborer."

"Do I need to know all the biographical low-down on this crook?" Hunter asked politely but impatiently.

"You only need to know that Pedro used to travel with his father on his jobs, especially as a young man. His father worked in the oil fields just across the border in Colombia, near the city of Cucuta. Pedro apparently became acquainted with Colombian drug-runners, and eventually worked with them. His frequent visits back and forth were well covered by his father's employment, so he was safe and reliable. He made lots of money, and eventually expanded his operations, first as a courier, then as a producer. Word is he's still growing cocaine in isolated areas of Venezuela, while expanding into other drugs, and other areas in Brazil, and even in Mexico and southern California. When he decided to become more than just a courier, he came into conflict with a lot of his former Colombian employers. There have been some bloody wars, followed right now by an uneasy truce. In these wars, he outgunned his enemies by purchasing state-of-the-art weapons from your friend here."

"So he's filthy rich," Hunter commented. "He's made his pile. Why is he so desperate to go after Edwards? That could be real risky for him."

"Because it isn't just money, and a hunk of drug turf, that he wants. While he was in Colombia, watching his father pump out that liquid gold, he started to hatch a scheme to be the owner of that oil, instead of one of the low-paid extractors. Word now is that his ego is on overdrive. The guy knows how smart he is, and is really enjoying the fruits of his successes. Now he apparently wants to get control of Venezuela's vast oil reserves and use the wealth and power deriving from them to forge a powerful Venezuela that would eventually be the first among equals in a United States of South America. He has even spoken about getting control of a nuclear arsenal and challenging the United States of *North* America's position as preeminent nation in the world. He has made discreet contacts through intermediaries to former Soviet nuclear weapons scientists and technicians—he may have the personnel in place for a nuclear program."

"But how's he gonna get control of that oil in the first place?" Hunter asked doubtfully. "Most of that stuff is buried around Lake Maracaibo, and they aren't selling off that real estate, even to drug dealers with cash to piss and burn."

"He knows that. He knows the nuts and bolts of the oil business really well. What he's done is use the drug money to take over the subsidiary industries—transit, pipelines, equipment production. And through an ingeniously complex set of convoluted financial arrangements, laundered two and three times, he has actually taken over a large portion of those industries. But he doesn't have enough yet. And he needs the easy money of the drug trade to keep buying in. Also, if oil becomes a less important commodity, his plans will be wrecked. So he has really compelling reasons for disliking one Michael Edwards."

"This all sounds a little far-fetched," Hunter commented, still doubtful. "Is the Venezuelan government just sitting around waiting for all this to happen? I would think they might have some idea of what's going on . . ."

"Enriquez, or Perez, has either bought, terrified or outright silenced the few who have tripped over his scheme, which is not all that easy to figure out. Our source on this is a person who has taken the hush money, and only very reluctantly, and very secretly, given us this information." The security man smiled mischievously. "We have him over a nasty barrel. But we also were able to confirm what he told us. The information is reliable."

"So he thinks he's gonna buy Venezuela and its oil, then run the world from Caracas," Hunter summarized.

"We don't even run the *whole* world," Fadiman added with a gleam in his eye as he rejoined them. "Just our little piece of it."

"We ready to catch some fish?" Hunter asked.

"Yeah," Fadiman replied.

"The boy is crazy," Hunter added casually.

"With *ambition*," Fadiman qualified. "He thinks he's Genghis Khan, or Napoleon. Well, we'll keep tabs on him. Because in the final analysis, he's still just a dumb punk."

Chapter 14

Early August, Election Year: Wednesday
Seattle, Washington

"THIS GUY DID A WHOLE INFOMERCIAL SUPPORTING ME?" EDWARDS asked in disbelief. Lusman, Saroyan and Edwards watched a videotape in Edwards' modest hotel room in Seattle as they prepared to begin a ten day, north-to-south campaign swing along the west coast.

"Yup," Lusman answered.

"It starts off okay, until it . . . deviates . . ." Saroyan observed soberly.

"I found this on one night, just flipping channels," Lusman told them. "I have no idea how long it's been running. I'm checking now to see where else, what other markets it's playing in. The only disclaimer on it is the weak one at the beginning, the one you just saw."

"Well is there a problem?" Edwards asked. "I mean, we encourage supporters, don't we?"

"Um . . . yeah," Lusman agreed uneasily. "But—"

"I don't want Michael to see this whole thing," Saroyan told Lusman. "Just show him the part . . . that shows the problem . . ."

"Here's the spot that really tells it," Lusman told them as he pushed the "play" button.

A wild-eyed young man in his mid twenties, with puffed-up curly blonde hair and dressed in psychedelic colors, was standing in front of a tall, deteriorating, brown brick building southeast of downtown Los Angeles. "This is America in the inner city, where more and more of America's economically disadvantaged have taken up residence. Let's talk straight—let's be real. Let's say what is happening in a way that doesn't lie. The people in these areas are getting *pissed*. It's obvious they'll *never* get their part of the American dream. We all see what's coming. Americans are going to learn to live with less. The resources of this planet have just about been depleted. And the people in these inner cities know that everything belongs to someone else, and nothing belongs to them.

"Look what Michael Edwards is proposing," the young man continued as he began to walk through the deteriorating area. "First, increase the gasoline taxes. That's right. Make it so these angry inner-city people can't afford to drive their cars into the more civilized neighborhoods. Second, he wants drugs legal, and cheaper. Make sure these people can afford to buy them. Let them all zonk out. Pacify them with cheap drugs. Then they'll forget what they don't have."

"What?" Edwards demanded.

Lusman stopped the video and hit the fast-forward button. "It goes on that way for half an hour."

Edwards was clearly disturbed by what he had seen.

"The guy doesn't just talk about turning the inner cities into zombie dens," Saroyan added. "He's like a philosopher-prophet, quoting Nietzsche and Nostradamus. He labels you as the first leader of the new age. He goes on to say that your agenda is to anaesthetize the lower and eventually the middle class as well, so society can be transformed into a new less-material, more-controlled situation, with the superior intellects of society rising to their potentials over the happy, drugged, ambition-less inferiors."

"I cannot believe this," Edwards told them emphatically. "How does he—"

Lusman interrupted. "Here," he said as he pushed the button for another clip, this one obviously closing the presentation.

The young man spoke earnestly, though still wild-eyed, as he made his point. "Michael Edwards is understandably reluctant to state his true agenda. He thinks you will turn away if you hear it. But I think we *need* to state it. We know what the future looks like without the Edwards changes. It will be roving bands of lawless thugs, taking the things they could never have a chance of possessing any other way. The stakes are high. And Edwards is the answer."

Lusman turned off the video.

"Who's bankrolling this nut?" Edwards asked. "It costs money to produce videos with these production values and put them on the air."

"We don't know for sure," Lusman answered. "We—"

"I mean it's so disgusting. It looks like some kind of a dirty trick to take away our lower *and* middle class support."

"We thought the same thing," Saroyan agreed.

"I had Carl Gregory check into it," Lusman added. "He found out that the guy leads an offbeat cult, usually with just a crude newsletter, distributed locally in the Montana and Idaho areas. But they recently got a huge load of money from a PAC with a bank account offshore."

"Offshore," Edwards repeated as his eyebrows narrowed in thought.

"It doesn't look like the Parker or Hampton organizations. It would be a blatant violation of campaign regulations—I don't think they'd risk that on a stunt like this."

Edwards was pondering.

"So," Saroyan continued, "I have our lawyers drafting papers to demand a much stronger disclaimer—"

"No," Edwards interrupted vehemently. "Whoever is behind this guy *wants* us to counter with a lawsuit. The publicity will make everyone in the country want to see this infomercial."

"We can't ignore this," Saroyan insisted. "This looks like one of our ads. People flipping channels, if they don't see the very beginning, will think that—"

"I'm not saying to *ignore* it," Edwards told him. "But you guys are missing another approach."

"Oscar and I—we feel the courts would be the best answer . . ."

"You couldn't come up with anything else," Edwards concluded.

"There didn't seem to be another—" Saroyan stopped himself and smiled. "No, we couldn't."

"We need to think of what the people behind this want, and what they *don't* want. They *want* publicity for this infomercial—a lawsuit would be perfect for them. Litigation makes great news. They *don't* want anyone to know who they are. That's why they're doling out money from a bank offshore."

"True enough," Saroyan shrugged.

"We need to get in touch with as many of the stations running this as we can. Tell them what we have, and tell them to pass along that we will give it *all* to the press and let them smoke out the rest, unless they run a crawling graphic throughout the entire broadcast that reads something like 'THE OPINIONS EXPRESSED IN THIS BROADCAST DO NOT REFLECT THOSE OF MICHAEL EDWARDS OR HIS CAMPAIGN AND ARE SPECIFICALLY DISAVOWED

BY HIM. THIS BROADCAST IS NOT PAID FOR OR IN ANY WAY SUPPORTED BY THE EDWARDS CAMPAIGN.'"

A grin crept onto Saroyan's face. "You're getting good," he commented. "It just might work. We'll give it a try."

Edwards nodded. He was certain his strategy would be successful. "Good."

"In the meantime, you and Phillips will hit the stump, speaking on a wide variety of issues until the Republicans start their little gathering," Saroyan commented.

"I've been thinking about this," Edwards told them. "The other parties have platforms. I think that rather than making this a set of speeches on isolated issues, we should tie these into my main theme, that we need to approach our current problems by turning loose the market and freedom, with government encouragement. I'm editing the speeches I have planned with this in mind."

"Sounds good," Saroyan agreed.

☼   ☼   ☼

AND EDWARDS DID ADDRESS A NUMBER OF ISSUES OVER THE NEXT FEW weeks. To defuse any ideas that he wanted to "anaesthetize" the inner city population, he had two speeches that he made to inner city audiences. First, he pointed out how taking the distortions of the drug economy out of the inner city would reduce the hold over the areas by lawless gangs, and give youngsters incentives to better themselves conventionally, without the temptations of the easy money of the drug trade. Government would use tax dollars from the sale of legal drugs to help rebuild areas and redirect the focus of areas victimized by the illegal drug trade. These would not be handouts, but seed money to stimulate the establishment of new local businesses, and to provide special educational needs. He was able to enlist the help of some lesser known, local minority leaders, who stood side-by-side with him as he addressed the crowds.

Second, he outlined three specific proposals for applying freedom and the market (Economic Activism) to the problems of the homeless and economically disadvantaged. First, he proposed working closely with local governments to create many more homeless shelters, even spartan, barrack-like residences, pointing out that for homeless people to get jobs and become financially independent, they had to at least be able to put an address on their job applications and have a place to bathe and change clothes to be presentable for a job or job interview. Second, he proposed legislation giving homeless people the means to borrow first and last month deposits, and security deposits for rental housing from the government, with a paycheck garnishment plan to pay back that money in financially feasible installments, pointing out that people living from meal to meal could scarcely come up with what was often over a thousand dollars just to move into a small apartment.

Third, he proposed expanding the concept of public schools by setting up adult schools at homeless centers to provide basic skills that adults might have missed learning when they were younger and less mature.

He also proposed applying Economic Activism to the problem by providing tax credits to businesses hiring homeless people who are then able to afford housing. He pointed out that society as a whole benefits as homeless people are reintegrated into the economy. He deliberately reversed the Republican phrase, "trickle down," and described how these newly integrated participants in the economy would create a "trickle up" effect as they earned taxable income and spent their earned dollars in the economy. And he pointed out that by giving the homeless more realistic chances of obtaining housing through these programs, the demand for rental housing would increase, causing a resultant increase in building starts, and therefore even more jobs. "Wouldn't it be fantastic if many homeless people became able to afford housing by getting jobs in the housing construction industry!"

He discussed two more major issues in the context of getting the American economic system in harmony with society's interests. First, he discussed crime, confirming that the truly evil of the world, those who seek to victimize others, should be punished, and society should be protected from them. He knew these stands were not new. But he also discussed an aspect of crime and the criminal justice system that had received little attention. That was the injustice the current system often did to crime victims. "Politicians will go on long and loud about how much compassion they have for crime victims. But what are we doing for them? We talk about criminals paying their 'debt to society.' But what about their debts to the individuals whose lives they may have severely affected?"

He stated that he would propose Federal legislation that he hoped would become the model for states as well. The legislation would reaffirm that victims have the right to seek civil judgments for damages caused to them by criminals. Those judgments would not be voidable through bankruptcy or any other similar procedure. The criminal would be required to pay this judgement back in installments, until it was paid off in full. Any estate of the criminal would go toward that judgement if the convicted criminal died. Any proceeds from books written by the criminal, especially about his crime, would go toward the judgment. In prison, the criminal would be given work that could generate income to satisfy these judgments. And probation or parole conditions would focus heavily on the convicted criminal's arrangements to continue paying the judgement. A failure to make timely payments on the outside would result in wage garnishment or even reincarceration. He pointed out that when governments stopped incarcerating the addict-victims of the war on drugs, there would be enough room in the prisons for parolees who had come up short on repaying their victims.

"Now I know there will be those who will bring up chain gang analogies. Some might even call this a form of slavery. The legislation would mandate that criminals working in prison to earn funds to compensate their victims would work no more than ten hours a day or sixty hours a week. But am I going to worry more about protecting the rights of some convicted rapist or murderer than insuring restitution to his victims? Any reasonable sense of justice answers that question."

The second major issue he addressed, with glee, was the health care system, because the approaches of the Democrats and Republicans seemed so typical of the problems with American government in the late 1900's. "Our nation's health care system has received an incredible amount of attention in the last 10 years. So how can both parties keep missing the obvious problem so thoroughly? I'll point up the problem with a little pop quiz, a two part-er. First, which of the following countries has the most people per physician? In other words, which has the least number of doctors to treat its citizens on a per-person basis? The United States, Albania, Mexico, Uruguay, or Canada? The United States has the most people per physicians with 611." He read off his notes. "Albania, often called the poorest country in Europe, has more doctors per citizen, with 574 people per physician. Mexico has 600 people per physician. Canada has 449, and Uruguay has 341.

"Part two. Which of these countries has the lowest number of hospital beds per ten thousand people. The United States, Bulgaria, Cuba, Russia, or Mongolia? I'll bet you're catching on. Again, the United States has fewer hospital beds per person than all of those countries! 51 beds per ten thousand. Cuba, supposedly a poor, Communist remnant in Latin America has 71. Bulgaria has 98, Russia has 137, and Mongolia has 127.

"The United States isn't even close to France and Germany in either of these categories. And Great Britain is close, though ahead of the United States in both categories. Japan has about the same number of doctors per person, but has significantly more hospital beds per person.

"It doesn't take a genius to figure out that if there are shortages of anything, including doctors and hospitals, then the price will be high, and there will be a wait for service, and difficulty with availability. Why do we have this situation in the United States? Don't we have enough people smart enough to be doctors?

"The fact is that the nation's most successful trade association, yes, *labor union*, the American Medical Association, uses licensing of medical schools and hospitals to control the supply of health care, and keep it scarce so that prices will stay high for the services of its members. We all know that it takes virtually straight A's through four years of undergraduate college to have any chance of getting into medical school. This is because there are too few medical schools, and the AMA makes sure the situation stays that way. I have an uncle who recently retired from a brilliant medical career. He healed many people—he enriched many lives during his nearly 40 years of practice. He would not have had even a slim chance of getting into medical school today, based on his school record in college, which was a 2.7, or B-minus average. Does it take straight A's in college to be a good doctor? My uncle often told me that the straight A students were sometimes the lousier doctors—they had a harder time relating to their patients.

"An Edwards administration will ask for the AMA's help in setting objective standards for medical schools, and then encouraging the numbers of schools and doctors to increase dramatically. If that cooperation is not forthcoming, then we will push for legislation to unloose this strangle-hold the AMA has over the supply of doctors.

"I am angry with the neglect of this fundamental issue by the major parties. The Republicans always implore us to let the free market handle matters, but their big supporters in the AMA have gotten the Republicans to turn a blind eye toward the AMA's blatant distortions of that free market. And the Democrats—they hand us hundreds of pages of rules and regulations, band-aid measures, turning the American health care system into one big HMO, with less freedom, less choice, less free market aspects, and then have the nerve to call it '*reform*,' while failing to reform the most fundamentally flawed part of the system!"

Edwards also indicated he would make it a top priority to utilize aggressively the recently adopted "line-item veto" for the President. "We have programs in our budget, products of old Congressional pals who long ago cut pork-barrel deals and are now themselves retired or deceased. But their programs live on forever. The President must exercise the power to lay these parasitical relics to rest or we will *never* get Federal spending under control. Congress will still have the power to override any veto the Congressional membership feels is unjust."

And, Edwards spoke to the young voters, charming them with his knowledge of their contemporary music. "It has impressed me that you are the children of those of us who were the flower children of the 60's, and the yuppies of the 80's, and of those of us who served in Viet Nam. You are the babies of the baby-boomers, coming of age. With the end of any meaningful threat of nuclear annihilation, I was certain that the new generation would feel less pressure, less fear, about the future. But when I listen to the music of the new generation, like 'Pearl Jam,' 'Alice in Chains,' 'Soundgarden,' and 'Rage Against the Machine,' I find it to be even more pessimistic than the music I grew up with. And I can see why. You wonder if we will leave you a world worth living in. I am here to try to get that process going *now*, with changes in the system that will allow us to live in harmony with this beautiful planet if we have the will to make the changes necessary. I hope you will have a chance to familiarize yourself with the ideas of this old veteran of the 60's, and that you'll join me in my effort."

With the hard work of both Edwards and Phillips, on the eve of the Republican Convention, Edwards had taken second place in all the major polls. With some variations, the polls showed Parker with 35%, Edwards with 26%, Hampton with 24%, and 15% undecided.

✿   ✿   ✿

Mid August, Election Year: Sunday
Atlanta, Georgia

"SO, SHOULD I PULL MY FISHING POLES OUT OF THE CLOSET AND SEE IF MY old buddy George Bush has room for another fisherman out there in Kennebunkport?" Hampton asked Covington Klondike as they studied the latest poll results. They were having a quiet room service dinner in Hampton's suite of the Atlanta Plaza Hotel, an easy walk away from the Omni Arena, part of the huge complex that included CNN. The Omni would host the Republican Convention beginning the following day.

"Third place," Klondike commented gloomily.

"I'm a God Damn incumbent President in third place."

"This convention is our shot to get a nice bounce right back to the top."

Hampton nodded. "What's the story with Frances Willis?"

Klondike shook his head. "She's not going to make any kind of unity speech," he told Hampton. "I think it's just as well she stays away from here."

Hampton nodded. "So do we hold on to old Burt for VP?"

"He'll step down if we ask him to," Klondike commented. "Probably retire from politics. He knows he could be a liability on the ticket."

"That's what he says. But don't kid yourself. He still wants to be President."

"He's a guy of national stature. But he's too old. He would have been okay eight, maybe even four years ago. But he's 69 years old now."

Hampton smirked. "It's just as well. He's a tough guy to work with, and he hasn't mellowed with age."

Now Klondike smiled knowingly. "Because he thinks he should have been President. Your sentiments about his temperament would be seconded by four ex-Presidents, two of them *Republicans.*"

"So maybe another woman? Florence Burleson?"

"Well, she's a high-profile lady from a big state. And she's been very loyal to you. But . . ."

"I know; she lacks experience."

"She does. And it's beginning to look like Republicans can't choose a proper running mate. Quayle, and then Willis and her resignation . . ."

"So we've got to go with a heavyweight, someone who'll know what's expected and impress the public as a choice of stature."

"That's right."

"Like Burt Dooley."

"Back to him."

"The best one for the job would be Paul Coleman."

Klondike sighed uncomfortably. "I think so too," he told Hampton uneasily. "He's popular. He's a former military man, a lot more famous than that Phillips guy. But . . . we got a call. We were told that Coleman is not interested in politics right now, and that it could embarrass us and him to offer him a spot on the ticket."

"Because he'll turn us down."

"That's the not-so-subtle point of the message."

Hampton smiled knowingly. "He's not interested in politics right now? Bullshit. That son-of-a-bitch has been running for President ever since he resigned from the military. He thinks I'm going to lose. *That's* why he's not interested."

"So it's Dooley."

"Call old Burt up and tell him he's still got a job." Hampton smiled again as he shook his head. "Coleman would have been such a nice shot at Edwards. It would have said to the voters 'look at this—all Edwards could get was this guy you've never heard of. The President pulls a famous former head of the Joint Chiefs of Staff.' That's the difference between dabblers and the real thing."

"Yeah," Klondike dismissed flippantly. "Don't kid yourself. Your opponent is Victor Parker. When Americans are in their voting booths on election day, they will not vote for a third party candidate."

"So we attack Parker and his ideas."

"Yes. We also need to attack the Democrats in Congress. But we have to be careful it doesn't sound like scape-goating."

"Yeah, yeah, we've discussed this before. Congress does sabotage me the way they say the Republicans sabotaged Clinton in 1995. But we can't say that . . ."

"Not that way," Klondike agreed.

"So, we attack Parker and his ideas, and the Democrats in general. We leave Edwards alone—he won't be a factor."

"Right. Except for one thing. We still think Edwards will help us by splitting the negative vote. So whenever we characterize the race, we describe it as a three-candidate race. And we'll want him on board at any debates."

"Sounds good. Get the word out on the strategy. I'll either sink or swim now."

And Hampton was able to "bounce" himself into second place. But the polls very clearly showed a close three-way race as Labor Day, the traditional beginning of the Presidential campaign, was just around the corner. The poll results were now Parker 30%, Hampton 29%, Edwards 27%, with 14% undecided.

✿   ✿   ✿

Early September, Election Year: Friday
Hollywood, California

"THE EDWARDS, HAMPTON AND PARKER CAMPAIGNS ISSUED JOINT statements today announcing a debate between the candidates for October 1st. All three have good reasons for wanting to face-off," the local newscaster announced on the television set in the east Hollywood bar on Fountain Avenue near Western. "President Hampton is behind, and needs to win a debate to rejuvenate his reelection chances. Victor Parker has a slim lead, but wants to capture more than just negative Hampton votes, and establish himself as a better choice to unseat the incumbent than Edwards. This would firm up and probably extend his lead if he is successful. And Michael Edwards, as a non-politician, needs to get on the podium with these gentlemen and look Presidential."

"Turn the fucking channel!" demanded one of the patrons, a heavyset, surly, drunken man.

"Hey, that's my man Mikey," Slick Naylor told them. "He'll mop up those crumb-bums. Leave it on."

"It's only a news brief," the bartender told them. "I got a ball game on here."

"Vote by vote, choice by choice, turn the fucking channel!" the heavyset drunk man demanded again.

"It's off," the bartender told him as the news update ended and the local baseball telecast resumed.

"Mikey's gonna kick ass," Naylor remarked with a macho swagger.

"You come in here all the time mouthing off about 'Mikey-this,' or 'Mikey-that,'" the bartender observed impatiently. "Stop acting like you're the guy's best friend, okay?"

"I was once."

"Bullshit," the bartender said angrily. "If you're gonna talk shit, then get the fuck out of here."

"You shouldn't talk that way to customers."

"I don't talk that way—to *paying* customers."

"I paid you off," Naylor insisted.

"You paid off about six weeks ago. You're in the hole again."

"I'll make good."

"Yeah? I believe that like I believe all your 'Mikey' shit."

"I *was* tight with the guy. A long time ago."

"People are voting for that guy for President. Hell, *I'm* voting for him. A guy like that has no use for anyone like you."

"Yeah? Well I got something on him. And they paid me off."

"You *what?*" Now the bartender was no longer simply annoyed. He was becoming seriously angry. "There's a difference between talking shit and *really* messing up. You're really messing up now, Slick."

"I'm telling you, it's true. They even sent me a real fancy lawyer to prove the cops framed me on that drug thing."

"If you're so tight with him, and he's paying you off, why can't you pay your fucking bar tab?"

"I'm out of money."

"Real big payoff, huh."

"I'm not shitting on this."

"Hey everybody! This is Slick Naylor, Mr. Smooth Operator! He's been getting paid off by Michael Edwards 'cause they were best friends and he has some dirt on Edwards!"

The patrons, most of them regulars, laughed at the bartender's announcement.

"So this is great news for everyone he owes money to, which is at least half of you," the bartender continued. "He says he'll pay you now."

"Wait a minute," Naylor requested tentatively. "I'm just a little short. I'm on the level about Edwards."

Snickers and chuckles again rippled through the bar.

The angry, heavyset, drunken man was not amused. He sauntered over to Naylor. "You owe me ten bucks on that Dodger game last week. Do you pay your bets or not, Mr. 'Smooth Operator?'" He shoved Naylor.

Another patron recounted Naylor's debt to him and also shoved him. Soon Naylor found himself being pushed around the bar by no less than five tough drunks. Their taunting laughter grew uglier.

Naylor had become desperate, almost in tears. "I'm not lying about this! I could bring that guy's whole campaign down! I'll pay you all back!"

He landed back with the heavyset drunk. "You're pathetic," he told Naylor disgustedly. "Find someone else to swallow your shit." The heavyset drunk flung Naylor very forcefully toward the exit door about ten feet away.

Naylor's face hit the door. He bounced back onto the floor. He grabbed his nose; blood flowed from his nostrils.

"Not like the old saloons," the heavyset drunk man told him, belittling Naylor's apparent suffering. "Those old-time doors would have opened right up and let you out. No give in these modern doors." He started toward Naylor. "Maybe if I try it again . . ."

Naylor crawled toward the door. "You guys'll see. I'm not lying." He tried to stem the flow of blood from his nose. "You'll see." He weakly moved through the door and out of the bar.

"'You'll see!'" the bartender mocked. "'I'm not lying!'"

The regulars settled back on their stools to watch the ball game.

Chapter 15

Mid September, Election Year: Saturday
New Orleans, Louisiana

"Big fucking operators," Enriquez said with a sneer as he sat down with Fadiman and Hunter at Le Cochon Rouge. "Real slick operators. We put out the word on the streets for dirt on Edwards and now every junkie and cokehead from Miami to Seattle has a story to sell."

"And the stories are all crap. We know," Fadiman said coldly.

"I could have told you this would happen," Enriquez stated haughtily.

"Then why didn't you?" Fadiman demanded.

"You guys treated me like I didn't know anything that could help."

"Well you know about street people. That's something I have very little knowledge of," Fadiman countered disgustedly.

"They come all stressed out and strung out, with information to sell." Enriquez continued his caustic rebuke, enjoying his reprimand of Fadiman.

"So we scratch that approach," Fadiman told them as he shrugged. "There's another one we had to scratch," he added to Hunter, deliberately addressing Hunter only. "You know that radical nut I found?"

"The one who supported Edwards, yeah," Hunter recalled. "I caught his commercial."

"I had to pull him," Fadiman told Hunter disappointedly.

"Too bad. That boy was a real hoot," Hunter said smiling.

"Edwards surprised me. I thought he'd scream bloody murder, go after the guy in the press, in the courts—he would have had the whole country watching the guy's show. Instead—" Fadiman gathered his thoughts. He nodded his head. "I underestimated him. And I was careless in the use of my resources. When we found out he had discovered a lot about the source of the guy's money, and he was going to the press with it—I know two or three sharp press people who could have put this together just on what Edwards already had. I won't underestimate Edwards again."

"Hey, you're such a smooth operator," Enriquez taunted.

Fadiman squinted irritatedly, but held his temper. "What we are doing here is not easy," Fadiman told him, in a controlled, brittle tone. "This is not like sneaking illegal drugs past an undermanned police force."

"So what I do is easy?" Enriquez demanded. "Dealing with cutthroats and hostile governments? If I made the kinds of mistakes you made, I'd be in prison . . . or *dead*."

Hunter shook his head. "You're showing a bad attitude here, son."

Fadiman reached down next to his chair and picked up a blue plastic sack labeled with the words "VIDEO PALACE" in red block letters. "I got something for you," he said to Enriquez with a slight smug smile on his face.

Enriquez took the sack warily and reached inside it. His expression turned hostile as he pulled out a plastic package, elaborately labeled with vivid images. "The 'Godfather Trilogy'?" he asked Fadiman with chilly disbelief.

"Yeah," Fadiman told him. "The Corleones figured out how to deal with the end of alcohol prohibition to keep making big money. You should try to learn some lessons from—"

"From a *movie*?" Enriquez demanded with angry disbelief. "From an American movie?" He threw the videocassettes on the table with such force that wine and water splashed out of the glasses in front of Fadiman and Hunter. "This is not acceptable. *You* have the bad attitudes." Enriquez stood up. "My association with you two pathetic patrones is over," he announced. He started to walk away.

"No more Mexican-Arab stunts," Fadiman warned.

"You fancy-pansters no longer have to worry about what I will do," Enriquez countered. "I will handle myself, without mistakes." He walked away.

The security man started to follow, looking at Fadiman for possible instructions.

Fadiman shook his head.

"He's wrong, you know," Hunter told Fadiman. "We do have to worry. Because if he gets tangled up in one of his schemes, he could be linked to us."

"He'd sell us out to save his own skin," Fadiman added.

"You still have that loose cannon insurance?"

"More or less. It's in place as good as I can get it."

"Why'd you give him the tapes?" Hunter asked curiously. "You must have known it was going to piss him off."

"I was trying to give him a message. He'll be hot at first. But when he cools down, maybe he'll be smart enough to curb his ambition and not try to overstep. That would be easiest for us. But if he doesn't, we'll be ready for him."

"We really throwing in the towel on this election?"

Fadiman shook his head reflectively. "Not yet. I still have one major card to play, and I have no idea how it's going to fall yet." He paused, then looked Hunter in the eye seriously. "But if it doesn't fall right, you might want to start preparing some lobbying strategies for the next Congress, under an Edwards presidency."

Hunter nodded.

Their meals arrived and they began eating.

✧   ✧   ✧

Early October, Election Year: Sunday
Hartford, Connecticut

"THE LEAGUE OF WOMAN VOTERS WELCOMES YOU TO THE FIRST DEBATE of the this year's Presidential Campaign, held here at the Hartford Civic Center," stated Harriet Ambrose, spokesperson for the League. The east-coast Connecticut location was chosen after tedious three-way negotiations. Hampton had only agreed to the location when Parker and Edwards agreed that they would hold the second debate in Nevada, Arizona or Utah. They tentatively agreed to hold the third debate in a southern state. The capacity crowd of 18,000 (increased from the usual 16,200 with extra seating added) watched attentively at the Civic Center. The crowd's sympathies seemed fairly evenly divided among the three candidates, though the Edwards supporters tended to be the most demonstrative, and Hampton's supporters tended to be the quietest.

The first half of the debate was the typical format of recent election debates where reporters asked questions and candidates essentially responded to the reporters. Candidates were allowed short comments in response to an opponent's answer, followed by a comment on the comments by the candidate who had been asked the question. The second half of the debate allowed the candidates to question each other. After the response, the other two followed up.

Parker's staff had shrewdly proposed Don Samuelson as a panelist. The Edwards Campaign either had to veto Samuelson, which would look petty and vindictive, or accept him and take their chances. Edwards was confident he could manage Samuelson's questions.

Samuelson's first question to raise eyebrows was addressed to Edwards about ten minutes into the debate: "Mr. Edwards, what would your administration's policy be toward Tajikistan, where civil war has torn apart that country and created terrible human rights violations?"

"Uh, Tajikistan . . ." Edwards seemed surprised. "As you are aware, this country has recently established what can only be described as a tenuous coalition government between Islamic elements and former Communists. In keeping with the principles outlined for foreign policy in an Edwards Administration, we should encourage this country to firm up democratic institutions, through regional and even United Nations auspices, and even more importantly, we should encourage the economic integration of the area through trade. We should *discourage* Russian unilateral intervention. And we should support religious freedom, standing in opposition to anti-Moslem bigotry, which has been used to fan the flames of this civil conflict." Edwards finished his answer with a strong, confident tone.

"Senator Parker?" the moderator asked.

"Mr. Edwards must be way behind events," Parker stated condescendingly. "President Niyazov has solid control over this country and has for some time. And we need to be concerned about Iranian influence in the region, and their efforts to encourage Islamic extremism. Otherwise, the United States need not be concerned with this fairly stable country."

Edwards' eyebrows raised and a subtle, private smirk came onto his face.

"President Hampton?" the moderator requested.

Hampton seemed confused. "Um, the policy of my administration has been effective . . . uh, has been effective in bringing stability to this situation. And we will continue to remain steadfast . . . steadfast in our concern over Iranian, uh, extremist Islamic influence in Turkestan, uh, Tajikistan. Radical Muslim terrorists must not be encouraged."

"And Mr. Edwards . . ."

Edwards tried not to look too smug as he moved in to mop up his opponents. "With all due respect, Senator Parker has confused Tajikistan with Turkmenistan. President Niyazov, whom he refers to, is the President of Turkmenistan; I had the pleasure of meeting him briefly during the preparation of the documentary I was involved with on former Iron Curtain ethnic groups. Tajikistan has only recently established internal peace and a stable government after years of complicated civil war between clans, religious groups, and contending former Communists and anti-Communists. We will hope that he doesn't confuse the other central Asian republics of the former Soviet Union. They have all taken very different approaches to life after the Soviet Union, and they all have their own unique situations.

"As to President Hampton's concerns about radical Islamic terrorists, that remains a serious international concern. But Tajikistan's Moslem leadership has shown no tendencies in this direction. They have consistently *rejected* the model of the Iranian Islamic state, preferring a secular state along the lines of our long-time ally, Turkey. In fact, in the early 90's, the major Islamic leader withdrew from the Presidential election, while he was leading in the polls, because he feared some of his more radical followers would push for an Islamic state. So in Tajikistan—"

"Time," the moderator interjected politely.

Edwards nodded. He had made his point.

Samuelson created another intriguing exchange about ten minutes later with another provocative question directed to Edwards: "Mr. Edwards, many commentators have accused you of engaging in pretty-sounding, abstract theories, devoid of a clear relationship with reality. One example is so-called 'cyclical consumption,' and 'linear consumption.' Would you please describe these ideas, and explain how they relate to the world we live in today?"

Edwards described the concepts clearly and concisely, relating them to his Regenerating Biosphere concept, and explaining how use of these concepts would lead to a world as materially prosperous as it is now, but in harmony with the environment. He ran out of time, but managed to get in one or two concluding sentences after time was called.

"Senator Parker?"

"Well," Parker chuckled, trying mostly unsuccessfully to be folksy, "I'm glad Mr. Samuelson brought up this 'circular consumption' thing.

Because it has been a mystery to me too. And people in this country don't know a 'consumption cycle' from a unicycle. We can't govern on obscure ideas like that. We need to stay concrete. We Democrats have led the fight to make industries responsible for their effect on the environment."

"Mr. President?"

"Government by theory. Yeah. That is exactly why Mr. Edwards is so dangerous. If his theories don't work, what will happen to all of us? Just listen to this 'circular consumption' malarkey. You want to stake our future on that? Or, do you want more rules and regulations like you'll get from Senator Parker and his people? That's the choice."

"And Mr. Edwards, your final response."

"Boy, there's a lot there," he said smiling. Edwards shook his head. "Unicycle? I thought we heard all those bad jokes at the Democratic Convention."

A slight giggle cackled through the audience.

"If '*cyclical*' and 'linear consumption' are such a mystery to Senator Parker, I'd like to refer him to little Dirk Schweitzman in Mr. Jackson's fourth grade class at Seminole School in Tallahassee, Florida. Dirk, and the entire fourth grade class, did a beautiful set of posters and presentations on the ideas that showed me they understood them easily and thoroughly."

Parker heaved an angry sigh as he stiffened noticeably. The camera caught his reaction in a demonstrative close-up.

"Both the Senator and the President complain about staking our future on abstractions. How about freedom? There's an abstract idea for you. Consumption and prosperity in harmony with the environment is an abstract goal, like freedom. I think these are noble goals.

"And Senator Parker says the Democrats have always 'led the fight' to make industry environmentally responsible. And that is exactly his problem. He sees it as a fight. I want to end this counterproductive conflict mentality—"

"Time," the moderator said.

"—and bring our industries into harmony with what is—"

"Time," the moderator insisted.

"—what is best for the environment."

The direct questions and answers among the candidates raised the temperature of the debate. Edwards got the tone started with his question to President Hampton. "Mr. President, how can the Republican Party call itself the party that keeps the government off our backs, and that champions free enterprise, when it is also the party that initiated the war on drugs, insisting that some drug addicts should be incarcerated and some shouldn't, when it is the party that insists a woman has no right to choose whether or not to bring a pregnancy to term, and when it is the party that subsidizes petroleum, nuclear power, mined materials, and even the highly addictive drug nicotine, found in tobacco?"

There was a twitter of laughter.

Hampton tried to flow with what he thought was the mood. "Was that a question, or a speech?" he asked.

"A question," Edwards replied smiling. "Would you like me to repeat it?"

Louder laughter rippled through the audience.

Hampton seemed flustered. "Uh, no," he answered as he brought his focus back onto the question. "Um, first of all, legalizing drugs is *nuts*. What kind of country will we be living in? Abortion is murder. We will not allow women, or male doctors for that matter, to have the 'choice' of murder. And we need to subsidize energy sources to keep this country prosperous. Republicans are still the party for freedom. Senator Parker will have us strangling in big government red tape and regulations. We need *more* Republicans in the Congress."

"Senator Parker?"

"Democrats also believe in the freedom of choice for women and are against subsidies for the rich and privileged. But we resist surrendering to the drug-lords by making drugs legal. We reject the rhetoric of a war on drugs. Instead, we envision the day when the cities of America are drug free, because the United States government cared enough to remove the conditions that tempt our citizens to use drugs."

"And Mr. Edwards, you may follow-up, or comment . . ."

"A couple of comments," Edwards indicated. "First, President Hampton asks what kind of a country we'll be living in with legalized drugs. It'll be a country where drug addicts are not criminals. Where we treat all drug addicts equally—cocaine and heroin addicts treated with the same principles as alcoholics and nicotine addicts. Where we will treat drug addiction as a health problem and not as a problem for our overcrowded prisons. And a country where druglords do not rake in millions of dollars in illicit profits that allow them to live like royalty and run some areas of our cities. The President implies that a choice between prohibition and drug legalization is a choice between an America with or without drugs. But we have prohibition now, and we are far from being a drug-free America.

"Senator Parker dreams of a drug-free America. So do I. And the only way we will truly achieve this goal is for our citizens to *choose* not to consume drugs. *Freely*. Legalizing drugs is not 'surrender' to the druglords. It simply removes the criminal tag from those who are victims of drug addiction, and removes the druglords' source of income."

Parker and Hampton both directed questions mainly to each other. But they each directed one pointed one to Edwards. Both dealt with Edwards' environmental ideas. Hampton's came first: "I want to ask Mr. Edwards; we are hearing from scientists who say there is no greenhouse effect. In the late 70's, these same climatologists now whining about the greenhouse effect were saying that we were about to enter a new ice age. We keep hearing doom-and-gloom on the environment—there's a new way we're all going to die every five years. All of this catastrophe-mongering that you have apparently bought into, Mr. Edwards, doesn't it kind of remind you of the boy who cried wolf? Should we base policy on these catastrophe-crazy eggheads who keep crying wolf?"

A slight ripple of chuckle sounded from the audience.

Edwards narrowed his eyes and grinned slightly. "Mr. President, if this is the story of the boy who cried wolf, then I'd like to remind you how that story ended. There *was* a wolf—the people ignored the final cries of the boy and tragedy followed."

Parker's environmental question was asked late in the debate: "Mr. Edwards, you have said repeatedly that Republicans lack compassion. But when you talk about phasing out gasoline and coal, you are talking about throwing thousands of people out of work. These are Americans who have labored in dark tunnels, on remote oil rigs off shore and in the ice of Alaska to bring energy to our homes. With the cavalier attitude of an impulsive amateur, you will have us send them to the unemployment lines. I submit that *you* are more insensitive than even the *Republicans* you label as lacking compassion. How do you answer for your plan to throw thousands out of work?"

"Senator Parker is forgetting that a key part of my proposals is that we *phase in* these changes," Edwards replied. "This will allow people to adjust, to end jobs through attrition instead of layoffs, to let people work toward early retirement, or make arrangements to learn new skills. I have previously suggested subsidies for education at all ages. This is why. Our changing world will cause many dislocations of occupations. And the fact is that study after study shows renewable energy industries are more labor-intensive than non-renewable energy industries; in other words, as the transformation progresses, there will be *more* jobs for our citizens, and cleaner and less hazardous jobs.

"I also submit that my approach of *gradual* changes, anticipated ahead of time, is much more compassionate than just allowing these industries to die when they become obsolete and we are choking on the wastes. Allowing the continuing use of filthy, polluting energy sources when a properly oriented economy can move us to cleaner alternatives shows a lack of compassion for the entire country, for the world, for the children in our cities who choke on the air, for the people in Miami, Cairo, and the floodplains of Bangladesh who will face rising waters year after year as global warming increases.

"And what about these coal miners? For years we have heard what a cruel occupation this is, with black lung, suffocating cave-ins, men forty years old looking like they are eighty. Now, when I come along and propose a way to phase out this occupation, this relic of a killing job left over from the Industrial Revolution, I'm accused of a lack of compassion! But these are Democrats, ladies and gentlemen. They never met a job or government program they didn't like. Never phase out the obsolete. If it isn't working, choke it with regulations. But for God sake don't *end* it. Somebody somewhere could still be making a living from it. Set up a new bureaucracy whose job it is to keep the obsolete relevant. And tax everyone with more than two dimes to rub together to pay for all of it. That is the Democratic politics of the late 1900's, and we have a chance to—"

"Isn't he out of time?" Parker complained to the moderator petulantly.

And the moderator had become distracted listening to Edwards' pointed response. "Yes. Time."

"No problem. I think I made my point," Edwards said with a polite, satisfied grin.

Another faint giggle twittered from the audience.

Edwards closed the debate first. "Ladies and gentlemen, I want to thank my opponents for debating me, and I look forward to more debates. It is clear what kind of choice you have in November. Republicans claim to have the party of the free market, and 'getting government off our backs.' But they often support laws that favor the rich, not the free market, and laws that intrude on private aspects of our lives. The Democrats claim to represent a broader cross-section of our citizens, with more compassion and evenhandedness. But the Democrats have also often tried to use government as a direct agent for solving problems, setting up regulations and bureaucracies that limit freedoms and sometimes actually make problems worse.

"I'll be honest. We could probably hang in for another four years with either of my opponents. We'd have more homeless, more degradation of the environment, and more dependence on scarcer and more expensive energy sources. But they are the safe choices for today.

"Unfortunately, they are *terrible* choices for the day of reckoning that must come. Yes, people have been predicting doom for a long time, and those predictions have yet to become reality. But we are seeing the outer edges of doom. We are getting the warnings. We need to make the adjustments *now*, when we can make them relatively painlessly, based on the transitional programs I have proposed. We should be a country run on the principles of freedom and free enterprise, tempered with compassion and vision. These two ossified political parties we have now are no longer capable of delivering that option. That makes *me* the safe choice for *tomorrow*.

"And ladies and gentlemen, I *can* win. As we've said, voter by voter, *you* will choose. Not pollsters or pundits. Cast your vote for me whether or not you think I can win. If you do, I just might win."

Parker and Hampton closed predictably.

The debate ended. The audience applauded, cheering for their candidates.

Edwards came backstage. Saroyan greeted him.

"You really did great," Saroyan told Edwards with almost a child-like giggle. "You really pissed-off Parker. He went into a snit—looked *terrible*. And I think you got some good ones in on Hampton too."

"Good."

"It'll be easy to get on every network news show and tell them how wonderful my candidate did."

Edwards smiled. "Go for it. I could use some *rest*." He paused. "Oh, can you believe Samuelson asking me about Tajikistan?"

"Yeah. And you were able to answer him. Where is the place, anyway?"

"Central Asia."

"You did a documentary on that area."

"The former Soviet republics, yeah."

"And Parker got the wrong country?" Saroyan asked, wearing a gratified grin.

"Absolutely," Edwards told him smiling. "Hampton figured out that one of us had it wrong, but wasn't sure which. So he tried to fudge it both ways."

"And stammered around with it," Saroyan added. "I wondered why he sounded so indecisive on it. Samuelson did you a favor on that one, without knowing it."

"I *loved* it."

"Well, I'm off to spin your praises," Saroyan told Edwards.

Edwards escaped to his nearby hotel room on Constitution Plaza.

Initial debate polls showed Edwards with a slight edge, and Parker with a slight deficit when neutral voters were asked to pick a winner. And analysts did not see the contest as a clear win for any of the candidates. But Parker suffered from the fact that the most intriguing bites from the debate were Edwards' quips at his expense. Edwards' referral of Parker to the fourth grade class, and Parker's mistake on Tajikistan were widely broadcast. Edwards' reply to Hampton's "boy who cried wolf" metaphor was also popular on the clip list. And as those bites were featured, it became clear that Edwards had decisively won the debate. In the days ahead, the victory became so obvious that Hampton and Parker now manufactured format issues and schedule problems to avoid another three-way debate with Edwards. This did not bother Edwards, because the polls now showed him in the lead: Edwards with 31%, Hampton with 29%, and Parker 28%, with 12% undecided.

✿   ✿   ✿

Early October: The Following Wednesday
Port Washington, New York

"I CAN'T BELIEVE THIS," OSCAR LUSMAN SAID TO ALICE BRAGAN AS THEY lay together in Oscar's bed. A late night rerun of the "The Simpsons" was just beginning, following the ten o'clock news. Alice Bragan was a thin, smallish young woman in her mid twenties with an olive complexion, and a confident, uninhibited manner that made her appear more attractive than her average looks should have allowed. They were spending a rare quiet evening together at Oscar's two bedroom apartment in the coastal Long Island community of Port Washington. "We are on an unbelievable roll."

"I'm finally convinced," Alice told him, kidding him, then tickling him.

"We're in the lead, and the lead is growing." Oscar shook his head. "Alice, I'm right in the middle of fucking *history*, right at the center of the power of the country."

"He's not elected yet."

"He's a lock," Oscar told her confidently.

"And you'll be the President's George Stephanopolis."

"You may laugh," Oscar confessed, "but as a teenager, I used to watch that guy, and I thought 'a guy that young doing that job. Maybe that could be me.'"

"Maybe it could," Alice agreed.

"And power . . ." Oscar turned toward Alice lustfully. "It's supposed to be—"

"It *is*," Alice assured him as she pulled him on top of her.

Suddenly there was a pounding on Oscar's front door.

They both sat up.

"What is that?" Alice asked.

"Probably a reporter," Oscar answered. He got up, grabbed his robe and headed out of his bedroom toward the front door.

The pounding sounded again.

Oscar opened the door.

Slick Naylor stood in the doorway with a silly smirk on his face. His nose was red and swollen, and slightly crooked.

Lusman felt a combination of anger, fear and profound nausea as he realized who his midnight visitor was.

"I need to talk to you," Naylor told him.

"We had a deal," Lusman reminded him sternly.

"Yeah. But I have a problem."

"Part of our deal is that I don't have to worry about your problems."

"I need to talk to you about that deal." Naylor continued to speak with patient confidence.

"The *other* part of our deal is that I don't have to *talk* to you, or *see* you, or have anything to do with you *again*."

"We gotta talk about this," Naylor insisted in an easy but persistent tone of voice. "Things have changed . . ."

"What're you talking about?"

"There's another buyer for my information."

"What?"

"I've got the word that there's some big bucks for someone who can deliver good Edwards dirt. Well, Oscar, we both know I can . . ."

"Do you have a short memory? We pulled your ass out of a tight sling. In exchange for saving your crummy little ass, you promised to get lost. I'm holding you to that promise."

"I never promised I wouldn't sell the information to someone else. I just promised I wouldn't make it public myself."

"Selling it to someone else *is* making it public."

"Well, that's . . . subject to interpretation. And . . . I'm interpreting it my way."

Lusman drew an angry breath as his teeth clenched and his jaw rose.

"I'm doing you guys a favor. I could have just sold the information. But I wanted to give you guys a chance to outbid the other buyer. You have been good to me, and I wanted—"

"Don't bullshit me. How much is your so-called 'favor' going to cost us?"

"I figure a hundred grand oughtta do it."

"Are you fucking crazy?" Lusman demanded, raising his voice as he flushed with anger. "One hundred thousand?"

"I know you guys can afford it. Edwards can afford it. I'm worth it, man. You're almost there."

Lusman pondered a moment. "Cash, I suppose."

"Well, yeah," Naylor replied through a smug grin.

Lusman sighed angrily. Rage grew within him as he nearly trembled. But he couldn't deny that Naylor was again a problem he would have to deal with. "It'll take some time to get it together. It'll be out to the coast next weekend. Be around your home. We'll contact you."

"I'd like to have the money before then."

"I don't care what you'd like. You want it? That's when you get it. You spill anything? You'll be doing time for extortion."

"Don't talk too tough," Naylor warned. "You got no right to be upset. I'm doing you guys a favor. And I really don't like threats."

"I told you, I don't care what you like. Just stay close to home next weekend."

"For a hundred grand? I'll be there. Glad we could get this worked out."

"Don't try to be my buddy, okay? Just get lost."

Naylor smiled. "You act like it's your money I'm taking. You're just spending *Mikey's* money to buy some peace of mind."

"And don't try to sell it to me. Our business is done. I don't have to talk to you again until next week." Lusman shut the door in his face, forcefully moving Naylor's foot out of the way in the process.

"Who was it?" Alice asked as Lusman returned and got into bed.

"My little headache is back," Lusman growled frustratedly.

"The guy? The guy who has something on Edwards?"

"Yeah."

"I heard you say something about a hundred thousand dollars."

"Yeah. That's the scum-bucket's latest fee."

"Are you going to pay him?"

"That's what I told him." Lusman smiled. "Let him try to collect it."

"He must have something pretty awful on Edwards."

Lusman exhaled quickly. "Some day I'll tell you about it."

"I'm dying to know *now*."

Oscar started to tell her. He needed to talk about this. But he stopped himself. He couldn't trust anyone with this. He was on the verge of emerging into the power center of the world. Occupying those positions was sometimes lonely. He would have to show the fortitude to handle this situation, without crying to his girlfriend about what a tough spot he was in. "I can't tell you," he said to her quietly.

"I won't tell—"

"Not *now*," Oscar insisted, losing his patience for a moment.

Alice stiffened at the harshness in his voice.

"Please," he followed, showing a vulnerability that contradicted his previous sternness. "Let me just try to get some rest and pretend this scummo is still out of my life."

They cuddled and Alice Bragan fell asleep.

But sleep came only in fleeting spurts for Oscar Lusman.

Chapter 16

Early October: The Next Day, Thursday
Sacramento, California

"SHE CAN'T DO THAT!" AN ANGRY PRESIDENT KEN HAMPTON pontificated to his staff at an emergency meeting in a small tent on the California State Fairgrounds where he was about to give a speech, trying to rally support in the state with the most electoral votes.

Covington Klondike hung up the phone. "Our source, who is totally reliable, says she's going to," he said calmly, but also with disapproval in his voice.

"Get her on the phone," Hampton commanded.

"I'm not sure—" But Klondike was interrupted.

"You can find her for the *President*, can't you?" Hampton insisted.

Klondike nodded to one of the aides who quickly went to a telephone in a corner of the room and spoke quietly into the receiver.

"This thing is going the wrong way," Hampton observed gravely, with agitation. "That Edwards is ahead, and pulling away."

"Their strategy has been—"

"Fuck *strategy*," Hampton insisted. "This guy would be bad for the country. We haven't gotten that word out. We treated him with kid gloves because we thought he'd help us beat Parker. Now he's beating *us*."

"We've got the—"

"I've got Frances Willis on the line for the President," the young aide told them.

"Good," Hampton said as he strode decisively to the phone. He took the receiver with a broad swipe of his arm. "Frances?"

"Yes, Mr. President," she answered calmly from the other end of the phone.

Hampton tried to moderate his tone, but was only partially successful. "You can't do it. You're committing political suicide."

"Can't do what?" she asked with feigned innocence.

"Come on, Frances . . ."

"Somebody on my staff has been telling tales. This isn't supposed to be public until tomorrow morning."

"Someone on your staff leaked this to us, and whoever it is did you a favor. Because now I can talk you out of this insanity."

"Can't you see politics in the United States is changing? Thank *God*. Edwards is remaking the political landscape, Ken. I'm just getting there ahead of—"

"The guy is *dangerous*," Hampton argued. "Forget riding the latest fad. He's not good for the country."

"I don't agree with you. I think he has some great—"

"What'd he do, offer you a cabinet post?" Hampton demanded cynically, in an increasingly harsh tone of voice.

"I believe I will be a front-runner for any one of a number of important posts with him."

"You're selling out your party, your *country*, for a demotion from Vice President to cabinet?"

"This is no demotion," she snapped back. "From token female, from the obscurity of being Ken Hampton's Vice President, to implementing the freshest agenda in maybe a hundred years."

"Don't throw away your future," Hampton warned.

"You're not worried about *my* future. You're worried about *yours*," she taunted. "I think we've spoken about this long enough."

"We'll speak until—" But Hampton was cut short by the click of the phone.

The room was absolutely silent. Aides watched with tense anticipation, as the President of the United States replaced the phone receiver on the hook after a former subordinate had just hung up on him. No one, not even Covington Klondike, was sure what to say. They would take their cue from the President's reaction.

But Hampton was not prone to rages. He gritted his teeth. "We've got no choice. We've got to gamble on the attack ads."

Klondike nodded.

"Parker's started his. Between the both of us, maybe we can knock this Edwards back down to size, before it's too late."

It was clear to everyone in the room that the emergency meeting was over. The discussion now focused on Hampton's upcoming speech. And Hampton and his staff were grateful for the advance warning when Frances Willis publicly endorsed the Michael Edwards candidacy on the following morning with an enthusiastic speech. The staff had time to craft a dignified, respectfully dissenting response to Willis's decision.

☼ ☼ ☼

Mid October, Election Year: Sunday
New York, New York

"OH, *THIS* ONE," MICHAEL EDWARDS RECALLED SMILING, AS HE, TERESA Edwards, Drew Saroyan and Oscar Lusman sat in the Edwards living room watching videos of the attack television ads that his opponents had arrayed against him.

The ad Michael was referring to was from the Hampton campaign. It showed a Michael Edwards look-alike sitting around on the White House lawn, wearing psychedelic 1960's-style clothes, surrounded by similarly attired people, male and female, all about Edwards' age. A Teresa Edwards look-alike was also present, dressed very provocatively.

The Edwards character was lying back on the lawn, looking up into the sky with a spaced-out expression, puffing on a joint. "We did it, man. Us hippies have finally taken over the country."

His companions cackled a stoned laugh as they passed joints and needles around.

"The whole country is stoned!" the Edwards character announced giddily. "Now no one will know, or care, whether our policies are working or not!"

"I think there's a crisis somewhere," an overweight, balding man stated, looking ridiculous in his 1960's attire. "Something about our troops on the carriers in the Mediterranean."

"Let it go 'til later," the Edwards character responded casually. "They're just guarding the oil. We don't need that anymore. We have—" He stood up dramatically.

His entourage watched him worshipfully.

"Sun power," he stated devoutly.

The entourage prostrated itself to the Edwards character as if in a primitive tribal ritual. "Sun-power, sun-power," they chanted in a trance-like mantra.

As the chant faded, but remained in the background, a narrator came on. "In these pivotal times, we must not choose our leaders frivolously, or we may suffer the consequences. Select a proven leader, Kenneth Hampton, to continue as our President."

A "HAMPTON FOR PRESIDENT" logo appeared on the screen.

Michael Edwards broke into a loud laugh.

Teresa looked at him, puzzled with his reaction to something that had made her angry.

"You haven't seen the latest polls," Michael explained to her as his laughter subsided.

"Michael has 35 per cent, Hampton 30, and Parker 26, with 9 still undecided. That puts Michael *up* another three points since these ads started running," Saroyan told her.

"And our research shows the attack ads are actually helping us," Lusman added. "Most voters, even those supporting Hampton and Parker, see the ads as desperation."

"We still have to react to them," Saroyan cautioned. "Don't forget what happened to Dukakis in 1988 when he tried to ignore Bush's attack ads. Just their repetition will have an effect eventually."

Lusman nodded. "I'll have the ad people begin some tough rebuttals, also taking them to task for attacking."

Edwards' expression became suddenly puzzled, then concerned. He shook his head. "No," he told them vigorously. "We don't respond by attacking. We'll look concerned about the ads. We might even end up giving these silly things credibility."

"We have to do something," Saroyan cautioned.

"This is what we'll do," Edwards told them. "First, in our infomercial, announce how the attack ads are helping us. Quote figures from Oscar's research. We could even *thank* Hampton and Parker for helping us and bringing so much humor to the campaign, and rate the ads for inventiveness and creativity. Second, Terese and I will go on a very publicly announced vacation. That will show how *un*concerned we are with these gutter tactics. We will announce that we need the rest to reflect on the awesome responsibilities that may lay ahead."

"Michael, this . . ." Saroyan gathered his thoughts to complete his cautionary response. "If you look like you're taking this thing for granted, like you're too cocky about it, there could be a backlash. I mean, this would be a rather arrogant approach, taking a vacation during the most crucial part of the campaign."

"Not arrogant," Michael stressed, "*confident*. I think the American people will understand the difference. And we have every reason to be confident. Frances Willis has publicly endorsed us. Wallace Trewillinger runs around the country talking about what a Secretary of State might do to implement the *Edwards* foreign policy. Media are picking a cabinet for me, speculating on what shape my administration will take. And they are talking about how Congress might deal with a third alternative candidate who has a mandate—whether my proposals will cruise through into law, or whether there will be total gridlock. Many say the *former* will occur. We *should* be confident."

"About Trewillinger," Saroyan asked. "Did you talk to him today?"

"Yeah," Edwards replied smiling. "I think he'd make a perfect Secretary of State."

"Maybe. But we know he'll try to take over—"

"I don't think that'll be a problem," Edwards assured.

"You set him straight?" Saroyan asked. "How did he take it?"

"I didn't come at him warning and scolding," Edwards explained. "I knew he wouldn't take that well—he's a man of stature, with a lot of pride. I used humor. I kidded him. I said 'you won't be sending over that Tyler Fullbright fellow to brief me on what entree you want served at Cabinet dinner meetings, will you? Because important decisions like food should be discussed directly with the President.' He laughed—what else was he going to do? We joked about Fullbright, how he was such a personable robot, and I said how sorry I was that I wouldn't see more of him, since I'd be talking directly to Trewillinger. 'Wallace,' I told him, and I was deliberately familiar with him, 'I think we will be able to accomplish some great things together.' And he answers 'yes, Mr. President.' He knew I was looking for him to show me that the 'joint presidency' idea was long buried in the past. And he did what he had to do." Edwards smiled again.

Saroyan nodded. Michael Edwards was on a roll. Saroyan wouldn't have contradicted Edwards' proposed strategies even if he wanted to.

"Where are we going?" Teresa asked her husband with girlish anticipation, obviously referring to their upcoming vacation.

"Nantucket," Edwards told her.

"Cold this time of year," Saroyan commented.

"We'll make it warm enough," Edwards said with a mischievous gleam in his eye as he shared a glance with Teresa.

The phone rang. Teresa answered their extension in the living room.

"Hello? . . . Sure." Teresa looked at Oscar. "It's your service. The lady sounds shaky."

Oscar scowled as he walked over to take the phone. "Hello? . . . Wait a minute, slow down . . . No, just take it easy . . . Okay . . . Just give me the number . . . " Oscar wrote as he listened. "Thanks . . . That's okay, you were right to call . . . Bye."

Lusman hung up. "Teresa? Can I use your phone in the kitchen?"

The request surprised Teresa, but she told him "sure."

Lusman quickly went into the kitchen, then punched in the numbers.

"Hello," Slick Naylor responded gruffly at the other end.

"Cool out, asshole. You'll have the money next weekend. There were some delays."

"You *fuckhead*. I fucking waited the whole dick-sucking weekend. You stood me up. You could have at least fucking *called*."

"You're going to lecture me on manners?"

"I'm going to lecture you on *reality*. I've got another buyer for my information. I'd rather do business with you. But don't jerk me around."

"I'm in no mood for your threats."

"Okay. I'll just tell you a little story. It has two endings. If I have a hundred K next Saturday, Mikey keeps his secret and maybe even goes all the way. If I don't have a hundred K on Saturday, I go to my other buyer on Sunday. By Sunday night, Mikey's secret isn't a secret anymore. You decide which ending, pal. I like the first ending better, but I can live with the second. Can you?"

"You'll have the money next Saturday," Lusman told him icily.

"Don't think you can jerk me around until after the election. That would be a big mistake, a mistake you'll realize you made a week from tonight."

"I got the message. Be home Saturday."

"*One more day* sitting around for you. That's *it*." Naylor hung up.

Lusman slowly returned the phone receiver to its place, grinding his teeth with nervous anger.

☼   ☼   ☼

Mid October: The Following Wednesday
Nantucket, Massachusetts

"WHAT'RE YOU DOING?" TERESA ASKED PLAYFULLY AS SHE WALKED down from the deck built on the back of their rented beach house on a private beach at the northwest end of Nantucket Island. Michael wore a sweat suit. Teresa wore a one piece swimsuit with a windbreaker jacket. Michael was returning from the water, a short distance from the back of the house, with a bucket full of sea water. "You can't build these things with dry sand." He had constructed an enormous sand castle almost three feet high. It stood above the otherwise dry, fine white sand on the beach. "You'll be lucky if it lasts to the weekend," Teresa told him as she walked down to where he was.

"'And so castles made of sand, slip into the sea, eventually,'" Michael sang, recalling the Jimi Hendrix song.

"It really looks nice," Teresa told him.

Michael smiled. "I have hidden talents."

"Building . . . that's something you seem to do well."

"And, everything 'slips into the sea, eventually,'" he told her philosophically.

"So why are we doing all this, Michael?" Teresa asked, not to argue, but to understand how he would explain himself in the context of his remark.

He motioned to the sand castle. "You say it's 'nice.' And I'm kind of proud of it. Do we enjoy it any less because we know it won't be here 'much past the weekend?'"

Teresa nodded. She understood. They stood a few moments, enjoying the castle, and enjoying the quiet, solitary time together on the beach.

Teresa shivered as a cat's paw blew off the cool autumn water.

Michael stepped over to her and embraced her. "You should be dressed more warmly," he told her.

She looked up at him with deep love, affection and even vulnerability in her eyes.

"Or," he said softly to her, "you should be *un*dressed warmly . . ."

Michael removed her windbreaker easily as he kissed her on the lips.

She pulled herself to him, wrapping her arms around him.

He pealed down the top of her bathing suit to waist level. The cold of the air made her nipples harden and stand up. He kissed them, first gently, then more vigorously. Teresa melted into him as she held his head to her chest. They tumbled to the sand where Michael worked to remove his own clothes while he continued to kiss and caress Teresa.

The sound of a jeep along the beach didn't catch their attentions until it was about fifty yards from them.

"Michael," Teresa tried to warn him. "Someone's . . . coming . . ."

"What?" Michael was totally naked, and Teresa was too, except for the swimsuit still down around her ankles. "Someone . . ."

The jeep was now 25 yards away.

"Shit!"

They untangled and started to sprint toward the back of the house. Teresa had forgotten that she had not finished removing her swimsuit from around her ankles, and lunged forward, beginning to trip. Michael grabbed her around the waist from behind, preventing a head-first fall into the sand.

From the view of the jeep-driver as he approached, it looked as if a naked man had playfully tackled a naked woman from behind. He couldn't see their faces. And as he zoomed by, he caught a view of their rear-ends, running toward the back of their beach house. The local man chuckled, never realizing he had caught a view of one of the Presidential candidates and his wife in a rather compromising moment. And though he hadn't often seen couples in such an embarrassing situation, this certainly wasn't the first time.

Michael and Teresa quickly recaptured the mood in the beach house, washing off the sand that had clung to them. They did not worry that the jeep-driver would compromise them in some way. He hadn't taken any pictures. And how could a man making love to his wife on a private beach, even if he was a Presidential candidate, be compromising?

✿   ✿   ✿

THE SUN SET OVER THE OCEAN AS MICHAEL AND TERESA SAT ON THE balcony in their robes. Michael had deliberately chosen a beach house to rent on the west side of the island because he knew Teresa enjoyed watching the sun go down over the ocean, as it did on the west coast.

"I can't believe how great this has been," Michael said to his wife. "I'm recharged, ready to campaign as hard as I have to on the home stretch of this thing."

Teresa smiled and gave her husband a quiet kiss on the cheek.

"And I gotta tell you, Terese, I feel like a new man, ever since the campaign."

"You just found the old one," Teresa corrected affectionately.

"I think we're going to win this thing. Then, the challenge really begins."

"If we lose now, it'll be because we gave it away somehow."

"Yeah. I don't think I could handle losing this election now—not after coming this far and this close."

"We're not going to lose," Teresa assured him.

✫   ✫   ✫

The Same Day
Stroudsberg, Pennsylvania

"YOU DON'T BELIEVE IN OFFICES, DO YOU?" LUSMAN JOKED AS HE walked toward Carl Gregory, waiting at a creek off a trail at a state park in the eastern part of Pennsylvania's Pocono Mountains. The air was biting cold, and the day slightly overcast. The trees and bushes had a wet, fresh smell to them.

"I believe in security," Gregory told him. "Offices are the least secure places in the world. Trust me on that axiom; I know from experience."

"Well it is important that no one eavesdrops on us."

"No way. Not out here."

Lusman drew a deep breath. "I have a special assignment. It involves a threat to the campaign. But it's something I haven't brought to Drew or Michael. The situation needs a special type of handling. It's got to stay between us."

"You have my word. If I can't help, I'll stay quiet."

"Good. I have a guy who's been extorting money from the campaign. He has something that could start a scandal. I had him settled out, but he keeps coming after me. I need him neutralized by Saturday, when he'll be waiting for a payoff."

Gregory nodded. "Killed?"

"Not necessarily. If you can scare him enough to lay off of us, then just do that. But it'll take a beating at least."

"Which is it? Dead? Or scared and beaten?"

"Use your discretion. If he doesn't buckle when you visit him, then remove him."

"Understood. We'll handle it for you."

"I'm feeling better just knowing you're on it."

Lusman gratefully gave Gregory all the information he needed to contact Naylor. Lusman felt great satisfaction to know that Naylor would answer his door, and instead of the expected $100,000, would find himself in perilous circumstances.

Lusman left and drove back across New Jersey to Manhattan.

Gregory had a longer trip to make. He drove his rented vehicle to Scranton where he boarded his helicopter. A few hours later, he landed at one of his eight residences around the country. This one was a small cabin with a heliport, just northeast of Bennington, Vermont, between the Taconic and Green Mountains. The colorful autumn leaves created a spectacular view from the air. Snow had just fallen the night before. Except for the heliport, his residence looked like a log cabin from the 19th Century, totally isolated by the lack of any meaningful roads or conventional traveling routes from 20th Century civilization.

Gregory exited his helicopter and walked into his cabin. He threw two logs into the fireplace and lit some kindling underneath.

He walked into an adjoining room which contained a huge bank of electronic attachments to a sophisticated short wave radio. He checked a notebook, then hooked a module up to his radio using some patch-cords.

"Chesire," he summoned. "Chesire. This is Mountain Man. Are you receiving?" As he awaited a response, he removed his army jacket. Then he began peeling off his fake beard, after which he removed his wig, revealing his totally shaved head. "Chesire?"

"This is Chesire," the voice on the other end of the radio replied. The voice sounded muffled and only electronic enhancement made it understandable, but not really identifiable.

"You scrambled?"

"Yes."

"So am I. This is a security broadcast."

"Understood. We are secure."

"You told me to get in touch with you if I ran across a scandal. I think I'm on to one."

"Fill me in."

"Their guy Lusman called me. He wants me to beat up or kill a guy who's been blackmailing them on some possible scandal."

"Any idea on the details?"

"No. He didn't offer details, and I felt pressing for them might have risked my status there."

There was a brief pause on the other end. "We may be able to work this without knowing what it is. You're supposed to beat him up or kill him?"

"I'm to use my discretion."

"Okay. Beat him up, but don't kill him. Make him mad. Don't do any permanent damage. Just make him feel awful, then pissed off."

"Got it."

"You traceable on this?"

"Not a bit."

"And can you keep that Enriquez character away from Edwards? We don't want to create another martyr with a hundred years of conspiracy theories, possibly involving *my* name."

"He's an amateur," Gregory assured him. "An amateur out of his element and off his home turf. He'll never get that close again."

"Good work, Mountain Man. Chesire out."

Zachary Fadiman put down his radio transmitter. His security man had handled another difficult assignment with brilliant professionalism. Fadiman turned off the light to his Virginia Beach townhouse basement and headed upstairs. He would have good news for Hunter at their next meeting.

☼   ☼   ☼

Mid October, Election Year: Friday
Maracaibo, Venezuela

"WITH APOLOGIES IN ADVANCE TO ADMIRAL STOCKDALE, A LONG-TIME associate of mine whom I admire greatly, I know who I am, and I know why I am here," Everett Phillips pronounced with dignified grace as he began his opening statement for the Vice Presidential debate. Ernesto Enriquez was watching on his television, linked up to a satellite dish on top of the mansion at his estate just west of Lake Maracaibo.

Phillips was referring to Admiral James Stockdale, who had started off his debate performance as Ross Perot's running mate in 1992 with the endearing pair of questions: "Who am I? Why am I here?" His charming but inadequate performance seemed to confirm the suspicion that Perot was a message candidate, not serious about winning or governing. Everett Phillips knew he had to stand face-to-face with Jeffrey Jefferson and Burt Dooley, and look as though he belonged with them. The Democrats and Republicans would try to prove he didn't belong, hoping to show once and for all that Edwards really was a fringe candidate.

"I am here to argue for the Edwards agenda, to explain why this is such a great opportunity, for all of us, to move this great country into a new era. And, I am here to show that I am qualified to be a heartbeat from the Presidency."

Ernesto Enriquez sat in a maroon leather couch, clutching a remote control, scowling as he put his feet on the glass coffee table in front of him and watched his forty inch big-screen television. It was 10:00 p.m. in Venezuela, one hour later than the eastern time zone in the United States. Enriquez was dressed in expensive, monogrammed, silk pajamas. Next to him, dressed in a robe, was Maria Romero, a young, stunningly attractive but simple girl from a Zulia village. She was restless. Enriquez focused his attention on the American Vice Presidential debate, hoping this event would somehow derail Edwards' chances.

"On the second part of my task, I will let you be the judge. As for the first part, the build in our support shows that many of you are agreeing with me on how the Edwards vision is the vision for America."

"Ernesto," Maria said seductively. This choice of television programs bored her. She stood up and moved in front of the television set. When she noticed Enriquez' attention was still focused on the television set, she removed her robe, leaving her clothed only in a short, sheer, light blue negligee, covering her only from well below her neck to the very top of her thighs.

Enriquez was irritated, trying to look around her.

"Support has come to us in other ways," Phillips continued on the television screen. "A recently completed independent economic study, not in any way associated with our campaign, has concluded that the Edwards plans for drugs and the environment are fiscally sound. In fact, some scenarios, based on computer simulations, indicate probable budget surpluses in less than five years."

"Come on, Ernesto," Maria insisted. "Aren't I more interesting than that old American?" With one quick motion, she stripped off her negligee and tossed it in Enriquez' face. She stood stark naked in front of him, still trying to block the television set. And she was an exotically beautiful girl, with a full, well-proportioned though fairly short body, with dark eyes, dark hair and a dark complexion that should have attracted any man older than thirteen or younger than a hundred and ten. But Enriquez continued to try to look past her.

She jumped in front of his line of vision playfully, changing position as he moved his head to look around her.

"We have also received support from all across the political spectrum, from liberals to conservatives, including respected police and city government officials—influential, intelligent and profound commentators have come forward in favor of Edwards' plan to phase out drug prohibition in America!" Phillips' intensity increased as he delivered the statement.

And that built Enriquez' anger to the snapping point. He wound up and threw his remote control at the television set.

Maria had to jump out of the way, flinging herself to the ground, landing flat on her rear-end, like a baseball batter trying to avoid a ninety-mile-an-hour fastball, high and tight.

The television set let out a small, harmless but noisy explosion as a flash of light followed by smoke came out of the hole made by the remote control.

"Look at what that guy made me do!" Enriquez exclaimed angrily.

Maria propped herself on her elbows, still lying on the ground, astonished.

Manuel Contreras ran in.

Enriquez was still ignoring Maria. He turned to Manuel. "This Edwards and his old general are going to win the American election," he complained.

Maria came up into a crouch and tried to cover herself.

Manuel smiled, amused with Maria's predicament.

Enriquez was still oblivious to Maria's embarrassment. "I will need your help," he said to Manuel ominously. "My American friends are of no use. Have you been in contact with the Cubans?"

Manuel nodded coldly. "Yes. I have what I need from them."

"And you have a man ready to go?"

"Yes. But I'd rather do this job personally."

"I know. But is your man capable?"

"Yes."

"Send him north. Put him in place."

"Yes."

"Ernesto," Maria insisted softly, but almost in a whine, "throw me my nighty."

Enriquez finally noticed her. "Hey, you stupid bitch, what're you doing running around naked in front of my friends?"

"Fuck you!" She stormed out of the living room, too angry to be further embarrassed.

"Hey!" Enriquez shouted after her. "Nobody talks to me that way! Especially not some little slut just off the fucking farm!" Now he stormed after her. Maria could have been in for the beating of her life as Enriquez prepared to take out all of his frustrations on her. But when Enriquez caught up to her, he finally focused his attention on her exotic beauty. Instead of a beating, they both expressed their frustration and anger with intense sex, almost as violent as they might have wished to be with each other just moments before.

Everett Phillips was not flawless in the debate, but he showed he did belong on the podium with the other two Vice Presidential candidates. He was well-prepared and knowledgeable on all the issues, and on the Edwards agenda. So he had proven himself to be a serious choice for Vice President, and the polls indicated voter beliefs along those lines. The Democrats and Republicans would have to find another way to beat Edwards. Or, they would have to hope he would beat himself. And this possibility was getting closer to reality than anyone realized.

☼   ☼   ☼

Mid October: The Following Sunday
Hollywood, California

"YOU GOT THE MONEY?" NAYLOR ASKED RUDELY AS HE GREETED CARL Gregory at the door. Gregory was in his long hair and beard costume, dressed in army-green, camouflage garb. With him were two expressionless companions. One was small and wiry, about five foot seven, wearing jeans and a body building T shirt, with a gold earring in his right ear. The other was larger and more obviously muscular, wearing army green sweat-pants and a red tank-top.

"Right here," Gregory told him as he tapped a briefcase he was carrying. "In cash."

"I'm not entertaining today," Naylor told him. "Just leave the money and take your friends with you."

"Not so fast," Gregory said as he forced his way through the door, his companions following. "We need to have a talk first."

"The money'll do the talking. If it's there, I'm quiet. If it's not, *I'll* do the talking."

"My principal needs to know what guarantee he has that he won't run into this problem with you again," Gregory told him.

"One time deal. I already talked this over with him."

"Yes, I know. He wanted *me* to do an attitude-check with you. He obviously wasn't completely happy with whatever you told him."

"An attitude-check. Hmmm. Well, life is a crap-shoot. That's my attitude. Guarantees are kind of tough. He'll have to trust me," Naylor responded blithely.

"Well, then I think we need to let you know what will happen to you if you ever become a problem again," Gregory told him casually. He and his companions surrounded Naylor.

Naylor finally began to become apprehensive. His attitude shifted, as if he had suddenly awakened to the true nature of his situation. "Wait a minute," he said worriedly.

Gregory shut the door as they pushed their way into Naylor's residence.

Gregory's larger companion grabbed Naylor's arms from behind and pulled them back so Naylor's chest jerked forward.

"Hey. This is not part of the deal," he said, almost starting to plead.

"We could bruise your ribs," Gregory told him, not responding to Naylor's changed attitude.

The small wiry man moved in front of Naylor as Naylor grimaced and struggled to fold in his now vulnerable abdomen. The wiry man slugged him in the mid-section rapidly three or four times.

Naylor gasped in pain.

"Or we could *crack* your ribs."

The wiry companion put brass knuckles on his fingers and hit Naylor twice on either side.

Naylor screamed. "Okay." He gasped for air. "You . . . made your point," he uttered through his pain.

"This demonstration is not over yet," Gregory told him. "Now we could drive a cracked rib into your lung . . ." He looked at the small wiry man and winked. "But not today. That could *kill* you."

"Alright!" Naylor was crying. "I won't . . . won't be trouble . . . not anymore," he pleaded. "Just leave the money. I promise, you'll *never* hear from me *again*."

"I'd like to take your word for that," Gregory told him, playfully taunting as he paused for a moment, allowing Naylor a slight glimmer of hope, "but I can't. The lesson is not yet complete. Ribs heal quickly. Now arms . . ."

The larger companion twisted Naylor's arm behind his back.

"God . . . oh God." Naylor was in intense pain. "You're going to break it!"

Gregory nodded.

The larger companion yanked the arm up. The bone in Naylor's arm cracked loudly.

"Ah! Come on, man! You busted it, you son-of-a-bitch!" Naylor moaned in pain.

"I could turn it into a compound fracture," Naylor told him casually.

The larger companion started to push up on the arm.

"Uh, uh . . . Uh! . . . Please don't!" Naylor whimpered.

"We'll save that for another time. I mean, your arm could get infected, then amputated . . . I would hate to see that."

The large companion flung Naylor to the ground.

Naylor groaned as he landed.

"Let me just mention what else we could do to you if you decide to become a problem again," Gregory continued. "The fingers can be exquisite pain centers when stepped on."

Gregory's large companion dug his heal into one of Naylor's hands.

Naylor screamed.

"There's another way to let your fingers do the throbbing," Gregory told him.

His two companions stood Naylor back up.

The small wiry man took Naylor's uninjured hand and rapped the backs of Naylor's fingers over the edge of a nearby table.

Naylor screamed.

"We're almost done with the lesson," Gregory told him. "I was trying to think of a reason we should leave your face without any marks. I can't think of a one."

"I've had enough," Naylor sobbed. "Just leave the money. I won't bother you."

"Sorry. We haven't completed a good professional job yet."

The larger companion backhanded Naylor. The wiry companion punched him in the jaw. They hit Naylor in the face and head five more times until they had beaten him almost senseless, but still conscious. They let go of him. He cascaded to the ground, face up.

Gregory dropped the briefcase he had brought so the corner landed right on one of Naylor's cracked ribs.

Naylor yelped and contracted into a fetal ball.

"No more trouble, shithead. Rest assured, next time we'll cripple you . . . or maybe even take a week or two to kill you. Don't doubt it for a second; we can do it." He kicked Naylor in the head, then again in the side. "We don't expect to hear from you again."

Gregory and his companions left Naylor.

Naylor lay on the floor for a long series of pain-racked moments. But his agony was somewhat alleviated by the briefcase lying next to him. He knew he could recover completely from all his injuries. And the beating in exchange for $100,000 was worth it. If only the pain would subside enough for him to open the briefcase. He even eked out a painful smile as he thought about the money. There he was next to a fortune, if he could just set aside the pain long enough to take hold of it.

Time wore on, short sprinkles of time that seemed eternally long to Naylor, as he tried to overcome intense pain to gather the strength to make the small movements necessary to check the briefcase. Finally, he managed to get his unbroken left arm in position to hold the briefcase. He brought his swollen right hand over to the latch. He struggled with the agony of a broken arm and at least two broken fingers on his right hand, but finally got the latches on both sides open.

The briefcase suddenly popped and crackled with the sounds of a string of blanks. They startled Naylor enough to cause his broken body to flinch. For a frightening flash of a moment, Naylor was afraid he had become the victim of a booby-trap. This flinch unleashed another wave of pain from his numerous injuries.

There was no money in the briefcase—only a note that read: "You were expecting $100,000? Forget it. We let you live."

Naylor was at first overwhelmingly depressed. He had nothing to show for his beating. But his depression started to convert to anger. And it was his anger that gave him the strength to get to his phone and punch in a call to 9-1-1.

When he knew the ambulance was coming, he gathered enough strength for one more call.

"Hello?" Oscar Lusman answered at his home.

"You . . . should've had 'em *kill* me," Naylor muttered weakly. "Mikey and you . . . you're gonna pay. I'll . . . you *mother-fuckers!*" Naylor no longer had the strength to sustain the phone call. He collapsed as the phone remained off the hook.

Paramedics found badly beaten and unconscious Bradford "Slick" Naylor at his home. They quickly transported him to a nearby county facility. He would remain nearly comatose for two days.

✧   ✧   ✧

Mid October: The Following Monday
Harrisburg, Pennsylvania

"HELLO?" A GROGGY MICHAEL EDWARDS ANSWERED. HE GLANCED AT the clock radio next to the bed of his Holiday Inn hotel room. It showed the time as 2:30 a.m.

"Michael, it's Oscar. I've got a real big problem. I've got to talk to you right away."

"What is it?" Edwards asked, still groggy.

"Not over the phone. I need to come see you."

"Where are you?"

"Home. I can be there in three to four hours."

"I've got a speech here at ten. Get here as quickly as you can."

"I'm on my way."

Lusman hung up the phone.

Edwards sighed and went back to sleep. He would find out about Lusman's problem soon enough.

Chapter 17

"THE GUY HAD A PICTURE OF YOU AND HIM TOGETHER!" LUSMAN insisted as he discussed the Naylor problem with Edwards. They sat together at a small table in Edwards' hotel room. Edwards was still dressed in pajamas. Lusman was dressed in jeans and a casual flannel shirt. "He had a picture of you and her signed by her, thanking you. He said he could have ten witnesses with the snap of a finger!"

Edwards shook his head. "If you'd come to me at the beginning of all of this, we could have shut the guy down. But now? We're in trouble."

"I thought you would have insisted on going public with it. You would have ruined your chances before we even got started. I felt what you were doing was more important than letting this slime-doggy shut us down."

Edwards paused. "I don't believe he would have shut us down. It's possible he would have hurt us momentarily."

"He would have strangled us in the crib."

"I'm not going to argue with you."

"Right. We need to discuss how to handle the situation the way it is now. The way I see it, we can deny any relationship with the guy. He's a sleaze. No one'll believe him."

Edwards heaved an irritated sigh. "We can't handle it that way," he told Lusman. "You've paid this guy off, spread out over months. You've had long distance telephone conversations with him. He's been seen with you. You had our security people beat the guy up. Oscar, what you did to the guy is a felony."

Lusman bit his lip.

"We're not going to cover up anything." Edwards paused. How was he going to explain what they needed to do? He gathered his thoughts a moment. "This needs to be handled the way Nixon *should* have handled Watergate. Do you understand what I'm saying?"

"Maybe . . . You better explain it to me."

"Nixon should have immediately admitted someone working for him had done something illegal, and cooperated fully with all investigations. He should have ended his relationship with any and all of his subordinates who had exceeded what was proper, no matter how important they were to him. He should have immediately stated that he did not condone the activity. Do you understand what I have to do?"

Lusman swallowed a lump in his throat, but tears still welled up in his eyes. "I think so."

"I like you, Oscar. You've been a great help to me. And I know this is a tough break. But . . . I wish you'd realized that *how* we win can be as important as *whether* we win."

"I screwed up," Lusman told him, now openly crying. "I screwed up big-time—I just hope I didn't screw *you* up."

"I don't know. I can't control that."

"I really am sorry."

"I only wish all the good you've done for us could somehow cancel this mistake out."

"I appreciate you saying that."

"It just doesn't work that way."

"I know."

Edwards paused reflectively. "You're going to have more problems than just losing your job."

"I know that too."

"I need to ask you one other question. What did Drew know about this?"

"He knew I had a guy claiming he could start a scandal on you. Drew didn't know any details, because I told him I had it contained."

"Thank you for that frank answer. So Drew won't lose his job over this."

"It wouldn't be fair if he did."

Edwards drew a deep breath. "Cooperate with the authorities, Oscar.

I'll be firing the security people. They'll also have to answer for this."

"I'll cooperate."

"Good luck, kid."

Lusman stood up and they shook hands. "I'll be voting for you," Lusman told him.

Edwards smiled.

Lusman left.

Edwards picked up the phone to call Drew Saroyan. After keeping his ten o'clock appearance, an anti-nuclear power speech delivered near Three Mile Island, he canceled the rest of his schedule through to the end of Tuesday. The Edwards Campaign needed to formulate a damage control strategy.

☼   ☼   ☼

Mid October: The Next Day, Tuesday
New York, New York

"SO YOU HAVE AN EXCLUSIVE FOR ME?" TED JESSUP ASKED AS HE entered Edwards' apartment at 6:00 a.m.

"Yeah," Edwards told him sadly as he ushered Jessup into the living room where they both sat down in front of juice and bagels. "A scandal is about to kick me in the teeth. I've called a press conference for four o'clock this afternoon. I'll be telling the public what I'm going to tell you now. I wanted to give you the whole story, before all the insanity starts to swirl around, because I know you'll be fair and accurate."

"Michael, what is it? What could you possibly have done?"

"I'll explain it to you. It'll be better if I take it from the beginning, the *very* beginning—back in the early 60's.

"As I think I've told you, back then I was an adventurous young kid in the Berkeley and San Francisco area, I did a lot of the things left wing radical kids did in those days. I went to protests. I went to concerts. And I did some drugs."

"This isn't one of those 'I-did-marijuana' scandals, is it?"

"I wish it were that simple. I knew a lot of different types of people back then. I'd say most of us eventually yuppy-ized. Some of us self-destructed and never made it out of the decade. Unfortunately, one guy, Brad Naylor, never quite made it out of the gutter. He ran a scam on Oscar."

"A scam . . . on . . . *Oscar?*" Jessup asked gingerly.

"That's the best way I can describe it. Back in those days, I also knew a girl, uh, Fiona McTavish. She died of a drug overdose—she'd mixed LSD and heroin, but it was the heroin that killed her. I was real close to her; we were all friends."

"Were you ever intimate with her?"

Edwards smiled. "There's a reporter's question. At one time, yes. But not at the time she died. She was really crazy. She was a poet and an artist who liked to get as close to the edge as possible and stay there as much as possible. I was a radical protest-type guy, but not as fond of the edge as she was."

"And she slipped off . . ."

"Yeah. It was quite a shock for all of us. This was before there was much publicity about drug overdoses, a few years *before* the deaths of Hendrix, Janis Joplin and Jim Morrison. And we were at an age when we felt absolutely indestructible. To see one of our own dead. . .

"Her death also got a ton of publicity. She was near the top of her class at UC Berkeley and was an absolutely gorgeous girl. She had been written up in the school newspaper as one of the really bright, promising intellectuals developing at the campus. So newspapers poked around and asked a lot of questions. They did a she-got-in-with-the-wrong-crowd story.

"When we discovered her body in a local park, there was a newspaper photographer there. He took a picture of me and Naylor, and about seven of our friends, standing and watching in disbelief as they wheeled Fiona away. There I am, part of that wrong crowd Fiona got in with, standing there with long, stringy, dirty hair, wearing worn clothes and a scraggly beard.

"Naylor showed Oscar a copy of that old newspaper picture to convince Oscar he knew me. Then he showed Oscar another photo. Now I'm not sure how he did this, because I haven't seen the actual photo, but apparently he took a group photo with me and Fiona standing together on Santa Cruz Beach, and made it look like a photo of the two of us alone. He then wrote on it what was supposed to be a message to me from Fiona, thanking me for a 'good time and great stuff.' I'm sure I was photographed with Fiona in groups a number of times at Santa Cruz. I'm also sure she never signed a photo and gave it to me. Naylor must have written the message himself.

"Then Naylor told Oscar he had ten witnesses who would testify that *I* sold her the heroin that killed her. The police tried to find the person who sold her the drugs; they had manslaughter, maybe even second degree murder charges pending. Naylor convinced Oscar they might reopen the case, particularly if a public figure such as myself were involved."

Jessup was puzzled. "Didn't Oscar know there's a statute of limitations involved?"

"For the drug sale, sure. But for murder, there isn't any I know of. Besides that, he convinced Oscar that the publicity alone would ruin me, whether or not charges were brought."

"As a good reporter, I have to ask you, did you sell her the heroin?"

"No," Edwards assured him. "I was never involved with heroin at all. But Naylor could have embarrassed me by linking me to that whole culture—at least that's what Oscar thought."

Jessup sighed. "It would have certainly put you on the defensive."

"Yeah."

"So you never sold any drugs back then. I suppose you did use . . ."

"I'll be honest, Mr. Good Reporter," Edwards told his friend with a smile. "I used marijuana for a couple of years. I dropped acid about ten times, always in small doses. On selling drugs—were you involved in that lifestyle at all?"

"Not really."

"I'll try to explain how it was. I mean, you might buy a lid of grass, make up a few joints, then sell a few to friends. I'd buy joints from friends the same way. So in that sense, I sold drugs. And, if I sold the whole lid as joints, I suppose I'd clear a small profit. But I wasn't doing this to make money. I wasn't what you'd call a drug pusher. My drug activity was just part of a youthfully adventurous lifestyle, a lifestyle I abandoned *completely* thirty years ago."

Jessup drew a deep breath as he reflected. "But I can see how someone might try to label you as a drug pusher, particularly in the current anti-drug climate, and in light of your proposal to legalize drugs."

"Oscar saw those problems too. Because he bought the guy off with money from my campaign."

"Jesus."

"It gets worse. He instructed my security people to beat up this Naylor guy when his demands got beyond Oscar's control. They tortured the hell out of the guy."

"Oh shit." Jessup was horrified. He swallowed hard.

Edwards didn't notice the extreme reaction of his friend. "Yeah," he continued. "The public will say the buck stops with me."

Jessup nodded, with a speechless, nauseated look on his face.

"Do you know where to reach those security guys?"

"Uh, no." But Jessup replied weakly, almost as if in shock.

"I had to fire Oscar. I told him to cooperate openly and honestly with any authorities investigating this. I'm trying to get hold of that Carl Gregory guy to fire his service and get the authorities in contact with him, but I can't find him."

After an uncomfortable pause, Jessup finally asked: "What will you do?"

"Tell everything in a press conference this afternoon." He handed Jessup a ten page press release. "We'll hand them this, then take questions."

Jessup nodded.

"I also had appointments yesterday with three different drug-testing companies. They tested me for *every* drug, including traces of LSD or marijuana. I'll present them to announce their results, without knowing the results myself."

"Yeah. Good idea."

"That press release gives the basic facts. I wanted you to have advance knowledge of the whole straight story from me because I know you'll have the best chance of being fair and putting this mess in context."

"I appreciate your . . . trust . . ." But Jessup seemed strangely distant.

Edwards interpreted Jessup's subdued mood as that of a caring friend sympathetic to his plight. "You know," Edwards told Jessup as he grinned ironically, "Naylor introduced Teresa and me."

"Really?" Jessup seemed able to shake his mood enough to be intrigued.

"Yeah. He was the kind of guy who was always a little bit out of control. He was fun to be with, but a little scary. One afternoon we were on Santa Cruz Beach when he wanted to show how fearless he was with women. He told me to pick out the prettiest girl on the beach, and he'd introduce her to me as if they were long lost pals. It started out as a lark to him, but that girl turned out to be Teresa. In her bikini, she looked like another beach bunny. But when she got dressed in her outlandish clothes, and started to tell me her perspectives on the world, she turned out to be one of the most amazing people I'd ever met. I fell for her—I've never gotten up. So I have Naylor to thank for that."

"But now . . . thirty years later . . ."

"Yeah." Edwards stood up. "I've got to get going. I've got a lot to do this morning."

Jessup remained seated. "Yeah." He finally stood up.

Edwards opened the door and exited to board a waiting limousine.

Jessup also exited, but more slowly. He stood outside Edwards' apartment building for almost ten minutes without moving. Finally, he trudged to a bench at a bus stop at the nearest street corner. He pulled out his cellular phone and an address book, then punched in a number.

"Hello?" Carl Gregory answered.

"You used me," Jessup told him with quiet but simmering anger.

"Who is this?"

"Ted Jessup."

"Oh. The media. Crying about being used."

"You beat up that blackmailer and sent him right into the spotlight. Who are you working for?"

"Not Edwards. Not anymore."

"I'm telling. I'm telling everything. How you got me to put you on the campaign. How you told me there was a drug cartel hit. How you made this scandal happen by infiltrating Michael's campaign."

"You're not telling anyone anything," Gregory told him confidently. "And I'll give you two reasons. First, and you should really consider the impact of this one; I know where to find you, and you have no idea where to find me. Even the cell-phone number won't be traceable to me in about ten minutes. You want to be looking for me over your shoulder for the next ten to twenty years?"

Jessup was chilled by this cold, undisguised threat.

"Second, you're going to look like a damned idiot if this comes out. I used you? The fact is, you were stupid enough to be used. How will it look to all your colleagues in the media?"

Jessup didn't respond.

"It's been nice for you. I've been a good source on a lot of things. And I appreciate how well our relationship ended up paying off for me. So though we won't be in contact again, I'd have to say that we both profited from—"

Jessup hung up. He labored to hail a cab. He would turn over the press release to Andrew Talbot, saying very little about his morning meeting with Edwards. He was ashamed.

☆   ☆   ☆

"THE STORY YOU HAVE BEEN HEARING FROM WWBS IS ACCURATE," Michael Edwards informed a packed crowd of reporters at the Rockefeller Hotel banquet room not far from Edwards' campaign office. Drew Saroyan stood stoically behind Edwards. Teresa stood proudly, though tired from her hurried trip back from California. "The press release details this entire matter. As you can see on page seven, I have been tested for a wide variety of substances, legal and illegal, in just the past six hours. Representatives of the three different companies doing these tests are here now to announce the results. I have not spoken with them since submitting to these drug tests."

The three representatives read off their long list of negative results for everything from sleeping pills to steroids. Of course, LSD, cocaine and marijuana were also negative.

"Now that you have these results, I am open for questions."

For the first time in his campaign, Michael Edwards was glad for the "horse-race" mentality of the media. Most questions were concerned with how his campaign would be affected by these revelations, and whether or not he could continue to mount a viable run for the Presidency. For Michael, these questions were easy to answer: "I will reveal everything I know about this entire matter. We will cooperate fully with all investigations—we will not hold anything back. After that, it will be up to the American people to decide whether or not we have a viable campaign."

A few reporters asked who knew what, when. Edwards answered patiently, then referred them to the passages in the press release that detailed dates and times of "who knew what, when."

Some also asked Edwards about his days with Naylor. He answered frankly, always reminding his questioners that he had not been a part of that lifestyle for thirty years, that he had not personally seen or met with Naylor for approximately the same period, and that he hadn't used any sort of illegal drug since then.

Finally it was over, and Edwards moved away from the podium.

He embraced Teresa with a firm and emotional hug. Their eyes glistened with tears.

"You did well, Michael," she told him as they moved out the side door of the banquet room, arms around each other. "I just wish there had been another way . . ."

"There wasn't," he told her gently but firmly.

"You know I agree. I just hope we don't get penalized for being in a world where not everybody would handle it this way."

Teresa hugged her husband as they moved out of the hotel toward a waiting limousine.

For the first time since the campaign had begun, Michael Edwards felt overwhelming weariness. His deflated campaign had lowered his usually energized mood, and his previous apparent immunity from fatigue, despite a hectic schedule, dissipated. He went home and slept for twelve hours.

Chapter 18

Late October, Election Year: Friday
New York, New York

"I'M GLAD ALL YOU REPORTER-PEOPLE COULD MAKE IT HERE TODAY," Slick Naylor told a large gathering of press representatives. He sat at a worn, portable, folding table in a courtyard between two towering office buildings in the Wilshire district of Los Angeles. Next to him sat a gaudily, casually dressed man in his mid forties, with kinky black and grey hair, very thin in front, but puffed up and unkempt where it was thick, toward the back of his head. They sat on cheap metal folding chairs. The press stood. "Because I know a lot of you wanted to talk to me while I was in the hospital, and I want to tell you everything I know about that scummy Michael Edwards who almost had me killed, who this country was almost ready to elect as President." Naylor's face was still discolored and puffy. His arm was in a cast, suspended in a sling, and six of his fingers were splinted.

Michael and Teresa Edwards, and Drew Saroyan watched the press conference nervously in the Edwards Manhattan campaign office as most networks televised it live.

"First, I am here with my attorney, Mr. Samuel L. Easler. We are suing Michael Edwards for one hundred million dollars." Naylor emphasized the number, slowing his words to dwell on each syllable. "Papers will be filed within the next week. Justice will be done. Second,

I have authorized my attorney to entertain offers for my life story, which will include the story of Michael Edwards and his years as a major drug dealer."

Edwards scowled and looked at Saroyan. Saroyan had been squirming uncomfortably. "If he overplays this," Michael told Saroyan, "he could help us."

"Maybe," Saroyan answered, unconvinced.

Teresa remained silent as she held a stack of papers and envelopes in her hands.

"I'm open for questions," Naylor told his audience.

"Did Michael Edwards himself get involved in the payoffs?" asked a reporter toward the front of the group.

"You bet he did," Naylor replied, almost too enthusiastically. "My old friend called me directly from his home, *many* times. He used that Oscar-guy only as a go-between. They're gonna make him take the fall. But that Oscar-guy was a nobody. A big fat nothing. I would have *never* wasted my time dealing with him."

Saroyan heaved a tortured sigh.

Michael grabbed some paper. "He's being the stupid asshole I remember," Michael stated confidently. He jotted down some notes. "Get someone to make my personal phone records available to the media. We'll make this guy a liar and end his fifteen minutes of fame right now."

"You didn't talk to the guy?" Saroyan asked.

"Of course not," Michael replied indignantly, almost angrily.

Teresa thought of something. "I think Oscar might have called him from here. Remember the night his service called here all freaked out? I think that was the Naylor guy."

Edwards nodded. "Let the media know that." He turned to Teresa. "Good thinking. That could have backfired."

Teresa smiled briefly.

"So Michael Edwards had personal knowledge of your information," another reporter stated.

"Absolutely. He knew I could ruin his power-trip run for the Presidency, with all the stuff I know about. He begged me to keep quiet. 'For the good of the country.'" Naylor whined the last phrase obnoxiously, a warped caricature of Michael Edwards.

"And what stuff *do* you know," another reporter asked impatiently.

"That Michael Edwards made his fortune dealing drugs, not fast food. He was a big-time dealer in Berkeley, and he's still doing it today. I have personally bought drugs from his organization just this year."

Naylor's attorney started to shift uncomfortably in his seat.

Naylor was oblivious to the building skepticism. He thought he had an audience wild to soak up scandal material on Edwards. And he meant to give them as much as possible, whether true or imagined. "And *Teresa* Edwards—she used to shake her cakes at every strip joint from North Beach in San Francisco to the Sunset Strip in Los Angeles."

"What!" Teresa exclaimed.

Now a squeamish expression crept onto the face of Naylor's attorney as he was even more noticeably uneasy with his client's performance.

"I *personally* took nude photos of her with Michael there coaching the poses, like a pimp. I sold the photos to at least ten magazines. Quite a first family we almost elected."

"Pictures?" one reporter asked. "What magazines? Do you still have copies of the pictures?"

"Uh . . ." Naylor now began to realize that he might need to do more than just offer wild, fantastic stories for the media to trumpet. "No, uh, I didn't keep them."

"What magazines?" the reporter asked again eagerly.

Naylor smiled sheepishly. "Folks, this was a long time ago. I don't remember which magazines. I was zonked out most of the time back then, on the drugs that Michael Edwards sold me."

"That . . . *ass*-hole," Teresa exclaimed in a barely-contained rage.

"Are there any pictures like that?" Saroyan asked warily.

Teresa's face flushed red, and Michael decided he had better answer before Teresa came after Saroyan and physically harmed him. "Drew, the guy is telling total lies about us. Teresa led a *protest* against Funny Bunny Magazine."

"That's right," she agreed emphatically, still insulted by the question.

"Of course," Michael added with a sly grin on his face, "one of their photographers came out to the protest and offered Teresa big money to pose."

"And I slapped his face so hard he was looking for the right corner of his mouth somewhere near his ear!"

Saroyan smiled, one of his few smiles in recent days.

"The guy is absolutely lying, and he is nuking all of his credibility. I will bet that by the end of this press conference, Naylor himself will cease to be a problem for us."

Naylor's attorney stepped in. "That'll be all for today," the man said cordially, but his smile appeared forced.

Naylor's attorney hurried him away from the makeshift set-up, leaving a bewildered and grumbling media contingent standing without much to show for their attendance at the brief press conference.

Michael nodded knowingly. "That's the end of Slick Naylor as a problem," he stated with quiet assurance. "The media hates being lied to, especially stupid lies that insult their intelligence. And they hate being manipulated, and treated casually, like coming out to a dramatically announced press conference and having it last five minutes." Michael chuckled. "He might have even created some help for us—he was so slimy that people might not be as angry with us for the beating he got. The media will finish off Slick Naylor."

Saroyan sighed. "I hope so."

"But the scandal he started in motion . . ."

Silence hung in the room a moment as they considered what Edwards was saying.

"So we have a decision to make," Edwards told them with tired resignation. "Do we stay in, or pull out?"

"*These* say you fight it out," Teresa insisted, waving her stack of encouraging faxes, e-mails and letters.

"I've read them," Edwards commented, "but we lost 21 points in three days."

"You have something important to say," Teresa replied, still insistent. "You owe it to those who are still with you to keep going."

"What does General Phillips say?" Edwards asked. In their short association, Edwards had developed deep personal respect for his running mate.

"He's coming in from the airport now," Saroyan told them.

"What do you think, Drew? What's your professional assessment?"

"There are some interesting aspects to all of this," Drew answered, with his mood now shifting slightly. "It's true we are now at 17 points." (The latest national poll results had Hampton with 32%, Parker with 30%, Edwards with 17%, and 21% undecided.) "But there's still a decent core of support. And the biggest jump was in the undecided voters—Hampton gained two points, Parker four, but the undecided jumped 12 points. It's as if your supporters left you, but can't make up their minds now. Have you lost them for good, or just temporarily? I don't know. And I'm relieved to see that Naylor's role is probably going to fade. Because if we have ended the bleeding from this wound . . ."

"So what would you do if you were me?" Edwards asked.

"Depends on what you want."

"Well," Edwards said, hesitating, "I got in this to win."

Saroyan stroked his chin reflectively. "I don't think you can win outright. Maybe if we had more time to recapture what we've lost . . ." He was still in the midst of reflection. "But I was looking at some of these poll results." He showed Edwards a partial list of state-by-state poll results, the ones he felt were the most important:

	Hampton	Parker	Edwards	Undec.
California	33	24	17	26
Oregon	28	29	16	27
Washington	27	32	15	26
Colorado	31	28	14	27
Pennsylvania	37	33	12	18
New York	29	35	14	22
Massachusetts	23	32	15	30
Connecticut	30	27	13	30
Minnesota	30	31	17	22

"Hmmm." Edwards pondered the results. "If we were able to latch on to some of that undecided vote—are you thinking I could win some of these states?"

"With concentrated media ads and appearances, yes."

Edwards nodded.

"Our chance is this," Saroyan explained, now on to a clear train of thought. "If we can win a few of these states, and if this election is close between Hampton and Parker, the whole thing will end up in the House of Representatives next January. Hampton should outpoll Parker, but the House will probably be Democratic. If they go partisan, then we get Parker, the second choice of the people. We would have two months to try to orchestrate a public campaign against Parker, against the second choice. The House has to choose Parker by a simple majority of state delegations. If we can get the first ballot deadlocked, I think the entire process might open up to a compromise candidate—Michael Edwards."

"That sure is a round-about approach," Edwards observed. "And it could throw the country into a bit of a . . . into some anxiety and confusion."

"That's the only realistic scenario that could end up with you winning," Saroyan told him. "I think the American people are in shock right now. They aren't sure exactly what to think about all this. You were in the lead. The American people were ready to choose you. Given two months to remember why they were on the verge of choosing you, they might look for a way for the process to choose you. We'll have that way available."

Edwards did not appear convinced.

"Michael, I don't understand," Teresa finally offered softly, with a confused tone. "What happened to believing? We still believe, don't we?"

"If we've lost the people . . ." Michael's voice trailed off.

Teresa was still puzzled.

Everett Phillips strode into the office, energetic and confident.

Edwards smiled fatalistically and stood up. "Glad to see you, Everett."

"Likewise. Sorry not to be here sooner, but I didn't want to break off my appearances in Pennsylvania. We've still got a chance there—if crowd applause is any measure."

"Not according to the polls," Edwards informed Phillips.

"We were just talking about what steps to take next," Saroyan added.

"Strategy changes?" Phillips asked, not completely understanding.

"It's obvious that this Lusman/Naylor situation has wounded us," Edwards told his Vice Presidential running mate. "We've got to decide what to do."

"What options are we discussing?" Phillips asked warily.

"Withdrawing," Edwards responded with quiet resignation.

"Really?" Phillips asked.

"And Drew also thinks we can win a few states, maybe throw this thing into the House, then try to win back the American public before January. It's certainly the long way around . . ."

"Hmmm," Phillips commented, mulling over the ideas.

The room was silent for a moment.

"Permission to speak frankly," Phillips finally requested.

"This isn't the military," Edwards answered. "You can always speak frankly."

"Good. Because I want to know who put together this *funeral*. If I'd known I was coming to a funeral, I would have worn black. I would have ordered flowers. I would have asked to say a few words about the dearly departed."

"It's not a funeral," Edwards countered. "But I think we have to be realistic—"

"I've got no problem with realism," Phillips replied quickly and forcefully. "But I just can't understand this hang-dog look when we have a lot of work to do." Phillips became more adamant, almost angry as he continued to speak. "We're acting guilty, like we really did something wrong! *Oscar* fouled up. We did the right thing by cutting him loose and telling the voters the truth! That shows that Michael Edwards, the man I am telling people should be President, has strong character, and the ability to make tough calls decisively. As a youth, you did some drugs. You're not a dealer. You never were. As a youth, I got drunk and thrown out of whorehouses on three continents! The people will forgive you! Did you sell heroin to that girl, Michael? Are you guilty? Is *that* why we're talking about quitting?"

"No. I don't know where Fiona bought the heroin."

"Okay. So why are we acting guilty?"

Edwards pondered Phillips' words, considering them carefully.

"Someone around here is making sense," Teresa commented.

"Damn it, Michael, does America need these changes any less now than it did a week ago?" Phillips demanded.

"Well, no."

"You're not asking the voters for favors. You're bringing them something they need. Now, because you had a little kick in the teeth, you're going to walk away? Because the fight got a little harder, you're not tough enough to continue? America needs us. You're serving your nation. How dare you try to back out! Are you a man capable of greatness? Or are you a spineless coward?"

Edwards was stunned.

Saroyan waited apprehensively.

Teresa smiled. She knew how much her husband respected Phillips, and that Phillips' challenge was the perfect answer to Michael's doubts.

Phillips stood his ground, narrowing his intense eyes as he directed them at Edwards, awaiting his response.

Edwards nodded slowly. "I believe my vertebrae are all present and accounted for, General," he finally responded quietly.

"I thought so, sir," Phillips replied, again assuming a supporting posture, but with a faint smile, aware that for a moment, he had been the leader.

"Count on it, Mr. Vice President—at least we'll do our best to get you that job." He paused for effect. "Because *I* intend to be *President*." He turned to Drew. "Let's get our butts back in gear."

Teresa nodded her approval.

Saroyan smiled.

"Awaiting your instructions," Phillips stated firmly and proudly to Edwards.

They all looked at Edwards.

"General Phillips, thank you. Someone had to remind me why I got into this. I won't forget again. We'll meet back here tomorrow at nine a.m. Drew, set up our itineraries. We're ready to hit the road in search of a victory."

That night, the host of the Tonight Show joked: "Slick Naylor's at it again. Now he says that Michael Edwards was part of the conspiracy to kill President Kennedy in 1963, that he started the Viet Nam War, that he was part of the Watergate cover-up, but worst of all that he invented synchronized swimming." Laughter was followed by prolonged applause. The book deal and lawsuit seemed completely ridiculous a mere twelve hours after Naylor's press conference.

☼   ☼   ☼

First Week of November, Election Eve: Monday
New Haven, Connecticut

"I AM HERE AT THE END OF A LONG, LONG ROAD," MICHAEL EDWARDS told a packed crowd at the Yale University Theater. Edwards' mood was intense. He knew he was speaking to a sympathetic crowd of students, volunteers, and other supporters. He knew it was his last major speech before the election. So he not only made his points, but he captivated the crowd with dramatic pauses, deliberate variances in the pace and volume of his voice, and artful gestures. He had become a virtuoso speech-maker, and like an athlete at the end of the season, he relished his last chance to excel at his skill.

He started with a recap of the key points of his candidacy. He then spoke frankly about the scandal that had threatened his candidacy, dubbed by the media as the 'Sixties-Gate' scandal. Referring to his drug usage in the 60's, he argued that if America wanted leaders who had made no mistakes, had no regrets or failed explorations, then America would have very few potential leaders to choose from. Candidates with no mistakes in their pasts were often uncreative candidates, childishly obedient, who had simply replaced their parents and teachers with media consultants and jaded mentors.

Guillermo Fuentes stood attentively, occasionally even cheering with enthusiasm. But if he carried out his assignment, Michael Edwards' speech would be his last appearance as a candidate, and as a live human being. Contreras and Enriquez had learned a great deal from Contreras's previous attendance at an Edwards speech, and Zoilo Metolitican's failed assassination attempt. Fuentes wore an Edwards campaign T shirt, and an "Edwards for President" badge. He also wore faded blue jeans, with stringy holes in a number of places. He had arrived early and taken a position at the front of the crowd, on the side of Edwards' probable exit route. They were aware that Zoilo's sudden movement forward through the crowd, and his conspicuous attire, had obviously drawn the attention of Edwards' security people. In fact, Fuentes was half Argentine, and the German and Italian blood of his ancestors mixed to give him a "Waspish" look—brown hair and green eyes to go with his tannish complexion. Contreras had chosen him carefully. And the plan was designed for him to walk away without anyone ever suspecting his mission.

Edwards continued his speech, arguing that his bold, frank handling of the scandal actually made him even more desirable as a President. "It's a sad fact that people who you count on will make mistakes. Sometimes, they make *bad* mistakes. *Good* people can make *bad* mistakes. The key for a leader is how he handles these mistakes. Does he try to cover them up, particularly when the acts of his subordinate are illegal or immoral? No. We've had too much of that in the last forty years. A leader has to do what I did. And that is how I would handle any similar situation as President. I think that my staff's awareness that I will not back them if they exceed what is proper, will set the proper tone for my administration. It was painful to let Oscar Lusman go. We have missed his hard work. But after what he did, I had no choice. And I believe I made the only choice that you, the American people, could possibly respect. Yes, I have the gall to argue that my handling of this 'Sixties-gate' scandal should make me an even more desirable choice for President."

Guillermo Fuentes looked down briefly at his right hand. He fussed with a brass ring that had a large, dark red stone on it. His ring finger was unaccustomed to this piece of jewelry, despite all the training and practice he had utilizing its unusual capabilities. He sensed Edwards was moving to the end of his speech, and he wanted to be ready for the split second he had rehearsed for months.

And Edwards was bringing his speech to a rousing conclusion. He attacked the notion that a vote for Edwards was a wasted vote because he couldn't possibly win:

"I'm going to tell you a story. Back in the early 60's, as a junior in high school, I was a dorky-looking, cerebral kid. I wasn't what you would call popular—I was the kid you called to help with your homework, not the kid you called on a Saturday night to have fun. I ran for student body president against one of the most popular kids in school. He'd never lost an election—since the Sixth Grade, he'd won eight or nine in a row. He was handsome, athletic . . .

"We both gave our speeches in front of the students. His was slick and polished, cute, but without much content. He'd won all his elections that way. I overcame my basic shyness to present some thought-provoking ideas for the early 60's, pretty tame stuff by today's standards. But my own circle of friends thought I had done rather well.

"At first, my peers' praise satisfied me. I had done my best, spoken my heart, and I had not embarrassed myself. But then I noticed that classmates I had never spoken to came up to me and said 'you don't have a chance in hell to beat Dave Stevens, but I'm voting for you.' I politely acknowledged these greetings, still not believing I would actually get more votes than this undefeated student politician. But as this greeting was repeated more and more frequently, I realized that if they all really *did* vote for me, I *would* win. Each greeting from the young voters fortified me more. Ladies and gentlemen, I *won* that election—I won it in a landslide.

"Now I have found over the last two weeks that many tell me they will vote for me, even though they believe I have no chance of winning. Will I dare to dream that a repeat of my high school student body election could be possible on a national level? You bet I will. And if you believe I am the best man for the job, I implore you to vote for me, even if you don't think I have a chance in hell of winning! Share the dream of our vision of the future! And share the dream that we will be chosen tomorrow to implement it!"

The crowd broke into a frenzied barrage of applause. Edwards stood at the podium for several more minutes, broadly smiling, inciting the enthusiasm, and taking it in like rejuvenating energy. Guillermo Fuentes sighed impatiently. When was the candidate going to shake hands with his supporters?

Edwards finally moved down from the podium toward the center of the front row of supporters, projecting an ebullient mood. Hands reached out for him. Fuentes knew his moment was coming. Edwards would make his habitual hand-shaking trek along the front row, moving toward the exit of the auditorium. Fuentes waited for his turn to engage in a deadly handshake with the candidate.

Edwards shook hands with a few in the center of the front row. But as the crowd began a boisterous, rhythmic chant of "Ed-wards for President," Edwards suddenly whirled around and moved in rhythm back up to the podium, conducting the chant with his arms. Fuentes sighed. How long was Edwards going to celebrate this crowd's adoration?

Finally, after almost a half hour, Edwards decided to make his exit. He was almost dancing as he moved down to the front row again. Fuentes' long wait made him nervous and anxious. He wanted to get this difficult job done. And he saw his quarry moving along the front row toward him. Hands reached out again to be shaken. Fuentes right hand, ring finger adorned with a red ring, was one of them.

But the exuberant Edwards was slapping hands, with both hands, not shaking them. He occasionally thrust his left fist into the air as he strutted confidently and quickly toward the exit. Why was he slapping hands? This was not in Contreras's plan. Fuentes would have to improvise. He resolved to grab and shake Edwards' right hand when it came to him. He could still complete his mission, despite Edwards' unexpected change in behavior.

Edwards arrived in front of Fuentes. His hand came toward Fuentes' hand as other hands also reached for him. Fuentes reached and grabbed. He could feel his grip on bare arm, just below the wrist, and he pressed his ring finger down. But in the quick instant of Edwards' hand-slapping routine, Fuentes had missed his target. A taller man, in his mid thirties, just behind Fuentes, had also reached for Edwards at that moment. And when he had stretched out his longer arm toward Edwards, he had blocked Fuentes' reach, and exposed his wrist as his jacket sleeve rode up his arm.

Fuentes grimaced. He had hit the wrong target.

The taller man pulled back his arm and shook it, annoyed with the sharp pinprick sensation he had felt just below his wrist.

Fuentes now knew it was damage-control time. He stepped back and looked for an escape route through the packed, standing crowd.

The taller man suddenly gasped and cried out as he grabbed his chest. His legs buckled and he crumpled toward the ground, falling into bystanders. He wore a look of utter disbelief as he called out "my heart. . . how . . . I think it's my heart!" He then caught a glance of Fuentes, who was trying to backpedal out of the area.

Fuentes had a grim, guilty look of worry on his face as his eyes met his victim's eyes. Suddenly, the taller man knew—not all the details, but he knew the pinprick pain in his arm was connected to his sudden chest pain, and that Fuentes was connected to the event. But the man was too weak to say anything more. As horrified bystanders tried to assist an apparent heart attack victim, Fuentes melted away into the crowd, and casually out of the area, safe with his secret, but short of completing his assignment.

The Edwards campaign would not learn of the death of this supporter until much later that evening. Edwards was saddened, and sent flowers and condolences to the family. He hoped that the excitement generated by his last campaign rally had not led directly to this man's death. Teresa, and Edwards' closest advisors, reassured him not to feel responsible for it, and he knew intellectually that he wasn't. He just wished this poor man had not been so unhealthy at such a young age that he was so easily prone to a deadly heart attack.

On election eve, the final poll results showed that Edwards was still well back in third place, though he had made some gains. The race between Parker and Hampton was very close: Hampton had 32%, Parker had 29%, Edwards had 21%, and 19% were undecided.

Chapter 19

First Week of November, Election Day: Tuesday
New York, New York

"MR. EDWARDS, DO YOU HAVE ANY PREDICTIONS FOR US?" ASKED A reporter in a crowd of them congregated inside the polling area at Roosevelt Junior College, a few blocks from Central Park on Manhattan's Upper East Side. Michael and Teresa had cast their votes at just after 7:00 a.m., for the benefit of the television news programs. They were smiling confidently, about to leave the polling place.

"I predict relaxation for Teresa and me for the next eight hours," Michael joked.

"Who's going to win?"

"The American people. This is the day they choose their President. Pollsters can measure all the opinions they want and pundits can make all the predictions they want. Today, it is up to the American people."

"Who do you think they'll choose?"

"Someone over 35 who's a citizen of the United States."

"Do *you* have a chance?"

"Of course."

"The polls show you at around 21 per cent. Can you win the Presidency with 21 per cent?"

"With 21 per cent? I can give you a straight answer to that one. I will not win the Presidency with 21 per cent."

"Will you get more than 21 per cent?"

"If we knew that, we wouldn't need to have an election now, would we. I'm patient enough to wait for the people to have their say." Michael and Teresa started to walk away.

"Your husband going to end this night a winner?" another reporter shouted at Teresa as she trailed Michael slightly.

"He's already a winner," Teresa answered, beaming. "I'm so proud of his effort, how well he fought this through."

Teresa and Michael finally moved past the reporters, exited the polling place, and entered a large station wagon, parked and running just outside, with Drew Saroyan waiting inside for them. A crowd of on-lookers applauded them. They both waved.

"Everett's driving over after he votes," Saroyan told them as the car started moving. "He says it'll relax him."

"That's—"

"Around 300 miles," Michael said, finishing Teresa's thought. "We'll meet him later. For now, I will enjoy the rest."

"Me too," Teresa added.

"When are the kids getting in?"

"Pauline is flying down from Boston after her last class, around three o'clock. Heather-Lynn said she had a meeting with one of her designers at noon, but that she'd come over to our hotel headquarters after lunch. All she has to do is take a cab. Keith had a late show last night in San Francisco. He's flying out here, but he won't get to New York until around eight or nine tonight."

Michael nodded. "It'll be good to see them; we haven't had much of a chance to check in with them lately."

Teresa also nodded with quiet but emphatic agreement.

☆   ☆   ☆

5:30 p.m., Eastern Standard Time

"Welcome to a preview tonight's Presidential election," Andrew Talbot of WWBS told his audience. He was sitting on the specially constructed election-night set. "With me is Delores Cushing, my co-anchor this evening," he added graciously. "And also commenting on the results will be Edwin Williams, from the Rogers polling organization, our expert this evening on public opinion. He will offer explanations of the results we will be covering this evening.

"The first polls close in about a half hour from now, in Indiana and Kentucky, and at that time we will begin to get results of the Presidential election. We will also cover House and Senate races, as well as looking at Governorships and some state initiatives of national significance. For the next half hour, we will preview what could be an historic evening, while introducing our anchor and reporting team, and also discussing what keys we will use to gauge tonight's results."

Michael and Teresa Edwards were alone in their hotel room, ready for a long night. Others would join them shortly, including Everett Phillips, who had gotten a late start from his Pennsylvania home.

Talbot went on to introduce reporters in the field at each of the major campaign headquarters. These reporters gave a predictable description of the optimism of the candidates. In fact, they interviewed Drew Saroyan who expressed confidence in a Michael Edwards victory. Saroyan knew this was unlikely, but he also knew it was his job to make such predictions on camera, especially since no polling place had even closed yet, and a large number of polling places would be open for much longer. So his appearance was one more opportunity to impress potential voters.

"Voter turnout is expected to have a major influence on this election result," Talbot continued. "The weather is unusually cold in most areas of the country, except in the west coast and gulf states. But there are no major storms that might influence voters to stay home. The Great Lakes area is still digging out from a moderate snowstorm that ended about 48 hours ago, but right now, it is just cold there, not stormy. Ed Williams, how will voter turnout affect today's results?"

"Well, as you know, Andrew, conventional wisdom is that a higher turnout favors the Democrats. But as with the Perot candidacy in 1992, the Edwards candidacy could also create a larger turnout. Voters discouraged by the conventional choices, who might not have voted at all, may come out to vote for Edwards. So a high turnout could mean a strong Edwards showing. And our information indicates that turnouts are running above normal almost everywhere."

"And another key to this will be the undecided vote," Talbot stated to Williams.

"Absolutely," Williams agreed firmly. "Our last poll for the Rogers organization indicated that the undecided vote was 19 per cent, the highest ever recorded for a Presidential election since modern polling began. And we also attempted to measure a factor we call 'voter volatility,' by asking how many times likely voters have changed their choices since Labor Day. Only 36 per cent of those surveyed indicated they will vote for the candidate they had decided to vote for on Labor Day. 37 percent have changed choices at least once, 19 per cent twice, and eight per cent, three or more times. This type of survey has not been done before, so there is no previous data to compare it to. But when we asked voters if their choices were more or less firm than in the last election, 52 per cent said "less firm," 19 percent said "as firm," 20 per cent said "more firm," and nine per cent had no opinion. Among the Hampton and Parker voters, the "less firm" choice was even higher. So the result today is the least predictable since perhaps as far back as 1948, when Thomas Dewey was prematurely declared a winner over Harry Truman, who eventually won the election."

"This could mean a long night for us here at the anchor desk," Talbot said.

"Not necessarily," Edwin Williams contradicted politely. "The President led the last poll, and despite Bill Clinton's successes in recent history, this country still leans Republican in Presidential elections. There are 11 states, representing 70 electoral votes, that have voted Republican every time since 1964. Spot the Republicans those 70. When you include five more that have gone Democrat only once since 1964, and haven't gone Democrat in over 20 years, add another 41 electoral votes, to spot the Republicans 111. Then add Texas, which hasn't gone to the Democrats since 1976, and we have 143 electoral votes that seem already spoken for. There isn't a single state that has gone Democrat every time since 1964—only the District of Columbia, with three votes."

"So if the President gets off to a quick start, it won't be such a long night."

"Precisely."

"Whether it's a long or short night, count on WWBS to take great care to be accurate when reporting results. Delores?"

"This may be a night of surprises," she said with some drama in her voice, "but not in Dixville Notch, New Hampshire. This small community, not far south of the Canadian border, has a tradition of all eligible voters casting votes at midnight in every Presidential election, then tabulating the results immediately."

As Delores Cushing continued her narrative, a crude, off-white placard stood on an easel, surrounded by a group of warmly and conservatively dressed people, mostly smiling. The placard displayed the results that Cushing would describe:

Ken Hampton (Rep)	17
Michael Edwards (Ind)	12
Victor Parker (Dem)	4
Stanley Green (Lib)	2

"Dixville Notch is certainly no bellwether," she continued. "Last election, the voters chose Ken Hampton. But in 1992, they chose President Bush overwhelmingly, with Ross Perot finishing second. Future election winner Bill Clinton finished fourth, with two votes, behind the Libertarian candidate."

"The candidates also voted early," Talbot said to her, then turning to the television audience. "Our cameras were there for each of them."

As these predictable segments ran, segments that Teresa and Michael had already seen more than once, Edwards said "He's doing a nice job. He has a good chemistry with his co-anchor."

"They seem a little scripted," Teresa observed.

"I'm sure Ted gave Andy a lot of help," Edwards replied. "It's his first election anchor. But he's handling himself well."

The phone rang. Edwards picked it up. "Michael Edwards."

"I'm over here at the Park-Tower," Saroyan told him above the hectic background. "I've done segments for all but one of the networks."

"We saw the one on WWBS," Edwards told him smiling. "Very nice job of telling them how confident we are."

"Yeah."

"Now what's the *real* word?"

"High turnout? High undecided? We've got a shot to put this thing in the House. If it's going that way, we won't know for awhile." Saroyan summoned his best Bette Davis imitation. "It's going to be a bumpy night."

"So look for—"

"Look for slow results, and root against a Hampton landslide, or even if we take a few states, it won't mean a thing."

"Okay," Edwards acknowledged. "We'll see where this whole thing is going to end up."

"I'll call you."

"Bye."

The phone clicked.

✿   ✿   ✿

6:00 p.m., Eastern Standard Time

"Ken Hampton wins the first electoral votes of the Presidential election—Indiana's twelve electoral votes will go to the Republican President. And Kentucky's eight votes are too close to call," Andrew Talbot told his viewers, ushering in the networks's coverage of the election results. "Welcome to the WWBS coverage of this year's Presidential election." The WWBS logo flashed onto the screen as some dramatic, fanfarish music underlined the headline nature of Talbot's greeting at the top of the hour.

Pauline and Heather-Lynn Edwards had arrived and sat with their parents. Everett Phillips and the two children of his who were scheduled to arrive were not there yet; Keith Edwards was also expected later.

The music died down. The camera view came in close on Talbot.

"Ken Hampton's victory in Indiana is not surprising, since Indiana is one of the most Republican states in the country," Talbot continued.

"Yes," Edwin Williams agreed. "Only Lyndon Johnson, in the election of 1964, won this state for the Democrats since World War II, and this is one of a very few states that voted against Franklin Roosevelt twice. And the state also relies heavily on coal and drives a comparatively high number of miles-per-capita. So Edwards' proposed increased taxes on so-called carbon-fuels had little appeal there."

"In Kentucky, there is a tight race between Victor Parker and Ken Hampton," Delores Cushing stated. "Democrats won the last two out of three elections in this state by close margins, but before that, five out of the previous six Presidential elections went to the Republicans. So Kentucky's electoral votes will be closely contested tonight."

"Edwards is also running a distant third in Kentucky," Williams added. "This is a coal-mining state with very little tradition of support for third-alternative candidates. They didn't even give much support to regional candidate George Wallace in 1968."

"So here is where we stand, very early into this election night," Andrew Talbot stated, referring to the graphic that summarized the current results:

Electoral Votes: 1 of 51 resolved (incl D.C.)			Popular Votes: 1% tabulated	
	Votes	States	Votes	%
Edwards	0	0	149,134	13
Hampton	12	1	562,121	49
Parker	0	0	435,931	38

At stake: 526.....
Needed to win: 270

(Candidates under 1% not included.)

"Thirteen," Michael said disappointedly.

"Remember what Drew said," Teresa reminded them. "We need to win a few states in a close election to get this into the House. We probably won't win it outright."

"Drew also said to root against a Hampton landslide. If he wins by eleven points, we can forget it."

✿   ✿   ✿

7:00 p.m., Eastern Standard Time

"The polls have closed in six more states, and we can now put two more in the President's column," Talbot declared, starting the hour's coverage of the election. "Virginia and New Hampshire will both choose President Hampton for reelection," he continued. "The President's quick and easy victories there could be a good sign for him."

The Edwards hotel room was filling up—Everett Phillips and his two large-framed sons had arrived. The only person still not present who was scheduled to be there was the Edwards' son, Keith. They expected him in a little over an hour. The room was quiet. These early results were not cause for much conversation.

"The race in Virginia was not particularly close," Williams told the viewers. "Since Johnson in 1964, Jimmy Carter was the Democrat closest to taking this state. The Edwards candidacy had no appeal here—there is little tradition for his kind of candidacy.

"But in New Hampshire, Edwards has polled well. Hampton's victory will be a fairly easy one, but only because Edwards and Parker split the anti-incumbent vote. New Hampshire has strong Republican roots, but voted for Bill Clinton both times he ran. Ironically, Edwards' strong showing there, nearly 30 per cent, has probably given President Hampton the state.

"In Vermont, we have a similar situation occurring, though the numbers are a lot stronger for Parker. Hampton has a slim lead over Parker, and Edwards is a strong third."

"He's quite close to second place, with 32 per cent to Parker's 33 and Hampton's 35," Delores Cushing added.

"That's true," Talbot agreed. "South Carolina, Georgia and Florida are too close to call right now," he continued. "And we are watching Kentucky, but still can't call a winner there either. So as of right now, Ken Hampton has built a slight early lead." The graphic showing the current results appeared.

Electoral Votes: 3 of 51 resolved (incl D.C.)			Popular Votes: 2% tabulated	
	Votes	States	Votes	%
Edwards	0	0	367,110	16
Hampton	29	3	1,078,385	47
Parker	0	0	848,942	37

At stake: 509.....
Needed to win: 270

(Candidates under 1% not included.)

✧   ✧   ✧

7:30 p.m., Eastern Standard Time

"We have three more poll closings and the first electoral votes for Victor Parker," Talbot announced. "West Virginia goes to the Democrats, as it has in every election since 1956, except for the Republican landslides of 1972 and 1984."

"This is simply not a good state for either President Hampton or Michael Edwards," Williams explained. "This state is a coal state, third in the country in coal production while 41st in land area. The Michael Edwards message of transition to renewable energy is not popular in this comparatively poor state—this transition would devalue one of its major sources of wealth. And as Andy mentioned, conservative Republicans are not generally popular there either."

"We may have a result from Vermont," Delores Cushing told them.

Talbot listened for a quick moment to his earpiece, then looked into the camera. "We do. President Hampton will just barely take this state, edging out Victor Parker. Michael Edwards will finish with over 30 per cent of the vote."

"If this were a larger state, we would not have been able to call it this quickly," Williams told them. "This was a very tight three-way race. This has been a traditionally Republican state, but in 1992 and 1996, the state was taken by Bill Clinton. The pattern tonight was similar to New Hampshire, but the margin of victory for the President is narrower."

"The polls are also closed in Ohio and North Carolina," Talbot added, "but we cannot give you results there yet. So as we approach the next hour, when the polls in 18 states will close, we still have only the very preliminary outline of what shape this election will take."

The graphic showed the current results as the WWBS coverage cut to a commercial:

Electoral Votes:			**Popular Votes:**		
5 of 51 resolved (incl D.C.)			4% tabulated		
	Votes	States		Votes	%
Edwards	0	0		780,109	17
Hampton	32	4		2,110,882	46
Parker	5	1		1,697,883	37
At stake: 501.....			(Candidates under 1%		
Needed to win: 270			not included.)		

Edwards sighed. "Up to a big *seventeen*. Am I going to finish with less than Perot in 1992?"

"Worry about it after those 8:00 results," Teresa advised.

"Yes," Phillips agreed. "There's still a long way to go."

Michael pursed his lips together, then took another deep, nervous breath. He knew they were right.

✧　　　✧　　　✧

7:55 p.m., Eastern Standard Time

"Thank you for that look ahead," Talbot said cordially to the reporter who had just highlighted the most newsworthy Congressional races on the west coast and in some Mountain Time Zone states. With the polls closed only in 11 states, the election coverage was still a hybrid between preview

and actual results. That would change in five minutes. Talbot turned to
Edwin Williams, then to Delores Cushing. "We still have no final result
in Kentucky, Florida, Georgia, South Carolina, North Carolina or Ohio."

"Not yet," Williams replied. "Ohio's going to be very close. And the
state has elected the winner in every election since 1960. So in a close
election, this state could make a big difference. As for the southern states,
demographics there have become more and more complicated. After the
Civil War, for nearly a hundred years, most of the South was fanatically
anti-Republican. But as the social turbulence of the 60's occurred, many
conservatives turned to the Republican Party, feeling the Democratic Party
no longer spoke for them. Some long-time politicians in the South actually
changed parties. Starting in the 80's, Democrats began to make a
comeback, forging a coalition of minorities, predominantly black, and
urban concentrations, which tend to be more liberal. And the elections won
by Democrats since 1964 have had significant southern state victories, with
many contests very close. So we are being very careful not to call those
states too quickly."

"Yes," Cushing added. "Most of us in this business remember that
some of the major networks called Georgia for Clinton very quickly in
1992, then had to withdraw the result when the race became uncomfortably
close. Clinton did end up taking the state, by one percentage point."

"Well, hold onto your seats, ladies and gentlemen," Talbot told his
audience with a beckoning smile, "because we have 18 more poll closings
in less than five minutes." He continued smiling as the camera angle pulled
back, and showed a graphic of the current results:

	Electoral Votes: 5 of 51 resolved (incl D.C.)		Popular Votes: 5% tabulated	
	Votes	States	Votes	%
Edwards	0	0	1,032,497	18
Hampton	32	4	2,581,242	45
Parker	5	1	2,122,354	37

At stake: 501.....
Needed to win: 270

(Candidates under 1%
not included.)

✷   ✷   ✷

8:00 p.m., Eastern Standard Time

"The polls have closed in 18 states, and Ken Hampton appears to be on a roll, capturing Illinois, New Jersey, and five other states," Talbot announced dramatically, ushering in the next hour of WWBS coverage. "Victor Parker will take three states. And Michael Edwards still has not won a state."

Michael slumped back in his chair.

Teresa fought back a tear.

"President Ken Hampton has added 66 electoral votes by taking Illinois, New Jersey, Connecticut, Oklahoma, Kansas, Maine and North Dakota," Talbot elaborated as the fanfarish music announcing the top-of-the-hour coverage faded out. "Victor Parker has added 36 electoral votes by taking Pennsylvania, Maryland, and the District of Columbia."

"Illinois is a big victory for the President," Williams told them. "This one was closely fought, and Edwards will finish a strong third. But ironically, many of the liberal/progressives who might normally have given Parker the margin of victory, have defected to Edwards. So Hampton, needing to outpoll Parker by at least two to one in the suburbs of Cook County to win the state, managed that task fairly easily.

"New Jersey is the other double-digit electoral vote state taken by Hampton. Parker will be about four to six points back. Edwards will finish a distant third in this state with major oil refining industries, with an older electorate not prone to voting for his type of candidacy, and with a relatively wealthy electorate, also prone to conservative choices.

"Connecticut has just enough conservatives to give President Hampton a slight edge. This is another state with a relatively older, richer population, with many working in the usually conservative banking and insurance industries. But this was a three-way race, and Edwards could end up second.

"Oklahoma was an easy victory for the President, Republican since 1964 for President, and rich in oil and natural gas, so not generally excited about Edwards' proposals to phase them out.

"North Dakota is another state that has voted Republican in every election since 1964. President Bush won North Dakota easily in his losing election of 1992. So did Bob Dole in 1996. Edwards is drawing some votes, but this rural state with large mineral reserves is simply not an arena for an Edwards victory.

"Maine has leaned Republican since 1968, voting Republican in every election until 1992 and 1996, when Bill Clinton took the state." Williams smiled. "It's interesting to note that this was Ross Perot's best state in 1992 and 1996. In 1992, he took 30 per cent there, only a point behind second-place George Bush. And Edwards will finish with around 30 per cent. But his push for recycling could hurt Maine's paper industry."

"We should also mention that Maine is one of two states that chooses electors by Congressional districts, with two chosen by district and two chosen at large," Delores Cushing added. "Nebraska has a similar system, with three by district and two at large. So a split in electoral votes in these states is theoretically possible. But we are certain that all districts will go for Hampton, so we can call all four electoral votes for the President. In 1992, one of these districts almost went for Perot."

Williams picked up again. "The Parker victory in Pennsylvania is particularly ironic. It appears that native son, Everett Phillips, actually drew rural conservative voters away from Hampton, giving Parker the edge. Pennsylvania is a classic swing state, with the Democrats and Republicans taking the state about an equal number of times since the end of World War II.

"Maryland is Parker's home state, and has only gone Republican three times since Eisenhower. Hampton will get a few more votes as the western counties and suburban results come in, but he'll still finish far short. Edwards will finish well back in third.

"And the District of Columbia has voted solidly Democratic ever since the Constitutional Amendment giving Washington D.C. three electoral votes. The closest result was in 1972, when Richard Nixon lost to George McGovern by slightly less than four to one. Clinton won in 1992 and 1996 by almost a ten to one margin."

"So, here's where we stand," Talbot stated as the latest graphic appeared. "Ken Hampton has added to his early lead, but still needs 172 electoral votes to be reelected."

	Electoral Votes: 15 of 51 resolved (incl D.C.)		Popular Votes: 6% tabulated	
	Votes	States	Votes	%
Edwards	0	0	1,238,996	18
Hampton	98	11	3,097,490	45
Parker	41	4	2,546,825	37

At stake: 399.....
Needed to win: 270

(Candidates under 1%
not included.)

"Eight other states where the polls just closed are too close to call," Delores Cushing added. "Massachusetts, Delaware, Tennessee, Alabama, Mississippi, Texas, Michigan and Missouri."

"And Edwards is a close second to Parker in Massachusetts," Talbot observed with raised eyebrows.

"Also very strong in the early returns from Michigan," Williams added. "He actually leads by three points there, though no one expects him to hold that lead."

"So a little less than one third of the states are now decided," Talbot observed. "To this observer, Hampton has a growing lead. Any trends you can point to?"

"President Hampton is holding together his victory coalition," Williams responded. "He is holding on to the states he won in the last election. So he has to be considered the favorite at this point. And Edwards is simply not a major factor, though he has split the anti-incumbent vote, and he will probably finish somewhere in the low 20's."

Michael Edwards squirmed in his chair. "He's taken eleven states—this means he's held his victory coalition together?" he demanded defiantly of the television set. "The guy needed *thirty-three* states to win by *four* points, you *robot*."

Teresa smiled. She was glad to see her husband feisty, instead of downcast, as he had appeared to be earlier.

✧   ✧   ✧

8:30 p.m., Eastern Standard Time

"The polls have closed in Arkansas, and that state will go to Victor Parker, giving the Democrats another victory for President in Arkansas," Talbot announced.

"This state has not voted for a Democrat for President who was not from a border state or from the South itself since voting for Adlai Stevenson in 1956," Williams said. "But Parker *is* a border state Democrat, and 1980 was the only year a Southern or border state Democrat *failed* to carry Arkansas. This is not a good state for national third alternative candidates, though Independent George Wallace carried the state in 1968. And this state produces a huge amount of virgin aluminum, something Michael Edwards proposes to tax, as he steers the country toward recycling."

"So Victor Parker is hanging on to his chances," Delores Cushing told them. "Former President Clinton still has profound influence in this state, and he and his wife definitely helped carry Arkansas with strong statewide campaign efforts."

"Here's the board right now," Talbot announced.

Electoral Votes: 16 of 51 resolved (incl D.C.)			Popular Votes: 7% tabulated	
	Votes	States	Votes	%
Edwards	0	0	1,525,801	19
Hampton	98	11	5,621,371	44
Parker	47	5	2,971,296	37

At stake: 393.....
Needed to win: 270

(Candidates under 1% not included.)

"We should look back at some of the states we haven't called yet," Talbot told his audience. "Florida was strongly contested by all three of these candidates, and though President Hampton has—" Talbot paused as he listened to his earpiece. "Well, I'm told we can call more states." He listened again. "Five southern states will . . . they will be split, with the two larger states going to Parker, and the three smaller states going to the President." His eyebrows raised. "And that will result in another 24 electoral votes for each candidate."

Williams hastily shuffled through his papers. "Yes, a lot of trends came together at once, so we are able to call these states. President Hampton has taken the strongly Republican Deep South states of Alabama, Mississippi and South Carolina. These states have voted Republican in every election since 1976, *against* both Carter and Clinton, Democrats from the region. Michael Edwards, and non-regional third alternative candidates, have little success in these states, though Wallace took both Alabama and Mississippi in 1968. But these were Anderson's and Perot's worst states.

"Victor Parker has taken Georgia and Tennessee. Clinton took Tennessee in both 1992 and 1996, and Georgia in 1992, losing to Bob Dole by only a point in 1996. These are states with larger urban centers, and more industry with more industrial workers, so tend to be more Democratic. Again these are not good states for an Edwards type candidacy. Anderson and Perot did close to their worst in these states also." He checked his notes. "But, well, George Wallace took Georgia in

1968."

"So the South is generally splitting again," Delores Cushing said, "which probably means a close election."

"But the Hampton coalition still remains largely in one piece," Williams added. "And he took 334 electoral votes to his opponent's 204 in the last election, with only a 52 to 48 per cent popular vote victory."

"Here's a look at the current results, with about two fifths of the states resolved," Talbot announced:

Electoral Votes: 21 of 51 resolved (incl D.C.)			Popular Votes: 8% tabulated	
	Votes	States	Votes	%
Edwards	0	0	1,835,550	20
Hampton	122	14	3,946,432	43
Parker	74	7	3,395,767	37

At stake: 342.....	(Candidates under 1%
Needed to win: 270	not included.)

But as fast as the graphic was displayed, Talbot was again speaking. Through most of the evening, he had maintained a slightly dramatic, but mainly dispassionate tone. This time, however, his voice was clearly excited. "We have two more state results, and one will make history," he proclaimed. The view quickly switched from the graphic back to him. "Massachusetts is going to go to Michael Edwards. He will take the state's 12 electoral votes."

Michael Edwards sat stunned for a moment, but slowly a broad, proud smile broke onto his face. He heard some howls of delight from others in the room, but his reaction was quieter. He breathed a huge sigh of relief. At least now, if he was only to merit a footnote in the political history of the country, he would have some hard electoral votes to show for his efforts.

"And Delaware will go to Ken Hampton," Talbot added.

"Well, we should discuss the Delaware result first," Williams told them.

"Where did Ted get this asshole?" Michael demanded.

"Didn't he play the robot in the old 'Lost in Space' TV series?" Teresa suggested.

"'Dan-ger, dan-ger,'" Michael said in a mechanical tone, imitating the robot-character Teresa had referred to. "'I might . . . have an emotion . . . red alert!'"

A giggle sounded. The quiet, nervous mood in the room had elevated with the Massachusetts victory.

"Delaware is the only state in the country that has voted for the winning candidate in every election since 1948, when Delaware chose Dewey over Truman. People in my business *love* this state," Williams explained.

"He's going to have an orgasm over Delaware," Michael joked.

There was another chuckle in the room.

"The state is a perfect national cross-section," Williams continued, "with the right proportion of urban, rural, suburban, and other groups of voters. It is a microcosm of the country. And that is why Delaware picks the winner so often. This result points strongly toward a Hampton victory tonight."

Michael scowled, then exhaled irritably. He knew this analysis could be correct, but he wanted to savor Massachusetts.

"Massachusetts is somewhat of a maverick state," Williams added. "It is strongly Democratic, and often votes against the national trend. In 1972, Massachusetts was the only state to vote for George McGovern—even his home state of South Dakota did not vote for him. And this state was certainly not part of the Hampton victory coalition in the last election. But, just the fact that any state has cast its electoral votes for Michael Edwards makes him one of the most successful third alternative candidates in the last hundred years."

"Yes, this is the first time since 1968 that a third party candidate has won electoral votes," Delores Cushing added, in a tone indicating she had prepared her remarks ahead of time, for just such a moment in the election coverage. "In 1968, ex-governor of Alabama, George Wallace, ran as an Independent candidate. His appeal was largely regional, confined to the Deep South. The last time a non-regional candidate won electoral votes was in 1924 when Progressive Party candidate Robert LaFollette won his own state of Wisconsin and finished second in 11 other states. He took 16 per cent of the vote. Before that, you have to look at Teddy Roosevelt's third party run in 1912. Roosevelt finished second to Democrat Woodrow Wilson. William Howard Taft, the Republican incumbent, Roosevelt's party before he formed the "Bull Moose" Party to run in this election, finished *third*."

"So with almost half of the states decided, here's what we have," Talbot stated as the familiar graphic was displayed:

	Electoral Votes:		Popular Votes:	
	23 of 51 resolved (incl D.C.)		9% tabulated	

	Votes	States	Votes	%
Edwards	12	1	2,271,493	22
Hampton	125	15	4,336,486	42
Parker	71	7	3,716,988	36

At stake: 330.....

Needed to win: 270

(Candidates under 1% not included.)

☼   ☼   ☼

8:55 p.m., Eastern Standard Time

"In five minutes, the polls close in 11 more states," Talbot told his audience. "That includes the 33 electoral votes of New York. Right now, we'd have to say that Ken Hampton has built a good lead, but that this election is far from over."

"Also, will Michael Edwards have any more surprises for us?" Delores Cushing asked. "And could these surprises deny Parker or Hampton a majority in the Electoral College?"

"Quickly, we should mention that we still do not have results in seven states where the polls have closed. Kentucky's polls closed almost three hours ago, but it's still too tight for us to call. Florida—we've been waiting for two hours, and though Hampton's lead appears to be building, we're still not ready to call the state. North Carolina's and Ohio's polls have been closed for about 90 minutes, and they are still too close to call. The last three Presidential elections in North Carolina were extremely close, after years of mainly Republican victories. The polls in Texas, Michigan and Missouri have been closed for about an hour. They are also too close to call, though Edwards has given up his lead in Michigan to Hampton. He now trails the President just slightly, with Victor Parker running a strong third. That state is still totally up for grabs."

"We'll be back after the nine o'clock polls close." Talbot looked down at his notes.

☼   ☼   ☼

9:00 p.m., Eastern Standard Time

"Ken Hampton wins three more states, and Michael Edwards takes his second state as the polls close in 11 states," Talbot announced, introducing the coverage for the hour.

"We got another one," Michael said smiling, as most in the room let out an approving cheer.

"Hope it's a big one," Phillips added.

"New York?" Teresa wished tentatively.

Michael nodded. "That would be nice . . ."

"Ken Hampton has taken his home state of Arizona, and the heartland states of Nebraska and South Dakota. And Michael Edwards has taken Rhode Island, his second victory in a New England state," Talbot elaborated.

"No surprise in Arizona," Williams explained. "This is Ken Hampton's home state, and it has gone Republican in every election since 1948, when Truman edged Dewey. Michael Edwards will finish second in this state.

"South Dakota is also solidly Republican, though George Bush carried the state by only four points in 1992 and Bob Dole carried it by three in 1996. South Dakota has been all Republican since World War II—the voters only went Democratic in 1964 for Lyndon Johnson. As we noted earlier, they rejected their home-state candidate George McGovern in 1972. This also means the Dakotas have voted together again, as they have in every election since World War II.

"Nebraska is also no surprise, solidly Republican for a long time. The only Democratic Presidential candidate to win this state since World War II was Lyndon Johnson. Nebraska chose Dewey over Truman in 1948, *and* over Franklin Roosevelt in 1940."

"And as we mentioned earlier, Nebraska has three electors chosen by district, and two chosen at large," Delores Cushing added. "Our results indicate that all five electors will go to Hampton."

"In these three states, Edwards is polling into the mid 20's, but will not win," Talbot added.

"Rhode Island has had a tendency to go for third alternative candidates, giving comparatively strong support to both Anderson and Perot," Williams now commented. "Otherwise, this has been a Democratic state—since 1956 the Democrats have taken all but the 1972 and 1984 elections. But Parker is an out-of-region Democrat, and the environmentally conscious, progressive Michael Edwards had enough appeal to carry the state."

"This gives Michael Edwards the most electoral votes since Teddy Roosevelt in 1912 for a non-regional third alternative candidate," Delores Cushing commented. "Robert LaFollette managed to take 13 electoral votes in a year that saw Republican Calvin Coolidge win a decisive victory. Edwards already has 16 electoral votes in what looks like it may be a close election. One of these candidates *must* capture more than fifty per cent of the electoral votes. That means 270 of the 538 up for grabs. If that does *not* happen, this election will be decided by the House of Representatives currently being elected. That situation hasn't occurred since 1824, the *only* time in our history that a candidate failed to carry a simple majority of the electoral college. In that election, the House chose John Quincy Adams, even though Andrew Jackson garnered the largest plurality of electoral and popular votes of the four candidates who ran. Henry Clay threw his support behind Adams in what was at the time a controversial move considering that Clay was eventually appointed by Adams as Secretary of State. Though both men denied any kind of deal, many cried foul, particularly Jackson's supporters."

"So, back in the present day, here's the board," Talbot said to the viewers. "Over half the state results are in, and President Hampton is just over half way to reelection:"

Electoral Votes: 27 of 51 resolved (incl D.C.)			Popular Votes: 12% tabulated	
	Votes	States	Votes	%
Edwards	16	2	3,303,990	24
Hampton	141	18	5,644,315	41
Parker	71	7	4,818,318	35

At stake: 310.....
Needed to win: 270

(Candidates under 1% not included.)

"In Colorado, Michael Edwards *leads* by four points," Talbot told his viewers. "And in Minnesota, one of the most Democratic states in the country, he is a very close second to Victor Parker. We have Louisiana too close to call, even though Hampton has a six point lead at this time. We may be able to call this state soon. New York—this may be a pivotal state, and is very closely contested. The initial results seem to favor Hampton, with a six point lead. But much of this early tally is absentee votes, which tend to go more Republican. The city tends to vote Democratic, but this is also technically Michael Edwards' home state, and he is expected to do well there. Any of these three candidates could win this state.

"New Mexico and Wyoming are too close to call—Wisconsin also.

"So we—" Talbot listened to his earpiece. "Yes. So we are not ready to call any other states yet. There are . . ." He paused a moment. "There are 14 where the polls are closed but where we have no final results yet. Let's turn to Delores Cushing for another look at the key House and Senate races."

Michael Edwards raised his eyebrows, looked at his wife, then at Everett Phillips. "We may take Colorado." He seemed reflective. "This thing really could end up in the House."

Phillips nodded. "That's our only shot at winning."

Michael smiled, but Teresa could read his mood.

"You aren't having any second thoughts are you?"

Michael's smile remained as he shook his head. "No. Second thoughts? No. But it is beginning to dawn on me just what a mess this could make."

"Not a mess, Michael," Teresa assured him. "It'll shake things up at a time they *need* shaking up."

Michael nodded.

Teresa glanced at Everett Phillips who flashed her an approving smile.

✧　　　　✧　　　　✧

9:15 p.m., Eastern Standard Time

"Ohio's electoral votes will go Ken Hampton," Talbot announced.

"That race is finally callable," Williams told them. "And this is a further indication that President Hampton will end this night successfully. Whenever the Democrats have won Presidential elections, since 1964, they have carried Ohio. Tonight, they *won't*. Edwards showed a lot of unexpected strength in Ohio, ironically helping Hampton. Because many traditional Democrats went to Edwards, as they are also doing in Michigan. That incidently, has made Michigan a tough state to call as well."

"And we can finally call Kentucky," Talbot told his audience. "This was a close one, but Victor Parker has taken it."

"And he needed it," Williams observed. "As with Ohio, Kentucky was taken by the Democrats the last four times they took the Presidency. It will end very close, but Kentucky is firmly in Parker's column."

"We're ready with results in two more states," Talbot said as his eyebrows raised and he nodded. "Hampton will take Louisiana, and Michael Edwards now has his third state—Colorado."

Williams smiled, intrigued with the Colorado result. "Edwards can now claim multi-regional victories. The fact is, Colorado was a great state for Edwards. The state has shown a willingness to go for third alternative candidates. And this state has moved from a mining-oriented economy to aerospace and service industries—mining now employs only one per cent of the work force. Coloradans drive comparatively low miles-per-capita, and they are *forty-ninth* in the country in solid wastes per capita, indicating a recycling mentality. This state is heading in the direction that Michael Edwards wants to take the country. It is no surprise that they would choose him.

"Louisiana has been a tough state to see patterns for. This state voted for Kennedy over Nixon in 1960, then Goldwater over Johnson in 1964. After voting for Wallace in '68, the state went Republican, except when voting for Carter and Clinton. This state was a part of all the recent winning Democratic coalitions—it is another blow to Victor Parker to lose this state. By the way, Edwards is doing better than expected there. He'll finish a strong third, with a great deal of support in the delta and marsh regions, presumably because of his environmental priorities."

"So Ken Hampton is inching closer to another four years, just 99 votes short of winning, while Michael Edwards continues to make election history," Talbot observed as a new results tally displayed:

Electoral Votes: 31 of 51 resolved (incl D.C.)			Popular Votes: 14% tabulated	
	Votes	States	Votes	%
Edwards	24	3	4,015,265	25
Hampton	171	20	6,424,424	40
Parker	79	8	5,621,371	35

At stake: 264.....
Needed to win: 270

(Candidates under 1% not included.)

✪ ✪ ✪

9:40 p.m., Eastern Standard Time

"Michael Edwards has just taken his fourth state," Andrew Talbot announced with the smile of a man who enjoyed bringing the unexpected results of an exciting event to an audience. "Minnesota now joins the Edwards group, coming from yet a third region of the country."

"Edwards' growing strength will only affect this election if Hampton loses key portions of his victory coalition from last election," Williams reminded the viewers. "Minnesota was not part of that coalition. This state has gone Democratic in every election since 1956 except the Nixon landslide of 1972. But this state was also tailor-made for Edwards. They elect their state legislators without party designation, so have a history of choosing candidate over party. And they also have a history of passing taxes for public services. So they have a political culture especially receptive to Edwards' True Costs and True Benefits concepts."

"We still do not have results in four large states, with 108 electoral votes—Florida, Texas, New York, and Michigan," Delores Cushing added. Keith Edwards finally walked in, looking tired, but pleased to join his family. Greetings and introductions were exchanged as the broadcast continued.

"New York is still a three-way race," Delores Cushing continued. "The President has a slight lead there. In Florida, President Hampton leads by—" But she broke off as she looked over at Talbot. She knew from her earpiece that Talbot would now pick up the broadcast.

"We are now able to call Florida," Talbot announced. "25 more electoral votes will go to Ken Hampton. We'll check with Ed Williams in just a moment on the Florida result. But let me complete Delores's update. In Michigan, Edwards has retaken a slim lead over Ken Hampton. And in Texas, we have Hampton with an increasing lead, though not ready to call yet. Ed?"

"Michael Edwards complicated the Florida result, taking a lot of the liberal/progressive vote that normally goes Democratic. But the Sixties-gate scandal and drug policy stances of Edwards were met with a lot of skepticism. Solar power and reducing greenhouse gases have become attractive issues in this state. But Edwards could not overcome his negatives enough to challenge for second."

Michael sighed. "We worked hard in that state."

"But not after the Naylor thing hit," Teresa reminded him. "Drew was right to give it up as a lost cause."

"Drew was right about something?" Edwards asked his wife in humorous disbelief.

"Sure," she answered without hesitation, and not acknowledging her skepticism about him throughout most of the campaign.

"Can we call—?" Talbot stopped his question. "No," he followed up quickly. "We'll be—" He stopped himself again. "Wait just a minute." He listened to his earpiece. "Texas is now decided. And this is another big boost for Ken Hampton, because we are projecting that the President will take this state by five points. Let's see—" Talbot seemed to stammer in confusion. "We'll hear from Ed Williams first, then look at the board. Ed?"

Williams quickly glanced at his notes. "Texas is indeed a *big* victory for Ken Hampton. Bill Clinton was the first Democrat to win the White House without carrying Texas, and he did it twice. But he also took Illinois, New York and California, among other large states. With Florida and Texas going to the President, you'd have to say it's only a matter of time before he wins this election."

"And as the board shows now, he's 42 electoral votes from a victory this evening," Talbot added as the latest results displayed:

	Votes	States		Votes	%
Electoral Votes: 34 of 51 resolved (incl D.C.)			**Popular Votes:** 18% tabulated		
Edwards	34	4		5,368,983	26
Hampton	228	22		8,053,474	39
Parker	79	8		7,227,487	35

At stake: 197.....
Needed to win: 270

(Candidates under 1% not included.)

Edwards slumped in his chair. "Ken Hampton, our next President."

"It's not over yet, Michael," Phillips assured him.

"Close," Michael said.

"He's got to *get* those 42 votes before I give up on this," Teresa insisted.

Michael smiled. "You're right, of course. Now we have to root for Victor Parker, don't we . . ."

"*And* Michael Edwards," Phillips reminded him. "We might have a shot at some more states."

Michael nodded. "We have to root for *anybody* but *Hampton*."

✿　　　✿　　　✿

9:55 p.m., Eastern Standard Time

"We have nothing new for you at this time," a wearying Andrew Talbot told his audience. "Specifically, New York is simply too close to call right now. We realize you may know that one network has called this state for Hampton. Hampton is surging back after losing his early lead, as the upstate results come in. We simply cannot call this state yet. All we can say for sure is that Edwards appears out of this race. He will not win the state, though he has taken over thirty per cent of the vote there. We are also still awaiting results in Michigan, New Mexico, Wyoming, Wisconsin, Missouri and North Carolina. In five minutes, we have poll-closings in five more states. Will these states give Ken Hampton the 42 votes he still needs to claim victory?"

"Very possibly," Williams answered.

"We'll be back to find out," Talbot assured his audience with a confident grin.

✿　　　✿　　　✿

10:00 p.m., Eastern Standard Time

"Ken Hampton has taken three more states, bringing him to the verge of winning this election," Talbot announced as the top-of-the-hour coverage began. "Victor Parker has taken one more state, but he is lagging behind as Hampton's lead in electoral votes widens."

As the logo and fanfare announced another hour of WWBS coverage, Michael Edwards decisively and fatalistically grabbed the phone. "Get me Drew," he said. "Drew. Anyone else call New York?. . . Hmm . . . Yeah. I agree . . . Okay. Give me a call." He hung up the phone. "One of the networks gave New York to Hampton. If New York goes to Hampton, we've got to go down to the hotel and throw in the towel. If the rest of the networks call New York for Hampton, we'll go down there, wait for the west coast polls to close, then . . ." He didn't finish verbalizing his thought. Everyone knew what he meant.

"Utah, Idaho and Nevada will all go to the President," Talbot told the viewers, expanding his top-of-the-hour headline statement. "With 13 more electoral votes, this brings Hampton to within 29 of victory."

"New York's 33 will do it," Williams commented.

"Give that man the Pulitzer—he's a *genius*," Michael blurted out.

"That's true," Talbot acknowledged to Williams through a forced, exaggerated smile. Michael smiled too. He could tell from the artificiality of Talbot's smile that he was not happy with the interruption. "Victor Parker will take the seven electoral votes in Iowa," Talbot continued. "Montana is too close to call right now."

"Well, again, Utah is no surprise at all," Williams commented. "This state has elected Republicans with huge margins in recent years, and hasn't elected a Democrat since Johnson in 1964. In 1992, Perot finished second to Bush—the anti-incumbent vote went to Perot over the Democratic candidate. And Edwards is also on his way to a second-place finish. This is a young state with a growing aerospace industry, so Edwards had some appeal there.

"Idaho is just about as Republican as Utah. But Edwards will actually be a close second to the President in this state. This is a young state that uses a lot of renewable energy, mainly hydroelectric. The silver mining industry could have some fear of Edwards proposed policies—that, and a general conservatism in the state probably prevented Edwards from making this his fifth state tonight. Parker will end up back in third place.

"Nevada is also a staunch Republican stronghold, though Clinton took the state by three points in 1992, with Perot a strong third. Clinton won again in 1996, by the even smaller margin of two points. It is interesting to note that Nevada has voted for the winning candidate in every election since World War II except for the close 1976 election when the state chose Ford over Carter. Edwards is doing extremely well in Nevada also. The state has a tradition of not legislating victimless crimes. Prostitution and gambling are regulated but legal. So Edwards' drug policies do not challenge Nevada's political culture at all.

"Iowa has gone from being consistently Republican, up until 1984, to being consistently Democratic, choosing the Democratic candidate in every election since choosing Dukakis over Bush in 1988. The Edwards agenda never had a lot of appeal here, except maybe close to the river."

"So as we approach the last group of poll-closings next hour, here is where the Presidential election stands," Talbot said.

	Votes	States		Votes	%
Electoral Votes: 38 of 51 resolved (incl D.C.)			**Popular Votes:** 27% tabulated		
Edwards	34	4		8,363,224	27
Hampton	241	25		12,080,266	39
Parker	86	9		10,531,466	34

At stake: 177.....
Needed to win: 270

(Candidates under 1% not included.)

Delores Cushing began an update on some high-profile state elections, eventually referring the audience to other reporters covering various regions.

"What about New York?" Michael demanded impatiently.

"Call Drew," Teresa suggested.

"Drew promised to call *me* when he hears something," Michael replied. "I'm tempted to flip channels to see if anyone else has called New York for Hampton."

There was a collective, almost unison groan from the Edwards children, who were familiar with their father's channel-flipping habits.

"Drew has the room with all the monitors," Teresa reminded him. "I thought we agreed we'd stay with Ted Jessup's people. If we start flipping channels, we'll lose track of *everyone's* coverage."

"Not the way I'll do it," Michael assured them. But he caught sight of his son Keith's expression. "No?" he asked Keith.

"I have memories of a lot of partially watched TV shows," Keith told him. "And *missing* the most important parts."

Michael saw that his two daughters were not jumping to his defense. "Alright," he finally agreed begrudgingly. "I won't flip. But I just want—" He gathered his thought. "If Hampton's going to win New York, then let's find out *now*. I'm tired of *waiting*."

Michael certainly spoke for everyone in the room.

Chapter 20

10:25 p.m., Eastern Standard Time

"This is a good time to summarize the situation in the eight states where the polls are closed and we have no results yet," Andrew Talbot suggested to his viewers. "As we recall, Ken Hampton needs 29 electoral votes to put him over the top. So New York's 33 will win him this election. Hampton started out leading, fell behind, then surged back. Right now, the President leads by two points with 36 to Parker's 34 and Edwards' 30. But just a half hour ago, his lead was four points. We are told that the results now filtering in are mainly from the boroughs of New York City, where Parker will be the heavy favorite. Will there be enough—" Talbot stopped in mid sentence as he listened to his earpiece. "I understand we are now calling New Mexico and Wyoming," he told the audience.

Graphics of those two states appeared as Talbot expanded his announcement.

"The three votes of Wyoming will go to the President, inching him closer to victory. But New Mexico will go Democratic, giving Victor Parker an additional five electoral votes."

Edwin Williams hurriedly shuffled through his notes. "Well, Wyoming is a traditionally Republican state, choosing the Republican candidate every time since World War II except for Truman over Dewey in 1948, and Johnson over Goldwater by a slim margin in 1964. Michael Edwards complicated this result, and he will do well there. But this is a state rich in oil, natural gas, uranium, and timber, all industries which could suffer with Edwards' policies. So though he'll finish in the high 20's or low 30's, he did not have enough appeal to carry the state.

"New Mexico is probably the least Republican state of this region, choosing Kennedy in 1960, and Clinton in 1992 and 1996, when most of the other states of the region went Republican. Among other factors, a growing Hispanic population that has become increasingly politically aware has led to more Democratic votes. And the Parker organization mounted a huge get-out-the-vote strategy that may well have won him this closely contested state."

"This has to be excruciating for the President," Delores Cushing observed with a whimsical gleam in her eye. "The signs all point to his reelection tonight, and the first 200 votes seemed to mount up so quickly. But the last 70 are dribbling in."

"Excruciating for *him*," Michael almost shouted.

"Yeah," Teresa commented. She smiled. "What about the poor man's *wife*?"

"And *children*," Heather-Lynn Edwards added.

"As the board shows, Wyoming has brought President Hampton to within 26 votes of winning this election," Talbot said, replying to Cushing's remark, "a bit closer, but still short of victory."

Electoral Votes: 40 of 51 resolved (incl D.C.)			Popular Votes: 34% tabulated	
	Votes	States	Votes	%
Edwards	34	4	10,921,520	28
Hampton	244	26	14,822,064	38
Parker	91	10	13,261,846	34

At stake: 169.....
Needed to win: 270

(Candidates under 1% not included.)

✿   ✿   ✿

10:40 p.m., Eastern Standard Time

"We're going to interrupt our report on the Senatorial elections to bring you some more Presidential results," Talbot announced excitedly. "We are finally able to call New York. President Kenneth Hampton may yet get those 26 votes needed for victory, but it won't be from New York.

Our projections are now certain. Victor Parker will win New York."

A few cheers came from the room, and Michael Edwards heaved a big sigh of relief.

"The upstate voters went solidly for Hampton over Parker as expected," Williams explained, "but there was a significant defection to Edwards in this relatively progressive state. Edwards ideas' were attractive to many of the suburban progressives, in a state with the lowest per capita BTU consumption in the country, and also a low miles-driven-per-capita. The resolution of this state came down to one factor—the defection to Edwards was stronger in the suburbs and upstate, where Hampton's support was, than it was in the boroughs, where Parker's support was."

"So President Hampton continues to wait as the west coast poll-closings approach," Delores Cushing added.

"With New York decided, here's where we stand," Talbot said.

Electoral Votes: 41 of 51 resolved (incl D.C.)			Popular Votes: 42% tabulated	
	Votes	States	Votes	%
Edwards	34	4	13,491,290	28
Hampton	244	26	18,309,608	38
Parker	124	11	16,382,281	34
At stake: 136.....			(Candidates under 1%	
Needed to win: 270			not included.)	

Edwards smiled. "That means one of the networks ate some major crow."

Teresa also smiled. "Which one?"

"I don't know."

"I hope it was Samuelson's crew," Teresa commented.

"Yeah." Edwards shook his head. "28 per cent—over one fourth. Maybe we *did* get something done."

Everett Phillips now added his smile. "And maybe we're not done yet."

"You know, I'll bet that network picked Hampton the winner of the whole thing," Edwards surmised. (Actually, the network in question, not Samuelson's, pulled back its New York projection before making the larger mistake of calling President Hampton the election winner.)

✧   ✧   ✧

10:55 p.m., Eastern Standard Time

"On the verge of the west coast poll-closings, we are able to call one more state, another one for Victor Parker," Talbot announced.

Edwards inhaled and exhaled with an exaggerated motion. "Hanging on by our fingernails . . ."

Teresa and Everett Phillips smiled.

Everett Phillips held up his hands—his strong, thick fingers were tipped off with closely cropped nails. "Not by *these,* I hope."

Now Edwards smiled as he listened to Andrew Talbot detail the latest result.

"North Carolina will go to Victor Parker. This is another 14 votes that will not go into President Hampton's column."

"And this state *was* a part of the Hampton victory coalition last election," Williams added. "This will be a 41 to 41 vote; Edwards will get only 18 per cent. But we are now able to say, with just over 80 per cent of the vote counted, that Victor Parker's 41 will be higher. Third alternative candidates do not traditionally do well in this state, though some support developed in tobacco regions. Legalized marijuana could rejuvenate tobacco-growing areas, slumping with the continually decreasing demand for cigarettes. Republicans have won his state in recent years, but by close margins. The Democrats finally broke through."

"Despite losing this state, the news is still favorable for Ken Hampton," Talbot continued. "He leads in Wisconsin and Missouri, two states we're not ready to call yet, but that represent another 22 electoral votes if he holds on. Michigan remains contested, but he has swept the Midwestern states of Ohio, Illinois, and Indiana. Michigan would be another 18 votes. And the west coast polls, with the huge, electoral vote prize of California, are about to close. California has voted Republican in every election since 1948, except when voting for Lyndon Johnson and Bill Clinton in solid Democratic victories. Close recent Presidential elections have had Californians voting Republican."

Williams nodded. "Yes, all the signs still point to a Hampton victory, though we cannot call it a certainty until all the votes are confirmed."

"Next hour could do it," Talbot said with quiet anticipation. "We'll be back in a moment."

The graphic showing the current results appeared:

	Electoral Votes: 42 of 51 resolved (incl D.C.)			Popular Votes: 44% tabulated	
	Votes	States		Votes	%
Edwards	34	4		14,133,733	28
Hampton	244	26		19,181,494	38
Parker	138	12		17,623,390	34

At stake: 122.....
Needed to win: 270

(Candidates under 1% not included.)

✿   ✿   ✿

11:00 p.m., Eastern Standard Time

"The polls have now closed in all but one of the fifty states—they just closed in the west coast states and Hawaii. We can call one state, but at this time, the Presidential election remains unresolved," Andrew Talbot declared dramatically.

"They call California for Hampton and we're done," Edwards observed.

"So they obviously didn't," Teresa added.

"Nope," Michael agreed, realizing that didn't preclude such a call in the very near future.

"Victor Parker will take Hawaii fairly easily, with Michael Edwards just barely out-polling President Hampton for second place in the state," Talbot continued. "The four more votes for Parker are not as important as the fact that this is four more votes that President Hampton will not get."

"That's absolutely correct," Williams agreed. "At this time there are eight states and 118 electoral votes still not decided. Even if Victor Parker takes all of those remaining votes, he would still finish 14 short of victory. So the only candidate who can win this election outright tonight is President Hampton. And he needs only 26 of those 118 votes.

"As for Hawaii, this state has only gone Republican twice since its history as a state, for Nixon in 1972 and for Reagan in 1984, both Republican landslide victories. The state embraced progressive candidate John Anderson more, compared to national averages, than populist Ross Perot. Edwards' policies had some appeal, but not enough to deny Victor Parker an easy victory there."

"In the all-important state of California, Ken Hampton has the early but slim lead over Michael Edwards," Talbot informed the viewers.

"Victor Parker is trailing in third place. With around four per cent of the vote counted, President Hampton has 37 per cent, Edwards 35 and Parker 28.

"Edwards is off to a lead in Oregon, and Parker has the early lead in Washington. We—" Talbot was interrupted again by something coming through his earpiece. "We are . . . okay, not yet . . ." He paused for an awkward moment.

"Say something, Andy, you look goofy," Michael advised his colleague.

Teresa giggled. "Would you be doing any better?"

"Hell yes," Michael told her with an overconfident smile. They both knew he didn't really know if he could have handled this complicated and sometimes dramatically surprising election any better than his young successor.

"We're getting some new results," Talbot finally explained. "But let's take a quick look at the board while we get our heads together here."

Michael chuckled as the graphic appeared. He knew his colleagues needed a quick off-air conference, but Talbot wasn't supposed to come so close to admitting it.

	Electoral Votes: 43 of 51 resolved (incl D.C.)		Popular Votes: 45% tabulated	
	Votes	States	Votes	%
Edwards	34	4	14,971,702	29
Hampton	244	26	19,101,189	37
Parker	142	13	17,552,444	34

At stake: 118.....
Needed to win: 270

(Candidates under 1% not included.)

The graphic lingered a little longer than it had normally been displayed earlier in the evening's coverage. The vote totals even changed once before Andrew Talbot came back on.

"In a stunning upset, Michigan will go to third alternative candidate Michael Edwards. This is another 18 electoral votes that will *not* go to Ken Hampton." Talbot was smiling broadly.

The Edwards hotel room made some noise of applause, but was relatively subdued. The result also stunned them. Michael leaned his head forward and widened his eyes almost as much as his smile, in happy disbelief.

Edwin Williams shook his head dubiously. "This is . . . I am really surprised," he finally said, groping for words.

"His robotic chips are overloading," Michael joked. "I can see smoke coming out of his circuits . . ."

Giggles filled the room.

Williams continued. "Our exit polls show that Michigan workers normally loyal to Democrats, blue-collar union workers, auto workers, voted with their pocketbooks. Edwards' policy of encouraging the purchase of electric cars could very well rejuvenate the American auto industry. And these same factories can be converted relatively easily to the production of windmills—several automobile manufacturers have indicated they might enter this area. Edwards policies would create an enormous demand for these products. So Michigan's workers chose a candidate whose proposals might create tangible demands for their work."

"And the auto industry favors the Edwards ideas over the regulatory approaches of the Democrats, and even Republicans," Delores Cushing added. "Instead of mandated standards, the industry is left to come up with the best designs that will succeed in the new marketplace, where there are tax credits for vehicles that use less gasoline."

"That is absolutely correct," Talbot agreed. "Michael Edwards made a number of speeches pointing out that his policies welcomed both so-called hybrid vehicles and purely electric vehicles. The hybrid vehicles run on both electricity and gasoline, and some government regulators have clashed with the auto companies over their development, feeling that the car companies are trying to avoid producing electric cars. The auto industry has argued that a purely electric car with the range and speed of a gasoline-powered car would be prohibitively expensive and technically awkward. A hybrid vehicle can travel for the first 50 miles on electricity, with the batteries then recharged as the vehicle uses gasoline to travel further. Most commuter trips are under 50 miles. And the vehicle can take the long trips without recharging constantly, or having huge arrays of batteries. In the Edwards scheme, there would be less of a tax credit for the purchase of a hybrid vehicle, because it uses some gasoline, but still some tax credit. This could serve as a transitional vehicle as electric vehicle and battery technologies develop. And as the gasoline tax phases in, consumers will be able to choose between hybrid and electric vehicles to deal with the escalating cost of fuel. Instead of having these innovators pitted against each other, Edwards feels his approach encourages all of them, and the creators of solar and hydrogen vehicles as well."

"This Edwards message obviously played well in Michigan, where the auto industry is tired of this regulatory wrangling," Williams added. "And Michigan was an important part of the Hampton victory coalition last election. I have to say, that unless he can win California, President Hampton may well have trouble securing 270 electoral votes tonight."

Michael Edwards wore his first real smile since the polls had closed in Indiana and Kentucky, just over five hours before.

"We should take a quick look at the House," Delores Cushing told her colleagues. "If the election ends undecided tonight, then it will be decided in the House of Representatives in January. There are still undecided races on the west coast and in other states. But based on what we know now, the Democrats will control somewhere between 230 and 245 of the 435 seats. They bounced back from the 1994 election to retake the majority, and they won't lose it tonight. This would seem to give Victor Parker the edge—"

"But they would vote by states, not by individuals," Edwin Williams quickly added, wanting to avoid any misunderstandings or mistakes. "To be accurate, we would need to—"

"Excuse me," Andrew Talbot interrupted cordially, "but we are now ready to call two more states, and this brings President Hampton to the brink of victory. Missouri and Wisconsin will both go to the President. That adds 22 votes to his total, leaving him only four votes short."

"This is like riding a God Damn roller coaster," Keith Edwards blurted out. "One minute we look real good, then the next minute we have happy Hampton looking good."

Michael nodded. "And you're the guy who just got here—think what the rest of us have been dealing with."

Williams nodded in response to Talbot. "Both of these states went to Hampton simply because Edwards took votes away from Parker. Missouri has gone Democratic in recent Presidential elections, and probably would have gone that way in this one as well. And the voters there don't usually go for third alternative candidates. But Edwards' environmental priorities got him support along the Mississippi River, some tobacco farmers liked his drug legalization policies, and the aerospace industry in Missouri also supported him. The state has a large Republican core of support that gave the state to Reagan twice, and to Bush in 1988. Edwards took enough votes away from Parker to allow that Republican core to prevail.

"Wisconsin has been solidly Democratic for President since 1984. But this is also a progressive state, with environmentally conscious policies, and with auto industries, creating a strong appeal for Michael Edwards. And Ross Perot *led* this state in 1992 just before he dropped out during the summer. This state might have gone to Edwards if it wasn't for the Sixties-gate scandal."

"Ed, there's one more state result in . . ." He paused for dramatic effect. "The four votes of Montana are now spoken for."

"Here it comes," Michael speculated apprehensively.

Teresa drew a deep breath.

Everett Phillips sat up and moved to the edge of his seat.

"This has been a Republican state in recent years," Talbot continued. "But tonight, as they went for Bill Clinton in 1992, Montana's voters have chosen Victor Parker."

Michael was again relieved, smiling, almost laughing at his own tenseness over something that was now totally out of his control.

"Dad, I'm gonna be a nervous wreck!" Keith Edwards complained good-naturedly.

"I should have remembered to have a piano in here for you to bang on," Michael replied.

"This is *worse* than a roller coaster, Daddy," Heather-Lynn Edwards added. "At least those end pretty quickly."

"You guys are a bunch of weeping wussy wimps," Pauline Edwards told them scornfully. "I think this is *fun*."

"Yes," Williams added to Talbot's announcement. "This state has been a Republican stronghold since 1964. But Clinton carried the state by two points in 1992. Edwards was a factor tonight, and some progressive influences have been felt in this state recently. But the substantial timber and mining industries in the state, and a high miles-per-capita-driven, undoubtedly made Edwards less appealing than Parker to remove the incumbent. And there was apparently a strong anti-incumbent mood in this state here again, as there was in 1992, despite the fact that Hampton is from this general region."

"We still may be on the verge of a decision," Talbot told his audience, "with President Hampton just four votes short of victory, and four states to get them from." The updated graphic appeared on the screen:

Electoral Votes:			Popular Votes:	
47 of 51 resolved (incl D.C.)			49% tabulated	
	Votes	States	Votes	%
Edwards	52	5	16,864,113	30
Hampton	266	28	20,799,073	37
Parker	145	14	18,550,524	33

At stake: 75.....
Needed to win: 270

(Candidates under 1% not included.)

☼   ☼   ☼

11:45 p.m., Eastern Standard Time

"The long night wears on," Talbot told his viewers. "Victories in either Oregon or Washington would have given President Hampton his reelection to the White House. But our projections show that Michael Edwards is going to win *both* of these states."

Michael's eyes widened and his face registered pleasant surprise, both with the result, and the swiftness of the announcement. He heard some cheers of delight, and a few "all-rights!" from those around him.

"Ken Hampton is clinging to a slim two point lead in California. And we still have Alaska's result to determine, when the polls there close in about 20 minutes. Ed, it looks like Edwards has strong appeal on the west coast."

"No doubt about it," Williams confirmed. "Both of these states have shown a tendency to support third alternative candidates—these were among the strongest states for both Anderson in 1980 and Perot in 1992 and 1996, and were stronger supporters of both of those candidates than California. They have also voted together in every election since 1948, except 1968, when Oregon voted for Nixon, and Washington voted for Humphrey. They have also voted Democratic for President since 1984. So they weren't part of the Hampton victory coalition. But the Wisconsin scenario could have replayed in either one of these states. Edwards and Parker could have split the anti-Hampton vote.

"Washington's aerospace industry helped Edwards to a fairly easy victory there, by six points. Oregon was slightly tighter for Edwards—the state has an older population, but is also strong in using renewable energy, particularly hydroelectric, and very strong in recycling."

"We'll keep tabs on California," Talbot added. "For now, here are the national results up to this moment:"

Electoral Votes: 49 of 51 resolved (incl D.C.)			Popular Votes: 56% tabulated	
	Votes	States	Votes	%
Edwards	70	7	19,273,272	30
Hampton	266	28	23,770,369	37
Parker	145	14	21,200,599	33

At stake: 57.....
Needed to win: 270

(Candidates under 1% not included.)

✩   ✩   ✩

12:00 midnight, Eastern Standard Time

"Ken Hampton has taken his 29th state as the polls close in Alaska," Talbot told his audience dramatically, almost playing with them as he paused before adding the key information that he knew was most important. "But he is still *one vote* short of victory."

"He took Alaska," Edwards observed. "It's down to California." He picked up the phone and punched in a number. It was late. He should have been tired. But he was functioning on nervous energy, and not even tempted by the need to sleep. "Drew Saroyan, please," he said into the phone. He waited to hear the rest of the network results.

"The three votes of Alaska will go to President Hampton," Talbot continued. "So this election now hinges on California."

"When was the last time California decided an election?" Delores Cushing asked with a smile of amazement. "If *ever*?"

"Certainly not in any modern election," Williams told them. "In checking our figures, we simply don't have enough information to call this state yet. This is a more conservative state than the other two west coast states that have already gone for Edwards. Parker is trailing both President Hampton and Michael Edwards. The state will go to one of them. The President still leads by a little more than a point.

"In Alaska, President Hampton was an easy choice. Perot ran strong there in 1992, but this state has gotten rich on oil. The citizens enjoy many advantages from the oil income. Edwards' policies had a lot of self-interest to overcome here. And since 1976, this has been a Republican state, going for Bush in 1992 against Clinton, even with 27 per cent of the vote for

Perot. In fact, 1992 was the first election since statehood that Alaska did not vote for the winner."

"We'll have our magnifying glasses on California," Talbot followed-up. "Here are the results up to now, with all but one state decided:"

	Electoral Votes: 50 of 51 resolved (incl D.C.)		Popular Votes: 59% tabulated	
	Votes	States	Votes	%
Edwards	70	7	20,305,769	30
Hampton	269	29	25,043,781	37
Parker	145	14	22,336,346	33

At stake: 54.....   (Candidates under 1%
Needed to win: 270   not included.)

Just as the graphic came on, Drew Saroyan came to the phone. "Yes," he answered.

Michael could hear the boisterous sounds of an excited group of people in the background. "Is Hampton going to take California?" Michael asked.

"Who knows?" Saroyan answered, glad to hear from his candidate. "What a night . . ."

"What about the other networks?"

"No one has called it."

"Should I come down there?"

Saroyan considered the question. "Yeah. Pretty soon. We'll need either a concession or a—" He stopped himself. "Stay put for now. If you have to concede, you'll need to call Hampton. You should do that from there."

"Yeah. I'd rather not try to call and eat crow while . . ." Michael started to get caught up in his emotions. "I don't want to throw in the towel surrounded by all those people who have worked so hard."

"I'll call you when all the networks call it the same way. I'd say to sit tight 'til then."

"Yeah. Sounds good." Edwards hung up. He heaved a weary sigh. "We'll sweat out California right here," he said to the occupants of the room.

☼   ☼   ☼

12:50 a.m., Eastern Standard Time

"Michael Edwards and Ken Hampton are almost dead even, and we still cannot call California," Talbot announced wearily. The first anchor team was slated to go home at 11:00, or when the Presidential election was resolved. Talbot was still at the anchor desk, after over seven hours of coverage. "It's Edwards with 35 per cent, Hampton with 35 per cent, and Parker with 30 per cent, as our graphic shows."

"Edwards has done very well in the country's largest state," Williams commented. "This is a state with a solid environmental record, with a large aerospace industry, and a state that has some tendencies to favor third alternative candidates, at least above the national average. It is also a comparatively young state, and younger voters have proven more likely to defect from the traditional political parties. This state is also 42nd in the country in BTU-per-capita consumption. This indicates that California's policies for energy conservation and renewable energy are in place. In fact, two of the state's major utilities *endorsed* Michael Edwards. This is in stark contrast to other states where utilities spent huge amounts of money to defeat him. So it is not surprising that he is doing so well. Will he do well enough? We still can't say, with almost 60 per cent of the votes counted."

"So here are the latest popular vote figures—the electoral vote figures haven't changed for almost an hour," Talbot said as the familiar graphic appeared:

Electoral Votes:			**Popular Votes:**		
50 of 51 resolved (incl D.C.)			**71% tabulated**		
	Votes	States		Votes	%
Edwards	70	7		24,435,756	30
Hampton	269	29		30,137,432	37
Parker	145	14		26,879,331	33
At stake: 54.....			**(Candidates under 1%**		
Needed to win: 270			**not included.)**		

Teresa, and most of the people in the room, had dozed off. But Michael felt a sudden surge of energy. He knew he was going to win California. He suddenly had no doubts. He didn't share his feeling of certainty about this premonition—it was pure intuition. But though the trend in the voting had been agonizingly slow, it seemed to be moving toward an inevitable shrinking of Hampton's lead. Edwards knew the lead would shrink away. He grabbed some paper and started making notes for the remarks he would make to his supporters shortly.

He paused a moment, then picked up a piece of paper with the phone numbers for the hotel rooms of Ken Hampton and Victor Parker. Edwards looked around the room. The only one not dozing was Everett Phillips. Edwards moved the piece of paper back and forth in front of his face contemptuously.

Phillips nodded and grinned.

Edwards smiled triumphantly as he crumpled up the piece of paper and flung it about five feet to his left into the center of a small waste basket.

Phillips' smile broadened.

They both knew that Phillips would not be eligible to be Vice President. The Constitution specified that only the top two finishers running for Vice President were eligible, and that the Senate decided the issue, voting individually, not by state delegation. But this moment was still their victory together.

✿   ✿   ✿

1:30 a.m., Eastern Standard Time

"Ladies and gentlemen, we finally have a winner in California," Andrew Talbot announced with drama, and not very well-disguised excitement. "And this will make election history. Because though both Ken Hampton and Michael Edwards will finish with 35 per cent of the California vote, we are now certain that Michael Edwards' 35 per cent will be the higher. So this election will not be decided this evening. Ken Hampton will end this night *one vote short* of the majority he needs."

"And as we mentioned earlier, you would have to think this result favors Victor Parker becoming our next President," Delores Cushing stated. "This will be a Democratic House of Representatives. If President Hampton does lose to Senator Parker in the House, he will be the first candidate for President since Grover Cleveland in 1888 to lose the Presidency to a candidate who received fewer popular votes than he did. In that election, Benjamin Harrison defeated the incumbent Grover Cleveland in 1888 but then lost the Presidency back to Cleveland in 1892. Cleveland is still the only President ever to lose office and regain it, and he actually won a majority of the popular vote three times in a row."

"But back to this election, I suspect a great deal could happen between now and January," Williams quickly interjected.

"That's for sure," Talbot agreed. "In the meantime, here's the final electoral vote tally, and the popular vote up to this moment:"

Electoral Votes: 51 of 51 resolved (incl D.C.)			Popular Votes: 77% tabulated	
	Votes	States	Votes	%
Edwards	124	8	26,500,749	30
Hampton	269	29	32,684,257	37
Parker	145	14	29,150,824	33

At stake: 0.....
Needed to win: 270

(Candidates under 1% not included.)

Michael Edwards did not jump up and down. He felt enormously overwhelmed by the magnitude of what had occurred. The people of the United States would now have to wait until January to determine for certain who would lead the strongest nation on the planet. For better or for worse, Michael Edwards knew he was the man responsible. Now the challenge to him would magnify. He wanted to make sure that what happened as a result of this outcome would really be "for the better." The evolution of events would now continue to depend on him, and a handful of other individuals charged with making decisions under circumstances without precedent.

He looked at his remarks, then nodded quietly. They would do for now. Broader considerations would wait until everyone had time to rest.

✿   ✿   ✿

2:20 a.m., Eastern Standard Time

"This has been a *phenomenal accomplishment*," Edwards pronounced emphatically in the huge, crowded hotel auditorium at the Park Avenue Tower Hotel. Though he should have been exhausted, he seemed as strong as ever. He was proud of this moment, and the people he was addressing. He had no trouble summoning the stamina to give them the kind of speech they deserved to hear. "This is an accomplishment I share with all of *you!*" Applause sounded loudly and enthusiastically. "And we share this with the courageous voters of this nation!" More applause sounded. "Write your

Congressmen. Insist that our agenda figure *prominently* in the administration of *whoever* is chosen to lead this nation!" Again the partisan crowd cheered wildly.

"I promise you, I will do *my* best over the next two months to keep our agenda in the public eye. The dream of a Regenerating Biosphere created through Economic Activism is very much alive tonight! Harmonizing prosperity with the environment is alive! Treating drug addicts as victims instead of criminals is alive! Summoning the power of free enterprise and the capitalist system to drive the transition into the next era of humankind, an era of prosperity and harmony among all people on this planet is alive!

"With *no party affiliation*, we have won *eight states*, including the most populous in the country! Our success has only begun. It's late tonight, so let's go home and get some rest. Then, tomorrow, we will begin the *next* phase of implementing a vision of America and the world that will serve us for generations! I'll see you as we begin the next phase of this great effort—I'll see you on the way to that dream! Thank you!"

Michael Edwards left the podium, but the celebration continued long after he had waved to the crowd and exited the building. Many of Edwards' partisans waited to see the final popular vote results, available at 5:20 that morning, Eastern Standard Time:

	Electoral Votes: 51 of 51 resolved (incl D.C.)		Popular Votes: 100% tabulated	
	Votes	States	Votes	%
Edwards	124	8	34,416,558	30
Hampton	269	29	42,477,088	37
Parker	145	14	37,858,213	33

At stake: 0.....
Needed to win: 270

(Candidates under 1% not included.)

☼   ☼   ☼

State by State Results for the Election

EDWARDS:

California	54
Colorado	8
Mass.	12
Michigan	18
Minnesota	10
Oregon	7
Rhode Island	4
Washington	11

(8 states, 124 votes)

HAMPTON:

Alabama	9
Alaska	3
Arizona	8
Connecticut	8
Delaware	3
Florida	25
Idaho	4
Illinois	22
Indiana	12
Kansas	6
Louisiana	9
Maine	4
Mississippi	7
Missouri	11
Nebraska	5
Nevada	4
N. H.	4
New Jersey	15
North Dakota	3
Ohio	21
Oklahoma	8
South Carolina	8
South Dakota	3
Texas	32
Utah	5
Vermont	3
Virginia	13
Wisconsin	11
Wyoming	3

(29 states, 269 votes)

PARKER:

Arkansas	6
Georgia	13
Hawaii	4
Iowa	7
Kentucky	8
Maryland	10
Montana	3
New Mexico	5
New York	33
North Carolina	14
Pennsylvania	23
Tennessee	11
West Virginia	5
D.C.	3

(14 states, 145 votes)

Part
Three

The
Result

Chapter 21

November: The Day After Election Day, Wednesday
New York, New York

"OKAY, WE PUT THIS THING IN THE HOUSE," EDWARDS SAID TO
Saroyan as they settled into a corner booth of the Park Avenue Bar and
Grill for a late lunch. The restaurant was almost completely empty, and
Edwards and Saroyan were some distance from the nearest occupied table.
As Edwards continued speaking, Saroyan placed a briefcase on the table
and opened it, taking out a yellow pad. Both men had dressed casually.
"We've made all the thank-you speeches and dealt with all the 'aren't-you-
proud-of-yourself' interviews. So what's on your yellow pad? What do we
do next?"

Saroyan smiled. "I jotted down a few ideas, instead of sleeping . . ."

Edwards nodded with a grin.

"We've got a chess match going. Or, more like a game of cards,
dealing with the screwball rules of the Electoral College. The three of you
have been dealt a set of cards—the Presidency may well go to the one who
plays his hand the most effectively."

"But some have better cards than others."

"And we have the weakest hand."

"Yeah." Edwards drew a deep breath of resignation. The euphoria of
throwing the election into the House, and winning success beyond the
expectations of the pundits and the naysayers was giving way to a stark,

morning-after reality. Ultimate victory was still against the odds. He was still probably destined to be a footnote in another Democrat versus Republican election, though a long and significant footnote.

"As I've said, our only shot at winning is for the House to deadlock, and you get chosen as a compromise candidate. The deadlock part of the scenario is the hardest." Saroyan looked at his notes. "The Democrats have a majority in 27 of the state delegations—they only need 26. The Republicans have a majority in 15 states. Eight states have delegations evenly divided between Democrats and Republicans. There are no provisions in the Constitution for tie-breakers for those delegations. And I know a number of Congressmen lean toward you. If those eight state delegations, split along party lines, have to abstain, and two Democratic states vote contrary to strict party considerations, we can get a deadlock. Ironically, we will not want any Republican Congressmen in the deadlock states to vote for you, or they could give a state to Parker that would have had a tie and been forced to abstain. We'll set meetings with Congressional leaders as part of our post-election strategy, but I'm getting ahead of myself . . ."

Edwards nodded that he was clear on what Saroyan was telling him.

"So we create this result with a couple of strategies. First, we create a public opinion groundswell. I've already seen polls that indicate you would have taken closer to 32 or 33 per cent if voters believed you could have won. We'll try to build on those numbers, maybe even leading to a poll that shows you would win if a new election was held. That might lead some Congressmen to defect from their parties, worried that their constituents might turn on them if they don't support you.

"Second, to build that public opinion, we keep pressing your agenda, trying to make you an increasingly attractive candidate. You'll go around the country, speaking for your agenda, lobbying for your *ideas*, not for yourself. We don't want to look like we're rerunning the election, but if people draw the conclusion that you would be the best guy to implement your ideas . . ."

"That'll be a fine line to dance on," Edwards commented.

"I have confidence in your soft shoe," Saroyan replied. "Our third strategy is related to making you look attractive as a Presidential possibility. We want to set up an Edwards administration, waiting in the wings. We don't want to do this with a huge fanfare, but quietly leak who is on board, and let *them also* lobby for your agenda. When people both in and out of Wash—"

"Wait a minute," Edwards disputed. "This sounds real arrogant. I'm choosing personnel for a job I finished third for?"

"There's a risk. But look who we already have—Wallace Trewillinger, Democrat, and one of the country's top foreign policy experts as Secretary of State. Frances Willis, Republican, on board for maybe Treasury, Attorney General or Chief of Staff . . ."

"You think they're still on board?"

"I haven't checked with them lately. But they already put their political eggs in your basket. I think they'll be right by our side. And Everett—we know he can't be Vice President. The Senate will have to pick either Jefferson or Dooley. But he's an ideal Defense Secretary, and I know *he'll* keep helping us."

Edwards smiled in agreement.

"By showing the kind of bi-partisan talent we can line up, we will look serious to the voters who are responding to the poll questions, and we will look viable as a Presidency to a House of Representatives looking for a compromise, bi-partisan President."

"And we have to take risks—we have the shittiest cards."

Saroyan smiled broadly. "And finally, we need to anticipate the other candidates' strategies and be ready to counter them."

"Okay," Edwards acknowledged. "And you have an idea what they'll do?"

Saroyan shrugged. "I know what *I'd* do if I were them. Hampton's hand isn't a lot better than ours. The Democratic Congress isn't likely to turn the Presidency over to him if there's a deadlock. They'd more likely turn to you, figuring they could control you more easily, and realizing your political philosophy is closer to theirs than to Hampton's. But Hampton's only one vote short in the Electoral College. If I'm Hampton's advisor, I'm telling him to try to get one of your electors to vote Hampton."

The traces of his previous smiles quickly drained out of Edwards' face as he sat, unnerved. This possibility had not occurred to him.

Saroyan continued. "He has to be very careful. Because if it looks like he's orchestrated a vote-shift, effectively stealing the election from Senator Parker before it gets to the House, he won't have a chance of getting anything done in Congress for the next four years."

Edwards exhaled loudly. "Didn't our people sign pledges?"

"Yes," Saroyan replied. "But no one knows how legally binding those things are. The damn election could litigate into the *next* Presidential election."

"We need to schedule meetings with all our electors," Edwards told Saroyan. "We've got to make sure they stay with us."

"And you need to run those meetings personally."

"Of course."

"Michael, you know Oscar picked a lot of those people."

"Yeah . . ."

"He'd know which ones might be iffy."

Edwards thought a moment about what Saroyan was suggesting. "How's he doing?"

"He's going into Lompoc in a couple of weeks, for two years."

"Sure is going quick with this."

"Things move fast when you plead guilty."

"I think . . ." Edwards stumbled a bit on his thought. "I think we have to leave him alone."

"What about a quiet, low-level contact for some information?"

Edwards shook his head. "Can't risk it, Drew. We're supposed to have cut ties with him. Polls show the American people respect the way we handled the situation. If we start fooling around with surreptitious contacts, and someone catches wind of it, which is likely, we'll have a public relations nightmare on our hands."

Saroyan nodded. "Parker's got the best cards," he continued. "If everything just runs its course, he'll be President. 27 states in the House of Representatives will put him in. But if I'm giving him advice, I would tell him to guard his flanks. And President Hampton stealing an Edwards electoral vote would concern me the most. I'd be contacting the Edwards people to express my concerns that all Edwards electors stay with their pledges. I'd offer legal help, advice, *anything* to keep the President from snatching an Edwards elector."

"So we can expect a call from someone with Parker?"

"By the end of the week, I would think," Saroyan confirmed. "Which could get awkward . . ."

"Why?"

"Because part of our strategy should be to portray Parker as unsuitable, and to portray you as a much better choice. That's our best shot at getting the House to deadlock."

"Yeah." Edwards understood. "Let's tone that aspect down. Hampton's people will keep up *that* barrage. We'd be better off looking very statesmanlike."

"I think you're right," Saroyan agreed as he nodded.

"And, we'll take any help on the elector situation that might seem appropriate."

"What have we got to lose?"

✿ ✿ ✿

The Same Day
Washington, D.C.

"I THINK SHANDRA FARLEY WOULD BE PERFECT FOR THE TRANSITION team," Parker told the small cadre of advisors gathered for a part-working, part-celebrating dinner in a private banquet room of the Maison Gourmet restaurant in southeast Washington, a block and a half from the Capitol. "She'll signal that the Parker Administration will be—"

"Senator Parker, excuse me," Will Runalli interrupted, trying to be polite.

Parker glared at him.

"I'm sorry," Runalli said, "but I really think that it would be a big mistake to consider this election result already set in stone."

Parker was impatient. "Nick says we have at least 27 states sewed up in the House. The President came up one vote short. So the House decides it. We're in."

"What if one of the Edwards electors shifts to Hampton?" Runalli asked.

"Then we sue that elector's ass into the next decade and tie Hampton up in so many Congressional investigations that he'll *beg* me to take the job from him." Parker wanted this discussion to be over. "Look, uh, Nick says he has all this covered. Talk to him about it."

"So how do we have it covered?" Runalli asked Nicholas Mueller.

"We have the best law firm in Washington setting up an impregnable case prohibiting elector defections," Mueller told him confidently. "We're going to work directly with the Edwards people on this to—"

"You're trusting this to the courts?" Runalli asked incredulously. He turned to Parker. "The lawyers can't *prevent* a defection. All they can do is sue if there *is* one. By then, it's too late. The election will already be stolen. You'll look like a child throwing a tantrum; you'll be accused of using the courts to gridlock the government when you finished second in the popular vote. You can't win this if it gets left to the lawyers."

"I hate fucking lawyers," Parker said irritably. He had consumed a number of glasses of champagne. He turned to Mueller. "Are we really in the hands of the lawyers?"

"I don't know any other way to play this," Mueller told Parker. "This crazy system . . . We'll be okay if we work with the Edwards people. And we get the lawyers to lay out their case *before* anyone defects, to show that it would be pointless."

"And President Hampton will hire his lawyers," Runalli countered. "They'll make out the opposite case. This is not a clear-cut issue. There are no precedents, no cases to look back at."

"We can't guarantee there won't be a defection," Mueller argued. "This is the best—"

"I *can,*" Runalli stated boldly.

"You can . . . *guarantee?*" Mueller looked at Runalli, then dubiously at Parker.

"How?" Parker asked.

Runalli looked around the table. "This is not the appropriate place to discuss the details."

Parker nodded. "Meet me after this conference; meet me over in my office at the Capitol."

"Um . . ." Mueller hesitated. "Uh, I won't be able to be there . . ."

"That's okay," Parker replied. "I know you have something going with your family. Mr. Runalli and I will meet alone."

Runalli was almost able to suppress a smile. He was back from his outcast status, poised to be at the right hand of the President-elect.

✧   ✧   ✧

"SO WHAT IS THIS 'GUARANTEE?'" PARKER ASKED WITHOUT PREAMBLE, as Runalli entered his office.

"It doesn't involve lawyers," Runalli replied obliquely as he shut the door behind him.

"What *does* it involve?"

Runalli remained standing. He kept his expression business-like. "These are things you don't need to know, and that you don't want to know."

"What?" Parker asked through a stern, suspicious look.

"Let me handle it."

"What kind of mess are you going to get me into?"

Runalli joked. "The biggest mess of all, the Oval Office."

"Mueller tells me you *can't* guarantee this."

"He's a good man. But he's a patty-cake player trying to handle a street fight. You can bet Hampton'll have a street-fighter working for him."

"Is anything you propose to do illegal?"

"I won't answer that, for *your* protection."

"I think that makes your answer clear."

"Do you want to be the next President? This election rightly belongs to you. If nobody fucks around with the system, you will be our next President. I'm just going to make sure things stay that way."

Parker was uncomfortable with this man. But he also believed Runalli was right. This was his moment, and President Hampton might try to take it away. Runalli was his protection. Parker hated Mueller's lack of certainty and enjoyed Runalli's confidence. "I could do a lot in this job," he thought out loud. "I've had so many ideas that I couldn't get launched as just another Democratic Senator fighting to put his agenda in front of a group of one hundred egomaniacs. As President . . ."

Runalli knew better than to interrupt.

"And the Republicans." Parker's face turned sour. "We don't need another four years of Republicans in charge of the Executive Branch."

Runalli waited patiently for Parker to complete his shield of rationalizations.

"Do what you have to do," Parker finally told Runalli quietly. "Just give me the details I need to know. And . . ." He knew he didn't really need to make his next comment, but he couldn't leave it unsaid. "Be discreet. Don't get us tangled up in something."

"I'll take care of it." Runalli paused. "And let's let Edwards pay for his own attorneys. He can afford it. He certainly had enough money to screw up this election."

"We don't need to help him?"

Runalli shook his head. "If it gets to the lawyers, it'll be too late. And we may need the money for other . . . activities."

Parker exhaled uncomfortably. "Keep us clean."

"Street fights can get dirty."

Parker didn't like this answer. He wanted more assurances. But this was the price of Runalli's protection of Parker's lifelong dream. "Good night," Parker said to Runalli.

Runalli smiled briefly, then left.

✩   ✩   ✩

Early November: The Next Day, Thursday
Washington, D.C.

"ONE VOTE SHORT," KEN HAMPTON LAMENTED AS HE AND COVINGTON Klondike sat down to their breakfast meeting at the Oval Office. "One vote short, but it might as well be a hundred."

"It never ceases to amaze me," Klondike commented, shaking his head. "You've got states like California, Indiana, Mississippi—states from every region of the country that vote Republican for President but put Democrats into the House. We're screwed if this thing runs its course."

"A bunch of geniuses—we kept thinking Edwards would take votes away from Parker. The damn guy ends up taking electoral votes away from *us*."

Klondike exhaled slowly.

"Well," President Hampton continued fatalistically after a short pause, "I'm thinking maybe we should go ahead and concede this thing, and get the transition started . . . for the good of the—"

"Mr. President, I'm not sure we should concede just yet."

"Why not?"

"Because you can still win this election. The House is not a guarantee for Parker. Some Democrats might be persuaded to vote for you."

Hampton grimaced in disbelief. "Turn against their own party to put a Republican back in the White House? You aren't serious, Cuv."

"There's another way," Klondike stated soberly. "It's . . . not exactly without potential problems."

"What is it?"

"If we can get one Edwards elector to change over to you . . ."

Hampton nodded, intrigued with this possibility that he had not considered. "And how do we do that?"

"We have to be careful how we encourage this," Klondike told him. "The Democrats will not take kindly to any hint that we created the defection."

"No kidding. I have enough trouble working with Congress now. Can you imagine?"

"Yeah. So what we do is get some influential people to call for the Edwards people, for the sake of the country, to break their pledges and vote for the candidate that was the clear popular vote choice in this country. We can get some media people to put out the suggestion. We can even leak that we'll release ours if Edwards and Parker will release theirs."

"What?" Hampton questioned in disbelief.

"Don't worry," Klondike assured him. "Parker and Edwards'll never go for it. But it plants the idea in the minds of the Edwards electors and gives us a rationale for accepting an election result based on a defection. Party loyalty keeps Parker's and our people from jumping ship. But Edwards' people . . ."

Hampton shook his head doubtfully. "So we're depending on Edwards electors to choose me? Have you forgotten how that guy trashed me over the last nine months? This sounds real nebulous, real iffy."

"We only need one." Klondike paused. "And, we can make it less iffy," he added quietly and evenly, with little emotion to betray the weight of his statement.

"Go ahead . . ."

"If an Edwards elector was smart enough to make the determination that we should return to power, then I think we have someone who deserves an important position in the Hampton Administration."

Hampton scowled. "And how do we communicate this . . . information . . . to Edwards' people?"

"Very discreetly, after a quiet investigation to determine who might be smart enough to make this choice. You see, someone might conclude that we are trying to bribe an elector if this is handled clumsily."

"Yeah. A whole Congress full of Democrats might just see it that way, and spend most of their time trying to nail my hide to the Capitol dome."

"What do you think?"

"I think it *stinks,*" Hampton stated impulsively. "But it's also our best shot. And nothing stinks more than this Electoral College system we're saddled with. Whether we win or not, I'm going to dedicate myself to making sure this archaic relic gets *dumped.* In the meantime . . ." He gathered his thoughts. "I took 37 per cent of the vote and 29 states. I won the God Damn election. And we can't let the Democrats back in the White House to mess things up for another four years the way their last two guys did. The country can't take it. So . . . go ahead. Put it in action. Find me an elector." And with those words, President Hampton had constructed his own shield of rationalizations. He sighed. "And for God's sake, be *careful.* If it gets out that we're trying to br—" He stopped himself. "To *influence* electors . . ."

"I understand."

The breakfast meeting moved to other matters, and the two men finally began eating their meals, which had remained untouched.

✪   ✪   ✪

Mid November, Election Year: Friday
Maracaibo, Venezuela

"MANUEL, MY FRIEND, PLEASE COME IN," ENRIQUEZ TOLD MANUEL Contreras. Enriquez was in his living room reading a newspaper. His stereo blared loud, contemporary rock music, with a raspy, rough electric guitar edge. The room, including Enriquez' couch, was littered with other newspapers from all over the United States. Some were strewn about, still in their neatly folded sections. Others were crumpled up in large paper-wads.

Contreras walked in, registering puzzlement at the condition of the room.

"Forgive the mess." Enriquez explained. "I have been going through these American newspapers."

Contreras nodded. "Anything useful?"

Enriquez threw down the newspaper he was holding. "They all say Victor Parker will probably win, but the result won't be confirmed until January." He sneered. "And some say there's a chance, a slim chance, but a chance, that after the election deadlocks in the Election College and goes to some place called the Home of the Representatives to be decided, the Democratics might give the election to Edwards as a compromise." Enriquez paused and looked at Contreras through a sinister stare. "That is not acceptable to us. We would actually prefer Hampton, because we prosper when the Americans try to take a hard line. They eliminate all the small-timers, and make it even more profitable for those of us with the skill and resources to do the job right."

Contreras nodded again.

"I need this problem handled once and for all. If Edwards were to become . . . unavailable as a candidate, then his votes would be released. Only one of them would have to vote for the Republicrat Hampton, and he would be in."

"Are we still trying to be so subtle with how we take care of this?"

"No. And I have decided you should finish this job personally. Watch that you are not followed. Make it look like someone else did it if you can. Make sure we can't be fingered. But take care of this yourself."

Contreras knew this was the closest Enriquez would come to admitting he should have let Contreras handle this task in the first place. "Can we count on any help from the Americans?" he asked, just to know his resources completely.

"My American friends feel that any assassination would be a poor idea," Enriquez explained contemptuously. "They are confident that Parker will win, or by some weird changes that I didn't understand, that Hampton will win. And they say Edwards is not so bad." He paused. "They do not have my priorities or my problems."

"No they don't," Contreras acknowledged.

"I don't share theirs either. The removal of Edwards is my only guarantee that he will not somehow win with the fluky American system. I like guarantees."

Contreras let a slight smile creep onto his face. "I will leave for the United States tomorrow. I will make sure no one is on my tail."

Chapter 22

Mid November, Election Year: Sunday
Houston, Texas

"You've been working on your drives," Hunter told Fadiman, impressed as Fadiman's first tee shot rolled down the fairway of the first hole at the San Jacinto Country Club. The ball came to rest only 25 yards short of Hunter's.

"Yeah," Fadiman acknowledged through an irritated squint. "I just think about that Enriquez guy, and I add 50 yards."

Hunter raised his eyebrows as he chuckled. "Maybe I'll try that."

They grabbed their clubs and started walking toward their balls.

"No caddies, no carts, wide-open grass," Hunter told Fadiman as they started their walks. "Good place to talk over some confidential subjects. Not so good for shoulders." He adjusted the clubs on his shoulder, obviously uncomfortable carrying them. "What's on your mind?"

"I wish I had never gotten involved with that Venezuelan lunatic," Fadiman told Hunter frankly. "My sources tell me he tried another hit on Edwards."

"What?" Hunter was unpleasantly surprised. He hadn't heard anything on the news.

"Well, a thirty-four year old man in pretty good physical condition shouldn't be dropping dead of a heart attack at a campaign rally."

Hunter now understood Fadiman's news. "I heard about that." He paused, not knowing if he wanted to ask the next question, but overcome by curiosity. "So, what *might* kill a thirty-four year old man, and *look* like a heart attack?"

"There's a poison the KGB once used for sensitive assassinations, especially in foreign countries. There's a case of a guy killed in London by a pin at the end of an umbrella that got some press a few years back. If no one does an autopsy within about 24 hours, it looks like the victim's heart goes out."

"You think your boy has KGB connections?" Hunter asked with disbelief.

"He's got enough money to dabble with former Soviet nuclear experts. Of course, he could have KGB connections. But he doesn't even have to go far from home if he has Cuban connections, which we're pretty sure he does."

Hunter paused, looking all around him carefully. "I see now why you wanted to have this discussion out here." He took in a deep breath, obviously not accustomed to carrying his golf clubs. "Seems to me that the punk is getting pretty sophisticated. He almost pulled this thing off."

Fadiman shook his head. "I mentioned the same thing to my security people. But they think he'll get more reckless now. He'll get frustrated and desperate, and try something much less sophisticated. He'll get cocky that he's tried twice and his efforts have not been detected. He'll get careless."

"We can't take a chance, can we?"

"We still have the same problem. If he gets tangled up in something, he'll sell us out."

"So what are you doing about this?" Hunter asked, figuring Fadiman wanted to tell him more than just the news of the latest attempt to kill Edwards.

"It's costing me a fucking fortune to keep an eye on the situation," Fadiman complained. "My security guy says that Enriquez' chief enforcer arrived in Miami yesterday. He was a bitch to follow—he's obviously looking for tails. We need teams to keep tabs on the bastard. Now he could be here on regular business—could be Edwards. We don't know—that's why we're watching him."

Hunter sighed. "So what do *you* think of Edwards?"

"I don't think he's such a bad guy," Fadiman commented. "But that doesn't really matter. He's not going to be President."

"Probably the Democrats get that damn Parker," Hunter said.

"Or Hampton. My Republican friends think there's a way he could pull this thing out."

"Hmmm. But Edwards won't take it."

"No way."

Hunter nodded as his pace slowed and beads of sweat formed on his forehead. "We had a meeting about him just before the 'Sixties-gate' thing hit," Hunter said, growing more short of breath. "I had some of these futurist people I have on the payroll do some scenarios."

Fadiman smiled. "You hired yourself some Alvin Tofflers."

"Yeah. It's the hip thing for a modern executive to do."

"I know. I have the overpaid eggheads in some of my publicly traded companies too. What did they say?"

"I was actually impressed—with the gritty detail of some of it." He drew a deep breath, trying to draw in enough air to finish stating his thought and continue walking with Fadiman. "They say we would survive—hell, we could make piles of money in some scenarios, if Edwards plans came into law. We'd just jump into the new industries." He paused to catch his breath.

"You gonna make it through 18 holes?" Fadiman asked through a good-natured smile.

"Shit no," Hunter told him frankly. "Let's pick up a cart when we get to the fourth tee." The fourth tee doubled back to the clubhouse where they could easily pick up a golf-cart before resuming their round.

"You gonna make it to the fourth tee?"

"I'll manage," he answered gruffly. "Anyway, on this Edwards, we also think we could get Congress to water down his policies."

They arrived at Fadiman's ball. Fadiman took a mechanical, compact swing and his ball landed just short of the green.

"That didn't look like an angry swing," Hunter joked.

Fadiman smiled briefly as he placed his iron back in his golf bag and picked up his clubs.

They walked the short distance to Hunter's ball.

Hunter put down his bag and selected a mid-numbered iron. His swing was broad and spirited. The ball soared high over the green, landing twenty yards behind it.

"Your angry swing?" Fadiman asked.

"Thought I'd be pooped," Hunter explained, "so I overswung." He picked up his clubs. "This'll be okay," he said as he settled the bag of clubs back on his shoulder. "Just gotta get used to it."

"So we don't have to stop in for a cart on the fourth tee?"

"Like *hell*," Hunter retorted emphatically.

They walked toward Fadiman's ball, in front of the green.

"So on this Enriquez problem, I think I may have a permanent solution worked out . . ." Fadiman's voice trailed off.

"How much do I need to know about this?"

"Only what you want to know."

Hunter nodded as he smiled. "As little as possible."

"There are just a few things *I* wanted to know, from *you*."

"Okay . . ."

"True or false; Edwards would be more dangerous as a dead martyr than as a live President."

Hunter smiled. "Probably."

"Choice A or Choice B: Choice A—we stop Enriquez and his people *hard* before they hurt Edwards. Choice B—we take a chance that Enriquez doesn't get caught, or lead investigators to us."

Hunter shifted the clubs on his shoulder as he considered the choices. "Wouldn't Choice A bring us a lot of trouble from friends of Enriquez?"

"We have a plan that would eliminate such a concern."

Hunter squinted, then grinned. "Eliminate?"

Fadiman didn't reply.

"Choice A is my favorite answer, as long as potential complications can be avoided." He paused a moment. "Must be one hell of a plan."

"My security guy is the best in the world," Fadiman told him. "And no matter how rich Enriquez gets, he's still an inexperienced amateur, in over his head."

"Amateurs can be dangerous."

"Yeah. Beginner's luck syndrome. Beginners get lucky because they approach an arena with a fresh perspective. They can catch a jaded, uncreative professional by surprise, by not following the rules that other professionals, even enemies, accept without question."

"That's exactly why they can be dangerous."

"Taking that into consideration, I still think we have everything covered with our plan."

Hunter smiled as they reached Fadiman's ball. "I'd say you usually have things under control," he said casually. "Go ahead and handle it."

"We won't act unless he makes a move on Edwards. But if he does . . ." Fadiman slowly broke into a triumphant, almost sinister grin. "He won't end up being more than a minor irritation."

Hunter smiled again.

Fadiman chipped his ball up to within four feet of the pin on the green.

"You do better *without* your angry swing," Hunter observed.

✡   ✡   ✡

Mid November, Election Year: Tuesday
Big Sur, California

"THIS ISN'T GOING TO BE A LONG SPEECH," MICHAEL EDWARDS ASSURED the audience seated in the packed, open-air amphitheater at John Muir State Park. The sweet smell of wet pine, and the thickness of moist air, permeated the area, noted for tall trees juxtapositioned with picturesque coastal views. The audience sat on slightly damp benches, well-bundled in heavy jackets to assure comfort in the 40 degree temperatures, not considered cold for November in many other parts of the country, but cold for Northern California. "I'm glad the weather cooperated today," he continued jovially. "We almost scheduled this for yesterday."

There was a slight giggle from the crowd, as they recalled the deluge of a rainstorm the day before.

"I thought this would be the ideal place to have supporters meet our electors," Edwards announced to his audience, explaining the purpose of the meeting. "All 24 of our northern California electors are here to shake your hands and share the victory *all* of us achieved in this state."

The 24 electors sat in two slightly curved rows of twelve chairs behind Edwards. Sitting just slightly left of center in the back row was Bennington Whittlebaum. He wore a cheap, green sports jacket, a worn white dress shirt, and faded green jeans. He also wore a high felt hat with a small yellow feather in the headband on the right side, trying to look 60's hip, but also trying to hide his thinning black hair. The most expensive items of clothing he wore stuck out in strong contrast to the rest of his wardrobe. First, was a shiny pair of brown cowboy boots. And second, was an elaborately decorated silk tie with a striking depiction of the destruction of a tropical rainforest. He held a thick manila envelope on his lap.

Whittlebaum looked smugly at the elector seated to his right, a pretty woman in her thirties whose pleasant looks showed through her simple attire, jeans and a long sleeve "Edwards for President" T shirt. "We're in the middle of *fucking history*," Whittlebaum said to her, trying to be quiet, but speaking too emphatically to be as quiet as he wished.

She smiled politely and nodded, but clearly wanted to listen to Edwards.

"We are still a formidable force in this election," Edwards stated firmly.

"Yes!" Whittlebaum blurted out as if his favorite football team had just scored a touchdown. A few electors looked over at him with forced smiles.

Manuel Contreras looked warily around from his position in the back of the crowd. He wore jeans and a Michael Edwards campaign T shirt. He had tried to take an inconspicuous position toward the back of the crowd, staying away from cameras that would be more likely to document his attendance if he was closer to Edwards in the front. And he knew he had been followed on some occasions since he'd entered the United States. So he kept a constant watch for unwanted companions. Contreras was frustrated, not just with dodging tails, but because he still hadn't determined how he would carry out his assignment. He had come to this rally to try to inspire his creativity.

Edwards continued his address. "There have been editorials written and spoken in the media suggesting that we concede, even suggesting that President Hampton concede."

"No way," Whittlebaum commented as if Edwards was addressing him specifically. "I've got the perfect answer right here," he told the woman next to him as he held up his manila envelope.

She eked out a polite nod and quick eye contact, but then turned her attention back to Michael Edwards.

"The pundits and so-called experts *again* have this election all wrapped up," Edwards continued to the audience. "They assume that all Democrats in the House will vote for Parker, and all Republicans will vote for Hampton. It's not even necessary for the process to continue according to the rules. Let the media get out their crystal balls and tell us what will happen—let them declare the winner. After all, their polls before election day showed President Hampton ahead and that we wouldn't carry a single state! So they're real *good* at this."

Laughter rippled through the audience.

"In fact, who needs these time-consuming elections?" Edwards continued in a light but sarcastic tone. "Let's just have the national media declare a winner. It would be so much more efficient." Edwards paused a moment. "Who needs these elections?" he asked quietly, repeating his question, but in a more serious tone. "*We* do," he boomed out. "This *country* does. Because our success shows that the *people* still choose, that pollsters and pundits do *not* tell us who will win—*we* do."

Applause responded to Edwards' statement.

Whittlebaum yipped and yowled exuberantly.

"Let's allow the House to decide this. That's what the system mandates. Let's encourage members of the House to vote for the best candidate—the Constitution says nothing about voting the *party* line. Let's encourage our fellow citizens to write their Congressional representatives. Let's state the case for our agenda. Just last week, Earth Assessment Report came out with a detailed analysis of our proposals," Edwards pronounced proudly as he held up a thick, bound paper document.

"Yeah!" Whittlebaum shouted. "I have that too!" He held up his manila envelope.

The electors in his area were growing impatient with his outbursts and cast disdainful looks in his direction. The woman next to him squirmed uncomfortably. Whittlebaum was oblivious to the increasing hostility he was provoking.

Contreras suddenly perked up as Edwards held up the E.A.R. document. His mind had been wandering, but the reference to this report suddenly focused his thoughts. He smiled victoriously. He knew now how he would carry out his assignment for Ernesto Enriquez. He would need to work out the details of his plan, and acquire some sophisticated materials. But he knew his idea was workable. He could resolve the matter within weeks. He moved forward as he looked back.

"He's here—he's watching," a tough-looking man said into a cellular phone as he watched Contreras. The man was wearing a green flannel shirt, and lurked back further from the crowd than Contreras, near trees that might be used to obscure him if necessary. "I don't think he's packing, but I'm not sure. Should we move in?"

"No," Carl Gregory's voice replied from the other end of the phone. He had parked in a van with tinted windows at a cafe just off the Coast Highway, three miles from the park. "He's not dangerous there. He'll want to complete his job and walk away. No way he can do that." Gregory paused. "But we know it now—he's stalking Edwards. Our people will want us to handle the situation." He thought another moment. "Watch him."

"That's not going to be easy. He's being real—" The man cut himself off. "Damn. He just looked back here and I think he made me."

"Okay. Stay in position until we move another team member in, then move out. I'll signal you."

"Right."

Edwards continued his speech. "This analysis from E.A.R. calls our policy proposals the most encouraging ideas from the mainstream political system *ever*. And they estimate that the impact of these proposals will have *immediate* positive effects on the environmental prognosis for the planet.

They have stated, as we have said repeatedly, that because these proposals call for a shift in priorities, not just another set of new regulations, they will bring *permanent* improvement. They compared this to the difference between going on a crash diet to lose weight, and changing the entire method of eating. With the diet, the weight comes back. Regulations are like the crash diet, because they don't change the patterns of consumption that created the situation. With new eating patterns, lost weight stays off, and the health improves. Our proposals amount to a new way of consuming. This analysis comes from a *respected, independent* group, committed to scientific analysis, and with an international reputation for objectivity and neutral politics. Let's make sure our Congressional representatives know about this!"

"They will, Michael! They will!" Whittlebaum shouted as applause followed Edwards' statement.

None of the electors looked back at Whittlebaum this time, as if they hoped that ignoring Whittlebaum would make the outbursts stop.

"What else do we have going for us?" Edwards asked rhetorically. "We have bi-partisan support from people of national stature and reputation. Wallace Trewillinger, Frances Willis and Everett Phillips have reaffirmed their support for our agenda in the most positive terms. We've added three more major supporters since then, all of whom would make fine cabinet members."

"Wait 'til he sees what *I* have," Whittlebaum said to the woman next to him as he nudged her with his elbow. "I'll be in that power structure." He held up his manila envelope. "Wait 'til he sees *this*."

"Are you here to listen, or be obnoxious?" she demanded irritably.

"I'm here to *contribute*," he insisted. "You should look at the stuff I'm presenting to him today."

"I'm here to *listen*," she snarled.

"You'll see. We're important, you and I and all the people sitting up here."

Another elector, seated in the row in front of Whittlebaum, now turned around. "Would you shut up!"

"You won't be telling me to shut up after Michael sees this," Whittlebaum replied defiantly, waving his manila envelope.

"And," Edwards continued, "we have a poll result that *really* makes our case. Voters in the last election were asked who their preference was for President, regardless of who they thought could win. Hampton polled 35, Parker 30—and Edwards also *thirty-five*!"

Applause swelled.

"And this poll has a three point margin of error," he added. "So we have the *right* to ask for our Congressional representatives to consider all of this when they choose a President in January."

More applause sounded.

Manuel Contreras looked back again. The man by the trees with the cellular phone had left. Contreras nodded. The man apparently hadn't been following him after all. He was free to carry out his plan. He'd accomplished what he'd set for the day. But he didn't want to draw attention to himself by leaving ahead of the crowd. He'd slip away quietly when the Edwards concluded his remarks.

"So let's all get together and enjoy the solidarity here," Edwards told his audience. "Meet our electors. Because we still have more work to do before we see the final result of our efforts. Thank you all again for your past support, and for your continuing support. We will need every bit of your help."

Applause again sounded as Edwards took his seat near the podium.

Saroyan, who had a seat next to Michael, stood and approached the electors. "Let's form some kind of receiving line," he suggested. "Right over here off to the side of the podium. We'll shake a few hands and maybe get a few good conversations going." The electors began getting up from their seats.

Saroyan moved to the microphone. "Michael Edwards and the electors will be in a line right over here to meet with you," he said in a functional, unemotional tone of voice.

Bennington Whittlebaum moved quickly out of the elector line to Michael Edwards. "Mr. Edwards?" he called out tentatively as he approached. "I'm Ben Whittlebaum, one of your electors?"

"Good to meet you," Edwards told him with a genuine smile. "I'll be talking directly to all of you electors privately in about two—"

"I know," Whittlebaum interrupted with nervous energy. "I just—" He stammered uncomfortably. "I just wanted you to know what an honor it is to be associated with you. And I think I can be of help." He thrust the manila envelope forward towards Edwards' chest. "These are some ideas I have. I hope—" He again did a conversational double-clutch. "I was thinking we could talk about these in the electors' meeting."

"Well . . . We won't have time to give these a proper look before this afternoon's meeting," Edwards told Whittlebaum with a courteous smile. "But Drew and I will go over your ideas in the next few days and get back to you to discuss them."

This satisfied Whittlebaum. "Thank you," he said with almost overstated pomposity. "I look forward to working with you."

"You electors have an important job," Edwards added.

"Yes. Well, we better get back and press the flesh with all the worker bees." He quickly moved into line with the other electors.

Edwards waited for Saroyan.

A few minutes later, with the receiving line set and functioning, Edwards and Saroyan shared a brief moment before joining the line.

"One of the electors gave me this," Edwards told Saroyan as he held up Whittlebaum's manila envelope.

Saroyan took the envelope. "Hmmm."

"He said he had some ideas."

"And it's from an elector . . ." Saroyan thought a moment. "Normally we'd give this to staff to review and comment on. But we better look at it ourselves and hold the guy's hand."

"He's a strange-looking guy."

"The one with the green coat, and the hat?"

"Yeah."

Saroyan sighed. "Some of the other electors complained about him—during just the few minutes I was setting up the line."

"I think he just wants some attention," Edwards concluded. "Let's give him some. We'll look this over tonight and figure out what to do."

"Right."

They headed to the line. For three hours, a celebratory attitude built as all these people with the same vehement views fortified each other and enjoyed their success in the November election. After this concluded, the 24 electors along with Edwards and Saroyan boarded three vans and went to a nearby restaurant, overlooking the Pacific Ocean, where they would have their private meeting. Teresa Edwards would join them there.

☼   ☼   ☼

"THE RESPONSIBILITY WE HAVE IS AWESOME," EDWARDS TOLD THE electors gathered around five round tables in the banquet room of the Big Surf Restaurant.

Bennington Whittlebaum had taken a seat at the same table as the young woman he had been seated next to previously. She had tried to pick a table away from him, but she chose her seat just before he walked in. Now she concentrated hard on not making eye contact with this man, while also concentrating on Michael Edwards' address as it continued.

"I wanted this group to see how many people are counting on us,"

Edwards continued. "I speak for the agenda. You electors speak for the voters who chose the agenda."

Edwards paused briefly. He and Saroyan had carefully crafted his next words, calculated to express a concern, without questioning integrities or sounding like they were applying pressure. It was Edwards' third meeting of this kind—the first two had taken place in Washington, then Oregon.

"Our people are concerned that strategists for President Hampton may approach you electors to try to convince you to change your votes. We have utmost confidence in *all* of you. We handpicked you carefully with the help of trusted staff people. But we want to know *immediately* if you are approached. We believe that any efforts by the Hampton campaign to influence you would be improper. This would be an assault on your integrity, a lack of respect for the pledges you have all taken. We will want to bring *any* such efforts to the attention of the American people if they occur."

Electors nodded.

"I told you we were important," Bennington Whittlebaum told his neighbor.

"I knew that before you told me," she acknowledged irritably.

"I'm working with Michael and Drew on some things," he told her casually. "I'd love to get your input over lunch some time. Maybe I can—"

"We're having lunch *now*," she told him with a chilly abruptness. "And I'm trying to listen."

"Yeah," Whittlebaum acknowledged, ignoring the chill in her voice. "I love hearing him tell us how important *we* are."

"The pledge you all took was an important one," Edwards continued. "The other electors are pledged to political parties. Your pledge is not to some traditional groups with strategically blurred ideological agendas. Your pledge is to a specific person at a specific time, advocating a clearly defined agenda. That makes your pledge more personal, more sacrosanct. We will work with you to make sure your pledge is *not* subject to outside pressures. We owe this to the supporters we met today, and to the millions of voters who signaled their desire for a new direction for this country by choosing *our* agenda.

"Thank you again for agreeing to be electors for us. And I will work to see our efforts pay off." Edwards sat down.

After applause, seafood lunches were consumed, and as the meals were finished, electors got up and moved from table to table, conversing, then eventually leaving.

Michael Edwards sat at a table with Teresa Edwards, Drew Saroyan, and three other electors whom they knew personally. Most electors approached this table individually before they left, exchanging handshakes and some words of mutual encouragement.

The table where Whittlebaum sat cleared the quickest. Whittlebaum was oblivious to the effect he was having on people. He interpreted the polite nods and lack of responses as agreement, even awe at his brilliance. When he felt he had sufficiently impressed his peers, he decided it was time to make his exit.

He approached the Edwards table. "So Michael," he called out loudly and familiarly as he approached the table, "I gotta get going now. Wife and kids, you know—they're waiting for me. Family values and all that." He paused, suddenly afraid he had put his foot in his mouth by quoting a recent Republican campaign slogan. "We're for that, aren't we?" he asked quietly and apprehensively.

"Of course," Edwards replied graciously.

"Of course," Whittlebaum repeated, regaining his blustering stride. "So I'll be talking to you guys—I'll be there for you." He waved as he left the restaurant, strutting away proudly.

There was a collective feeling of relief in the banquet room that was obvious to the fifteen people remaining.

"Strange guy," Teresa commented.

"Yeah," Drew agreed.

"It's his day in the sun," Edwards observed casually. "He'll probably never be in another situation like this. He likes the attention."

Saroyan held up the manila envelope. "You can bet this is a pretty flaky package."

Edwards drew a deep breath and nodded. "We can't ignore it, or *him*, until after December 18th."

"I know," Saroyan answered.

✩   ✩   ✩

"IT'S JUST ABOUT ALL CRAP," SAROYAN TOLD EDWARDS. THEY SAT AT A small table in Michael's Santa Barbara hotel room. They had scheduled the meeting with the southern California electors for the following day up at a resort in the hills just south of Santa Barbara. Teresa Edwards was at the University of Santa Barbara, speaking to a particularly enthusiastic group of student supporters.

Edwards tossed a sheaf of papers down on the table and rubbed his eyes wearily. He looked at the digital clock in the room—it read "11:38."

"He either restates our stuff, and tries to call it his own, or he is totally off the wall."

"He offers a plan to use the IRS to pressure oil companies to go along with your tax plans," Saroyan told him.

"Jesus."

"And the guy sent us his *resumé*," Saroyan continued. "He's some kind of buyer for a gardening supply chain. That, and a list of twelve books he's read, qualifies him for Interior or Agriculture, as the *Secretary*—that's what he says . . ."

Edwards eyes popped open in disbelief.

"He says that his lack of experience in government is made up for by his charisma with people, and his total understanding of the Edwards agenda. But he promises that as Secretary of the Interior, he'll stick it to all the miners and forestry people who have supposedly been ruining the country."

Edwards shook his head. "He obviously doesn't understand us at all."

"He has also promised to spy on the other electors, to ferret out defectors."

"Him? *Spy?* Every one of the northern California electors hates his guts. They wouldn't confide their *shopping lists* to him. So, what do we do?"

"We get one of our really good people. Tracy would be good for this—she's got a real pleasant voice, sexy over the phone. We'll get her to call him back right away. Maybe a quick call to him will distract him from the fact we aren't calling him personally. She'll have to diplomatically nix the spy idea. I don't want him telling fellow electors, or the *media*, that we're spying on our own electors. Otherwise, she'll talk him up; treat him like a trusted advisor, even give him inside information we don't mind having him blurt out around town. No commitments, and certainly no promises on government posts. She can just tell him that those decisions can't be made yet, but that all good people will be considered."

"Okay," Edwards agreed. "But how does she explain why we're not contacting him directly?"

Saroyan nodded. "That'll be tricky. I think Tracy can handle it." He thought another moment. "He's got to understand how busy we are. We'll have her assure him that she is working directly with us, and let slip some inside information on our itinerary. Unless I miss my guess, this guy just wants to be able to say he's got access to us. He wants to brag about it. Two minutes with the guy, and no reasonable person will believe it. But as long as *he* believes it, we won't end up alienating him."

Edwards nodded, then frowned. "Is there any way we can replace him?"

"I'll put our lawyers on it," Saroyan replied. "But I don't think so. I'm sure we'd have to prove the guy was nuts or dangerous."

"He *is* nuts," Edwards insisted.

"I think you'd have to show the guy is really *insane,* divorced from reality; you know, thinks he's Jesus Christ, or Napoleon, or Darth Vader—doesn't know what century he's living in."

Edwards understood. "Hold off on the lawyers. See if Tracy can manage this."

"Okay. Well, another elector meeting tomorrow," Saroyan said as he stood to leave. "Three states down, five to go after this one." Saroyan smiled wearily as he left the room.

✷   ✷   ✷

Late November, Election Year: Monday
Washington, D.C.

"SO, HOW'S MY CAMPAIGN COMING ALONG?" PRESIDENT HAMPTON asked Covington Klondike as Klondike entered the Oval Office, first thing in the morning.

Klondike took a seat in front of the President's desk, putting his briefcase on the floor next to him as he faced the President. "Nothing new to report," he replied.

"Do we have any Edwards people willing to defect?"

"No. Not yet."

"We've got 28 days before they turn in their votes," Hampton reminded Klondike emphatically. "If we're going to resolve the election this way, we better find someone *soon.*"

"I realize time is short," Klondike replied. "But we have to be very careful about this. Edwards is meeting with every single one of his electors *personally* and asking them to contact him immediately if our people approach them, with the idea that he'll splash it all over the media."

"So he's anticipated us . . ."

"Absolutely."

"Damn."

"What we're doing is making very careful contacts. Our people are striking up casual conversations, trying to get a feel for these electors.

We've made subtle contact with just over half of them now. That's how we know what Edwards has been telling them."

"And what do we have from these contacts?"

"There are two or three we *might* approach, but they're not guaranteed. There's a risk they could report our approach to Edwards."

"Which he would promptly splash all over the media."

"Exactly. We're still trying to get a more secure . . . opportunity."

"If we don't, we'll have to take a chance on one of the two or three that might defect."

"That's right. And we'll have to do it soon."

The President nodded. "This is so damn frustrating. Am I going to be here next term or not? When I talk to a world leader about policy and issues, are we having our last conversation with me as President? Should we start working on some new legislation to send down to the boys on Capitol Hill, or should I go renew my fishing license? It's a piss or get off the pot situation, and it isn't getting any clearer."

"We're trying to get this resolved," Klondike assured him. "We've leaked the call for releasing electors. People working with us, and people sympathetic to us, are calling publicly for electors to be released from their pledges so the true choice of the people can be selected."

"Would it help if *I* publicly called for the electors to vote their consciences?"

Klondike shook his head. "The cynics in the media would *bury* you. They'll say you're only calling for the pledge releases to try to steal the election."

"Which is partly true, though I don't know if you can call it 'stealing' when we got more votes than the other guy."

"You can't look like you're soliciting electors or the Democrats will go ballistic and the last four years will look like a love-fest compared to the next four years."

Hampton knew they had discussed this before, and that Klondike's assessment was as correct now as it was then. "It's just so hard to sit here and do *nothing*."

"You need personal distance from any defection."

"I know."

"You know, part of this current strategy of subtle contacts with these electors has led to another strategy, less reliable, but still a possibility."

"And what's that?" President Hampton asked warily, not sure if he wanted to hear about an even less reliable strategy.

"Well, in the process of befriending the Edwards electors, our people may be able to gain influence with them. We may simply be able to convince one or more electors to switch over to us. Of course, we won't know for sure if we've been successful, but as long as we're making contact, why not include this? Some of our people can be very charming and persuasive."

"I'm sure they are." But the President certainly preferred a more guaranteed strategy.

Klondike glanced at his notes. "There's another matter that has come up," he told Hampton.

"Election related?"

"More or less," Klondike replied shrugging.

"What is it?"

"It's a matter of some sensitivity—it concerns the FBI investigation of the attempted assassination of Edwards, and some information that has come to us."

"Why is it sensitive?"

"You may not want to know the details . . ."

"Well, give me a general idea."

"We have some disconnected facts that might indicate . . . that one might look at and conclude . . . well, that an objective party might think we should tell Edwards about."

"So, tell him."

"These same facts could be politically helpful to him, and harmful to . . . to others."

"Mmm-hmmm."

"And the outcome of withholding the information could be very advantageous to us."

"So, then maybe we should withhold it."

"If the public finds out we had this information and withheld it, we could—"

"I don't know what-in-the-hell you're talking about," Hampton interrupted. "You're going to have to give me more to go on."

Klondike drew a deep breath. "The FBI has finally gotten results in on the fingerprints of the dead assassin. He's a Mexican national who lived in the Sinaloa province for the four years just previous to his attempt to kill Edwards. It took awhile to get the international fingerprint results, but this is a positive I-D. He has a record for selling marijuana—he was distributing it as part of some offbeat religion."

"How does that help Edwards?"

"He was apparently tending a huge marijuana plantation for some big-time Venezuelan coke and grass trafficker."

"Venezuelan?"

"I know. Not a country you really think of in connection with the drug cartels. But their problems with this increased throughout the 90's, and this guy is one of the slickest people—the DEA reports that he's in and out of this country all the time, but they have nothing on him."

"Okay . . ." Hampton still wasn't certain what concerned Klondike.

"This means Edwards' claim that drug dealers are threatened by his policies would seem to be confirmed by this development."

"How solid is the link between the dead guy and the drug guy?"

"It's pretty well established, but nothing that could be proven in court."

"Then who cares? We can't comment on investigations in progress. If there is good evidence of the link, then we'll have a duty to let people know. Otherwise, we'd just be passing along speculation."

"There's one more thing."

"What?"

"There's a report from the Secret Service that a Venezuelan national, on a questionable passport, has been seen at Edwards functions. On a hunch, I ran the name past some people in the DEA. They couldn't match the name, but the description matches Manuel Contreras, the main muscle for the same Venezuelan drug trafficker connected to the assassin. And when I asked DEA about it, they verified they tracked the guy to an Edwards speech once."

"You figure this means that the Venezuelan drug-lord is gunning for Edwards?"

"It's possible."

"Who else has this?"

"No one else has put these two pieces of information together."

"And if something happens to Edwards? If he gets killed?"

Klondike shrugged casually. "His electors would obviously be released from their pledges. You'd need one of 124 to take the election."

Hampton mulled over the situation for a few more moments. "What we have here is a lot of speculation," he finally commented.

"Informed speculation, but speculation, true."

"There are no charges pending against this Venezuelan man you say is now in the country?"

"The muscle guy? No. Lots of suspicions, no charges."

"In fact, we don't even know for certain that this Venezuelan guy checking out Edwards is really associated with the drug-lord."

"Not absolutely solid, no."

"So we're supposed to contact Edwards, or even the media through a press conference, with all this speculation that drug-lords are stalking him? Turning him into a crusading hero beset by evil drug dragons?"

"No. I guess not." Klondike now knew clearly what the President's wishes were.

"I would say that even putting the Secret Service and the FBI together on this could be inappropriate. What does it say about our attitude toward our South American friends if we harass their citizens and assume they're all drug dealers? The vast majority of them aren't, you know."

"I think I understand how you want this information handled," Klondike told President Hampton.

"Good." Hampton narrowed his eyes and pursed his lips, again in thought. "Oh, and Cuv?"

"Yes?"

"Please leave the investigation of the attempted assassination, *and* the protection of Michael Edwards to the appropriate agencies. You concentrate on my campaign."

"Yes sir."

"We wouldn't have the problem of what to do with the information if we didn't have it."

Klondike nodded.

"Get me my God Damned 270th elector."

"We'll keep working on it."

Chapter 23

Late November: The Next Day, Tuesday
Bayside Beach, Maryland

"They're getting real frustrated," Runalli assured Parker as they held a private meeting in Senator Parker's home on a high cliff overlooking the Chesapeake Bay. The Parker home was large enough to be comfortable, but was not so large that it radiated wealth. Senator Parker had money, but he was well aware that it was not "politically correct" for a rising liberal Democrat to live in opulence, unless your last name was Kennedy. "They haven't found an elector, and Hampton's getting annoyed."

"How reliable is this information?" Parker asked.

"Absolutely reliable."

Parker nodded. "You've got a spy inside the President's organization."

"Sort of."

"You have a friend."

Runalli smiled. "Senator, if you really want to know the source of this information, I'll tell you. But I believe you'd be better off *not* knowing."

"Every time you say that, I get more and more nervous."

"Don't like street fights, do you."

"I don't like not knowing what's going on. You say you have reliable information. I don't know how reliable it is. Then you tell me I shouldn't know how it's being gathered. Too many question marks, Will."

"Hypothetically, Senator Parker, soon-to-be President Parker, suppose the method used to gain this information is illegal? Would you still want to know how we're getting it?"

"Hypothetically?" Parker squinted uncomfortably, with a twinge of anger and frustration. "I suppose I better not know."

"Do we need to discuss this any further?" Runalli asked.

"Don't get caught," Parker told him sternly.

"Get caught doing what?" Runalli asked innocently.

"Whatever you're doing to get this information."

"I didn't say I was doing anything."

Parker glared at Runalli. "It doesn't take a moron to figure out that you're into something slimy—countering Hampton slime with our slime."

"You got that right. We have some juicy stuff on our dear President right now. If by some fluke he *does* steal the election, we can make him look real bad. But for now, we should hold that in reserve."

"What 'stuff' do you have on Hampton?"

"If I tell you, you'll want to know where I got it. It involves government agencies, and—"

"Don't tell me anymore," Parker interrupted abruptly. "If this blows up, I hope you're ready to fall on the grenade for this party, and for the Parker organization. Because I'll deny any knowledge of what you're doing."

"No one's going to have to fall on any grenades," Runalli stated casually. He paused. "You should be more grateful to me," he told Parker, smiling, but with some seriousness.

"I will be grateful to you when this is *over*, and I'm certain I haven't been buried by one of your schemes."

"Fair enough," Runalli replied. He got up to leave. "Guys like me get in the mud so guys like you can stay clean. And I like the mud. Just remember me when you're taking the oath of office."

Parker exhaled a nervous breath. "I'll have no choice."

Runalli smiled as he headed for the door.

Parker didn't get up to see him out. He tightened his lips nervously. He had been an outspoken, rising young Democrat in the early 70's, when he stated confidently that the Watergate scandal revealed Richard Nixon's hidden character defects. Parker now wondered what hidden character defects this current situation revealed in him.

☼   ☼   ☼

Late November, Election Year: Wednesday
Concord, Massachusetts

"I'M GOING TO GET YOU FOR THIS, DREW," TRACY ZELLER SAID WITH A good-natured sweet smile and a joke in her voice as she entered the living room of the bed and breakfast the Edwards Campaign had stayed in the previous night. The campaign was euphoric, with only one more elector meeting to go in Rhode Island on the following day. They had just finished the meeting with the Massachusetts electors in an outdoor gathering area at Walden Pond, surrounded by the high green trees that philosopher and environmentalist-ahead-of-his-time, Henry David Thoreau, had once made into his backyard when he built his cabin there.

Tracy Zeller had worked her way into more and more important tasks for the Edwards campaign, simply through efficient competence, demonstrated in every previous assignment given to her. She had lost nearly all of the timidity she once demonstrated as someone who started out answering the phones for the campaign (she was the one who had taken the call from Frances Willis during the selection process for the Vice Presidential candidate). She had even lost about 20 pounds.

"How is our friend Bennington Whittlebaum?" Saroyan asked, immediately aware of the subject of Tracy's gentle chiding.

"Well, like I told you, it was tough at first, because he was not happy to be talking to me. And I still have to be careful."

"I know," Saroyan acknowledged through a patient smile. "And you have every right to tell me again how you turned on the charm and won the jerk over."

"Just want to make sure you appreciate me," she replied, again through a pleasant, cordial smile. "Giving him the inside scoop on our itinerary is making him feel very important."

"I figured that would turn the guy on," Saroyan said to Edwards confidently.

"So he calls me at all of our exotic locations almost every day to pass along his . . . ideas."

"Off the wall stuff?" Edwards asked.

"Yeah. It's kind of tough sometimes. I have to dodge telling him he's crazy, or his idea is stupid, by saying things like 'that could have implementation problems,' or 'that sounds like a second-term project.' But some of the time he's just recycling our own ideas and claiming them for himself. That's easy. I just thank him for the idea and pretend he thought of it, then come back and say how much we all liked the idea."

"Any problems with this?" Edwards asked.

Tracy Zeller drew an apprehensive breath. "He keeps on asking if we went over his resumé. It's pathetically inadequate, but I can't tell him that."

Edwards and Saroyan waited for her to elaborate.

"I told him we're considering all good people. And—" She hesitated a moment. "I told him we have him listed in our personnel charts as Special Advisor to the Edwards Campaign."

"I don't want to misrepresent to him," Edwards commented.

"My idea," Saroyan told Edwards. "I figured a high-sounding title like Special Advisor that really means nothing would massage the guy's ego and give him something to brag about. No one will believe him, but as long as *he* does."

Edwards nodded.

"It's just going to be tough, because I think he's going to call me every day."

"I really thank you for what you're doing," Edwards told her sincerely. "This is a thankless job that we appreciate, but that you'll never really get any recognition for outside of this small circle."

"I know." She smiled. She was glad the man at the top of the ticket appreciated her efforts.

"Sounds like you still have it under control," Saroyan said to Tracy Zeller. Then he asked Edwards "Do we need to check with the lawyers about legal means to replace him?"

"I think Mr. Special Advisor to the Edwards Campaign is under control."

"I'd still like to know more about him."

Edwards drew a deep, irritated breath. "Out of the question."

"We can contact Oscar very quietly," Saroyan told Edwards. "But I'd like to know how the hell Oscar picked this nut. I thought he was so careful."

"I remember," Tracy added. "He had trouble with California. There were over 50 spots to fill and he's from the east coast. He commented to me that he was using acquaintances, and friends of friends, and that he wished he knew some of them a little better."

"So if Oscar doesn't know the guy, what good would it do to contact him?" Edwards asked.

Saroyan couldn't argue with the logic of the question.

"Keep on handling it the way we are now," Edwards stated, putting a bottom line to the discussion. "It seems to be contained. Let us know if there are any problems," he said to Tracy specifically.

"Of course," Tracy replied. She left the room.

"So, what's next?" Edwards asked Saroyan.

"Statesmanlike appearances, firming our endorsements, keeping tabs on the electors as well as possible. And we have meetings with Congressional people set for the week after next."

Edwards smiled. "And keeping our fingers crossed that everyone votes the way they should in mid December."

"Yes," Saroyan agreed.

☼   ☼   ☼

Late November, Election Year: Sunday
New York, New York

"IF THERE IS *ANYTHING* I CAN DO FOR YOU, PLEASE, ALL YOU HAVE TO DO is page me. My beeper number is on my card," Thornton Cornet gushed to Cherise LePlume as he drooled and handed her his card. He was a gaunt, well-dressed but unattractive man with crooked teeth and a pruny, weathered face. He covered up his lack of regular bathing with overpowering doses of after-shave lotion. He had stubby grey whiskers and looked older than his 52 years. The apartment they stood together in was a plush, well-furnished apartment on the seventh floor of 15.

"Thank you," Cherise LePlume replied with a seductive French accent, but in perfectly understandable English. "And thank you again for coming out like this on your Thanksgiving weekend." She was a gorgeous young woman, tall and leggy, thin, but with all the proper curves. Her short brown hair framed an exotically beautiful face. She had dressed in a white blouse and jeans—the blouse was loose and unbuttoned to breast level while the jeans were skin tight. "Sorry I am not so familiar with your American holidays."

"No problem," Cornet answered, overselling his helpfulness. "*Any* time."

"You are very kind."

"I can see why you're a model," he told her as his blood pressure seemed to rise with each word he spoke.

"Yes, well I do a lot of work in New York, so I need a place to stay," she explained to him.

"This is a good place. You know, a bunch of famous people live around here. Michael Edwards, the Presidential candidate? He lives across the street." He pointed out the appropriate window.

"Really?" she replied with genuine surprise. "Michael Edwards?" She giggled. "I do not follow American politics."

The man apparently needed a cue to stop looking at her and leave.

"Thank you, monsieur. I need to settle in."

"Of course. Well, anything I can do . . ." He flashed a quick smile and left.

She waited one or two minutes, glancing warily around the apartment, particularly at the door. She then reached down into her purse and pulled out a small cellular phone. She punched in a number. "He's gone," she said in an accent that was not French, but southern United States.

Five minutes later, Manuel Contreras was in the apartment with the pretty woman.

"Maybe I *should* be a model," she told Contreras in her twang accent with a gleam in her eye.

"We picked you for this because you could be one," Contreras told her.

"Yeah? Picked me for what?"

"Don't ask too many questions."

"Okay. I have only one more question. When do I get my payment?"

Contreras's face broke into a lascivious grin. He moved slowly toward her and took hold of her shoulders gently with his hands. "After we do just one more thing . . ."

She pulled away angrily. "That was *not* part of our deal. I am *not* a prostitute."

Contreras laughed a belittling snicker. "Yeah. You're a model from Paris!"

She backed up, trying to increase the space between them. But she ran out of space and found herself pinned against the wall.

"You're getting caught up in your role," Contreras taunted. "A high-class model from Paris?" He laughed, not out of humor, but to intimidate. "You're a *coke*-whore from New Orleans."

"I don't have sex for—"

"You'd do it," he said confidently. He backed off. "But you're right—we didn't agree to anything extra." He moved toward a satchel he had brought with him into the apartment. "And it looks like you did a real nice job. That horny old guy got things set up in a hurry."

Cherise heaved a huge sigh of relief.

Contreras tossed her a baggy of cocaine.

Her eyes widened with delight.

"Don't get caught with that stuff," Manuel cautioned her, smiling. "I hear it's illegal."

She smiled slightly.

He tossed her a wad of cash. "Plane fare. We'll contact you in New Orleans if we need you again."

"Okay." She headed for the door.

Contreras sidestepped into her path so that she walked into him. "It would have been good," he told her suggestively as he put his arm around her and moved his face close to hers.

"No thank you," she told him politely, but with a touch of fear.

"I'm not a rapist," he told her as he stepped aside to allow her a clear path to the door.

"Bye," she said, leaving the apartment as quickly as she could.

Contreras smiled. Let her be afraid of him. If by some fluke this apartment, which she had paid for in cash under a phony name on the rental documents, was actually traced to her, she would still fear linking herself to Contreras.

On the street below, a van circled the block around the apartment building. "I'm not sure what he's planning," the same operative who had followed him at Big Sur said into his car phone. "He just went into an apartment."

"Keep reporting," Carl Gregory's voice said through the other end of the phone.

"It's a little difficult right now. This part of the city has no street parking, and if I keep circling . . ."

"Understood."

"I have the son-of-a-bitch wired. Stupid idiot. He doesn't even know it."

"What's he doing?"

"He just had a girl rent an apartment for him so he can't be traced to it, right across from Edwards' apartment."

"Park as close as you can and keep tabs on him with the wire."

"What about moving in now?"

"No," Gregory replied decisively. "We don't know what his plan is yet. Maybe he's already put it in place and is there watching to see it come off. We need to watch him and find out what he has in mind."

"Right."

"He thinks using some girl to rent the apartment will keep him out of it?"

"Looks that way."

"I'll bet the idiot isn't even wearing gloves, and that she didn't either."

"Didn't see any going in."

"The FBI will crack this guy open in 48 hours. We've got to snuff this thing. Keep tabs on the wire. We'll bring more people in to help out with the surveillance, and maybe try to establish our own post at the apartment building."

"Acknowledged."

Manuel Contreras walked to the window and looked across the street with a confident sneer. He formed his right hand into the shape of a pistol and pointed his index finger at Edwards' window. He made a shooting sound as he lowered his thumb, pulling some sort of imaginary trigger.

He picked up the same cellular phone Cherise LePlume had used and left behind. He quickly punched in a long series of numbers. "This is your delivery service—everything is in place for your Christmas present to be delivered. We are certain of a complete delivery by Christmas at the latest, depending on the availability of your customer. We will be able to complete delivery the next time he comes home . . . Yes, the basics are in place. A few items need to be gathered . . . Right. Bye." Contreras disconnected his call.

The operative quickly reported this latest telephone conversation, Contreras's side only. The "basics" were "in place."

✪   ✪   ✪

Early December, Election Year: Friday
Santa Cruz, California

"I'M GLAD MY ADVICE IS SO MUCH HELP TO THE CAMPAIGN," BENNINGTON Whittlebaum said magnanimously. "Tell Michael I'm here for him. Hang loose, babe." He hung up the phone with a grin of total satisfaction on his face. He was playing in the big leagues—the world would discover his genius soon. He sat back in the chair of his desk, facing the doorway of his tiny "study" in the two bedroom house he and his wife rented in Santa Cruz, California, the small coastal community, known for counter-culture and white sandy beaches.

"'Hang loose, babe?'" his wife Molly sneered in disbelief as she eavesdropped on the tail end of the conversation. Molly Whittlebaum was attractive, but with a tired face, hard eyes and a hollow, unforgiving expression that had evolved from her general weariness with a disappointing life and a loveless, respectless marriage. Her blonde hair frizzed in tangled puffs around her head. "Is that your new girlfriend?"

"That is Tracy Zeller from the Edwards organization," he corrected sternly. "I was giving advice that will be used by Michael Edwards—"

"Oh yeah. He's been hanging *real* loose lately. I saw him hanging off—"

"The lady is *not* my girlfriend."

"Too bad," Molly snapped. "I thought being an elector was going to bring women after you in droves; you'd dump me—I think you said something stupid like 'a bad habit.'"

"The women are there," he told her insistently. "I'm working on it."

"Which means they all think you're as big a dork as I think you are," she countered. "The only man in the country who has a wife who *wants* him to cheat, and he can't pull it off." She smirked. "You should pull it off for all the use it gets." She giggled.

Bennington Whittlebaum shook his head. "You are history, bitch. When I'm accepting my *cabinet post,* you can stay and *rot* in this dump, and make your junior high jokes to the fucking winos down on the Boardwalk!"

"What a speech! How long did you rehearse that one? Don't waste my time with your next masterpiece. I'm not buying into any of your silly fantasies."

"Fantasies?" he repeated with astonished indignation.

"If you weren't an elector, these people would be sending you the same form letters you've gotten from everybody else you've tried to latch on to."

"That's right. Somebody finally had to listen to me! And when they did, they found a wealth of—"

"They found an idiot who needs to be handled."

"You have no idea—"

"You lucked out—can't you see it? You happened to be gathering signatures one day when Oscar Lusman just happened to be there. He needed names for the elector sheet, and you didn't look like the loser you are that day. He obviously didn't know you very well."

"We had a long conversation," he insisted.

"After you vote in Sacramento, these people won't know you. You're so pathetic—you don't even see it." She walked away.

He followed her. "I'll get Tracy on the phone right now. She'll tell you—"

"If you're so important to those people, then why aren't you speaking directly to Edwards? Why aren't you out there with his entourage? Why are you talking to flunkies, Mr. Secretary of the Interior?"

"I've got the inside track on that job," he insisted. "And Tracy is *not* a flunkey. She's in the inner circle. I'll get her on the line. She'll tell you."

Molly stopped and turned toward him. "You can't reach her right now. Didn't she give you certain hours when you can call?"

"That was to make sure we could get together—she knows how busy I am."

Molly's skeptical eyebrows shot up.

He stormed past her toward the phone in their living room. "She'll take my call." He punched in the number.

"She won't take your call," Molly predicted confidently.

"We'll see." He waited for someone at the phone number he had called to answer.

"Winston Hotel," the operator answered.

"Tracy Zeller's room," he stated.

"She's in a meeting," the operator answered politely.

"In the hotel?"

"Yes sir. May I take a—"

"This is Bennington Whittlebaum," he told her in an austere, self-important tone, as if the name should mean something to her. "Please interrupt the meeting and tell her I am on the line."

"I can't do that," the operator told him politely but insistently. "If you will leave a—"

"Young lady, I am one of the most important advisors to the Edwards campaign. It is *imperative* that I speak to her *now*."

"You're an advisor?" The operator sounded puzzled. "I thought they were . . . aren't they all meeting tonight?"

This was the last thing Bennington Whittlebaum wanted to hear. He gritted his teeth. "Not *all* of them," he told her. "My beeper number is 408-555-1465. Have her page me right away."

"Of course, sir."

He hung up.

His wife's I-told-you-so expression belittled Whittlebaum without words. But she couldn't resist an extra taunt. "Oh, you mean somebody might actually use your pager?"

"Fuck you, bitch!" he shouted at her. His face flushed red with a violent rage, and he started toward her.

Molly backed up cautiously.

Her obvious shift to fear defused Whittlebaum. "You think I'd hit you?" he demanded. In all their unhappy years together, he'd never tried to intimidate her physically. But he enjoyed the sudden superiority he had attained as a result of his momentary loss of temper. "Maybe I will." He grabbed a coat out of the closet as Molly continued to keep a cautious distance between them. "Maybe I'll come home and beat the crap out of you." He stormed out of the house.

Bennington Whittlebaum walked rapidly toward a small club about three blocks from his home. It was more than a local bar—musicians and writers gathered at the club and performed for each other. Whittlebaum had often retreated to it when frustrated by his relationship at home. As he walked, he wasn't sure what made him the angriest, his wife's insistence that the Edwards campaign was patronizing him, or that she had almost convinced him it was true.

It was still early, only around a quarter to eight. So Whittlebaum was able to find a small table he could occupy by himself. He nursed a Cognac and checked his beeper at least once every five minutes to see if it was working.

Three singers were rotating fifteen minute sets, offering guitar and voice songs to a generally appreciative crowd. Whittlebaum sat and stewed, not really hearing any of the music. Why hadn't he gotten a beeper page? Was his wife actually right? He desperately needed another answer.

✿   ✿   ✿

TRACY ZELLER WEARILY WALKED THROUGH THE HOTEL LOBBY, AFTER A marathon meeting with the Edwards campaign staff, during which they discussed every single state elector, including Bennington Whittlebaum. They had reserved the following few days for meetings with Congressional leaders and their staffers. So it had been necessary to hold a late night meeting to discuss the elector situation.

Tracy Zeller had assured Edwards and Saroyan that Whittlebaum was under control. She had spoken to him just before the meeting and she told them they could still count him as a loyal, enthusiastic supporter. Edwards and Saroyan had praised her for her handling of the delicate situation.

She moved to the front desk in the hotel lobby. "Any messages?" she asked the white-haired, elderly male clerk on duty.

"Room?"

"6-37."

He went to the boxes. "Yes," he said as he returned. "There's one." He handed it to her.

She saw the name and number. She was tired, and did not recognize that this was not Whittlebaum's home telephone number. And Whittlebaum usually called her, so she wasn't familiar with his number anyway.

"What time was this message taken?" she asked.

"I don't know," the clerk answered. "They usually put the times down, but these night clerks sometimes get a little lazy." He looked at the message again. "And that clerk has gone home."

"That's okay," she said, dismissing the concern. "I already spoke to this guy." She crumpled the message and walked away from the desk, depositing it in a nearby waste basket.

☼   ☼   ☼

WHITTLEBAUM SEETHED AS HE LOOKED AT HIS DIGITAL WATCH: "9:32." The only reason he didn't move was because he didn't know what to do next—he was only certain that he did not want to go home and tell his wife he hadn't received a call from Tracy Zeller.

Matt Harper walked in. He glanced over at Whittlebaum seated alone, radiating anger and hostility. Harper had dressed in jeans and a T shirt, the politically correct attire for this Santa Cruz night club near the college, but not Harper's normal attire. He had carefully selected these clothes for his visits to the club and charged their purchase to his expense account. He had let his beard grow—the stubby blonde hairs were still a few weeks away from coalescing into anything respectable. His hair remained neatly styled.

Harper approached the host, a balding man in his early fifties.

"You told me to call you if he came in," the host said to Harper in a cautionary tone. "But he looks *pissed* tonight . . ."

"Mmm." Harper considered what that might mean. He reached into his pocket, pulled out a fifty dollar bill and handed it to the host. "Thanks again." He moved toward Whittlebaum's table.

Whittlebaum had his arms folded, as if to put up a silent "stop, no vacancies at this table" sign.

Harper walked right through it as he took a seat across from Whittlebaum at his table. "Hey Ben!" Harper greeted enthusiastically. "How's my man inside the Edwards organization!"

Whittlebaum looked at him with a stern, unwelcoming expression. "I'm not into company tonight, Matt. Please find another table."

"What's wrong?"

"What's wrong?" Whittlebaum was tempted to answer the question. But he held back. "Nothing. I just need some space."

"I can imagine. With all the stress of advising the Edwards people . . ."

"Yeah. The stress. It's—" He cut himself off. "Stress."

"So you need some time to think over the next problem that—"

"I have my *own* problems," Whittlebaum snapped. "I'm more than just some Edwards worshiper! Now can you back off?"

"I'm sorry," Harper said sincerely. "I never meant to imply you were a . . . an 'Edwards worshipper.' I know you're one of the people who's working to make him great."

Whittlebaum was silent a moment, then exhaled deeply. "I'm sorry. I shouldn't be coming down on you." He forced a smile through his dejection. "I'll buy you a drink." He motioned for the waitress.

Harper settled more comfortably into his chair.

"I'm just in a bad mood," Whittlebaum explained.

"I can understand the bad mood," Harper told Whittlebaum sympathetically. "This whole political scene is making me nuts. Before I met you a few weeks ago, I was a Hampton supporter. Now, after hearing from you about what Edwards stands for, I've been looking at him. He's not like the other politicians. He's a new type of guy, innovative . . ." Harper searched briefly for a key word. He found it. "But most of all, he's *accessible*." He had built the phrase to lean on the last word, hoping to provoke an emotional, gut-level response from Whittlebaum.

It worked. Whittlebaum snorted cynically. "Yeah, he's . . . 'accessible,'" he repeated with sarcastic disgust.

"Well isn't he? I mean, he's been open to your ideas. You're a guy he didn't know until a few weeks ago."

"I *thought* he was open. But now? I'm not so sure."

"Really . . ." Harper left a gap of silence.

"They . . . I don't know." Whittlebaum stammered. "I'm just one of over fifty electors in California—one of over a hundred in the country. Hell, I'm one of 34 *million* voters for him."

Harper smiled. "Yeah. It's tough to be one of an admiring crowd." He chuckled strategically. "It's ironic." He shook his head. "The guy who really needs just one insightful person—" He deliberately cut himself off before completing the thought. "You wouldn't want to hear about that."

Whittlebaum swallowed the bait hard. "Ironic? What? Who needs just one person?"

"I thought that would be obvious," Harper told him. "Sometimes I still hang out with people connected to the Hampton organization back over the hill." ("Over the hill" referred to the upper middle class, generally conservative communities of Los Gatos, Monte Sereno, and Saratoga.) "They mentioned how nice it would be if just one Edwards elector chose Hampton. So you could be *real* significant to Hampton."

"How? He doesn't even know me. And if I switched my vote, what would he care? He wouldn't need me at all."

"But you're significant to him *now*. And I would think he'd want to meet with someone as smart as you, who can see the political landscape accurately and make an astute decision."

"Maybe. But I don't know his people. I wouldn't even know who to approach."

"But *I* do," Harper told him with a helpful smile. "I could set up a meeting—I'll bet their top guy would come out to see you personally within forty-eight hours."

Whittlebaum responded with attempted nonchalance. "I'll meet with him. No commitments, of course."

"Let me make some calls—I'll get back to you."

Whittlebaum's eyes squinted decisively. "I'll give you my *beeper* number," he said. "Call me tonight." He stood up. "I'd better be getting back to the wife."

"Of course."

☼   ☼   ☼

KLONDIKE WAS AWAKENED BY THE CALL FROM HARPER. HE congratulated Harper on a job well done and woke up his travel agent to book the first flight out of Washington D.C. to San Francisco the following morning, which on the east coast had technically already arrived. He woke up a few other associates to lay the groundwork for the meeting.

Whittlebaum's beeper went off as he and his wife were getting ready to go to sleep for the night. They set the meeting for two nights later. Whittlebaum beamed a smile of supreme satisfaction as his wife watched and overheard his conversation in amazement. His elector status was going to pay off for him after all. After he'd finished making his wife regret her treatment of him, he'd unceremoniously dump her for one of the young, beautiful women who congregate around men of power. Whittlebaum raised his chin proudly in the bathroom mirror as he brushed his teeth. He knew his day was finally coming.

Chapter 24

Early December: The Next Day, Saturday
Bayside Beach, Maryland

"I THINK THEY'VE GOT A GUY," RUNALLI TOLD PARKER GRAVELY AS they met privately at Parker's home, just after breakfast on Saturday morning. They were in the same study where they had met almost two weeks earlier. This time, both men were more casual and familiar with one another, though they both still measured their words to each other carefully.

"What do you mean, they've 'got a guy?'" Parker asked as he sat back in his office chair, wearing monogrammed pajamas.

"They have an Edwards elector in California they think they can get to defect," Runalli answered.

Parker felt a wave of nausea. For a split-second, he thought he might be physically ill. He inhaled and exhaled deeply, trying to calm his suddenly jumpy stomach. "How solid is this?"

"It's not a done deal yet, but it's close enough that we need to have a strategy."

"What do you mean it's 'not a done deal yet?' Is the guy going to switch his vote or not?"

"We can't be sure. But—" Runalli paused. "There's a good chance he will. He's put himself into a position to be enticed into it."

"Enticed. You mean bribed? Can we prove it?"

"Not easily. Our source of information—it's reliable, but it could prove embarrassing."

"I know," Parker replied with gruff impatience.

"We're leaking what we know to the media, but they may or may not be able to substantiate it quickly enough to do us any good."

"I see." Parker didn't like his next question, but he had to ask it. "What 'strategy' do you recommend?"

"We have to neutralize this elector's decision," Runalli told him with a calculated, methodical tone of voice. "There are a variety of ways to do that. Some we need to discuss; some we don't . . ."

Parker frowned. "I am very uncomfortable with your strategies that we 'don't need to discuss.' I'm telling you now how we'll handle this. I want these Hampton strategies leaked to the press. No one'll stand for the President bribing electors. We'll get a special prosecutor involved and run that son-of-a-bitch—"

"Do you want to win this thing or not?" Runalli interrupted combatively. "I'm sick and tired of having to explain this shit to you."

"Don't you talk to me that way," Parker scolded.

"A quick Civics lesson," Runalli lectured, ignoring Parker's admonishment. "If President Hampton steals this election, and you get him investigated and tossed, the guy that becomes President is the *Vice President.* Or, you could argue that the whole election is invalidated and throw the thing into the courts where it will go on and on for months, making a lot of Constitutional lawyers rich. Even then, with all the judges stacked into the courts by Republicans for most of the last thirty years, you could lose that court battle. If you want a clear path to the Presidency, this thing must go to the House. I can get it there. Your strategy might, but might not. You should stand back and let me do my job."

"I don't know what your job is," Parker responded uneasily.

"Simple. To make you President of the United States. Victor Parker. Into the history books. One of a very select group of Americans. And with power, maybe the most power of any one person in the world. My job is to give all that to *you.*"

Parker hated the fact that he had no response to Runalli's argument, by now a very familiar one. He still would have liked to say that morally, he would not permit illegal or unethical maneuvers to win. But he knew such a stance would be naive and self-defeating when it was obvious that Hampton was not playing by such lofty principles. "What 'strategies' do you need to discuss with me?" he asked coldly and quietly.

"I need to be able to deal with this elector," Runalli told him. "I need to be able to offer him an important position working with your administration. Something high-sounding."

"Jesus." Parker again drew a long breath and exhaled it. "Yeah. Okay."

"And . . . I need some money, mid six figures, that we can get at, untraceable to—"

"Are you fucking crazy!?" Parker demanded. "A straight payoff? You've got to be out of your mind!"

"I need that option. And there could be expenses that we need to pay. . . to people who don't take checks and don't give receipts."

"You're *nuts*. How do you propose to get away with this?"

"By laying it off on the Edwards people."

Parker stiffened.

"I have it set up so I can lay off the embarrassing options on the Edwards people."

Parker shook his head. It occurred to him that once you enter a room and decide to stay, there is no way to be just a little inside the door. "I hope you know what you're doing."

Runalli smiled. "I was *born* to win a fight like this. You've joined up with the right guy at the right time."

Parker wasn't sure what to say. He wanted to get back on familiar territory: making speeches, setting policy, doling out the huge bounty of the Federal government. The strategy of leaking to the media about Hampton's behavior was in his comfort zone—Runalli's intrigues were not. "Maybe," he finally replied to Runalli's boast. "I just get unsettled when I think that you'd probably be just as happy directing President Hampton's end of what you call a 'street fight.'"

"Never," Runalli responded with exaggerated indignation. "We need Democrats running the country." He fought a smile, but it crept onto his face slightly.

"I'll have the money available for you; contact Mueller first thing tomorrow morning. If we have to buy this guy with a job . . ." He paused. "Just be careful. We could easily get tangled up in this."

"I'll handle it. Don't worry."

"Yeah."

☼   ☼   ☼

Early December: The Next Day, Sunday
Santa Cruz, California

"WAIT HERE," KLONDIKE SAID TO HARPER AS THEY PULLED TO THE curb outside Bennington Whittlebaum's rented house. Klondike had paid cash for a commercial plane flight under an assumed name, and was staying with Harper instead of at a hotel. He wanted to make sure there was no documentary evidence of his visit to Bennington Whittlebaum. "Thanks for your help on this thing. And for the inside scoop on this clown."

"My pleasure. Remember, the guy is starving for some kind of power and recognition."

"And he's a bit off kilter."

"Yeah."

Klondike emerged from the car on this dimly lit, narrow street. He had dressed in slacks, a sports shirt and tweed jacket. He carried his briefcase. When he shut the car door, he heard a dog start barking. As he walked toward Whittlebaum's front door, he noticed the cluttered appearance of the neighborhood. He spotted a few derelict cars along the curb—one was even up on a front lawn. Yards were cluttered with boats, surfboards, bicycles, and other junk. Klondike grimaced with distaste as he reached the front door of the house, with its faded white paint.

He knocked on the door.

Molly Whittlebaum answered the door.

"Covington Klondike here to see Ben Whittlebaum," Klondike said in a business-like tone, hiding his irritation that Whittlebaum himself hadn't answered the door.

"I'll get him," she replied. "It was *his* idea that I answer the door." She left him standing outside and went to summon her husband.

"You told him I had you answer the door?" Ben Whittlebaum asked his wife caustically as she approached him in the small, cluttered living room. Whittlebaum was wearing a T shirt and jeans, but was freshly bathed and groomed, with his hair still wet. "I told you to bring him in here."

"Go answer your own doors," she countered sharply.

"I'll remember the *help*," he promised her angrily as he got up from his seat. He headed for the front door.

Molly Whittlebaum headed for the bedroom. The door shut quietly behind her.

Whittlebaum's concentration diverted to Klondike as he approached him, still standing outside the front door. "Mr. Klondike," he greeted. "Please come in."

"Thank you." Klondike stepped in, wondering for a moment when he had last entered such a modest residence.

Whittlebaum ushered Klondike into the living room and showed him to a seat across the coffee table.

Klondike sat down and placed his briefcase on the coffee table. "So, Mr. Whittlebaum, a mutual friend says you're a man of some sophistication, ability and influence, whom I might want to speak to . . ."

"I'm an Edwards elector," Whittlebaum blurted out, like a man who had won the lottery and was in a hurry to claim his prize.

Klondike moved slightly in his chair, and tried mostly successfully to contain his irritation with Bennington Whittlebaum's lack of finesse. He'd have to nurse this neophyte through their mutual courtship. "Mr. Whittlebaum, I think we have to be very careful how we handle the elector situation," Klondike told him diplomatically. "That's why I want our meeting to be secret. While my friend assures me you are a brilliant young talent whom we should consider putting to work for us, someone else might think we are contacting you just because you are an elector for Michael Edwards."

Whittlebaum considered Klondike's statement. "Yes," he said. "I agree that we must be careful. And I can tell you, I have been listening to commentaries calling for electors to vote their consciences. After all, the President got the most votes. Is it fair that Parker will be President? Here I am in a position to make a difference, to enforce justice. Am I serving my country faithfully if I fail to use my position to enforce justice?"

"I can see you have a sharp political mind," Klondike told him, satisfied with this shift in Whittlebaum's approach. "Mr. Harper told us this."

"And he told you I might change my vote to President Hampton?"

"He mentioned that as well. And that further demonstrates the insight and astuteness that we could use in the Republican Party."

"Would you come to see me if I wasn't considering changing my vote?"

"Of course," Klondike replied quickly. "But the trip will be wasted if you don't, or if one of you Edwards people doesn't change his vote, because we'd be out of power."

"True." Whittlebaum paused and smiled slyly. "And I'd hate to see you waste a trip out here."

"Never a waste to unearth young talent."

"Or guarantee an election victory."

"Sometimes things work out symbiotically that way."

"Yeah," Whittlebaum answered cynically. "How would you plan to put me to work if . . . if some elector turns . . . if an Edwards elector switches over to the President?" he asked awkwardly.

Klondike flashed a charming smile as he opened his briefcase and pulled out his business card. "This card has my *private line* on it," he told Whittlebaum as he handed him the card. "You call me in about six months after we take office and I promise you—"

"*Six months?* After us electors vote, you won't . . ." He stammered, but gathered himself. "Guys like you change jobs so quickly. I'd hate to lose my connection with you—personal relationships are so important in politics."

"Yes." Klondike paused. "You see, the problem is that if you take a job with us immediately, it could look like a payoff. So the six month waiting period—"

"Mr. Klondike, if I'm going to change my vote with the idea that President Hampton will stay in power, I won't wait six months. That's out of the question."

"The six month waiting period would be an absolute must if you are going to work directly for the President. Now if—"

"The six month waiting period will cause me to rethink my position," Whittlebaum stated bluntly. "I need a commitment to at least an Under Secretary Cabinet position—an appointment *immediately.*"

Klondike held his facial expression intact, but his stomach surged with acid as he became aware that this man did not have a firm grasp on reality. "Mr. Whittlebaum," he explained slowly, lowering his voice, trying to maintain a charming tone, "you must be smart enough to know why we can't do that. Because you are an elector, the Democrats in Congress would parade you in front of a Congressional committee and question you day and night. We need to use your talents more subtly. A guy like you will be able to work your way into one of the big spots in a very short time."

Whittlebaum nodded. "What do you have in mind?"

"This isn't a deal, Mr. Whittlebaum. I'm not here making offers and accepting counteroffers. That would be improper and unethical."

"I understand, but—"

Klondike cut him off and continued before Whittlebaum could redirect the conversation. "I think I know how we could employ your talents," he stated as if the idea had just occurred to him. "Senator Stephan of Utah is a close friend of the President. I know he's looking for a good Special Assistant, a liaison to—"

"Work for a *Senator*?" Whittlebaum blurted out. "When I hold this election in the palm of my hand? I think you have underestimated me, *and* the power I hold at this moment in history. Now I expect—"

"It would help immeasurably if you would not interrupt me," Klondike suggested. "Now if you are trying to get me to pay you off for changing your vote, I must decline any such exchange. We must not couch our contact in those terms. I've explained this . . ."

"You just want to help a bright guy get a good job."

"And help out my *party* by bringing good new blood on board."

Whittlebaum seemed to have regained his composure, and asked reasonably, "So how will you ensure my future, Mr. Klondike? And how will you make sure your party gets use of my talents? Six months is a long time. I could easily get lost in the shuffle by then."

"I think I can make you feel very good about your future," Klondike assured him. "But you must be patient. Please listen closely to what I have to say about working for Senator Stephan."

"Okay," Whittlebaum acknowledged skeptically.

"I am certain that Senator Stephan will offer you a contract for three years on his staff as a paid consultant, liaison to the White House. You will tell him you have to clear up your own work situation before you can start, which I'm sure is true."

"It's *not,* but go ahead . . ."

"The six month thing is important. Now in your position with Senator Stephan you will be working with the White House every day. We cannot promise you anything in writing. But if you distinguish yourself, you can expect us to grab you, even before your three year contract has expired."

Whittlebaum tightened his lips and squinted in thought.

Klondike was pleased he hadn't heard an immediate rejection. Whittlebaum was thinking it over. As he did, Klondike continued the sales pitch. "This is a hell of an opportunity for you."

Whittlebaum finally responded. "I was hoping my future could be assured a little better than that . . ."

Klondike sighed. "Well, there is one other matter," he added, moving to what he hoped would be the deal-maker, though he had wanted to avoid casting this element into the package. But it was clear he needed a clincher. "Your courage to follow your conscience and change your vote will make you the target of serious litigation. We will, of course, encourage those who admire you to contribute to your defense. But we would also like to advance you 300,000 dollars to pay for legal expenses while the other contributions come in. This money would be sent to you in cash, untraceable to us, because again, we wouldn't want our payment to be misconstrued. We admire your principles, and your courage to vote your conscience. But others . . ."

"The money doesn't mean that much to me," Whittlebaum replied sincerely. "But maybe you're right. I will have legal expenses." Whittlebaum again thought for an awkwardly silent moment.

Klondike resisted the temptation to fill the moment. Whittlebaum appeared to be seriously considering this proposal, trying to talk himself into it. Klondike needed to give him a chance to do it.

"Send the contract from Senator Stephan, and the money," Whittlebaum finally said to Klondike. "My conscience is . . . I feel good about voting my conscience, knowing that my future is so well set."

"Good," Klondike replied smiling. "Well, I'm still on east coast time, so I hope you'll forgive me if I head back to my hotel room for some rest." (There was no need for Whittlebaum to know he wasn't staying in a hotel.)

"Sure."

Klondike stood to leave.

"Please get me the items we discussed by the end of the week," he told Klondike, "or I'm not sure how my conscience might . . . how my vote—"

"They'll be here by messenger; Tuesday, Wednesday at the latest," Klondike assured him, cutting off the awkward, clumsy threat. "I'm glad to be able to offer this opportunity to such a sharp young man." He turned, took two steps, then turned back. "Of course, if your conscience told you to stay with Edwards, we would be out of power and there would be no job with Senator Stephan as liaison to the Hampton White House. And we wouldn't be of much assistance for your future." Klondike smiled broadly, just as he uttered his most ominous statement. "In fact, I'd say the future for you would be very bleak if you accepted our help, but we failed to retain power."

Whittlebaum's expression became slightly apprehensive.

"So we understand each other?"

"Yeah." Whittlebaum appeared to accept the deal, and the potential consequences of reneging. "Tell Senator Stephan to expect me in Washington in June—tell him to include moving expenses in my employment package."

"Good."

"You and I and President Hampton will have lunch, maybe in the Oval Office?"

"It'll be our pleasure," Klondike lied.

✿   ✿   ✿

"THE SON-OF-A-BITCH IS OURS," KLONDIKE TOLD HARPER AS HE arrived in the car where Harper had been waiting for him.

Harper started the car motor.

"I don't have to tell you how quiet this has to stay."

"No."

"The President will need a favor from his friend from Utah."

Harper nodded as he smiled knowingly. "He's the one who'll have to deal with that jack-ass?"

"Yeah. The small price we Republicans will have to pay to stay in power."

Harper's eyebrows raised as they traveled up Highway 880 (known by longtime residents as Highway 17) to Harper's home in the Almaden area of San Jose.

✿   ✿   ✿

Early December: The Next Day, Monday
Washington, D.C.

"THE MEETINGS WENT ABOUT AS WELL AS WE COULD HAVE EXPECTED," Saroyan assured Edwards as they took their seats at a single table in a private room of the D Street Cafe. They had arranged to enjoy a late afternoon meal in a small private dining room. Some Secret Service men sat in the regular customer area. Appearances in public places had become public events. They needed some privacy to assess their efforts.

"We know that most of these Congressmen will vote party on the first ballot," Saroyan continued. "What we've done is set up some good lines of communication with a bunch of these people in case this thing stalemates."

"I wish we could have met directly with more of them," Edwards commented.

"Not during an end-of-the-year recess," Saroyan reminded him. "Michael, I know you're used to approaching people directly and laying all your cards face up. But in this situation, it's just as well that we have cultivated staff people. If we'd met directly with a lot of Congressmen, it would turn into a media event, and we might force people into inflexible positions of party loyalty because we've put them on the spot publicly. These staff people will go back to their bosses. Based on our meetings, I'm sure some of them will lay the public relations groundwork for supporting you in the event of a stalemate."

"So you feel we had some good meetings—for me, it was hard to tell."

"It was what they *didn't* say. Not a single one closed the door to supporting you, or spoke disparagingly about your agenda. They left their options open. And over half made apologies that the Congressional representatives couldn't meet with you personally. They are taking you seriously—you are still considered a factor."

Edwards nodded. "So if the House deadlocks . . ."

"We still need some breaks. But we have a shot."

"Especially with the polls that show that I might actually win if the election were held today and decided by popular vote."

"These polls are looking very good, and they're on a trajectory in your favor. Your public appearances have been dignified and statesmanlike. I think we'd have to say we're playing our hand as well as we can right now."

"The electors seem to be locked down."

"It looks that way," Saroyan agreed hesitantly. "We've been staying in touch with them, and we feel a good rapport with almost all of them."

"*Almost* all?"

"It's hard to tell when you're dealing with personalities. Some people are not enthusiastic by nature. And it's tricky to question loyalties directly."

Edwards drew a deep, nervous breath. He wished the situation could be more certain.

Donald Samuelson walked into the main room of the D street Cafe. He had dressed in casual clothes, blue jeans and a blue Pendleton shirt. He pulled off his gloves and undid his thick coat as he took a seat, escaping from the cold autumn air outside.

Samuelson had not become a top reporter with a major network by having poor observational skills. He immediately noticed two tables, with white-shirted Secret Service agents sipping their drinks, but with an on-duty aura to them. After he saw the owner of the cafe walk into the private dining room a few times, he became curious.

The next time Samuelson saw the owner exit the banquet area, he quickly went toward him. "David!" he greeted. "How're you doing?"

The Secret Service agents saw him go by, but they recognized him as a reporter, and saw he had gone to greet the owner. So they did not move to stop him.

"Don," the cafe owner acknowledged. "Out for a little stroll?"

"Yeah. They got you working on a Monday?"

"Occasionally. And, the Redskins don't play tonight."

"Well, good to see you," Samuelson told him as he shook his hand.

Samuelson turned back toward his table, but moved slowly. The owner moved much more quickly toward the kitchen.

Samuelson suddenly turned and headed into the private room. He saw Edwards eating his salad and Saroyan eating his soup.

Saroyan saw him first. "Aw Christ. Listen, this is a private meeting."

Samuelson smiled. "I *knew* you guys were back here."

Edwards turned, then grinned, almost admiringly. "The Secret Service guys."

"And David shuffling in and out of here. I knew Parker and Hampton weren't hip enough to know about this place."

"Probably not." Edwards looked at Saroyan. "Those Secret Service guys have got to dress down, Drew. We've been trying to tell them that."

"Yeah." Saroyan turned to Samuelson. "You found us. Now give us a break and leave us in peace."

"Wait a minute," Edwards said graciously. "We're *always* willing to talk to the press, no matter how unfairly some of them have treated us." Edwards stood up. "Have a seat."

Samuelson sauntered up to an empty seat at their table. "You guys don't know a friend when you have one," he replied as he sat down.

"A *friend?*" Saroyan asked in disbelief.

"Absolutely." Samuelson paused a moment. "This conversation is off the record. As far as we're concerned, I was never even here today, and I never saw you guys."

Saroyan looked at Edwards.

"Okay," Edwards agreed. "What're you about to tell us that has to be off the record?"

"That I admire you more than you can imagine," Samuelson said to him. "I admit that after you trashed me last year, I was pissed. But you put yourself on the line. I was impressed. All that chatter about visionaries—you *meant* it, and you *acted* on it. Hell, Michael, I *voted* for you."

Edwards flashed a dubious look. "Wait a minute. You took pot-shots at us, Don. If all my 'friends' were like you, I'd have never gotten past my first campaign tour."

"Let's talk about that," Samuelson suggested. "I couldn't endorse you—I would have, but the network doesn't do that. So if I wanted to help, I had to be subtle. You didn't need much help. But a little push here and there . . ."

"Like that commentary on past editorials Michael has given, stringing together offbeat, out-of-context comments over ten years old," Saroyan added with suspicious cynicism.

"Your campaign was fading into the background," Samuelson explained with casual confidence. "It needed some controversy to get back into the public eye. I felt it *should* be in the public eye. And I knew you could shake off those radical stances. That commentary got people talking about you again."

Saroyan breathed deeply. He was still not convinced, but he had made a similar point at the time of Samuelson's commentary. "Explain the *debate* then," Saroyan requested, still suspicious.

"I served up some smoking ninety mile-an-hour fastballs, but right down the middle of the plate," he answered smiling. "I knew Michael could handle them. They looked high and tight, hard and nasty—but they were fat. Like the Tajikistan question—hell, I got the Tajikistan question from *your book*."

A smile of realization crept onto Edwards' face. "Not too many people remember now that I did that book, and the series for PBS."

"Not many knew in the first place," Saroyan commented wryly.

Edwards smiled. He knew well that the PBS series, while critically acclaimed, was not a ratings success.

"I looked *real* mean on that one," Samuelson added. "And you nailed Parker, almost Hampton too. You were always getting knocked on your foreign policy experience. But *you* were the one who looked sharp on that one."

"I'm buying it," Edwards said, now with a smile on his face.

"I almost buy it," Saroyan added, perhaps not wanting to give Samuelson complete satisfaction.

"Well, it's true—off the record, as we said. When I walk back out that door, I'll be back to my role as tough reporter. But I'm rooting for you, Michael. And I can say with assurance that a number of your former colleagues are too."

Edwards nodded his appreciation.

"I also know you guys must have your hands full with the maverick electors, so I'll be on my way."

Edwards shook his head nonchalantly. "Those reports about maverick electors are just rumors."

Samuelson looked apprehensive and hesitant. "I'm not sure where you're getting your information. We have what we consider reliable information that at least one of your electors, maybe more, are going to defect and vote for President Hampton."

Michael Edwards' light mood vanished.

"Who?" Saroyan asked with icy anger in his voice.

"We're not sure," Saroyan told him quickly. "But even if we find out, I'm not really at liberty to share that information."

Saroyan's jaw rose as his lips pressed together.

"Well, what *are* you at liberty to share?" Edwards asked.

"We're working on a story that there have been some major shenanigans going on with your electors, definitely involving Hampton's people, probably involving Parker's people as well. But we're still trying to confirm some of the details. We've got some shadowy sources who have definite axes to grind. By the way, even your organization has been accused of applying subtle pressure on your—"

"I object to that characterization of our efforts," Saroyan countered indignantly. "We've had some solidarity meetings—"

"We *have* applied pressure," Edwards contradicted quietly and frankly.

Saroyan flashed an expression of profound disbelief at Edwards.

"We're off the record here," Edwards added candidly. "Yeah. It's called *peer* pressure. We got electors to meet the rabid supporters they represent, to give them a sense of responsibility and loyalty."

Saroyan seethed.

"That's what our information indicates," Samuelson continued. "And the public won't find anything wrong with what you're doing. The other two—well, if we can confirm even some of what we're hearing, their actions are *definitely* improper."

Edwards nodded. But this didn't help him discover which electors he needed to be concerned with.

Samuelson stood up to leave, but seemed to hesitate, as if he had one more question. "Good luck with this situation," he offered sincerely as he extended his hand and he and Michael shook hands. Saroyan remained seated. "Michael," he asked hesitantly, "can I count on you as a background source for information on your campaign's activities? In other words, can I have direct and confidential access to you?"

A slight smile broke onto Edwards' face. "Yeah."

Saroyan cleared his throat, expressing audible irritation.

Edwards ignored him. "You have a pen?" he asked.

Samuelson handed Edwards a small pencil.

"Here's my private line," Edwards told him as he wrote on a packet of sugar.

Samuelson took the packet, then took a another packet and wrote on it. "And here's mine." He handed Edwards the packet.

Edwards shared a knowing look with Samuelson, and was certain the two newsmen understood each other. They did not need to say anything else. Samuelson left the banquet room.

"Are you *nuts*?" Saroyan blurted out the instant Samuelson was out the door.

"No," Edwards told him quietly with a smirk. "He's on the level. And he knows, without us having to say a word, that the information door will swing both ways, or it won't swing at all."

"Michael, the guy has been after your butt. You can't just—"

"No," Edwards interrupted, shaking his head confidently. "He told us the truth in here."

"You can't believe—"

"You know, Drew, your problem with this is that you've spent your entire career mistrusting and distrusting people from the media. You're not seeing this clearly. I may be running for office, but I'm still one of his kind. I know he's on the level."

"I hope you're right, because—"

"I'll deal with him. Don't worry about it. We've got other problems."

Saroyan sighed. "Like some electors," he muttered through gritted teeth.

"Start with that weirdo from California—get Tracy to call him."

"Yeah," Saroyan acknowledged menacingly through a squint. "If it's him, or *whoever* it is, I'll make their life a *living hell*."

"Within the bounds of peer pressure."

"Right," Saroyan replied perfunctorily. "Listen Michael, you handle Samuelson. *I'll* handle the disloyal electors."

"Just be careful. You sound too angry."

"Don't worry. But I *am* angry. We've worked too long and too hard for some jerk to screw us on a whim."

Edwards shook his head. "I guess this puts an end to my trip home."

Saroyan thought a moment. "No it doesn't. Personal contact didn't discourage these people. What good would more of the same do? Don't break off your schedule until we find out exactly what's going on. Go ahead and spend a few days at home with your wife. You need the rest."

Edwards nodded. "Keep me posted. We need to bring everything we can out into the public eye. That should keep any sleazy, back-room deals from sticking."

"I'll let you know when we get something solid."

The two men continued eating their salad and soup, just as the restaurant owner arrived with the main courses.

✪   ✪   ✪

Early December: The Following Wednesday
New York, New York

"AND PRESIDENTIAL CANDIDATE MICHAEL EDWARDS RETURNED HOME TO New York today for a brief visit," the pretty television co-anchor reported as she summed up her relatively short report on the activities of the three major Presidential candidates. "He is expected to handle some routine personal matters before resuming his schedule of rallies with supporters and electors. He and campaign manager Drew Saroyan described their recent Washington meetings with Congressional representatives as successful opportunities to share views. When asked about the rumors that one or more electors could defect to President Hampton, they both emphasized how loyal all their electors are."

The television screen cut to a shot of Edwards and Saroyan together, addressing reporters at an airport.

Manuel Contreras's attention was diverted to the window of the apartment he had rented across the street from Edwards' residence. He had almost completely drawn his curtains shut, with six inches of space not obscured. So Contreras had a clear view of the Edwards building entrance from the angle he was watching, using a mounted pair of binoculars.

He looked in the binoculars. "So where is he?" Contreras grumbled out loud. He was tired of monitoring news reports on Edwards' activities and watching the Edwards building. He was wondering if his plan, now meticulously set in every detail, would ever get started.

But his evaporating patience was finally rewarded. He saw a black limousine pull up to the front of the building, and watched two Secret Service men emerge from it. After they'd glanced around the area, Michael

Edwards emerged from the limousine and entered the building. He was home.

Manuel Contreras smiled. It was time to get to work. He walked over to a desk that had been supplied with the furnished apartment.

Contreras reached into the wide middle drawer and pulled out a padded mailing container with some labels. There were three laser-printed mailing labels on an 8 by 11 backing sheet. They all had Michael Edwards' name and address in the area for the "addressee." The return address was for Earth Assessment Report, "E.A.R." Obtaining these labels had been ridiculously easy for Contreras. He had gone to the headquarters in disguise, masquerading as a person interested in their activities. While the representative left his desk to get a receipt for Contreras's $200 cash contribution, Contreras had easily pilfered the blank E.A.R. mailing labels.

Contreras turned his attention to the padded mailing container. It had a string on one side, imbedded in the padding, which would be used to open it. Contreras opened the container and noted where he had previously cut into it, exposing the string from the inside by cutting away a small portion of the inside padding.

Contreras now went to the drawer on the top right of the desk. From it, he pulled out a large paperback book entitled *Before and After the Iron Curtain*, by Michael Edwards. This would be Contreras's private joke, because he was using the book for its size and shape, and if his plan worked, no one would ever know what book was in this package. He opened the book which he had almost completely hollowed out.

Contreras went to the bottom right drawer of the desk and pulled out a small coffee can. In it was a clay-like substance which was completely safe at the moment. But soon, this plastique explosive would become very dangerous. He packed the clay tightly into the hollowed-out book.

Contreras then reached into the bottom drawer on the left side and pulled out a clear plastic zip-locked baggy. In the baggy was a small tube-like device with a thin piece of string tied to a loop on the top of it. The device was all glass, except for the plastic loop at the top of it, and the sharp plastic edge attached snugly to the bottom of it. The tube itself contained three compartments with inert substances all separated by small barriers within the tube. A yank on the string at the top of the loop would cause those elements to combine, creating a chemical spark and flame. That would set off the plastique explosive. The absence of metal in the device would pass any metal detector tests without a second try.

Contreras tied the string at one end of the tube to the exposed string in the padding of the mailing container. He then took the hollowed-out

382 ✿ Richard Warren Field

book and grunted briefly as he realized he had not totally completed his preparations. He went to the bathroom and got a razor blade. With the razor blade, he cut away a small portion of the top of the hollowed-out book, almost at the right edge. This left the clay-like substance exposed for a width approximately the same size as the lower edge of the plastic tube.

Contreras slid the book past the tubular device tied to the inside of the mailing container, and made sure he had situated the book snugly within the container. He then forced the lower edge of the tubular device into the exposed clay-like substance.

Now Contreras became extremely careful. He had just armed this package-bomb. If the string at the top of the tube was pulled before he could complete delivery to his intended victim, Contreras would be the victim of this bomb, not Michael Edwards. And there was enough explosive in this package to take out two or three rooms of the apartment building where Edwards lived.

Manual Contreras carefully sealed the opening of the package with many staples, and heavy tape. He wanted to make sure that the only practical way to open this package was by pulling the string on the outside. Actually, there was a good chance that opening it and removing the book without using the string would also set off the bomb. But the string-opening would be foolproof.

Contreras delicately attached one of the laser-printed labels to the package. He had printed three, just in case there was a problem with adhesive wrinkling, or bending as he removed the labels from the adhesive backing. He had no trouble placing the first one perfectly. The mailing container was stenciled in bright, block-red letters, at a 45 degree angle to the label, stating "RESULTS OF NEW RESEARCH." Underneath that, in hastily scrawled handwriting were the words "Michael, this really helps your campaign, look it over and call me."

Contreras set the package down carefully on top of the desk and went to the apartment closet. He had packed all his clothes except for one lone suit on a hanger in the closet. Contreras took it out and dressed in it. It was the uniform of a National Express delivery-person.

Now he grayed his moustache, and colored his hair salt and pepper, instead of its usual black color. He applied some subtle make-up to age his face. The cap on his head, that came with the uniform, would further obscure his appearance.

Contreras took the package, boarded the freight elevator in the apartment building he was in, then exited the building. He walked across the street and entered the lobby of the Edwards apartment building.

Contreras approached the doorman at the front desk.

"May I help you?" he asked.

In a thick, street-sounding New York accent, Contreras told him "Yeah, I just got a rush delivery for Michael Edwards. I hear he just got in. I'm supposed to get this to him right away."

"I'll see that he gets it," the doorman acknowledged politely. "Do you have something for me to sign?"

Contreras's mood sank for a moment. He labored not to let his face register his anxiety. All the preparations, the meticulous planning—but he had overlooked this one detail. He had no credible ledger or receipt for the host to sign for the package. Contreras had to think fast. "When we do a person-to-person job like this, we don't get a receipt," he stated casually. Contreras turned to leave.

The doorman accepted the answer without stopping to think about whether or not it really made sense.

Contreras moved quickly, but not too quickly, back across the street. He knew it would be at least a few minutes before the package was delivered to Edwards upstairs. But he expected that the source of the material indicated on the return address, and the note on the package, would cause Edwards to open the package immediately.

Contreras returned to his room, took off the uniform, removed his make-up and hair dye and dressed in some casual clothes. He prepared to leave quickly. He carefully packed away the National Express uniform. He had tried to think of some way to destroy it without a trace before leaving. But every idea he came up with was more conspicuous than simply taking it with him and disposing of it the first opportunity after leaving New York.

Contreras again settled in at the window, with a view of the Edwards apartment across the street. He had packed away the binoculars. If his plan worked, he would not need binoculars to witness the results. He also turned off the lights and pulled the curtains totally shut except for the window he was using, which had the curtains only slightly open, just enough to see the Edwards' building. He wanted his apartment to appear unoccupied.

Contreras watched and waited, with a mischievous gleam in his eye.

Chapter 25

The Same Day
San Francisco, California

"WHAT'S THE ELECTOR SITUATION?" MICHAEL EDWARDS ASKED Saroyan over the phone, as Saroyan relaxed a few minutes on the bed of his hotel room before his next meeting.

"We can't get that Whittlebaum guy in California to return Tracy's calls," Saroyan informed Edwards disgustedly. "And we're getting what I would describe as equivocation from a few of the other ones."

"Damn."

"I'm surprised Parker's people haven't been in touch with us on this," Saroyan observed. "They have as big a stake in this as we do, maybe bigger."

There was a pause, and Saroyan heard some papers rustling in the background.

"Do we need to contact them?" Edwards finally asked. He sounded as if he was speaking from across the room.

"Yes. We should present a united front, make a joint public statement that if electors defect, there will be a challenge. We need to make President Hampton think twice about whether or not he wants the grief we'll give him."

"Except this is really his only chance." Saroyan heard the sound of paper ripping.

"Yeah." Saroyan paused. "Michael, I'm having trouble hearing you."

"I'm on the speaker phone. I was trying to open some of the personal mail that stacked up here. I'll pick up. I think I can open this package with one hand."

"Okay."

"Damn!" Michael yelled.

"Michael?"

"I cut myself on a staple," Michael explained. "My copy of D. Leif O'Kieran's latest book came—they want me to do the foreword."

"He's the guy who coined the phrase Economic Activism?"

"Yeah."

"Do it," Saroyan advised confidently. "Our PR campaign is moving along," he continued, "but it won't mean a thing if one of those electors hijacks this election for Hampton."

"I know."

"I feel like we've got to do more," Saroyan said resolutely.

"Like what?"

Saroyan thought a moment. "I'll come up with something."

"Keep me posted." There was a brief pause. "Bear with me a second," Edward requested. "I've got a big package here that's full of staples."

Saroyan smiled. "If it's one of those padded ones, try yanking the string." Suddenly there was a loud banging sound. "Michael?" he questioned. "Michael!" he demanded more firmly. He heard scraping noises. "Michael, what's going on?"

Just as Saroyan began to formulate some serious worries, Michael Edwards came back on the line. "Sorry," he apologized sheepishly. "When I opened the package, I dropped the phone."

Saroyan breathed easier.

"Some publisher got my home address and sent me a book. It's got this wicked cover—a monstrous cow taking bites out of a tropical rain forest. The title is *Fast Food Forests*—it's stenciled in blood-dripping letters." There was a brief moment, presumably to allow Edwards to study the package further. "They're looking for a quote. I don't recognize the author's name—I really don't have the time."

"And you really aren't a radical environmentalist. You don't want to be associated with anything too far out."

"True." Edwards paused a moment. "Well, that's all the mail. I'm going to give Teresa a call."

"I'll check in with you later, when I know more."

"Good."
"Bye."
"Good-bye."
Saroyan hung up the phone.

✿   ✿   ✿

MANUEL CONTRERAS FIDGETED IMPATIENTLY AND IRRITABLY IN THE darkness of the apartment. The only light came from sources outside the building: street lights, lighting from other buildings, and the headlights of passing cars. He never believed he would still be waiting for results at night. What had gone wrong? If someone on Edwards' security team had intercepted the bomb, then Contreras would want to leave soon.

He watched the local television news on a portable set he pulled from his small traveling suitcase. He played it at a low volume. If anyone had detected the attempted assassination, no one was reporting it in the news media.

Contreras scowled. He'd wait a few more hours.

Suddenly Contreras heard furious horn-honking and even the faint sound of angry voices, carrying through his closed window. The activity first startled, then annoyed him. He moved up to the window so he could look out and down. He smiled as he saw two cars parked, one in front of the other, with the doors flung open, and the two drivers nose-to-nose in a furious argument. A brawl seemed imminent.

"New Yorkers," Contreras commented with amusement as he settled back to his previously established viewing position.

But seconds after he made himself comfortable, he was jolted by a blinding light in his face. As he reflexively shielded his eyes and turned toward the light, he heard a package hit the floor next to him. He looked down in horror to see that the corner of the padded envelope he had delivered to Edwards' apartment building earlier that day was actually on fire. He grabbed the package with the idea of flinging it away from himself, maybe even out the window. His action was more reflex than reflection. But when he put his hands on the package, he immediately felt searing pain to both his palms. He flung the package down, but still felt a jello-like, gooey substance burning his hands. He tried to scrape it onto his pants, but only succeeded in transferring the burning sensation to his thighs. He tried to scrape his hands on the floor. Somewhere in the back of his mind, he must have known that an ominous presence was creating these circumstances. But the intensity of the pain, and the sudden burst of activity after such a long, boring wait, had distracted him from considering "who." His focus was still on trying to determine "what," and more urgently, "how" he could stop it.

As he positioned himself on his knees, trying to scrape his hands off on the floor, he felt a forceful blow to his chin, which sent him flying to his back. He had been kicked hard with a heavy boot. A flashlight shone into Contreras's face. He held up his still-burning hands to shield his eyes.

"You were looking for this?" Carl Gregory's voice taunted as he held the hollowed-out book, with the explosive removed.

Contreras grimaced. "Who the fuck are you? Secret Service? I want my fucking lawyer." He still managed to show some arrogance through his pain. "You've violated my Constitutional rights. Police fucking brutality, man."

"Police?" Gregory mocked through a belittling smile as he pulled out a huge pistol and pressed the barrel against Contreras's temple. "You should *wish* for the police. I'm here protecting a client, not Edwards, who wanted me to make sure these amateur plans of yours didn't work out."

"Amateur?" Contreras still managed some indignation through his growing realization of his helplessness.

Gregory moved right into Contreras's face as he continued to press the gun barrel into the man's forehead. "Only a fucking amateur takes a hiding place that has a lock any third rate burglar could pick, and then fails to put something on the floor, not even *newspapers*, to warn himself of an approach! Only an amateur gets distracted by a street fight! And the fucking bomb—invented by the Japanese Revolutionary Front who stopped using it because it only works about *one fifth* of the time. Whoever sold that thing to you is laughing his ass off."

"I'm not no fucking amateur," Contreras told him, trying to sound tough, but seeming pathetically silly.

"What else are you?" Gregory demanded. "We've been watching you shop all over town for a week. It wasn't real tough to figure out what you were up to. And when you delivered that silly bomb to the clerk at Edwards' apartment—I'm a very convincing Secret Service agent. And you didn't even ask the guy for a receipt! When I showed the guy an I-D, and told him the package could well be a *bomb*, he was real glad to part with it."

Contreras did not reply.

Gregory backed out of his face, and pulled the gun back, but kept it trained on Contreras's head.

Contreras fought the burning pain in his hands which superseded the dull throbbing in his jaw as the most pronounced pain tormenting him.

"You *are* an amateur," Gregory told him disdainfully. "You should see yourself." He forced a superior laugh, intended to emphasize the ongoing humiliation.

"Am I under arrest or what?" Contreras asked. He stared at his hands, hoping there was some way to make the pain go away.

"Under arrest?" Gregory laughed. He noticed Contreras's preoccupation with his hands. "How do you like the stuff I put on the outside of your package? Ever heard of napalm? Jelly that burns and never comes off? This is the 1990's version of it. Illegal for governments to use. But like I keep telling you, I'm not working for any government. That stuff is *not* going to come off your hands. I've got a neutralizing agent . . ." Gregory paused playfully. "Oh. Yeah. I left that down in my van."

Contreras didn't respond to the explanation. He would not give Gregory the satisfaction of watching him accept or admit his humiliation.

"The question is this. Are you interested in living through this night? If you are, I'll help you out with those hands, and give you your *only* escape hatch. If not, well, we can discuss alternatives with my buddy here." Gregory circled the barrel of his pistol slowly around Contreras's head, then jammed it up one of Contreras's nostrils.

"I've got people who will be here," Manuel threatened weakly through a nasal twang. "You don't know who you're messing with."

"You definitely have that backwards." Gregory pulled the gun back. "Look Manuel, I'm telling you, there is one way I can let you survive this thing. But you've got to go along with me."

"Nobody talks to me that way," Manuel told him recalcitrantly. "*I'll* let *you* survive."

"Have it your way. Come on," Gregory said, motioning for him to get up.

"Shoot me now."

"Okay." Gregory casually pointed the gun at his temple.

☼   ☼   ☼

TWO HOURS LATER ON THE RAILROAD TRACKS IN THE SOUTH BRONX, near Hunts Point Sewage Treatment Works and with a fairly clear view of the Riker's Island Penitentiary on the East River, an old Cadillac exploded. The authorities were on the scene within five minutes. They found remnants of Contreras's luggage. They also found an unidentifiable body. A charred watch with an engraving referring to Manuel Contreras, a

Venezuelan national with known ties to South American drug interests, was the best clue to his identity. A bridge and gold tooth were also found, though the body was too charred to give investigators a complete dental chart. Within about a week, the Venezuelan dental records of Manuel Contreras confirmed that what they could identify of the dental-work was his. Though there was no way to be certain, the presumed cause of death was the explosion. The authorities suspected a drug-related murder. But there were no clues to the perpetrators.

Ernesto Enriquez was frustrated. He was suspicious of the circumstances of Contreras's obliteration, but didn't know how to pursue those suspicions. And he had no one else he trusted to remove the Edwards threat. He would have to await the results of the "crazy American system" he only slightly understood and didn't trust at all.

✩   ✩   ✩

Mid December, Election Year: Thursday
Washington, D.C.

"ANY REPORTS OF A MESSENGER?" RUNALLI ASKED INTENTLY INTO THE phone as he sat in his small, cluttered Washington D.C. office.

"We'll call you, Will," the gruff voice on the other end of the line insisted.

"But you're in position to document it."

"Yes," the voice responded with weary insistence as if this question had been answered many times before.

"He must be getting antsy."

"I don't know. But I know someone who is."

Runalli exhaled an anxious breath. "Yeah. I'm . . . I'm coming out there. I want to be ready to pounce on this Whittle-bum character the minute he thinks he's in fat city."

"Come on out. We'll show you the set-up. He'll be on tape, getting the delivery, and we even have a shot at catching him on film with the money."

"I'll be on the red-eye tonight." Runalli hung up the phone. It was hard to make chess moves or handle a street fight from across the continent. The battleground for Will Runalli at this point was in Santa Cruz, California.

✧   ✧   ✧

Mid December: The Next Day, Friday
New York, New York

"JUST OVER A WEEK TO GO; HAVE WE LOST ANY OF OUR PEOPLE OR not?" Edwards asked Saroyan as they sat down for a croissants and juice breakfast at Edwards' home.

"No one's admitting it. But a few have given us guarded answers. And that Whittlebaum guy—he won't return Tracy's or *my* calls."

"We have to go see him."

"Michael," Saroyan said in a tone of voice that clearly indicated he did not like this suggestion.

"I know the guy's a nut. But he still has the power to single-handedly wreck this entire election for us after a year of effort and millions of dollars spent. I have to face this guy down. If I don't, and he sells out, I will always wonder."

"You can't go out to the guy hat-in-hand. Jesus, Michael, you're a Presidential candidate."

"And he's an elector who can deny us our shot in the House in January. We'll do it quietly. But we will go out and see him."

"Let me send someone—"

"I've decided. The guy's probably been tampered with. I want to look him in the eye and ask him what's going on. Set it up."

"We may not be able to 'set it up.' The guy isn't returning calls."

"So let's not set it up. We don't want him alerting the media."

"Just show up on his doorstep?"

"Get someone to confirm he's there. Then we'll head over."

"Okay. Some time early next week," Saroyan acknowledged, not completely agreeing, but resigned to Edwards' decision. They moved on to other more routine matters.

✧   ✧   ✧

The Same Day
Santa Cruz, California

"I GOTTA SHOW YOU SOMETHING," AN EXCITED BENNINGTON Whittlebaum said to his wife as she emerged from her car, just arriving home from work. He had hurried out the front door to greet her in the cracked white cement driveway in front of their rented house.

"Give me time to breathe a little," Molly Whittlebaum requested irritably as she shut her car door and walked past him.

"You'll wanna see this," he assured her with a knowing smile as he followed her.

She stopped just short of opening their front door. "What is it?" she demanded impatiently.

"In the bedroom."

"I've seen *that,*" she countered caustically. "I'm not interested."

"Not sex," he told her, now becoming impatient himself. "I'm telling you, you'll wanna see this, Molly."

"If you touch one button or zipper on *either* of us, I'll scream and kick you where you'll squeak like the little twerp you are."

"You might change your mind," he told her playfully as he followed.

"Not likely."

She arrived at their small, cluttered, dusty bedroom ahead of him, and stood just inside the doorway with her hands planted defiantly on her hips. "Okay. What is it I have to see?"

"Just a second," Whittlebaum told her as he walked around her and picked up a worn leather satchel.

Molly gave her husband a belittling look, as if to ask what silliness he would inflict on her now.

Bennington Whittlebaum smirked. He turned the satchel upside down, over their unmade bed. Thirty bundles of green currency flopped into the middle of the light blue sheets.

Molly's eyes widened dramatically. She was stunned silent for a moment with disbelief.

Bennington enjoyed the reaction. He savored it.

"Is it . . . real?"

"Unless the President's staff has taken up counterfeiting," he replied casually. "And we're moving to Washington the middle of next year."

"How much?" She barely even heard the comment about Washington.

"Three hundred thousand."

Molly still wasn't sure what to think. Finally she asked the question that was really on her mind. "How? *Why?*"

"The Republicans are very happy that I'm considering changing my vote to Hampton," he told her slyly.

"This is . . . ours?" she asked tentatively.

Bennington Whittlebaum moved toward her with a manipulative look in his eye. "Sure. We're *married,* aren't we?"

Molly drew a deep uncomfortable breath, then flashed an uneasy grin. "Of course," she told him, but not convincingly.

Whittlebaum took her by the shoulders and kissed her hard. He pulled her over to the bed and gently, but unequivocally, pushed her onto it. She landed in the middle of the money. Whittlebaum waited to see how she would respond to his forceful actions.

"Ours?" she asked again, more confidently, with her smile growing.

He nodded.

"Let me see how this much money *feels,*" she told him, smiling seductively.

Bennington waited to see what his wife had in mind.

Molly unwrapped three of the bundles and tossed them a few feet above her head. Bills fluttered around her as she giggled. Molly removed her clothes as she told her husband "Shower me with the money."

As Molly took off her clothes with an alluring, seductive expression, alternating between a playful smile and a look of desire, Bennington Whittlebaum took the wrappings off the rest of the bills and showered her with them. She was still in very good shape—thin, but well-proportioned and firm. She had exercised fanatically to compensate for her lack of a sex life in recent years. Bennington Whittlebaum could scarcely contain himself as she moved from slow, fluid movements, to more rapid, wild movements. Whittlebaum flung the bills more exuberantly as Molly's dance became more vigorous.

Molly finally flopped back onto the bed, face up, stark naked, but covered with the bills and out of breath.

Bennington started to fling off his clothes in uncontrollable anticipation. But a loud knock at the door interrupted him. "Forget it," he stated decisively, clearly worked up.

Molly didn't argue as she scooped up more money onto her body.

"We know you're here!" an insistent voice shouted from outside the door. "We're not leaving until you answer!"

"Shit!" Whittlebaum sputtered frustratedly. He was down to his jockey shorts. And Bennington Whittlebaum was a little thin, but basically attractive. He was actually better looking without clothes—with clothes, his obnoxious personality began to assert itself.

The pounding on the door became even more insistent.

Whittlebaum pulled up his pants, still down around his ankles. He didn't put his shirt back on. He would dismiss these intruders and return quickly. "Don't go anywhere. I'll be right back."

Molly rolled in the money as if it was a freshly raked pile of leaves. "I'll be right here," she promised.

Whittlebaum stomped from the bedroom to the front door. He flung it open. "I hope you assholes have something God Damn important, because you are *not welcome* here right now."

"My colleague and I have something very important to discuss with you," Will Runalli said without a smile. A large, brutal-looking man stood next to him. His huge forearms were folded across his chest and he glared contemptuously at Whittlebaum.

"What do you want?" Whittlebaum asked coolly.

"I'm Will Runalli with the Victor Parker organization," he told Whittlebaum, beginning his explanation with an introduction. "And this is Gus DeBarres with the Edwards campaign."

"Campaign? The election's over. I'm an Edwards elector. I don't need any and I'm not giving any," he stated curtly as he reached for the door.

"We're not here for contributions," Runalli told him quietly but insistently. "We need to have a little heart-to-heart with you."

"Make an appointment," Whittlebaum told them tersely.

"I think you need to see us *now*," Runalli insisted. "Mr. Klondike preferred to talk to you in riddles." He quieted his voice almost to a whisper. "I will speak bluntly and directly. We were here with surveillance cameras when a large amount of cash was delivered here today, and we know why. Do you really want us to have this talk out here where your neighbors can hear everything?"

Bennington Whittlebaum pursed his lips and wordlessly widened Runalli's and DeBarres' entrance paths by opening the door.

The two men entered.

"Let's make this quick," Whittlebaum told them as he led them to his living room, the same place where he had met with Klondike the previous Sunday.

They all sat on the worn living room furniture.

"As I said, I am a very frank man," Runalli told him. "We have very good intelligence on the Hampton people. We know for a positive fact that you have agreed to change your vote to Hampton in exchange for 300,000 dollars and a job with Senator Stephan from Utah. The money was delivered today."

Whittlebaum wished he wasn't sitting in stunned silence, but he didn't know what to say. Runalli seemed to know the situation so well that he would feel silly trying to deny it. But if he wasn't going to deny it, how was he going to handle this man? His indecision froze him, extending the awkward silence.

"These people think they have bought you, but they risk—"

"The money is for possible legal expenses in case you people challenge my right to vote my conscience," he finally blurted out feebly.

Runalli smiled contemptuously. "Yes, I know what the denial line will be. Mr. Klondike will say they spotted your talents and decided to put you to work. They sent the money for attorney's fees—you don't even have an attorney on retainer yet. It might have worked if all this had been exposed in six months and you had actually been challenged in court. But these excuses will be laughed right out of Washington. Hampton will jettison Klondike like so much useless ballast. And you'll have nothing."

Whittlebaum quietly fumed. Why couldn't he ever get just a few moments of sustained triumph? His nude wife was waiting compliantly for him with the money. Now he would lose the money, *and* his wife's briefly rekindled affection. "So why don't you just expose this," Whittlebaum demanded.

"Believe me, we seriously considered it. But my source for this information—as you can see, the source is infallible. But my source could also prove embarrassing if exposed . . ." Runalli allowed an awkward silence to follow again.

"So what is *your* answer?" Whittlebaum demanded, trying to throw the challenge right back onto Runalli.

"There are three answers to this," Runalli told him ominously. "The *least* attractive is public exposure. You lose, probably removed as an Edwards elector. We lose our source, and therefore our ability to prevent Hampton's people from approaching someone else."

Whittlebaum nodded.

"The Edwards people have their approach," Runalli commented. "You lose—*big*. We don't." Runalli looked over at DeBarres.

"It's simple," DeBarres finally said gruffly, speaking for the first time. "You die, beaten to a fucking pulp by an intruder in your home, robbing your money . . . your *bribe*."

Whittlebaum felt a chill, but also disbelief. "I know Edwards' people well," he challenged. "I've never seen *you* before."

The man stared ominously at Whittlebaum. "I've never met Mr. Edwards personally," he told Whittlebaum. "I work with Drew Saroyan—I used to work with Oscar Lusman." He flashed a twisted smiled. "Mr. Saroyan has a short fuse for people who fuck with his man. You saw what we did to that drug dealer."

"And it almost ruined his campaign," Whittlebaum reminded DeBarres, trying to be tough, but betraying some nervous apprehension.

"We didn't finish that son-of-a-bitch off—that was our mistake," DeBarres told Whittlebaum through an unsettling, sadistic squint. "We won't make that mistake again. I'll handle your traitorous little ass myself."

"But we don't like bodies," Runalli quickly added.

DeBarres made it clear from his expression that Runalli might not speak for both of them. He made sure Whittlebaum caught his facial expression by fidgeting in his seat until Whittlebaum looked over at him. He glared at Whittlebaum who looked away quickly.

"Bodies are too messy," Runalli continued. "Too much suspicion. So we have a third idea that will benefit all of us. You start work for Victor Parker *tomorrow*. You'll be a special assistant to the President-elect, right in the center of power. You'll be helping the transition team immediately. Moving expenses—they can be provided. And the beauty of it is you don't have to change your vote. You do what you're supposed to do, and get everything from us that President Hampton was going to give you, *without* a waiting period. And there's no risk, because you're not changing your vote."

"But Hampton's people will know. They'll know I was paid off not to change."

"And what will they do with that information? To disclose it, they have to acknowledge their own behavior. They can't. And us? We got to know you and decided to hire you. Nothing improper. We're not asking you to change your vote to Parker."

"Moving expenses?" Whittlebaum asked. He was still thinking of his wife, and her reaction to the Hampton money.

"It's got to be credible—I think we could manage about 25 grand for a cross country move."

"I just got *three hundred* grand from Hampton's people."

Runalli's face became stern, almost angry. "This has to be a credible transaction," he lectured. "Mr. Whittlebaum, I had hoped you would embrace my win-win proposition. I am not happy with this dickering. You see, I have a problem. I can't be with you when you cast your vote. So when I leave here, I must be convinced that you will cast it for Michael Edwards. Or, I'll let Mr. DeBarres here enforce *his* answer. It's a sure thing. Messy, but sure."

"My wife's here," Whittlebaum told him, addressing his comment to Runalli, not DeBarres. "You're willing to kill *two* people?"

"What does she look like?" DeBarres asked with a sinister grin. "This job might turn out to be fun."

"Convince me," Runalli told Whittlebaum.

"I don't like being threatened," he told them. But his voice contained more fear than the toughness he was trying to project.

"Mr. Whittlebaum, we're giving you an opportunity to benefit from this situation, instead of . . . *not* benefitting."

"I don't know if I could have worked for Republicans," Whittlebaum finally said. "I'm a liberal at heart, even a radical. I'll be much more comfortable working with a Victor Parker presidency. Okay. Where do I report to work?"

Runalli smiled. "Our San Francisco office. Monday morning. You're on the payroll starting today." He handed Whittlebaum a piece of paper. "Here's the address. We'll make arrangements to move you to Washington. You'll be meeting with future President Victor Parker in less than a week."

Whittlebaum now smiled. Sure they'd threatened him. But isn't this what he wanted? Edwards had sluffed him off to an aide. Hampton had sluffed him off to a Senator. This was clearly the best possible outcome for Bennington Whittlebaum. "I'll be there bright and early."

Runalli stood up. "Good," he said jovially. "I'm glad we could work this out."

Whittlebaum showed his guests out.

He poked his head into the bedroom. His wife had fallen asleep, still covered with money. He smiled. He'd take care of one loose end quickly, then wake her up gently. He was sure that $25,000 and an immediate move to Washington would still impress her. And they could still use the Hampton money to finish what they'd started, before he returned it. Who would know?

Whittlebaum went to his desk, retrieved a business card, picked up the phone and punched in a number.

"Hello," Covington Klondike answered at the other end after three rings.

"You're working real late tonight, Mr. Klondike."

"Who's calling?"

"Ben Whittlebaum."

"You can't call me," Klondike told him emphatically.

"There's been a problem. I had to."

"How did you get my number?"

"You gave it to me at our meeting."

"This is my private line," he explained grouchily. "I have it forwarded to another line in my home. Don't you understand that you've now made a phone record, a traceable contact, between us? You *idiot*."

"You're the idiot," Whittlebaum countered. "Someone is totally on to your game. One of Parker's smooth-talkers, and one of Edwards' goons was—well, they have convinced me to change my mind. I'm joining Parker's transition team tomorrow. I'll send the money back. Now I've gotta go . . ."

"Wait a minute!" Klondike insisted. "Don't send the money." Klondike paused. "You really *are* in over your head, aren't you . . ."

Whittlebaum was taken aback by this rebuke. This was probably the most cutting insult that Klondike could have leveled at him. "I can't . . . keep the money . . ."

"You are such a *fool*," Klondike told him. He decided to run a calculated bluff. "Do you think you're the *only* one about to turn?" he asked him in a caustically belittling tone. "Do you think we'd rely only on *you*?" He laughed. "This job you're taking with Parker—it'll disappear after the electors vote! Because President Hampton is going to win in the Electoral College." Klondike's voice became hard and stern. "And only *reliable* people will get jobs with his administration."

Whittlebaum bit his lip. He was glad this was a phone conversation. He was in total confusion, and on the verge of tears. His day in the sun was turning into a nightmare.

"You better figure it out," Klondike warned mercilessly. "Because you don't want to piss off powerful people."

"But I—" Whittlebaum began timidly. He had put himself in a position where he was absolutely certain to infuriate someone.

"We expect you to hold to our arrangement," Klondike stated tersely, now ordering Whittlebaum, not making suggestions. "We'll see you out in Washington to start work for Senator Stephan around the middle of next year. Don't disappoint us." The phone clicked.

Whittlebaum was glad the call was over. But the dilemma the call had created for him was not. The only advantage of being off the phone was that he could now suffer this dilemma privately, with time to think, and without some hostile presence waiting for him to come up with a response.

But as his wife walked into the room, wearing her light grey robe, he realized he wouldn't be alone with his dilemma quite yet.

"You're sending the money back?" she asked coldly as she folded her arms.

"I don't know," he told her indecisively, his eyes still glistening as he continued to hover near tears. "I'm in some deep trouble."

His wife radiated an unsympathetic look. She snorted disgustedly, turned and walked out of the room. A few moments later, Whittlebaum heard their bedroom door shut. It was a clear communication that whatever his "deep trouble" was, he was on his own with it.

Whittlebaum successfully fought off his tears. He needed time to think. He'd made mistakes dealing with these big league political operators. But he was now, in his uncluttered solitude, able to salvage some confidence, and work out his solution to this dilemma.

Chapter 26

Mid December: The Following Saturday
Washington, D.C.

"IT'S GOT TO BE A BUG," KLONDIKE INSISTED. HE WAS IN HIS OFFICE, about three blocks from the White House.

Klondike was speaking to Lester Crowley, a chunky, short, red-headed man who appeared to be a cross between a computer nerd and a street punk. He walked through the office with a metal detector and various other devices in a satchel hanging from his shoulder. He was now looking carefully along the wall of Klondike's office. "If there's a bug in here, we'll find it," Crowley replied in a scratchy, high-pitched voice.

Klondike watched him a moment before looking back at his desk as if to review some papers. But he was still distracted by Crowley, who crept slowly through the office, checking every crack and crevice, every irregularity or potential irregularity, for some clue that someone had violated the security of the office. Depending on where he was looking, he ran his metal detector over the area he was examining, or thumped on the wall, or ran other electronic detectors and carefully examined the readings.

"There's nothing in your office," Crowley told him, betraying a twinge of surprise and frustration. "I've got permission from building management to check the air ducts and other places adjoining your office that could have a bug. It won't be a pleasant job, but that's the next step, and the only remaining possibility."

Klondike shook his head. "It's *got* to be a bug. Is there any other way they could be getting their information?"

"Doesn't sound like it. From what you're telling me, the stuff they've been getting is too good for. . . well, is there anybody who goes with you on all your appointments and has total recall of all conversations?"

"No," he answered, but he actually considered the idea for a quick moment before dismissing it.

Crowley paused a moment in thought. "Some of this information was about meetings outside of the office," he said, restating information he had already obtained, making sure he understood.

"Yeah . . ."

He looked directly at Klondike, now appraising him as if he was one of the cracks and crevices in the office. "What do you always have with you?"

Klondike looked back impatiently. "I change clothes every day, including underwear and socks," he answered sarcastically.

"What about your watch?" Crowley asked.

Klondike looked at his wrist. "I wear two or three different ones."

Crowley's eyebrows raised. The watch Klondike had on was expensive enough; Crowley could only imagine two or more interchangeable with this one. "Let me see your wallet," he requested politely, but not deferentially.

Klondike reached into his pocket with an exaggerated sigh.

"Keys too," he added, ignoring Klondike's obvious disapproval.

Klondike begrudgingly handed both to Crowley.

Crowley examined them, frowning in thought as he concentrated. He pulled every credit card and picture out and examined each one meticulously.

Klondike became more and more annoyed as Crowley continued to linger over each item of his private possessions.

"Does all this stuff look familiar to you?" He handed the wallet and items back to Klondike, with the items now out of their positions in the wallet.

Klondike took them and looked them over. He hadn't considered the possibility of a bug in his wallet. "Yes," he replied, now disgusted with the idea. "These things all belong here. Come on."

Crowley shook his head. "I don't know."

Klondike hurriedly jammed the contents of his wallet into his pocket. "I was hoping to tell the President I had an answer to the security problem here," he complained. "Unfortunately, I *don't*."

"I'll let you know if there's anything in the building structure."

"Yeah," Klondike acknowledged unenthusiastically. He stood up. "I'm running late to a meeting." He grabbed his briefcase.

"I'll keep working on—" Crowley stopped in mid-sentence. "Just a second. You take your briefcase everywhere?"

Klondike was reaching the end of his patience. "Of course. You think I have a bug in my briefcase?"

"Let me look at it and I'll tell you."

Klondike raised his jaw as he drew a deep breath of condescension. "The President does not like to be kept waiting," he stated haughtily.

Crowley remained unintimidated. "It won't take long to check this out. And maybe you'll have your answer for him."

Klondike handed the briefcase to him without further resistance.

Crowley examined the outside with his usual thoroughness. He then laid it on its side, and just as he was about to open it, he looked at the handle. He nodded. He ran his metal detector over it, then smiled. "You can report that the mystery is over," he stated with just a hint of pride in his voice.

"I can?"

Crowley pulled a Swiss Army knife out of his pocket and used the largest blade to slice through the brown leather handle. "This is very good," he commented admiringly, but also implying he was very good for detecting the device. He tore apart the handle and pulled out a small, metallic, cylindrical object, silver, with some clear parts also visible.

He handed it to Klondike, who took it with guarded sheepishness.

"Someone went to a lot of trouble, getting access to your briefcase, then matching the handles. This is an impressive professional job. Someone with a lot of expertise, and probably very expensive, did this job."

Klondike nodded. "The Democrats can't afford people like that . . . ."

Crowley shrugged. "From what you tell me they had to have access to the information to act on it the way they did."

"Edwards and Parker, working together."

"It's possible," Crowley said as he packed his gear. He gently took the device back from Klondike. "We'll go over this thing and I'll get you my report."

"Okay." Klondike paused. "Thanks."

A brief but victorious grin flashed onto Crowley's face as he left the office.

Klondike felt his anger and frustration rise. To hell with the meeting! (Not with the President, though he had tried to lead Crowley to believe it was.) He threw his handle-less briefcase onto his desk and plopped down into his chair. He acted on impulse, an impulse that he might have second-guessed if he'd given it a moment's thought. He twirled his rolodex, picked up his phone and punched in a number.

✿   ✿   ✿

"COVINGTON KLONDIKE ON LINE THREE FOR YOU," NICHOLAS Mueller's secretary told him through his speaker-phone intercom as he sat at his desk reading a book.

Mueller was intrigued. He punched line three and picked up the phone. "Hello."

"Mueller," Klondike stated gruffly.

"Right here. What's on your mind?"

"Listen, you and I have been on opposite sides of the fence, but we work in the same business, and I'd like to think I know you a little bit. What the fuck is going on over there?"

"What are you talking about?" Mueller asked testily.

"I just found a God Damn bug in my . . . my office. And either you people or Edwards' people are doing it—and if it's not your people, they're certainly getting and *using* the information from it."

"I really don't know anything about this."

"The hell you don't," Klondike challenged. "This crap went out after Watergate. You guys get caught doing this, and you're in some deep fucking shit."

"Then why don't you call a press conference?" Mueller countered calmly. As long as he maintained his cool, he had the advantage over Klondike, whose anger had him a little out of control.

There was a silence. Did Klondike regret making this call? "Let's just say that if I see anything like this again, I will," he finally replied.

"I'm telling you, Cuv, I don't know anything about it. And I doubt if the Senator does either." He hesitated. Now he was about to say more than he should. But the pride of one professional speaking to another stepped in. "I gotta be honest with you, because you and I have been in this business a long time, and we'll probably face each other again. In this campaign, I'm not the one calling the shots right now."

"Aw come on, don't try to lay this off on some underling."

"I'm not saying it's an underling. A guy's been called in. Don't expect me to say any more."

"Okay." Klondike paused. "You might want to reassert your influence before shit really hits the fan for your candidate."

"I might."

"Talk to you later."

"Right."

Both lines clicked.

Mueller knew why Klondike didn't call in the police or the media. The bugs had uncovered some damaging information, probably proof that Hampton's people had been tampering with electors. Maybe it *was* time to reassert his influence. But could he outmaneuver the street-fighter right now by going directly to Senator Parker? He shook his head. He didn't believe he could. He would have to use another approach, distasteful to him, but the only practical alternative to doing nothing, as he watched the electoral process degenerate. He checked his rolodex and picked up the phone.

☆ ☆ ☆

Mid December: The Next Day, Sunday
Santa Cruz, California

"THIS IS WHERE HE LIVES?" EDWARDS ASKED QUEASILY AS SAROYAN pulled their rented car over to the curb across from Whittlebaum's residence. There was a light on, visible through the front window of the house. Edwards glanced at the digital clock just to the right of the speedometer—it read "11:13 P.M." "And he's there?"

"If he didn't leave in the last ten minutes," Saroyan assured him. "He finally came home from some beatnik place nearby."

"Beatnik?" Edwards chuckled.

"Some place where artsy-fartsies sit around and pontificate or sing with their guitars at each other—at least that's the way my man describes it."

"Well, let's go," Edwards suggested, not looking forward to the task ahead, but knowing there was no reason to put off what they had come to do.

Saroyan pulled out a small microcassette recorder and slipped it into the left side pocket of his sports jacket.

Edwards looked at him disapprovingly, soliciting an explanation.

"We need to start thinking about putting together a case to have him removed as an elector by the courts. If he goes as far off the wall as I've been hearing this guy is, this could be evidence to use against him."

"But isn't this illegal, without his consent?"

"You're thinking of telephones. As long as one party gives consent, we can record him in person."

Saroyan had not totally convinced Edwards. And Edwards still hoped to reason with Whittlebaum. The cassette recorder seemed like the first step in a declaration of war. But Edwards did not object any further.

They got out of the car and walked toward Whittlebaum's front door. Saroyan knocked loudly.

There was no response. In fact, the light showing through the front window of the house went dark the moment after Saroyan knocked.

Saroyan knocked again, pounding forcefully.

Again, there was no response.

"Ben Whittlebaum! It's Michael Edwards!" Edwards called out. "We came out here to talk to you! It's very important!"

After another silent pause, Saroyan said "I *hate* this. Standing out here on someone's porch. You're a Presidential candidate!"

"I'm a Presidential candidate who will have no chance if this guy—"

"Go away!" Bennington Whittlebaum ordered loudly through the door. There was a near-hysterical edge to his voice.

Edwards suddenly saw the wisdom of bringing the microcassette recorder. He pointed at Saroyan's pocket.

Saroyan nodded. He pulled the recorder out of his pocket, flipped it on, then returned it to his pocket.

"Ben!" Edwards called out familiarly, "We need to talk! We need to find out if people have been tampering with you! We will—" But Edwards was interrupted.

"You take your goons the hell out of here! I'm not talking to you! I'm not talking to *anybody*!"

"We're . . . alone! We don't have any . . . any 'goons!'" Edwards was puzzled by Whittlebaum's reference.

"I'm no drug dealer! No one's gonna beat on me! You tell Oscar and his thug-boys—his brown-shirts! I'm no punching bag! I'll have you all in a cell right next to Oscar!"

Edwards looked at Saroyan. "Listen!" he called to Whittlebaum. "You sound a bit crazed! You sound . . . unbalanced! We'll get you help! But I've got to warn you, Ben. We're taping this! We'll go into court and—"

"I don't care what you're taping! You're not the only one who can record things! I . . . the whole thing is in a letter! In the event I die—that's what it says! Open in case I die! And it's all there! Your goon! Your threats! Parker's threats! So leave me alone!"

Saroyan shrugged, looking as mystified as Edwards. "He just gave us consent to record him. So, there'll be no controversy about using this tape."

"I don't want to do it that way," Edwards insisted. "I want to find out what he's talking about."

"He may not . . . he may not be real clear on it."

"Ben!" Edwards called out again. "There aren't any goons! Someone . . ." He paused to try to think of a way to reach Whittlebaum. "If someone has been threatening you, *we* want to—"

"I have a gun in here, God Damn it!" Whittlebaum interrupted in a fearful frenzy. "I'll blow anyone away who comes through that door! You're not gonna trick me into letting you in! I'm not some target-practice for muscle-bound goons!"

Saroyan now caught the Whittlebaum fear, contagious through the door. "Michael, I think we ought to be going."

"We're not trying to trick you!" Michael called back through the door. "Someone has obviously—"

But he was cut short by the nearly deafening explosion of a gunshot. Both Edwards and Saroyan jumped back from the door.

"That was a warning!" Whittlebaum screamed. "The next one won't be!"

"Okay," Edwards said to Saroyan. "We're out of here. We'll call the police from the car—"

"You can't do that," Saroyan insisted. "The media attention will kill us, and we're not even sure if this is a police matter. The guy fired a gun inside his house."

Edwards wondered if there wasn't something more they could do about the situation that evening, but could not argue with Saroyan's points.

As they walked hurriedly to the rental car, Saroyan told Edwards "I'll get the lawyers on this immediately. The guy's obviously either nuts, or he has been tampered with, with someone applying some nasty pressure. I'd bet on the first. But either way, he's been tainted in some way, and we can question his ability to serve as an elector. Even though there's no legal precedent, I think we can get a Federal Judge to remove him. We've got a week."

Edwards nodded fatalistically, now resigned to this path as the best alternative for dealing with Whittlebaum.

"He's going to be tough to serve with papers."

"Yeah." But then Edwards had an idea. "Drew, he has to show up in Sacramento to cast his vote. If he ducks service before then, we'll serve him there."

"That might be too late."

"We serve him with a temporary injunction, and have a Federal Judge standing by to hear it."

"And what Federal Judge is going to do that for us?"

"None I know of," Edwards answered casually. "But Parker, and the Democrats, might just know one."

Saroyan smiled. "I'll contact them and get that going."

They drove quickly away from Bennington Whittlebaum's home.

✿   ✿   ✿

Mid December: The Next Day, Monday
Washington, D.C.

"IS HE GETTING THE PAGES?" RUNALLI ASKED IMPATIENTLY AS HE SAT IN his office, speaking on the phone. He looked at the digital clock on his desk—it read "4:53." At 5:00 he was due to call Senator Parker with an update on their situation, and he wanted to solidify his information before their conversation. As usual, clutter surrounded him. His tie dangled loosely from his neck—the top button of his shirt was unbuttoned.

"I don't know," the woman on the other end of the line told him politely, but starting to lose patience herself. "We don't really check on that."

"Is there some way to check on it?" Runalli asked insistently.

"Hold the line," she replied, obviously intending to consult someone else.

Runalli seethed, ready to explode as his impatience escalated into angry frustration. He tapped on his desk as he waited for what seemed like a long time to him, but was no more than two minutes.

"Sir?" a firm, gruff male voice said.

"Yes."

"You have some question about whether the pages are getting through to our customer—uh, Bennington Whittlebaum?"

"Yes," Runalli replied emphatically, tired of restating his request.

"We can't divulge that information," the man told Runalli tersely. "We take messages and refer them. Beyond that, we—"

"Do you know who I am?" Runalli demanded with pompous insistence. "Have you ever heard of Senator Victor Parker? The man who may well be the next President of the United States? I work directly with him."

"Sir—"

"We have an urgent need to talk to Bennington Whittlebaum immediately. Now please tell me if—"

"Sir, I don't care if you're the Pope of Rigatoni Provolone. We don't work for you. We work for Mr. Whittlebaum. If he is not answering your pages, then that is his choice."

"At least tell me if he's getting them."

"I can't do that."

"Your cooperation will be taken into consideration when we take office—"

"Good-bye." The phone clicked.

Runalli sneered as he put the phone on its receiver. In three more minutes, he had to report to Senator Parker. He decided to get it over with now. Nothing would change in the next three minutes. He punched Number 1 of the stored telephone numbers in his telephone's memory. Victor Parker's private line was ringing.

"Yes," the Senator answered.

"Well, we still have a few loose ends on the Whittlebaum situation," Runalli told Parker.

"What does that mean? Where do we stand?"

"That Whittlebaum guy still hasn't showed up for work in San Francisco. But we're pretty sure he will. There's obviously some wrinkle that's come up, and we—"

"And you still can't even get him on the phone."

"No," Runalli answered.

Senator Parker was not happy with Runalli's "loose ends." "It sounds to me like that guarantee you gave me back in November may not be such a sure thing."

"We have Mr. Whittlebaum agreeing to—"

"That was last week. It looks like your 'agreement' fell through."

"I still have other options."

"Sounds like you might want to consider a different one."

"I will."

"In the meantime, I have Nicholas Mueller working with Edwards' lawyers. They have an angle on this thing that . . . that might be more effective than whatever it is you're trying to do."

"The lawyers? Senator, I—"

"Mr. Runalli, I'm going to let *both* of you work on this. The *results,* not the rhetoric, will show me who knows what he's doing."

"Yes, Senator."

The phone clicked.

Runalli stiffened. His confidence that he could guarantee Victor Parker an indecisive Electoral College and therefore a January vote in the House of Representatives had dissipated with his loss of reliable information on President Hampton's contact with the electors. Rumors abounded about other defecting electors, but his investigators could not pin anything down. Runalli would have to settle for that uncertainty. But he needed to know what was happening with Bennington Whittlebaum. Whittlebaum had been on the verge of ruining Runalli's efforts. Had Runalli successfully turned him around, or was he still a threat? Runalli couldn't control all the uncertainty. But he could make sure that if his efforts were thwarted, it wouldn't be by Bennington Whittlebaum. And maybe the rumors about the other defections would come to nothing.

Runalli had to try to get some answers. He thought a moment, then picked up the phone, punching in a number he had on a rolodex card in front of him.

"Hello?"

"Mrs. Whittlebaum? This is James Buchanan with Capitol Movers. Your husband called us about your move. Uh, I need to talk to him, about his order . . ."

"Order?"

"Yes. For his move . . . out here to Washington . . ." Runalli was fishing, tossing out statements and hoping for informative reactions.

Molly Whittlebaum's mystification was a partial answer. "He's already contacted movers? For our move next May?"

Runalli felt a cold chill shoot up his back. "We were led to believe he'd be moving almost immediately."

"Oh no," she told him assuredly. "He starts working for some Senator—from Utah? I think from Utah. But not until May."

"I need to talk to him about his order," Runalli told her politely, hiding his reaction to the unpleasant surprise he had just been handed. "Can you get a message to him, or tell me how I can call him?"

"I won't be able to reach him until the electors vote. He's trying to avoid some people." It was obvious from her tone of voice that she didn't take her husband's concerns seriously. "He thinks people are after him. He says that after he votes, they'll have no reason to come after him anymore.

So he left town, and didn't say where he was going. He didn't even tell me. He thinks I'll tell someone."

"Well, we'll call him after the vote, then."

"Can I take a—"

Runalli ended the call. He turned white as the blood drained from his face. Whittlebaum had been coaxed back to Hampton, and he had barricaded himself against any further influence. Now Runalli would have to move to his fall-back option. He had planned for it. But it was a risky and unsavory last resort. The street fighter would have to pull out all the stops now.

He punched in another phone number. "Please have a talk with Mr. Whittlebaum," he said into the telephone answering machine that answered with a beep, and no greeting. He hung up the phone and thought for a quick moment about the irony of the instructions he had just given, instructions to "talk" to a man who had closed himself off from any further discussions.

☼   ☼   ☼

BENNINGTON WHITTLEBAUM TRIED TO GO INTO HIDING. HE FLED TO THE California coastal town of Pismo Beach. But two mornings later, front pages across the country would carry the story that Edwards elector Bennington Whittlebaum had been murdered shortly after eleven o'clock in the evening, the victim of an apparent robbery attempt that had gotten violent.

Chapter 27

"WHAT DO WE KNOW ABOUT THIS?" MICHAEL EDWARDS ASKED DREW Saroyan as they began an early morning meeting at Edwards' New York apartment. Michael and Teresa Edwards sat in the living room.

"The guy turned up dead," Saroyan told Michael casually. "Now we can replace him with someone reliable."

"You aren't just a little bit concerned about this?" Michael asked, not understanding Saroyan's attitude.

"Of course I am. But first things first. We'll get a reliable elector to replace him. Then it's up to the authorities."

"A guy *died,* you know," Michael stated indignantly. "You're just a little too happy about it for my taste."

"I didn't know the guy—he wasn't a close buddy. He was a pain in the ass who pissed people off. I don't usually mourn those kinds of individuals."

"Drew," Michael addressed him with solemn seriousness, "you have to promise me that our people have nothing to do with this."

"No one I know."

"Damn it, Drew, don't equivocate."

"No orders were given by anyone I know of to eliminate this guy. Can I promise you that one of our people didn't do it on his own? How can I?

The guy was really obnoxious. He could have rubbed one of our supporters the wrong way."

Michael lowered his chin and shot a piercing glance at Saroyan to show his dissatisfaction with Saroyan's lack of firm responses to his questions.

"Maybe the guy was not as crazy as we thought he was," Saroyan added. "Maybe someone *was* after him."

"Yeah." Michael's mind drifted to a related issue. "We've got to share our tape recording with the authorities."

"Wait a minute, Michael—"

"If we *don't* share it, we look like we're hiding something."

"You're not considering one very important possibility."

"What's that?"

"That maybe he *was* killed by a street punk. Why should we finger ourselves as suspects by showcasing Whittlebaum's crazy ramblings to the police, and to the media, if he really was killed in a robbery attempt that got carried away? We met that guy. I could see him mouthing off to some would-be robber and getting himself killed."

"The tape could be evidence in a murder case—"

"*Could* be, Michael. *Could* be."

Michael drew an apprehensive breath.

"If their investigation points to a political motivation, then we'll turn over the tape," Saroyan added.

Teresa nodded. "He's right. We don't want to get so overly noble that we go out of our way to shoot ourselves in the foot."

Michael squinted as he pondered. His wife tended to be skeptical of Saroyan's advice. Her concurrence definitely influenced him. "Let's see where the investigation goes," he finally said. He paused another moment. "And I guess we can call off the lawyers."

"On the Whittlebaum matter, yeah," Saroyan agreed. "But I think we should keep them working on a litigation alternative in case another elector defects."

"Yeah. Okay." Edwards was not enthusiastic. "Just don't let them run up too many hours on this. A litigation approach would be a long shot."

"True."

"So replace Whittlebaum—try not to look too pleased about it. Then we wait for the electors to vote, and the Pismo Beach authorities."

"That's pretty much our strategy. We'll try to see most of the electors before the vote." Saroyan stood up. "I'll leave you guys with the rest of the day." Saroyan left the Edwards apartment.

☆   ☆   ☆

The Same Day
Washington, D.C.

"BRING ME UP TO DATE," PRESIDENT HAMPTON REQUESTED IN A concise, business-like tone as he sat behind his desk. Klondike had just entered the Oval Office for an early afternoon meeting.

"Not much more," Klondike told him wearily as he took a seat across from the President.

"I'm assuming we have a regiment of FBI agents digging into this by now."

"Um . . ." Klondike was tentative. He read the President's mood as impatient and intolerant. "Uh, they're having a jurisdictional problem. This is basically a local murder—"

"It's *tampering* with a *Federal election*," he insisted.

"We don't really know that," Klondike told him diplomatically. "It could be what was originally reported—a robber got carried away. The FBI is in touch with the local authorities and if—"

"We're waiting for some Podunk Beach police department to tell us if this is election tampering or some street crime? No way, Cuv. Get on this yourself. Talk to Justice. Talk to the Director. I told you, I want a regiment of FBI agents on this. The American people deserve to know if their election has been tampered with."

"Yes sir."

"Now what are our chances without this Whittlebaum character?"

"Iffy. Our people may have influenced a few to turn, but there are no guarantees."

"Great," President Hampton quipped with caustic sarcasm. He stiffened. "If Whittlebaum was killed by someone connected to Parker *or* Edwards, I want the whole God Damn thing exposed, and the sooner, the better."

Klondike nodded. "We can try to make it impossible for the House to choose Parker."

"Exactly. And justice. In the United States, we don't murder people to win an election."

Klondike grinned. "True."

"I want daily progress reports on this, Cuv. And tomorrow, I want to hear that FBI agents are crawling all over that Piss-and-moan Beach place."

"Yes."

Klondike left quickly.

✿   ✿   ✿

Mid December: The Following Friday
Arlington, Virginia

"UNCLE EMMETT'S FINAL RESTING PLACE," NICHOLAS MUELLER commented as he moved up toward Donald Samuelson. Samuelson stood, looking down at a white headstone labeled "Emmett Townsly: February 16, 1916 - December 7, 1941." They were just off a path among the grassy rolling hills of gleaming bright white headstones in the Arlington National Cemetery. It was a chilly, sunny day, a day when people could see breathy wisps of steam coming out of their mouths as they spoke. The trees on the grounds had already lost the multi-colored leaves of autumn, and their branches stood bare and frost-covered.

"Yeah," Samuelson commented reflectively. "I haven't been here in awhile." Samuelson turned around to meet Mueller's eyes. "How did you know about my uncle?"

"You do mention him in your autobiography," Mueller answered, as if the question was stupid and the answer was obvious.

"My autobiography."

"I've picked you, Mr. Samuelson."

"Yes. Complete with the cloak-and-dagger meeting. But picked me for what?"

"No one can know I've met with you," Mueller stated with profound gravity.

"Okay."

"People know I come out here sometimes; it's on my way home. So it's not out of the ordinary that I would stop by here. But this is also a place where it is easy to spot someone watching or following."

"You like to come out *here*?"

"I like to stop by the eternal flame at John Kennedy's grave. I like to think his ideals are still burning in me. And for more inspiration? There's the Washington mansion." Mueller motioned to a structure dominating a nearby hill that looked more like a Greek temple than a home for mere mortals, complete with thick white round columns in the front, visible even at this distance.

Samuelson smiled. "Built by Washington's son, *after* George Washington died."

Mueller also smiled, sheepishly. "Okay. That's true. But this place really is a special place to me. I've been . . . Something needs to be. . . . Someone needs to know what I know." Mueller seemed to have trouble finding the words.

"Somebody over at the Parker organization has been chopping down some cherry trees, and they *can* tell a lie," Samuelson guessed.

"Yeah." Mueller looked down at the headstone he and Samuelson had been standing at. "Your mother's brother had a lot of courage to do what he did at Pearl Harbor."

"Are you trying to tell me that what you're doing here takes a lot of courage?"

Mueller shook his head sadly. "No. Not at all. I'm not the kind of a guy who runs into a burning, sinking ship to try to save people who are probably not saveable. I'm much more cautious. I'm a bookworm, a thinker, a philosophizer . . . a ponderer. Your uncle would probably have called me a coward."

"So . . . you don't have his courage. Whatever we're here to do, let's do it. It's cold out here, and this place closes at five." He looked at his watch. "It's four-fifteen now."

"You remember Watergate? 'Deep Throat?'"

"Yeah. People *still* don't know for sure who he, or she, was."

"Exactly. I'm here to be your 'Deep Throat.' No one is ever to know who I am. I mean you are not even to tell your people back at the network. You and I will be the only ones who will ever know."

Samuelson nodded. "I'll have to confirm your information through other sources."

"Fine, fine, you do whatever you have to do. But I want your word as a journalist that—"

"I *never* reveal a confidential source."

"And I will set the conditions as to when and how I will release the information I'll give to you."

"Mr. Mueller, this is getting tiresome. If you put too many conditions on—"

"Don't try to haggle with me on these ground rules," Mueller interrupted firmly. "We'll do this my way, or not at all. I know you're gonna want this story."

Samuelson drew a deep breath. "Okay, Mr. Throat. It's your show.

What have you got?"

"The electoral process has been perverted by all three of these so-called candidates. The American people have to know. One of our own people masterminded buggings of Hampton's campaign leaders. I've seen the tapes. And Hampton's people bribed an elector to switch his vote from Edwards to Hampton—that's proven on the tapes. And Edwards' people probably—"

"You've heard the tapes?"

"Some of them. The guy who has them is such a slob." Mueller did little to hide his disgust. "He doesn't even have them locked up. I guess he figures no one else knows about them."

"And how do *you* know about them?"

"I snooped around his office after the murder."

"Whittlebaum's murder?"

"Are there any other election-related murders you know of?" Mueller quipped derisively.

"Do you know anything about the murder?"

Mueller became very guarded. "Not a lot."

"But something."

"Let me put it this way. I'd be very surprised if this was just a street crime. I think you'll find Edwards' people, or our people, or *both*, had something to do with it."

Samuelson shrugged, dissatisfied and disappointed. "This is what you have?" he asked in disbelief.

"I'm 'Deep Throat,'" Mueller reminded him. "I've given you facts. You'll have to do the leg-work to get your story. I'll try to steer you when I can. . . point you in the right direction."

"This is not Watergate, and I'm not Woodward-Bernstein. Votes are going to be counted on this in a few days. There's no time for these games. I can't use any of this. I need more. I need something besides statements I can't attribute, statements that sound almost like opinions and inferences. I need the raw facts."

"You're lazy, Mr. Samuelson. It'll cost you this story."

"If what you say *is* verifiable, then it'll cost the American people if it doesn't—"

"I'm not a hero," Mueller countered. "I told you, I'm not your uncle."

"There's not much I can do with this."

"Then I guess we've wasted a trip out here . . . "

"Get me the tapes."

"What?" Mueller could not believe the audacity of the request.

"Or copies—they would give me something substantial . . ."

"You're not just lazy, you're *crazy,*" Mueller chastised angrily. "And you could get me killed."

"You tell me the guy doesn't lock them up. On a weekend, or when he goes out of town, slip them to me."

"Forget it."

"You want this story to get out? This is the quickest way. The tapes will verify everything you've been saying."

"You get the story out on the buggings, and you'll smoke the tapes out."

"That won't work!" Samuelson insisted. "Damn it, Mueller, I keep telling you, this isn't Watergate! What is the one thing about Watergate no one could understand? Why didn't Nixon destroy the tapes? They incriminated him and his people. They proved he was a liar. Why did he keep them? If I hint that anyone knows about these tapes, that mistake won't be repeated. They will be *gone.* That's why I can't report this story, not without more confirmation. Maybe I can get another source in your organization to verify the tapes exist. Or maybe I spook everyone and the tapes are turned into road-fill. I need to hear the actual tapes. If I hear them, I can write the story, whether they're eventually destroyed or not."

Mueller pondered. "You work with what I've given you," he finally replied. "I'll get in touch for another meeting."

"With the tapes?"

Mueller's tight facial expression visibly demonstrated his irritation with Samuelson's pushiness. "Work with what you have," he repeated, spitting out each word individually, as if making sure he was clear this time. "We'll discuss other information at our next meeting."

"I need—"

"I'm setting the rules. Like you say, it's getting chilly out here. And the place closes at five. We can't walk out together. I'll leave first." Mueller walked away abruptly.

Samuelson waited for a few moments at his uncle's headstone. He allowed a smile to creep onto his face. How would Uncle Emmett, the family hero who had died before Samuelson was born, have felt about a nephew breaking one of the biggest stories of the last hundred years? Samuelson knew that he might be about to do just that, if he could flesh out Mueller's allegations.

✧   ✧   ✧

December: The First Monday After the Second Wednesday
Sacramento, California

"WE ARE INTERRUPTING OUR REGULARLY SCHEDULED PROGRAM FOR A special news bulletin," Andrew Talbot stated to his television audience. Michael Edwards and Drew Saroyan watched anxiously in their Sacramento hotel room. Talbot tried to project objectivity, but Edwards could see he was unhappy with the story he was about to report. "As everyone in the country knows, this is the first Monday after the second Wednesday in December, the time Constitutionally designated for state electors to meet in their state capitols and cast their votes for President. We have just learned that two, maybe three electors pledged to Michael Edwards have cast their votes for Kenneth Hampton."

"Damn!" Edwards was angry, and for now he used his anger and frustration to shield him from the dejection that might well set in if this result proved to be the conclusion of his election effort.

Saroyan sat quietly. The dejection seemed to hit him immediately.

"This is a monumental story," Talbot continued, "because this election will now go to President Hampton, instead of the House of Representatives, where Senator Parker was likely to be chosen. And because of this story's importance, we have taken careful measures to confirm it. For more on that, here's WWBS political consultant, Edwin Williams."

"Thank you, Andy." Williams was almost clinical with his explanation. "We have three separate sources confirming two of the defections, and two sources confirming a third defection. We cannot be specific about the states. Our sources have access to information that has been described as 'sealed,' and it is unclear if revealing that information is unlawful for these sources. To give the specific states would potentially reveal the sources."

"Weasel," Edwards said disparagingly.

Saroyan was amused. "One media guy to another . . ."

"Shut up," Edwards ordered. He knew he would be reporting the same result in the same way if he had still been on the WWBS staff. But he wasn't interested in objectivity and fairness to the messenger of bad news.

"But these are reliable sources," Talbot reiterated.

"Absolutely," Williams replied. "And we will not be able to determine which electors defected, unless individual electors come forward, or someone through subpoena or court order, compels their identities to be made public. When the votes are officially counted on January 6th, there will be no reference to who cast them."

"I'd love to know which bastards betrayed us," Edwards pronounced irritably.

The phone rang. Edwards picked it up. "Hello?"

"Michael, did you hear—"

He cut off Teresa's question. "Yes," he told her abruptly, then followed with a softer "Yes, I did. Can you come out here?"

"I'll be on the first plane I can get." She paused. "Are you okay?"

"No," he replied. "But I'll be better when you get here. Drew and I—" He paused. "We'll get all of our meetings out of the way before you arrive."

"Good." She paused. "I love you," she finally told him softly. "And I think that what you've accomplished is . . ." Her voice trailed off.

"I took it pretty far, didn't I," he said to her affectionately, finishing his wife's statement.

"No one could have taken it further."

"Thanks. Oh, and I love you too."

"See you soon." The phone clicked.

The WWBS report continued. "So is the election over now? Has President Hampton won?" Talbot asked Williams.

"If no one contests this result, yes," Williams answered definitively. "There have been rumors of some irregularities with the electors, and if Parker or Edwards choose to challenge the result, then . . ." Williams gathered his thoughts. "There aren't really any applicable precedents to this situation. In 1877, Republican Rutherford B. Hayes ended up as President after a very controversial electoral commission awarded him the disputed electors from the 1876 election. But that result was embroiled in the politics of post Civil War Reconstruction."

"Spare me the history lesson," Saroyan requested of the television set.

But Edwards waited to hear more detail. "Let me hear him."

"It doesn't apply to us," Saroyan told Edwards.

"Can you explain to our viewers how that election was resolved?" Talbot requested.

Williams chuckled. "Trying to distill some complicated history down to essentials without oversimplifying? I'll try. Samuel Tilden, the Democratic candidate, appeared to have the election won with a significant electoral vote majority, and a small popular vote majority as well. But the Republicans disputed the results in four states. In the three southern states of Louisiana, Florida and South Carolina, they claimed blacks were unlawfully kept from voting. In Oregon, they claimed the Democratic Governor had acted improperly when he disqualified a Republican elector and replaced him with a Democrat.

"Congress appointed an electoral commission to resolve the dispute—it consisted of five from the House, five from the Senate, and five from the Supreme Court. Congress chose four of the Supreme Court Justices, two Democrats, and two Republicans. Those four Justices were asked to pick a fifth Justice. They chose a Republican, but he started off favoring Tilden. He was eventually replaced, and the commission awarded the disputed votes to Hayes, giving Hayes a one vote victory only two days before inauguration day.

"But there was more to this than just the action of the commission. Historians basically concur that moderate Republicans and southern Democrats cut a back-room deal. Republicans agreed that they would withdraw Federal troops from the southern states and allow them to control their own affairs again. This essentially meant that white southern Democrats would be back in power. In exchange, Democrats would not protest a commission finding that favored the Republicans. So the electoral commission was simply ratifying the deal.

"This proved to be a short-sighted deal for the Republicans. They took the White House, but the southern Democrats retook control of politics in the South. Blacks were excluded from voting by various schemes, all the way into the mid 1960's. For the better part of a hundred years, Democrats dominated politics in the South, with the Republicans only reasserting themselves in the 1960's and 70's. For the southern Democrats, this was a great deal. It is unlikely that New York Democrat Samuel Tilden would have been as quick to withdraw troops from the South.

"So we can see why this may not apply to the current situation."

"Thank you, Ed." Talbot turned to the television audience as the camera focus narrowed to him only. "We'll have more on this story in a special report during our news broadcast tonight at 6:30."

Edwards picked up the remote control and turned off the television. "Looks like that litigation long-shot is our only shot," Edwards told Saroyan.

"Yeah." Saroyan remained subdued, almost paralyzed.

"I want a report from those lawyers in three days—an objective pros-and-cons assessment of what we might be able to do. That history lesson you didn't want to hear might give us a shot. There's a precedent for an electoral commission, in the event of irregularities. I think this situation qualifies as having some irregularities surrounding it. Maybe an electoral commission is just what we need to get to the bottom of it."

"Okay." Saroyan started to return from his temporary paralysis. Work was his best medicine. Edwards had just given him some.

"FBI meeting tomorrow?" Edwards asked.

"Yeah. In San Francisco. We'll give them the tape. I already told them what's on it."

"So they really think this was an assassination?"

"I don't know what they think. They're not saying much. But I do know they got ahold of Whittlebaum's 'in-the-event-I-die' letter. It points fingers at us, and at Parker's people. The FBI's talking to everybody right now—fishing, I'd say."

Edwards looked seriously at Saroyan. "Drew, are there too many holes in this battleship to plug up? Are we going down?"

Saroyan drew a deep breath. "I don't know. Let me . . . this is a bad time to decide anything. We've been . . . we've taken a nasty blow here today."

"I know."

"I think we should set a meeting with our core supporters; Everett, Wally Trewillinger, Frances Willis—anyone else you feel should be part of our . . . decision-making process. Let's see how everybody feels. It'll take a few days to put it together. The dust'll settle a bit by then."

"Good idea."

"I'm going to go . . . relax in my room," Saroyan told him as he got up to leave.

"Okay. See you downstairs for dinner?"

Saroyan looked at his watch. "In about two and a half hours, at six-thirty. But make it here in your room. I don't think we want to face reporters right now. At dinner, we'll put together a statement, something to the effect that we're waiting for the *official* results." Saroyan left quickly.

Edwards smiled. That last thought expressed by Drew Saroyan told Edwards that he was emerging from the "nasty blow." Edwards settled back for a two hour afternoon nap.

Chapter 28

Mid December: The Following Thursday
New Orleans, Louisiana

"I'M GLAD YOU GUYS ASKED ME HERE," ENRIQUEZ TOLD FADIMAN AND Hunter as he polished off a huge ice cream and cake dessert, wolfing it down. "I hated to think we had hard feelings."

"Friends can have honest disagreements," Fadiman said calmly. "As long as they level with each other. As long as they're *honest* disagreements."

"I agree completely," Enriquez told them as he continued wolfing down his desert. "That's why I leveled with you guys about why I didn't like Edwards."

"We appreciate just exactly how honest you've been," Hunter added.

"Hear anything from your friend Manuel?" Fadiman asked.

"Manuel," Enriquez responded disgustedly with his mouth still almost full of ice cream. "He got himself killed, the idiot. He's a lap-dog. I've got another one already. Dogs don't live as long as people. They follow you blindly, then eventually die off."

Fadiman and Hunter were silent.

"You guys're sharp," Enriquez told them with obviously insincere flattery, filling in the silence. "I can learn a lot from you. I'm glad I took your advice and left Edwards alone. We ended up with our guy."

"We're glad you took our advice, too," Hunter acknowledged,

sounding as insincere as Enriquez did.

Enriquez was finally through with his dessert. "I really hate to eat and run, my good friends, but I have to catch a plane to Mexico City. Come down and see me in Venezuela." He stood up.

Fadiman also stood up. "We might just get down there some day."

"We'll go out on Lake Maracaibo," Enriquez told them.

Enriquez shook hands with both men. He left the table and headed out of the restaurant.

Fadiman pulled a pocket transmitter out of his inside jacket pocket. "Mountain Man. Is our guest with you?"

"Yes. He heard it all. He's with us," Carl Gregory said from a nearby parked vehicle.

"Come on in."

Shortly after these instructions, Manuel Contreras and Carl Gregory were ushered to their table. Contreras had bandages on both hands, but his fingers were exposed, and the hands did not appear to cause him any pain.

"Manuel," Fadiman greeted. "I see your hands are getting better."

"Good as new in a few weeks," he replied without a trace of irritation or vindictiveness.

"And let's see the dental work," Fadiman requested.

"I like this a lot better than what I had in here before," Contreras told them as he opened his mouth and showed off his new bridge and tooth. "And I got a new watch out of the deal too."

"Has Mr. Enriquez' car been brought up to specs?" Fadiman asked coldly, with simmering anger just under the surface.

"Yes," Carl Gregory answered. "But I don't think the car will last until it's next scheduled service."

Fadiman smiled a cruel, superior smile.

"I gave our friend here the opportunity to handle the body work," Gregory told them through an enigmatic grin.

Contreras smiled knowingly and pulled out a small remote-control detonator with a bright red button.

"I don't want to know anything more about this," Hunter told them seriously.

"The only thing we have to know is that *this* lap-dog is gonna outlast its master," Fadiman commented wryly.

"You aren't interested in oil, are you, son?" Hunter asked Contreras.

"Oh no," Contreras replied through a streetwise smile. "I can't make enough money with *that* stuff. Mr. Gregory here has convinced me that oil investments are not healthy—I mean, economically speaking. I've decided that the organization should sell off its interests in the oil business. Besides, my expertise is in . . ." He paused a moment to find the right English words. "Pharmaceutical products," he finally said, still smiling. "And I don't even have anything against Michael Edwards. Because I have been studying your Joseph Kennedy, and I will be ready to be the Joseph Kennedy of my time if anyone is ever in a position to change the legal status of my products. That is, Joseph Kennedy without the political ambitions."

"Enjoy your new job," Fadiman told him casually. "Just be careful—it can be dangerous."

"And say a prayer for John Doe 46871 out of the New York City morgue," Gregory joked.

"I'll send flowers to his grave—easy enough to do—he's buried under my name." Contreras stood up. "Well, I have a car to repair, so I better get going. And no offense, but I don't think we'll be seeing each other again."

"I agree," Fadiman responded.

"Don't do the body work here," Gregory reminded Contreras.

"I know exactly where I will . . . do the *repairs* on the car," Contreras told them confidently. "He will go to his Miami mansion before returning home. I don't care what he says—he is not going to Mexico City tonight. There is a girl there he always sees when he is in this part of your country. And the mansion is the perfect place for my . . . car repairs." Contreras gave a slight casual wave as he left the restaurant.

Fadiman and Hunter sipped their after dinner brandies.

"CIA ops is going to owe me for this one," Fadiman commented. "They were just starting to see the Enriquez clouds on the horizon and trying to figure out what to do about it. I'll have a marker to call in from some very good people to have as friends."

Hunter raised his glass. "Here's to coming out on top."

Fadiman smiled. "To this great system of complicated political relationships and media people who think they're using *you* when you're really using *them*. Like Ted Jessup over at WWBS."

Hunter laughed. "Oh, and here's to Michael Edwards, a man of vision."

Fadiman smiled again. "A man of great ideas—for somebody *else's* lifetime."

They clinked their glasses and laughed as they drank.

Three mornings later, the Miami papers carried a story about a wealthy foreign businessman killed by a car bomb. They speculated about drug involvement, or even the volatile politics of South America, as possible catalysts for the murder. They said the police had no suspects.

Manuel Contreras appeared the next day, ready to take over Enriquez' operations. And with his knowledge, power and brutal will, Contreras had little trouble stepping in with few questions, and even fewer challenges.

✡   ✡   ✡

Late December, Election Year: Saturday
Washington, D.C.

"SORRY TO DISTURB YOU, MR. PRESIDENT," KLONDIKE STATED apologetically as President Hampton entered the room in a sweat-suit, obviously drowsy. They were in the Oval Office, not far from where the President slept. And it was clear the President had been sleeping, not working, right before Klondike had asked to see him. Klondike stood to greet the President. "But the FBI has had a breakthrough on the Whittlebaum assassination, and I wanted to let you know about it right away."

"That's okay, Cuv," he replied as they both sat. "I'm supposed to be taking some time off with my family for the holidays," he mentioned, offering an explanation for his casual appearance. "But I wanted to stay in town until I had a little more definitive information on this. I am, however, getting some rest."

Klondike smiled. "You deserve it. And this news might help you rest a little easier, though it's not *everything* we want, at least not yet."

"But something has been determined."

"It was almost certainly a political hit," Klondike told him. "I'm not sure how much detail you want . . ."

"As much as you've got. I want to get a sense of how solid the findings are."

"Okay," Klondike nodded. "After that note surfaced, with the handwriting verified, agents contacted campaign officials from both Edwards' and Parker's organizations to see what they knew about possible threats against Whittlebaum. The Edwards people produced a wild tape recording where Michael Edwards and Drew Saroyan are sent away from Whittlebaum's doorstep with a gunshot! So either Whittlebaum was a paranoid lunatic, or someone else was applying some heavy pressure."

"Any evidence he *was* mentally unbalanced?" the President asked.

"They had part of the 'regiment of agents' you requested check that out," Klondike said as he smiled.

President Hampton also smiled.

"He was not well-liked, and possibly had some inflated ideas of himself. But no one interviewed about his personality or character described him as being paranoid, or having any unreasonable fears."

The President nodded.

"This impressed the investigating agents. Why would this man suddenly turn paranoid over night? They figured someone probably *had* threatened him, someone who knew he was considering changing his vote, and that when that someone couldn't get him to guarantee he'd keep his pledge to Edwards, he was assassinated. But their interviews didn't turn up anything. So they decided to work it backwards. They assumed Whittlebaum's note was accurate—some combination of Edwards and Parker people did have him killed as he feared would happen. But Whittlebaum was hiding out. How would they find him?

"The agents figured the guys doing the hit would be slick professionals. They'd check to see if he had left a charge-card trail. So the agents contacted all the credit-reporting agencies to see if there were any formal inquiries for information on Whittlebaum. It came back empty. But would a pro leave a trail like that? So they called back and asked about *informal* inquiries. That took longer, but was doable because computer transactions of any kind at these places leave a record. And someone in one of the agencies did look at Bennington Whittlebaum's file. The inquiry was done on an unassigned terminal with a generic password, so the individual in the credit-reporting agency who made the inquiry has not been identified yet. But the credit records showed that the stupid fool had charged his hotel bill and two restaurant bills to his Mastercharge."

"I thought we paid the man three hundred thousand dollars cash," the President recalled.

"I don't know." Klondike shrugged, unable to explain Whittlebaum's actions. "Without a good lead on the specific person who made the credit card inquiry, obviously an employee who's picking up some extra money selling information on the side to people who don't want their inquiries recorded, the agents tried another route. They identified the time of the computer inquiry, then checked phone company records for *incoming* long-distance calls. They figured whoever called for the information would want it immediately, before Whittlebaum changed locations. This kind of phone company information would have been real difficult to come by ten or twenty years ago, but today, it's just a matter of asking a computer the right question. It's all stored somewhere. Well, they came up with around fifteen numbers in that general time frame. They were able to link all but one of the numbers to legitimate inquiries, or other company business. The fifteenth number came back to a New York City phone booth, next to the restroom of the Park Avenue Bar and Grill. That is one of the favorite meeting places of Michael Edwards and his campaign people."

"Edwards? Himself?"

"Not likely. In fact, it appears he was out of town. But phone company records show a short call from that phone booth to Lompoc—the number came back to the minimum security prison."

"What?"

"Oscar Lusman is an inmate there."

"Lusman—the guy who had the drug dealer beaten up?"

"Yup. He denies taking any calls. And no one at the prison remembers him getting any calls. But someone may be clamming up."

"So it looks like Edwards' people . . ."

"Someone associated with them. Because the next call went to a phone booth in Berkeley, just down the street from the headquarters there. And then another call from *that* phone booth to Lompoc."

"Any links to Parker?" Hampton asked. That was the result he was hoping for.

"Not yet."

"But still possible . . ."

"I'm not sure. But they were able to get some more information. The FBI investigators figured the call to Berkeley was probably the call to the killer. And the killer had to be around the phone booth to take the call. They canvassed local merchants, some of whom weren't enthusiastic about helping. But they got a composite sketch on a guy who was hanging around the area of that phone booth when the call came in."

"And they figure that is a sketch of the killer."

"They took it a step further. They checked car rental agencies—no one remembers seeing him. That would be pretty stupid, and they figure this guy is not stupid. He either had a car rented for him by someone else, or took a bus. No one at the possible bus depots remembers him—they checked with a couple of bus drivers as well.

"So they took the composite sketch down to Pismo Beach. They had their artists do some alternative sketches, figuring the guy might have used a disguise. And guess what? The one with the moustache and darker hair got three I-D's from people around the murder area the night that it happened. So we have him—we know what he looks like. Now it's a process of weeding through mug-shots, or trying to get someone to come forward and say who he is. I almost forgot—they also checked with Edwards and Parker people. Some of the Edwards people remember a guy looking a lot like this guy doing some volunteer work recently for the Edwards people in the Bay Area, stuffing envelopes. But no one was able to come up with anything specific on the guy. Other possible trails are being checked; charge-card trails, hotel registration desks in the area—but he's probably too slick to leave anything like that behind."

"And that's where we stand."

"Yes."

"Tell them they've done a nice job," President Hampton instructed Klondike sincerely. "Have them call a press conference. Get that composite splashed all over every front page in the country. And this potential link to Edwards needs to come out."

"A press conference? In the middle of an investigation? The usual procedure is not to call the press in until they are ready to announce an arrest."

"President's orders," Hampton told Klondike. "This case has important national implications. The people deserve to know what is happening." Then he flashed a sly grin. "And with Edwards linked to this dastardly crime, it will soften all those protestations that the elector defections were unfair. It might even look like those defectors had great insight. And it shows Edwards to be a man who, at best, cannot control his people—not a fit man for the Presidency." He paused as his lips formed a tight, tense line. "I just wish it was *Parker*."

Klondike nodded. "We may yet tie his people into this. But right now, there are no links, except for Whittlebaum's beliefs."

"Yes. Well, good work. You and the FBI. Keep me posted." He thought a moment. "I'll have a very important role for you during my second term. You've done an absolutely stellar job of engineering my reelection, when it looked like we—hell, when I was talking about conceding!"

Klondike smiled.

✿   ✿   ✿

Late December: The Following Wednesday
New York, New York

"WELCOME TO THE NOTORIOUS PARK AVENUE BAR AND GRILL," Edwards greeted with a gallows humor grin as he stood looking down a long table of about twenty supporters. Among them were Teresa, Drew Saroyan, Everett Phillips, Frances Willis, Wallace Trewillinger and three Congressmen, two from Minnesota, and one from California, who had been elected on an Edwards-type platform. They were meeting at 9:00 a.m. for breakfast, about two and a half hours before the restaurant was scheduled to open. "This turned out to be our most practical meeting location," he told everyone. "And, this is where we do our best scheming and plotting, at least according to these reports I keep hearing."

A nervous laugh twittered through the group.

"I want first to tell all of you that despite all those reports on an *ongoing* and *incomplete* FBI investigation, no one associated with my organization had anything to do with this terrible murder of our elector. Drew and I have personally questioned our people about the guy in that composite. Maybe he did one or two days of volunteer work for our Bay Area office. Even that is shaky. But he is *not* one of ours. It was unfair for the FBI to release partial information like that."

"Unfair, but predictable," Willis told them quietly. "They work for the President, and this news certainly helps him."

"True enough," Edwards agreed somberly as he sat down. "And that's why I called you all here today. I wanted to get your thoughts, on how or whether we should continue."

"I would like to remind everyone here that the electoral votes have not yet been counted," Trewillinger stated with dignified eloquence. "The media do not decide elections, especially on the basis of anonymous sources."

"Absolutely," Everett Phillips added with stern firmness.

Edwards drew a long breath. "I appreciate that. And in principle, I agree with you. But the information seems to be overwhelming. So while I agree that the result isn't officially in yet, as a practical matter, we have a good idea what it will be."

Teresa squirmed uncomfortably in her chair.

"All right," Trewillinger spoke first. "Let's assume, for the sake of argument, that this predicted result is accurate. It would be clear that electors failed to vote the way their voting constituencies mandated. At the very least, an explanation from those electors should be demanded. And to those 34 million plus who voted for your candidacy, Mr. Edwards, to those who chose *you*, we owe it to them to request, no *demand* an investigation into all the circumstances surrounding the disloyal shifts of allegiance by the electors in question. A special electoral commission, such as the one appointed for the 1876 election, should be appointed to look into the matter thoroughly."

"People I've talked to will be disappointed if we don't ask for someone objective to dig into this," Phillips added.

Edwards nodded. "We have attorneys, one of the best Constitutional Law firms in Washington, standing by with papers to serve the minute the results are official. But the litigation approach, as Drew and I call it, can't work in a vacuum."

"We can talk about demanding details from electoral commissions all we want," Willis interjected shaking her head. "But what do we need to win? Even if we undo this result, we need the House to look to *us*. Right now, most of the country thinks you lost control of your people again—this time someone working for you was involved in a murder. The House can't look to us right now because the American people won't look to us."

"That is the challenge," Edwards agreed.

"I will not tell you to quit," Phillips stated, almost angrily. "We need to fight back. We're being defeated by partial investigations and unnamed sources. Let's convince the American people to look to us again. Before that unfortunate murder, polls showed they wanted us."

Trewillinger nodded. "It's an uphill battle. So was your campaign. Mr. Edwards, I will also not be a defeatist. I will be realistic enough to say that this is a challenge. But great leaders are not forged out of comfortable times. They prove themselves during adversity. This is your chance to do just that."

Edwards nodded. "Point well taken. Thank you."

"I'm enjoying the eloquence I'm hearing here," Willis told them frankly. "But you have to consider withdrawing as an option. If there's no chance of success—if the people don't want you anymore—it's an option, a practical one. Because in politics, public perception can become reality, even though it isn't even close to the accurate truth. But if there is a chance, and if we can win back those we may have lost, then you would be letting down a lot of people if you took the withdrawal option."

"I appreciate all the advice I have gotten here today," Edwards told them sincerely, though somewhat subdued. "Let's have some breakfast."

Animated talk, including juicy war stories and lively debates on every topic imaginable filled the nearly empty restaurant, making it sound almost as boisterous as if all the tables were occupied. But Michael Edwards was quiet, absorbed in thought. And Teresa was also uncharacteristically quiet, trying to contain her dissatisfaction.

✧   ✧   ✧

"IT'S A GOOD GROUP OF PEOPLE, MICHAEL," SAROYAN TOLD HIM AS HE stood with Michael and Teresa Edwards after the last of the group had left. Saroyan was signing the check. It was almost 11:00.

"I feel good about bringing them together. I'm just not sure I should continue to put us all through this. Frances Willis was right. She—"

Teresa finally could not contain her discontent any longer. "Drew, could you go pay the check or something? I need to talk to Michael alone."

The force of the request almost compelled Saroyan's answer. "Sure." He walked toward the restaurant host to deliver the signed charge slip.

Michael was taken by surprise. "Are you upset with me?" he asked incredulously.

"You can't keep doing this to people, Michael," she told him bluntly.

"Doing . . . *what* to people?"

"Trying to talk them out of supporting you."

"What?" he asked.

"It almost seemed like you were trying to talk everyone into telling you to give up."

"That's *ridiculous*. That is *not* what I was doing. We were—"

"*Two* of your top people told you they were *refusing* to advise you to quit. That implies they thought you were leading them in that direction."

Michael thought a moment about what Teresa had said. She was right. Both Phillips and Trewillinger had phrased statements just that way.

"Michael, I know you, better than any of these other people. You want everybody to love you. You feast on public admiration—you did as an anchorman, and you have as your support in this election has grown. But every time it starts to look like people may be questioning their admiration for you, you go into this pout. You want to go off and cry by yourself somewhere, 'nobody loves me anymore.' If people dare to think about withdrawing their admiration, you want to run away. Because that hurts you. It hurts that they don't trust you, that some of them left you."

"That is me," he agreed honestly. "Remember when the ratings fell off back in '96? I talked about retiring?"

Teresa smiled. He was listening to her and clearly understood what she was saying. "And when you lost all those supporters after the Naylor thing," she reminded him.

Michael nodded. "Maybe I'm not tough enough to do this," he said reflectively.

"You're doing it to *me* now!" Teresa told him sharply.

Michael was startled by the outburst, but realized she was right.

"Michael," she commented tersely, almost scolding, "if you are a *leader*, then *lead* these people. Are you really so blind? Didn't you see you had a table full of people who want to fight? But they can't do it without you. And they weren't sure they had you today."

Michael winced. Then he finally said, "They really are with me, aren't they . . ."

"If you really need me to answer that, then you haven't—"

"They are," he followed up, now sounding more decisive. "It's part of the process for me to question things, Teresa."

She looked at him, discouraged that he may not have taken her words to heart.

"But you are right. If you keep asking the wrong questions, eventually you might end up getting the wrong answers."

"That's right."

"Am I in or out? I told them I would decide by the end of the week."

"Stay in, Michael," Teresa advised gently. "Stay with it all the way, no matter what."

"Play all nine innings, even if it's a laugher."

"This isn't a baseball game."

"Or a 'laugher.' Some very serious matters are at stake."

"Yes."

Michael said nothing. He looked over toward Saroyan who now rejoined them.

"I've got a meeting with Don Samuelson tomorrow," Edwards reminded Saroyan. "What do you think about me telling him that we had a meeting about me possibly ending my effort—let him put it out to test public reaction."

Teresa rolled her head and stomped away disgustedly.

Saroyan shrugged. "Sure. The old trial balloon."

"Did his network call the Electoral College for Hampton?"

"I think so." Saroyan tried to recall. "I'm not sure."

"Hmm." Edwards was certain they must have—he believed all the networks had called it that way. But he could not remember any specific reference to it on their broadcasts.

"What time's the meeting?" Saroyan asked.

"3:00."

"We'll meet afterwards. Call me."

"Okay."

✪   ✪   ✪

Late December: The Next Day, Thursday
New York, New York

"NICE PLACE," SAMUELSON TOLD EDWARDS AS EDWARDS USHERED HIM into his living room.

"Thank you."

"We're alone?"

"Yup. No Saroyan. I felt he could be a distraction."

"And you can handle yourself, can't you?"

"I don't know," Edwards replied grinning. "Have a seat."

Samuelson took a seat on the couch. Edwards sat in an easy chair.

"Drink?" Edwards asked.

"Maybe later."

"So, any particular topic you wanted to talk to me about?"

"What do you know about the demise of one Bennington Whittlebaum?"

"I wish I knew more," Edwards answered honestly.

"Someone working for you didn't get carried away?"

Edwards started to feel insulted, but realized this was a reporter's question. "I really don't think so," he replied, shaking his head with earnest sincerity. "We've gone over this with our people—we have searched hard for the guy in that sketch. The best we can come up with is that someone who looked a little like him was stuffing envelopes for a day or two out in California." Edwards paused. "There's something else you should know about that whole situation, something the FBI never mentioned in their press conferences. We turned over a tape of a visit we had with Whittlebaum—"

"Who's 'we?'"

"Drew and I. We visited Whittlebaum. Alone—no 'tough guys.' We taped him as he ranted and raved about how we were threatening him."

"You taped him?"

"To use in court to get him disqualified as a nut-case."

"Very interesting."

"I ask you, Don, would we visit the guy and tape it if we were going to have him killed?"

"You have a copy of that tape?"

"Sure. I'll get it to you."

"Thanks."

"Don, I'll tell you, and this isn't for attribution, because I can't prove it. But someone is trying to lay this off on us."

"Who?"

"Come on. Who else needed to prevent my electors from turning?"

"You mean Parker."

"Someone in his camp."

Samuelson nodded. "It's not that far-fetched." He grinned, then began to boast. "I have a source over there that you wouldn't—" He stopped himself as his grin broadened to a smile. "I almost forgot that you're a candidate—I'm so used to thinking of you as a fellow journalist."

"That's okay. You got a good source over with Parker?"

"Yeah. And that's obviously all I can tell you. But I think you'll like the story when it comes out."

"Good. You might also want to know, from a 'high-ranking source with the Edwards organization,' that I held a meeting with my core supporters yesterday. We had serious talks about withdrawing from this thing."

"Really."

"Yes. No final decisions have been reached, but—"

"The old trial balloon gambit," Samuelson interrupted smiling. "Well, you should know how to do it. I'm sure you've been on the receiving end often enough."

Edwards shrugged. He wasn't going to try to deny it.

"Do we have it exclusive?"

"Yeah. That and the tape are all yours."

"I'll float your balloon—if you really want me to . . ." Samuelson smirked, as if he knew something Edwards didn't.

Edwards didn't respond immediately. Had he missed something?

"You know, you really are losing the old journalistic instincts. There's a question I was sure you were going to ask me. Michael Edwards, the journalist, would have asked by now . . ."

"I thought *you* were supposed to ask the questions."

"You can ask questions. It's permitted."

"I . . . can't think of a thing." Edwards smiled and shrugged.

"Aren't you curious why we haven't reported that President Hampton has won in the Electoral College?"

So his network hadn't called the election for Hampton. Edwards held the smile, never hinting that he had been unsure of this situation until just this moment. "Oh, *that* question," he responded nonchalantly. "Why haven't you?"

"Because I have another source," Samuelson told him. "I'll describe this source as a friend, a close friend trying to save me and the network some embarrassment. I'm only allowed to use this information to prevent an inaccurate report. I can't be more specific than that. But I can tell you, there will be a lot of egg all over a lot of faces on January 6th, including that robot Williams over at your old network. Because these people have missed a *major* possibility."

"I hear a lot of commentators now saying the election should be conceded to Hampton, in the best interests of the country, to begin an orderly transition to another Presidential term. Just a few weeks ago, they were anointing Parker."

"They're all going to look stupid."

"Most of my people seem to want me to keep fighting."

"I'd say you have good people, with good instincts."

Edwards nodded as he thought a moment.

"So, do you still want me to float that balloon for you?"

Edwards smiled as a look of realization came onto his face. "You came here to tell me . . ."

"Not *me*," Samuelson said with playfully protested innocence. "I came here for a story. The tape you gave to the FBI, and your visit to Whittlebaum a few days before his murder; those are good."

"Well I've got another one for you."

"Hey. My lucky day."

"You can stick a pin in that trial balloon. Instead, you can report that Michael Edwards, candidate for President, called his core supporters late this afternoon, right after we get done here, and told them—he told them he would stay in this race *all the way to the end*. And you can report that the Edwards campaign also issued a statement—I'll be issuing it shortly to all media—that results aren't final until they're *official*. We're *not* withdrawing. We did not kill Bennington Whittlebaum and resent any implications, based on partial investigations, to the contrary. And we still feel we can accomplish a great deal if we are fortunate enough to prevail."

"So the phone calls are exclusive."

"Yes. And yesterday's meeting."

Samuelson stood up. "I think we've both had a rather good day today."

Edwards stood up and shook his hand. "Yes. I believe so."

"But we both have a lot of work to do," Samuelson said as he headed to the door.

"*Lots,*" Edwards agreed as he showed Samuelson out. "Stop by again."

"Call me with a story." Samuelson left.

Edwards smiled. At that moment, he knew he would never withdraw from the race before it concluded. He would marshal his forces and confront the obstacles, no matter how formidable they appeared to be. After all, the race had to play out to the end so he could find out the secret Samuelson had alluded to.

Chapter 29

Late December: The Following Saturday
Manistique, Michigan

"THEY HAVE TV'S AND NEWSPAPERS EVEN OUT HERE IN THE boondocks!" Grady Dunn complained to Will Runalli as they sat on worn, faded chairs in his small rented cabin just east of Indian Lake State Park. A fire blazed in the fireplace. The wood floor had worn rugs covering some of the floor surface. And out of one small window near the front door in the living room, there was a view of the snow-covered ground with tall green trees projecting into the sky, and a hint of the shore of Indian Lake in the distance. Grady Dunn was the real name of the muscular young man who had visited Bennington Whittlebaum with Will Runalli at Whittlebaum's Santa Cruz home. "What happened to *Edwards'* people getting blamed for this?"

"It would have worked if you hadn't hung around long enough to be described."

"I got made by those witnesses because of all those phone booths you had me hanging around," Dunn protested.

"I thought you were a professional who could keep himself out of the way."

"Don't start up on me," Dunn warned, now more angry than scared. "This is *your* stupid plan."

"It might still work, if you stay calm. Now I have some more cash—"

"How much? Enough for me to leave the country?"

Runalli placed ten twenty dollar bills on a table next to his chair.

Dunn grabbed them. "Two hundred bucks?" he commented in angry disbelief.

"This is not a good time to get a lot of cash from the people I work with."

"I don't think *their* problems compare to *mine*."

"No one knows about your problems but me. And believe me, we want to keep it that way. If I start grabbing for big chunks of cash right now, eyebrows are gonna be raised."

"What am I supposed to do? That damn sketch is in every newspaper in the country!"

"Just sit tight. They can't do anything with that silly composite sketch. But if you get nabbed, and they start putting your picture, or you in person, in front of witnesses who still have fresh recollections. . ."

"I'm going crazy out here," Dunn told him frantically. "The guy in the Lake Market gave me a real funny look. Someone's gonna spot me."

"I'll get somebody we can trust to bring in—"

"Just get me enough money to slip over the fucking border," he insisted impatiently.

"Canada?" Runalli asked unenthusiastically. "They have a very good extradition agreement with the United States. And their people have newspapers and televisions too. If we need to get you out of the country, we'll set you up right. Lots of cash, and a country where the extradition procedures aren't so smooth."

"I don't speak Mexican," Dunn quipped.

"Spanish."

"What?"

"They speak Spanish down there."

"Whatever. I'm not going to a place where I have to learn some third world language."

"If you leave the country, that's exactly the type of place you'll go to."

Dunn folded his arms and snorted sullenly.

"And you took a real chance by *calling* me and leaving a *message,*" Runalli scolded. "Don't do that again."

"I was afraid you'd forgotten about me."

"Look, we both want the same thing. We want to make sure you are *not* caught. I'm not gonna forget about this problem, and hope it goes away."

"I'm not a *problem.* I'm a *person.*"

"Like Bennington Whittlebaum . . ."

"Don't threaten me. I can take you down."

"That would not be a smart thing to try," Runalli countered as he glared at the man. "I take care of my friends. You know how I deal with my enemies. You're my friend. We'll keep it that way. Just stay put here. I'll even get your food delivered. Just think of it as a vacation, all expenses paid. Relax."

Dunn nodded, but he was clearly unconvinced.

Runalli smiled, as if to smooth over their problems. "It's tough. But you'll be rewarded. Just hang in."

"I'll try."

"Do it. You're a pro." Runalli left.

Dunn moped around the cabin. He did not like being forced to trust a man whom he knew first-hand was untrustworthy.

✿   ✿   ✿

New Year's Eve, Election Year
Arlington, Virginia

"MR. THROAT. GOOD MORNING. HAPPY NEW YEAR'S EVE. SOMETHING IN your bag I might be interested in?" Samuelson greeted as Mueller approached with a small, dark blue athletic bag. Again, Samuelson waited at his Uncle Emmett's headstone, this time just after Arlington National Cemetery opened at 8:00 a.m.

"These are the rules," Mueller stated resolutely, without any ice-breaking small talk. "They are not negotiable. You must promise you agree *in full* with *all* my conditions *before* you accept delivery."

"I'm listening."

"You can have these tapes for your review until four o'clock tomorrow afternoon. We need to meet back here at that time for you to return them. No one else is to review them with you. No one else is to know of their existence while you have them. And you must wait 24 hours; no, make that 48 hours after their return, before you run any stories on them—"

"48 hours?" Samuelson repeated, almost moaning.

"I must have a chance to get them back where I got them."

"I see."

"You may take notes, but you are not to make any copies of these tapes. You may refer to them in your story, even quoting them, but you can't even *hint* how you got access to them."

Samuelson sighed impatiently. "Is this all really necessary? I mean—"

"It *is* necessary. I'm asking for your word on this, Samuelson. I'm taking a big chance here."

"Your career will be safe, because no one will figure out how I got these. But I have to be able to copy them, and get some assistance reviewing them so—"

"My career? You really don't get it. They've *killed* a man. I've got a wife and kids. I'm not just risking my career here."

"You're running into a burning, sinking ship . . ."

"With all due respects to Uncle Emmett here, I hope I'm not being *that* stupid. I'm taking precautions."

Samuelson considered the situation. "Okay. You win. No copies. Just me. I'll get a cassette deck with a variable speed and live on coffee and Coca Cola until tomorrow afternoon. And . . . I guess I'll miss watching the Rose Parade this year."

Mueller let a slight smile creep onto his face. "Okay."

"There's something else, isn't there . . ."

"What makes you think that?"

"You said 'they've killed a man.' Who killed a man?"

"I'm not ready to—" Mueller stopped himself. "That subject is closed to our relationship."

"Come on, Throat. You found something out. The tapes are part of the story. But you know more . . ."

"I know too fucking much," he blurted out, obviously conflicted between fear and conscience about what to do with his knowledge.

"So share it. It's only dangerous to your safety if you're the only one who knows. Let's get it out. No one will know how I found out. Then you're safe again. You won't know 'too much,' because everyone else will know."

"Go over the tapes. I'll . . . I'll maybe open this subject up to you tomorrow afternoon."

"You're getting too cautious," Samuelson warned. "You know you're going to decide to tell me. Sooner will be better. I can start confirming it right away, and end your exclusivity."

Mueller turned away, then back. "You won't run it unless you can confirm it?"

"I told you."

"I doubt you'll be able to confirm it."

Samuelson could tell Mueller was almost bursting to unburden himself. He let silence act as a magnet, drawing the words out of Mueller.

"I know who the guy is," Mueller stated with quiet intensity. "The composite."

"You've got an I-D on Mr. Composite?"

"Yeah."

"Who is he?"

"Some kind of bodyguard, or Mr. Fix-It used by—" Mueller stopped himself. "Used by another member of Senator Parker's staff."

"What does Runalli use him for exactly?"

"I didn't say Runalli."

"But it is him."

"I didn't say that."

"I don't blame you. The guy's a prick-and-half. Just tell me—if we run a story saying Mr. Composite worked for Runalli, would we have the defense of truth in a libel action?"

Mueller snorted disagreeably. "No one'll testify for you. Not *me* . . ."

"Okay. So we'd lose because we couldn't prove it. But the story would be true, right?"

Mueller raised his head, then exhaled. He nodded quietly.

"What're you gonna do with this little hydrogen bomb you're carrying around in your pocket?"

"I don't know. I don't know the guy's name. I was gonna call in an anonymous tip, but I don't know the guy's name."

"I can't really run this the way it is now. It's too . . . vague. But if I know the FBI has been tipped that a guy working for Runalli is Mr. Composite, then I might be able to—" Samuelson cut himself off as an idea occurred to him. "You know, one of the other staffers has to know this, and probably a whole bunch of them."

"Not likely," Mueller contradicted. "I saw him once, when he picked up two hundred grand I was asked to transfer to Will Runalli. Runalli didn't bring the guy to meetings."

"You funneled two hundred grand in cash to Runalli?"

"On Senator Parker's orders, yes."

Samuelson could barely believe what he was hearing. "That's how the Watergate guys got caught," he reminded Mueller. "You could be criminally liable for—"

"Which is why you can't use the stuff about the cash."

"Oh, come on," Samuelson objected. "That's one of the juiciest things you've given me. It ties Parker directly into the whole thing."

"You use it, and you're cut off. No tapes, no *nothing*," Mueller stated tersely. "I'm not going to put myself in jail. This meeting is over." He turned to walk away.

"Wait a minute," Samuelson pleaded as he saw the tapes sauntering away with Mueller. "Okay. But . . . I'm going to keep asking you when I can use this," he gently told Mueller.

"As long as you accept the probability that I'll keep saying never."

"I'll accept that."

"Good."

"Well, I have a lot of listening to do . . ."

"Mr. Samuelson, can the FBI match a phone number to a person or a place?"

"In a hummingbird heartbeat," he told Mueller definitively. "Why?"

"Runalli got a phone call, a message that upset him so much that he left in the middle of a staff meeting and flew out of town. When I . . . when I snuck in to borrow these tapes, I saw the number. It's somewhere in Michigan."

"You want me to slip this information to a contact I have in the FBI?"

"Will he push for the source?"

Samuelson shook his head. "Not if he ever wants to do business with me again. He won't need to know if this gets him the guy. They've got other witnesses to make this case once they have a flesh-and-blood guy instead of Mr. Composite."

Mueller handed him the number, then passed him the satchel full of tapes.

Samuelson smiled. "I'll see you tomorrow afternoon."

"Right."

"How about I leave first this time," Samuelson suggested. "I've got to make every minute count."

Mueller smiled and nodded.

☼   ☼   ☼

New Year's Day, The Year After Election Year
Detroit Michigan

"THAT'S HIM?" COVINGTON KLONDIKE ASKED FBI INSPECTOR DAVIS Tucker as they arrived at a two-way pane of glass looking into an interrogation room in the FBI headquarters located in Detroit, Michigan. Grady Dunn was dressed in a thick cotton shirt and blue jeans. He sat quietly, and though he tried to project calm toughness, he fidgeted when left alone. He was alone in the room now, puffing anxiously on a cigarette.

"Just in from Sawyer's."

"Sawyer's?"

"The K.I. Sawyer Air Force Base up on the peninsula," Tucker explained. "We found the guy up at Indian Lake. These stupid guys. They think going to some out-of-the-way place is the best way to hide. Let me tell you, in small towns, they notice the strangers *quicker*. We got a tip that the guy was up in the area. So we canvassed the area, and in 24 hours, we had five people confirm he was up there, just off the composite. All we had to do then was check every place that wasn't occupied by a long-time resident. That wasn't too difficult. There aren't too many people up there. And in winter, there aren't many visitors. He answered our knock, looked us in the eye, and said he wanted his lawyer."

"Anything from him?"

"Just a little. He said it was off the record when I told him we had witnesses in both Berkeley and Pismo Beach who could I-D him. He's hinting at a deal. He admitted he took the calls at the Berkeley phone booth, and called the Lompoc Federal Prison, though he says he doesn't know why he was asked to do that. That explains the call from Berkeley to Lompoc, but still doesn't explain the call from the Park Avenue Bar and Grill. And he said he won't talk about Pismo Beach without a deal."

"But *what* can he deal?"

"I don't think he can deal Parker. But a guy in the Parker campaign— he won't name him, but we think it's Will Runalli—he can deal that guy, and I think if we push him, he will. Oh, and it looks like he'll exonerate Edwards' people. He says he was asked by his superiors with Parker to do some volunteer work for Edwards."

"What's next with him?"

"The State of Michigan wants to check his record before letting us take him out to California. We should have something any time now."

"Will you guys arrest him?"

"Yeah. Justice is drafting the complaint right now. But we'll make it official in California, later today."

A thin young agent walked up to Tucker and handed him a sheet of paper.

"Thank you," Tucker acknowledged.

The young agent nodded and walked away.

"Interesting," Tucker said. "He's going to California. No wants here. But that old misdemeanor is still sitting there."

"Misdemeanor?"

"Yeah. He beat up a guy back in the early 80's. Sent the guy to the hospital. He got six months in County for his trouble." Tucker put his thumb up to his mouth as he thought for a moment. "We've got an agent putting together some background on him."

"I'd like to be able to tell the President all I can."

"I know." Tucker spotted an agent in the hall. "Stewart?"

"Yes sir," another young agent replied.

"Where's Drake?"

"In conference room seven."

"Thanks." He turned to Klondike. "It's just down the hall." He smiled. "No funny mirrors there. You need anything else from this guy?" Tucker asked, motioning toward the pane of glass and Grady Dunn, still sitting alone in the interrogation room.

"No."

Tucker led Klondike down a plain white hall to the conference room. They opened the door and entered.

"What have you got?" Tucker asked her. "This is the President's special assistant, Mr.—"

"Klondike," Monica Drake acknowledged with a courteous smile. She was an attractive, though not head-turning gorgeous, young African-American woman in perfect physical condition with a sultry deep voice. "I've only had time to pull up the court file," she told them. "But I can actually tell a lot from that, and even start to map out a strategy."

"Okay," Tucker replied.

"This is a big strong guy with a bad temper. His father was a college professor. From the sentencing report prepared by the Probation Department, his father was rich in prestige, but not in money. Young Grady grew up in tough blue collar neighborhoods with the sons and daughters of UAW line-workers. He ended up doing six months in County."

"Any records from County?"

"Yeah. Lots of fights. And from what I can see, he didn't lose many of them, if any at all. I'll tell you what I think. The guy figured if he was tough enough to pound his fellow inmates at County, he should put his talents to work. This was the 80's, right? The age of turn-a-buck, who-cares-how—he worked himself up to a high-priced, sophisticated professional strong arm. And he really did his job decently on this one. He didn't realize an army of our agents would drop everything to take a crack at it."

"So what is your proposed strategy?"

"Custody with the little brats in the State Pen," she told him. "County jail's a picnic. This guy needs to know what he's in for if he's going to do real time. With that hanging over him, he might deal."

"Does he look like he can make bail?"

"Not on his own. And his outside sources will have to hide their interest. That'll take time. We should have him at least a day, maybe two or three."

"Okay. Thanks, Drake. Nice job. Keep filling this guy's background in." He turned to Klondike. "We'll have to be careful. We don't want to deprive him of his Constitutional rights. But I think we can bring a strong dose of reality to Mr. Dunn while he is our guest. If Drake is right, it should be enough to get him to give up Runalli."

"You guys have it well under control," Klondike told him contentedly. "I'll tell the President."

☼   ☼   ☼

IT TOOK GRADY DUNN A LITTLE OVER 24 HOURS TO DECIDE PRISON LIFE would not be a happy prospect at all. They couldn't transfer him to a California State Penitentiary. But they did place him in custody with some inmates of that caliber. Grady Dunn made a deal to give up Will Runalli for a guarantee of three years in the county jail on a reduced charge. The people in charge of the case reluctantly agreed, believing this was the only way to identify those responsible for masterminding the crime, and then bringing them to justice. FBI agents quickly followed Dunn's statement with visits to officials with Victor Parker's campaign organization.

☼   ☼   ☼

January 3, The Year After Election Year
Washington, D.C.

"MR. RUNALLI, IT APPEARS YOUR ABILITY TO CARRY OUT YOUR DUTIES has been severely compromised," Senator Parker told Will Runalli in a slow, stately tone of voice. Runalli had just walked into the room and exchanged hello's. But Runalli was immediately uncomfortable as he saw that Nicholas Mueller was standing at Parker's side, behind his desk. Runalli also noticed that the usual chair across from the Senator's desk was not there, and Mueller also had no chair to sit in. Senator Parker intended this to be a short meeting. No one was going to be in there long enough to sit down. "And, we feel you may want time to prepare yourself to respond to this investigation," Parker continued. "So—"

"Hold it," Runalli interrupted abruptly. "You guys are panicking. We can still step away from this thing." He looked at Mueller. "Senator, why is Mr. Mueller here? He has never attended any of our private meetings."

"He's here as a witness," Parker explained frankly.

"I see." Runalli flashed a hostile squint at Mueller. "Senator," he said, turning his focus back to Parker, "it is *vital* that we close ranks. This is no time to—"

"I did not call you here to listen to any more of your advice," Parker told Runalli bluntly. "In my judgement, you can no longer be effective as my . . . as a campaign advisor. I'm asking for your resignation."

"And if I don't offer it?"

"I will dismiss you."

"Not a hot idea, Senator. You don't really wanna do this . . ."

"Mr. Runalli, we need you to do the honorable thing. The time has come for you to fall on this grenade—for the Party, for my campaign that you have consented to serve."

"I refuse to do that when we can still wiggle out of this."

"The only reasonable way out is for you to take responsibility for your actions. In our judgement, to 'wiggle out of this,' we need to remove the cause of this situation—*you.*"

"You could go down with me, Senator."

"Is this your 'guarantee,' Mr. Runalli?"

Mueller flashed a gratified grin at that question.

"These people are talking about murder," Runalli stated plainly. "In California, that carries the death penalty."

"You shouldn't have done it."

"You weren't saying that before. You were saying that I should do whatever I have to do. I told you we were in a street fight, and—"

"You *bastard*," Parker blurted out, dropping all formality. "You implied you kept me uninformed for my protection, so I could deny specific knowledge at a later time. Well this is it. This is where you protect me. You tell everyone I knew *nothing,* nothing about threats, or thugs . . . or *murders.* You were an overzealous staffer, too eager to please. I knew *nothing—*"

"You knew about *cash,* Senator."

Parker was temporarily speechless.

Mueller stiffened.

"Yeah. Now that I have your attention." A slight, snide grin appeared, then disappeared from Runalli's face. "But don't worry. *I'm* not interested in discussing this with anybody . . . not as a loyal member of Victor Parker's campaign staff."

"Fall on the grenade, Runalli. That is your assignment now. Take one for the cause you've pledged to serve."

"No way," Runalli replied defiantly. "If I'm fired, I'm fired. But I'm not gonna be the fall guy. I'll plead the Fifth. I'll hedge and dodge. And I know you gentlemen won't interfere with my efforts, because you would hate to see me start discussing any details about cash. If it starts to look real bad, I'll see you for car-nee-val, in *Rio*. Good luck, Senator. It's every man for himself, now." Runalli walked out.

"I knew he wouldn't do it," Mueller commented quietly to Parker.

"And now we're stuck doing it his way, whether we want to or not—and without him. We'll have to deny everything, and hope nothing can be proven."

"It'll be tough."

"It's the only way." Senator Parker sat down.

Mueller pulled a chair up to his desk.

"Edwards announced he'll ask for a complete investigation of any electors who did not keep their pledges to determine if anything improper was done to induce them to shift," Parker continued. "I think we should join their request."

"They may not be anxious to work with us, given that we tried to frame them for Whittlebaum's murder."

"Deny our involvement. Deny we sanctioned Mr. Runalli's efforts, if they press. And stress our common goal."

"Okay."

"On the subject of money . . ."

"Yes?"

"Do you recall any large cash disbursements to Mr. Runalli?"

Mueller looked carefully at Senator Parker and read his face. "Not at this time."

Senator Parker smiled. "Me neither. Not at this time." Senator Parker became quiet and reflective. "We need to win this, not just for our stated platform, but because we need to take hold of the power of the Presidency. If Hampton retains it, he will pick at this nasty sore until all the ugly pus comes gushing out."

Mueller nodded. The Senator was right. But Mueller knew that one more card would fall before the stage was set for January 6th.

Chapter 30

January 4th, The Year After Election Year
Washington, D.C.

"There's only one thing to do," Hampton announced with caustic venom. "Give Runalli immunity. Get him to deal Parker. I don't care what you have to do. We've got two days to soil Parker with this mess." He and Covington Klondike stood in the White House media center, in a small room on the third floor of the White House. Hampton and Klondike were standing and viewing one of a bank of video monitors. Hampton held the video remote. The television screen was frozen on the image of Don Samuelson.

"We can't do that Mr. President—"

"Of course we can. This is well within Justice's discretion."

"Mr. President, I don't mean *legally*. I mean *politically*. The public will be screaming that we have over-politicized our approach to both the legal system and the election system. There has already been criticism that we gave too much to Dunn to get Runalli. We can't make a deal with Runalli just to—"

"We have to make Senator Parker look a lot worse than we do. Right now, we *both* look bad. I need a distraction. I want it to be *him*."

"You'd make the situation worse," Klondike explained. "We know that Runalli can't deal Parker for the murder itself. Everything in the FBI investigation indicates that Parker didn't know about it. He *chose* to be ignorant, but he didn't know. Runalli, on the other hand, is knee-deep in the murder. How do we justify letting a second murder suspect off the hook with immunity, just to get some embarrassing lesser charges to hang on Senator Parker? We don't even know if Runalli can deal anything on Parker that would be considered criminal."

The President sneered and hit the play button on the videocassette remote control. He knew Klondike was right, but didn't want to acknowledge it right away.

Samuelson picked up from where his broadcast had been frozen: "—tapes reviewed by this reporter are absolutely definitive. Covington Klondike of the Hampton organization, with a clear implication of approval from the President himself, bribed elector Bennington Whittlebaum to shift his vote from Edwards to the President. They paid Mr. Whittlebaum three hundred thousand dollars under the pretense of 'future legal fees,' and promised him a Washington job with Senator Frederick Stephan from Utah. The actual recording of Klondike's discussion with Whittlebaum was among the tapes I listened to.

"And there is also a clear decision taken *not* to warn Michael Edwards that his life might be threatened by an assassin working for drug-lords from South America. Clearly, that fact would help bolster Edwards' claim that *his* drug policy would be the most effective way to win the so-called war on drugs. And perhaps more sinister than that, there is a clear discussion that if Edwards was killed, the election would almost certainly end up going to President Hampton."

President Hampton hit the pause button again, freezing Samuelson's image just as his name was said. "Do you think that jerk has copies of the actual tapes?"

Klondike thought a moment. "No. Or if he does, he's not in a position to use them. But I'd say he doesn't have them. If he did, they'd be playing those things, with the words spelled out—you know how they do it."

"Yeah," President Hampton acknowledged as he thought. "And you'd have to figure those tapes have been destroyed by now."

"No way Runalli would keep those things lying around after this."

"So we have some flexibility to spin this our way."

"It's a bit of a gamble, but it's unlikely someone will trot those things out to contradict us."

"Unless it's a trap," Hampton said, still reflecting on the situation.

"By Samuelson?"

"No. By whoever's feeding him. Maybe they want us to try to spin this the wrong way, then blind-side us with the tapes."

"I suppose that's possible," Klondike contemplated. "But I doubt it. Someone from Parker's group let Samuelson in the back door. And Parker has already issued a statement denying everything. They're denying bugs, links to Whittlebaum's killing." Klondike smiled. "They're defying someone to prove this stuff. They wouldn't do that with the proof still lying around somewhere."

"So we can still spin this thing our way."

"Yes. I don't see the risk as all that great."

"Okay. Release a statement. Samuelson's story takes everything out of context. We held up the information on the supposed assassination threat because the information was very shaky. And we were in contact with Whittlebaum at *his* request. It was *his* idea to change his vote. We met and liked the guy, and decided he'd be good to recommend to somebody's staff. That was after he made up his *own* mind to change his vote."

"Do we have to admit to any of this?"

"A lot of this is verifiable through other sources. If we get caught denying things that are obviously true, this thing'll drag on. Let Parker make that mistake. When we start our second term, we're gonna dog that guy and all his people until we have all of this out. Unless . . ." President Hampton's mind considered another concern. "Unless they have those tapes."

Klondike smiled.

"But for now, all we want to do is look palatable to the American people, so there won't be an uproar when the results become official, the day after tomorrow."

"Right."

President Hampton hit the stop button on the remote, and then the rewind button. "I've seen enough of this thing," he commented with weary disgust. "Have it stored somewhere."

He tossed Klondike the remote and left the room.

☼   ☼   ☼

January 6, The Year After Election Year
Washington, D.C.

"MR. EDWARDS, WILL YOU LODGE A PROTEST AGAINST TODAY'S results?" asked one of a group of swarming reporters from all media as Michael Edwards and Drew Saroyan worked their way along a path which led to the eastern staircase up to the principal floor of the Capitol Building. The path cut through a tree-lined lawn, with the lightly-colored building rising above the lawn in the background. They headed toward the Columbus Portal, a set of bronze doors adorned with carved images depicting events of the explorer's voyages to the Americas. The doors opened into the Great Rotunda, with a round ceiling almost 200 feet in height. The votes would be counted in the Senate chamber—Saroyan and Edwards would enter by the North Door. They would be given seats in the south gallery, facing the Chair, reserved for the most prestigious visitors to the Senate.

The state governments technically forwarded the results of the state elector votes to the President of the Senate, to be opened in front of the House of Representatives. In effect, this meant the entire Congress would be present. And it would be the new Congress, the one that had just been elected.

Vice President Burt Dooley would preside over the process. He had pushed for the counting to be held in the Senate Chamber, even though joint sessions were often held in the House Chamber. Edwards was arriving about 30 minutes before the session was to begin.

"Let's wait until the results are in before we discuss a protest," he replied as he and Saroyan kept moving.

"Do you have any comment on the alleged murder of your elector Bennington Whittlebaum by people from Senator Parker's organization?" another reporter asked.

"No. We will withhold comment on this until all of the facts have been established. It is in the hands of the proper authorities. It is not my place to comment until all the facts have been confirmed."

They started up the two-tiered set of white steps leading to the entrance.

"Can you find *any* cause for optimism, given that it appears well-established that President Hampton will win this election today?"

Edwards stopped on the fifth step up. He stood higher than most of the reporters, with just a few to his rear.

Saroyan smiled. Here was a potentially open-ended question that Edwards could steer in whatever direction he wished. He knew his candidate couldn't resist.

"Do I have cause for optimism? You bet. Every major poll taken in the last 24 to 48 hours shows that the American people, by anywhere from seven to ten per cent, would choose *me* to be President. *I'm* the one who took the high road over the last two months. I'm proud of that."

"But those same polls show that most voters are reconciled to President Hampton as the winner of the election. Voters see Senator Parker as the worst transgressor," another reporter countered.

"Resigned but not getting their first choice," Edwards replied.

"If the President is confirmed as the winner, will you protest?" yet another reporter asked.

"Didn't I answer that question already? Ask me a new one or I'll have to start back up these steps."

"You're just going to sit in the gallery?" a reporter asked from behind him.

He turned. "That's as close as they'll let me get. I've worked too hard to remain aloof in some hotel room and watch the whole thing on C-Span."

"I think it'll be covered by some other stations," a reporter from behind the small crowd wisecracked.

"Think so?" Edwards smirked.

"What is your comment on information that drug-lords were trying to kill you?" the same reporter asked.

"It shows *they* know what the doomsday weapon of the drug war is, even if my opponents in this election don't. Look, you guys are starting to reach. I think you're out of questions." He turned and started moving again, taking a step.

"What are your feelings as you head in?" called out a reporter trying to keep the questions and answers flowing.

Edwards stopped and turned again. "That's a nice one to finish on," he complimented. "I've worked very hard on this—I've had a lot of ups and downs. But I'm here. I'm proud of that. I'm still here fighting, because my cause is worth fighting for. And I want to leave you with one final thought. Anything can happen in there. Don't think you guys have written the bottom line on this yet. I'll talk to you all again later." Edwards turned and picked up his pace with a brisk walk. It took Saroyan a few steps to match the new pace. Though reporters continued to call out questions, Edwards ignored them.

✢   ✢   ✢

"PURSUANT TO ARTICLE TWO, SECTION ONE, AND AMENDMENT TWELVE of the Constitution of the United States of America, this will be the time appointed to unseal the results as submitted by the state legislatures. We have confirmed 51 results, the states plus the District of Columbia, and we will proceed alphabetically. I will open the envelopes, read the summarized result, then pass it to designated representatives from the House of Representatives for verification."

Edwards and Saroyan sat nervously transfixed in the gallery, a balcony looking down on the large, high-ceilinged room, facing Burt Dooley. Dooley stood at a marble dais, with a carved chair behind him. Whatever surprise Donald Samuelson had been keeping to himself remained unknown. Edwards didn't have a hint of what it could be. But whatever it was, it had better come clear in the next half hour.

"Alabama," Vice President Dooley called out perfunctorily as he opened the envelope. "Nine votes for Kenneth Hampton.

"Alaska." He opened that envelope. "Three votes for Kenneth Hampton.

"Arizona . . . eight votes for Kenneth Hampton."

It was the Edwards states that were of concern to Michael Edwards and Drew Saroyan. And California, the one that made them both the most nervous, with 54 electoral votes as a large target for wooing defectors, would be the first of those states to have its result announced.

"Arkansas . . . six votes for Victor Parker.

"California." The Vice President opened the envelope.

Michael Edwards held his breath.

"Fifty-four votes for Michael Edwards."

Edwards smiled and exhaled.

Saroyan tapped Edwards on the back, also relieved.

"Colorado . . ."

"So it was only Whittlebaum in California," Edwards commented.

"Maybe *anywhere,*" Saroyan added.

The Vice President took a moment or two longer than usual with the Colorado result, then read the result with little emotion. "Seven votes for Michael Edwards, one vote for Ken, uh, Kenneth Hampton."

A murmur rippled through the gathering. It began to swell as Vice President Dooley reached for the next envelope.

Michael Edwards slumped into his chair.

Saroyan whispered "Damn!"

"Order, please," Vice President Dooley requested calmly. "We need to get through the rest of these."

Edwards and Saroyan would be similarly disappointed two more times—one of Michigan's 18 electors, and one of Oregon's 7 electors also cast votes for President Hampton instead of Michael Edwards.

"We'll file that protest," Edwards told Saroyan with grim determination as the state results neared the end of the alphabet.

"No meeting to check with our supporters?"

"No," Edwards answered firmly. "I think I know what they'll want. And I am here to *lead* my supporters, not follow them."

Saroyan flashed a gratified grin.

"Texas . . . thirty-two votes for Kenneth Hampton," the Vice President continued. "Utah . . . five votes for Kenneth Hampton.

"Vermont . . ."

"Utah," Edwards groused. "That Senator Stephan should be one of the *first* on the hot seat when they investigate this thing."

Vice President Dooley lingered on Vermont. He had established an almost rhythmic patter, and his departure from it caught almost everyone's attention—attention that had drifted since the elector defections had been announced. Dooley handed the result over to the House's representatives first, but retained a sheet of paper. Then he said, with a brittle voice, "Vermont's electors have abstained."

Edwards' eyes widened.

"Un-fucking-believable!" Saroyan blurted out in ecstasy.

"We just got three back," Edwards observed, also with uncontained delight.

"More accurately, Hampton just *lost* three. This thing is *not* over!"

The Vice President did not pick up another envelope. "The Vermont delegation enclosed a statement they wish to make public. Though it may be out of order, and a little lengthy, I'm going to make it public now. In light of their action, I think it should be heard."

He held the piece of paper where he could read it easily. "It's addressed to the President of the Senate, members of Congress and President Kenneth Hampton, Senator Victor Parker and Mister Michael Edwards:

"We were pledged to vote for Republican candidate Kenneth Hampton. With this action, we are not violating that pledge, but withholding it. Because despite our belief that President Hampton is the best candidate, we believe even more in following the rule of law. We have been disturbed by persistent rumors that electors have been induced to violate pledges and distort the result of the election. Whether we like the Electoral College system or not, it is the law of the land. If it is inadequate, then we should change it. The Constitution provides clearly for that process. But we must not allow nameless, faceless individuals, answerable to no one, to circumvent the system at whim, and with questionable motivations. The result of this election should be a resolution in the House of Representatives. Withholding our pledge will not change this result. But if three or fewer electors choose to put themselves above the system, our action will prevent their success.

"Vermont was the first state to join this great union after the original thirteen colonies ratified the Constitution. We were an independent republic from 1777 until we became the 14th state on March 4th, 1791. We were then, and are now, a small state. The rule of law guarantees that we will never have our unique way of life taken away by some tyrannical majority. Vermont is still a land of small communities, cabins in the forest, and quiet, uncomplicated lives. We will assure our existence and identity by zealously maintaining our principles over the needs of the moment. Our apologies to President Hampton. But one Republican president is not as important as these principles.

With solemn sincerity,

The Vermont electors"

The Vice President passed the note to the House's representatives. Without any further comment or delay he continued processing the results. "Virginia . . . thirteen votes for Kenneth Hampton."

"I'll be damned," Saroyan commented with a look of genuine surprise on his face.

"And we know one thing," Edwards added. "One of those Vermont electors is a close friend of Don Samuelson."

"Yeah."

"There's still one of our states left, though. If Hampton got to one of my electors in Washington . . ."

"Washington," the Vice President called out.

Edwards and Saroyan held their breaths one more time.

"Eleven votes for Michael Edwards," he announced. "West Virginia . . ."

"This thing is going to the House," Edwards said quietly. "We need to get all of our people working on this."

"Right."

As the results from West Virginia, Wisconsin and Wyoming were dutifully reported, a murmur started through the crowd, quickly rising into pandemonium as reporters and Congressional aides rushed around and out of the building. Vice President Dooley had to call for order more than once before completing his task at the podium.

"The final results," Vice President Dooley announced wearily, masking his disappointment by showing apathy, "are as follows: Kenneth Hampton, 269 electoral votes; Victor Parker, 145 electoral votes; Michael Edwards, 121 electoral votes; and three abstentions." He paused a moment as he looked at his notes.

"Try not to look *too* disappointed," Edwards commented wryly, mostly to himself, but as if addressing Dooley.

Saroyan was talking quietly into a cellular phone.

"Pursuant to Article Two, Section One, and the Twelfth Amendment, and by prior agreement, we will adjourn this meeting. Since no candidate for President or Vice President received the 270 electoral votes necessary to constitute a simple majority, two special legislative sessions are now scheduled. At 11:00 the Senate will meet to vote for Vice President. And at 2:00, the House of Representatives will convene to vote state by state for President. This meeting is adjourned." He banged his gavel and walked away from the podium.

"I've reached Everett and Wally," Saroyan told Edwards. "They're on their way down. We'll meet them at the G Street Cafe—I'm arranging for a private room over there."

"Good."

As the hall emptied out, Congressman Phillip Lake of California sat quietly in his seat. Most others had left, many hurriedly, to deal with the results: scheduling caucuses, making phone calls, checking poll results in their constituencies. But Phil Lake did not need to make a mad dash out of the hall. He was 65 years old, distinguished looking, tall with thinning hair and only slightly pudgier than three decades earlier when he had started in Congress. And he knew what he was going to do. He had made his decision fully believing that he would not have to implement it. But what would forever be known as the "Vermont Turnabout" forced him to take what in his mind was the only course he could take, and keep his self-respect.

Congressman Lake stood, now in a virtually empty hall, and started to leave. But he looked up and saw Edwards and Saroyan in the gallery.

Chapter 31

January 6, The Year After Election Year
Washington, D.C.

"CONGRESSMAN LAKE." MICHAEL EDWARDS STOOD UP TO MEET HIM. Saroyan also stood. They both extended their hands and the Congressman shook Edwards' hand first, then Saroyan's. The chamber was nearly empty—the three men had the gallery to themselves.

"Pretty interesting result," Lake observed to Edwards.

"Never a dull moment," Edwards commented.

"I'd like to have a few words with you."

Edwards' eyebrows raised and he shrugged casually. "Sure. Let's sit down."

Saroyan moved to the next row up by stepping over his chair, and sat behind Edwards. Lake sat next to Edwards.

"Mr. Edwards, I want you to know that in our caucus today, I'll be voting for you. I can't promise many of my colleagues will. They'll be afraid of offending the Democratic Party establishment. But I'm not. The Democratic Party establishment has offended *me.*"

Edwards looked at him seriously. "You've been a Democratic Congressman ever since I can remember."

"Since I was elected in 1972, the year of Watergate," he added disgustedly. "We Democrats are supposed to be incapable of that kind of behavior."

"Not some Democrats."

"Yeah. Listen, uh, do you need someone in your corner out there on the floor?"

Saroyan squirmed in his seat uncomfortably.

Edwards played his reaction down. "Are you . . . applying for the job?"

"Yes. I think I could be of some help."

Saroyan interrupted. "Uh, Michael—could I have a private word with you?"

Edwards looked at Congressman Lake.

Lake shrugged.

"Just a quick moment," Edwards said to the Congressman politely.

Saroyan and Edwards moved a few rows up and spoke quietly. Saroyan asked, "Do you think we should trust this guy?"

"You think he's—"

"I know Parker has pulled a lot of crap on us, and this could be a way for him to sabotage our efforts one last time. This guy Lake has been a Democratic stalwart for over thirty years, if you count his pre-Congressional days in the California State Senate."

"But if he's on the level, he could make the difference for us."

"Michael, I don't know how to advise you on this. You'll have to make up your own mind on his sincerity. I just wanted you thinking about the possibility of double-dealing. Let's talk to him some more. Then you have to call it."

"Okay."

They rejoined Lake, who seemed almost hurt by the brief private discussion.

"You could be a lot of help to us, Congressman," Edwards remarked, following up on the earlier comment made by Congressman Lake.

"Call me Phil. I have to tell you that I can only be of help on this thing if it gets past the first ballot. Then Senator Parker's support will start to erode. I'll be down there, making sure it stays eroded, and flows to you."

"We agree," Saroyan stated with detachment. "An inconclusive ballot is the first essential step. And unfortunately, it looks like Parker's got a Democratic majority in at least 26 states. How do we get around that?"

"Exactly 26—I've done a careful count. And there are apparent deadlocks in eight states; they'll have to pass their votes. Those deadlocks have to hold. They'll save the first ballot for us. Because I don't think all 26 states'll toe the Party line for Mr. Senator Victor Parker. I can't promise my state for you, but there are a few key ones to watch. If they don't back Parker, we can squeak through that first ballot without a result. Then the fun starts."

A smile crept onto Saroyan's face, even though he didn't want one to.

"Which states?" Edwards asked.

"Watch Delaware. This is a one-Congressman state. He might just feel the way I do. I'll try to talk to him before two o'clock. Indiana has a six to four split favoring the Democrats. But one of them could decide he or she can't stomach Parker. This is a state with a lot of Republican voters, and casting a conscience vote on this might be a good way for a young Congressman to carve out an identity for a future Senator's or Governor's race."

"Any others?"

"Oregon," he advised. "It needs to *stay* deadlocked. They have five Congressmen there, and right now, the vote looks like two for Parker, two for you, and one for Hampton. If one of yours changes his mind . . ."

Saroyan's cellular phone rang. He quietly took the call as Edwards and Lake continued speaking.

"Oh, and I think one of the Rhode Island Congressmen is going to vote for you," Lake continued. "He said he would when I saw him at a luncheon last Friday. If he does, that'll deadlock Rhode Island and pull it out of Parker's column."

"We took Rhode Island in the election," Edwards recalled.

"That's right." Lake smiled. "Seems like that was a *long* time ago."

Edwards turned to Saroyan.

"We've got a call from the two Senators who ran on our platform. They want to know who we might recommend for Vice President, since Everett is ineligible."

"Tell them to cast a symbolic vote for him anyway," Edwards stated audaciously. "It's the least we can do for Everett after all the—"

"Excuse me," Congressman Lake interrupted, "but I would like to make a recommendation to you on this."

"Jefferson?" Saroyan asked knowingly, then casting a cynical glance over at Edwards.

"No," Lake told him emphatically. "My information is that this will be a very close vote in the Senate. It would be better for you if *Dooley* was chosen Vice President."

Saroyan smiled as he thought over the statement. "He's right." He nodded slowly. "You *are* right—this could be the key to the whole thing."

"What?" Edwards asked.

"I'll tell you in a minute," Saroyan replied. "Let me advise our Senators." Saroyan again spoke quietly into his cellular phone.

"Join us for lunch and explain it to me," Edwards requested politely. "We're having an inner circle meeting over at the G Street—"

"With all respects, no thanks," Lake declined courteously. "I have a lot to do if I'm going to give you my best shot at getting this to a second ballot. Look me up after it's over, if we're still in it."

Edwards stood up. "Thanks."

Saroyan was now off the phone. He also stood up.

"My pleasure," Lake said as he stood and started to walk away.

"Phil," Edwards called to him slyly. "You haven't asked us for anything in return."

"I haven't, have I," Lake responded through a smile, intended to say more than his words did.

And Edwards read him correctly. Lake hadn't asked for anything. He had deliberately avoided even the hint of a reward. He wanted to demonstrate his sincerity, and he had now won both Edwards and Saroyan over. "Talk to you this afternoon," Edwards said to him.

Lake nodded as he resumed walking away.

☼   ☼   ☼

"HERE WE GO," EDWARDS COMMENTED TO SAROYAN WITH A FATALISTIC grin on his face as they took seats in the gallery of the House Chamber. There were no reserved seats here, and no special gallery designations. Medallions of all fifty states decorated the walls. Otherwise, it looked similar to the Senate Chamber, including the Speaker of the House's dais and chair. "It's all in the hands of those people down there on the floor."

"And really up to just a few of them."

"I feel better about our chances with Congressman Lake down there."

"Maybe . . . I'm not sure what he can do." In the next few minutes, they would both find out exactly what Congressman Lake could do.

This would be a game of "chicken" for Democratic Congressmen. They risked their constituents' wrath if they voted for their party's currently unpopular candidate. And they risked their futures in the Democratic Party if they voted for Edwards and Parker ended up in the White House. So the smart move was to vote Parker on the first ballot and see which way the wind was blowing. Edwards and Saroyan expected most of them to play it safe—a career in Congress was not something to risk easily. But they hoped that just a few would deviate from years of traditional party politics to express the public will they had theoretically been chosen to express.

Unfortunately for Edwards, as the first ballot progressed, it was clear to everyone that almost all the Democratic Congressional representatives were making the safe, smart, first-ballot choices. As the trend became more obvious, the chances for a deviation from party loyalty were shrinking.

"Oregon," the Speaker of the House called out. Speaking with a decisive voice, he was conscious of the historic implications of the moment.

"Oregon cannot make a choice at this time, Mr. Speaker. We do not have a plurality for a preference," an anonymous voice from the floor stated.

"Mark it as an abstention," the Speaker requested.

"At least Oregon stayed deadlocked," Edwards observed, trying to keep alive a sliver of optimism.

Saroyan shook his head. "If everything goes according to script, Parker comes out of this with 26 states, and the first ballot is the only ballot."

Edwards drew a deep, nervous breath.

"Pennsylvania," the Speaker queried.

"Pennsylvania votes for Victor Parker," was the response.

"Rhode Island."

There was no immediate response.

"Rhode Island," the Speaker called out again, this time more impatiently.

The delay had Edwards and Saroyan searching the floor for Rhode Island's location. It was Saroyan who spotted it first. "Phil's down there," he told Edwards.

Edwards now spotted Congressman Phil Lake having what appeared to be an animated discussion with two men right next to the microphone. Edwards still believed that Congressman Lake was sincere. But if he wasn't, they would probably find out right now. And there was no way for Edwards or Saroyan to listen to or interfere with that discussion.

"Rhode Island, will you please make yourselves heard," the Speaker requested with a calm tone, but underlying impatience.

The pop of a microphone coming on sounded, simultaneously with Phil Lake's animated voice stating over the loudspeaker system "don't let him bully you, kid." The microphone quickly popped, and was off again.

If the microphone had stayed on, the rest of the people in the hall would have heard Lake remind the young Rhode Island Congressman that Edwards had taken his state, and that if he neglected his conscience for his career on such an important vote, maybe his career wasn't worth preserving.

"Rhode Island, we—" The Speaker's latest prodding was interrupted by the microphone popping on again.

"Mr. Speaker, Rhode Island will have to abstain. We are deadlocked on a choice," an older male voice finally announced disgustedly.

Edwards glanced briefly around, then over at Saroyan. "That was it, wasn't it?"

"Could have been," Saroyan replied cautiously, not wanting to claim the desired result until it was official. "If there are no more surprises. . ."

There were no more surprises during the first ballot. The Speaker, a staunch Democratic Party stalwart, quickly read what were for him very disappointing results: 25 states for Parker, 15 for Hampton, and 1 (Minnesota) for Edwards, with nine abstentions due to delegation deadlocks. "Since the first ballot has failed to give the Constitutionally mandated majority of 26 states to any candidate, we will need to reconvene for a second ballot. The Chair fixes the time for the next meeting at 5:00 this afternoon. The Speaker urges delegations to break any deadlocks and make their choice. We are adjourned for now." He banged his gavel and left the podium.

Saroyan and Edwards waited in the gallery. They saw Phil Lake hurrying across the floor on a route that would take him up to them.

"By the skin of our teeth," Lake commented with a relieved grin on his face as he approached Edwards and Saroyan.

"Rhode Island," Edwards commented knowingly.

"And the son-of-a-bitch almost chickened out when his buddy told him he'd be through as a Democrat," Lake told them.

"Thank you, Congressman," Edwards acknowledged sincerely.

"Like I said, it's *Phil*. And now we might be able to crack into this party-line bullshit and get some more states."

"How does it feel down there?" Saroyan asked him.

"You're gonna get more support," Lake told both of them. "I doubt we can actually take it on the second vote, but I think I can deliver my state."

"Good," Edwards responded.

"Still only counts as one," Saroyan reminded them.

"That's true. But we have another great card to play now," Lake replied with a strong hint of pride sneaking into his voice.

Saroyan smiled. "Vice President."

"Exactly," Lake agreed. "Now that the Senate has chosen Burt Dooley as our next Vice President, by one vote, we have a real good *partisan* argument. If the House stalemates and cannot choose a President, then the Vice President becomes President. With Parker not really publicly viable, and not able to grab the Presidency on the first ballot, we can argue to these Democratic Congressmen that they are choosing between Michael Edwards and Burt Dooley. If they continue to vote for Parker, and the thing stalemates, they get Dooley. And after almost 40 years of some real bruising partisan in-fighting with that guy, no one's gonna want him. So I'll see you gentlemen a few minutes before five. Because I've got to go sell this argument to as many Democrats as I can, before they go to their caucuses."

"We'll see you then," Edwards agreed.

Lake hurried off.

"What should *we* be doing?" Edwards asked.

"If we didn't have Phil Lake, we'd be trying to contact those staffers we met with in December. But. . . let Lake push our cause. I think he's proved we can trust him."

"Of course we can trust him."

"So we let him carry the torch. He knows these people. And it's always better to have someone else pushing you. We'll wait and see how this will translate into results on the second ballot."

☼　　　☼　　　☼

"COME TO ORDER," THE SPEAKER OF THE HOUSE SHOUTED. THE DIN OF animated chatter was as loud as it had been at any time since the House had gone into session to finalize the results of the election. "Please come to order," the Speaker requested insistently as he pounded his gavel more forcefully.

The din finally began to spiral down.

"This is the time fixed for the second ballot for President. We will call out each state in alphabetical order and await a report of the preference of the state by a designated spokesperson. Alabama."

"Alabama chooses Victor Parker."

"Alaska."

"Mr. Speaker, Alaska votes for President Hampton."

"Arizona."

"President Hampton."

"Arkansas."

"We also choose President Hampton."

"California."

"California continues its support for Victor Parker."

"*Damn,*" Edwards cursed as the state results continued to come in, at a faster pace than the previous vote, now that everyone was acquainted with the process. "Phil still can't get us California."

"We may have a problem," Saroyan told Edwards gravely. He was doing a quick tabulation as he heard the results. "We should have seen this coming." He gritted his teeth as the Speaker continued to call for the results. "If you pick these things apart weeks in advance, you can spot problems like this. It should have been obvious. But we came here this morning thinking electoral commission, or just generally about a first ballot deadlock."

"What is it, Drew?" Edwards asked, getting impatient with Saroyan's bleak references and oblique statements.

"There. There it is again," Saroyan stated as his apprehension seemed to grow. "Louisiana. Called for *Hampton.*" He turned to Edwards. "The state delegations are splitting their votes between you and Parker. In some states, that's giving *Hampton* the plurality, and therefore the state."

Edwards' face went white. "How bad is this?"

"He's already gained six states. Five more, and *he* has 26."

Edwards sank back in his chair. Then he smiled as he saw Phil Lake racing around the chamber from group to group. Edwards was sure that Lake had also spotted the problem, and was running around trying to remedy it somehow. But it might be too late.

Saroyan kept careful count of the states calling out Hampton as their choice.

"Texas votes for Hampton."

Twenty-One.

"Utah chooses President Kenneth Hampton."

Twenty-Two.

"Vermont casts its vote for President Hampton."

Twenty-Three.

"Virginia votes for Ken Hampton."

Twenty-Four.

"Washington casts its vote for Michael Edwards."

Still twenty-four.

"West Virginia again votes for Victor Parker."

Still twenty-four.

"Wisconsin chooses Michael Edwards," announced the proud voice, apparently knowing that this state vote ensured another ballot, and denied a victory to President Hampton.

Wyoming's vote gave Hampton one more state, but this was one state short, reminiscent of the one electoral vote Hampton had needed to win the general election.

"We're okay," Saroyan told Edwards, "but we dodged a bullet."

Edwards nodded.

"The official results are as follows: 25 states for Ken Hampton, nine for Victor Parker, eight for Michael Edwards, and eight abstentions. We will convene one last time today to try to resolve this matter. The Speaker fixes the next meeting time at 8:00. We're adjourned." He pounded his gavel and walked away quickly.

✰   ✰   ✰

"HONESTLY, PHIL, I CAN'T UNDERSTAND YOUR OPTIMISM," EDWARDS told Phil Lake as they sat around a table in Edwards' Washington hotel room having dinner. Michael and Teresa Edwards, Drew Saroyan, and Phil and Jenny Lake were all present. "The big shift was to Hampton, not to me."

Phil Lake was wolfing down his food. He seemed extremely energetic, almost hyperactive, as he discussed the day's results. "This may be the best thing that could have happened," he told them.

"What?" Edwards asked in disbelief.

But Saroyan just smiled. He knew what Lake was thinking. He enjoyed working with such a seasoned professional, performing at the peak of his potential.

"This will scare the Democrats; almost all of them would prefer Edwards to Hampton, and *all*, without any doubts, prefer Edwards to Dooley. I'll be down there trying to convince them to rally around you. And I'll tell you, from what I'm seeing and hearing, we'll get quite a few."

"Enough for 26?" Edwards asked.

"I don't know," Lake replied. "I hope so. Because I see this third ballot as crucial."

"Absolutely," Saroyan agreed. "The third, and fourth if it's needed. Because if it begins to look like Michael can't close it out, they might try to rally back around Parker, trying to take one or two of ours along."

"They'll remember that they almost took this thing in ballot number one," Lake added.

"So hopefully we'll get *our* 26 tonight." Edwards remarked.

"I think we'll be in the 20's," Lake assured them. "I'm certain a lot more will rally around you to avoid splitting the vote. But I can't guarantee you the 26 we need. I'll be working on it."

"Is there anything *we* could be doing?" Edwards asked.

"If they'd give us a little more time between votes, we could try to cut some deals," Lake replied. "But I barely have time to see and talk to everyone we should contact. There's no way I have time to negotiate anything."

"And the problem with deals is that you have to live with them later," Edwards told them. "I know of more than one politician who ended up being ineffective one-term office-holders because the commitments they made to get them into office worked against their agendas."

"Well, there's no time to put anything together anyway," Lake commented, heading off a potential argument. Congressman Lake had spent most of his life making deals. This was not an abhorrent process to him. And he suspected that Drew Saroyan had cut a few in his career as well.

✩   ✩   ✩

"CRAP," SAROYAN BLURTED OUT AS HE CHECKED HIS PAD. HE AND Edwards again sat in the gallery of the joint-session chamber. "We're gonna be two or three short."

"We just took Texas," Edwards remarked. "That was Hampton's state, last ballot."

"Texas is a perfect example of what's been happening in a bunch of pivotal states," Saroyan informed him. "The Democrats stuck together for the first ballot, split between you and Parker in the second ballot, allowing the Republicans to give the state to Hampton, then rallied around you for the third ballot. We just haven't managed to take *enough* states. We're gonna leave here tonight with the momentum, but still without the prize." Saroyan tossed his pad on the seat next to him as the Speaker called the last few states and recorded the results.

"The Speaker reports the following results: 23 states for Michael Edwards, 16 states for Ken Hampton, three states for Victor Parker, and eight states abstaining." He put down the small piece of paper and looked out at the gathering. "Well, we'll take another stab at it tomorrow morning at ten a.m. Good night." He barely banged the gavel before he left the podium.

"I want to talk to Phil Lake," Edwards told Saroyan. "We need to make good use of the next twelve hours."

"I'll try to get his attention," Saroyan commented wryly as he looked out on the floor and saw Congressman Lake racing around, starting and finishing conversations all over the hall.

✧   ✧   ✧

"OKAY, SO LET'S TRY TO SUMMARIZE THIS," EDWARDS SUGGESTED wearily as he, Drew Saroyan and Phil Lake sat around a table in Edwards' hotel room. The digital clock read: "1:03." They had littered the table with crumpled papers, empty coffee cups and soda cans, and sheets of notes scattered around, some in piles, and some loose and out of place. "Can we get three more states?"

"The short answer is yes," Phil Lake replied succinctly, still strong and vibrant despite the late hour.

Edwards was glad for a "short answer" from Congressman Lake. The man seemed to have an endless knowledge of all of his fellow Congressmen, and an indefatigable source of strength for relaying that knowledge. Edwards felt both admiration and gratitude for Lake's contributions, but now they needed to tie his information together into something they could use.

"And you don't think we need to try to make some deals for the last three states?" Edwards asked, not thrilled with this possibility, but wanting to know.

"I don't think we have to," Lake replied. "There's still some play in those states. There's still some support left to mine. If we—"

"Um, I think I may have a summary of all this," Saroyan interjected. He had been quietly writing, without contributing to the discussion, for about ten to fifteen minutes. "I'd like Congressman Lake to comment on its accuracy."

"Sure," Lake said helpfully.

"First, there are 16 states that are Hampton's and will remain that way just about no matter what. They don't care if there's a stalemate—they'll take their fellow Republican Dooley as President if the House can't agree on someone. And maybe, if support starts to flow back to Parker, they can pull it out for Hampton when the delegations begin splitting between you and Parker again. There are no incentives for these states to shift their preferences.

"Second, there are five stalemated states that we probably can't mess with. In fact, from what Congressman Lake here says, we particularly want Colorado and Kansas to *stay* deadlocked, because a Parker-Edwards split vote could give one or both of these states to Hampton."

"That's correct, so far," Lake commented.

"Third, that leaves six states for us to go after—we need *three* of them," Saroyan continued.

"Right," Lake agreed.

"Three are stalemated, and might give us a shot. Maine has a Democrat and a Republican. The Democrat has already gone to Edwards. You think the Republican could."

"He's a progressive Republican—he's philosophically not far from you on a number of issues. And he and Dooley do *not* get along."

"Louisiana is a possibility because one Democrat is still voting for Parker, so the delegation is split three to three with one for Parker. If the Parker man shifts to either one, he will decide the state's choice."

"Correct," Lake verified.

"And in Hawaii, we have the same situation as in Maine, with a Republican who might shift."

"I'll talk to him," Lake promised.

"Then there are three states still with Parker: Alabama, Kentucky and Maryland. With Democratic majorities, you'd think they'd be anxious to knock the Republicans out by uniting with us. But they will be a tough sell."

"Very tough, since some of those Democrats are more conservative than anyone," Lake added.

"So we need to concentrate on those six states," Edwards observed, "but probably most on Maine, Louisiana and Hawaii."

"Yes," Lake replied, "and we need to keep our support from flowing away from us. With that in mind, I'd like to hold a breakfast meeting with as many Congressional supporters as I can. I believe the meeting should be without Michael, Drew or any other high-positioned authority. I want to have very frank conversations with all of them."

"Good. Send us the bill," Edwards praised enthusiastically. "Now let's get some sleep."

Chapter 32

January 7, The Year After Election Year
Washington, D.C.

"HOLD IT DOWN," PHIL LAKE REQUESTED, TRYING TO BE POLITE, BUT also trying to break through the cacophony of opinions shared by animated voices. Edwards had arranged for them to have exclusive occupancy of the G Street Cafe. "Please! I just want to close with a few thoughts!" His requests were having virtually no effect on the noise. He picked up a knife and tapped it loudly against his nearly empty water glass. The last hit shattered the glass.

That got almost everybody's attention, and the noise tapered down.

"Thank you," Congressman Lake said to the group of almost two hundred. "I've heard various concerns expressed here. We've exchanged views. Now I would like to express my main concern, that while we bounce back and forth between Victor Parker and Michael Edwards, we end up with Ken Hampton through the back door, or Burt Dooley if we can't make up our minds.

"So I'm asking you to hold on during the fourth ballot. Don't drift away just yet. Give us our shot at finishing this thing today. And if you're still wavering, think about how switching back to Victor Parker, given what he has apparently been linked to, will look to the voters in two years when you're trying to get reelected. It's best for *all* if this matter is settled *today*, with Michael Edwards on the way to the White House.

"Thank you for letting us buy you breakfast this morning."

✿   ✿   ✿

"WE ARE IN THE DRIVER'S SEAT," BURT DOOLEY TOLD HIS BREAKFAST audience, most of the Republican Congressional membership, assembled in the Paul Revere banquet room of the Hotel L'Enfant, a few blocks from the Capitol building. This gathering was quiet. The participants seemed almost reluctant to say very much. And the events of the previous 24 hours created a tense mood. "All we have to do is *stay together.*" Dooley let this statement sink in.

"Our numbers experts have looked at this. Edwards cannot get the last three states unless one of *us* goes over to him. Everyone else is locked down. If we stay that way, our party will retain the White House!"

Dooley intended the remark to draw applause. After a slight pause, there were a few scattered handclaps.

"I've seen that old fool Phillip Lake, Mr. Liberal Loudmouth for more years than my tired ears like to recall, running around like a beheaded turkey, trying to talk everyone into voting for Edwards. And I know he's talked to some of you. He's really enjoying himself—this is the most important thing he's been asked to do since he got to lead the pledge of allegiance for Bill Clinton's harem. Don't let this fool suck you into his game. Because fools won't go far in *my* administration—or President Hampton's," he added, almost as an afterthought. "And disloyal fools—that would be two big strikes and you're out; out of *this* man's Party, that's for sure. There's one in Connecticut that, as far as I'm concerned can call himself a Republican, but better not come to us for *anything*. He handed Connecticut to Michael Edwards.

"So this is solidarity. We will prevail, because we will stick together while the Democrats will be the fools without loyalty. I'll see you at the Capitol."

There was polite applause. After all, Burt Dooley was a leading figure in the Republican Party, and even had a chance to become President. But not all of those who were present appreciated these remarks. Some resented them. Dooley didn't care. As long as they feared reprisals for "foolishness" and "disloyalty," the meeting would have served its purpose.

✿   ✿   ✿

"I'M FINISHED," VICTOR PARKER LAMENTED, CLEARLY SINKING INTO depression. He was reacting to the numerous empty seats in the banquet room of the Blue Moon restaurant, about a block away from where many of his fellow Democrats were having breakfast with Congressman Phil Lake. Some were at this Democratic solidarity breakfast, but less than half of those expected.

"Not necessarily," Mueller responded, reacting to Parker's bleak comment. "If Edwards can't get this done on the fourth ballot, our people will slide back to us. We were one Rhode Island Congressman from taking this. We'll get it to slide back to that situation again, then twist *both* arms and maybe even one of the legs of that damned Congressman "

"You think we'll actually get that opportunity?"

"It's possible. It all depends on whether Edwards can finish it this morning. If he can't, we'll be back in it. It'll take a few votes to get it back to where it was on the first try. But we could do it."

Parker sighed. So maybe there was still a chance. And Parker needed to prevail, not just to fulfill a lifelong ambition, but because control of the Presidency would make life after the conclusion of the election less difficult. He had no doubt that even as President, the activities of his campaign staff, and his own role in those activities, would be scrutinized. But as a losing candidate with no political power, his position would be much more difficult.

☆   ☆   ☆

"HOW CAN THAT WILLIAMS GUY SHOW HIS FACE?" PAULINE EDWARDS demanded as she and her parents sat in their hotel room watching the live broadcast of the results. Pauline was the only Edwards child present at this point. The other children had arranged to join the family later in the day. Television cameras were in the room as well. Drew Saroyan was also present. They had decided to take a lower profile, because it was more dignified than waiting in the gallery, and because Phil Lake was on-site protecting the Edwards interests.

Edwin Williams was commenting on the fourth ballot for WWBS. Only Don Samuelson's network had not been caught off guard by the previous day's events. That network had been in place with commentators and coverage strategies right after the Senate had finished counting the electoral votes. WWBS, and the other major networks, now had all of their coverage in place, on the following day.

"I'm serious," Pauline insisted. "He's the one with the 'sources—' the one who said Hampton was for-sure the winner."

"No one remembers that now but us," Edwards commented wryly.

"Louisiana has become the second state to shift from a deadlock to Edwards," Edwin Williams said, commenting on Louisiana's just-announced vote. "Hawaii was the first when Hawaii's Republican Congressman apparently threw his support to Edwards. So Michael Edwards needs only one more switch to get to 26—he had 23 on the third ballot."

A graphic showed the current breakdown of the results:

House State-by-State Vote for President:

	Votes/States	
Edwards	9	
Hampton	4	Needed to Win: 26 of 50
Parker	2	18 of 50 decided
pass	3	

"And now Maine has just shifted to Edwards," Williams stated with slight excitement leaking into his demeanor.

The graphic changed slightly:

House State-by-State Vote for President:

	Votes/States	
Edwards	10	
Hampton	4	Needed to Win: 26 of 50
Parker	2	19 of 50 decided
pass	3	

"That is three shifts . . ."

"So if he holds on to the rest of the states which supported him on the last ballot, he will be selected by the House as our next President," Andrew Talbot clarified for the television audience.

"All right Dad!" Pauline cheered.

"We've got to sit through 31 more states," Michael reminded his daughter.

"But it's looking good," Saroyan told her smiling.

Teresa also flashed a confident smile.

And their confidence seemed appropriate as the results continued without Edwards losing any support. His three-state gain remained intact as the roll call reached South Dakota.

"South Dakota is one of seven states with only one member of the House of Representatives," Williams commented. "These states can be the most volatile, because all you need is for one person to change his mind. No time-consuming caucuses or negotiations. So they can shift allegiances in a hurry. But in this case, South Dakota has stayed with Edwards."

The graphic showed the current tally:

House State-by-State Vote for President:

	Votes/States	
Edwards	21	
Hampton	12	Needed to Win: 26 of 50
Parker	3	41 of 50 decided
pass	5	

The WWBS broadcast featured the live sound from the House of Representatives chamber.

"Tennessee," the Speaker called out.

"Tennessee is now deadlocked," the spokesperson announced.

"We just lost one," Saroyan told them all disgustedly.

Edwards exhaled, frowning silently.

"That delegation was two for Parker, three for Hampton and four for Edwards—one of the Edwards people must have gone back to Parker," Williams guessed. The usually cool and calm Williams was almost starting to pant, exhibiting the same kind of excitement that a sports commentator might show when broadcasting the seventh game of a World Series in the bottom of the ninth, or the last two minutes of a close Super Bowl game.

"Texas," the Speaker called out.

"Texas selects Michael Edwards."

"Utah."

"Utah again proudly casts its vote for Kenneth Hampton."

The graphic changed after each result to update the numbers:

House State-by-State Vote for President:

	Votes/States	
Edwards	22	
Hampton	13	Needed to Win: 26 of 50
Parker	3	44 of 50 decided
pass	6	

"We need one back," Edwards commented nervously.

"Maybe this one," Saroyan predicted.

"Vermont," the Speaker called out.

"Vermont votes for Michael Edwards."

"We got it!" Edwards blurted out.

"I'll be damned," Saroyan commented, registering some surprise, even though he had mentioned the possibility.

"One of those states with single members in the House of Representatives," Edwin Williams stated quickly. "He has been under intense pressure from his local media, constituent telephone calls and telegrams to support Edwards in light of the attempted manipulations of the electors. Many in the state have been proudly inspired by the example set by their own electors, and this has no doubt had an influence on the lone Congressman, a Republican, from this state. This is what we meant by watching these single-representative states. But now, there is only one of these left. He is Clement Hurdlaw of Wyoming, in Republican politics for over 40 years, and about as solidly Republican as a Congressman can get. He has been known to tell stories about his role in getting Wyoming to choose Dewey over F.D.R. in 1944, though he was only about 20 at the time."

"Virginia," the Speaker summoned.

"President Hampton," the fatalistic voice responded.

"Washington . . ."

"Michael Edwards again," replied a cheerier voice.

With three states left, the graphic showed that Edwards needed two of them. But West Virginia and Wisconsin had chosen him in the previous vote, so his chances looked good:

House State-by-State Vote for President:

	Votes/States	
Edwards	24	
Hampton	15	Needed to Win: 26 of 50
Parker	3	47 of 50 decided
pass	5	

"West Virginia," the Speaker called out.

"West Virginia votes again, uh, returns to voting for Victor Parker."

"Shit!" Edwards blurted out.

"Dad," Pauline scolded gently, pretending to be shocked.

"We'd been hearing that these Congressmen were swamped with telegrams, both from the coal-miner's unions, and the coal-producing companies of the region, after the state voted for Edwards yesterday evening. One or more of these Congressmen obviously gave in to the pressure," Williams explained.

"Can we withstand a fifth ballot?" Edwards asked Saroyan, trying to think ahead and distract himself from the disappointment of having success so close to their grasp.

"I don't know," Saroyan equivocated. "It feels to *me* like we've peaked. So I have to worry what everyone else will think."

"And Wyoming," the Speaker called out, soliciting the result from the final state as the graphic on the WWBS screen read:

House State-by-State Vote for President:

	Votes/States	
Edwards	25	
Hampton	15	Needed to Win: 26 of 50
Parker	4	49 of 50 decided
pass	5	

Clement Hurdlaw stood proudly in his stitched brown suit and string tie. He had a weathered, tanned face, and was entirely grey, though he still had some traces of rugged handsomeness through his generally aging, craggy appearance. He cultivated the almost stereotypical image of the cowboy-gone-to-Washington, though he had never worked near a ranch in his life. He looked carefully at some notes he had been keeping, then looked up assuredly. The long-time Republican stated firmly, with a touch of fanciful satisfaction in his voice, "I'm gonna cast Wyoming's vote for Michael Edwards."

A hush came over the chamber, which quickly gave way to an evolving din of animated chatter.

"Was that it?" Edwards asked cautiously.

"Did he say . . . Edwards?" Saroyan asked incredulously.

The television cameras focused on the podium, which was momentarily silent. They did not catch a little drama, still evolving on the House floor.

A young Wisconsin Congressman, no more than thirty-five years old, wearing an immaculately tailored European suit and sitting closest to the

Wyoming Congressman, looked at Clement Hurdlaw with a puzzled expression.

Hurdlaw understood the young man's confusion, and was a friendly, gregarious man, definitely willing to explain himself. "I'll go back to Hampton on the fifth ballot," he stated casually. "I just wanted to send a message to that grouchy old bastard Dooley—some of us don't like threats, especially made over breakfast. And we aren't all afraid of him."

"Well you showed him," the young Wisconsin Congressman commented casually, with a touch of whimsy. "You just gave the Presidency to Michael Edwards."

"No I didn't," Hurdlaw countered confidently. "Three went over, but two went back."

"You lost count somewhere . . ."

Hurdlaw considered this comment as he looked up at the podium. He recalled that all the other final ballot results were announced immediately. This time, there was a delay. That must have meant they were double-checking a final result. He really had lost count. Panic suddenly seized him. "Mr. Speaker!" he called out frantically. The din of chatter absorbed his summons. "Mr. Speaker, I wish to be heard!" he called out again, more forcefully. There was still no response.

Only the young Wisconsin Congressman was watching the older Wyoming Congressman. He smiled knowingly. "I wouldn't do that," he commented quietly to Hurdlaw.

Hurdlaw looked at him, still somewhat panicked, and now looking like he had no clue of what to do next, with the failure of his attempts to get the Speaker's attention. He hoped the Wisconsin Congressman would explain himself.

"Unless you want to look like a damned *idiot,*" the young Wisconsin Congressman explained, "you better make this look like the most momentous decision of your life."

The panic drained out of Hurdlaw's face as he realized this young man had just given him some very useful advice. He smiled. "You're wise beyond your years, son," Hurdlaw told the young Wisconsin Congressman quietly. "This'll be our little secret."

"Fine with me," was the casual reply. "I've been supporting Edwards since the second ballot."

Hurdlaw sat back down, to make sure no one followed up on his just-stated request to be heard.

The Speaker of the House finally came back to the microphone. His voice sounded tired, but he still attempted to capture a sense of the history of the moment. "The Chair confirms these results: Michael Edwards, 26 state votes; Kenneth Hampton, 14 state votes; Victor Parker, 4 state votes; and six states abstaining. Pursuant to the rules stated in the Constitution, the Chair declares that Michael Edwards has been chosen President of the United States for a term beginning on January 20th, and ending on January 20th, four years from that date. May God bless President-elect Edwards as he leads this great nation for the next four years." The Speaker banged his gavel. "We are now adjourned."

Edwards sat stunned. "We did it," he stated, almost in shock.

Saroyan was almost teary-eyed. "Yes sir. Congratulations, Mr. President."

Teresa and Michael both stood and embraced, exchanging an affectionate kiss. Pauline let her parents have a quick private moment, then came over and hugged her father first, then her mother.

"Who's the guy from Wyoming?" Edwards asked, still intertwined in an embrace with his wife.

"I don't know, but I have a feeling all of us will know more about him shortly," Saroyan commented.

"Yeah." Edwards paused. "Set up a press conference. Make it in two hours. I'm going to write the most magnanimous acceptance speech ever heard."

"There he is." Teresa pointed to the television screen.

Clement Hurdlaw was just beginning an impromptu press conference on the steps of the Capitol building. Reporters squeezed in on him, holding microphones and maneuvering cameras to try to get unobstructed views of the veteran Republican Congressman as he spoke. And he spoke with thundering drama in his voice, as if he was recounting a biblical epic. "Last night, I had a dream," he was telling them. "My new baby granddaughter, who is three months old now, and who I met for the first time over the Christmas break, was ten years older. I was lying on my deathbed, up in an old cabin in the beautiful little tree-covered hills my state is famous for, where I plan to retire to when my service to this country has concluded. She asks in the dream, 'Grampa, what did you do for *my* future? What did you do in your years in politics to make the world better for *my* children, and my *children's* children?' When I woke up, the dream struck me as a revelation. I had been thinking of my *own* future when voting for the choice of my Party, not my *granddaughter's* future. So I asked myself, who would be the best for *her* future? Clearly, the answer was Michael Edwards. He believes in the basic concepts of freedom and the free market, and his policies follow those ideals. I knew I'd be risking *my* future by defying my Party. But I had my *granddaughter's* future in mind. So I am gratified that my humble vote put him in office. And I will look forward to working with him."

The performance was convincing. Many were touched, including Michael Edwards, who made a note to contact him with the idea that he would be a very important man in Congress to the Edwards Administration. Only one Congressman, a young, well-dressed one from Wisconsin, went into a long, vigorous laugh when he saw a tape of the press conference that evening.

✿   ✿   ✿

The Same Day
Dallas, Texas

"I'LL SPELL IT FOR YOU," BEAUREGARD HUNTER RAGED INTO THE PHONE as he and Zachary Fadiman sat together in Fadiman's elegant hotel suite enjoying a private meal. They had just finished watching Hurdlaw's press conference on television. When the election had gone unresolved after January 6th, Fadiman and Hunter decided to meet to watch the outcome together. "Hunter! H-U-N-T-E-R! Beauregard! You tell him his silly dreams just cost him a million dollars worth of support for his next campaign!" He slammed down the phone. "It's the mountain air—they're *all* wacko."

Fadiman was much less demonstrative, but clearly unhappy.

"So now you've got Everett Phillips to deal with . . ."

"And you've got *President* Edwards and his oil taxes," Fadiman reminded Hunter, "a man who will be immune from a lot of the normal pressure points we can bring to bear."

"There are ways to deal with our problems."

"Of course. He has to get Congress to go for this stuff. They still *are* mere mortals who need *money* to be reelected, and crave power and more power. And if that doesn't work, we may need the talents of my security people."

"I won't be the only one who will be a bit unhappy about what this man wants to do. Some of my friends may be interested in your alternative approaches if things start to go down a rocky road."

"Could be expensive . . ."

"I wouldn't expect you to work for free," Hunter assured him smiling. "It's just nice to know we could have alternatives."

"I'll be here."

"Good." Hunter stood up. "I'll get back to my family." He shook his head, with a slight smile of disbelief sneaking onto his face. "God damndest thing; who'd have thought it. Some old geezer has a dream—an old geezer who *I* bought and paid for *personally*." Hunter left the room.

Fadiman turned off the television and began packing.

☼   ☼   ☼

The Same Day
Washington, D.C.

"NICE SHOT," DREW SAROYAN SAID.

Edwards had just banked a paperwad off the corner of his hotel room wall into a wastebasket below it. There were other paperwads lying around the wastebasket, indicating that Edwards' aim had not been so accurate on other occasions.

"I've had lots of practice," Edwards told him through a disgusted glare. "I'm glad we put this speech off until tonight. I'm trying to get it just right, and I'm not there yet."

"No speechwriter for this one."

"Why would I start now?"

"You have been a unique politician to work with . . ." Saroyan looked like he wanted to say something more, but decided not to. "I'm sorry to bother you right now. I'll come back."

"It's okay. I think I need the break. What's on your mind?"

"I feel funny bugging you with this right now."

"It's okay, Drew."

"You sure?"

"Absolutely."

"So," Saroyan said to Edwards with a smile of familiarity, "is there something for your campaign manager to do, now that you have actually been elected?"

"Of course," Edwards assured him cordially. "We'll find something for your talents."

Saroyan appreciated the gracious answer. But the answer brought to mind another, maybe more important question. "I wonder if you have anything for someone whose talents involve winning elections."

"You could still be a great deal of help to me."

Drew Saroyan realized that he had not yet considered his post-Edwards career, particularly in the context of an Edwards victory. He was evolving his own ideas about the situation as they spoke. "I could be of help. But do you realize, I've been your right hand man, the most inner of the inner circle for a year? When you take power, I can't retain that spot . . ."

"Probably not. I need someone with a ton of actual governmental experience, and preferably a lot of connections in Congress. But there are still press relations and—"

"I don't want to stop working with this," Saroyan told him as his feelings about the matter crystallized. "I have a feeling the excitement has only begun. But I think my role is over. I did my best to serve your effort, but you don't need me any more. And to hang around in some ceremonial job while others take my place in the inner circle would be too hard for me to accept. I think I have to move on."

"I would miss you."

"But you see what I mean."

"I do. I'll offer you the best position I think would be of help to us, and you can decide if—"

"No," Saroyan interrupted gently. "Anything less than the inner circle would feel like a demotion to me, even though you would be trying to make me the best offer. I have relished this opportunity, the most exciting of my life. But it is now over, and time to say good-bye. I'll try to stop—" He shook his head. "I almost said I'll try to stop by for lunch. But I think you'll be busy the next four years."

Edwards nodded. "We'll stay in touch."

✿   ✿   ✿

"AS YOU ALL KNOW, I HAVE ALL THE MONEY AND NOTORIETY ANY HUMAN being could want," Edwards told the media conglomeration gathered to witness what was not really a press conference, but a victory speech, given in a huge banquet room at the hotel Edwards had been staying at during his visit to Washington. He finally delivered his acceptance speech at 9:00 that evening. Edwards had wanted it to be just right, and delayed making it until he was satisfied. And he had successfully delivered a warm, conciliatory speech. "So my *only* reason for taking this office is to serve all of *you,* to leave this job having accomplished something positive. Fate has put me in a unique position to accomplish a great deal. To those of you who supported me at the ballot box in November, and also joined me between then and now, I will try with every molecule of my being to justify your faith in me. To those of you who did not support me, I will try to allay your fears, and win your support with the positive effects of my accomplishments. Because this is a great country, with a history of monumental accomplishments, and if we can harness the boundless energy turned loose by freedom and a system that encourages creativity, we will prove that our greatest successes are ahead of us. I humbly wish to be a small part of making that happen. Thank you." He walked away from the podium to enthusiastic applause from his supporters who were present. He ignored the questions attempted by members of the press—the supporter applause virtually drowned them out anyway.

Michael Edwards stepped over to his wife and embraced her, joined quickly by all the Edwards children, now present for this historic occasion. As his embrace of his wife expanded into a family hug, Edwards thought about the ecstasy of winning a great struggle, and obtaining an unlikely result that was exactly what had been sought. But his thoughts then drifted to something his father had told him during his childhood. There had been a major financial setback for the Edwards family. An investment that Michael's father had begged to be a part of had failed, with a huge financial loss to the partners. Michael's father had felt proud, nearly elated when the partners had accepted him to join them. And now, in the context of near bankruptcy, Michael's father told his eight-year-old son: "Sometimes our biggest challenges occur when we get exactly what we want. Be careful when life gives you what you want. Because success is rarely absolute, just as failure is rarely fatal." Michael suspected he would think of those words often as he dealt with the challenges that were sure to follow the historic result of this election.

Epilogue

Late April, The Year After the Election: Thursday
San Luis Obispo, California

"THE CLERK WILL PUBLISH THE VERDICTS," JUDGE ORRIN DAGGETT announced disgustedly. He didn't look at the defense table, or even at the prosecution. He sneered and looked down at his notes.

Judge Daggett's attitude encouraged Will Runalli as he stood next to his attorney Elwood Kaplan in the crowded San Luis Obispo County courtroom. But Runalli maintained a poker-faced, respectful expression.

"The jury finds the defendant not guilty of murder. The jury finds the defendant not guilty of conspiracy to commit murder," the clerk read robotically.

Judge Daggett squinted as a brief murmur rose and dissipated among the spectators. "Does either counsel wish to have the jury polled?"

"Yes," the prosecutor answered immediately, not successfully cloaking his disappointment with the verdict.

Kaplan whispered to Runalli, "Good, you remembered. Do *not* celebrate."

"It's hard," Runalli replied quietly, barely moving his lips. "Damn fucking incredible. You did it."

"Let *me* talk to the reporters."

"I know."

The twelfth juror finally ended the polling process with her affirmation of the unanimous not-guilty verdict.

"The Court thanks and excuses the jury," Judge Daggett muttered insincerely. "The defendant . . ." He drew a frowning breath. "The defendant is free to go." He pounded his gavel and fled from the bench.

Reporters quickly rushed toward all the major participants, including Will Runalli and his attorney.

"My client is gratified that the criminal justice system has vindicated him with respect to these unprovable allegations. Other than that, he has no comment," Elwood Kaplan told the inquiring reporters forcefully as he and Will Runalli worked their way out of the courtroom toward a private conference room.

"You're a magician," Runalli told Kaplan gratefully as they shut the door to the room.

"Yeah. I made your troubles disappear."

"Almost. What about federal charges?"

"No news, which is good news. That's why you need to zip your lips and take a low profile. Right now, you're the villain of the election who got off, *not* because he was innocent, but because he had brilliant legal representation. Good for *my* career—not good for you if someone decides you're a little too smug about beating this thing."

"What about the book deal?"

"In the *millions*," Kaplan told him. "But we don't dare sign for another six months, maybe longer."

Runalli nodded slowly. "And there are no statutes against me writing a tell-all book about this?"

Kaplan shook his head. "You were found *not* guilty. You can write whatever you want. The statutes you're thinking about refer to criminals profiting from their crimes. You weren't convicted."

Runalli smiled. "Okay. Millions? I'll wait."

"And you'll have me read it, to make sure you don't create any evidence against yourself for any future prosecutions."

"Of course." Runalli smiled again. "I'm not going the route of some of the other bad guys of this election."

"At least not prison, like Lusman."

Runalli shrugged. "He'll be out for good behavior in less than a year from that country club prison. Then he'll do *his* multi-million dollar book."

Kaplan nodded.

"Anybody know what happened to the guy who got Lusman in trouble—the guy who got the shit kicked out of him?"

Kaplan laughed out loud. "His attorney dropped him right after that silly press conference. And I hear that attorney is one of the sleaziest in L.A.—supposedly will take any client with a pulse. After that Naylor character lost his attorney, he disappeared in a hurry when the cops started asking him about extortion."

"Disappeared." Runalli grinned. "So did 300,000 bucks . . ."

"Yeah." Kaplan looked intrigued. "The little mysteries of this election."

"Do you think the widow Whittlebaum might be interested in a wise-ass, washed-up political asshole?" Runalli asked with a mischievous gleam in his eye.

Kaplan shook his head with a disgusted smile. "You figure she's got the money?"

"Who else? Maybe she can help me pay *you*."

Kaplan shrugged. "I'll get my end when we get your book deal signed." He tapped Runalli on the shoulder as he headed toward the door. "In the meantime, I've got plenty of business from all of the publicity of defending *you*."

Runalli moved with him to the door. "So what do I get for that?"

"My sincere and undying gratitude," Kaplan told him with apparent relish.

Runalli smiled reluctantly. "How nice."

"All right," Kaplan said seriously, as if he was a quarterback calling a play in the huddle. "I'll be in touch when this thing has died down enough to discuss setting the book deal. Let's get past these reporters as quickly as we can."

Runalli nodded. "Let's get out of here."

They moved quickly and resolutely through the door.

So no one would ever pay for the murder of Bennington Whittlebaum. And no one ever came after the Whittlebaum bribe money. By the time Runalli thought of approaching "the widow Whittlebaum," the money was already disappearing. Molly Whittlebaum, in her grief and anguish, took the $300,000 cash, which the Republicans were in no position to reclaim, and moved to Hawaii. She opened a macadamia nut cookie stand which she called "Mrs. W's." She hoped to duplicate the success of the Mrs. Field's cookie chain, but ended up losing all her money and marrying a used car salesman on Oahu.

The man who had almost destroyed Edwards' historic campaign, Slick Naylor, disappeared into homeless anonymity. As Edwards stood for inauguration, Slick Naylor stood shivering in the winter cold at a freeway off-ramp, clothed in rags, holding a sign that no passing motorist would have believed from looking at his pathetic appearance: "Will work for food."

President Edwards did indeed ask for his Justice Department to investigate all aspects of the Presidential election for potential criminal conduct. They looked at Runalli closely. But since Runalli's efforts appeared directed toward preventing elector defections, and no one could develop hard evidence of criminal activity that would hold up in court, the consensus at Justice was that Runalli was untouchable as long as he kept his mouth shut.

President Edwards had much higher priorities than even a moment's thought about Will Runalli and the election Runalli had tried to steal for Senator Parker. Edwards faced performing one of the most complex jobs in human history under unprecedented circumstances. He was discovering that winning The Election had been simple, compared to navigating the intricacies of personalities, rivalries, pitfalls, and traps that would make up the challenges of The Administration.

We'd love to hear from you . . .

We encourage our readers to write us with any comments, positive or negative—the more controversial the better. We'll feature the most intriguing comments at our web site. A book like *The Election* is bound to generate some lively discussions, and we would love to provide a forum for them. Our address for correspondence, and for contacting the author, is:

IFT Infortainment Publishing Company
P.O. Box 571752
Tarzana, CA 91357-1752

Web site:
http://www.infortainment.com

Author e-mail:
rfield@infortainment.com

Publisher e-mail:
ift@infortainment.com